Fiona Walker

Fiona Walker now writes full-time, dividing her days between a jolly home in the country and her chaotic flat in Hampstead.

Praise for *Snap Happy*

'Walker's style is up-beat and wisecracking, whatever the emotional weather' *The Express on Sunday*

'. . . hate to love via a one-night stand, misunderstandings and a barrel load of one-liners. You'll love every minute of this book' *Company*

'Fiona Walker does it again with her latest serving of whimsical banter and feisty characters . . . Fast, furious and fruity' *19*

'A good choice for a light and frothy summer beach read' *Miss London*

'Sunshine, a garden chair and the latest Fiona Walker novel – what more could one ask? *Snap Happy* is the perfect choice for summer reading with its fun mix of romance, misunderstandings and handsome men . . . For every woman who dreads putting on last year's bikini this summer, *Snap Happy* is a great antidote' *Coventry Evening Telegraph*

'. . . a rollercoaster of emotional tangles that are vintage Fiona Walker' *Bolton Evening News*

Snap Happy

Fiona Walker

CORONET BOOKS

Hodder & Stoughton

First published in 1998 by Hodder and Stoughton
First published in paperback in 1999
by Hodder and Stoughton
A division of Hodder Headline PLC
A Coronet paperback

A CIP catalogue record for this title is available
from the British Library

ISBN 0 340 68227 2

Typeset by Palimpsest Book Production Limited,
Polmont, Stirlingshire
Printed and bound in Great Britain by
Clays Ltd, St Ives PLC, Bungay, Suffolk

Hodder and Stoughton
A division of Hodder Headline PLC
338 Euston Road
London NW1 3BH

For the angelic Ealing broad, the half-Dane Highgate dame, the craft Thatcham tochter and, of course, for the tall poupee with whom I make whoopee.

Chapter One

Juno's throat was so dry that every quick breath seemed to suck her lungs sharply into her ribs like flags whipping against their poles. She touched her upper lip with her tongue and tasted salt from the light film of sweat there.

'They're a good crowd tonight,' Bob said encouragingly as he moved in beside her with a fresh bottle of Ice, anticipating his next compère's slot. 'They even laughed at one of Eric's dead-Tory jokes, so they must be pretty undiscriminating.'

Juno glanced at him briefly, too nervous to speak. Even in the half-light between the bar and the stage, his popping-out eyes gleamed with mirth as he shot her a cheer-up wink. It would be so easy to be a great stand-up comic like Bob if my face were funny already, she mused.

Bob Worth had been on the London comedy circuit for almost a decade and was a regular compère in the upstairs function rooms of pubs and clubs in the West End, where he bounded up to a mike stand night after night to deliver his own unique brand of off-the-cuff, off-the-wall humour. It was popularly believed that he would have made it big-time were he not so regularly off-his-face too.

Somewhere in the depths of her leather trousers, Juno distinctly felt a twang as her teddy poppers gave way. There was no time to dash to the loo to re-pop them – the queue was already out into the bar, and Bob was sinking his Ice fast as he geared up to leap on stage and introduce her. She wondered briefly if anyone would notice her having a quick re-popping delve in the gloom where she was standing, but decided it wasn't worth the risk. One or two laddish audience members were eyeing her occasionally, sensing fresh blood about to be thrown Christian-like on to the stage.

Why do I do it? she thought wretchedly. Why do I put myself through this?

Up on the small, raised rostrum which was acting as the stage, a droopy student with a ginger goatee beard, which clashed disastrously with his hyper-fashionable carrot orange Diesel surf-shirt, was giving a long, observational spiel about other students eating his Coco Pops. Hardly anyone in the audience was listening to him. Only his close friends and supporters laughed. The crowd had started to feel restless, their glasses empty. People were already slyly creeping off to the bar to get their rounds of drinks in before the rush started.

'Got any friends in tonight?' Bob asked distractedly as he glanced at his watch and winced. Everyone on the bill so far had overrun their allotted time.

Juno shook her head. She could usually guarantee that her brother and Triona, his tempestuous girlfriend, would be inhabiting the front table, along with various loudly cackling friends who were just as likely to heckle mercilessly.

But tonight was different. Sean was currently airborne over the Atlantic, heading for New York where he was planning to spend six months working as a freelance photographer. Triona was holed up in her flat crying her eyes out as a result, and Sean's loyal band of friends would see no point in turning out to support the little sister of the man they called the Top Shot, when the great man himself had deserted them. Her own friends were banned from her occasional slots at comedy clubs because she became even more hopelessly nervous with them around.

The student had moved on to the theft of his Low-Fat Flora now. Bob pressed his forehead to Juno's shoulder and groaned.

'Jesus, I hate doing this, but he was only offered five minutes and he's already done quarter of a fucking hour.'

'Is fucking time different then?' Juno asked through chattering teeth as she realised her cue was almost upon her. 'Like a quarter of an ordinary hour, only shorter? Are we talking Greenwich Male Time here?'

Bob cocked his head and wrinkled his long nose. 'That sort of feminist humour's going out of fashion, babe – too oblique. Stick to the family and friends material.'

Juno felt even more hellish. Bob usually humoured her enough to laugh at her nervous pre-act gags, an act of charity few of the hardened, regular compères afforded her. But tonight he simply handed her his half-smoked fag and stalked on stage to reclaim the mike.

'Terrific stuff! Rory Hanson, ladies and gentlemen – a star of the future. And if the future is as orange as his shirt then I personally am planning to kill myself tonight. Let's hear it for him – Rory Hanson!' He more or less elbowed the confused student off-stage and then adopted a conspiratorial stance, allying himself with the audience, long nose wrinkling, eyes narrowing against the wall of cigarette smoke as he scanned them all. The crowd respected Bob, were intimidated by his manic stare, acid humour and sheer physical presence.

'I said to him before he came on tonight that he had no more than five fucking minutes.' He rolled his eyes and shrugged. 'But you know what young lads are like, girls – to you it might be five minutes of boring fucking, to us it's half an hour of unbelievable fucking and boring and grinding and sending you to heaven and back, impaled upon the greatest seven inches of love piston that ever came out of the womb, went back in it again, came out, went in, came out, went in, came – and then rolled over and farted. You women have PMT, we men have GMT – Greenwich Male Time. And I think we all agree that Rory didn't come too soon tonight – he simply stayed too long.'

The lads beside Juno jeered, some of the girls in the audience shrieked with giggles, and Bob had them exactly where he wanted them: paying attention once more, stopping halfway to the bar or the loo to listen again, to laugh in shocked delight and exchange big grins with their friends.

Juno inwardly smarted with jealousy and pique that he'd stolen her Greenwich Male Time joke and, worse than that, made it appear screamingly funny to all around. But a few seconds later she almost forgave him.

'Now I might be planning suicide later tonight but, boys and girls, there is one last thing I want to do before I die – and that's watch our next act. She's one damned fine bit of totty. She's sexy, she's funny, she's yet to give up the day job but I think you'll agree when you see her that this lady is made for the night – for sin, for laughs and, most of all, for your enjoyment. Let's hear it for the divine Juno Glenn!'

Buoyed up by the introduction, Juno picked up her faithful squeezebox. To flattering whoops and catcalls, she wound her way towards the rostrum and decided at the last minute to inject a bit of physical energy into her routine by jumping Bob-style on to the stage.

Laughter is a comedian's addiction. The bigger the roar, the higher the fix. The communal cackle that greeted Juno's arrival on stage at that moment was the largest of her life, the loudest, longest and most gut-busting she had ever received. People were literally weeping. It was her best punch-line by far, yet she hadn't uttered a word.

Jay Mulligan sat in the back of a black cab with his biker boots up on a leather holdall, staring through the windscreen ahead at streams of red tail lights on the M4.

An office block gleamed beneath an arc of floodlighting to the right. Compared to the sky-scrapers of Manhattan, it looked squat and disproportionate. To the left, a dingy yellow rectangle of light bulbs flashed the time and temperature from a dirty grey concrete wall. Jay saw 21° and shuddered in horror before realising this was Centigrade, not Fahrenheit. Even so, he felt cold and clammy and badly in need of a hot shower.

The journey to North London took far longer than he had anticipated. The parts of the city he saw on the way appeared pretty small-scale and grubby – dimly lit pubs on street corners with dusty window boxes, row upon row of tiny houses with paint peeling from their doors, those squat office blocks and narrow streets with dinky little traffic lights.

'What's this area called?' he asked.

The driver didn't hear him, so he tapped on the glass in front until it slid to one side.

'This place – what's it called?' Jay repeated, staring out at pavements crawling with gaggles of young drinkers shuffling past shuttered shops and all-night fast food cafés.

'Camden, mate,' the driver sniffed. 'A dive. That's the canal to your left there. Full of needles and johnnies.'

All Jay could see in the dark was a low wall and beyond it a large brick building with 'Dingwalls' painted on the side, which vanished as they swooped under a metal bridge and roared through the traffic with a splutter of diesel engine.

When they finally made it to Belsize Park and located the right road, the driver clocked the affluent-looking street and became chatty.

'Nice road this.' He nodded along the row of stucco-fronted town houses with their flower-filled balconies and porticoed front doors below. 'Don't that Liam Gallagher bloke live in one of these?'

'Pardon me?' Jay was fishing through the pockets of his leather jacket for his wad of sterling.

'You staying with friends while you're over here?' The driver started to heave some of Jay's luggage out on to the pavement.

'Uh-huh – I've done an apartment-swap with a guy.'

'Nice.' The driver whistled. 'Your gaff must be pretty choice to swap with one of these places.'

'My what?'

'Your gaff. Your house, mate.'

'I live alone – I don't have a house-mate.'

Jay tried not to think too hard about his huge, airy loft with its wooden floors, sparse furnishings and vast darkroom. Places like his were gold-dust in TriBeCa, and he hated leaving it – and especially his Bengal cat, Bagel, who was hell to live with but a better burglar deterrent than three Dobermanns and a Colt

.45. His only solace was that Sean Glenn was a great guy who not only loved the apartment as much as he did, but also doted on the most violent feline in America. Jay guessed his place was in safe hands.

Out on the pavement, he handed over a pile of notes and searched through the pockets of one of his kit-bags for the keys that Sean had left at the British Airways desk in Heathrow for him, along with a note explaining that his dog, Rug, was being looked after by his parents, but that Jay would have to take care of Poirot and Juno himself.

'That's nothing compared to the task I've got with Bagel,' the note had read, 'but I'd better warn you that Poirot bites if he's in a bad mood, and that both he and Juno make a hell of a lot of noise and mess if left alone too long.'

Jay was slightly confused by this. He knew that Poirot was a macaw that talked dirty, but he wasn't too sure what species Juno was. He guessed it was another bird, possibly a second parrot, but he was surprised Sean hadn't mentioned this when they'd met in New York last month to discuss the swap. He'd gone into every other detail about the place – from the dodgy boiler to the days the cleaner came and what sort of wax polish she liked. Jay, by contrast, had simply bought in some extra cat food and cancelled his mail delivery. He found it easy to leave places behind – he'd been doing it all his life.

The house which Sean Glenn's apartment was in looked much the same as all the others in the road – tall, narrow and austere. It had a glossy black front door with a brass knob set in the centre and, to the left, three bells – one for each apartment. Sean's was the top one, but the only thing written in the small box to the side of it was, 'Don't ring before midday'.

Jay let himself into the gloomy communal hall, which had a low oak table covered with uncollected mail, at the centre of which a chipped vase was housing a few dusty pieces of dried grass, a broken pen and a plastic wind-twirler on a stick. The carpet on the stairs was loose and bald and, thanks to timer lights that gave a guy less than ten seconds to climb three levels, Jay risked his life as he staggered back and forth with his luggage and equipment. At last getting everything to the top, he let himself in, further appalled that the door, which was clearly fitted with three locks, had been secured with only one little automatic latch.

Inside, his mood lightened as he took in the size of the place.

The hallway, which he encountered first, had a high, slanting glass ceiling through which seeped a combination of city glow and moonlight to throw a clutter of sports equipment into high relief. Straight ahead were open double doors leading to a huge room lit by the dancing blue glare of a colossal illuminated fish tank, and by two tall, uncurtained windows the size of garage doors. Unable to locate a light switch, Jay tripped his way through the half-dark towards them and realised that they overlooked a large garden, beyond which stretched rooftops and terraces towards central London. In the far distance, he could see the pin-prick gleam of lights from tower-block windows several miles away. To his left was a panelled glass door which clearly opened out on to some sort of balcony, and to his right was a wide arch through which several green or red power lights winked and vast swathes of zinc gleamed, telling him this was a kitchen.

The fish tank was letting out the occasional faint burble and, glancing across to it, he spotted an extremely ugly reptilian face peering at him quizzically. Perched on what appeared to be a tower of kid's plastic building blocks shaped like a sunken ship, and looming out of the surface of the lumines-cent water, was a turtle of some sort. It was the size of a shoe box, had flippers shaped like lily petals, a beaky snout and strange, hooded eyes on stalks which made Jay flinch in revulsion.

'Jeez, you're a seriously ugly individual.' He wandered across to it, tripping over what appeared to be a pizza box en route. 'Guess you must be Juno. Now where's Poirot?'

Beside the tank was a tall light shaped like a movie lamp. Crawling around its base, Jay located a foot switch and threw it, turning back to look around.

It was undoubtedly one of the most beautiful rooms he'd ever seen. And also one of the messiest.

The walls were painted a deep, vibrant green so intense it almost blew his head off. They were covered not with the photographs he'd expected but with hundreds of framed caricatures and cartoons, all originals, and some bearing names which even Jay had heard of – Steadman, Scarfe, Searle. There was even a tiny Hogarth sketch. He was amazed. The floor – what little of it he could see – was of polished ash floorboards, so silvery grey it seemed to be cast in pure metal. A fat, rust-coloured silk sofa the size of a family car dominated the centre of the room, facing a fireplace with a grey marble mantel so laden with candles and framed family photographs it was almost cracking under the weight. Dried wax of every colour dripped decadently from its rim like icicles seeping over a winter gutter. Under each of the enormous windows, a heavy oak table shouldered its way into the room, gleaming like wet tar with polish.

The rest of the furniture was also minimal, very old, and beautifully proportioned. And almost every piece of it was covered in fast-food litter, wine bottles, drink cans, brimming ashtrays and clothes – what appeared to be women's clothes. Skimpy women's clothes. The same went for the floor, the sofa, the protective cover on the fish tank, the old-fashioned painted radiators and even the palatial parrot cage beside the balcony window. Wandering over to it, Jay peeked beneath the sleeve of a red satin blouse and saw a scraggy red parrot bearing the same expression as a grumpy lush awoken at six in the morning by a neighbour asking for sugar. Blinking evilly, it opened its beak, poked out a grey tongue and shrieked, 'A tenner on the three-fifteen!' before lunging violently at the side of the cage.

Jay hastily dropped the sleeve of the blouse and backed off.

Opening a door beside the cage which he assumed to be a bedroom, he encountered the boiler Sean had told him about, covered with yet more female clothes – most of them lacy undergarments. Jay knew from talking with him that Sean had a girlfriend called Triona who was furious that he was going to the States for six months, but surely vandalising the flat with fast-food containers and pantyhose was kind of weird.

The kitchen was so full of junk and dirty dishes that he backed straight out again, hardly taking in the high-tech gadgets and pots of fresh herbs on the window sill. The smell of old Big Whoppers decomposing in their plastic containers was too much.

Back in the hallway, he peered in trepidation through each of the four remaining doors. One led to a huge, plant-filled bathroom, in which the steam of a recent shower and a sweet scent still lingered, swamp-like. Two were bedrooms: one large, neat and impersonal, like a luxury hotel suite awaiting its one-night stand, the other smaller and cluttered with books, clothes and dirty mugs, and dominated by a cast-iron bed that looked not only slept in, but sex-marathoned in too. A twisted wire coathanger lay in the centre of its creased cream duvet like a man-trap.

The final door was Jay's release from this confused arrival. He could forgive Sean any amount of messiness and mad girlfriend revenge when he looked through it. Inside was a darkroom of glorious technicality. Jay only wished he would need to use it while he was in England – but that was about as likely as his ever meeting the extraordinary subjects of the photographs Sean Glenn had left behind on his drying racks.

It was past midnight when Juno got home, and she was somewhat baffled to find all three bolts on the flat door double-locked, necessitating a lot of key-rattling, cursing and fiddling to get inside. She couldn't remember leaving the place that way, but she'd been hellishly distracted when she'd rushed out earlier.

Kicking off her boots as she wandered through the hall, she was even more perturbed to find that the place looked tidier than she'd left it.

She stopped midway into the sitting room, baffled. Then

she remembered that their cleaning lady, Simmy, had promised to call in and give the place a quick once-over before the photographer Sean was flat-swapping with arrived tomorrow. She must have let herself in after Juno had left for the club.

Relieved that she'd solved the mystery, Juno untied the borrowed shirt from around her waist and looked down at her stomach, where one paltry button restrained her bulging spare tyres from their desired escape route. They'd made it through the zip – blasting it like explosive through a safe door – but the riveted fly button had held firm, unlike the poppers on her lace teddy. At least she was wearing knickers underneath, she mulled dejectedly. She'd heard of a duff joke, but to her knowledge no one had, as yet, been laughed off stage for a muff joke.

Disgusted with herself, she peeled off her ruined leather trousers and dragged the defective teddy over her head without a second thought. The relief was exquisite, especially as the agonisingly tight, sweaty trousers had creased the flesh of her thighs until they resembled raw, pinched pastry, and the waistband had pressed the fabric of her teddy so tightly to her belly that it had indented its pattern and she was now wearing a temporary red lace belt. She kicked the trousers hard across the floor and headed through to the kitchen for a juice, pausing briefly to blow a kiss at Uboat, who was balancing on her plastic reef and looking lovingly at her.

'I know you love me, darling,' she sighed, wondering if she could resist slobbing in front of late-night cable TV before heading to bed.

She did a double-take when she opened the fridge. Not only were there about twenty cans of Diet Coke inside which she was certain hadn't been there earlier, but yesterday's half-eaten curry take-out, which she'd been looking forward to finishing, had disappeared, along with her yoghurt and avocado face-pack mix and half a whiffy St Paulin her friend Lydia had brought back from France the previous week.

'And where's my chocolate penis disappeared to?' She peered deeper inside.

'Who the fuck are you?' demanded a furiously angry voice behind her.

Spinning around in fright, she took in the glorious sight of a long-haired, narrow-hipped Adonis wearing nothing but a towel. Burglars don't wear towels, she told herself logically, noticing that he also had a pair of scuffed biker boots on his feet.

'I'm Juno,' she squeaked nervously. 'Nice outfit.'

Jay backed off in horror. With the steely blue light of the refrigerator behind her, this mad woman was standing there in nothing but a pair of cream lace panties.

'*You're* Juno?' he managed to croak.

'I'm afraid so. Don't tell me – you're Jay?' She was desperately trying to cover herself up with a carton of Covent Garden soup and a packet of ready-mixed salad. 'Welcome to London. Now, if you don't mind, I think I'll go to bed – it's been a long day.'

Squeezing past him, she fled into the messy bedroom and slammed the door behind her.

Jay kicked shut the refrigerator and headed for the phone to dial his own apartment in New York.

It was eight in the evening there, and Sean clearly hadn't arrived yet. Jay listened to his own voice up until the beep and left a furious message, demanding to know why Sean had left his flat in a complete mess with an incumbent mad woman in it. Feeling better, if still confused and slightly freaked, he headed back to bed, carefully locking the door behind him.

Chapter Two

'And your teddy flap flew out of your flies?' Lydia shrieked. 'In front of all those people? On stage?'

'Poked out like some sort of obscene tongue.' Juno groaned as she remembered. 'It was so awful. The zip had completely bust so I couldn't do it up again. I just pretended it was part of the act, but I went down like a blue movie at a funeral after that. Then, when I got home, this mad American bloke leapt out at me.'

'You *what*? In your flat?' Lydia was horrified, her beautiful face suddenly wide-eyed with concern.

Juno nodded. 'I practically died of fright – he appeared from nowhere, like a pervy stalker or something, wearing just a towel and biker boots. I thought my hour had come.'

'Who was he? Did he run away? Did you call the police?'

'No.' She sank her face into her hands with a low moan. 'It was the guy my brother's doing a flat swap with. Jay Mulligan – the photographer from New York. I thought he was arriving tonight.'

'Jesus!' Lydia giggled. 'What's he like? Did he say much?'

'Not a great deal.' Juno kept her hands over her eyes.

Lydia's office chair creaked as she sank back into it again. 'But he saw the funny side when he realised who you were?'

'Um, not exactly.'

She rubbed her eyes and resurfaced, peering blearily at Lydia. 'He was still in bed when I got up for work this morning. I left him a note to apologise. I guess I'll have to formally introduce myself again tonight. I just hope he recognises me with my clothes – '

'Invite him along to your birthday meal!' Lydia interjected excitedly. 'Then we can all meet him. Is he good-looking?'

'I'm not sure.' Juno tried to remember the vision in a towel she had gazed at in fear and amazement the previous night, but she'd been too terrified and then too embarrassed to take him in properly. She seemed to recall he had longish fair hair, sinewy shoulders and one of those Celtic band tattoos around his right bicep, but his actual face was impossible to picture apart from two glaring eyes, which had flashed a lot of white before averting their gaze from her naked flesh.

'He has a nice torso,' she remembered vaguely.

'In that case you'll *have* to invite him tonight,' Lydia said determinedly. 'We have absolutely no single men coming apart from Jez, and at least three single women – four if you count Lulu the Zulu. He has to fancy one of us.'

Juno managed a weak smile, knowing full well whom he was expected to fancy. With her slithering white-gold mane and playful eyes as blue and intoxicating as curaçao, Lydia was the siren of the group, and few resisted her charms.

'I thought you were going to bring . . . um . . . Claude?' Juno asked, struggling to remember the name of Lydia's latest amour – a small, beetle-browed French flautist with an athletic tongue.

'I'm going off him a bit.' She wrinkled her beautiful nose. 'He's so boringly possessive.'

Juno sighed, shooting her friend an amused shock-horror look. Lydia's high turnover of boyfriends always became either 'boringly possessive' or 'ridiculously jealous' after a while. Understandably, as Lydia was a woman whom almost every man she met wanted to wine and dine, then bed and breakfast.

The tall, angular product of a former 'fifties tennis icon and a six-foot Swedish au pair thirty years his junior, Lydia looked like a Gucci girl and ate about as little to maintain a figure so lithe that her ribs showed even through a fur coat.

Her Timotei-girl, white-blonde hair was – unlike Juno's – as natural as her white-hot sex appeal. She had extraordinary energy for someone who consumed fewer calories than the skinniest members of the Royal Ballet. She and Juno had known one another for almost five years, had shared a grotty flat in Camden for two of those, and were now inseparable friends despite an oil and water contrast between them which went way beyond the tall, slim girl with short, fat friend visual joke.

'How old is he?' Lydia was still checking out Jay's suitability.

'Late twenties,' Juno guessed, wincing as she realised that this was a bracket in which she no longer belonged.

'Rich?' Lydia never minded appearing obvious – life was too short and so were most of the men she dated. Her particular penchant was for small, intense dark men who – unable to believe their luck in attracting her attention in the first place – charmed her like mad and then became wildly jealous when she treated them badly.

'Not sure,' Juno laughed. 'But there was a lot of very expensive-looking camera equipment piled up in the sitting room this morning and he'd set up one of those flashy little laptops with lots of wires poking out. I thought it was a bomb at first.'

'Oh, please invite him along,' Lydia implored, blue eyes dancing with excitement. 'I've never dated an American.'

'He might not be straight,' Juno told her.

'Of course he is.' Lydia pooh-poohed the suggestion, twiddling a long strand of glossy hair around her pen and gazing thoughtfully at her computer screen. 'I bet he's devastating – New Yorkers have a reputation for machismo. I'm going to have to pick up my Joseph trousers from the dry cleaners after all. You'll have to wear your new top, of course.'

'Mmm.' Juno glanced dubiously at the small bundle of lacy fabric sitting on top of a pile of crumpled wrapping paper on her desk. Lydia's gift was amazingly generous, as usual – a whisper of a designer shirt in feather-weight chiffon lace. She'd called it 'a birthday present to show off your birthday suit' but had, as ever, completely neglected to visualise what Juno would look like in it.

Juno was dreading another encounter with Jay Mulligan if she sported it – she had a feeling he'd seen far more than he wanted to of her birthday suit already. A generous size sixteen, with breasts straight out of a Russ Meyer movie and hips you could rest pints on, she knew that the lace top would emphasise all her worst bulges. It would look far better on Lydia, with her sculpted frame, pert little ice cream-scoop tits and long, slender neck. But Juno would wear it to please her friend tonight, even if it did mean looking like a bundle of King Edward's in a greengrocer's net.

'I'm thirty,' she groaned, ignoring the phone that had starting ringing on her desk. It was a statement she had been repeating all day in the hope that it would eventually start to sound better.

'Not even at your sexual prime.' Lydia didn't look up from her computer screen. She had been cheerfully rebuffing her friend's mantra with encouraging little truisms since nine o'clock that morning.

'You've been at your sexual prime for almost a decade and you're still only twenty-seven,' Juno pointed out. 'I'm already over the hill and have yet to achieve an orgasm with a man in the same room. At this rate I'll have taken to marital aids before marriage.'

Laughing, Lydia's eyes crinkled up in delight and she gave up on her game of computerised Solitaire. 'Are you going to pick that up?' She nodded at Juno's phone.

'Nope.' Juno leant back in her chair and sighed. 'I'm too depressed. Say I'm in a meeting with my maker.'

'It's not being thirty that's getting you down.' Lydia pressed three buttons on her own phone to intercept the call. 'It's being a miserable, unshagged old bag. Juno Glenn's desk . . . it's Lydia here. Oh, hi, darling – how are you getting on?' She settled back with a smile on her face and shot Juno a wink.

Watching her crabbily, Juno realised that her caller was clearly male and eligible enough to be called 'darling', which made him one of two people – her brother Sean or her ex, John. The thought that it might be the latter made her clench her hands in trepidation. There'd been no card this morning, but she'd guessed he might call. It was just his style – remembering her birthday when it was too late to catch the post, and then calling to announce schmoozily that he'd got her a card and present and wanted to meet for a drink to give them to her.

His half-hearted attempts to resurrect their relationship were almost more hurtful than his initial announcement that he'd been seeing someone else behind Juno's back and wanted to live with her. Not easy when saddled with a joint-mortgage on a small Clapham terraced house that was in negative equity. Juno had been so shell-shocked and angry that she'd done totally the wrong thing by packing her bags and leaving the two of them to move in together there, instead of staying put and waiting for him to move out. She'd just slunk across London into Sean's spare room and hidden there for days on end, crying so much that her brother – a vat of tea and sympathy at first – had finally developed compassion-fatigue and complained that she was causing a damp patch on his polished wooden flooring.

Now, two months later, Double D Debbie had walked out on John and he was trying to crawl back into Juno's life. Not that he was trying very hard. When he could be bothered – which was about once a week, usually around midnight when he'd been in the pub all night – he would phone up and tell her that he loved her and needed to see her. Suspecting that he only wanted a shag, Juno would be soothing and sympathetic and tell him to phone back the next day so that they could meet for lunch or a drink to talk about it. After she'd hung up, the prospect of such a meeting always preoccupied and flustered her far more than she was ready to admit, and she would start to dwell lovingly upon the good times they'd had, conveniently blanking out the agony at the end. But he never did call the next day, and another week would go past before the phone rang again in the middle of the night. The last time he'd called, he hadn't even bothered to mute the sound on the pornographic film he was watching in the background as he'd offered to pay her cab fare to Clapham. Juno sometimes wondered if he called Double D Debbie before or after he called her.

'No, still single,' Lydia was giggling. 'You know me – why settle down when there's always a lovely new man out there to settle up for me?' She shot Juno a look which clearly said that she was happy talking for as long as it took.

Juno whispered: 'Is it John?'

When Lydia nodded in response, she mimed cutting her throat and mouthed, 'I'm not here.'

Escaping to the office loo, she found to her horror that she'd had ink all over her hands when she'd pressed them to her face and now looked as though her cheeks and forehead were covered with some sort of ritualistic tribal tattoo.

Back in the office, Lydia had hung up and was again playing Solitaire with her computer whilst chatting to Finlay from advertising sales, who was squatting on Juno's chair opposite her, spinning round and round on the swivel like a child.

'Hi, sugar,' he greeted Juno cheerfully, not stopping his pirouettes. 'Happy Birthday.'

A beautiful Scottish drug addict straight out of the Ewan McGregor *Trainspotting* mould, Finlay was completely hopeless at his job but too good a supplier of Colombian angel dust for the ad director to fire. All the female members of staff adored his bountiful bounder's charm and sweet, hapless inefficiency. He possessed the face of a cherubic toddler, which was totally incongruous with his tall, skinny frame. His hair was a floppy blond mop of Little Lord Fauntleroy curls, his wide-set eyes huge, thick-lashed and the palest silver-grey, his lips as plump and pink as marshmallows. Only the broken nose and chipped front tooth hinted of a misspent youth and lost soul. He barely ever sat at his own desk. He just drifted around the office like a beautiful stray dog, pausing to be patted and admired or to flirt and play.

As he whizzed in circles on Juno's chair his head continually faced front like a ballet dancer's, only twisting around at the last second. All the time he smiled and laughed and blew Lydia kisses. Juno watched him in awe, wondering whether his boundless energy came from cocaine or the fact that he was still under thirty.

When he finally drifted off to scrounge biscuits from Uma, the cuddly production department secretary who adored him like a prodigal son, Juno reclaimed her seat – which was now so low to the ground she was staring at her top drawer. She cranked her way back up until she could once again see Lydia over her In Tray.

'Oh, there you are.' Her friend smiled at her sweetly. 'That was Sean on the phone. He's just had breakfast in the coffee bar Jay recommended on the corner of the block, and says that the waitress there looks like Winona Ryder. He wanted to know if his watch is still in the bathroom at home. He thinks he left it on the side of the bath. Also, he asked me to tell you not to run around naked in front of Jay in future, because apparently you freaked him out last night. What else? Oh, yes. He said Happy Birthday. Bugger – I've just missed an ace.'

'That was Sean?' Juno gaped at her.

'I told you it was.' Lydia looked up innocently.

'I asked if it was John!'

Lydia cocked her head patiently. 'Go back to that mirror you've just been staring into, mouth "John" and then "Sean", try to spot the difference and then come back and tell me about it.'

Juno gritted her teeth. 'I'm going to lunch.'

'Don't tell me Mel's taking you out for your birthday?' Lydia giggled. 'That *is* generous!'

Mel was the office block's notoriously mean security guard, a neckless ape with bad breath and a crush on Juno, which he had once flatteringly announced was because 'big women are better in bed'.

'No, he gave me a potted fig.' Juno dragged a comb through her hair. 'I'm meeting Triona.'

'Better not mention the Winona Ryder lookalike then.' Lydia was still buzzing her mouse around as she settled red cards on black. 'So how come you stripped off in front of this Jay guy last night? I know you're always moaning on

18

about being desperate for a shag, but I think that's a bit keen, Joo.'

'I was giving him a good old British welcome,' she muttered. 'Waving the Union Jacksy.'

Chapter Three

Juno's office was located at the northern end of Tottenham Court Road, just a few minutes' walk from Triona's tiny, eccentrically decorated Fitzrovia flat. It always astonished Juno that her brother's girlfriend could pack so much into it. Triona was so tiny and doll-like that she danced between the over-loaded' fifties tables, inflatable Ruth Aram chairs and kitsch lava lamps like a will o' the wisp, barely even disturbing the air as she passed. Being large-legged and clumsy, Juno was always terrified of inadvertently knocking something over and starting a domino effect.

She was therefore hugely relieved when Triona suggested eating out at the little Italian restaurant along the street.

'I just invited you up here first to give you these,' she explained, handing over a large wrapped package with a smaller one balancing on top. 'The big one's from Sean – he asked me to give it to you today. You'll see why I thought you should open it here rather than the restaurant in a minute.'

'Is it that bad?' Juno took the parcel in trepidation. Last year her brother had given her an inflatable male sex doll called Randy Andy. Six months later, Sean had dressed him up as Santa Claus for Christmas and driven him along the M40 in the back of his car, much to their parents' amusement when the plastic stranger had arrived on their doorstep with tinsel attached to all his vibrating parts. Juno had been appalled, as had the dogs who had launched into a savage attack. Randy Andy was currently in the barn of her parents' house with a slow puncture.

Triona grimaced and scratched the incredibly short crew-cut which she dyed a different colour every three weeks. 'It's not one of his best, but he was in a rush because of New York.' She narrowed her eyes, still furious with Sean for leaving her behind. 'Pig.'

Beneath the retro' seventies wrapping paper was a large yellow plastic toy box with THIRTIES EMERGUNCY KIT emblazoned on one side.

'He apologises for spelling emergency wrong.' Triona bit her lip to hide a smile. 'But he ran out of Letraset Es and the shops were closed.'

Sean had packed the box with an array of tasteless items – a pair of zip-up sheepskin granny boots, a heated massage pad, a set of Carmen rollers, some hair dye especially designed to hide grey, leaflets about Saga holidays, an Omar Sharif *Play Bridge* video, several Daniel O'Donnel compact discs, a jar of Estée Lauder time-defying capsules, a bottle of gin, and three pairs of support tights. Nestling at the bottom of the box, beneath a pamphlet advertising a Harley Street cosmetic surgeon's radical new Facial Peel technique, was a self-help book on growing old.

Saying nothing, Juno carefully repacked each item and closed the lid with a plastic click.

'It's the thought that counts,' Triona said carefully.

'Yes,' muttered Juno, 'and if Sean really works on it, he may be able to count to six in a few years' time.'

'God, I miss the silly sod.' Triona kicked the toy box in irritation. 'I was so furious with him last night for leaving me behind that I collected together all the stuff he'd left here and jumped up and down on top of it wearing stilettos.' She waggled her own small package at Juno and winked. 'And, remember, I'm already thirty-seven.'

'That's not the point,' Juno sniffed despondently, taking it from her. 'You're far younger than me in spirit.'

The second package contained a fake snakeskin g-string and matching balcony bra.

'What do I need with these?' Juno laughed in amazement, pulling out a triangular nylon pad from one of the bra cups. 'My boobs already arrive at a party ten minutes before I do.'

'It's our latest line.' Triona tried not to look miffed. 'I had to order it 'specially in your size. It'll look magnificent, and besides, you have to take the pads out to smuggle your drugs into clubs these days. No bouncer can tell the difference between a foam rubber support and three grams of coke.'

Triona Eastford and her ex-husband ran Soho's infamously trendy lingerie shop, Fame Fatale, which had such an inter-national reputation that it was considered one of the area's top tourist attractions. Not only did they stock the sauciest collections from the designer houses, but also created their own-label garments which were pure fantasy.

An unstoppable party animal, Triona was a well-known figure on London's club scene where her gamine frame popped up at only the most controversial and exclusive of clubs, wearing only the most cutting-edge of clothes – which were usually more cut than cloth.

Her business partner and ex-husband, Marky Eastford – a startling red-head with pierced lips – had trained as a fashion designer at nearby St Martins in the 'eighties and married Triona in a Las Vegas Elvis chapel when they were both still students, a few months before he came out of the bisexual closet and moved in with a then chorus dancer from *Cats*. But by this time Triona was already pregnant with their son, Bolan, who now divided his time between London and California, where his 'second father', the former chorus dancer, was one of the biggest-grossing Hollywood stars of the moment. In one of the most peculiar twists of logic Juno had ever known, he and Marky were no longer a couple, but the actor had won partial custody in an American court, and Bolan was so attached to him that Triona and Marky had done nothing to fight it. Consequently, the boy spent a large part of the year floating around a Beverly Hills swimming pool on a lilo shaped like a limousine while both his biological parents lived and worked in London. The arrangement seemed to suit everyone ideally.

Throughout the 'eighties and 'nineties, Triona had dated a host of famous men, most of whom had at least two registered addictions, three ex-wives, several houses and a problem child. Since coupling up with Sean – who had come to photograph the Soho shop for a piece in the *Face* – she had settled down to her longest known spell of monogamy. She had also started a one-woman crusade to squeeze Juno into crotchless French knickers and baby-doll nighties, continually pronouncing that barely there undies were as sexy on big women as they were on skinnies.

'I'm sure they'll look fantastic – thanks.' Juno gave her a guilty kiss. 'D'you mind if I leave them here and collect them another time?'

'Of course not.' Triona was already turning on her answerphone and hunting for her keys in anticipation of leaving. 'I'll drop them round tonight on my way to Trash. I'm picking up some friends in Primrose Hill, so you're almost next door, and it'll give me a chance to collect those Westwood mules I left in Sean's room last week – I've just got to wear them tonight.'

Juno hid a smile as she realised Triona was heading for one of the biggest, seediest and hardest to enter nights in the clubbing calendar. So much for crying over Sean. Having danced on his clothes last night, she'd clearly decided to put her crazy taste in shoes to better use and party on without him.

'I won't be in,' Juno suddenly remembered. 'We're all going to The House for a meal.'

'I'll let myself in with my own keys, then.' Triona turned on the burglar alarm and hustled her out of the door. 'I'll just leave the stuff, grab my shoes and say hi to Poirot and that revolting reptile dinghy of yours.'

'And Jay,' Juno muttered darkly as she waited in the hallway.

'The photographer?' Triona joined her, pulling the door shut and shrugging into a tiny Alexander McQueen jacket at the same time. 'Is he already here? I thought he was arriving on the red-eye tonight?'

'So did I.' Juno pulled a face.

'What's he like? I didn't get to meet him in New York.'

'I don't really know yet,' Juno confessed. 'Quite short and gingery, I think.'

'Sounds a bit grim.' Triona started to pick her way down the stairs on five-inch rubber platform Doc Marten's. 'I'll give him a wide berth later. Aren't you going to ask him to The House with your cronies then?'

'I might.' Juno followed her, racing to keep up. 'I don't think I gave him a very good first impression, to be honest.'

'Oh, he'll learn to love you,' Triona laughed, moving incredibly stealthily given the heels. 'Sean obviously thinks he's a superstar, although he did have a few reservations about letting him use the flat.'

'He did?' Juno yelped in alarm, still scuttling after her and almost flying down the bottom five steps.

Already standing on the mansion block's marble hall floor, Triona looked up from examining her second post.

'What sort of reservations?' Juno asked nervously. All sorts of possibilities were flashing through her mind now. A drug addiction? A criminal record? He had a tattoo, after all. Mind you, Sean had several, as did Triona. Sexual perversion? A history of mental illness? Hatred of women? Or perhaps he liked wearing their clothes? She'd noticed her red satin shirt was missing that morning, plus several other things she was certain she'd left in the sitting room. *That* was it.

'Don't tell me he's a transvestite?' she groaned.

Triona burst out laughing. 'Now *that* is classic Juno.' She hooked her arm through her friend's. 'Only you could come up with that. Let's talk about it over lunch.'

'Sean says he's one of the hottest photographers in New York,' Triona explained through a mouthful of antipasto a few minutes later.

'Sean would say that.' Juno spat an olive pip into her palm

24

and washed the pulp down with some Orvieto. 'My brother's got an ego the size of China.'

'Not Sean, you prat – Jay. Apparently every picture editor worth his salt beef on rye in New York knows Jay's number by heart. He is to reportage what Meisel is to fashion – you name somewhere you wouldn't want to take your summer holiday and he's been there in the past five years: Zaire, Afghanistan, Bosnia, Algeria, Tibet, Angola.'

'You're kidding me, right?' Juno swallowed an olive whole in surprise.

'His nickname's the Jaywalker because he doesn't care where he goes to get a good shot, and he takes ludicrous risks. He's legendary for having nerves of steel, for hanging around a war zone ten minutes after everyone else has scrammed and getting the pictures the rest of the pack know they would have died for. And he almost has, several times – next time you encounter him in a towel, check for bullet wounds.'

'Wow!' Juno whistled, starting to wonder exactly who she'd flashed in front of last night. 'So what's he covering over here? Not the Labour Party Conference, I'll be bound.'

'Not unless he's had a tip-off from his friends in the IRA.' Triona shrugged.

'Now you have to be fucking kidding!' Another olive sailed down whole and Juno started coughing frantically.

Triona patted her hard on the back. 'I wouldn't put it past him – or rather Sean wouldn't. He brought the idea up when we were trying to figure out what Jay wanted to come to England for. He wouldn't tell Sean a thing – completely blanked him out when he asked. And a lot of these Irish Americans are decidedly pro the Cause, you know. Particularly in New York.'

Her eyes starting to run, Juno fought to clear her passageway and spluttered, 'Are you suggesting I'm sharing a flat with a terrorist?'

'No, Juno, of course I'm not,' said Triona dismissively. 'I haven't a clue what he's doing over here – nor has Sean. All we know is that he's told his agency in New York that he's taking six months' sabbatical – i.e. the only thing he's planning on shooting is the breeze. Not a great move when you've just held one of the most successful exhibitions ever housed by the ICP.'

'What's that?'

'The International Center of Photography. Uptown New York. We're talking big, big time here. Sean can only dream of that sort of league. Jay's done other work as well as reportage – special commissions, thematic studies, portraits. Did you know Mapplethorpe actually asked Jay to shoot him before he died of AIDS? Can you imagine that? *Mapplethorpe*.'

Juno's jaw was swinging now. 'Mapplethorpe asked Jay Mulligan to kill – '

'A photograph, Juno. He asked him to take his photograph.'

'Oh.'

'Go to the Dillon's on Long Acre and look at the photography books. I bet you a tenner he's in there. And he's single, you know.' Triona grinned wickedly.

'You do surprise me.' Juno widened her eyes hammily. 'Aren't there women out there who love tending graves? I'm sure they'll snap him up next time he's off on a jaunt to jaywalk through Rwanda.'

'Sean says he's just your type.' Triona's dark green eyes glittered.

'Thanks, but I'm not sure the visiting hours at the Maze would fit in with my schedule.' Juno pulled a face. 'I can't believe my brother would willingly let a strange man, possibly a key member of an active cell, come and plot unknown treason from within our sitting room. You know, there was something that looked suspiciously like a bomb on the table this morning. I thought it was a laptop, but now I'm not so sure.'

'I wish I hadn't said anything.' Triona poured her some more wine. 'I thought you'd be as fascinated as I am.'

'I bet he's in the darkroom making triggering devices as we speak. It's perfect for it.' Juno crunched another olive manically. 'I hope he doesn't use one of my bloody alarm clocks – it's hard enough getting up in the morning as it is.'

Realising that Juno was winding her up, Triona threw a piece of ciabatta at her and laughed.

'You're thirty, hon.' Triona's witchy little face was all smiles. 'From now on you're going to have to get a lot more sleep – preferably with a younger man. Jay's twenty-seven.'

Chapter Four

He was clearly out when Juno arrived home that evening, rushing to get ready for her night out because, as ever, she was running desperately late.

Setting the taps in the bathroom running, she galloped through to the bedroom to fetch her towel, then slowly backtracked as something occurred to her.

'No watch,' she muttered, searching every surface in the bathroom. 'Sean's watch isn't here. He said he'd left it on the side of the bath.'

After a quick check that Jay was definitely not in the flat, she nipped into the darkroom to nose around.

'Sean, you bastard!' she wailed as she immediately came face-to-face with a large picture of a familiar kipper tie nestling between two glistening orbs of flesh.

He had left the blow-ups from a recent drunken photo-shoot hanging on the drying racks. In them, Juno, Triona and her friend Souxi, and Sean's mate Horse, were re-enacting Abba in all their gruesome disco tat. They'd done it whilst spending a weekend in Cornwall where Sean and Horse liked to surf, and had smuggled themselves into the local Butlin's camp to do a *Muriel's Wedding*-style impersonation for the Talent Contest. Unfortunately they'd forgotten to bring along their backing tape and, trying 'Thank You For The Music' a cappella had proved an irony beyond the audience's comprehension. They had been booed off stage.

Triona looked predictably gorgeous as Agnetha, in a blonde fringed wig and crocheted sequin skull cap, her slim, tanned legs stretching endlessly from white hot-pants. Souxi was similarly minxy as a Japanese Freda, with red-sprayed, crimped hair and a silver space suit. Even Horse – who was a dope-smoking freelance music journalist with a bandy body and Jim Morrison manners – made a passable Bjorn. But Juno, dressed in an old velvet suit of her father's with flares as wide as the M25 even after they'd been taken up ten inches with staples, looked diabolical as Benny. Sweating heavily and wearing a fake beard that had given her a rash for weeks afterwards because Sean had glued it on with Copydex, she looked frighteningly like Peter Sutcliffe. The arms of the suit came down so low she also resembled a chimpanzee, and the jacket clearly wouldn't do up at the front, where her boobs had burst through a cheap frilly shirt so that her bra was in full view – a red rubber one Triona had insisted she wear. To her fury, Sean had taken six or seven close-ups of her cleavage.

'Bastard,' she repeated, ripping up the worst of the boob shots. She was so spitting mad that she made only the most cursory of inspections for evidence of bomb-making activity (there wasn't any) before stomping back to her running bath. Her mood wasn't improved by finding that she'd forgotten to put the plug in.

Trying to calm down, she switched on the stereo and had a manic dance around the flat to the latest Pulp CD, not noticing that for once it was clear-going underfoot, without the usual debris of clothes, magazines and fast-food containers. She opened a bottle of wine in order to indulge in a quick drink while she was having her bath, but was still so distracted about the booby Benny mug-shots that she carried the entire bottle into the bathroom, forgetting to dispense any of it into a glass. Nor did she remember to collect her towel from her bed.

After a quick soak and a scrub, she slugged some of the bottle into the tooth mug and noticed a new line of toiletries abutting her own gunky collection. They were unfamiliar American brand names and included moisturiser, toner and shave balm.

Juno stared at them in wonder. She had never known a man to use moisturiser, and hadn't a clue what shave balm was. Out of interest, she tried some out on her legs, over which she'd just dragged a blunt Bic. It smelled delicious – like freshly cut grass. Fascinated, she got carried away and used up almost half the tube before remembering how late she was going to be.

Just as she was racing from the shower to her bedroom wearing a small bleach-stained hand towel and carrying the bottle of red wine, Jay let himself through the front door, clutching a wad of newspapers. Juno was too slow to make a run for it. They met just inches apart on the hall carpet.

'Hi,' he muttered uncomfortably, taking an inordinately long time to remove his key from the far side of the door, behind which most of his body was still sheltering. He politely averted his gaze from her bath-heated flesh.

Juno stood rooted to the spot, momentarily blown away by what she was looking at.

She hadn't appreciated quite how glorious he was the night before. He wasn't particularly tall – maybe five nine or ten – but he was beautifully built, and his hair was the most mesmerising colour, like pale golden treacle on buttered toast, almost down to his shoulders and falling in long, unkempt layers at the front so that it mingled seductively with his pale lashes. He was not conventionally handsome either, but possessed the most staggering pair of eyes Juno had ever encountered – long, slanting and the same yellow-gold colour as that lion's mane hair. The combination was devastating.

Shooting out broody, disconsolate vibes, he looked the height of bad-boy-from-the-Bronx chic, and also a dead ringer for Mickey Rourke as an IRA man in *Prayer for the Dying*. As he inched his way through the door, Juno took in the heavy, scuffed knee-length leather jacket, white t-shirt, faded Levis and chunky biker boots. It was pure anti-hero. She wondered if he'd just made contact with his cell leader – perhaps meeting in a dingy Kilburn pub to drink Guinness and discuss the Cause?

'Hi there, Jay,' she greeted him in what she hoped was a spontaneous and husky rasp, aware that she must have been staring unblinkingly at him for several seconds and freaking him out somewhat. 'I don't know what it is about you, but I only have to look at you and I feel naked.' She shrugged, pulled a comic face at her pathetically scanty towel, and grinned goofily.

It was a very weak crack and he clearly didn't get it. In fact he started to back behind the door again, golden eyebrows curling towards one another worriedly. They were gorgeous eyebrows, she noticed – strongly delineated, sootier in tone than his hair and curving above his drop-dead sexy eyes with the exquisite geometry of a Beardsley sketch. Juno had always been a sucker for eyebrows. In her critically attuned estimation, his were one up from Christopher Plummer's, one short of Dirk Bogarde's. Scorching eyebrows in fact.

'Sorry – it was just a joke,' she said hastily, realising that she'd have to do some conversational donkey work to stop herself from looking a complete ass. 'Listen, why don't you pour us out a couple of glasses of this,' she waggled the wine at him, 'and I'll just get dressed? Then we can have a quick chat before I have to go out – although you're welcome to come along if you're free. It's just a meal with some friends of mine. We should get to know each other better.' She winced, realising how crass that sounded.

'I don't drink,' he said flatly, taking the proffered bottle with some difficulty as he tried to keep a hold on the papers in his arms.

'You must get awfully thirsty,' Juno said cheerfully.

'Huh?' Not for a moment did that smooth, wide mouth break into a smile. It was a wonderfully sensual mouth – the top lip shaped like the shank of a cello, Juno decided light-headedly – not entirely symmetrical, but exquisitely proportioned nonetheless.

'You must get a bit dehydrated,' she muttered vaguely, still contemplating his mouth. 'Not drinking.'

The lips twitched irritably. 'I meant, I don't drink alcohol.'

'Oh.' Juno was instantly appalled. She was stuck with a tee-total flatmate for six months. It would be torture. 'Well, in that case, I'll have it back.' With a forced, jokey laugh, she snatched back the bottle rather clumsily, making him drop most of his newspapers, and causing her tiny towel to plunge dangerously from beneath her elbows. Yelping in alarm, she shot through her bedroom door and closed it behind her.

For a moment she barely breathed as she heard him gather his papers with a crisp crunch, and then head through to the sitting room.

'Shit!' she whispered, finally letting the towel drop and taking a huge swig straight from the bottle. 'He thinks I'm a bloody loony. I've got to make up for this.'

She was supposed to be meeting her friends at Bar Room in Hampstead at eight. It was already twenty to, but she knew they'd give her at least an hour, if not more. She was notoriously late for everything, and the table at the nearby restaurant, The House, wasn't booked until ten. That easily gave her enough time to convince Jay what a terrific, sane person she was, and persuade him to come along and meet the gang. Lydia, for one, would die of happiness when she saw him.

She pulled on a pair of black waisty pants and said a silent apology to Triona before clipping together her favourite front-loader bra, which she'd nick-named her 'robustier'. Most of Juno's bras gave her the ultimate plunge neckline – they were falling apart and so tight that she fell out of them. This one looked decent enough to show under the lace shirt Lydia had given her. Then she groaned.

The lace shirt was still in her handbag in the sitting room. Not only that, but the linen trousers she had intended to wear with it and had washed that morning were still lying wet in the plastic laundry skip, waiting to be hung out to dry.

To give herself time to think, she slapped on some make-up and combed through her damp hair, wincing as she realised how many dark roots were showing through. She made a mental note to go to Boots first thing the following morning and bulk-buy hair bleach.

'This is ridiculous!' she told her reflection. 'You're a thirty-year-old woman.'

It was already eight, she wasn't dressed, her friends would any minute now be arriving at the bar to wish her a Happy Birthday, and she was hiding in her room plotting the best way to retrieve her clothes in front of a strange man who had nice hair and questionable political leanings.

Then her eyes alighted on the Peruvian birthing smock her parents had given her for her birthday, telling her it would make a nice night-shirt. Now that *was* cool.

Jay spread out all the papers on the floor of the sitting room, which he had cleared earlier, and then sat back on the sofa without looking at them at all. The turtle was peering at him again, perching on a rock this time. It freaked him out. As did the foul-mouthed macaw, which he was convinced had mange.

'Fuck off!' screeched Poirot, and then did an impersonation of an incoming call that made Jay get up and head for the farthest oak table, on which sat a huge digital fax-phone.

The bird had been doing the ringing trick all day, and no matter how often he heard it, Jay still kept picking up the damn' receiver and saying 'hi'.

'Tenner on the three-fifteen!' Poirot chortled, edging along his perch and cocking his head to look more closely at Jay.

He shut his eyes and listened to the dialling tone for a moment or two, wondering whether to call Sean and announce he was flying back tomorrow and to get the hell out of his apartment. But opening his eyes again, he looked straight out at that glorious view of London, sharp and crisp in the foreground where the falling sun cast long, monochrome shadows across the gardens and roof terraces, then misty and mysterious farther out, where the tower blocks receded into a haze of pollution. He knew he had to stay. He had no choice.

He wandered through to the kitchen to fetch himself a Diet Coke, and stiffened as he realised that Juno had dumped a half-eaten kebab straight on the zinc surface, along with a corkscrew and wine bottle foil. He'd spent close on two hours washing up, scrubbing and cleaning the dirt out of every crevice earlier. The girl was a total slob. He scooped the lot – corkscrew included – into the swing bin and headed back through to the sitting room.

'Still changing!' announced a bright voice, and he stopped in amazement as he saw a plump figure in a huge, beaded blue sack dress sidling out of the room, clutching a flimsy piece of lace to her chest.

Almost through the door, her head popped back into the room. She only had one eye made-up, he noticed.

'Er – I don't suppose you know what happened to the clothes that were lying around on the floor in here, do you?'

'Sure I know.' He gave her a withering look. 'They're in the wash tub.'

'But some of those are dry clean only!' she yelped.

'I didn't say I added powder and water, did I?' he muttered. 'I just put them in there as there was no closet space anywhere.'

'Oh – good thinking.' She winked and disappeared into her room.

Jay went for a pee and found his tube of shave balm lying half-empty in the sink with the cap off, and the tooth mug full of red wine.

As he washed it out, he could hear music suddenly start up in the sitting room – some sort of awful Britpop drone, which he detested. He wondered vaguely if he should stay put and have a long soak in a hot tub, but decided that wouldn't be the greatest way of trying to get on with this girl.

When he walked back in, Juno was dancing opposite Poirot waving a glass of red wine in her hand. The scraggy red parrot was bobbing up and down excitedly on his perch, shrieking 'Fuck off!' in between phone impersonations.

'It's all so beau-oo-tif-ewel,' sang Juno in a surprisingly tune-ful voice, far too carried away with her Small Faces singalong to notice Jay watching her from the doorway.

He had to admit she looked pretty reasonable with her clothes on. She looked better than that – she looked something close to what the Bronx homeboys called a butter babe: plump, pale-skinned and curved like a ripe yam. His old man used to call women like Juno '*zoftig*'. And there was no denying she dressed to emphasise her voluptuous, fleshy contours rather than to hide them. The nip-waisted purple satin jacket was unbuttoned to reveal a lacy black shirt with plunging neckline. A pair of amazing striped velvet 'seventies flares hugged her generous hips in all the right places and led down to high patent leather boots with dinky wooden heels inset with metal. Most women of her size would have looked ridiculous, but matched with Juno's cheeky smile and glossy blonde bob, the effect was of a girl who just wanted to have funky dress sense and almost got away with it.

She had a soft, sweet face under all the make-up, Jay realised. Her eyes were huge and the same flecked grey as a roan pony.

'Those boots are really neat,' he said, wandering into the room.

'Cheers.' Juno waggled the glass at him and her dance ground to a halt.

Jay cleared his throat and sat down on the sofa again. She had a funny way of looking at him – she'd done the same in the hallway earlier. It was unsettling.

Juno was in fact calculating just how to approach this potential IRA connection. She decided to arm herself with information first.

'Seeing what the other photographers are up to?' She pointed to the spread-out newspapers as she headed to the oak table closest to the kitchen.

'Something like that.' Jay swept his hair from his eyes.

She picked up a packet of cigarettes and drew one out, watching him closely. 'So do you do the same sort of work as Sean – magazine commissions and the like?'

'Sometimes, yeah.' He shrugged.

God, he was hard work! Juno brooded. And far too sexy to be true. She adored the way his t-shirt sleeves were rolled up to the shoulder, revealing the faded blue Celtic band tattoo on one upper arm. She longed to ask him where he'd had it done, but was trying to sound fascinated by his photography right now. Banging on about his tattoo might sound a bit shallow by comparison.

She popped a cigarette between her lips and gazed at him quizzically. 'And are you covering stuff for the American press agencies while you're over here?'

'Kind of.' Jay was looking at her mouth rather than her eyes, and Juno felt light-headed with a sudden free-fall moment of pure lust. His long, yellow eyes were seriously disturbing, and that sinewy body draped over the rust-coloured silk of the sofa – ludicrously flattering to his colouring – was desirable enough to make a girl dizzy.

You don't fancy him, Juno, she told herself sternly. It's just that you haven't had sex in three months. And the danger element turns you on. Plus he's gazing at your lips.

He shifted uncomfortably on the seat cushions. 'Listen, this might sound kinda anal, but I'm not keen on passive smoking.'

'That's okay – I'm not very keen on it either.' Juno calmly lit up. 'Buy your own, you tight bastard.' She grinned and winked, grateful that her moment of wantonness had been so boringly quashed.

Jay was speechless.

'This place is looking fantastic,' she said, eager to ingratiate herself and avoid a smoking debate. 'You must have been hard at it with the Marigolds all day.'

'Huh?'

'Or did Simmy come after all?' She realised that all the ashtrays had gone missing and wandered through to the kitchen to fetch one.

Jay's voice was tightly controlled, but anger still drilled each word into Juno's skull. 'I cleaned the place up. It looked like a dump.'

She cleared her throat before walking back through to face him again. 'Well, I wasn't expecting you to arrive from the States until tonight.'

'Evidently.' He gave her a withering stare, aimed more at her cigarette than her face.

'Listen, I know I haven't been very – '

'And I'm sorry, but I cannot live with that floating frisbee over there.' His eyes slid to Uboat's tank. 'Can't it be moved?'

'How dare you call Uboat a frisbee!' Juno yelped. 'She's a Florida soft-shell turtle and she's beautiful.'

John had bought Uboat as a present for her twenty-eighth birthday. Two years ago to the day. He had wanted to get her an iguana, but the pet shop had mercifully run out. It had been just a few weeks after they'd moved in together, and they were still at the stage when they baby-kissed while making tea and made love on every new piece of furniture – even Ikea self-assembly coffee tables. That was long before John had complained of being too tired, too drunk, too stressed or too upset about the football results to get it up. Long before he'd wandered in reeking of CKOne, and Juno had complimented him on his new aftershave, not realising it was Double D's perfume. It was only after it was all over that she'd noticed that the bottle he'd bought as a decoy and placed in the bathroom cabinet had never even been opened.

Uboat was the only worthwhile thing she had salvaged from the relationship.

'Turtles are unhygienic.' Jay was still glaring at her broodily, utterly unrepentant. Juno felt her jaw clench.

'Let me get this right.' She perched on one of the scroll-sided altar stools by Uboat's tank so as not to contaminate him with her smoke. 'You don't do alcohol or fags or drugs or turtles or much else apart from Diet Coke, Mr Muscle and Fairy liquid, am I right?'

'Huh?' Jay scratched his chin against his shoulder and looked at her, beautiful brows furled. It was one of the most indolent, sexy gestures Juno had ever seen – pure James Dean.

He was so cool, he was going to give the sofa freezer burns in a minute.

'Is that why you're called Jay?' She cocked her head. 'After the little checked blue cleaning cloths and the fluid?'

It was as though she'd asked him whether his penis was deformed. Jay sprang off the sofa and marched towards her so fast that his nose was practically against hers before she had time to react.

'Let's get one thing straight, lady,' he snarled, his New York drawl ridiculously thick and menacing because his voice was shaking so much, 'I'm called Jay because I am. Period. We're gonna have to share this place for the foreseeable future, and I figure that means we should try to get along. So the sooner you cut out the wisecracks and start treating me like a normal human being, the easier you're gonna make it on yourself.'

Juno flinched nervously. The outburst had been totally without warning. He was starting seriously to scare her. 'First time I've been called a lady in ages,' she said feebly, inching backwards on the stool.

'Will you cut it out?' Jay turned away in despair, pushing his hair from his eyes. 'Jeez, I knew before I came here that the English think foreigners are stoopid and that you all have a sense of humour that ain't funny, but I never thought I'd find myself shacked up with Britannia herself. Christ, you're all so fucking superior over here, you'd think you still had an Empire.'

Juno's eyes flashed warily. 'What makes you say that?'

'Huh?' He looked back at her.

'Why did you say we think we still have an Empire?'

He sighed in exasperation. 'Juno, I don't wanna get into politics right now, okay? You're going out and I've got work to do.'

'What work?' she demanded, starting to get into the swing of her cross-examination. She'd always fancied herself as a barrister, but had been put off by the grey granny-perm wigs.

He pulled back his chin and stared at her in disbelief for a moment before saying in a low, almost amused tone, 'I'm a photographer, Juno. I take photographs – click.' He did a quick mime and then splayed out his fingers, eyebrows raised, condescension creeping into his voice. '*Capisce*, Juno?' He pronounced her name 'Dyoono', she noticed.

'*Capisce*, Dyay.' She tried for a hearty smile, but it came out hugely sickly and suggestive. Then, trying a bit of psychological game-play, she cocked her head and added casually, 'Are you planning on visiting Ireland while you're so close?'

He screwed up his forehead, trying to relate to the sudden change of tack. 'Why should I?'

'I thought all you Irish Americans loved tracing your Celtic roots.' She was rather regretting taking this potentially explosive line now and tried to interject a bit of light-hearted personal interest. 'I have a grandmother in County Sligo. She's Catholic, of course.'

'Is she?' His jaw was quilting with irritation.

'Great old soak.' Juno nodded fervently. 'I stay with her occasionally. It's a very pretty area – lovely scenery to photograph. And wonderful old characters, too. You should pop over there and shoot some people – I mean, rolls. Shoot some rolls.'

He moved towards her again so quickly that for a terrifying moment, Juno thought he was going to make a grab for her throat. But instead he dropped to his haunches in front of her and gripped her shoulder with his hand, his startling gold eyes level with hers and perilously close. They were glittering with irritation.

'Okay, Juno, here's the deal,' he said quietly. 'I've tried to explain this once, but I guess you didn't understand. I'm in England for a purpose – I've come here to do something. Now that might take a week, a month, whatever. And until I get it done, we have to share this apartment.'

She swallowed noisily and flinched as he took the cigarette from her fingers and ground it into the ashtray beside her, his eyes still holding hers with their intense yellow glare, his hand still pinned to her shoulder. What he'd just said filled her with dread. She longed to know what the 'something' he had to do was; it sounded ominous. She was finding it hard to breathe normally now.

'While I'm here,' he went on, a heavy hint of irony lacing the New York drawl, 'I do not want to travel to Ireland and take photographs of your alcoholic grandmother. Or debate fucking politics. Nor do I want to spend half my days cleaning up after you. I don't have the time, do you understand?'

She wasn't entirely sure how her messy laundry fitted into this. 'Not really, I – '

'It's simple, Juno,' he butted in, scratching his chin on his shoulder in that menacing, sexy gesture. 'You're obviously a great girl, I can see that.'

'You can?' she gulped nervously.

'Sure,' he said flatly, not smiling. 'It's just I've got to work from this place, and I get kinda distracted if I've got someone like you in my hair all the time.'

'You do?' Juno was totally intimidated now, and not at all sure whether what he'd just said was intended to be flattering or not.

He nodded, squeezing her shoulder with his hand and tipping his head back so that he could study her face. His stare was so serious and direct that Juno had to curl her toes to stop her knees from shaking. She was certain he was checking out which side to start pistol whipping if she asked any more questions.

'You have mascara on your cheek,' he told her.

'Do I?' she gulped, intensely relieved that it was something so mundane. 'Where? Can you wipe it off for me?'

She hadn't intended anything intimate by the suggestion, but there was something about the slow, deliberate way he lifted his thumb to her face and brushed the smudge away that turned her stomach inside out with excitement. Three parts fear to one part lust ripped through her belly like kerosene under combustion, and she fought a sudden urge to pull his hand to her lips.

At the same moment the phone rang. Juno jumped so violently that her heels played castanets on the wooden floor. Jay's hand didn't even flinch.

Seeming in no hurry, he wiped the last of the mascara from her face, eyes still intently focused on their task.

'That's better.' He tipped his head back again, shaking his butterscotch hair from his eyes. 'You wear too much make-up, you know.'

God, he was anal! Juno smarted with hurt pride. If she weren't quite so scared, she'd clobber him.

Poirot was going berserk now, screaming obscenities between rings. The phone droned on monotonously in accompaniment. Whoever it was knew that the machine would switch itself on and pick up eventually.

'Can you answer that? I'm already late.' Spotting her duffel bag on the sofa, Juno slipped from her stool and made to fetch it, but Jay grabbed her arm and she froze with nerves.

'Friends?' he asked, a hint of a smile lifting the edges of his mouth, but not enough to form a crease in the stubble-dusted skin.

'I never watch it myself,' she muttered, 'but I think it's on Channel Four at nine-thirty. There's a listings magazine some-where if you want to check.' She pulled away and bolted.

She was almost through the door by the time Jay finally picked up the call.

'Hey – it's for you!' He turned back to her. 'Someone called John.'

'Tell him I'm not here,' she muttered, untangling her bag strap from the knob.

'But you are here, Juno.' He gave her an exasperated look.

'Not any more – watch.' She slammed the door after her.

Galloping down the stairs, she encountered Triona coming the other way, carrying the 'Emerguncy' kit.

'You look great!' Triona stopped in her tracks and whis-tled.

Juno smiled gratefully then gaped at Triona's Red or Dead bondage dress which was made entirely from treated fish-skins and clear plastic D-rings. 'And you look staggering – like the little mermaid in her transitional phase. Not sure about the trainers, though. Maybe without socks?'

Triona laughed. 'I'm picking my shoes up here, remem-ber?'

'Of course. I'm sorry I can't stop – I'd offer you a drink, but I'm killingly late as it is.'

'S'okay, I can help myself.'

'You'll have to get approval from the teetotal arsehole first.' Juno jerked her head upwards to indicate the flat door. 'And whatever you do, don't light a fag. He'll get out the fire extinguisher. There's nothing these Yanks love more than a good ol' Country and Western hose down.'

Triona pulled a face. 'I take it you haven't asked him along tonight?'

'He says he has to stay in and wash me out of his hair.'

'I'll put in a good word for you.' Triona winked. 'You wait – when you get home tonight, he'll welcome you with open arms. Promise.'

'Thanks, but the last thing I want to see is his arms stash,' gulped Juno in an undertone. 'I half believe Sean was right, you know,' she whispered. 'He's bloody shifty about what he's doing over here. And he hates the British. He was banging on about the tyranny of the Empire just now.'

'Really?' Triona's witchy face lit up. 'In that case, I'm going to introduce myself straight away. This is thrilling! I wish Sean was here – he'd love all this.'

'Sean,' Juno pointed out, 'is the reason all this is happening. My life could be in danger for all he knows. And Uboat's imminent future is threatened, too.'

'That, as the Americans say,' Triona started to haul the 'Emerguncy kit' up towards the second landing, 'is turtle-ly awesome.'

Chapter Five

Even though she was almost three-quarters of an hour late, Juno found that only two of her friends were resident in the slick Hampstead wine bar. Pressing her nose to the glass panel in the door to make them laugh, she waved happily at Elsa – a petite, curly-haired fireball of energy who was a disc jockey at one of London's trendiest FM stations, and the only person Juno knew who could distinguish between hard groove bass, techno funk, garage, drum 'n' bass and jungle.

Elsa's partner, Euan, was equally formidable. Tonight he was wowing the ultra-cool clientele of the bar with his neon blue fake fur frock coat, snakeskin trousers and side-burns so long and narrow it looked as though his eyebrows had slipped down his face. A tall, lean Glaswegian with a buzzcut head and more body piercings than an African tribal elder, he was a journalist for London's top listing magazine, *The Outing*. Between them, he and Elsa could almost guarantee free tickets to the funkiest function of their choice, yet often preferred to stay at home and watch *Emmerdale* whilst indulging in a Domino pizza. They were ludicrously domesticated, and Juno thought they had the best relationship in the world, although Euan's encyclopaedic knowledge and usage of drugs frightened her more than she cared to admit.

The bar was frantically busy. As she pushed open the door, a host of beautiful, arrogant male faces turned to size her up. And, as usual, when they quickly sized her as a wholesome size sixteen to eighteen, backs were immediately turned and conversations resumed.

Elsa and Euan were standing at the bar, the bottle of wine between them already almost empty.

'Happy Birthday!' They greeted her with a simultaneous kiss on both her cheeks so that for a second she was in a strange couple sandwich of leather and fake fur.

'We tried to get a table, hon, but the place was already heaving by eight,' Elsa apologised, pulling back her explosion of brown corkscrew curls so that she could roll her expressive grey eyes.

'S'okay, we can move on once everyone gets here.' Juno gazed around, and spotted Lydia coming through the door from the lavatories where, judging by her perfectly applied lip-liner, she had just been for some repair work.

'Jez was here a minute ago, but he's pushed off to buy some fags.' Euan was extracting a birthday card and a small wrapped gift from deep within the fake fur.

'Isn't there a machine in here?' Juno looked around.

'Yup, but you know what he's like – he's such a fashion victim he's only smoking Ducardos Long-Tipped Light Menthol or something at the moment,' Elsa laughed, sweeping her mop of curls from one shoulder to the other and causing a minor gale in the process.

'The big jessie thinks they make him more attractive.' Euan raised a pierced eyebrow. 'Add to his sophisticated charm.'

'A ciga-Rhett Butler?' Juno giggled, taking the present that he was now waggling at her. 'Thanks, guys.'

'Jez is more of a Scarlet Pimpernel if you ask me – hi, Joo.' Lydia swanned up, kissing Juno on the cheek and leaving behind a perfect Cupid's bow lip-print. She smelled deliciously of CKBe. 'That shirt looks fantastic on you – I knew it would. You look sensational, Joo.'

'Thanks.' Juno smiled humbly.

Lydia, dressed in a tight black satin Gucci shirt and white silk jersey trousers that clearly revealed she was wearing no knickers, looked absolutely devastating. A couple of rogues had already moved in to either side of her at the bar and were angling for an eye-meet, but she was far too preoccupied stuffing matchbooks into her handbag to notice.

'Isn't your new flatmate coming?' Elsa asked her. 'Lydia says he's gorgeous.'

'She hasn't even met him yet!' Juno laughed in exasperation. 'And no, he's not – coming or gorgeous. He's totally anal. He's staying at home to dust the CDs, put them in alphabetical order and then catalogue them.'

Elsa was watching her through her veil of corkscrews, grey eyes clever and knowing. They had been friends since college and Elsa could, Juno knew, read her as easily as a book she'd memorised as a child. Thankfully, she was far more subtle than Lydia, and said nothing in front of Euan, but she had clearly decided that not only was Jay very gorgeous indeed, but that Juno probably fancied him rotten.

'Shame he's not coming,' Euan was saying. 'We've got loads of free passes to Trash tonight. Come along with us later, Juno,' he urged, peering at her over his trendy black-rimmed Joe Ninety specs to reveal two very red-rimmed eyes. 'There's bound to be a few celebs knocking around, and we can get you into the VIP lounge if you fancy a couple of lines to celebrate your birthday, hen.'

'Thanks.' Juno pulled a face. 'I've got far too many lines as it is.'

Elsa laughed. 'I know you think that charlie is God's way of telling you that you earn too much money, but I had a g on my thirtieth courtesy of the toot fairy here,' she patted Euan's fake fur arm, 'and I felt better than ever. If you've got to take in a bloody deep breath to blow out all those candles, you might as well have fun doing it, hon.'

Juno watched as one of the rogues offered to pay for Lydia's round. 'I prefer scoring punch-lines, thanks all the same,' she said priggishly.

'You're such a killjoy, hen,' Euan protested, pressing his top teeth to the stud in his lower lip and pulling a face. 'You'll happily do half an hour of stand-up – which to my mind is like sticking your head down the altar and asking someone to flush – but you won't do drugs. You might be funnier if you were high,' he pointed out, calmly pursuing his pro-drugs campaign. It wasn't intended for a moment to be critical, but Juno still felt absurdly hurt.

'How did last night's gig go?' Elsa shot him a warning look and poured herself the last of the wine. 'Or shouldn't I ask?'

'Not if you want an answer that doesn't include the words "feet", "on", died' and "my".' Juno turned gratefully as Jez bounded noisily through the door, dragging someone behind him.

'Look who I found nervously wandering around Hampstead clutching an *A to Z* and a rape alarm!' he bellowed cheerfully, causing most of the bar to crane around and do just that.

Juno burst out laughing as she saw Lulu glowering with mock disapproval from the doorway. Lulu was the last woman in the world who would wander around clutching a rape alarm. She marched everywhere purposefully, a pair of personal stereo earphones attached to either side of her face and a book glued to her nose. Juno often wondered how she managed to find her way anywhere.

'Happy birthday, you old bat,' she hailed Juno in her booming Middlesbrough rasp before stomping over, long black coat-tails flapping. Lulu wore her vast military great coat throughout the year – even tonight when the temperature had yet to drop below twenty and the girls were all taking the opportunity to bare their flat midriffs and flash their pierced belly buttons. Juno was convinced that the reason women with pierced navels were inevitably so thin was because the little silver rings somehow stapled their stomachs too. With this in mind, she had debated going through the cosmetic puncturing process herself, but suspected they'd require a harpoon and an industrial bolt to do the job.

'I'm so glad you could come.' She gave Lulu a hug which largely involved hugging herself because, inside the great coat, there wasn't very much of Lulu at all.

'Yeah, yeah, cut out the soppy shit, pet,' Lulu laughed

gruffly and elbowed her away so that she could delve into her cavernous duffel bag. 'Now I'm opposed to the giving of presents on political grounds, as you know. But I'm making an exception in your case because you'll slag me off on the circuit if I don't.'

'Sure,' Juno giggled, knowing her friend wouldn't dream of turning up empty-handed.

Lulu was a full-time comic whose aggressive delivery and overtly militant, feminist material sometimes marginalised her audience, and often made enemies of men. She was also, however, screamingly funny, and had a loyal following in London and Scotland, if not in her native North East. At first Juno had been terrified of her but, finding that she was often on the same bill, had tried hard to make friends and break through the snappy, snarling veneer. She'd done it for the challenge at first, but had ended up with a match-less friend. Lulu didn't give herself easily, but beneath the brusque rudeness, she had a heart the size of South Shields, just as beneath the enormous coat and cloud of back-combed, crazy-coloured blue hair, she was a tiny vole of a woman with big blue eyes, a dusting of black freckles and a snub little nose which would have looked more at home on Violet Elizabeth Bott.

'One family-sized vodka!' announced a cheerful voice as Lydia thrust a dripping glass over Juno's shoulder before registering that Lulu had arrived. 'Oh – hi there, Loo. Sorry, I didn't realise you were here,' she greeted the little virago with wary affability. 'What would you like to drink?'

'It's okay, I can get my own,' Lulu muttered, trying not to show distaste at being addressed by the nickname she only tolerated from Juno. The 'Joo'/'Loo' thing was an old private joke which she loathed Lydia muscling in on. If Juno hadn't told her off so often in the past for bawling Lydia out about it then she wouldn't hesitate now.

'Don't be ridiculous, Loo,' Lydia insisted cheerfully. 'Is white wine okay? I've already bought a bottle, so I can easily get another glass.'

'No, I'll have a Newcastle Brown, pet.' Lulu smiled wickedly. 'And no glass.'

In truth, most of Juno's friends were frightened of Lulu, however much she made them laugh. The only one who genuinely seemed to adore this sharp-tongued addition to their circle as much as Juno was Jez.

Even now he was appropriating a bar stool for her to sit on, and then taking her bag in a theatrical show of gentlemanly charm. He adored fussing around her in a way he seldom did for the others.

If Juno didn't know better, she would say he fancied Lulu. But she had known Jez longer than most – he'd lived in the flat below hers almost a decade ago, and now claimed to be the only person who'd ever had to look up to hear what she was saying. Juno had got to know him during a long, cold winter in which he'd had no hot water in his flat and had regularly trooped upstairs to use her bath. Before long, they were such firm friends that she would sit on the laundry basket and chat to him while he sponged and scrubbed. In those days he'd been an impoverished music student.

Now Jez Stokes – a bouncing scouser – was the famously short, wiry bass guitarist from the legendary Britpop band, Slang. This kudos, combined with a sense of humour that was as acute as his arse was cute, lent him enviable pulling power. He was a staggering draw for overdeveloped, underage girls, yet he was surprisingly ugly. He had a face like a featherweight boxer's, with a gloriously off-centre nose, split lip and blond eyebrows so cross-hatched with scars they looked as though they'd been braided. But the rough, barrow-boy exterior belied a super-quick mind and wit, just as the fact that he was one of the earthiest, most accomplished flirts in town belied his true sexuality.

Jez appreciated Lulu because her humour had the same split-second timing as his own. And Lulu, for all her anti-male tirades, worshipped Jez. It was one of the few things she and Lydia had in common.

'You're looking gorgeous,' he told them both now. 'And

so am I. Don't you think Lydia's getting fat? I'm certain she's been pigging out on the Ryvita crumbs again, girls.'

Juno laughed and then felt guilty as Lydia shot her a hurt look, clearly feeling victimised, if mildly flattered by the insinuation that she was, in fact, extremely slim. She had just bought Lulu a Newcastle Brown and stolen a bowl of pretzels from the bar to offer her as well. Juno smiled gratefully and shot her a wink, but Lydia was again being distracted by a pouncing admirer proffering a cigarette.

'Thanks, but I've got my hands full,' she apologised, trying to squeeze past him and get close enough to Lulu to pass on her offerings.

Several other men had also tried their luck with Lydia by the time the rest of Juno's friends arrived. The next to turn up, Ally and Duncan, were hugely apologetic that the babysitter had delayed them. A rock-solid couple, Juno had known and adored them since she'd first met them on the comedy circuit several years ago, when Duncan had run a club called The Delivery, and Ally – a some-time actress, some-time waitress – was his resident compère. Now writing sit-coms full-time for the BBC, Duncan had left the smoky club behind him, and Ally was for once enjoying 'resting' between roles as she proof-read Duncan's scripts and looked after their six-month-old baby, China, who was as sooty blonde and sweet-natured as her parents.

They gave Juno a magnum of champagne for her birthday. Along with the Lazy Fish corkscrew Euan and Elsa had given her, a tin of spliffs from Jez and Lulu's gift of a bottle of brandy, Juno was feeling conspicuously alcoholic and very overloaded by the time her friend Odette arrived, panting her apologies.

'Couldn't get a cab – I brought you some Jack Daniel's 'cos I know it's your fave. 'Fraid I didn't have time to wrap it, babe.' She handed over a Thresher's bag and kissed everyone hello. 'I can only stay for a starter at the restaurant 'cos I've got to show my face at a drinks party with J. Walter Thompson before ten-thirty, then I'm taking some clients to the late show at JoJo's.'

Odette had been at college with Elsa and Juno, and was now a commercials director who earned huge amounts of money which she never had time to spend. Working twenty-hour days, she lived alone in a huge warehouse conversion by the Islington Canal, which was clinically tidy and impersonal because she was there less often than her cleaning lady and hadn't the time to furnish it fully. It was nicknamed the Zen Den (a pastiche of a grotty flat Juno and Lydia had once lived in, nicknamed the Cam Den) and perfect for parties since there was nothing in it to get broken. Despite looking like Linda Lusardi in a DKNY suit and possessing a bank balance with more zeros at the end of it than an astronaut's altimeter, Odette was also far too busy to have relationships.

Her quota of friends complete, Juno relaxed into the evening and allowed the vodka Cokes to sink down. Standing between Lydia and Odette, she found that three rogues had sidled up and were starting to stake them out – catching their eyes and smiling, listening in to the conversation and then paralleling it with their own banter. They soon began to invade the group physically, boy/girl, boy/girl, so that each had an individual target. It was classic group matchplay, perfectly executed.

One had clearly decided to lay claim to Lydia, and was by far the most eager to ingratiate himself. A tall, slick Media Suit with ash blond hair and crinkling blue eyes, he was much more successful than his predecessors had been with her, mostly because he was much more persistent, and pretty soon he had engineered a one-on-one conversation. Poor Odette was then pounced upon by her new drinking neighbour, a bully-boy rugby player with huge shoulders and a booming laugh. Juno watched in fascination as he homed in on her with the subtle opening line, 'Nice tits!'

Suspecting he wouldn't get too far, Juno turned to find herself beside a short, doe-eyed man with a head of unkempt black curls, two days' growth on his dimpled cheeks, and a vast checked shirt which was far too big for him and turned back at the wrists. He was probably older than he looked, but had the gauche charm of a young boy heading out on his first pub crawl. He looked so lost and out of place that she felt rather sorry for him.

'Short arms.' She smiled, holding up her own folded-back cuffs. 'We're genetically programmed never to buy pornography from newsagents.'

For a moment he looked as though he hadn't really taken this in, and then he laughed – an unexpectedly gruff, sexy sound which made Juno smile even more widely. He was really rather cute and had very nice teeth, she noticed.

'I'm Bruno.' He held out a hand to shake hers, and she found herself clutching a lot of checked shirt. His accent was delectably soft and Irish.

'Juno.' She grinned.

'We sound like a pair of Marx Brothers, Juno and Bruno.'

She liked the way he coupled their names together. He was growing more attractive by the second, especially those huge seal-pup eyes with their ridiculously long lashes.

'This must be a Marxist meeting place. Don't tell me your friends are called Groucho and Harpo?' she asked, noticing that Lydia was already at the whispering into the ear and giggling stage with the blond Suit. She really was a phenomenally good flirt.

'No, it's worse than that.' Bruno's eyes twinkled. 'They're called Kevin and Darren. Good Irish names, those. Somehow they're not so popular over here, so they're not.'

'Are they Irish too then?'

'Not exactly.' He dropped his voice to a whisper. 'They're just doing the accent because it works with the girls. Kevin's is a bit ropy if you listen in.'

True enough, Kevin the rugby player was telling Odette about the wonderful world of computerised post-production edit suites in an accent that not only jumped from Ulster to Cork, but also detoured through New South Wales and Texas.

Juno laughed. 'And you?'

'Sure, I'm the real thing, so I am.' He held up his pint of Guinness as though it was proof, his eyes fixed on hers. 'Say, have you got any Irish in you?'

Juno knew the joke far too well.

'Not right this moment, no,' she laughed.

They chatted on for ten minutes, and Juno started to like him more and more. It turned out he worked with the other men at a post-production house in Soho. He had a lovely, self-deprecating sense of humour, and they seemed to have such an acutely twinned angle on things that they finished sentences for one another several times and then laughed in surprise. All the time those big baby-calf eyes engaged hers then danced around the room, drinking in everything before returning to her as he added a point to one she'd made or asked her something about herself.

Flushed with delight, Juno noticed Lydia looking over at them. She tried to catch her eye for a girl-to-girl wink, but Lydia didn't seem to notice.

'Your friend seems to have fallen for the rogue brogue over there.' Bruno was following her gaze.

'Don't be too sure.' Juno watched as Lydia turned back to the blond Suit and laughed at something he'd just said. 'She's pretty choosy.'

'Is she now?' He carried on watching Lydia for a moment then turned back to Juno. 'So what are you all doing here tonight? Is this your local bar or something?'

'We're celebrating someone's birthday,' she said vaguely, unwilling to admit to being thirty. 'Here, I'll introduce you to the others.' She was dying to know how he'd cope with Lulu. It was something of an acid test.

They all took to him straight away, she noticed happily. Another good sign. Best of all was the way Lulu laughed almost as uproariously at his jokes as he did at hers, and he didn't seem to take offence at all when she called him 'a filthy bogtrotter' at one point.

As he chatted easily to Elsa and Euan about a club they had all been to, Juno threaded her arm through Lulu's and squeezed it.

'Gerroff the wool, you soft bitch.' Lulu turned to her, grinning as she dropped her gruff voice to a whisper. 'Nice. I approve. Ha he asked for your number yet?'

Juno knew there was no point trying to fob her off with a lot of bravura guff about not being bothered, especially as she was in a hurry to get back to Bruno, who was obstinately failing to look in her direction for an eye-meet. 'Not yet. I hope he does. He's lovely, isn't he?'

'So you fancy your chances then, pet?' Lulu's blue eyes twinkled.

'No! Well, a bit, maybe.' Juno shrugged, still looking across at Bruno who was staring into mid-distance now. He really was gorgeous. 'I think he's quite shy.'

'You should take the initiative for once, pet.' Lulu let out her deliciously filthy, low, rasping laugh. 'Make the first move. Act upon it.'

'Act upon it?' Juno fretted worriedly. In her limited experience, acting upon impulse meant wearing sickly-sweet body-spray and hanging winsomely around flower stalls, not grasping the nettle. The only man she'd ever asked for his phone number had given her the old *Swapshop* one as a joke.

But Lulu was adamant, clapping her tiny, pale hands together briskly. 'Yes. Act upon it, you soft bat. So get back to your sweet little Irish piece and I'll get you a bloody big birthday drink. Two buttons have gone on the front of your shirt by the way, pet, so I'd cross my arms if I were you.'

Bruno seemed delighted when Juno found him again. 'I've been looking around for you. I've just heard you and Lydia have *the* most amazing job.'

'Oh, yes?' Juno smiled, knowing what was about to come. For once she didn't care. Those big, dark eyes were drinking her in so attentively that she could happily talk about it all night.

The thing about birthdays, she reflected headily in the loos half an hour later, was that one was never short of a drink. She had just enjoyed a rather spectacular, if low-key, flirtation with Bruno with whom she shared not only a sense of humour but also a remarkable number of tastes, history and memorised Blues Brothers jokes. He had yet to ask for her phone number, but she guessed it was only a matter of time. She was certain he'd been lightly stroking the back of her neck with his fingers at one point, which had felt simply delicious.

Applying her lipstick dreamily, she wondered whether the restaurant would mind squeezing three more in around the table. If she invited the trio along, then the numbers would be even for once, and she could carry on her lovely, chatty conversation with Bruno. She kept expecting him to ask her on a date, and was almost certain he would. Cocking her head, she studied her flushed, excited reflection, with its plump kiss-me mouth and glittering eyes. A siren in her sexual prime winked back, smacking her freshly painted lips. God, she loved being thirty.

'There you are!' Lydia slammed her way through the door, also luminous with excitement. 'I've been looking for you everywhere. Girly goss, girly goss!' She rubbed her hands together conspiratorially and then twisted round to perch on the unit beside the sinks.

'So do you fancy him?' Juno asked, taking in Lydia's glowing skin and lipstick-free mouth which hinted of a hasty, stolen kiss somewhere. 'He obviously adores you.'

'Oh, did you notice?' She looked incredibly pleased.

'Couldn't help but,' Juno laughed, groping through her handbag for her mascara.

'Did he say something to you then?' she giggled, pulling her fingers through her rumpled white-blonde sheet of hair.

'To me?' Juno creased her forehead and looked up. But Lydia was peering at Juno's chest in alarm now.

'You've lost a couple of buttons, Joo!'

'Yes, sorry – they just popped off,' she apologised. 'I'll sew some others on tomorrow.'

'It doesn't matter – I'll get you another one next week. God! I wish I'd had a chance to talk to him alone,' Lydia sighed in frustration, staring up at the ceiling. 'It's been maddening.'

'Let's invite them along to The House.' Juno bit her lip happily at the prospect.

'Oh, they've already left.' Lydia looked down at her again,

pulling her 'that's life' face. 'Bruno wanted to say goodbye, but we couldn't find you.'

'He's gone?' Juno almost poked her eye out with the mascara wand.

'Yup – just now.' Lydia leant forwards and wiped away some mascara from Juno's nose. 'Off to a party or something. They said we could go along after we've eaten, but I don't really fancy it, do you?'

For a split second, Juno felt a strange shudder come over her. Then she shook it off and focused upon the idea of a party. She adored parties, particularly ones full of sexy strangers.

'It'd give you a chance to suss Darren out some more,' she pointed out, suddenly desperate to go, still picturing poor Bruno being dragged away under protest, unable to find her to say farewell and demand her phone number. It was a tragedy.

'Spare me!' Lydia laughed, taking a Lancaster lip-liner from her tiny handbag. 'I thought I'd scream if he mauled me any more out there. And that phoney accent was diabolical.'

'But I thought . . .'

'Little Bruno was laughing so much, he almost fell over, did you see?' she went on, twisting around on her haunches to face the mirror, and starting to draw lines around her lovely, curling lips. 'He kept waving at me from behind your shoulder. Thank God Darren didn't notice.'

Juno watched Lydia complete the line then start to fill it in with Chanel lipstick. A great ball of dread and *déjà vu* nausea was churning in her belly. I thought he was stroking my neck, she remembered sadly.

'But you just said you fancied him.'

'Like mad, my dear,' giggled Lydia, her voice distorted from pulling her mouth open. 'He's my type, isn't he? His eyes are to die for, and he's so funny, plus – and wait for this – his father is a bloody movie star.' Her voice laced with relish, she named one of Ireland's best loved wild men of film. 'Darren told me. He's worth a *bomb*. We're going to meet up on Sunday. He's offered to take me to the Groucho Club – he's a member like Jez, can you believe it? – says it'll be our illicit Marxist meeting place. He's so witty.'

'Darren?' Juno knew she was clutching at straws, but couldn't bear to let go.

Misunderstanding the emphasis, Lydia rolled her eyes, blotted and started another coat. 'Well, he wanted my number just now, but I fobbed him off by taking his. The trouble is, he's Bruno's boss at Imagic Eye, and a total bastard from what he proudly told me about himself tonight, so he was pulling rank out there. Ten seconds after they all left, Bruno raced back in pretending he'd left his fags, pulled me to one side, planted a kiss like you would not believe, and arranged our date. It was all hugely exciting.' She caught Juno's eye in the glass, her own glittering like hot, blue flames.

'This happened just now?' Juno feigned mutual, delirious excitement then stopped herself when she spotted a mad-eyed thing in the mirror which bore a scary family resemblance.

'Romantic or what?' Lydia nodded. 'I'm so sorry you missed it, Joo. You'd have loved it, it was such a hoot. But I can tell you, I was as amazed as anyone. When Bruno left it so late to make his move, I thought he wasn't interested after all. I even thought he fancied you for a bit.'

So did I, she thought bleakly.

'I was a tad pissed off to be honest, because he'd already chatted me up earlier,' Lydia said, with a tiny edge of accusation in her voice as she claimed first refusal.

'He had?' Juno carried on gazing at her own reflection. Her face was no longer flushed at all. She looked as though she'd plunged it into a bucket of iced water like a freshly hammered horseshoe.

'Yes.' Lydia was tweaking imaginary smudges from the corners of her mouth with long, manicured nails. 'It was when I was buying Lulu that bottle of Newcastle Brown, remember? He was standing at the bar.' She rubbed her lips together to distribute the red gloss. 'He just burst out laughing and asked me if it was my usual, because I looked like more a Tennant's Extra girl to him.'

Juno closed her eyes for a second. She could picture the scene only too well.

'That laugh is just so killingly sexy,' Lydia went on. 'When Bruno disappeared back to his friends, I thought I'd lost my chance, especially when his revolting boss decided to chat me up. But he kept catching my eye and just carrying on looking, you know?' She was blissfully unaware of Juno's frozen face as she reapplied some eyeliner.

'I can imagine,' Juno sighed. She'd seen Bruno looking but had thought nothing of it – everyone gazed at Lydia because she was so beautiful, like an exquisite painting hanging in a room that continually draws the eye. Juno had grown resigned to John ogling her friend continually when they'd all been out together in the past.

'What did he say to you?'

'About what?' Juno thought over all the jokes they'd exchanged about being a short teenager, about the early episodes of *Brookside*, about commuting on the Northern Line.

'About me,' Lydia laughed, and then turned to her in horror. 'God, Joo!' She put a hand to her mouth in embarrassment. 'I'm sorry. You didn't think – '

'Hell, no.' Juno shook her head so urgently she felt slightly dizzy. 'He told me he thought you were gorgeous.' He had, and Juno had agreed because it was true.

'Oh, you are sweet!' Lydia hugged her tightly. 'Thank you. Actually, I could tell you didn't fancy him at all.'

'You could?' Juno backed away and looked at her, trying to nod knowingly.

'Mmm.' Lydia nodded too. 'It was obvious from the way you were crossing your arms in front of your chest and firing out jokes to keep him at a distance. He's not your type at all, is he?'

'Absolutely not,' Juno agreed hollowly, suddenly realising how lousy her flirting technique must be. It seemed she didn't even have one. The only thing Bruno had wanted to pick up when they were chatting was her one-liners.

Chapter Six

The first thing Juno heard as she climbed slowly up the stairs to the flat were the faintest strains of classical music.

Realising that this meant Jay was still up, she sagged against a banister, summoning up a friendly smile to walk in with. It almost cracked her face. Smiling was the last thing she felt like doing.

She slotted her key quietly into the Yale lock and took a deep breath.

He was sprawled, fast asleep, on the sofa. Still in the hall, Juno paused for a moment to marvel at the way his golden-treacle hair seemed darker – almost russet – in the dim light from the sole lamp in the room.

The music was dancing along in a merry, frivolous tempo and Jay shifted slightly in his sleep as though disturbed by such melodic cheeriness. His head was resting in the crook of his arm and Juno could see that his hair had become caught in the steel links of his watch strap. She also noticed how bitten down his fingernails were – they were so well gnawed that there was almost nothing left of them, like tiny staples embedded in skin that was roughened by so much contact with photographic chemicals. She wondered what angsts of his own he mulled over while sinking his teeth into them. Taking in his obvious beauty, she was certain they were nothing like her own humiliation of that evening.

It was then she realised with a leaden thud of guilt that

she must have left all her birthday presents in the restaurant.

She'd excelled herself in there, she remembered with a guilty stab. The gang had teased her mercilessly about being thirty and consequently assumed that her quiet, sad mood was as a result of that. Determined not to be a glum party pooper, Juno had come up with the only distraction she knew – humour. And she'd used her new American flatmate as her fall guy. Poor Jay – conked out on the sofa – had no idea how much she had talked up and exaggerated their brief, tempestuous acquaintance to make her friends laugh. She'd told them he was a tidy, turtle-hating terrorist. She'd hammed up the nude fridge encounter like mad. She'd made herself as much the butt of the jokes as Jay, but still felt hugely bad about what she'd done – stitching him up to leave her friends in stitches.

Suddenly she didn't feel at all like scuttling to bed for a solitary sob, however easy his slumber made her quiet, tearful retirement. The night had been far too hellish to go to bed on without added comfort calories and alcoholic oblivion. She wanted another drink and a vast cheese and pickle sandwich, and she wanted them now.

She only wished Jay wasn't here. His physical perfection seemed to mock her from its passive reign over the centre of the room.

Everything in the fridge had been serried into food types and encased in several layers of hygienic cling-film, foil and self-seal bags. Juno's hardened lump of fortnight-old Cheddar took ages to locate and then proved impossible to unwrap from its multitude of layers. She cursed Jay under her breath as she twisted and tugged at the plastic film without success. Finally she gave up entirely and settled for a mayonnaise and pickle doorstep which she carried back into the sitting room on the palm of one hand.

As she tried to creep past him again, she realised that Jay had opened one eye and was watching her.

'Hi.' He yawned and stretched lazily. 'Good night?'

Juno nodded vaguely, not wanting to blurt out the truth. She was hardly about to tell a complete stranger that her beautiful best friend had yet again scored with someone she fancied.

He had clocked the sandwich now. 'I thought you were going out to eat?'

'We did.' She shrugged. 'And now I'm staying in to eat. I like variety. Do you want some?' she croaked, offering him a bite of the ungainly doorstep. A great lump of pickle chose that moment to dive towards the floor where it landed on what appeared to be a discarded copy of *Cheers!* magazine. Juno gazed down in astonishment and found that the *Londoners* soap star, Belle Winters, was smiling up benignly from a tiger-striped, eight-seater sofa in her sumptuous Buckinghamshire home, one eye obscured by the pickle patch. Wondering what on earth Jay was doing reading *Cheers!*, she suddenly had the ludicrous vision of the nation's favourite ageing sex kitten as a potential IRA target.

'Nah – I've already eaten.' Jay was trying to raise himself up on one elbow and had found that his hair was attached to his wrist strap.

While he was busy untangling himself, Juno hovered uncertainly. If she plumped herself down beside him, he might feel obliged to make conversation, she realised. It was really far too late for that, and she wasn't in the mood.

'You must be shattered,' she said. 'I guess you'll want to push off to bed. Don't mind me.'

'I'm not tired,' he murmured, untangling the last strand and looking up at her with those yellow eyes. 'I'm still on New York time. Besides, I'm pretty insomniac.'

'I'm prettier in pink myself.' Juno yawned widely, hoping he'd catch on to it and yawn too, then realise he was jet lagged and desperate for duvet diving.

He either chose to ignore her joke, or didn't get it, still looking at her seriously. 'You're the one who's gotta be beat – after all, you were working all day, weren't you?'

'If you can call it that.' Juno shifted uneasily. His eyes were really quite disturbing. If she wasn't feeling so utterly depressed, she might gaze into them rather lustily at this point. Gold, slanting and thickly lashed, they had a way of eating into her skin which made her feel more than just stripped, they made her feel X-rayed. Remembering the way he had touched her face earlier, she felt an involuntary shudder of excitement.

'What is it you do?' he asked, jumping slightly as Uboat's tank burped.

God, he was going to make conversation, Juno realised. But his sexy, cool gaze was unfriendly and appraising – like a school examiner's. The last thing she needed was an argument about cleaning rotas.

'I – er – sort of help out with people's personal problems,' she muttered, perching on the farthest arm of the sofa and taking a vast bite out of her sandwich.

'That sounds kinda epic.' His eyebrows shot up again, but he didn't pursue the topic. Instead he went straight for the jugular. 'Not a great night, huh?'

Juno balked so much that she almost choked on a pickle lump. The sandwich was truly disgusting without cheese, and she had to chew for ages before she could force herself to swallow it.

'What makes you say that?' she asked cagily.

He pressed his chin thoughtfully into the knuckles of one hand, not taking his eyes from hers. 'Just a hunch.'

'Quasimodo had one of those, and look where he ended up.'

'Your lover playing you up, huh?'

She felt her teeth grinding gently against one another as she took in his condescending, therapist's tone of voice.

'I don't have a lover,' she said, tossing the sandwich on to the coffee table.

'No?' There was something even more condescending about that.

'I have lovers,' she announced hot-headedly, not caring whether it was true or not. 'In the plural. I'm practising casual sex at the moment. It's like sex with my ex-boyfriend only more regular and with more commitment.' It was a standard line from her act and guaranteed to get at least a weak laugh.

Jay didn't even smile. He just raised one gold eyebrow, the malt whisky eyes unblinking.

Juno wasn't quite sure how it happened, but they stared at one another for a full minute, saying nothing. Throughout, she coped valiantly with every manner of inner biological horror, from rumbling stomach to burping urges, to a sudden and horrifying desire to break wind, but refused to give in to speech or to look away. This was a fully fledged battle, and she was determined to win.

It was the phone that finally called time. Juno looked at it in relief, then slowly realised something was missing. She glanced worriedly towards Poirot's cage, over which Jay appeared to have draped her Peruvian birthing smock.

'It was the only thing I could find that was large enough to cover it up,' he apologised.

Suddenly Juno could hear Sean's voice and jumped up in excitement, ready to apprehend the call, before she realised it was just her brother's old intercepting message on the answerphone explaining that he and Juno were out. Halfway across the room she stopped, instinctively knowing who the caller would be.

'Juno flower, it's John,' announced a deep, creamy Yorkshire voice, tinged with the slackening effect of one too many Ruddles. 'Are you there? Juno? Obviously not.' There was a long pause and she could distinctly make out the soundtrack of *Reservoir Dogs* in the background. Then there was a sharp intake of freshly lit smoker's breath. 'Listen, I'm not sure if that Yank passed on the message – who is he, by the way? – but I called earlier. I wanted to wish you a Happy Birthday, flower. I was hoping you might still be up – might fancy coming over here. I've got you a present . . . um . . .' There was another lengthy pause, and Juno was certain she could hear Tim Roth wailing 'I'm fucking dying' before John spoke again. 'It's here if you want it. So am I come to that. Call me.' The line went dead.

Juno was still stranded between the sofa and the phone, her heart somewhere perilously close to her wind-pipe. Had Jay not been in the room, she knew she would have picked up. Tonight, for once only, she would have accepted that taxi ride to Clapham. She'd have crawled into their old bed as willingly as an old diva slipping into the heroine's costume before curtain up. She'd have made love with John – terrible, lack-lustre, beer-sodden love, no doubt, but with the gratification of being sexually desired nonetheless – and then she'd have waited and willed him asleep. Once he was breathing deeply and grunting dreamily, she'd have pressed her face to the warmth of his shoulder like a child with a comfort blanket and allowed herself to feel safe for a few precious hours until the sobriety of morning told her how foolish she'd been.

Tonight, if she'd been alone, she'd have done it. Instead she was cooped up with a stranger whom she found almost as irritating as he was frightening. And in the pit of her stomach, she also knew she was still here because she found him sexually attractive, and that was no longer true of John.

'What did you think of Triona?' she asked in an artificially bright voice, turning back to Jay, determined to regain a sense of normality.

'She's just like Sean described.' He was watching her over the sofa back, his face in shadow.

'And what did he say about her?'

'That she was indescribable.'

Juno smiled and nodded. 'That's Triona.'

She headed through to the kitchen for a drink, pouring out three inches of vodka and looking at it.

'Live a little,' she breathed, watching an air bubble pop on the surface and remembering Lulu's words earlier that evening. 'Act upon it, pet.'

She downed the lot in one and poured herself another before walking back through.

The whole thing had been a bit too spontaneous. Halfway to the sofa, Juno realised she was on the threshold of a gagging and spluttering attack as the vodka swept around the entrance to her oesophagus like a bowlful of washing-up liquid trying to get down a plughole.

'Are you okay?' Jay was watching her with concern as she tried hard to swallow and breathe at the same time.

'Fine.' She managed to get the slug down and then coughed as it blasted fumes back up. She cast around for a suitable position from which to 'Act upon it'.

Jay was still dominating most of the sofa in a sinewy sprawl of creased Levis and crumpled t-shirt. Looking up at her, his eyes didn't blink or shift, and Juno suddenly realised how alone and precarious she was right now. He was possibly as uncertain of her as she was of him, yet there was something that gave him the advantage and that fact not only vexed her, it scared her too.

'I think I'm going to have a bath,' she announced suddenly and then wondered why on earth she had said it. She'd already had one bath this evening. She felt like Blanche DuBois dodging the sexually potent Stanley in *A Streetcar Named Desire*.

Jay looked mildly surprised, but made no comment as she hastily headed for the bathroom to set the taps running.

Stooping to the floor, Juno pressed her forehead to the cool enamel and felt the steam rise up to flatten her hair.

'Please let him go to bed,' she muttered under her breath, tipping the vodka from her glass into the frothing bath.

Gathering strength, she added half a bottle of relaxation Radox to the bubbling water and crept to the mirror to glimpse the ravages of the evening before her reflection steamed up too much to be truthful.

Watery eyes and an itching nose had rendered her smudgy-lashed and glowing in all the wrong places, but her make-up had done her proud and she wasn't looking too much like an extra from an early Michael Jackson video. In fact she looked a hell of a lot better than she felt. She tugged off her clothes and pulled on Sean's old green towelling gown from its hook on the door, wishing she'd noticed it there earlier that evening. It was remarkably soft and fluffy.

'Don't tell me he's bloody fabric-conditioned this along with tidying up,' she murmured under her breath as she stopped the taps and headed back into the sitting room to fetch her cigarettes. 'He thinks he's Lenor Cohen.'

He was still on the sofa, reading *Cheers!* again, his eyes

scanning the Belle Winters At Home spread as devoutly as an Islamic wannabe scouring the illustrated Koran.

'That suits you.' He looked up and took in the bath robe.

'Tell that to Sean.' Juno collected her cigarettes from the pocket of her jacket, which was slung over the back of the sofa. 'He always says I remind him of something out of *One Flew Over the Cuckoo's Nest* wearing this.'

'I only bought it last week,' Jay said smoothly. 'My old bath robe was kinda skunky.'

She turned to gape at him, letting what he'd just said sink in.

'This is *your* dressing gown?'

'Yup – I guess this is what you English mean by giving someone a good dressing gown. I never understood that saying, but now I've finally figured it out.' For the first time he smiled.

The effect was so absolutely devastating that Juno wanted to step back. His face was like a distant, seductively beautiful valley which had suddenly grown more approachable and more enchanting the moment the sun came out. She wanted to run towards it like Laura in *Little House on the Prairie*, pretending to be an aeroplane. God, she regretted that vodka. She could even hear the theme tune now – da-da-da-da-da-dum-dum, da-da-da-da-da-dum, DUM DUM – DUM DUM.

DUMB! She tried to pull herself together.

'I'm sorry, I thought it was Sean's dressing down – I mean, gown.' She was fighting to be cool, but something about that incredible smile was moulding the dressing gown so tightly around her hot body that she was in danger of exploding.

'Triona said you believed in share and share alike,' he murmured, sweeping the hair from his eyes. 'I thought she was talking about investments.'

Juno had no idea why she said what she did next – just as she'd no idea why she'd announced she was going to have a bath. But, in both cases, she regretted it the moment the words rushed past her lips in hot air and hot-headed embarrassment.

'I also share baths,' she joked lightly. 'So come along and hop in if you like?'

She expected him to be embarrassed, to be angry, to tell her to get lost. Now that he was growing accustomed to her sense of humour, he might even dismiss it as a joke. Instead he stayed motionless on the sofa, eyes glued to hers.

'Are you making a pass at me?' he finally asked, rubbing his chin against his shoulder in that sexy, defensive way which made her stomach plunge down the lift shaft of lust.

Juno had never felt so depressed or reckless in her life. She was absolutely certain he was going calmly and coolly to tell her he didn't find her sexually attractive; he certainly wouldn't be the first. She was equally desperate for some sort of reassurance, however shallow, male and temporary. She needed proof she could, after all, still pull. And she needed an excuse not to get a taxi to Clapham tonight.

'Well, if I'm taking a mass, I'm in the wrong outfit and all out of wafers,' she croaked. 'So I guess I'm making a pass.'

He didn't move. Nor did he stop staring at her. Juno started to sense that she had made a major misjudgement for the second time in a night.

'I don't like faucets on my back,' he murmured.

Imagining this was some sort of New York slang for pushy fat women desperate for a shag, Juno nodded sympathetically and started backing away.

'Dreadful predicament,' she agreed. 'Not exactly Farrah Faucet – more Juno force-it-far-too-far. Sorry. Worth a try, huh? I'll make myself scarce, shall I?'

'Please don't run away again, Juno.' He got up in one fluid movement and followed her to the door. 'I'll take the faucets.'

'You'll what?' She wavered uncertainly, ready to bolt.

'The taps.' Jay pressed the back of a long, chemically callused finger to her burning cheek and she almost expired on the spot. 'I'll take the taps.'

Juno reeled. It was the finger that did it. It was like hot branding iron to flesh, the realisation was so sudden. She no longer belonged to John. She belonged to something far more carnal – her own sex drive. Jay's touch could hot-wire it into high revs as easily as a teenage hooligan, while John had held the keys for years and never even found the ignition. A pulse in the depths of her pelvis was giving such a spectacular drumroll she had no choice but to press the accelerator herself.

Barely thinking, she raised herself up on tip-toes and pressed her lips to his wonderful cello-curve mouth. It was like kissing molten chocolate as his mouth yielded into the most exquisite, warm opening. She simply had no idea where to stop. The more she drank in, the more he gave and the sweeter it tasted.

Drawing breath before she suffocated with pleasure, she laughed in delight and gasped, 'Talk about tapping into something sensational.'

Chapter Seven

With the bathroom lit by just two fat candles that flickered dimly from the top of the medicine cabinet, Juno wasn't worried about how ghastly she might look, splashing around like a pink baby hippo. She was feeling decidedly Degas, and very much admired. The swig of vodka she'd downed earlier was firing her belly just as Jay's wandering touches were reducing her pelvis to molten ore. He was surprisingly gentle and tentative as he explored her wet body with those long, callused fingers.

Now that she'd actually got him into the bath with her, Juno felt far more confident and in control, her nerves disappearing as quickly as the bubbles around her and Jay's warm, slithery bodies.

'That feels good,' she murmured, watching indulgently as he pulled the crook of her ankle on to his shoulder and ran a loofah along her thigh. The rough texture made her shiver. She could feel the leather thong wrapped around his neck pressing into her calf. From it hung a pendant shaped like a shark's tooth.

'Is that real?' She tried to reach for it, but almost went underwater as her bottom slipped.

'Sure.' He lowered her ankle gently back into the water. 'It's a wolf's tooth.'

'A wolf? Wow. Does that mean something?' Juno was fascinated, instantly imagining him living as one with native American Indians, and being adopted into a tribe as an honorary brave called Wolf's Bite.

'Like what?' He cocked his head. 'I'm not an animal dentist in my spare time if that's what you mean.'

'No, I mean is it spiritual?'

Jay's lips curled in amusement. 'I bought it from a street trader on the Lower East side. It's a fashion accessory, Juno.'

'Oh.' She felt a bit prattish for asking. Then she remembered her earlier suspicions and Triona's idle chat over lunch.

'Juno, what are you doing?' he asked a moment later.

She glanced up from examining a strange, circular silver scar just below his knee. 'Looking for bullet wounds.'

'Why?' He looked perplexed.

'Oh, I just thought you might have some, that's all.' She shrugged casually.

He said nothing, just reached out a warm, soapy hand and stroked her cheek, cocking his head to one side in concentration as his barley-pale eyes examined her face, his thumb tracing every hollow with extraordinary delicacy. It was a hopelessly romantic gesture. Juno suddenly felt so aroused they could have been sitting in a Jacuzzi. She was amazed the water didn't start boiling around her.

When he finally looked away, she closed her eyes and wallowed in a few seconds' delirium before she remembered the scar.

'So is this one?' She reached out and traced the soft, hairless silver skin by his knee with her finger.

'One what?' he sighed tetchily, his mood seeming to darken in an instant.

'Bullet wound?'

He looked away, staring intently at the wash basin.

'Yup,' he finally muttered flatly.

'Wow!' Juno gaped at it in awe. 'How did you get it? Have you any others?'

He continued glaring at the basin with narrowed eyes, a muscle starting to leap in his cheek.

'Yes, I have others,' he replied slowly, a steely edge to his voice. 'But I don't give tours.'

Juno wanted to badger him to show and tell all, but

something in his set, defensive face dissuaded her. She wasn't so sure that sharing a bath with him had been such a great idea. She'd thought she was going to swim with the dolphins, but instead she'd dived into a tank with a shark. She suddenly wanted to swim for safety.

As though realising he'd unsettled her, Jay slowly ran a finger from the nub of her ankle to the hollow of her thigh, tipping his head to watch its progress.

'You sure as hell talk a lot.' He pulled damp, treacle-coloured tendrils from his eyes and looked up at her with an awkwardness that was almost timid.

Gazing back, Juno said nothing, just to fox him.

She had been lying back indulgently while Jay washed her feet, but now she spun around so that she faced forwards like an oarsman rowing stroke in a two-man sculling competition. Great splashes of water slopped out on to the bathroom floor as she moved.

'What are you doing now?' He leant away in alarm as a minor tidal wave approached him.

'I want you to sponge my back.' Juno settled beneath the bubbles again and reached for the huge fun-sponge which Lydia had given her last Christmas, and which was shaped like a groping hand.

'Sure.' Shifting behind her, Jay wrapped his legs either side of her waist and started to kiss away the ruffle of scented bubbles which had formed on the nape of her neck. The wolf's tooth was tickling the top of her spine now. At the same time his hands slipped around the liquid warmth of her wet sides to her breasts, which he picked up in wonderment, letting their weight rest on his palms.

'You have great tits.'

'I've never been much of a bird fancier myself,' she murmured, tracing the foam on his knees, letting her fingertip surf through the bubbles and stroke the soft, sandy hairs beneath. They were the same treacle colour as his hair, she noticed, and turned the same deep auburn when wet – like burnt caramel.

'Huh?' He never seemed to get her jokes.

'It was my birthday today,' she sighed, dropping her head forward as he rubbed the sponge across her shoulders.

'You didn't tell me.' The sponge dived beneath the water, letting out a fizzing sound as Jay squeezed the air from it.

'It's not something I was keen to advertise.'

'How old are you?' He slid the sponge up the deep groove in the centre of her back.

Juno curled her toes and crossed her fingers beneath the water. 'Twenty-five.' She could feel a great blush flash-burn her face, but kept her head low and wriggled back against him to hide her embarrassment. 'Please don't stop.'

'I like this dip in your back.' He traced the sponge back down the groove. 'Most women have knobbles here.'

'Well, I'm dippy.' Juno pressed her fingers between his toes.

'I've just started to figure that out.'

They stayed in the bath until their fingers were wrinkled and their bodies squeaky clean yet moist with the sweet sweat of anticipation.

'This water's getting kinda tepid,' Jay said. 'It's almost British beer temperature.'

'And it's gone just as flat,' Juno agreed, taking the cue.

Standing up to reach for a towel, she felt a great shy shudder of nerves and uncertainty ripple through her again, mirroring the waves and whirlpools her sudden movement had just caused in the bathwater below.

Still lying in the bath, Jay was looking up at her through those narrowed, startling eyes. They reminded Juno of a wolf's – pale gold, distant and dangerous. No wonder he liked wearing the tooth around his neck. He was a wolf in wolf's clothing. Despite a heat-pinkened body, the lean length of him was both imposing and intimidating. As well as the Celtic band tattoo on his right arm, he had a small icicle tattooed on his shoulder – a crude, lop-sided navy blue pattern that looked as though it had been undertaken with nothing more than a bottle of ink and a knife.

She pulled a towel around her and stepped out. 'Let's go to bed.'

Jay stayed put, yellow eyes unblinking as he watched her. 'Yours or mine?'

Juno felt like saying 'each other's' as a joke, but suspected it wouldn't be wise. Instead she caught sight of her pink face and bedraggled hair through the steam of the cabinet mirror and, totally distracted, murmured, 'Whichever – you choose.'

'Well, yours is kinda loaded down with stuff. And my sheets are clean.'

This was all getting a bit domestic, she realised in panic. She was supposed to be acting the wild seductress, not housekeeper. She'd be suggesting they fetch their cocoa and hot water bottles in a minutes. She'd better get in touch with her inner femme fatale, and quick.

Edging closer to the mirror, she decided that her inner femme fatale would undoubtedly recommend some hasty smartening up. Her hair looked a total mess and she appeared to be developing a pre-menstrual pimple on her chin.

'Yours then.' Keeping her back to him, she eyed the shelves above the sink in the hope that she'd left a spare tube of concealer or some powder there which she could stealthily apply under the pretext of cleaning her teeth or something, but there was nothing suitable to hand. Her tart sack was in her bedroom. She'd just have to think up an excuse to go there. Finding a comb might be a good idea while she was at it.

'I need to get my diaphragm,' she announced before she had a chance to think what she was saying.

In her bedroom, she groaned out loud and head-banged the bed a few times. How completely unsexy, Juno! First you start organising the sleeping arrangements like a girl guide leading a Brownie camp, and then in a fit of vanity you head off to get a diaphragm which you now recall you stuck pins into one night last month to stop yourself giving in to John's tempting offer of a reheated Indian take-out and a chat at one in the morning. You twit! Talk about spontaneous seduction. You're simply not cut out to 'act upon it'. You're no It Girl. You're a zitty twit, girl.

Her confidence was to blame. She hadn't so much as

exchanged a phone number with a man since John, let alone body fluids. It was all very well being mouthy and headstrong when fully dressed, but the moment her kit was off, she became a nervous, joke-firing chatterbox. Her body would be screaming 'Yes, yes, yes!' but her mouth kept jabbering 'There was an Englishman, a Scotsman and an Irishman'. She found Jay wildly sexy, went dizzy at the prospect of being a reckless seductress tonight, of leading him to bed with a knowing smile and a head full of naughty ideas, but she wasn't sure she was up to the job. A part of her wanted him to be masterful and take over. Yet for all his cool, truculent allure, he seemed intent on playing follow-my-leader.

I am going to get in touch with my inner femme fatale, Juno told herself firmly. I'm going to be as breezy, abandoned and devil-may-care about sex as Lydia is. I am doing this for my own personal entertainment and pleasure, as a mature, sexually liberated woman who can be dominant and selfish in bed, who has a high libido and a positive body image. Must just cover up that spot first . . .

A loud gurgling from the bathroom told her that Jay had pulled the plug on the bath.

'Juno – are you okay?' she could hear him calling from the hallway.

'Fine!' She hastily slapped some loose powder on her chin.

Spinning around, she saw that he was standing in the doorway wearing his fluffy green bathrobe.

'You look kinda pale.' He shouldered the door frame and started to towel his wet mane with the robe's hood.

'It's the light.' Juno looked up at the glaring overhead spots and winced. She knew from experience that they were far from flattering. During one of Sean's particularly raucous parties recently, she had walked in to find his friend Barfly sprawling naked on the bed in the vague, paralytic hope of some action. Under the bright halogens, he'd looked more like a corpse laid out for a post-mortem than an object of desire. She'd slept on the sofa.

She swept hastily to the door and cranked the dimmers to

low, over doing it in her haste so that they were momentarily plunged into darkness. As she tried to twitch the dials into a more ambient state of brightness, she subjected Jay to a lengthy strobe-like disco show of flashing lights. She hoped he wasn't epileptic.

'I thought we were going to my room?' he said in alarm.

So we were, Juno realised, just as she got the room to an uncannily flattering state of light. Sean had no dimmers in his room, she remembered. It was either operating theatre bright or pot-holer's paradise.

This was all getting far too technical, she realised – she'd moved from house matron to lighting engineer. She had to get this seduction back on schedule. Calling inner femme fatale . . . come in, inner femme fatale, your time is up, your blood is up and your lights are dim.

'Jay, lover.' She wrapped her finger around the wolf's tooth and dragged him closer. 'Where's your sense of spontaneity?'

But just as she stretched up to kiss him, tapping into a brief free-fall moment of that sublime lip-synching feeling, the tooth came away from its silver fitting in her fingers and something scratchy sprang out of its hollow centre.

'Ugh! It's full of hair!' She dropped it in horror.

'Shit!' Jay squatted to his haunches so fast that he head-butted Juno's knees. A moment later he was gathering both tooth and hair from the carpet, meticulously pulling every strand of the strawberry blonde lock into his palm, along with a good deal of Juno's own split ends, toe-nail clippings and general epidermal by-product.

Squatting down beside him to help, she scrabbled underfoot too, but only managed to scrape up some carpet fluff and a Quality Street wrapper.

Jay rammed the hair back in place and fitted the tooth into its setting. There was something about the hard line of his jaw that told Juno she'd just made a major blooper.

'Whose hair is it?' she asked nervously.

'You ask too many fucking questions,' he muttered, face once again adopting its shuttered, unfriendly look.

Juno stared at him for several seconds, weighing up her options. Tempting as it was to call the whole thing off at this point, he was far too desirable to scrap with over a bit of blonde frizz. They were so close that she could smell the toothpaste on his lips and the Radoxy cleanliness of their skin.

'Only one way to shut me up,' she murmured.

'What's that?' Jay's eyes narrowed, still unfriendly.

'Kiss me, you secretive bastard,' she smiled. 'Let's not split hairs.'

His lips hit hers like a force nine gust on a cliff top. One moment all had been calm, then the next his hands were pressing her cheeks so that her mouth yielded and was suddenly filled with the cool, muscular slither of his tongue. Rocked back on her heels, Juno felt his hands slip into her hair and cradle her head as he pressed her back still further.

The sexual kick was fantastic. The physical exertion less enjoyable.

She'd never dreamed he would respond to her suggestion with such exciting, eager passion.

God, I'm not supple enough for this, she realised in alarm as her hip bones groaned under the strain of a near back-flip and her stomach muscles twanged like dried-out elastic bands. Jay's long, sinewy body was hard against hers now, pushing her down yet further, one taut forearm sliding around to her shoulder blades to support her weight.

Feeling his kisses deepen and her pulses leap in response, Juno was enjoying herself too much to want to stop, but her knees had started to creak like woodwormed joists in a storm. As she sank lower, she could distinctly make out the sight of a long lost bra in her peripheral vision, nesting between an old suitcase and a stack of magazines behind the door. She closed her eyes to the sight and enjoyed the sparring of two hot, greedy tongues coiling together like randy eels. But Jay's hip bone was digging into one of her thighs and her left ankle was twisting awkwardly beneath her bottom.

'Hang on a sec,' she murmured into a lot of athletic tongue, lip and tooth action.

'Just . . . er . . . trying to free . . . ouch . . . my foot.' She wrestled free from Jay for a moment and pulled out the twisted ankle which had now gone completely dead.

'Sorry.' He backed off.

Now that her leg was free, Juno realised that the rest of her body was almost melting into the flat below. Her nipples were fizzing, her belly writhing and her lips buzzed from kissing him. Any second now she expected her nose to light up like the patient in the boardgame Operation.

The towel she'd been wearing was trapped around one thigh, her tangled hair caught up in her wicker laundry basket and her new spot was pulsing painfully from a sand-papering against Jay's stubble. But none of that mattered as she gazed up at him, longing to be kissed again, her heart pumping an adrenaline and pheromone cocktail into every erogenous zone of her body. He was looming over her like a wild tribesman – all tattoo and wolf's tooth and serpentine wet tendrils, yet so poised and still and uncertain, he almost looked nervous.

Then Juno's eyes widened in astonishment. Not only was he the most beautiful and dangerous thing she had seen in ages, but he had an erection from heaven. It was glorious – as sleek, pink and inviting as an ice-cream, as tight and powerful as a rower's forearm and as straight and proud as a skyscraper from his native New York. She'd never seen anything quite so spectacular – and she had more than her fair share of manuals with diagrams that could give a girl unrealistic hopes.

'D'you want to stop?' he asked reluctantly.

Terrified that the glorious vision would start to subside, Juno shook her head frantically and decided she had to seize the initiative once more. And it wasn't the only thing around here she wanted to seize.

'Not if you don't want to.' She remembered John's tip about holding a penis as one would a Gameboy joystick. His tips were inevitably analogies of sport or television. But in this context it really was a thoroughly new and invigorating experience. Game on . . .

'Would you like *me* to stop?' she asked. ('Push the foreskin back, get a tight grip, play with the red button at the top like you're zapping aliens. Atta girl.')

Jay groaned and closed his eyes.

('The aliens are coming from all sides, Juno baby. They're gonna get us unless you shoot the little fuckers. We're doomed.')

'Was that yes or no, Jay?' ('The aliens are retreating – ease off the trigger, flower.')

'No – don't stop. Please don't stop.'

('They're re-forming troops! And they've brought back-up with them. Jesus! There's millions of them out there! Hold on tight. *Hasta la vista*, green slimies!')

'Christ, that's fantastic,' Jay moaned, starting to kiss her throat distractedly. 'Jesus H. Christ, that's fantastic.'

'The H. stands for horny.' Juno dropped her chin until she found his mouth against hers. He almost devoured it, breath coming faster and faster against her upper lip.

Juno was beginning thoroughly to enjoy herself.

She pushed him to the floor. As she straddled her legs around him, he looked up at her with something close to idolatry. Given those pale, predatory eyes, this was a moment to savour.

I could get used to this, she thought headily, dropping her face to his belly. Boy, but he smelled good. And tasted better. When she dipped her tongue into the salty ink-well of his navel, the lightest traces of scented bathwater were still trapped inside.

When he'd really wanted to nettle her, John used to say that plump, talkative girls gave the best head – their tongues being the most regularly exercised thing about them. Right now Juno didn't much care. She knew this was something she was good at and thoroughly enjoyed. Unlike the skill of holding the erect male member in her hand, which had been an art it had taken her years to perfect (like symmetrical pottery or smooth gear changes), giving head came as naturally to her as stroking a purring cat whilst eating a Galaxy bar in front of *Blind Date*. And Jay was purring like a revving tank.

'Christ, that's good. Jeeeeesus! Kerr-ist. Jesus H. That's so good.'

Juno had always been a sucker for encouragement.

'Jee-eez! Oh, boy.' His voice was hoarse and soft at the same time – like verbal mohair. It was an incredible turn on. Juno forgot the carpet burns on her knees and the breeze from the hall hitting her bum and tried out her *pièces de résistance*. The 'catching dribbles from the rim of a melting Cornetto' followed by the 'lightly flicking froth from a cappuccino that's still too hot too drink' and finishing off with the 'probing the crease of a chocolate-covered cashew'. That last one was a killer.

Jay, who had been trying to run his fingers through her bath-tangled hair, almost pulled her head off as he let out a low growl of pleasure. The result was cunnilingus-interruptus as, pulled backwards by the knots, Juno found herself staring at the ceiling and wincing slightly at the sharp tugs at her scalp.

'Sorry,' Jay breathed gruffly, his slanting cheeks high with colour as he pulled her face back to his, kissing her gently on the lips, then the chin, then both dimples one after the other. Disentangling his fingers, he ran both hands down to her bottom and pulled her higher on to his body so that she could feel the soft down of his balls between her legs and the taut shaft of his penis against her pubic mound.

'Did you put your diaphragm in?' he breathed as he stretched up to kiss her ears.

Juno tried to ignore the fact that the question sounded unpleasantly clinical. She couldn't.

'I think we should have fully protected sex,' she retaliated in an equally antiseptic tone. She suddenly had visions of herself and Jay wrapped head-to-foot in cling-film coated with spermicidal jelly, trying to get into bed like two randy mummies.

'Why are you laughing, Juno?' Jay looked perplexed as he rested his head back on the carpet and peered up at her.

Juno tried to keep her giggles in check and pressed a few more kisses to his mouth to calm herself down and get back in the swing. She wasn't going to try this wild seductress lark again in a hurry, she decided. It was the best fun she'd had in ages, but she kept losing the plot. Not that she wanted to stop for a moment. She felt wonderfully randy, randier than ever before – just strangely detached and headstrong with it, almost out of control.

'Have you got a rubber then?' he asked between kisses, arching up against her, his glorious pink possession getting dangerously close to entering the ball unmasked.

Juno wriggled against him, for a moment not caring as she was swept away on a rip-tide of reckless abandon. She wanted him inside her now. She wanted to keep this sublime sensation thrumming between her legs and not break it in order to scrabble around in the bathroom for an out-of-date Durex or dig through her handbag for a lager-and-lime-flavoured glow-in-the-dark novelty condom she'd bought for a joke in a pub loo. Her period was due either tomorrow or the next day. She was bound to be safe, wasn't she?

'Have you got a condom, Juno?' he repeated, the head of his cock tantalisingly close now, almost stroking her labia like a skilled, persistent thumb.

Damn, damn, damn! Juno wanted to wail aloud. I could come, she realised. If we go for it now, I'm going to come. And I never did that with John. Never even felt this bloody close. Any minute now my entire body is going to enter nuclear melt down and he wants me to be back in a jiffy *with* a Jiffy.

'I've got my diaphragm in,' she breathed, easing herself closer around him. Saying a silent prayer of apology for fingers-crossed foolhardiness, she tilted back and sank down, feeling the thick, smooth shaft get sucked up inside her.

Madness made her demanding. It also made her feel as turned on as an electricity showroom in the January Sales. She was gambling like an idiot hooked on scratchcards. And she was so, so close to winning. As she put her own hand between her legs, she felt selfish and high and oh-so-damnably good. Letting her fingers press and caress where his flesh couldn't, she experienced such a heady cocktail of physical sensations that she moaned aloud.

'You're so beautiful,' Jay murmured hoarsely. 'You feel so good.'

His hands were on her breasts now, alternately teasing her nipples, palming the soft flesh around them and then grabbing great hunks like a prospector running gold-filled sand through his fingers. Juno pitched back on her haunches until his arms were at full stretch, and moved him deeper inside her. Bang, bang, bang . . . dive, dive, dive. God, it was delicious. He was so clean and new and novel. It was like wearing a new dress.

Suddenly she had a vision of herself in something ludicrously expensive, ridiculously flattering, absurdly chic. She was Liz at *Four Weddings*, Cinderella at the ball, Lydia at just about anything. She was fresh and beautiful and envied. The dress slithered off. She was coming . . . coming . . . coming . . . going . . . no, still coming . . . oh, boy, was she coming!

'Wow – oh – wow – oh – WOW!'

No amount of holding her own had prepared her for this. Thirty years of life, sixteen years of conscious sexual experimentation, twelve years of active sex, a decade of sex manuals, six months of therapy (curtailed due to finances), several weeks of cyber-sex on the company's Internet relay chat link-up, two or three extremely erotic dreams about Malcolm from *Neighbours* . . . Nothing compared to this. This was head-to-toe electro-impulse therapy, centred right where it counted. Counted with an O. Several Os.

Juno's first truly interactive orgasm (those I'll-show-you sessions with John didn't count) was something close to perfection. Close to but not spot on. Spot on would have been Jay coming shortly afterwards – at the same time was perhaps too much to ask. However, Juno – as sore as a burnt finger in certain regions by now and regrettably positioned for fuzzy friction – found herself still plunging and bucking gallantly above him for more than twenty minutes.

She was suddenly experiencing a stuck-to-the-ceiling sensation of aloofness. She supposed it was her fault for getting so high on lust that she flew up there in the first place.

In all her overawed and, on reflection, wildly selfish, self-discovery, she had rather neglected Jay's side of the deal. He looked delighted enough right now – groaning and tensing ecstatically beneath her, his sexy yellow eyes staring intently into hers, his beautiful, angular face high with colour and glistening with sweat, sinewy shoulders quilted with muscles as he pressed back on his elbows to move deeply inside her – but Juno had a sudden feeling of drenched self-loathing and guilt as she rode him home. It was something to do with their being strangers, with knowing what brought him off before she really knew what turned him on. As she squatted forwards and pushed faster and harder, she realised she was using the same tricks she had on John. They had taken her years to glean and perfect. Now she was simply repeating them mechanically for Jay just because he was male. She didn't know him at all.

As he finally collapsed back, breathing as hard and fast as a marathon runner who grips his knees after the tape's broken, Juno found she couldn't kiss him. He was still inside her, his sperm was trickling out of her, and she couldn't kiss him. It seemed too intimate somehow.

His long, rust-coloured lashes were almost veiling his eyes, cheeks soaked with a red-wine flush, the sardonic mouth was smiling in amazement and the pendant wolf's tooth was under one neat, pale ear (three pierced holes in the lobe, no earrings; one silver sleeper on the upper rim – another new sighting). He looked as formidably sexy as he had two hours earlier, but she wanted to apologise rather than eulogise.

She could still feel the warm afterglow of her earlier ecstasy teasing the tips of her toes and the pit of her navel. An insistent pulse tickled the core of her cervix like a bee collecting pollen from a stamen. Yet as Jay stretched up an arm to pull her down for a kiss, she jerked her head away and eased him from inside her.

'I need to find a tissue,' she muttered, getting up and walking to her dressing table. She felt numb. Used and using. Cheap and paying the price. Easy and hard as nails.

'Juno,' he called, still lying by the door, head propped on his elbow.

She ignored him until she had cleaned herself up and binned

the tissue. She really was feeling extraordinarily cool about this, she realised. Cool as in frosty. Far from relaxed.

When she looked across at him, she felt marginally less cool – he had rolled over on to his belly and was looking up at her with his chin pressed to crossed wrists. There was something about the position – and the way it showed off both his wide, sinewy shoulders and his tight buttocks – that made her feel perhaps tonight hadn't been such a mistake after all. She'd bedded – or rather floored – something extremely desirable. And, with a lurch in her guilty stomach, she realised she still desired him. Coming hadn't made the lust go. It had increased it tenfold.

'What is it?' she asked shakily.

'Juno, don't try to love me,' he said, yellow eyes watchful and guarded.

'You what?' she gulped, completely taken aback.

'I don't want you to try to love me,' he repeated calmly. 'People don't. They just don't. Promise me you won't, Juno.'

'Sure.' She forced a cheery laugh. 'As long as you promise not to fall in love with me.'

'I'm serious.' He looked away nervily.

Tipping his head, he pushed the floppy gold forelock back from his forehead until his fingers were interlaced at the nape of his neck, knuckles showing white with tension. 'You've got to swear.' His voice was muffled. 'And you've got to mean it.'

Juno stared at him in astonishment, saying nothing. Was this some sort of weird PC American thing? Like the consensual sex forms women were asked to sign before a date just in case they cried rape the next day?

He looked up again, raking her face for an answer.

'Okay,' she said slowly, hardly able to believe the absurdity of the situation. 'I swear I will not fall in love with Jay . . . um, what's your second name again?' she asked with pointed irony although she knew it perfectly well.

'Mulligan.'

'. . . with Jay Mulligan,' she finished sarcastically, tempted to add 'conceited bastard' after his name. 'Satisfied?'

Saying nothing, he stood up and walked towards her.

Cupping her face in his hands, he tilted his head so that his forelock flopped against her nose and kissed her with unbelievable tenderness. It was a mesmerising kiss, one that went straight in at number one on Juno's chart. The sort of kiss that would haunt her lips for ever, revisiting her mouth during restless, sultry dreams and then slithering away the moment her eyes opened. If ever one kiss could make someone fall in love, then this was it.

Jay kept his hands cupped around her face as his cello-curve lips robbed hers of their sweet, greedy pleasure. Touching her forehead with his so that their eyes were too close together for her to see straight, he suddenly smiled. 'May I sleep with you tonight? I wanna lie beside you.'

Juno hadn't a clue what to say. She simply hadn't a clue. The first thing that came to mind was the first thing she said – and that took some time.

'Get into bed, Jay. My bed. We'll lie together tonight if that's what you want. We can always tell the truth tomorrow.'

Chapter Eight

Juno found it hard to sleep, and when she did, was wracked with peculiar dreams in which Jay metamorphosed into other people – John, Bruno from the wine bar, Malcolm from *Neighbours*.

Staying awake was less disturbing and gave her the chance to mull over what she'd done. Part of her was rather proud of her wild-child antics; she'd always known she had a siren's streak inside. Yet another part of her was deeply ashamed and very confused. Was it truly sordid to sleep with a man one hadn't even dated? A man who scared one slightly? And, even worse, someone she'd only really hit upon because she'd been rejected earlier in the evening and wanted to feel better about herself.

In her singularly single pre-John years, Juno had gone to bed with several men she had barely known, but each had been in the context of a brief relationship of sorts – they'd at least been through the formalities, like swapping edited life-stories in a wine bar, eating a meal or two at Bella Pasta and watching a Woody Allen movie together. She'd only ever had two fully fledged one-night stands, and both had been self-hate disasters, but neither had been with someone she then had to live with for six months afterwards. She had a feeling she could have just opened a can of worms big enough to bait every fishing hook in England, when all she'd really wanted to do was fish for compliments.

Beside her, Jay slept fitfully, turning often, breathing irregularly and muttering aloud at times.

She was getting more accustomed to his face now, and allowed herself the indulgence of examining it at length in the early hours of Saturday morning, when the steely white light of late dawn cast it into high relief.

Juno watched him for almost half an hour.

At one point his eyes opened, quite suddenly and unexpectedly, and he stared straight at her with unnerving focus. Then he reached out a hand – warm and dry from the fug of the duvet – and stroked her face with exquisite tenderness, before sliding it to the nape of her neck and running a thumb along the bone at the top of her spine. As his fingers relaxed against the tendons of her throat, his eyes closed again.

She woke very lazily from the most delightful dream. Jay – or was it Malcolm from *Neighbours*? – had been kissing his way very slowly up her thighs. Delicious. She could still feel cool lips against warm, sleepy skin. Mmm. And damp hair brushing her belly. Mmmm, mmm. And a recently shaven chin burying itself deeply into the soft flesh at the very tops of her legs. And that tongue was doing unbelievably real-feeling things now that it was lapping its way closer to her much-neglected love bud. Too unreally real. This just had to be real.

If I open my eyes this won't be happening, she thought dizzily. If I open my eyes this won't happen. Only it's happening right now. Ready or not, here I come. God, I never knew it was this easy! What have I been doing wrong all these years? Here we go . . . whoopee! Hallelujah! Fizz, bang, whoosh, whizz, wham, bam, thank you, Uncle Sam.

'Good morning, pretty lady.' Jay's face appeared between her breasts. He pressed a smooth chin to her collar bone, and smiled up at her. He was wearing jogging clothes, she noticed. Used jogging clothes. 'I brought you some breakfast. Hope you're feeling hungry.' The thick lashes blinked slowly and he watched her face with those dangerous yellow eyes, now brimming with mirth.

'Famished,' Juno said in a very warbly voice, still fizzing all over from the aftershock of the chemical explosion that had just taken place inside her body.

'The park here is great,' he enthused as he jumped out of bed and fetched the tray. 'I gotta swim in those natural pools, man.'

Blinking, Juno peered at him over her duvet. Was this chatty, smiling charmer of a wake-up call the same moody, taciturn, sexy terrorist she'd gone to bed with last night? She pinched herself and winced with pain. She was certainly awake.

'Hampstead Heath?' She elbowed her way into a sitting position and gazed disbelievingly at his gloriously tight bottom. 'You ran as far as the ponds?' It took her forever to walk there. She normally got a cab.

'That what they're called?' He carried the tray over with care. 'Yeah. I went there. And up to that big stately house. What's its name? Kenwood? Great place.'

Juno nodded. 'Sean takes Rug up there a lot – he likes to bark at the tourists. Rug sometimes joins in too.'

'Rug?'

'Sean's mutty old dog – Mum and Dad are looking after him.'

'Oh, right.' He grinned. 'I like dogs. He shoulda stayed here. I like someone to jog with.'

He was so high and happy, Juno found it utterly unexpected and totally infectious. The pale eyes crinkled like gold leaf rubbed between fingers when he laughed, the symmetrical face creased with sudden asymmetric life, the tense-lipped mouth loosened into a ravishing smile. He was no longer the ice-cool Bronx hoodlum with possible IRA connections. He was, just for now, her new lover, in her bed, feeding her breakfast. The feeling was beyond sublime. She longed to call the girls and brag.

They remained in bed all morning, dropping crumbs amidst the Saturday supplements and the creased duvet cover. As Jay pored over the papers – and he seemed to have bought the entire English range – she napped and dozed and rolled over on to a pile of rejected Appointments and Cars sections. Considering he was so unfamiliar to her, she found him remarkably easy to sleep with.

She woke at lunchtime, feeling far more refreshed. In fact she was ravenously hungry once more – quite a feat after the all-time calorific breakfast she'd scoffed earlier. Beside her, Jay was stuck into an *Independent* article about political refugees while at the same time listening to *Any Questions* on the radio. She was amazed he took such an active interest in British politics. She wondered if that was what he was covering for the American papers while he was in the UK. Either that or something more sinister lay behind his interest. But she tucked any fears of possible mortar attacks firmly to the back of her spinning, happy head.

He looked quite gorgeous in the midday sunlight which cut into the room at an acute angle from the tall, thin windows beside the bed. It cast his hair in highly polished copper and bathed those pale shoulders in tawny tones of brandy butter and *crème anglaise*.

Juno wondered briefly, and rather vainly, how good she was looking right now. She had a very romanticised image of them lying together as viewed by an outsider – perhaps by Triona dropping in unannounced to borrow a few of Sean's videos. Jay was all russet mane and tattooed blond skin, while she was softer, golden-haired and more rumpled. A fleshier Julie Christie perhaps? The image was rather appealing. She pondered it for a few more minutes, envisaging her peachy skin, sexily dishevelled tresses and wanton curves. The whole concept made her feel randy again. She stealthily removed her hand from beneath the pillow where it had been resting and slid it over the *Daily Mail* magazine, a Scott's of Stowe catalogue and the *Guardian* review.

Soon the *Independent* was being merrily crushed beneath Juno and Jay as they touched and tussled their way towards pleasure. Like two tramps on a park bench indulging in frottage beneath a newspaper eiderdown, they ripped and shredded and creased and crunched.

★　★　★

When Juno ventured into the bathroom later for a pee and caught sight of her face in the mirror, she barely recognised herself. A red-chinned, baggy-eyed, thatch-haired wild woman stared back. This was no Julie Christie vision fresh from a warm, sinfully creased bed. This was closer to the missing link.

The spot on her chin had swelled up and trebled in size; it matched the rampaging stubble rash perfectly. And last night's mascara was all over the place – it hadn't just leaked into her crow's feet and smudged sexily beneath her bags, but had splattered on to the side of her nose, her forehead and even into her eyebrows.

Worst of all was her hair. It looked as though something had been nesting in it overnight. Something that had then given multiple birth, *Alien*-style.

She looked diabolical, and was now aching so much from her sexual excesses that she was walking like a cowboy after a pan-American cow-herding record attempt. She was so stiff that climbing over the bath rim to have a shower took several attempts.

With warm water plastering her tangled mop of hair to her scalp and rinsing away the mascara, she tried a few pelvic floor exercises and winced. Lydia had told her to do thirty a day and revolutionise her sex life. Seeing as she hadn't had an active sex life for the past few months (and not much of one in those last weeks with John before that) she'd lapsed in her daily tense-and-relax shower routine. Now she decided it was time to catch up big time.

Ten floor exercises later she realised someone was moving on the other side of the shower curtain. Someone who was a blur of golden-treacle hair and clover-honey skin. Someone who was getting in with her.

Oh, the bliss of having one's hair washed by a lover. It didn't matter that Jay commented on her split ends and used enough conditioner to make an Old English Sheepdog look like an Afghan Hound; his long, bony fingers moved so sensually through her hair and massaged her scalp so expertly that she was wriggling with lust before he'd even started to rinse.

Aware of the spot and the splatter-effect mascara, which was probably heading for her chin under the blast of water, Juno kept her back to him as he kneaded the base of her neck and pressed his long, lean belly to her spine. The water was getting cooler all the time (the old boiler generally packed up if forced to work for more than ten minutes). But as he moved from her hair to her nipples, she wouldn't have cared if she was standing under Niagara Falls in winter. By the time Jay had rinsed most of the conditioner from her hair, the water was only lukewarm.

As Juno leant down to the taps to crank up the hot water output, she felt him take a firm hold of her buttocks and before she knew it he was inside her, thrusting from behind like a pneumatic drill and filling her up so completely she almost head-butted the tiled wall in front of her.

It was absolutely thrilling. Her balance on the slippery enamel was precarious, and soapy water was now running from her back through her hair and dribbling into her eyes, but what Jay was doing was far too sensational to put a stop to. She gripped tightly on to the taps and abandoned herself to blind danger and wet pleasure. After a few minutes they were screwing under a deluge of freezing cold water.

And I thought cold showers were supposed to dampen your libido, Juno thought giddily.

They ate lunch on the roof terrace, sitting at the slatted wooden table with napkins on their laps and polite conversation on their lips. Juno thought it ridiculously formal to swap platitudes after the amount of body fluids they had exchanged in the past twelve hours, but Jay seemed suddenly distant and rigidly civilised again. She kept finding herself taking the piss and wanting to giggle.

'Is this a main course or a sexual inter-course?'

It was a sweltering day. The sun, almost directly overhead, was like a blinding flame-thrower, and Sean's much-nurtured potted bays cast thin shadows, along with the furniture. Wearing lime green jeans and a faded Stussy t-shirt, Jay helped himself to piles of ham and salad and ate like a hungry foxhound competing with his pack.

Juno watched him for a while, wondering at his capacity to throw back food and Diet Coke without apparent pause for breath. Then, deciding to see how he'd react, she toyed with her fork and, waiting for one of his can-swills, playfully speared a hunk of brie from his plate before popping it into her mouth.

'What the fuck did you do that for?' He turned on her, only the slightest hint of humour sweetening the outburst.

Juno chewed away cheerfully.

'There's still thirty degrees of brie on the board.' He nodded irritably at the sweating cheese.

'I think you'll find it closer to forty.' She peered at it intently. 'Shall we get out a protractor and check? Or are we talking temperature here?'

He rolled his eyes disparagingly and continued to bolt back his food.

'Why d'you eat so fast?' She toyed with a salad leaf.

'It's how I eat.' He spoke with his mouth full. 'You got a problem with it?'

'No, it's fascinating.' She propped her chin on her hand. 'I just thought perhaps you grew up in a big family – mealtimes were a competition to get the most grub? I had friends like that at school.'

'Oh, yeah?' More Coke was swilled back.

She nodded. 'So do you have many brothers and sisters?'

He started scooping up salad, his fork in his right hand American-style.

'I got six elder sisters.'

'Wow!' Juno whistled. 'Bet you had fun trying to get in the bathroom in the morning. So you're the youngest?'

He tilted his head guardedly. Juno got the distinct impression he didn't want to talk about it.

'Have you lots of nieces and nephews then?' she asked, becoming more interested the less he was willing to divulge.

Jay chewed for a long time before answering, his eyes

narrowed and evasive. 'My sisters and I fell out. I don't keep in touch with them. I think they got a few kids between them, yeah.'

'You fell out with *all* your sisters?' Juno gulped. 'What did you do? Murder your parents?'

'Something like that,' he muttered, looking more and more uneasy. 'Listen, can we talk about something else? I don't like talking about my family.'

'Sure.' She swallowed nervously and decided to lay off the subject. 'Let's talk about the weather or something personal like that.'

He polished off his can of Coke and reached for another. 'You could tell me what a twenty-five year old is doing with a big box with 'Thirties Emergency Kit' written on it.' He suddenly gave her that disarming, devastating smile.

Juno bit her lower lip awkwardly. God, he'd rumbled her, the sod. Why had she lied about her age when the flat was full of cards saying Happy Thirtieth?

'Nothing like planning for the future,' she murmured vaguely.

'I prefer older women.' He was still smiling as he pressed the cool can to his brow.

'I'll introduce you to my grandmother sometime,' she muttered sulkily, getting up and wandering to the balcony railings to look out across London's heat haze of pollution.

She felt his hand creep under her dress and slide up her leg. When she glanced over her shoulder, she saw that he was still smiling, those mesmerising eyes crinkled against the sun. Suddenly her grumpiness was erased by the realisation of just how gorgeous he was. Her groin bubbled like a rising soufflé, frothing over with desire and happiness.

'Do you want to go for a walk on the Heath?' she asked, squirming as he stroked the back of her knees with his knuckles.

'Not especially.' He squinted up at her.

The sun was directly behind her and he must be able to see every bulge and curve of her body's outline through her dress. Juno longed to shuffle into the shadow of a potted bay, positioning herself carefully so that the bulbous clipped growth eclipsed her bottom.

'What do you want to do then?' She hoped he'd say 'talk about us'. She was dying to know what was going on in his head, what he thought of her, how they had ended up in this situation, but she wanted him to introduce the topic.

'I want to go back to bed.' His fingers were sliding higher.

'Are you tired?' Juno cocked her head playfully, although she wasn't altogether certain she was wrong. He couldn't be feeling randy again, could he? Didn't men have a limit on these things? John certainly had.

'Nope.' The fingers were tracing the seam of her knickers now.

Delightedly realising she was indeed wrong, Juno reached out to take his other hand and lead him inside the flat, but he withdrew it and picked up a plate.

'Let's just clear away lunch first.'

'You what?' Juno wrinkled her brows in astonishment. The suggestion hardly smacked of spontaneous seduction. 'Can't it wait?'

'No – it'll be covered in flies in spit time if we leave it.' He was already expertly stacking crockery.

Juno let out a deep sigh and shrugged. 'Okay, but on one condition.'

'What's that?' He scraped her almost untouched salad back into the bowl.

'That we wash up in the nude.'

Chapter Nine

They spent the remainder of Saturday in bed, only getting up to visit the loo or fetch a drink. It was the first time in years that Juno failed to set the video for *Blind Date* or rush out and buy a lottery ticket. The phone rang occasionally and was picked up in the sitting room by the machine where Poirot's furious squawks drowned out the caller's message. The sun dropped out of sight and was replaced by a deep, red glow on the horizon. Juno felt the sky was blushing at the scandalous amount of sex she was participating in.

Later, she made him lie on the hearth rug while she massaged him. As she worked her way very leisurely along the length of his body, she noticed another soft, circular cicatrix like the one on his knee, this time on his right shoulder blade by his armpit, and a long, thin stripe of scar tissue across his left hip. She longed to ask him about them, but was certain it would darken his mood once more.

'You're seriously good.' He stretched out luxuriously under her oiled, agile fingers and groaned with pleasure.

'I took a course once.' She pressed the balls of her thumbs into the base of his spine with practised skill. 'I thought of doing it as a career – combining it with stand-up comedy – but it didn't work out.'

'Why not?'

'Most people want massages in the evening. Home visits after work. It clashed with any comedy gigs I got.'

He tilted his face towards her. 'Sean never said you were a comedienne.'

'Trying to be – I still can't afford to give up the day job.' She rolled the angle of her wrists into his buttocks, as much for her own pleasure as his. They dipped divinely in just the right spot. Michelangelo couldn't have sculpted them better.

'So what is it you do during the day?' He propped his chin on his crossed wrists. 'You were working on Friday, right?'

'How come you can ask me questions like that but I can't ask you?' She poked a playful finger into the soft flesh of one perfect buttock.

'Because,' he flicked the hair from his eyes and regarded her thoughtfully, rubbing his chin on his shoulder, 'you'll answer them. You like talking about yourself. I don't.'

Juno bit her lip and smiled. At least they were having a conversation of more than three consecutive sentences for the first time that day. She guessed her job was a fairly ideal entry level, even if she did hate talking about it.

'I'm an agony aunt,' she confessed with the usual attempt at self-parody.

'A what?' He squinted quizzically over his shoulder.

'I write advice columns for magazines. Several in fact, although not under the same name. I answer people's sexual and emotional dilemmas.' She pulled another face, ever the clown who knew her career was a sham.

'Jesus!' Jay rolled over on to his side so that he could look her straight in the eyes. 'Are you some sort of analyst then?'

'God, no.' She sat back on her heels and wiped the oil from her hands on to her thighs. 'I got into it by accident.'

'You did?' He looked even more astonished.

'I used to be a temp,' she explained. 'I did typing for some quick cash while I was first trying to break into comedy.

'A few years ago, I got a fortnight's work at a magazine publishers called Immedia – they produce all those free magazines you get handed at the tube. Do you have the same thing in New York?'

'At subway stations? Yeah, commuters get tons of pulp stuffed in their faces.'

'Pulp's a good word for the stuff Immedia produces,' Juno sighed. 'There's a title for every day of the working week. One of them had a problem page – *Career Girl* it was called; it's folded now. All the letters on the page were made up, and everyone in the office had to take a turn to be Betty Unwin – that was the column's fictional agony aunt. Doing "The Betty" was universally loathed. No one could be bothered to do it that week, so the job fell to me. The temp.'

'And you made it all up too?' He cupped her cheek with one hand – that strangely intimate gesture which made her stomach feel as though she was belly dancing in a Jacuzzi.

Juno cleaved to his touch.

'All lies?' He stared into her face.

'Yes.' She screwed the top on the massage oil. 'I suppose I must have made up some pretty scurrilous problems because it caused quite a stir. The fake letters were usually well-worn old chestnuts about having a crush on the boss or trying to get one's boyfriend to propose. To be honest I don't think anyone checked the page before it went to print apart from the copy-editor, and she was a raging drunk who'd been fired from *Tatler*. So I spiced it up a little and no one in the office cared enough to notice until it was being handed out at Holborn. By then it was too late.'

'So what did you write?' He was up on one elbow now, fascinated.

Juno thought back, trying to remember that first silly week of thinking it was all a one-off joke that didn't matter. 'Well, there was one about a man who could only achieve an erection if his girlfriend enveloped him in bubble-wrap and popped the bubbles by sucking them,' she recalled with a giggle. 'And another was from a woman who said she couldn't stop herself farting for fun on the tube in rush hour just to see the reaction on her fellow commuters' faces.'

'You're kidding?' Jay's eyebrows were almost on top of his

head as he brushed the hair from his eyes to gape at her. 'You didn't get fired?'

She shook her head. 'Betty got a post bag full of letters the next week. Considering hardly anyone ever reads those free magazines, let alone writes letters in to them, the editor almost flipped over with joy, and told the group publisher to put me on a salary. It didn't matter that half of them were complaints and the rest from cranks. I was hired and problem pages were introduced into almost every free-sheet magazine they publish. I've been doing it for over four years. I'm now Edna Dougherty, Claire Frankel, Brian Bevan and Greta Rayson. And I freelance for the *News on Sunday*'s "Ask Annie" page, plus doing the odd stint on cable TV.'

'And do you still make all the problems up?' Jay looked enthralled.

'Ninety per cent of them. I change my style according to the magazine, but it's largely sexual.' She blushed as she realised that last night's stop-start seduction – however glorious its final denouement – had hardly demonstrated the copy-book skill of a sexual expert.

But Jay was still laughing delightedly. 'Jesus, this is fucking insane! I love this shit, man. I love it.' He lunged upwards and kissed her hard on the mouth. 'You have gotta be the most interesting woman I've met in years.'

'Really?' Juno spoke with her mouth full, suddenly finding herself fizzing all over with happiness like a Refresher dropped in lemonade. Most people thought her job was ludicrous and immoral. On the whole, so did she.

'I sure do.' He was rolling her beneath him now. 'First, you turn up naked in the kitchen here, then the next day you act as if you're all attitude and drill me like a journo, later you seduce me – '

'Sedoose,' Juno laughed, mocking his accent.

'Yeah,' he laughed, sliding between her legs. 'Seduce. And now you tell me you lie for a living. It's fucking crazy. I think I could get seriously into you, Juno.'

'I think you're already inside me, Jay,' she laughed as his warm, oiled body moved against hers.

Thoroughly overexcited by the spectacle of two nude humans mounting one another amongst the scatter cushions, Poirot started screaming out betting tips and old Bernard Manning jokes.

'That parrot's putting me off,' Jay complained as he started to lose his sublime rhythm in and out of Juno. 'I keep expecting him to give us marks out of ten.'

'He's a mocking bird,' she laughed, stretching up to kiss him quiet. She was learning fast.

Behind them, Poirot bobbed up and down in time and let out a serious of jealous screeches. 'The mother-in-law's a dragon! Tenner on the Coral Stakes!'

Stretching out on the rug later, Juno played with a strand of Jay's hair and propped herself on one elbow so she could look at his face. He was lying flat on his back, staring at the ceiling. She longed to ask him what he was thinking, but knew that was the height of crassness. She also longed for a cigarette but she wanted to stay put and delve a little first. She was wary of broaching a personal topic, but impatience was getting the better of her. She had a feeling that if she didn't ask what was going on between them soon, it would have already gone and the chance would be forever lost. He had, after all, just said he could get seriously into her – just a few hours after making her swear not to fall in love with him. She was desperate to know why he'd done that. Was that his usual technique? It was a bit odd to say the least. Most men rolled over, farted and fell asleep. Perhaps he should be gently told it wasn't normal.

'Jay . . . can I ask you something?' She pressed her lips to his shoulder. He smelled of soap and deodorant, with a heady underscent of perspiration and sex.

'Yeah?' His eyes slid towards hers but didn't lock with them. She knew straight away that he had read her predictable mind and indeed thought she was going to ask him what he was thinking. There was a tell-tale look of dread on his face – his lips had tightened, brows furled. She had seen the same look many times before on John's face – the 'oh-no-here-we-go' response to what he had always described as her 'Freudian gym-slips' or, in kinder moments, her 'bad hair-brained days'.

'Do you want me to put some music on?' she asked instead.

The face relaxed.

'Sure – whatever.'

'What would you prefer?' Remembering his classical CD the previous night, she hoped he didn't suggest Wagner. All those fat women bellowing about war and wearing Viking helmets. Now that *was* a bad hair day. She'd had a short-lived Bjork phase herself, knotting her hair into two little tufts that looked like scraggy horns and consequently getting called 'Ermintrude' all night in a wine bar.

'I don't care, you choose.' Suddenly sounding irritable, he gazed broodily at the ceiling again.

Really, he was impossible to read, Juno decided as she flipped through Sean's high-rise pile of 'seventies punk CDs, interspersed with the very few she had been able to wrest from the Clapham flat (John had only let her take the ones he didn't like). She wondered if Jay would like The Beautiful South and decided against it. 'You Keep It All In' was a bit too pertinent, and 'Song For Whoever' was asking for trouble. He might think of her as a 'whoever'.

Juno wished she understood what was going on in his head. One minute he was laughing and open, almost childlike in his heady enthusiasm; the next he was clamped up, shuttered and utterly insular. She still hadn't figured out what triggered his 'on' moments – it wasn't just sex. Sometimes today it seemed to be what she said or the way she looked at him. What was increasingly clear was that the instant she seemed likely to ask him anything personal, he grew grumpy and incommunicative.

She settled for Lloyd Cole as he was safe and mellow. Soon 'Rich' was quirkily telling the story of a glamorous 'fifties movie star turning to the bottle and losing her stardom, reputation and money.

Juno settled back down beside Jay and wondered whether she should hit the bathroom for another clean up. It was becoming something of a regular stop-off. She couldn't remember ever having this much sex. She vaguely recalled the detectives in *Basic Instinct* shining some sort of ultra-violet light on the death bed at the start of the film. It had illuminated all the semen, indicating a sexual marathon before the victim breathed his last. If someone flashed the same light over Sean's flat right now, they'd call in the contract cleaners.

Adopting the same position as Jay, she stretched out alongside him so that their flanks connected, and shuddered happily at the sensation of skin touching skin. Why clean up when you want to get dirty again as soon as possible? she mused, although she was starting to have doubts that he could keep up the pace. She hoped men didn't get tennis elbow or housemaid's knee in the underpants region – a sort of rutter's cramp. As it was, she was currently walking as though she'd just ridden down Ben Nevis on a mountain bike.

He had gone very still beside her as he listened to the song, she noticed. He seemed to be straining to hear every word. Juno strained too and laughed.

'He's great, isn't he? His songs are so clever, that's what I like about him.'

Jay didn't immediately respond. He waited until the song had ended and 'Why I Love Country Music' was beating its sardonic way into the room.

'What made you choose that track?' he asked quietly.

Juno twisted her head towards his and raised an eyebrow, but it was lost on him as he remained staring at the ceiling.

'It's the first track on the album.'

'Good song,' he muttered sarcastically.

'I'll put something else on if you like.' Juno suddenly felt embarrassed by her taste in music, and not for the first time. Men always thought it was diabolical; John had almost weed himself laughing the first time he espied her record collection, complete with its seven-volume Carpenters set and well-worn 'Barbra Streisand Sings Love Ballads' EP.

'No, keep this on.' He closed his eyes and stroked her thigh absent-mindedly. 'I want to listen.'

Forced to listen along too, Juno decided that Cole was neither safe nor mellow. She must have played the CD a thousand times, loving the mood, picking up on the odd witty soundbite here or clever phrase there, but she had never listened as she did now. 'Pretty Gone' told of what appeared to be a one-night stand, 'Grace' of a twenty-eight year old who was looking rough and old and drank too much, 'Brand New Friend' pretty much summed up what she wanted to wheedle out of Jay. She stuck it as far as 'Lost Weekend' before she could hold her silence no more.

'Is that what this is?' she asked, propping herself up on one elbow.

'Huh?' He seemed to be swimming back from miles away as his eyes blinked open.

'Is this a lost weekend?' She suddenly felt rather silly and over-analytical for asking. Listening intently to lyrics made one feel a bit too damned self-dramatising to be healthy, she decided. It was Slade and Status Quo from now on.

'Are we in a hotel in Amsterdam?' he asked after a brief pause for thought, listening carefully to the lyrics.

'Not that I'm aware of,' she admitted.

'Well, then.' His eyes slid across to hers again and this time locked on target, searching intently. She couldn't tell if there was humour in them or something far more puzzling.

They were lying in near-darkness. The only light came from Uboat's luminescent tank and from the huge windows over which they hadn't yet drawn blinds. The last traces of sunset in the darkening sky soaked the room in a great claret stain, spilling on to his face so that those yellow eyes were deepened and warmed, lending them a sympathy which had been absent until now.

Juno felt a great romantic twang inside her – like a violin string breaking, a rose stem snapping, a champagne cork popping. For a moment, it was glorious. Yet the feeling, however powerful and moving, was closer to profound loss than to bowled-over love. What she was experiencing, she realised, was not just the giddy rush of falling for a stranger; it was the realisation that she was once and for all out of love with John. This sublime deliverance was liberating and enthralling. It was also terrifying and unfamiliar.

'Do you want this weekend to be lost?' Jay asked eventually.

Juno watched his face, uncertain how to reply. She didn't want to blacken his mood yet further by suggesting they lift the love ban and lower the emotional drawbridge. What she was experiencing right now was far too sexy and exciting to risk losing.

'I don't think so.' She kissed his chest lightly. 'I think we're still finding it right now.'

He nodded and a faint smile flickered across his lips.

'Sure.' He ran a hand from her belly to her right breast which was hanging pendulously above his ribs, while the left one dived towards her armpit. Juno wished they wouldn't obey gravity quite so much. She'd read somewhere that one's cleavage was starting to droop when one could hold a pencil under a tit whilst standing up. She reckoned she could get three marker pens and a clipboard under hers, no problem.

'Your ex,' he said, playing with her nipple like a worry bead. 'John, isn't it?'

'Yes.' Juno suddenly felt rather chilly. She was getting goosebumps on her bum. 'What about him?'

'How come it ended?' His fingers moved across to the other nipple and started twiddling fretfully.

'He went off with someone else.' She shivered uncomfortably.

He stared unblinkingly at her face. She expected him to respond, to say something – express sorrow, anger for her, surprise, anything. But he stayed silent.

Lloyd was getting particularly depressing about children with bad complexions and greasy hair in 'James' now. Juno felt decidedly self-pitying.

'I was abandoned,' she announced rather dramatically, again

regretting her tendency to derive her moods from popular music.

Jay continued staring at her. Still he hadn't blinked.

'So was I,' he muttered so quietly that she could barely hear him over the music, although his face was just inches from hers.

Trying very hard not to be offended that he'd so shamelessly turned the topic to himself, she mustered a sad smile. 'Did you love her very much?'

'I never got the chance.'

Juno didn't understand what he was driving at. *Never got the chance*? Was he talking about being stood up on a date here? Having an unreciprocated crush? Perhaps a one-night stand or something equally banal? She hardly felt it compared to the years she had invested in her relationship with John, and the hurt she had endured when he threw it all back in her face for Double D Debbie.

'I want to love her very much,' he whispered.

So he was hooked on another woman, Juno realised sadly. Some mystery witch who hadn't even given him time to love her, whatever that meant. Sharp splinters of jealously scatter-gunned her chest and she decided she didn't want to know right now.

Watching his clenched face, she stroked his cheek absent-mindedly. She didn't know what to say so decided it was her turn to remain silent. She was starting to feel seriously cold now, too. The French windows were still open on to the roof terrace and a breeze was catching their naked bodies in its bracing slipstream.

'I can't figure out what I feel for her.' He pressed his hands to his face suddenly, muffling his muttered undertone. 'Love, hate, emptiness . . . I just can't figure it out.'

There was another aching silence. Juno wanted him to repeat what he'd just said, she wasn't sure if she'd caught it right. She was pretty certain, however, that he'd just said something about feeling empty. Now that she could relate to.

'I'll cook us some supper,' she suggested brightly, sitting up. 'There's tons of stuff in the freezer.'

He opened his eyes and looked up at her.

'You want to cook?'

She nodded enthusiastically, deciding to adopt a chummy lightness for the moment, although it was a pretty tall order when naked and goosebumped all over like a Braille porn magazine.

'I do a mean chilli.'

'Chilli?'

'Now you come to mention it, I'm freezing. I'll get started, shall I?'

Juno prided herself on her cooking. She was something of a whizz in the kitchen, having played sous-chef to her mother for years. But it was not easy to chop and chiffonade and pound and parboil with Jay watching – and criticising – throughout.

His attitude to hygiene bordered on the obsessive, she decided, as he insisted she sterilise her chopping board for the third time.

Having scoured her room for something casual to throw on that would make her look absurdly sexy and chic, Juno had settled for the Peruvian birthing smock, but was now far from certain that it suited her. It was also incredibly impractical – so long that she kept tripping over the hem whilst carrying a knife, and with vast bell sleeves which drooped into the chilli sauce and trailed through the chopped onion, scattering it on the floor like pungent confetti.

It was past ten in the evening and her stomach was rumbling like an old washing machine. She supposed it was because she wasn't smoking. She was dying for a Marlboro Light, but if she tried to light one now, Jay was bound to tell her how unhygienic it was, puffing away during food preparation. She couldn't nip into her bedroom for a sneaky one in case the chilli caught and burned.

When she slopped some rough red Fitou on to the sizzling mince, she hit upon an idea.

'I don't think we've anything but cooking wine in the flat,' she sighed, flapping a few cupboard doors open and shut in a pretence of searching. 'Could you pop out to Oddbins and buy something? I'll give you the money.'

'I told you, I don't drink.'

'Well, I do.' She spooned far too much chilli sauce into the pan, now positively twitching at the prospect of a cigarette.

'Okay, okay.' He headed off to put on some shoes. 'What type do you prefer?'

'Red, under a fiver and over thirteen per cent proof.'

'A connoisseur then?' he called from the sitting room.

'Sewer, yes,' she mocked his pronunciation.

The moment he'd gone, Juno turned off the heat under the chilli pan and bolted out on to the roof terrace where she puffed headily, like an office worker taking an illicit break.

Halfway down her cigarette, she closed her eyes and groaned loudly, allowing sense to creep back in.

'What am I doing?' she started to laugh bitterly. 'What the hell am I doing out here?'

This was her lost weekend of lust and self-indulgence. She was supposed to be taking control, letting go of her inhibitions and grasping the nettle. Instead she was pandering to Jay's health fixation and getting stung for all she was worth.

Cigarette still glowing, she marched back inside and flopped on to the sofa, propping her feet on the coffee table and sighing contentedly.

Which was where Jay found her ten minutes later, dragging on her second consecutive cigarette and twiddling with the tassels on her birthing smock.

'What are you doing?' he demanded, depositing the thin plastic bag on the table with a clank.

'Having a fag break.' She smiled sweetly. 'The meat needs to relax.'

He gazed at her in momentary astonishment. 'Is it feeling tense?'

'It helps tenderise it.'

'Oh.' He looked blank for a second and then peered censoriously at her cigarette. 'I thought I told you I loathe smoking.'

'You did.' She took a final puff then stubbed it out.

'Well, why the heck are you smoking?' He seemed genuinely offended.

'I just thought I'd get a quick one in while you were out.' She looked up in surprise. 'It's nothing personal. I'm an impassive smoker.'

The moment he headed for the bathroom, she nipped to the kitchen, put the pan back on the heat and poured the remainder of the bottle of Fitou into it. That should loosen him up, she thought with uncanny foresight.

The resulting meal was perhaps a touch sloppy by her exacting standards but undeniably tasty. A purist like Juno might also grumble about the quality of the mince, but Jay seemed genuinely impressed, if still slightly sulky over the cigarette débâcle.

'Where did you learn to cook?' he asked as he helped himself to thirds.

'My mother writes cookery books,' she said, helping herself to more wine. 'She's quite famous in the UK – has her own television series, *Judy Glenn Cooks the Books*.'

'Wow!' Jay raised his eyebrows. 'No wonder you're so good. What does your father do? Apart from test recipes.'

There was an edge to his voice that Juno failed to pick up on.

'He composes music – scores for films and TV mostly.' She cast her fork aside and fingered up a few grains of rice from the table beside her plate. 'And he lectures in music at various colleges to bring in extra cash. I think he feels rather emasculated that Ma earns so much more money than he does. He might be a bit of a hippy but he comes from a long line of macho-men, so it goes against genetics.'

Jay nodded thoughtfully, as though this struck a chord with him, eyebrows veering towards one another until they almost kissed.

Juno took what she assumed to be her cue. 'What do your parents do?'

'My father was a construction worker. My mother brought up me and my sisters. They're both dead.' He rattled out the words as though they meant nothing.

Juno was thrown for a moment, trapped between acute embarrassment and appalled fascination.

'How long ago did they die?' she asked quietly.

'My old man died eleven years ago, when I was sixteen.' He didn't look at her as he responded in the same flat, indifferent monotone.

'And your mother?'

'My old lady? This year. I'm not sure when. Round February, I think.'

'You don't know?' She almost spat a mouthful of wine over him in surprise.

'She was ill for a long time,' he muttered. 'I wasn't allowed to visit her in hospital – or invited to the funeral. I only found out she'd died in April.'

Juno's eyes were watering from being stretched so far. She took another big gulp of wine and coughed it down. 'Why weren't you allowed to visit her?'

He looked up, eyes dull, face impassive. 'She hated me,' he said simply. 'Now can we change the subject?'

'Sure, sure,' Juno spluttered hastily, her head spinning with this new, tragic angle on Jay's elusive, contradictory personality. 'Tell me how you got into photography.'

He pursed his lips for a second. 'I meant, change the subject away from me, Juno.'

Which rather killed the conversation. Usually extremely eager to talk about herself non-stop for hours with only occasional loo breaks, she suddenly found herself tongue-tied.

'Er – what do you suggest we talk about?'

'We don't have to talk at all.' He gave one of his shrugs.

'Do you want to listen to some more music?'

'Nope.' He leaned back in his seat.

'Watch TV?'

'Nope.' He watched her thoughtfully.

'Do the washing up?'

'Nope, that sounds kinda dull.'

'What then?'

'We could make love, I guess.' One sandy eyebrow lifted. 'We haven't tried out my bed yet.'

Christ, he was insatiable, Juno thought excitedly as she started to grin lasciviously across the table at him. If they carried on like this, his pride and joy would drop off.

He might not be great at talking, she thought dizzily twenty minutes later, but boy could he use his tongue to bend a girl's ear.

In the darkened sitting room, Poirot chewed another bead from the Peruvian birthing smock that was covering his cage and spat it out sulkily. He was so demoralised he didn't even join in when the phone rang. Moments later, Sean's voice was talking into the empty room. Poirot cocked his head and listened.

'Hi, guys, hope you two have made friends. Have you found my watch yet? I've also left my phone charger and the spare battery in my room – it's in the socket by the bed. They don't sell them out here so can you Fedex it to me along with the Tag? Cheers. Also, I forgot to mention, I left a load of Rug's food in the freezer – it's the minced stuff in the bottom drawer. Whatever you do, don't eat it. You can take it to Ma and Pa's next time you visit if you like, Joo. That's all, folks.'

Chapter Ten

It was about two in the morning when Juno – caught in the giddy mid-heaven between waking and sleeping – remembered that she was lying on a sex-saturated bed having maintained her reckless diaphragm lie for over twenty-four hours.

She felt her stomach hit her spine with a sickening lurch. But at least her period was due today, wasn't it? She knew she wasn't very good at keeping track of these things, but she was pretty certain it was this weekend. Rubbing her face with her hands to regain some clarity, she reasoned that she was feeling this all-time high of a sex drive because she was pre-menstrual. She was bound to be okay. She'd even stocked up on tampons in Safeway last week.

Feeling slightly calmer and far more awake, she propped herself further up the pillow and peered through the darkness to the far wall of Jay's room. She could just make out the framed Studio 54 poster for which Sean had paid a ridiculous amount of money at auction because it had a faded felt-tip pen squiggle on it that was reputed to be Andy Warhol's signature.

I'm living a little, she told herself. Andy would approve. Then it suddenly hit her like a pen in the eye: AIDS.

A few moments of Benetton ad death-bed scenario later, and she'd quickly quashed the idea.

This is the sort of thing Triona does all the time, she reflected. Or at least used to do, before Sean came along. She was always having unsafe sex in the eighties – not to mention taking copious amounts of drugs – and she's the healthiest woman I know. I have unprotected sex on one weekend with a hygiene freak and I'm convinced I've got an HIV baby on board. It's ridiculous. I must calm down.

By three in the morning, she had worked herself into a frenzy of worry.

Sound asleep beside her, Jay hadn't the slightest idea of how many times she had nearly prodded him awake to ask after all his previous sexual partners.

It was still pitch black outside but the dawn chorus was already going mad, as though belting out 'Land of Hope and Glory' on the last night of the Proms.

By three-thirty, she had crept into the sitting room and was rifling through her bag for the number of the nearest Marie Stopes Clinic.

'I need emergency contraception and an AIDS test,' she announced in a hysterical whisper to the calm-sounding voice at the other end of the line. It was only then that she realised it was a recorded message telling her of the clinic's opening hours and emergency twenty-four-hour helpline.

Juno slammed the phone down and looked at her watch. She knew she had seventy-two hours after sex in which to take the morning after pill. As the first coitus uninterruptus had taken place so gloriously in the early hours of Saturday morning, she still had bags of time.

She lit a cigarette and inhaled deeply, watching with half an eye as Uboat waddled on to her battlements to eye-ball her.

Suddenly she felt a great cramp rip through her belly, almost sawing her in half with pain. At almost the same moment a resounding clap of thunder rattled the tall windows and silenced the premature twitters of the dawn chorus.

'Are you telling me something?' She looked up at the ceiling in what she hoped was penitent gratitude.

From beneath his cage-cover, Poirot let out an almighty squawk.

As the first heavy droplets of rain started hammering on the roof terrace, Juno crawled to the bathroom to fetch her

Nurofen and sweat out the monthly agony with a smile on her face for once.

Half an hour later, the smile had gone. Never had she known such pain. Now she was sure there was a God up there, to cast moral judgements and punish her for her lapsed Catholicism and lousy will-power.

Cramps were tearing through every tissue of her womb, which seemed to have grown inside to encompass most of her body. She was drenched in cold sweat, her teeth chattering, stomach heaving. She had developed terrible diarrhoea as well and had not moved from the bathroom for almost an hour.

Outside, the storm was still raging, although the rain was no longer drumming quite so hard. The booming thunder seemed to have moved on to Hampstead Heath to terrify the multitude of celebrities in their gothic mansions. Dawn should have started to break, but the clouds were so low and dark that the slanting panes of glass above her head were still coal black.

Juno shuddered as another spasm of agony clutched her belly and rocked her innards. She squealed with pain and clenched her eyes closed. As it subsided, she distinctly heard a groan from the other side of the bathroom door.

Sitting on the loo with a clutch of toilet tissue in her hand, she gritted her teeth, cocked her head and listened.

There it was again – a low, throaty groan. More of a sexy growl, in fact.

'Juno?' whispered a hoarse voice. 'Are you in there?'

His tone was deep and clearly trying to be seductively gravelly, she realised. Oh God, not now, she thought.

'Let me in,' he growled, voice urgent.

Does he never let up? she thought weakly. Is he suffering from some sort of medical condition? Recurring priapism or something?

She couldn't even move from the loo. The idea of Jay trying to get a jump right now would have been laughable if she didn't feel so rough.

'Go away,' she croaked. 'I'm ill.'

There was silence and Juno assumed he'd headed back to bed, but then he spoke again. This time the voice came from lower down the door – as though he was squatting on the floor to look through the key-hole.

'Juno, please let me in.' He sounded desperate. She guessed he must be feeling truly lusty. He was like one of those monkeys who have sex every ten minutes to appease their insatiable craving, even rogering a hole in a tree trunk if there's nothing better around.

A knife-like cramp cut through her stomach and speared her spine.

'I can't,' she howled, doubling over and biting her knee. 'I think I'm getting my period. I'm in agony.'

'Me too,' he hissed.

Juno propped her chin on her knees and creased her forehead in surprise as she squinted towards the door. He was getting weirder by the second.

'Are you telling me you've got a period too?' she spluttered.

'No, dumbass,' he groaned, moving even lower down the door until Juno suspected he was trying to spy on her through the gap at the bottom where the carpet left room for a howling draught. She pressed her knees together modestly.

'What then?' She mopped her sweating face with her hunk of loo roll. 'Because I'm really not in the mood, Jay.'

At that moment, she was plunged into darkness. Guessing he had hit the light switch – which was on the other side of the door – Juno rolled her eyes as she heard him say, 'You've given me something . . .' His voice trailed off into another rasping growl.

Suspecting he was proudly about to announce the size of his current horn, Juno clutched her stomach tightly and clenched her teeth to match.

'I can't help you,' she croaked. 'Just go back to bed and hold your own. And turn the light back on in here.'

Jay let out a huge, angry moan from the other side of the door.

'Food poisoning!' he wailed. 'You've given us both food poisoning, you bitch. The power's just shorted out and I can't see a goddamned thing. Now, for fuckssake, let me in before I ruin the carpet out here.'

There was bathroom intimacy and there was embarrassing over-familiarity. As Jay raced to the loo to throw up, sounding like a supermodel the night before the first Paris show, Juno backed hastily out and headed to her room to collapse on the bed. She felt weak, drained and nauseous, but far better than she had in hours. Outside the storm had finally moved away and the sun was splitting through the dark, distant clouds to dry out the rinsed street and perk up the flattened flowers.

Her bed smelled of stale sex and sweaty bodies. Juno longed to strip and change it, but she didn't have the energy. She was absolutely exhausted and absurdly depressed.

'I did *not* give us food poisoning,' she said out loud, trying to generate a spark of anger inside her, but sadness still reigned. He'd called her a bitch. The word rang in her ears like tinnitus.

Last night, as she'd cooked, she had been overexcited and full of lusty potential. She'd also been desperately distracted and in need of a cigarette. But she was certain she'd done nothing wrong. She'd cooked chilli for years – since her student days. It was one of her specialities. Jay himself had even commented how delicious it had been. She could cook it blindfold.

Yet it seemed that whatever it was in the food that was bad, it had also soured their brief trust.

Listening to a distant moan from the bathroom, Juno closed her eyes and chewed her lower lip unhappily. There was no denying it, they were hardly made for one another. The slightest upset and they seemed not only to get on each other's nerves but to go for each other's throats. Arguments between long-standing lovers were one thing; scraps between near-strangers who'd got to know one another's bodies before they exchanged second names were more dangerous.

Juno slept fitfully for a few hours, dreaming that Jay was trying to administer colonic irrigation to her whilst they were travelling on a crowded number 13 bus.

At lunchtime, she crawled out of bed in order to watch the omnibus of her favourite soap, *Londoners*. She felt incredibly weak and dehydrated.

In the hallway, the bathroom door was wide open and the ventilator fan was rattling like an infirm flamenco dancer getting to grips with her castanets. Jay's bedroom door was firmly shut.

Poor Poirot was still covered up and refused even to look at Juno when she pulled the birthing smock from his cage. Feathers fluffed and back hunched, he shuffled as far away from her as his perch would allow and gave a feeble telephone impersonation, directed pointedly at the wall. In amongst the droppings below him were a large number of brightly coloured beads. Juno fed him and then Uboat, who flapped her flippers in welcome and poked her long Gonzo snout out of the tank with joy.

The *Londoners* omnibus was already underway when Juno flicked on the vast flat-screen television in the corner of the room. Lily Fuller, landlady of the Green Man – played by legendary sex kitten Belle Winters – was conducting a loud argument with her wayward daughter, Sandra, on screen.

'*You listen to me, my girl. No Fuller 'as ever married a Sullivan. You know the feud between our two families.*'

'*But I love 'im, Mum. I love Liam.*'

Keeping half an eye on the battle of the bottle-blondes, Juno wandered over to the answering machine. Neither she nor Jay had picked up a call in twenty-four hours. The display was flashing an angry, unlucky thirteen.

Knowing that most of the messages were probably from her friends, Juno guiltily pressed 'Play' and headed to the kitchen to drink several pints of mineral water.

The debris of the night before's chilli-fest was still strewn across the surfaces. Although it was congealed and slightly honky, it didn't look capable of wrecking a weekend love-tryst quite so horrifically as it had.

She downed a final glass of water and listened as Odette and

Ally spoke one after the other on the machine in the other room, wanting to gossip about Friday night. There were also messages from Lulu offering her comps for a comedy club on Saturday night, Elsa saying that she and Euan would be in Bar Humbug in Brixton if Juno wanted to go along, and Jez asking her what she was doing for Sunday lunch. All were now too late. Along with these, her mother had called to check that she was 'still alive', Bob Worth had rung to offer her a last-minute cancellation slot at a new comedy gig called Laughing Gear on Wednesday night, and Triona had rung to say 'hi'.

Juno felt a familiar flinch of distaste as she heard the words, 'Juno, it's John. Are you there, Juno? Obviously not . . .' His razor-sharp patter never differed.

She listened with half an ear as Sean waffled on about his phone charger, not hearing the end of the message as the kettle started boiling to a shriek. After Sean, there was a late-night call from Lydia panicking about what to wear to meet Bruno the following morning: 'Joo, it's two a.m. D'you think a leather cat suit is too much for a Sunday lunch drink? Shit! You're probably at your parents', aren't you? Perhaps I'll call Jez . . . he'll still be up.'

Only one was for Jay. It was the final message and its contents – and caller – intrigued Juno so much that she abandoned any attempts at making tea and wandered back through to the sitting room to play it again.

'Jay, it's me . . .' Female voice. Soft, husky and American. Very Agent Scully. 'I know you told me not to call, but I had to. I'm so sorry we had that fight. Listen, please come home. I don't want you to do this. None of us want you to do this. You might get hurt real bad. Come back to New York and we'll talk it over, baby.'

Mindlessly, Juno pressed the 'Save' button on the answering machine and wandered back into the kitchen. There she pressed her forehead against the handle of an overhead cupboard and took a deep breath.

The mystery message leaver was clearly She-who-would-not-let-Jay-love-her. And the urge to wipe that message was so, so strong. Juno stared accusingly at the answering machine from the kitchen arch. Why wouldn't it just go wrong? Blow a fuse or something? The messages were digitally recorded, after all, and not committed to a tape. She chewed her nails and wondered whether to wipe them now, but couldn't bring herself to do something that mean.

'I'm just too fucking conscientious,' she cursed, heading for the shower.

Under the lukewarm blast of water offered by the dodgy boiler, she started to work out a second scenario. The message was possibly from another New York cell member, trying to dissuade Jay from a dangerously suicidal terrorist mission: 'None of us want you to do this. You might get hurt real bad.' He could be planning to martyr himself for the Cause.

Juno decided to skip conditioner and listen to the message again. Dripping water everywhere, she padded damp footprints back into the sitting room and leaned over the answering machine. The message indicator was reading 'O'.

She glanced over her shoulder to the hallway. Sean's – or rather, Jay's – door was still closed. She pressed 'Play'.

'Seeery, you have *noo* messages. Time: one thirty-seven pee-eem, Sernday,' the voice simulator announced, sounding like a California crack addict.

'Shit!' Juno gnawed her lip. She must have pressed the wrong button, and deleted the message instead of saving it. Now she'd have to tell Jay about the bloody thing. Not only that, but she'd been dying to hear it again. Shit, shit, shit!

She threw on some clothes and headed towards the shops for a chocolate fix.

Jay was glued to the final few minutes of the *Londoners* omnibus when Juno returned. He had clearly been working on his whizzy little computer which was whirring quietly on the oak table beside the fax machine, an aquarium screen saver filling its flip-top VDU with swimming fish.

Right now he was stretched out on the sofa, however,

watching as Sandra Fuller and Liam Sullivan stole an illicit kiss behind the eel and pie shop.

'I lav you, Liam. I'm gonna marry you worever Mum says.'

'I lav you too, Sandra. Let's run away togevva. 'Ave your bags packed tommora – I'll meet you first fing outside the Man.'

Clutching her Budgen's carrier bag to her chest, Juno watched the closing seconds of their passionate embrace, and then saw the shot of Lily Fuller spying on it all from behind a bus stop where she was crouching commando-style in tiger-print satin camouflage, puffing menacingly on a fag. The next moment the familiar plinky-plinky theme music took over and credits began to slide up the screen.

'Do you get *Londoners* in New York?' she asked as Jay stretched his arms behind his neck and noticed her standing there.

'Only on cable. It's not real popular out there. Too depressing.'

Juno was immensely relieved that he was still talking to her. 'I suppose there are rather a lot of brown Dralon sofas in it.'

'It's got a bigger following than the other English soaps because of Belle Winters, I guess.' He rubbed his chin on his shoulder awkwardly, glancing up at her.

'Of course, she made all those cult Sci Fi films in America in the 'sixties,' Juno remembered, deciding that Jay had to be a closet fan. This was also good news as Belle was short and blonde with a pneumatic cleavage and a tendency to run to fat. She had once been an alcoholic, Juno recalled cheerfully – and she still smoked extra-long menthols in almost every *Londoners* scene. No wonder he's been so rampant this weekend, she concluded cheerfully. I'm just his type.

'How're you feeling?' she asked in a suspiciously Cockney accent, although she managed to stop herself from adding 'darlin'' to the sentence.

'Lousy.' He rubbed his forehead, still looking pale and pasty.

'Up to *pain au chocolat* and the Sunday papers?' She waggled her bag as a peace offering, wondering quite how to broach the topic of the deleted message.

One sandy eyebrow twitched upwards in a derisory fashion, and Juno noticed for the first time that he was already surrounded by the Sunday papers, and not just by the *Observer* and the *News of the World*, which was what she had bought, but by every single national paper.

'I went out earlier for a swim. You were still in bed.'

'You've been swimming?' Juno felt physically weak at the notion, the plastic bag slipping several inches through her hands.

'Yeah. I needed to.' He flipped off the *Londoners* theme tune with the remote control. 'I couldn't just stew in bed all day.' It sounded like a criticism.

Juno took it as one. 'I think I must have had slightly worse symptoms than you,' she said evenly, knowing that would rile him. 'It took me longer to recover.'

'Bullshit!'

'So you're not feeling up to a *pain au chocolat*, I take it?'

'No, I'm fucking not.' He stalked over to his laptop.

'Fine – all the more for me.' Juno headed into the kitchen for a plate. Damn! They were at each other's throats again.

Something struck her as different, but she was feeling too testy to take much in as she dumped her bag on the floor and fished out her crumbly sweet treats.

Back in the sitting room, Jay was hammering out a tattoo on the keyboard of his laptop.

'I'm just going to make some calls in my room,' she told him, reaching for the cordless phone on the wall.

'No, you're not.' He carried on typing. 'I'm using my modem on the telephone line.'

'Oh.' She slotted the phone back on its cradle. 'How long will you be?'

'A few hours.' He didn't look up. 'I'm setting up a connection to the States. I gotta have it up and running by the morning.'

'A few *hours*?'

'Yup.' He didn't sound remotely apologetic.

'But I've got loads of calls to return,' she moaned.

'Tough. You should've returned them earlier. Anyway, there's nothing urgent, is there?'

Juno gritted her teeth. 'How do you know?'

'I listened to them.' He started rattling his mouseball around.

'You can't have.' She stared at the back of his head. 'I deleted them by mistake.'

'This morning, dumbass.' He sighed irritably. 'I listened to them this morning.'

'Oh . . . right.' Juno realised that he must have heard all her messages, including the John ones.

'I guess what Sean said explains how come you poisoned us both,' he muttered under his breath, still not looking around.

'What?'

'Didn't you listen? You fed us both dog food, Juno!'

'I did what?' She was appalled.

'You got the meat from the bottom drawer of the freeze cabinet, right?'

'Yes – so what?' Juno wished he'd look at her instead of peering into his computer screen.

'It was dog food,' he said icily. 'Sean said so in his message.'

Juno started to giggle.

'I don't think it's particularly amusing.'

'Amoosing, no.' Juno giggled even more as she mimicked his accent. 'Not very amoosing at all. More likely to be equine than bovine. You could say I was being neighbourly, really. Horsing around. Talk about making a dog's dinner of things!' She giggled even more, because his still, crouched back was making her nervous.

'No wonder you can't fucking cut it as a stand-up,' Jay hissed under his breath.

'You what?' Juno found it hard to stop giggling. 'What did you say?'

Finally he turned to face her, peering critically over his shoulder. 'I'm not surprised you can't yet afford to give up your office job. Your humour is so puerile and unfunny.'

Juno closed her mouth, the odd giggle still rippling through her chest and dying in her throat. 'Who told you I couldn't give up my job?'

He didn't answer.

'Who told you?' she repeated, although it didn't really matter. After four years on the circuit, it was still the bitter truth, and something she was deeply ashamed of.

Still, Jay said nothing. He simply turned back to his computer and started tapping away again. Then he muttered, 'You did, Juno.'

At that moment, she decided she hated him. She couldn't even bear to be in the same room as the supercilious, secretive bastard. She had just started to slope towards her room with her chocolate croissants when he called over his shoulder, 'Aren't you going to thank me?'

'Thank you for what?'

Glancing coldly over his shoulder at her, he jerked his head towards the kitchen. Juno wearily plodded back to take a look.

It was spotless – all the debris cleared away and the surfaces sparkling like a Jif advert. No wonder he was picking on her; he must assume she was taking him totally for granted. And she had, after all, fed him dog food the night before, there was no denying it. Turning back to the sitting room, she was about to say thanks and apologise for being a bit crabby when he dropped a bomb at her feet.

'I think I should move out. I'll try to get somewhere else by the end of the week. I can't live here with you, Juno.'

She gaped at him, but he was once again watching the little cursor dancing around the screen in front of him.

'What about . . . ?' The words petered out in her mouth like a melting wafer. What had she been going to say? she wondered. What about us? She couldn't bring herself to say it. There was no 'us' she realised – just a few sordid sessions playing at being lovers. They'd barely even spoken, couldn't communicate, had nothing in common, could get it on without getting on. They hadn't even been out of the flat together. All they seemed to be able to do was have sex or argue.

And now that sex was off the agenda, it hardly made for domestic bliss.

'Listen, I'm sorry about what happened between us,' she said, walking towards him. She was still clutching her plate of croissants, she realised, like some sort of pathetic peace offering. She longed to dump it somewhere, but Jay had stacks of discs and cables all over the table and she daren't place it amongst them for fear of incurring even more disapproval.

'Sorry about the food poisoning . . . or the fact we slept together?' he asked flatly.

'I think both were unfortunate mistakes, don't you?' Juno said untruthfully, because she was pretty certain it was what he wanted to hear. 'Can't we just agree that it's all my fault, that I took advantage of you, tried to kill you and then irritated the hell out of you? Surely we can draw a line under all this and I'll just steer well clear of you until John sells the house and I get enough money to move out. It might only be a couple of weeks. There've already been a couple of people interested and – '

'You took advantage of me?' Jay butted in, his jaw slack with disbelief, one corner of his mouth curling up in defensive mock-amusement.

Juno blinked. He was being competitive, she realised. His little Bronx macho mind was incapable of accepting the idea that a woman could do such a thing – and certainly not to him. Well, it was my wild weekend, not his, she thought furiously. It might have gone more pear-shaped than my thirty-year-old bottom, but it was still me who initiated it.

'I was drunk on Friday night,' she said hotly. 'And I was exceptionally pissed off at being thirty, and about what's happened with John, and . . .' She was about to mention the Bruno/Lydia scenario but hastily changed her mind. 'You were here and available and very attractive at the time, so I made an error of judgement which I let go on too long, and I apologise for it. Can't we leave it at that?'

His jaw remained slack and one eyebrow twitched. 'I guess I should have listened to what you told me then, huh?'

'What was that?'

'You said you were into casual sex, remember?' he said acidly. 'Like sex with John only more committed you said. I thought it was a joke. Guess I didn't figure you were quite so liberated. Turns out you were all along. So tell me,' his eyes narrowed, 'exactly how many lovers have you had and how certain can you be that they're all safe? 'Cos I don't fucking trust you, baby. Right now, I wish I'd never laid a finger on you.'

A *pain au chocolat* flew off her plate and disappeared under the table as Juno jerked back in surprise.

'The feeling's entirely mutual,' she spluttered.

'So tell me, where's the best place to get a blood test around here?'

'A blood test?' she balked. 'Are you suggesting I've given you something?'

'Given the fact you're such a fucking slob, you're practically alcoholic and – from the sounds of the messages I heard this morning – you keep some bad company, I'd say it was worth checking out, wouldn't you?'

'Bastard!' she hissed. 'Get out! Get the fuck out of this flat.'

'I've changed my mind.' He leant back in his chair. 'I'm going nowhere. If anyone should go, it's you.'

'I'm not fucking budging,' Juno stormed.

'Fine.' He turned back to his computer. 'Whatever – you keep out of my way, and I'll keep out of yours.'

'Suits me!' she announced shrilly and set off with her one remaining croissant towards her bedroom.

'Juno, wait!' he called, making her spin around in just a split-second of hope.

'Two house rules.' He watched her levelly. 'You don't smoke in the apartment, and you clean up after yourself.'

She gritted her teeth. 'In that case, I have one of my own.'

'Which is?' He sounded like an impatient headmaster eager to boot a trouble-maker out of his office.

There was an awkward pause. Damn! Juno couldn't think of anything clever and witty to say, so she blurted out the first thing that came into her head.

'You don't . . . um . . . *talk* to me,' she spluttered childishly. 'I hate the sound of your voice. You sound like a bad de Niro impersonation.'

He nodded calmly and turned back to his computer.

The only sound from the Belsize Park flat that night came from Poirot. Given total freedom of speech to a silent auditorium, he let rip with his most obscene repertoire and told Jay he was a loser more than twenty times.

Sitting in her room sulking, Juno couldn't agree more.

Chapter Eleven

On Monday morning, Juno overslept because all her alarms were switched off. Falling out of bed in a state of panic at eight-thirty, she found that Jay was firmly ensconced in the bathroom showering away his early-morning jog. Hopping from foot to foot on the other side of the door, she demanded to know how long he'd be. When there was no answer, she remembered her stupid house rule and gave up. She was running disastrously late as it was. She had no clean underwear because she hadn't done any washing that weekend, and her office swipe card had yet again gone missing (she lost it on average once a month, usually when she was pre-menstrual).

This necessitated going in to work with dirty hair and a funny walk because she was wearing the bottom-flossing g-string Triona had given her for her birthday. Worse still, she had to negotiate with Mel the flirty security guard in order to get into the office at all.

He made a lot of fuss about having to search her before he buzzed her into reception.

'You'd forget your head if it weren't screwed on to your neck,' he told her, with his customary line in original phrases. As ever, he managed to make it sound deeply suggestive, emphasising 'screwed' with a knowing wink.

'I haven't forgotten it, Mel, I've lost it.'

'Your head or your swipe card?' He cackled at his own wit.

'Both,' Juno said truthfully.

'I'll give you one if you want,' he leered. 'How 'bout tonight?'

'Sorry?'

'You free?'

'No, I'm outrageously expensive. Overpriced, even.' Juno bolted, not bothering to wait for the lift.

Panting upstairs, she encountered Lydia in a Monday morning mood. Dressed in her everyday office wear – a crotch-length pinstripe hipster skirt which could almost have doubled as one of the publisher's kipper ties, and lime green see-through shirt – she gave Juno a dirty look over her desk monitor.

'Your phone was engaged for hours yesterday!' she moaned, already playing a heated game of Solitaire on her PC. 'I almost came round to batter your door.'

'It tastes better in a crispy crumb coating,' Juno said sulkily, heading for her desk, where even her potted fig was looking decidedly droopy.

Lydia cocked a pale eyebrow, not getting the joke. 'I even tried that ringback thing – you know, dialling five and waiting for the other line to clear – but when it finally called me back, it was almost two this morning and bloody woke me up. I'd completely forgotten I'd used it and found myself saying hello to your answerphone. By the way, you should change the recorded message – it's still Sean's voice, *and* he gives out his mobile number.'

'I think he can still use his phone in the States,' Juno said vaguely, going through the post on her desk. Then she remembered with a guilty twitch that she was supposed to be searching for her brother's watch and phone charger to post on to him.

'You don't know how badly I needed to speak to you.' Lydia's big blue eyes were wide with censure and appeal.

'I do know and I'm sorry.' Juno threw down her pile of post and headed to the percolator in the office to pour them both a coffee. 'But now I'm here, you can tell me all about it.'

'Not sure if I want to now.' Lydia pulled a face. 'And I'd prefer lemon tea, thanks.'

Juno placed the mug of coffee on Lydia's desk anyway, cramming it in between a silver-framed photograph of her beautiful mother and a furry hedgehog that an admirer in accounts had left there recently.

'In that case, I'll tell you about my weekend, if you like.' She sagged back into her desk chair and took a deep breath, preparing herself for a confessional spillage of grand proportions.

'Okay, okay, I'll tell you about the date.' Lydia hastily wheeled her chair closer, assuming Juno was about to launch into a long, boring tale of washing her whites and teaching Poirot a new blue joke.

Juno sipped her coffee and tried not to feel too put out.

'He really is gorgeous,' Lydia sighed, sinking her chin into the palms of her hands and gazing dreamily at Juno. 'I just love that Irish accent. He has this wildly sexy way of dropping his voice so that you have to lean in really close . . .'

'This is Bruno, right?' Juno rubbed her eyes tiredly.

'Who else would it be?' Lydia tapped a bongo beat on her desk impatiently. 'Wake up and smell the coffee you just poured me, Joo.'

'Well, there's Claude . . .' she suggested. She always muddled Lydia's lovers up.

'Oh, I dumped him on Saturday.' Lydia waved a hand dismissively. 'I never two-time, you know that. It's cruel.'

'Sorry.' Juno couldn't help but smile. 'Silly me. Where did you go? The Groucho Club?'

'No – some Irish pub in Highbury that he likes. It was a bit rough, actually.' She wrinkled her nose. 'I'd've preferred a decent brasserie or something more intimate. We ended up sitting in a beer garden on wet chairs – it ruined my silk Joseph trousers.'

'You changed your mind about the leather cat suit then?' Juno smiled into her mug.

'Oh, that would have been far too hot,' Lydia said airily.

'So I settled for my pale blue Josephs and a string bikini top – more subtle, I thought. I wish I had worn old catty, though, at least my bum would have stayed dry. I looked like I'd weed myself for the first hour.'

'At least it was sunny,' Juno pointed out, starting to giggle. 'It was a beautiful day once the storm passed.'

'I know, but tans are out this year,' Lydia said simply, as though there was no other reason to sit outside. 'And the food was incredibly greasy. My chicken salad was literally swimming in fat, and they'd never heard of rocket or radicchio.'

'Have they never lived?' Juno winked. 'So what happened between you two?'

'Oh, Joo babes, I like.' Lydia pressed her very white top teeth to her plump lower lip and smiled wickedly. 'I like a lot.'

'And him? As if I need ask.'

Lydia giggled too. 'Well, he did keep saying he loved me which I thought was a bit excessive.'

'So what else did you two talk about?'

'Oh, the usual things – our jobs, where we live, places we like to go, films we've seen, music we dig.' She shrugged.

'Got much in common?'

'A couple of things.' Lydia thought back. 'He likes "Sleeper". And we've both got very sensitive nipples.'

'You *slept* with him!' Juno spat a mouthful of coffee straight on to a letter from a middle-aged accountant wanting advice about his sexual obsession with his vacuum cleaner. She'd forgotten how much Lydia took sex for granted. To her, it was as easy as breathing, whereas Juno found it more like an asthma attack – rare, potentially deadly and hell to recover from.

Lydia looked at her blankly. 'Of course I didn't. We listened to "Sleeper" then had sex together. There's a difference. I'll only ever sleep with men on the second or third date, you know that.'

'Oh.' Juno felt rather taken aback, and more than a little hypocritical given her own weekend bonkfest. 'Good for you.'

'He lives in Islington – only five minutes from the pub – and I wanted to see his house.' Lydia grinned mischievously. 'As it turned out, his flatmates were both out so we had the place to ourselves. One thing led to another and . . .'

'You bonked the night away.'

'Afternoon actually.' Lydia tasted her coffee and pulled a face as she realised it had no milk in it. 'I was home in time to catch the latest Ruth Rendell and have a gossip with Nat.'

Lydia lived in a vast Maida Vale flat bought for her by her doting father, and supplemented her income by renting out the spare bedroom to an eccentric design student called Nat who redecorated it practically every month. His room was currently crafted to resemble the inside of a Bedouin tent, which Juno personally felt made it look as though it was swathed in one large, stained sheet. This didn't matter much, as he was so ludicrously in love with Lydia that he never brought women back to the flat.

'And was it good?' Juno mentally calculated that Lydia was getting laid at around the time she had her first heated argument with Jay.

'Ecstatic,' Lydia shivered. 'Seriously dirty, but totally divine.'

Juno, who had thought her own sexual encounter was pretty wild and adventurous, suddenly felt very stuffy and prudish.

'And are you seeing him again?' She realised that, in her state of shock, she sounded like a nosy old mother.

'Have to, I guess.' Lydia shrugged.

'You'll have to?' Juno eyed her thoughtfully. 'So what did you nick?'

Pulling her chin back in mock pique, Lydia finally looked up from the little cards whizzing about her screen.

Juno cocked her head. 'What did you steal, Lyds?'

'Oh, just some CDs and a watch.' She batted her big blue eyes innocently.

'Nothing much then.' Juno grinned. 'What sort of watch?'

Lydia jiggled her wrist from which swung something far heavier than the usual Cartier. It was a man's Tag Heuer – vast, professional and capable of withstanding a marine depth of several hundred metres. Scuffed and well used, it looked strangely familiar.

'It's a bit like Sean's.' Juno looked at it. 'Not a good indicator of Bruno's taste.' Then she noticed a strip of blue gaffer tape around the strap. 'Jesus, Lyds, that *is* Sean's watch!'

'Nonsense – it's Bruno's. It was on his sitting-room window sill.' She sniffed her wrist dreamily. 'It even smells of his aftershave.'

'Ralph Lauren Sport?'

Lydia nodded, tweaked blonde eyebrows shooting up.

'And does it have "Surf, Shag and Shit" engraved on the reverse?'

Lydia's wrist was so narrow she didn't even have to unclip the watch to flip it over. 'Christ! How did you know that?' she gasped as she read the words.

'It's Sean's watch,' Juno said decisively. 'Don't ask me how it got there, but it's definitely Sean's.'

Somehow Juno didn't get round to telling Lydia about what had gone on between her and Jay over the weekend. Her friend was so high from her date that it was virtually impossible to get a word in edgeways. Plus Juno had to catch up like mad to complete the agony page for *Weekwork* magazine and to file copy for the *News on Sunday*, who liked her contributions well in advance of going to print. She also called Bob Worth to confirm her comedy gig on Wednesday.

'It's upstairs at the Cod and Cucumber in Finsbury Park,' he told her. 'Door-split, I'm afraid.'

'Sounds salubrious. Why are you doing it? I thought you'd left all that behind you years ago.'

'The promoter's a mate of mine. Nice bloke. You'll meet him there.'

Lydia wasn't keen to do any typing in her current state of euphoria. Instead she chose to drape herself over the photocopier and chat up Finlay the charmer from advertising sales, who was looking typically poetic in crumpled white jeans and a satin shirt the same pale, creamy gold as his wild locks.

Juno watched them with half an eye as she typed up her own copy with two fingers and lousy spelling. Finlay had joined the sales team at roughly the same time as Lydia came to work at Immedia. Upon the arrival of these two exquisite – if inefficient – creatures, there had been a marked improvement in personal hygiene and dress sense from both male and female members of staff, but neither of the beauties had noticed as they only had eyes for one another. In that classic way that staggeringly good-looking people have of cleaving together like members of a separate species, Lydia and Finlay had become as thick as thieves over the past few weeks, and yet he was one of the few men she rarely spoke about during her 'girly goss' sessions with Juno in the loos. As far as Juno knew, the relationship was wholly platonic and purely confined to the office and the occasional shopping trip during the lunch hour when Finlay acted as 'surrogate boyfriend', waiting outside fitting rooms to give his opinion on an outfit Lydia was buying for a date with someone else.

'Why don't you fancy him?' Juno had once asked. 'He's so gorgeous and you two flirt all the time.'

'Of course I fancy him,' Lydia had laughed. 'Like *mad*, Joo. Christ, don't you?'

'So why not do something about it?'

'Joo, he's gay. Anyone can see that.'

'Have you asked him?'

'No, I just know. I feel comfortable with him. We flirt, yes, but it's not sexual. He's never once made a move. I know when a man wants to sleep with me, and believe me, he doesn't. Do you know how refreshing that is?'

Juno had thought about this for a while. 'I can safely say I'm pretty familiar with men not wanting to sleep with me. And refreshing wouldn't be my first choice of adjective.'

Lydia was back at her desk and playing Solitaire again by the time Juno suggested they escape to buy lunch in a nearby deli and sit out in Russell Square to eat it. Chattering excitedly all the way, Lydia was still consumed by the watch intrigue, believing that the kismet coincidence was somehow a lucky omen for her relationship with Bruno.

'The only possible explanation is that he must know Sean and have borrowed his watch, or muddled it up somehow,' she mused as she nibbled unenthusiastically on a lettuce and rye sandwich. 'Could they play squash together or something?'

'Sean hasn't played squash in ages.' Juno was speaking with her own mouth full of avocado and bacon double mayo on ciabatta. 'Besides, Sean phoned from the States on Friday to say he thought he'd left it behind in the bathroom, didn't he?'

'Perhaps Jay's got something to do with it?' Lydia suggested, suddenly fastening upon an idea. 'Perhaps that's how come the watch was in Bruno's flat. They might know one another.'

'Jay?'

'Think about it, Juno.' She shrugged, discarding her half-eaten sandwich. 'He's the only person who's been in the bathroom other than you, and possibly Triona, since Sean left.'

'Are you suggesting Jay has somehow met up with Bruno in the three days he's been in the UK and given him a manky Tag belonging to the guy he's borrowed a flat off? Pretty coincidental, not to mention illogical, don't you think?' She swatted a wasp out of the way.

'Well, you yourself said he was an odd fish.' Lydia took a swig from her little bottle of mineral water. 'I think it's all fascinating. I'm going to ask Bruno about it.'

'Won't you have to admit you've nicked the watch?'

'That's the whole point of stealing it in the first place, Joo. I'll just say I put it on by mistake and arrange to give it back – over dinner.' She started digging around in her bag for her mobile phone.

'And the CDs?'

But Lydia was already dialling a number into her tiny flip-phone. She tipped her dark glasses on to her long, straight nose and grinned as the call rang through.

'Bruno, it's Lydia,' she cooed, her voice changing tone completely as she spoke to him. It was now soft, deep and seductive. 'Yes, wasn't it lovely? Were you? That's nice.'

Juno swallowed the last of her ciabatta with a large gulp of Lilt and lay back in the sunshine as Lydia chatted to Bruno for several minutes. Oh, the effortless way in which she spoke to him – laughing cheerfully, not asking too many questions, giving away just enough about herself to fascinate, yet all the time keeping the conversation fluid and pause-free. Given similar circumstances, Juno knew she would have been uptight and defensive, shooting out jokes as covering fire. Come to think of it, in similar circumstances, Juno would not have called at all. Wasn't it supposed to be Date Death to call him the next day? Even worse to steal things from his flat as an excuse to see him again. That was the blissful thing about being Lydia; not only could she get away with flouting The Rules, she in fact used far older rules, minxy tricks which dated back to courtiers and concubines. And because she was so beautiful, men didn't even notice they were being manipulated by a pro.

'Tonight would be lovely,' she was saying, 'but I have my aerobics class at seven-thirty and then I swim for an hour. After that? Well, having a shower, I guess . . .' She wrapped her perfect lips around the water bottle neck and took a long swig before speaking again. 'Sure, you can join me there if you really want.'

God, she's frisky today, Juno thought bitterly, closing her eyes. A bit bloody up-front too. She thought sadly of returning to the flat to share a tense, broody silence with Jay. So much for being a liberated seductress. She knew she should tell Lydia all about the Jay fiasco, but felt absurdly defensive and secretive now that it had all gone so wrong. Compared to her friend's copy-book seduction of Bruno, Juno was only too aware of her own failings. When Lydia had asked after Jay earlier, Juno had just mumbled something vague about his being 'in and out' all weekend, which didn't seem too much of a lie.

'Bruno says he never wears a watch,' Lydia announced when she finally flipped her phone shut and threw it into her bag. 'He's going to come to my aerobics class later. Isn't that too divine?'

'So he didn't know anything about it?' Juno was perplexed.

Lydia shook her head, peering at her over the tortoiseshell rims of the dark glasses. 'I guess it must be something to do with one of his flatmates. I'll try and find out some more tonight. Meanwhile, you ask Jay whether he's picked it up by accident or something.'

'We're not really talking at the moment,' Juno admitted. 'We had a bit of a row over – um – the bathroom rota. He's very petty like that.'

'In that case,' Lydia smacked her lips keenly, screwing the cap back on the water bottle, 'I am definitely going to have to meet him. I'll come round tomorrow night for a drink. You need a mediator as soon as possible.'

'An immediator?' Juno grinned.

Chapter Twelve

Sitting in the empty, open-plan office after Lydia had left along with the rest of the Immedia staff, Juno tried to concentrate on writing copy, but her Flying Toasters screen saver kept sweeping across her monitor as she sat lost in thought for minutes on end. She was starting to blame herself more and more for the situation she was in with Jay, for the stupidity of their lovely, lusty, lost weekend, for the childishness of her comments afterwards, for the reason she was sitting in the office now instead of heading home.

Before John, Juno's heart had been on a love-life support machine of hopelessly one-sided crushes and occasional dates with men she didn't fancy.

As a teenager, she'd been a scruffy little ball of cuddly, mad-cap energy and daring, who'd do anything for a laugh, whom everyone liked but no one ever fancied. Yet inside, she had almost burned her heart away with secret, frustrated passion as she squandered hours of red-hot day-dreams and white-hot sleepless nights on one long, painful, unrequited crush after another. Those crushes were always hopelessly unrealistic, always wasted on the best-looking sixth formers at school or the hunkiest of her brother's friends – those broad-shouldered, floppy-haired, self-confident boys who always asked out her prettier, quieter friends and broke her heart without knowing it.

At university, as she grew in confidence and style, she

became the wackily dressed funny girl who partied hardest and hugged tightest. She still fell head-over-painted-Doc-Marten's for those campus gods who only dated the prettiest girls, but actually started trying to do something about it too, making a move across the crowded student union dancefloor, cornering a hunk at a beer-and-hash party, inviting herself round for coffee at his digs with a packet of Hobnobs and a tight top on. They humoured her, they laughed at her jokes, they seemed to like her, but they always rejected her – sometimes gently, occasionally harshly, often hurtfully, but almost always unknowingly: 'I'm glad you came round, Juno, I just have to ask you something – is your friend Elsa/Odette/Gilda free, because I've fancied her all term?' was quite a common one.

So the unrequited crushes for hopeless causes had raged on unabated until to her amazement she'd suddenly found that she herself had become an object of desire – albeit with a distinctly cult following. She found she attracted quiet, intense, bespectacled science boffins whom she didn't fancy. They'd trail around the campus after her at a distance, send her anonymous love notes on computer paper, stare lovingly at her from across the dining hall, shyly ask her friends if they thought they stood a chance with her, and then ultimately – stuttering, blushing and not looking her in the eye – they'd pluck up courage to ask her out. Juno hadn't wanted to admit how like her they were. She'd been embarrassed by them, had joked about them with her friends, but ended up snogging them anyway because no one else wanted her, because she'd felt sorry for them and because – with the heartless optimism of youth – she'd thought they would be good to practise her kissing technique upon in anticipation of that heady day when she became a swan.

But she never had become a swan, nor had she yet learnt to cope with rejection like water off an ugly duckling's back. Throughout her sociable, independent, career-drifting twenties, she'd endured lovelorn, dateless, crushless months, occasionally punctuated by a chance flirtation in a pub or at a party (usually with a shy spectacle-wearer). They were sweet, shy, easily intimidated men whose names she now got muddled up because she'd talked about herself so much that she hadn't bothered learning anything about them. They'd laughed too much at her jokes and been too shy to touch her body. She'd fancied one or two of them in a mild, flattered kind of way, but it was nothing like her white-hot, wet-dream crushes.

She sometimes wondered whether she simply went on these faceless, nightmare dates to give her something to talk about to her friends – that priceless little support-group of sanity, the 'gang'. Friends like Elsa, Odette, then Ally – and later Lydia – whom she kept totally separate from her bizarre love-life, but to whom she dished out the grisly low-down, to their continued delight. The weirder the man, the funnier the story. She'd regale them with tales of dates-from-hell that would leave them in cramps of tearful laughter, and leave her feeling happy because she'd entertained them.

That, she felt, was her role in the gang. People dined out on her love life in those days. It wasn't uncommon for Elsa or Jez or Lulu to introduce her to someone at a party and for them to say, 'Juno, did you say? Aren't you the one who once climbed out of the loo window in the Oxford Arms to get away from a mad Canadian computer engineer who'd just told you he was heavily into bondage and then flashed his pierced penis at you under the table? *That* Juno?' In truth it had hurt like hell to be considered such a loser in love; she'd wanted to be like Elsa or Lydia with their whistle-stop love affairs which broke hearts and beds all over London. But she'd wanted to be involved too, and her hopeless crushes weren't enough to entertain her friends – they were boring after a while, like describing a dream you'd had the night before. Perhaps in those pre-John days, Juno reflected, she also dated anyone who asked her out so that she could join in with the gang's smutty, graphic, girls-only, wine-bar conversations about sex.

Occasionally – if they still fancied her after that first, gabbling date, and a surprising number did – she had gone to bed with one of the better-looking faceless dates, for much the same reasons she had once snogged those shy undergraduates. It had been fumbling, sweaty, self-conscious sex which improved her technique and lowered her self-esteem. She had lost her virginity that way, offloading it with the same relief as giving away an embarrassing Cliff Richard CD.

The relationship hadn't lasted. None of them ever did. The ones that remained keen – and, after she slept with them, Juno found they often did – ended up leaving lots of unreturned messages on her answerphone, or with embarrassed flatmates who fobbed the caller off while Juno cowered on the sofa shaking her head madly. Sooner or later they all gave up, leaving her feeling mean and silly and cowardly and sad. Nowadays she still screened almost all her calls. It drove her friends mad, but it was a hard habit to break.

And all this time, throughout what Elsa and Odette had nick-named her 'nerd-date years', the fierce, self-destructive crushes on unattainably beautiful men continued. They grew fewer and further between as she stopped drifting and settled into a steady job, as her social group tightened, as coupling up and cohabiting began in earnest all around her, as life became more routine. She searched madly for crush-victims, rubbernecking her local streets, favourite bars, business associates. But she met fewer hunks on which to hang her confused little heart; there was less breadth of choice – big raucous house parties full of strangers gave way to small, chummy dinner parties, nights on the town to evenings in the local pub. Her social circle closed intimately, warmly, in on her like a bear hug. But her self-obsessed passions needed a vent. Once or twice she found, to her horror, that she was developing crushes on friends' new boyfriends, but she'd hastily hidden them in the darkest recess of her psyche and quietly sweated through sleepless nights until the fever passed.

It was then that she'd started out on the London comedy circuit, channelling her passion and energy and self-hatred into her material. Comedy was, or so she'd always been led to believe, an ugly business. And Juno was always being told she was funny. She just put the two together and knew where she belonged. But it was much harder to break into than she'd anticipated. The biggest rejection of her life came when, for the first time ever, people didn't laugh at her jokes. For weeks, she sweated through open-mike slot after try-out night and panned at them all. Her friends may have fallen about cackling at her every anecdote, but audiences who had actually paid money to be amused didn't find her very funny at all. She was just too damned nervous and bitter and aggressive. It took a lot of set-backs, hard work, steeled nerves, angry tears and self-determination to develop the gentle, naughty-girl, self-deprecating patter which worked for her today. And during that time, as she'd struggled her way into better venues and on to better material, the crazy crushes – however brief – didn't go away.

She and Lydia moved into the Cam Den together, and her beautiful, irresistible, flirtatious friend dated one gorgeous man after another – cute, clever charmers whom Juno would meet for the first time when they wandered out of the bathroom first thing in the morning, wrapped in nothing but a fluffy towel and a shy, sexy smile. Living with Lydia was a scream: late gossipy nights, wild evenings out, slobby Sunday afternoons dissecting their lives. Juno had never known anything like this, an itching, infectious disease of a friendship which tickled her all over, which was both dangerous and such, such fun. But Lydia's myriad lovers inevitably became Juno's friends too as they rolled up at the flat with a bunch of flowers and two tickets to the opera to find Lydia still in the shower, or not back yet, or out with someone else – often necessitating a lot of hasty fibbing on Juno's part. Lydia treated men appallingly but Juno was always around to make them snacks, pour them drinks, give them fags, tell them funny stories, and dream that it was her they had come to see, not darling, feckless Lydia.

Then John came on the scene and everything changed. He'd heckled her during a gig in a pub in Camden – one of the first where she'd really gone down well. Halfway through her set, he'd shouted 'Get your tits out' (not a great start, especially as it was her most common heckle). For a moment, she'd stared at him, mike in hand. Huge, sexy, blue-eyed, exquisitely eye-browed, and a classic hunk-crush subject, he'd had just one flaw – a penchant for wet-look gel. Juno had leapt upon the weakness. 'Nice hair, big boy – what d'you do . . . swim here?'

He'd come up to her in the bar afterwards and chatted her up. *Really* chatted her up – the sexy banter, the smile, the body-language, the self-belief, the blue-blue eyes razoring off her clothes – and those had been the days when she'd performed stand-up in baggy, faded black t-shirts, leggings and dusty pumps. It wasn't when he'd said 'You're dead funny,' that Juno had fallen for him, nor was it when he told her he'd fancied her from the moment she'd answered him back. It was when he'd said, almost in surprise, 'Christ, you really are beautiful.' She had wanted him so much then that she'd discovered a new gland in her body which pumped out pure longing.

She recalled the night she had phoned Elsa and screeched that she had found the living embodiment of Alan Davies and Neil Morrissey and what's more he could blow the theme tune to *Rhubarb and Custard* into his pint with his nostrils through two straws (one of his many pub tricks). She remembered dancing around the streets beside long-suffering friends as she sang hits from *Grease*, did hand-stands against walls, wolf-whistled at strangers, and became a total 'John says', 'John thinks' boyfriend bore. And that was after just one date.

At first, she simply hadn't been able to believe someone so good-looking had wanted to spend so much time with her, had wanted to hold her hand, put an arm around her shoulders, or stroke her cheek in public. His giddy, little-boy enthusiasm had been so unexpected and uncommon. She'd known that she was sharper than him from the start, both in tongue and mind, but she hadn't cared. Her friends had warned her that he was a charmer, an incorrigible flirt, that he was shallow, that he'd let her down, that she could do better, but Juno didn't listen. After the nerds, John was a paragon of demonstrative physical contact and emotional honesty. A hunk fancied her back at last. This beautiful, beefy northerner had fallen in love with her and taken her with him. He never wore wet-look gel again.

After years of rejection and disappointment, finding requited love at last had been a revelation. It had for so long seemed as impossible as solving a pyramid puzzle – knowing that other people could do it in twenty seconds didn't make it any easier to crack. She'd never realised that being in the first stages of love was essentially just having that all-too-familiar stonking crush on someone who had an equally stonking crush on you in return, and what's more you could tell them all about it as *well* as telling your friends. It was so simple in those first few giddy weeks. It was like the forty seconds of freefall before the parachute opens when you can look around and admire the view.

She wanted that feeling back. She wanted to tandem jump into love again and enjoy every second of the ride. But she knew she didn't want it with John. Their three-year fall had already landed with a limb-breaking, heart-rupturing jolt, miles away from the big white cross of happy-ever-afters.

On Friday night, Juno had seen Jay as just a better-looking version of the nerds, a return to her pre-John years but with post-John hindsight. She'd seen him as someone she could sleep with for an experience and for reassurance, because he was available, and sexy, and she was lonely and slightly pissed. That is, until he had touched her body and made her libido fizz up like a firework shooting from its sleeve. Until he had clammed up so much about his personal life that he just had to contain a pearl deep inside. Until he had rejected her too, just as Bruno had, just as John eventually had.

Now Jay was looking dangerously like hijacking the infamous Juno crush and she hated him for it. He'd seen her vulnerability a mile off. He'd even made her promise not to fall in love with him. He had probably only slept with her in the first place because she'd presented herself on a plate to him like a free snack. Now he hated living under the same roof as her, and she was developing a crush on him. God, but she loathed him!

Chapter Thirteen

Jay and his laptop were not in the flat when Juno got back from work. With the place to herself, she felt it was her chance to stake her claim. He had hogged the phone line and the sitting room the previous night, so she wasted no time in securing them for herself now. Within minutes, she was in her birthing smock, on the sofa, in front of *London Tonight*, halfway down a gin and tonic and chattering to Elsa on the phone.

'Sorry I haven't returned your message sooner.' It was her standard greeting – she said it roughly twenty times a week to different friends. 'How was Brixton?'

'Same as ever, hon. Full of Beemers, dreamers and two-pot screamers. More to the point, how's your rude Yank? We were all talking about him. You were so funny when you were describing him on Friday night.'

Juno only faltered for a second. 'Oh, Elsa, we are talking *nightmare* scenario . . .'

By the time she had called Jez, Ally, Lulu, Odette (who was, as ever, still at work, in a meeting and unavailable apart from a message service), and her mother, Juno felt as though she had honed her Jay-sniping and 'flatmate from hell' material to a fine peak. Darling, acerbic Lulu had added some cracking suggestions. Juno was definitely going to make it part of a new comedy set for Wednesday night, and started to make notes while she waited for her Microchips to heat through in the kitchen. She hadn't told anyone that they'd slept together, of course – just listed Jay's more impossible habits and played down her own involvement in their current stand-off – a stand-off tailor made for stand-up. Guilt was nibbling at her, but she batted it away. He'd said some foul things, had called her a bitch. And he had, after all, only made her swear not to love him. He'd said nothing about hate.

Pouring herself a glass of wine and changing channels in anticipation of her Monday night *Londoners* fix, Juno dialled Triona.

'What's this I hear about you being horrible to Jay?' She was light-toned but clearly annoyed.

Juno's pen stopped mid-jot and she cocked her head against the phone.

'Who told you that?'

'The man himself. I met him for lunch today. He said you two weren't talking.'

'Oh. What else did he say?' Juno swallowed anxiously, trying to ignore the little hope gland that was pumping inside her heart, desperate for a scrap of positive information to cling to.

Triona didn't oblige. 'He said that you almost killed him on Saturday night.'

Disappointed, Juno wondered if he'd been referring to the energetic sex or the chilli.

'You fed him dog food, Juno.' Triona started to laugh despite herself. 'Sean can't believe it – I spoke to him earlier, promised him I'd try and patch things up between you two, in fact. He's going to call you himself tonight and tell you to be nicer to Jay.'

'Can't wait.' Juno made a mental note to turn on the answerphone. 'How was Trash?' She changed the subject, realising that Jay hadn't said anything about their sex marathon, just whinged about her cooking.

'Oh, the usual,' Triona hedged. 'Lots of charlie, lots of charlies and even more cha cha cha. I saw a couple of friends of yours – Euan and Elsa.'

'Elsa mentioned she'd bumped into you.' She'd also mentioned the fact that Triona had been so stoned she'd lost her fish skin dress in the loos and was later spotted dancing in a flesh-tint body-stocking and pop socks.

'Listen, we gotta slam dunk the receivers now – *Londoners* is starting,' Triona said as their favourite soap's theme tune started playing in stereo – in their respective sitting rooms and down the line to one another. 'Are you doing any stand-up this week?'

'Wednesday, some place in Finsbury Park. The Cod and something.'

'I'll try and get to see you there – bring the boys. Barfly's been asking after you.'

'I'm flattered.' Juno took the phone through to the kitchen to fetch her Microchips. 'Don't feel you have to come. I get the impression it'll be pretty low key.'

'The lower the key, the better I sing,' Triona laughed. 'See you there.' And she rang off.

Juno left the phone on the draining board and slid her hot little box of chips straight on to a plate. With the ketchup bottle under one arm and the Saxa tub under the other, she headed back into the sitting room just in time to see Belle Winters as Lily locking her daughter Sandra into her bedroom in order to prevent her eloping.

At the same moment Jay let himself in through the front door.

Resolutely refusing to look up as he walked into the room, Juno stretched herself out as randomly as possible on the sofa, encompassing at least two-thirds of its width with a casually propped leg here and a flung-out arm there to claim total ownership. The position was in fact incredibly painful and difficult to maintain – even more so when trying to eat Microchips – but she gritted her teeth and remained spread out as she heard him walk across the room behind her, heading for the oak table where he put down his computer and camera cases with a series of thuds.

Juno had a slug of wine and tried to concentrate as gutsy little Sandra Fuller slid open her sash window, threw out her overnight case and started to lower herself on to the rusty corrugated roof of the Green Man's delivery yard. Her concentration was severely challenged, however, as Jay moved closer to the television and lurked menacingly by the far sofa arm.

Juno was spread out as widely as she could. She tried to get a toe on to the arm to claim possession of that too, but she simply wasn't long or supple enough. Damn those years of skipping yoga! Within a couple of seconds, she saw in her peripheral vision one of Jay's hard, tight and enviably round buttocks sliding on to the arm, closely followed by the other.

Juno sulkily devoured the remaining Microchips as Sandra dropped the last few feet into the Man's delivery yard, landing on a pile of old mixer crates and crisp boxes. Meanwhile Liam Sullivan was waiting on the pavement beside the Man's tatty front façade, glancing sporadically at his watch and telling a black cab driver to keep the meter running.

Jay was practically sitting on top of Juno's feet now, his arm reaching out towards the coffee table, eyes glued to the screen where Liam looked forlornly up at the darkened windows of the Man and sighed in despair. This, given a face like a King Edward potato and a neck the width of the Old Kent Road, was no mean feat of acting.

A light flickered on above him, a sash flew up and a bleached blonde head loomed over the window boxes, clutching her candlewick dressing gown demurely to her ample chest.

'Get out of 'ere, you no-good layabout! She ain't coming out, you hear?'

At that moment, Jay's bottom finally landed on Juno's feet and he grabbed hold of the remote control.

'Ouch!' she wailed as her ankle crunched into a scatter cushion.

'Jeez!' He leapt up, at the same time gripping on to the remote control so tightly in surprise that the channels started changing as quickly as slides shuffling through a faulty projector. 'Shit!' He looked at the television, then the control, and hastily turned it back to Londoners.

'Sorry, Juno, I didn't see you there,' he said tersely, cranking up the volume on the set until the walls were shaking and Poirot was screeching delightedly. Jay perched back on the sofa arm once more, watching the screen intently.

As Lily's screams and Liam's booming yells almost deafened her, Juno cradled her injured foot in her hands, eyes smarting in pain.

How could he not have noticed her? She thought furiously. It was impossible. She'd been aware of his every move since he'd walked in, even though she hadn't actually *looked* at him. Bastard. He was winding her up.

After a few seconds, she allowed herself a stealthy glance in his direction. He was gazing at the television with almost manic concentration. Sliding her eyes towards the screen, Juno saw Belle Winters giving one of her regular demonstrations of gloriously high-camp acting. She might have the candlewick on and the hair-rollers in, but she was still in full make-up, had a very flattering face-light to emphasise those high cheekbones, and was showing just a hint of lacy nightdress as she loosened her grip on the dressing gown and heaved her chest in maternal distress.

'My Sandra's only seventeen,' she screamed over the dusty geraniums. 'She ain't seen nuffink of life. You leave her alone, you pervert!'

Juno pressed herself towards the far end of the sofa and stewed sourly as Jay continued to watch the *Londoners* action. She didn't want to admit it, but she was starting to suspect that he really hadn't noticed her before he'd sat on her feet. The sofa was very high-backed and in order to take up as much of it as possible, she had been forced to lie pretty flat across it. If he'd been as engrossed in *Londoners* as he was now, it was perfectly plausible he could have walked in, copped the TV action, wandered over to the sofa arm and distractedly groped for the remote as he slid into a more comfortable position.

She pressed her tongue to her upper teeth and narrowed her eyes in irritation. And he'd *spoken* to her, she realised with disgust. An act she had strictly forbidden.

It was only when the episode ended and the familiar plinky-plinky *Londoners* theme tune boomed out into the room louder than ever that he moved. He swiftly stood up, collected his computer carry cases from the oak table and – without looking at Juno or saying a word to her – walked into his room and slammed the door behind him.

Later that night, the answerphone intercepted another call.

'Juno, this is your brother speaking – tall bloke, likes surfing. Remember me? Are you there? Listen, it's Monday night, I know you're de-waxing your ears and plucking your chin, so pick up the phone. Juno? Christ, you're a pain in the seat region, wild child. Why do you screen every call? These machines were designed to take messages, not to be crouched over and monitored to decide whether you want to speak to the caller. And while I'm on the subject, can you please change the outgoing message? Contrary to popular belief, I hate hearing the sound of my own voice. Incidentally, have you been checking on my –'

'I surrender.' Juno picked up. 'You leave such boring messages that it's more painless to hang up on you.'

'At last!' His familiar cackle blasted into her ear. 'Were you listening all this time, you sow?'

'No, I was trying to watch a tribute to Lucille Ball on the box but I couldn't concentrate. I guess nothing changes – you even talk over the television programmes I'm trying to watch from the States.'

He laughed delightedly. 'Same little sister as ever. It's lovely to hear your voice too.'

'I miss you. How's it going?' she asked grudgingly, picking at a scuffed corner of the oak table.

'Slow, but I'm starting to feel my way around. I've been a bit of a tourist so far to be honest. Jay's flat is simply fantastic.'

'I'm sure it's very clean,' she sniffed.

Sean took a deep, diplomatic breath. 'You two don't get on?'

'Oh, we get on . . . on one another's nerves.' She glanced towards the hallway and Jay's closed bedroom door.

'Give it time,' Sean soothed. 'I'm certain you'll hit it off eventually. Triona thinks he's terrific – can't stop talking about him. And I seriously liked him when we met here. He's a shit-hot photographer, totally straight down the line, and he's got a lot of soul.'

'Arsehole,' Juno agreed.

'He's shy.'

'Yeah, and I'm a virgin.'

'I'm serious.' He sounded it. 'I know the affliction is completely alien to you and your friends, wild child, but some people are burdened with this thing called self-consciousness. They're awkward around super-quick wits, particularly women. People like you scare them.'

'D'you think so?' Juno bucked up at the idea of scaring Jay. So far he'd been the one doing all the scaring.

'Absobloodylutely.' It was one of Sean's catchwords.

'Cheers.' She took it as a compliment.

He sighed in exasperation. 'I've got to go – this call is costing me a fortune and I'm already burning C-notes like tinder out here. You will try and make more of an effort, won't you?'

'I'll try.' Juno crossed her fingers. Looking up, she saw Jay stalking out of his bedroom and heading for the kitchen, head hanging, shoulders high in self-defence like a misunderstood hooligan.

'I hope so,' Sean was winding up. 'I'll call you soon. Hurry up and send my bloody watch – I'm wearing a Ronald McDonald freebie at the moment. Hardly streetcred.'

'About your wat—' Juno started, but he had already rung off.

Jay was banging about purposefully in the kitchen. Juno hovered by the oak table, wondering whether to make conciliatory moves. The idea that he was shy hadn't occurred to her before. She suddenly felt a great gush of excited guilt for her own thoughtlessness.

She saw him move to the freezer opposite the arch to extract something, tight bum rising gloriously as he stooped for the lowest tray. His nondescript, baggy grey trousers were crinkling over tractor-soled lace-up boots, he was wearing a faded purple baseball shirt over a frayed white sweatshirt, but he was still cooler than the chilled products he was rootling through.

Then she saw what he was taking out – it was the neat, half-pound bags of unlabelled mince-like dogfood. One by one he placed them on the surface beside the freezer. Once he'd cleared them all he slid in the tray, closed the freezer door, gathered his booty, and moved out of sight. Seconds later the hot tap was gushing loudly and the waste disposal unit was crunching through them.

'Shy and retiring, my arse!' Juno muttered beneath the clatter from the kitchen as she started sloping towards her own room. 'He's a sly, tiring arsehole.'

When she re-emerged later to fetch herself a cup of tea and raid the biscuit tin, she could hear Jay talking on the phone in his room, his voice muffled by the door.

'Get your tits out, hot stuff!'

'Shhh, Poirot baby,' Juno hushed the foul-mouthed macaw and tried to listen in to Jay's conversation, but she could only catch snatches.

'. . . I'm not in that line of business any more. I told you that on Friday night . . . yeah, it was great to see you too, buddy . . .'

Juno's eyes narrowed. So he had been out on Friday night after all. Perhaps Lydia was right. There was a possibility he'd worn Sean's watch by mistake and lost it, or perhaps done something more sinister with it, which had led to its turning up in Bruno's house.

'. . . I seriously don't do that shit any more . . . I don't care how much money's involved . . . it's not why I'm over here . . .'

Juno crept closer to his door, wincing as a floorboard creaked underfoot.

Jay sounded quite irritated, his husky drawl tightening harshly. 'It's too dangerous, man. I got too much at stake. I don't need that kind of exposure right . . .'

'You're a loser! Thirty-three-to-one, double carpets. Fancy a quick one, you slapper! Eh? Eh?' Poirot bobbed on his perch excitedly.

What had Jay been saying? That he was in England to do something dangerous? Juno chewed her nails anxiously, giving the parrot a dirty look over her shoulder. Then she froze in horror.

'. . . I told you, I don't want to shoot her unless I have to – I just need to figure a way to get past her heavies. I thought your guys might know her routine . . .'

Ohmygod! Juno bit her thumbnail clean off. Triona had been right all along. He was talking about a terrorist target, wasn't he? He was some sort of assassin after all.

'. . . haven't got much time. I thought I could take things slow when I got over here, but there's been a development. Now I have to act real fast or this thing will blow up in my face . . .'

A bomb! There was a bomb in the flat. Juno's eyes darted towards the darkroom door.

'Sure, I'll meet them if you think it'll help, but I don't want word getting out any further, *capisce*? I gotta sort my head out over this, figure out a plan. Things are getting complicated. Someone's on my back. I can't say much right now but I think they know too much about me already . . .'

Juno started backing away from the door in a panic. He was talking about her. He *had* to be talking about her.

There was a loud clatter as she fell over Sean's golf clubs.

'The mother-in-law's a moose! Twelve-to-one on the nose. You're a loser!'

'Juno? Is that you?' Jay called out.

She darted into her room and clicked the door to, heart pounding so violently she felt as though she'd run a marathon, not the length of the hall carpet. I am living with a gunman on the run, she realised in awe, hating herself for being so excited by her adrenaline-rush of terror. Nothing this thrilling had happened in Belsize Park since Chris Evans moved out and Oasis moved in.

Don't be ridiculous, Juno, she told herself firmly. It's probably a perfectly innocent conversation with his agent.

Ah! Her inner femme fatale countered, locking her bedroom door as quietly as she could behind her and adopting a film noir Soviet accent in her head. But what sort of agent?

Chapter Fourteen

Juno and Jay hadn't exchanged a word in twenty-four hours when Lydia, intent on inspecting the new flatmate, descended upon Belsize Park with a bottle of Pinot Grigio and a teetering stack of tubs of glorious-smelling food fresh from the Rosslyn Hill delicatessen. Juno had tried all day to put her off, but Lydia was undeterred.

'He can't be that bad – I'm sure I'll like him,' she'd insisted airily, and then spent most of the afternoon out of the office having her scalp aromatherapy massaged by a Japanese hairdresser she had heard about and then visiting her gym.

So when she bounded upstairs to the flat, she looked even more stunning than usual. Freshly clipped, manicured and powdered, she radiated health, CKBe and perfection so vibrantly that Juno wanted to put on shades and dim the lights as she opened the door to welcome her in.

'You're heaven scent.' She sniffed appreciatively and feigned delight, realising worriedly that – due to their current silence – she hadn't even warned Jay of the impending visit.

Lydia kissed both of her hot, pink cheeks, leaving war-stripes of lipstick. Then, off-loading her cartons into Juno's arms, she breezed into the sitting room proffering her bottle of wine.

It was only watching her rear-view that Juno realised what Lydia was wearing. Her small, high bottom was encased in what appeared to be a nylon string bag of the sort that usually contains oranges; the latest fashionable must-have – D&G mesh cycling shorts which only the most perfect figures could take. Beneath them, the flimsiest pair of flesh-coloured bikini pants only just served to cover her modesty. Matched with a shiny white t-shirt which appeared to be from the Ladybird toddlers' range, and a pair of knee-length white patent leather boots, she looked the height of designer babe, It girl chic.

'Hi – you must be Jay!' she almost sang as she homed in on the sofa where he lay prone in front of CNN.

'S'me, baby.' Jay didn't even look up.

Despite hating him at the moment, Juno couldn't help but admire his infuriating cool.

As she plodded towards the kitchen with the delicatessen tubs, she saw Lydia fiddle awkwardly with the white Versace sunglasses she was wearing on her head while the other hand waggled the wine bottle she was carrying like a majorette with a baton.

'Jay, this is my friend, Lydia,' Juno grunted reluctantly, too kind to leave her stranded by the sofa, but equally aware that addressing words directly to him represented an enormous climb down.

As she passed behind Lydia, she saw him finally glance up. Scuttling hastily into the kitchen, she dumped the tubs on a surface and gritted her teeth, determined not to feel jealous.

On seeing Lydia, those yellow eyes had widened as though an ophthalmologist was pulling back the lids to administer soothing drops. Juno hadn't hung around to monitor his expression beyond that.

She busied herself opening a bottle of cheap Merlot. In the sitting room, she could hear Jay and Lydia falling into conversation – awkward at first; the stilted, staccato monosyllables of the newly acquainted, followed by the overlapping conversational flood of the eager-to-impress.

Juno carefully peeled the foil from the neck of the bottle, located three glasses which were remarkably smear-free (she suspected Jay had been through the cupboards with a glass cloth) and then killed time by nosing through the tubs.

Because Lydia didn't eat more than a thousand calories a day

– and ninety per cent of those were rice cakes – she had hopeless taste in food. The array that confronted Juno was undoubtedly pricey and individually delectable, but in combination it was decidedly quixotic.

Along with fat, black olives, artichoke hearts and fennel in oil, there was a huge square of Tiramisu, some raw calves' liver, a jar of rabbit pâté, a carton of fresh tapenade and a family-pizza-sized gorgonzola. Juno carefully placed the calves' liver to one side and peered into the bread bin. In its very depths were two French Toast slices, a mouldy Bath bun and half a packet of stale tortillas. There was no bread in the freezer, and no salad in the fridge. Juno suspected that even her creative culinary skills would be stretched to make the given ingredients gel together into palatable fare.

She could hear Lydia telling Jay that she'd brought 'lots of goodies' for them to eat.

'I got that calves' liver so that you can do that wonderful thing with basil you did for all of us a couple of months ago,' she called through to the kitchen. 'The night Ally and Duncan came, remember? Their first outing after Africa was born.'

'China.' Juno gritted her teeth. That 'wonderful thing' had taken hours to prepare and involved marinating the liver in a vat of reduced sherry, chopping acres of basil and emulsifying a dairyload of cream in clarified butter – none of which she had in the kitchen now. In the past week, she had shamelessly neglected Sean's herb bed by the window and all but the dill was currently doing an impression of raffia. The fridge was bare apart from Diet Coke, skimmed milk and a four-pack of yoghurt vitamin drink that appeared to be called Yukkaie.

She tipped the antipasto into a bowl and dumped it on the tray along with the wine bottle, glasses and a can of Diet Coke which she shook vigorously.

Lydia had settled into the sofa beside Jay when Juno walked back through. She was more specifically osmosing into the sofa, Juno decided, since every taut, sleek inch of her that was in contact with the rust silk upholstery was sinking seductively into it as though glued, stitched and tacked there like a decorative motif.

'Of course, the whole thing is very copacetic,' Jay was saying in his husky drawl, totally ignoring Juno as she slammed the tray on to the tiles of the coffee table.

'Sure,' Lydia breathed, turning to Juno and grinning. 'D'you mind opening this, Joo?' She held out the Pinot Grigio. 'Only I prefer white.'

'Sure,' Juno mimicked her breathy little voice and, grabbing the wine, stomped back into the kitchen.

I will not be crabby and childish. I am not jealous. I love Lydia lots, she told herself as she yanked the cork so violently from the bottle that it crumbled.

I can't look at Jay, she realised in shock five minutes later as she perched on the medieval altar stool by Uboat's cage and sipped her Merlot defiantly. This wasn't just because he was still dripping from the fountain of Diet Coke which had come up to meet him when he'd pulled the tab on the shaken can – his lion's mane was now divided into sticky tendrils, his satsuma orange t-shirt stained iodine brown at the front. Juno couldn't look at him because he was looking at Lydia. And if those yellow eyes could eat, drink, binge and feast upon a face then that was what they were doing with Lydia's perfect bone structure right now. They were, in fact, pigging out.

Apparently unaware of the admiration, she was picking pieces of cork from her wine glass and glowing at Juno lovingly, blue eyes prismatic with misdirected enthusiasm. Having clearly elected herself mediator, she'd wasted no time in steering the conversation towards 'the flat', 'the flatmates' and mates generally.

'Juno and I shared a place for a while,' she was telling Jay. 'But then she met John and they decided to live together, leaving me on my own.'

This wasn't strictly true, as Lydia's father had bought her a Maida Vale flat several weeks before Juno and John finally made the commitment to live together. But he had insisted that the place be decorated before his daughter moved in, and so Lydia was still languishing in the Cam Den when Juno left it to move to Clapham.

'You still live alone?' Jay asked enviously.

Juno picked at the trimming on her altar stool and longed to be somewhere else entirely – hanging off a precipice by her fingernails perhaps? Trapped in a zoo cage with a rabid grizzly bear? Standing on the terraces wearing the Everton strip with a bunch of Liverpool United fans?

'I live with a guy called Nat.' Lydia winked at Juno encouragingly, clearly bemused by her silence.

'Is he your lover?' Jay took a suck of Coke from his can.

'Not currently, no.' Lydia laughed. 'God, you Americans are all very up-front, aren't you?'

'I can't say.' He shrugged easily. 'I don't know all Americans individually.'

Lydia laughed in delight. 'Juno was a great house-mate,' she said eagerly. 'She cooked like a dream, never complained if I stayed out all night, never borrowed my clothes and liked the same soaps as me on the box. I'd say you're on to a good thing, Jay.'

'Sure am,' he muttered tightly.

'Of course the sex is pretty deafening, but you're okay as she's not seeing anyone at the moment, are you, Joo?'

This was clearly intended to be a throw-away joke, but neither Juno nor Jay laughed.

'More antipasto?' Juno offered through gritted teeth as she thrust the bowl under Lydia's nose.

'No, thanks.' She took the bowl and offered it on to Jay. 'Like I said, Juno's a terrific cook – her mother's something of a national culinary icon.'

'So I gather.' He speared an artichoke heart with a cock-tail stick.

'Has Joo cooked for you yet?' Lydia asked.

Juno was staring fixedly at the artichoke. Jay was holding it in front of him like a medical specimen.

'I'll put some music on, shall I?' she bleated, dashing

to the stereo and firing up whatever was already inside the CD player.

Some sad, melodic strains started filling the room. They were hauntingly familiar. Juno suddenly wished she'd bothered to listen to her father when he'd waffled on about music all those years ago – trying to teach her and Sean to recognise classic works, when all they'd wanted to do was bed-bounce to 'Remember You're a Womble'.

'This is lovely.' She headed back to her stool, frantically trying to remember what it was so that she could show off. 'Is it Fauré?'

'Isn't it the theme from the Rover advert?' Lydia turned to Jay as the music was joined by a chorus of rather grim-sounding choristers.

He cleared his throat. 'It's Mozart's *Requiem*.'

To the accompaniment of a slicing violin section, the choristers trilled their way through the *Requiem Aeternam* without interrupting Lydia's happy patter much, although the more dramatic vocal flourishes made both Juno and Jay flinch.

'Tell me about New York – where do you live? Do you share?' She was happily asking questions to which Juno had found it impossibly hard to get straight answers just a few days earlier. 'Were you brought up in the city? What do your family do? Are there many of you?'

Amazingly Jay answered, if only in single sentences. 'I live in downtown Manhattan now, but I was brought up in Woodside – that's in Queens – until I was a teenager when my family moved to the Bronx.'

'Gosh!' Lydia was spellbound by the danger of it all. 'Isn't there a crack dealer on every corner and a drive-by shooting every half hour?'

'That's the South Bronx.' His face remained dead-pan. 'Where the gangs hang out. We moved to East Tremont. It's a pretty rough neighbourhood in places, but nothing like the South.'

It was when the *Dies Irae* kicked in that conversation became more laboured. The volume was cranked up very high and the tragic music seemed to bounce off the walls and storm around the room like a maddened ghost.

Juno sloped back to the kitchen to try and do something sensational with the calves' liver. Whatever she did, she was pretty certain Jay would refuse to touch it. As she chopped a couple of wrinkled shallots and glugged olive oil into a pan, she heard Mozart being replaced by Garbage – undoubtedly Lydia's choice. She doused the sizzling shallots in Merlot along with a handful of peppercorns, watching them jump on the bubbling red sea like little bouncing bombs. For a brief moment, she wondered rather guiltily if she should call Lydia through and warn her to lay off the subjects of religion and politics when talking to Jay, but decided that would be pointless. Lydia never talked about religion and politics.

Singing along to 'Queer', Juno danced her way into the recesses of the freezer, bum waggling behind her as she stooped. Ah, ha! Tucked behind a catering pack of economy fish fingers and a bag of spinach was her secret ingredient.

'This is absolutely delicious – try some, Jay.' Lydia held her fork so close to his mouth that he had no choice but to open up before the slither of liver tipped into his lap.

'It's good.' He sounded relieved as he chewed cautiously.

Garbage had made way for Portishead now. The sexy, grinding music filled the room, which was already swirling with complicated cross-currents as the sun dropped beneath the tall windows, its splash of orange sliding slowly into the crevice of the ceiling.

Only Lydia was joyfully eager to paddle among those currents.

'I love these potatoes. How did you do them, Joo? I'll try them out on Nat.'

'Oh, they're pretty simple.' Juno watched as Jay stealthily helped himself to a spoonful of calves' liver which he'd flatly refused ten minutes earlier. 'They're basically *dauphinoise*, but I used the Gorgonzola instead of Gruyère. And instead of nutmeg, you use . . .'

Lydia was beaming at Jay again. He was staring at her runway-long thighs.

Juno tried a brief pause. No reaction.

'. . . finely chopped pickled wildboar sweetbreads and a light sprinkling of chives.'

Aware that she had lost her audience, Juno stuffed her mouth with spinach and walnut sauté. It was probably no bad thing that they didn't know what the secret ingredient was anyway, she mulled. For in with the potatoes and Gorgonzola, she had heaped some joke garlic ice-cream which Sean had brought back from the Isle of Wight recently. It was foul with a wafer and a flake, delicious with potatoes. If he knew, Juno suspected Jay would throw up.

'Have some more.' She thrust the serving dish at him, still unable to look him in the eye. Instead she peered intently at the Diet Coke stain on his chest.

Now Lydia was telling him what a joy Juno was to work with. 'It was so good of her to get me that secretarial job at Immedia. The money's a joke, of course, but our boss is *sweet* about time off . . .' All the time she kept crossing and uncrossing her long, silk-skinned legs so that the orange-mesh shorts rose into the crease of her hips. Juno was certain Jay didn't take in a word of her eulogising.

Juno knew, with a punctured heart, that Lydia wasn't just flirting with Jay out of habit – she fancied him like mad. And he wasn't exactly fighting her off.

Portishead were singing 'Glory Box' with sexy abandon. Juno felt her chest shrink like a balloon suddenly released at the neck; she could almost hear her lungs squeal as the air was forced out.

'You okay, Joo?' Lydia turned towards her in sudden concern.

Buttocks tightening so hard upon her altar stool that she was lifted up several inches, Juno nodded fiercely.

'You're not feeling crampy or anything are you? Only you said this morning that your period was coming.'

'I feel fine, thanks.' Juno gritted her teeth.

'Juno gets appalling PMT.' Lydia winked at Jay. 'I'm sure you'll grow accustomed to finding sacrificial headless chickens in the fridge once a month at full moon.'

'Huh?' Jay looked non-plussed.

'PMT – Post Modern Tension,' Juno quipped flatly. 'I get pissed off living with reconstructed males.' That was going to be scrapped from tomorrow night's new set, she decided hastily as Lydia and Jay both looked blank.

'Oh, PMS.' There was a corrective tone in Jay's voice. 'Sure, a couple of my sisters suffered from that. You should try Evening Primrose Oil.'

'For frying or for salad dressings?' Juno snapped. 'Finish off those potatoes. Shame to see them going to waste.'

'Your waist, you mean,' Lydia laughed.

Juno tried not to look put out.

'You should come to aerobics with me sometime if you're really keen to lose weight.'

'I'm not,' Juno snapped.

'I don't know what you're worrying about.' Lydia hastily tried to make up for her gaffe, taking a minute sip of Pinot Grigio. 'You always look gorgeous – like the ripest, sweetest fruit. Don't you think so, Jay?'

Taking a long, slow toke at his Coke can, he shrugged and said nothing.

The silence was so unbearable that Juno spluttered out the first thing she could think of to fill it.

'So how was Bruno last night?'

'Sweaty.' Lydia wrinkled her nose. 'He's not very fit – he almost passed out when we did the high-impact leg workout, and he decided not to swim at all – just watch from the restaurant.'

Most men would, Juno thought to herself.

'Lydia's seeing a man called Bruno at the moment,' she announced quickly, still not looking at Jay. She was determined to quash any hopes he might hold that Lydia was available – however hard Lydia herself was trying to impress that fact upon him.

'If you call two shags and a few phone calls "seeing".' Lydia gave Jay the benefit of her big-eyed wink now. 'And the weirdest thing is that you know one of his flatmates, don't you? Will Pigeon?'

'Who?' Jay looked amused at the name.

'Yes, who?' Juno was equally perplexed.

'Will, the ticket tout.' Lydia put down her glass of wine and turned to look at Jay. 'Works around the West End selling everything from the back row of *Starlight Express* to debentures at Wimbledon. I thinks he deals in other lines as well – thin, powdery ones, if you get my snow drift. He has the best contacts in town, according to Bruno. Gossip columnists call him the Dream Ticket. He knows who's seeing what, eating what or snorting what, with whom and where.'

'Sure I know of him,' Jay said with tight-lipped irritation. 'Who doesn't?'

'I don't,' Juno chirped nervously, desperate to change the subject. She had a feeling they were entering very danger-ous conversational territory. 'Now would anyone like more spinach?'

'I knew it!' Lydia gasped, ignoring her friend as she seized upon the connection. 'So that's how he got hold of Sean's watch. Did you do a deal with him?'

Juno closed her eyes and almost dropped the spinach dish as she realised Lydia had been doing some detective work behind her back.

'Sean's watch?' One of Jay's perfectly arched eyebrows lifted disdainfully.

'Bruno says Will brought it home.' Lydia turned to Juno for confirmation, but she still had her eyes closed. 'Something to do with a deal, he reckons, but Will won't tell him more. He's always getting paid in odd ways – jewellery, other tickets, insider share information . . . you name it.'

'More liver?' Juno offered desperately. She had forgotten to warn Lydia off the subject of the watch. Right now, she didn't care how her brother's battered Tag Heuer had ended up in Bruno's flatmate's hands, or whether Jay was involved. It was pretty small fry compared to shooting terrorist targets and whatever else she had overheard him discussing last night. He already thought she 'knew too much'. The underworld worked in mysterious ways, and she had no intention of joining it – ten feet under and no longer of this world. She had a feeling that playing Tag with Jay was as dangerous as playing Catch with a pinless hand-grenade.

'And what's all this baloney got to do with me?' Jay was looking mildy bemused. He didn't look like a man whose long-term assassination plans had just been rumbled.

'I love the way you tark,' Lydia giggled, mimicking his accent. 'Do all New Yorkers sound like you?'

'Sure, identical – even the women.' He pulled a 'wise-up' face.

She wasn't in the slightest bit deflected. 'Juno and I thought you might have something to do with the fact that Sean's watch – which he was supposed to have left on the side of the bath here – turned up at Bruno's flat, which is also Will's. Will the ticket tout. Dream Ticket.' She re-emphasised the sobriquet.

'Oh, yeah?' Jay was typically unresponsive.

She nodded earnestly. 'What is really *weird* is that I only met Bruno on Friday night. Amazing coincidence, huh? And he's Irish, you see, so we thought . . .' Her voice petered out.

'You thought what exactly?' Jay's eyes glinted with anger.

'Oh, that you might know him. But he says you don't.'

'I don't,' he said flatly, yellow eyes suddenly resembling two recently struck matches.

'Quite.' Lydia cleared her throat. 'But you do know Will.'

'I know *of* Will,' he corrected slowly.

Sensing an atmosphere as dense as Mercury, Juno gathered their plates and started to slide towards the kitchen.

'So let me get this right.' Jay was looking at Lydia with narrowed eyes. 'Sean's watch goes missing from this place, yeah?'

'Mmm,' she nodded encouragingly, poised to guide him through the story again.

'And turns up in another guy's apartment – some guy you've just started dating?'

'Mmm.'

Juno had almost made it into the kitchen.

'But he knows nothing about it, except that he claims it came from a deal his sleazeball room-mate made on some street corner.'

Lydia gently but encouragingly corrected him. 'Well, not in quite those words, no. He actually said – '

'And you reckon that because I'm some low-life New York harp, I stole the watch and did a deal with this Dream Ticket character. For what exactly? Information? Nose candy? Front row seats at *Cats*?'

'Cost more than a scratched Tag Heuer,' Juno muttered, nipping into the kitchen.

'Juno! Get your ass back out here!' Jay yelled.

She ignored him and, humming loudly, started to rinse the plates.

A few seconds later, he loomed in the doorway. 'What exactly have you been saying about me?'

'Huh?' She turned on the waste disposal and fed the last of the spinach into it.

Marching over to the sink, Jay turned it off where it spluttered to a rattling halt.

'Did you tell your friend out there that I stole your brother's watch?' he hissed in an undertone.

'No!' Juno bleated, staring intently at the stain on his chest.

'Then what?'

'Well, it went missing. And turned up at Bruno's. And he's Irish, and – '

'What's all this shit about me being Irish? I'm American, for Chrissake!'

Watching him rake his hair from his eyes in that now familiar, oh-so-sexy gesture, Juno suddenly realised he was only furious because she'd embarrassed him in front of Lydia. She was also starting to suspect he wasn't a terrorist after all.

She squared her jaw. 'Well, yes, I thought it was a bit

far-fetched too. In fact I told Lydia so, but she was convinced there was some kind of coincidence behind it all.'

'Okay, Juno.' He sighed, rubbing his eyes tiredly. 'I don't give a shit what the deal with the watch is, I'm not involved. I never saw the sumbitching thing and I never want to see it. As far as I'm concerned that's the end of it. Next time you wanna make up stories about me, consult a fucking lawyer.'

'Oh, piss off,' she snapped angrily.

'Yeah, and screw you too!'

'You fancy him, Joo!' Lydia threw her fluffy hedgehog at Juno.

'Do not.' She batted it back with her mouse pad.

'Well I do.' Catching it, Lydia kissed its nose. 'I adore argumentative men. He's so brooding and angry, isn't he?'

Not a great conversation for nine in the morning with the publisher e-mailing a demand for a meeting every two minutes and peering beadily at her through the venetian blind in his office window, Juno decided.

'But he was so rude to you!' she bleated. 'He walked out on you while you were talking. And he was bloody horrible to me.'

'Well, you *did* practically accuse him of larceny and terrorism.' Lydia had moved from Solitaire to Hearts today and was staring in single-minded concentration at her screen.

'It was you who brought up the subject of the bloody watch.' Juno was unfolding paperclips with manic speed. 'Anyway, you can't fancy him. What about Bruno?'

'I think he's becoming a bit keen.' Lydia wrinkled her nose. 'Anyway I only said that I fancy Jay, not that I'm going to do anything about it. I just knew you'd react like this. You've got a honking great crush on him.'

'Have not!' She gritted her teeth.

'So are you saying I've got your permission to go after him?'

Juno glared at her In Tray, heart crashing at the prospect. 'Juno?'

She glowered at her potted fig, wondering whether to spill all the details of the lost weekend to her reckless, indiscreet friend who had undoubtedly enraptured Jay more in an hour than she herself had in three days with her kit off and her bed bouncing.

'Juno?'

She squinted barbarously at her pen-holder, wondering whether to drop heavy hints that he might be a hitman. She doubted telling all would make the slightest difference now that they had met and the blue touch paper had been lit.

Lydia was growling like a winsome poodle puppy – forepaws to the floor, eyes sparkling, eager to frolic. 'What d'you say? Can I play away with Jay?'

Juno scowled at her signed, framed photograph of Jimmy Saville (there was a Naff Old DJ Pic competition going on in the office and she was currently well behind Finlay who had Tony Blackburn). Old Jimmy's marbles-in-crêpe-paper eyes and waggling cigar seemed to be willing her to make a stand, to refuse, to say Jay was all hers to play with, however much she'd screwed things up with him so far.

'Be my guest.' She shrugged. 'Now, if you'll excuse me, I have a meeting.' She stomped off to see their group publisher, Gordon Wilson-Croft, otherwise known as GWC or the Great White Chief.

Five minutes later, she was back, shaking all over, any thought of Jay temporarily obliterated.

'What's up, Joo?' Lydia looked up from her game of Hearts and immediately swung her office chair into action, wheeling around to Juno's side of the desk and holding up a packet of fags.

'It's a no smoking office, Lyds, but thanks.' Juno batted them away. 'I've just had my first official warning. One more and I'm outta here.'

'A warning! What for?' Lydia was the picture of indignation.

'Missing deadlines, sloppy copy, moonlighting for the *New On Sunday* during office hours with office resources, taking too long for lunch, too little time to think up new ideas. And all for sixteen poxy grand – Jesus!' She tore several leaves from her potted fig.

'Poor Joo.' Lydia stroked her shoulder. 'He's a bastard. You work like a slave.'

Juno knew that wasn't true, but was too grateful for the support to say anything. She was equally aware that a great deal of the blame for her recent fall from favour could be laid firmly at Lydia's DKNY-trainered feet. It was Lydia who failed to type copy in time, who encouraged the long lunches and kept Juno continually distracted with gossip and chatter when she should have been working. On the days which she took off, Juno got twice the work done. She knew she should say something about it, just as she had tried to say something to GWC, yet he had pooh-poohed it so contemptuously she couldn't bring herself to continue. He adored Lydia, fancied her like mad, in fact. In his eyes she could do no wrong. Whereas Juno was a lazy, blowsy, overweight liability. The only thin thing about her these days was her novelty factor. She knew it was her own fault, that she should delegate more, keep Lydia in check, but she was frightened it would ruin their friendship.

'This'll cheer you up.' Lydia pulled a mock-glum face. 'I just phoned Jay up to ask him out for a drink tonight, and he turned me down. Said he already has a date.'

Juno looked at her in horror. 'You did what?'

'Asked Jay out – just as friends, seeing as he's a stranger to London. I thought it'd be a nice gesture,' she said with total conviction. The only person Lydia ever lied to was herself. 'Anyway, he told me he's busy. Fast mover, huh? I wonder who she is . . . ?'

Chapter Fifteen

'My flatmate's an American. Last night I offered to cook. I said, "Fancy chip butties tonight?" He said, "I don't even know the guy" – no, that won't work. Shit!'

Juno looked up as the tube train hissed to a juddering halt and the doors rattled open. Kentish Town. Tufnell Park was the next stop and she still hadn't worked out how she was going to start her set. She had plenty of new material, but quite how she was going to knit it together defied her. The butterflies were already flying formation loop-the-loops and dives in her belly. Her hands were damp and clammy, her knees juddering, her breath quickening. The woman opposite had been peering at her in concern around an *Evening Standard* since Camden Town, clearly thinking she was a muttering crack addict or something. Juno noticed she'd discreetly moved her handbag from between her feet to her lap in self-protection.

'My new flatmate's an American. He pledges allegiance to the flag over his Pop Tarts and speaks a foreign language. The other day he said he wanted to orally interface with me. I had my kit off and was lying on my bed before it occurred to me he wanted to have a conversation . . . Jesus, that's even worse.' Juno smiled nervously at the *Standard* woman who looked hastily away and cleared her throat.

She glanced at her watch. Bob had told her to get to the pub by seven-thirty; it was already ten to eight. She wished she'd spent less time getting ready, but most of her clothes seemed to have shrunk recently. Dresses wouldn't go on either over her head or over her hips. Juno had tried to convince herself that this was the penalty one paid for having an hour-glass figure – nothing would fit over the curvy parts to reach the narrow band in the centre – but the fact that the buttons of three pairs of trousers had stubbornly refused to do up rather belied that theory.

In a panic, she had resorted to a black Lycra mini dress which was straining every fabric molecule of its stretch-to-fit guarantee. When she sat down, it corrugated her belly into neat little bands of flesh like a stack of shiny black sausages. Although it was regulation female comic black, she knew it was neither androgynous nor sexless enough to try for the 'I'm one of the lads' look, so she'd gone for all-out Gayle Tuesday innocent tart appeal with Baby Spice bunches and pink glitter eyeshadow. Judging from the looks she was getting, she had a pretty shrewd idea that the outfit made something of a statement. It positively screamed 'Loony Trollop'.

She'd also forgotten to bring her squeezebox with her. It wasn't too much of a problem as, being forgetful, she regularly arrived at gigs to realise she'd left her beloved accordion at home. Nowadays she could perform equally well without it – often better. But the songs were a good stand-by if the audience was unresponsive, especially when she was trying out new material.

'It's only Tufnell Park,' she told herself, getting up and lurching towards the door as the train started to brake at the platform. The sparkly platform-soled trainers had been a mistake too, she decided as she tripped out of the sliding doors.

An *Evening Standard* was discreetly lowered and she was stared at by her concerned commuter friend as she tugged down her short Lycra skirt and headed for the way out.

The Cod and Cucumber was a newly 'reinvented' theme pub just behind Holloway Prison, with austere pebble-dashed grey walls befitting its location. The interior designers had clearly been aiming at understated, utilitarian chic, but the result was more reminiscent of a 'seventies soup kitchen, with dingy low lighting, industrial fittings, fixed benches and a high, zinc-covered bar. In it a few theme-hardened locals – who would drink there whatever the fixtures – were clustered around the bar along with what were clearly new incumbents with razor-sharp suits, fashionable shirts and the latest in trendy haircuts: the unflattering one-inch demob buzz cut. The pub was a third full at most, and there were only two women in the bar at all.

'Hello, darling, you working tonight?' leered a local.

'Yes!' Juno beamed before she realised what he actually meant.

Scuttling to the other end of the bar, she spotted several Day-glo posters offering COMEDY TONITE and felt her heart sink. 'Starts 8 p.m.' had been crossed out in felt pen and replaced with '8.30'; there was no billing – just 'Well-known stand-up Bob Worth introduces some of London's hottest new comics. Carlsberg half price all nite'. It was hardly Jongleurs.

A droopy youth behind the bar pointed her towards a set of stairs above which a sign read 'Toilets and Function Room'.

'Is there a difference?' she muttered, heading towards them.

At the top, a lopsided trestle table had been erected in a tight corner and was being presided over by a shaven-headed hippy chick who was counting a very small amount of loose change into a plastic ice-cream container, beside which was a very thick book of cloakroom tickets with just three or four missing, and a thinner book entitled *Didactic Polemics in European Literature 1947–80*. The girl didn't even look up when Juno approached.

'That way,' she murmured, pointing to the left with a thin wrist lassooed in leather thongs.

'Sorry?'

'The lavs are that way,' she said in a bored voice, clearly used to repeating the same directions many times.

'I'm here for the comedy. Are you front of house?'

'You are? I am!' The girl dropped the pile of pound coins she was counting and looked up in amazement. 'Great! It's a fiver, or three pounds concession. Is it just you, or have you got friends coming too?' She was almost beside herself with anticipation as she picked up the ticket book and fingered several pages.

'Just me.' Juno shrugged apologetically. 'And I'm one of the acts.'

'Oh.' The girl's face fell. 'You'd better go through and find Frank then.'

'Frank?'

'The promoter. You don't know him?' She gave Juno a wary look, clearly detecting a freeloading ligger.

Juno shook her head. 'Bob Worth got me this slot.'

She looked impressed. 'You must be good. He's with Frank – big table at the back. Easy to spot, it's the only one with people sitting at it.'

The Function Room was even dingier than the pub proper, with low Artex ceilings, nicotine-stained walls, mirrored pillars, sticky-topped mismatching tables and a very small bar at which a lone barman stood dutifully by the Foster's pump despite the lack of custom.

Of the dozen or so tables placed in front of the small scuffed black stage with a mike and stand on it, only three were occupied. A young couple sat necking at one and a group of cackling lads occupied another which was at the lip of the stage. Hecklers. Juno shuddered. She could recognise them a mile off, and judging from the multiple stalagmites of empty pint glasses littering the table, they had been gearing themselves up for the verbal fight for quite some time.

'Juno, you slack bitch – at last!' Bob bounded out of a dark corner in which several glasses, watches and whites of eyes glittered ominously.

He gave her a hug and steered her towards the gloom.

'Fucking shit turnout, huh?' he muttered in an undertone as they walked. 'We all want to scratch the gig, but Frank's insisting we do the bastard thing. He's promised the landlord it'll go ahead.'

Frank turned out to be a thin, bearded weasel of a man with lots of gold rings, darting brown eyes and a habit of brushing the nub of his thumb along a damp lower lip as though moistening it to count a wad of notes. Dressed in a white nylon polo-neck and a tight blue mod suit which showed lots of white sock, he looked just like a petty crook from an early episode of *The Sweeny*. Reeking of Egoïste, he sprang up from the table to greet her.

'Juno – a pleasure.' He proffered a gold-encrusted hand with unselfconscious insincerity. 'I don't like women comics as a rule, but Bobby boy tells me you're good so I'm giving you a shot. You never know, treacle, if I like what I see, we might do some business. Drink?'

'Thanks – a Budvar.' Juno winced as her hand was pumped in his like a lactating udder. Then he headed for the bar with a bantam cock's swaggering walk. She turned to Bob in confusion. 'I'm sure I know him from somewhere.'

Bob gave her one of his winks. 'Didn't I tell you this was a Harry Frankel gig?'

'Jesus!' Juno clutched a chair for support. 'No, you didn't. Frankel?'

'Fersure. Pretty low key by his standards, but he's behind it nonetheless.' Bob offered her a fag. 'I thought you'd appreciate the intro. Like the sparkly trainers by the way. Very Wizard of Oz.'

'Thanks,' Juno said numbly, allowing her shaking cigarette to be torched by Bob's flame-throwing Zippo.

She glanced at Frank, who was making a mobile phone call and ordering drinks at the same time, talking loudly and self-importantly, clicking his fingers and generating enough nervous energy to power a small town. Harry Frankel was one of the longest established promoters on the London comedy circuit, organising gigs in pubs, private clubs and small venues from Lewisham to Harrow, Kingston to Walthamstow.

A Soho-born Jew with more chutzpah than Eric Hall, he had procured cabaret line-ups since the working men's clubs of the 'sixties, and was renowned for loathing female comics, black comics, gay comics and comics who worked in 'character'. Anything comic in fact, Juno privately suspected. She had always despised his reputation and everything he represented, but there was no doubt he was a fairly powerful player at the lower end of the live comedy spectrum.

'Took a lot of persuading to get him to agree to use you tonight,' Bob told her, heading towards a chair at the 'comics' table. ''Specially as he's never seen your act, but he heard about your flash the other night and said he always thought strippers and comics were the best combination for a good cabaret line-up, so he'd try you out as a favour. Now who do you know out of this lot?' He nodded at the chain-smoking gaggle of nervous wrecks huddled around the dark, crisp-littered table.

'All of them,' Juno groaned with mock-horror as she slid into a vacant chair. 'Hi, boys.'

'All right, Juno baby – I hear you're the stripper tonight, yeah?' She was greeted by Gary Blumfield, a cocky, buzz-cut football fanatic who was far funnier and more endearing off-stage than on. His ladsy, *Loaded* brand of humour contained innumerable references to 'bints and beer', and he ended every sentence with 'yeah?' in place of a full stop. Juno hoped he wasn't on first as he tended to turn an audience into stone – even a stoned one.

'Hi, Gary. Yes, I'm stripping again. Glad that joke's not wearing too thin yet – still a tenth of a millimetre to go,' she said flatly.

'Yeah, yeah.' He swigged from his pint and peered at her boobs through the taut Lycra. Because she was nervous, her nipples were sticking out like glacé cherries on cup-cakes.

'Things are picking up, boys – and girl!' Frank announced pointedly as he darted back to the table with a tray of drinks, the cloud of Egoïste eclipsing the rising fog of fag smoke and swirling mist of stage-fright. 'More punters are queuing outside, despite the fact your bald little dyke of a girlfriend's on the door, Fergie boy.'

'Milly's no' a dyke, you wanker,' muttered Fergie Walsh, a bleach-blond Scottish punk whose oblique, anarchic humour was inaccessible to all but a very few. He always wore his kilt, an SNP t-shirt and sixteen-hole Doc Marten's to deliver his bizarre and psychotically energetic set. 'And they're probably just queuing for the shit-box out there.'

'Now, now,' Frank tutted, and flashed teeth as large and yellow as a llama's. 'Give it half an hour and the place'll be heaving.'

'I'm heaving already,' moaned Pete Jenkins, a likeable, self-deprecating English teacher. His nervy, public school manner and gentle humour were often far too subtle for a drunken, gee-ed up crowd and despite witty observations and a glorious eye for the absurd, he regularly bombed. 'Must have another pee.' He dashed off.

'That poor boy couldn't deliver a joke if it had a stamp on it,' Bob sighed ruefully, watching Pete sprint for the door and almost crash into a giggly pair of girls teetering in the opposite direction on platform trainers. Nudging one another self-consciously, they headed for the table farthest from the stage, sniggering as they spotted the hecklers.

'Whoopee, the totty's arrived, yeah?' Gary leered, looking up from Juno's breasts.

Great, she thought, as she removed the glass from the top of the bottle Frank had placed in front of her. I'm stuck at what is destined to be the Gig From Hell – make that Unpaid Gig From Hell – with a bunch of sexist comics I don't find funny, apart from Bob, and a promoter who could get me enough work to give up the day job so long as I prove to be the first woman in history he finds amusing. Pushing the glass to one side, she took a huge swig straight from the bottle neck and almost choked.

'Got you some Passion Fruit Hooch.' Frank patted her knee as he perched on a stool beside her. 'I don't like to see girls drinking beer. Now, I don't know if Bob's told you, but I don't want you to do any filthy material – nothing about sex, or periods, or women's problems, although jokes about being fat are fine. Just leave the smutty stuff to the boys. You've got a hole in your tights, by the way – I'm sure you've brought some spares so I'd slip into them now while you've got time. And another thing . . . Hang on – ' He answered the mobile phone that had started shrilling from its executive clip on his trouser belt and started chattering into it about a gig in Dalston later that night.

'What's the running order?' Juno glanced at the piece of paper Bob was fingering.

'Whereabouts would you like to go, slapper?' He grinned, picking up a pen.

'Second from last.' Juno perked up.

'Damn, I was hoping you were going to say first.' He tucked the pen behind his ear. ''Cos that's when you're going on.'

She almost crowned him with a Hooch bottle, but needed what was inside it too much. Going first in a line-up was the least-liked position – you were a warm-up man, test pilot and fall guy all at once. For such a macho, action-hero role, Juno was continually surprised to find that it was a position regularly reserved for the token female on an otherwise all-male bill.

Gary and Fergie were both moaning about how dreadful the line-up had been at Finnegan's Wake on Monday night. It was a gig where many top comics tried out their new material in low-key surroundings to see whether it worked or not and was often the setting for a top-drawer line up.

Bob mouthed at Juno, 'Jealous as hell.'

Still annoyed about the running order, she looked away, swigged her Hooch and brooded about her set. Thank God she had all the new anti-Jay material to use tonight. She wasn't certain how much of it was truly funny, and had been planning to put just the best bits at the end after some tried and tested repartee. Given Frank's veto on sex, periods and 'women's problems', however, and without her trusty – if dated – squeezebox songs to fall back on, she was only left with a couple of fat girl jokes, an overused spiel about children's television in the 'seventies, her growing-up-with-hippy-parents set and bitching about It girls – all of which was as stale as week-old French bread.

A long-haired man with a Meatloaf t-shirt and a beer gut lumbered on to the stage and tapped the microphone a few times before shambling off to preside over a small table with a very primitive lighting board placed on it.

As Frank had predicted, the paying public were starting to arrive at last. Although there were still more empty chairs than full ones, the Function Room gradually began to look less like the inaugural meeting of an agoraphobics' self-help group. At least six tables were occupied and the barman was pouring more than one pint simultaneously as a small but demanding queue formed at the bar. Among them, the gang of lads were buying two pints each, Juno noticed worriedly.

'Are you doing Edinburgh this year?' Bob was asking Fergie.

'Yeah, a couple of half-hour sets at the Pleasance – in the Cabaret Bar. You?'

'A week at Guilded Balloon. Got a sponsorship deal with some alcopop called Speedball.'

'You're sorted, you jammy bastard! Did you know Jerry Maloney's tipped to win the Perrier?'

'Christ!' Gary butted in indignantly. 'Haven't we already heard enough fucking paddies doing material about gay priests? What is this? A Murphia conspiracy? Mick Collins should win it, he's a fucking top man.'

'Just 'cos you think you're like him,' Fergie scoffed, 'which you're not, incidentally. Mick actually makes people laugh.'

Juno tried not to listen in. She hated the build-up to a gig – it was why she was always deliberately late, trying to arrive just minutes before the start. The smoky, nervy, bitchy pre-show atmosphere in a green room, dressing room, or at comics' tables, always unnerved her. The gossiping, sniping rivalry and ladsy badinage was for many a vital component of getting keyed up for their set, but Juno found it hard to contribute, especially as it often involved bragging about how many bookings one was getting, university tours in the pipeline, plus radio work, press interviews and very occasionally television. Juno seldom had anything lined up beyond the following week. Male comics could also be a pretty misogynistic bunch, and she was regularly excluded from conversations. If there was another woman on the bill, they'd almost inevitably chum up. Nights like tonight could feel very lonely.

By twenty-five past eight, Frank had taken several more phone calls, Pete Jenkins had visited the loo so often he'd been nicknamed Sissy Titus by Gary, and Bob had started a fresh packet of Benson & Hedges. Fergie was now buried behind a copy of *Marxism Today*, flicking his ash over its top leaves on to the table in the hope that the ashtray was somewhere near.

Juno had played nervously with the hole in her tights so that it had doubled in size and was laddering like mad. Tugging at her skirt hem she realised that it wasn't long enough to cover it. She'd just have to take the stupid things off and bare her stubbly, fake-tanned legs in front of the paying public.

'Just going to the loo.' She clambered through the bunched stools and chairs which were grid-locking the comics' table.

'Don't be long, treacle, we start in five,' Frank called after her. 'And change those tights, eh?'

On the other side of the Function Room doors, Fergie's shaven-headed girlfriend was only on to page four of her cloakroom ticket book and hadn't got much further with *Didactic Polemics*. Her ice-cream box now contained a few bank notes, a chewing-gum wrapper and a packet of Rizlas.

In the loos, Juno yanked off her tights and threw them in the swing bin before assessing herself in the mirror. The Baby Spice pigtails were looking decidedly lop-sided now and her mascara had run to give her panda eyes, but she decided to stick with it for the bombed Lolita look. It had a vacant kind of sex appeal to it. Her dress really was far too tight; in the unflattering overhead lighting it looked more like spraypaint than fabric and the seams were straining to their limit. Frank might get his strip after all, she realised. At least it gave her a fantastic cleavage. She only wished Lulu or Triona was around to cheer her along.

'I live with an American,' she told her reflection. 'That's like living with a Canadian only without the sense of irony.' She scrunched up her face. 'Too subtle.'

She put on another layer of bright pink lipstick and smacked her lips together.

'I live with a house-proud American IRA terrorist. He's

great at unblocking the loo, but I wish he'd put the lid down after he's set the timing device.'

Several more fivers were in the ice-cream container when she finally ventured back towards the Function Room.

'Are you Juno Glenn?' Fergie's girlfriend looked up from *Didactic Polemics*.

'Wish I wasn't. Why?'

'Some friends of yours have arrived – they were asking after you.'

'Great.' Juno perked up, suspecting it would be Triona's mob. 'I think you'll find the sequel is even better.' She nodded towards the book and headed into the throng.

The room was more than half full now, the sensory padding of smoke, chatter and movement making it appear even more so. Juno caught the briefest glimpse of her brother's girlfriend waving from the bar before she was almost floored by a blast of Egoïste. Frank was positively panting with hyper-energetic excitement.

'Thought you'd done a runner.' The chunky sovereign ring on his middle finger was pressed into the crease of her elbow as he steered her towards the table where another Hooch was waiting, this time already poured into a glass. 'Now you're on in two shakes of a camel's scrotum, treacle, so start breathing deeply – those fantastic tits deserve a jiggle. We've got a bit of a VIP situation going on tonight.' He tapped his nose, brown eyes darting frantically over her shoulder. 'Won't tell you who in case you get nervous – I know you girls can get in a bit of a tizzy when there's a celeb around. I'll just remind you to lay off the Tampax references – and no swearing on stage neither. Leave that to the lads. Keep it bubbly and clean.'

'The jacuzzi of comedy, that's me,' Juno muttered, straining around to see who he was talking about, eyes smarting from his aftershave.

'Attagirl.' Frank pressed her down into the chair in front of the glass of Hooch and then took a call on his mobile.

Directly in front of her, Juno could just make out Triona's

shock of blonde hair settling at a table to the left of the stage. She was accompanied by her chi-chi accessory of a friend Suoxi, a tiny Japanese fashion victim. Already waiting at the table were the sprawling, beery figures of Barfly and Horse – two of Sean's oldest cronies. Juno bucked up as she realised she had a few partisan plants in the meagre crowd.

Barfly was as beefy, burly and surly as Horse was tall, gangling and free from both muscle power and aggression. Whereas Barfly had been known to head-butt lady pensioners for queue-jumping in a post office he wanted to hold up, Horse would ask them their life stories and say 'no shit' a lot with empathetic – if dim – understanding. Barfly was passably sexy in a terrifying, bullying kind of way – yet underneath he was as romantic and old fashioned as a Whitney Houston ballad; Horse was a beautiful, tragic surf-junkie whom women adored, and yet he treated them with the thoughtless disrespect of a child letting his guinea pigs starve to death in an excrement-filled cage. The fifth son of an East Ham print-worker, Barfly had played truant from his special needs school from the age of eight, and absconded from a detention centre at fifteen; Horse, whose father was a high court judge, had attended Charterhouse and then Christ Church where he'd been sent down for dealing coke. Barfly, despite having more criminal connections than the central police computer, had never been to prison. Horse had served three years for possession of heroin with intent to supply. They loved one another like brothers, Juno never understood why.

There were two other people sitting at Triona's table whom she couldn't make out because they were hidden behind a mirrored pillar. In front of them all was a forest of frothing Budvar bottles and in the centre of those a bottle of tequila. Juno sipped her sugary Hooch and longed to join them.

Pete turned jumpily to her. 'You know who's in tonight, don't you?'

'Don't tell me – a reviewer from the *Tufnell Park Advertiser*?' Juno had a shrewd idea that Frank's idea of a VIP was anyone wearing a tie.

'Piers Fox.' He wiped a sweaty upper lip. 'Came in while you were in the loo.'

Juno howled in delight. 'That's the best joke I ever heard you tell, Pete!'

'Thanks. Squizz the table by the bar and see if I'm wrong. Gary asked him along, didn't you?'

'Might have.' Gary shrugged nonchalantly, milking the kudos. 'But I reckon he's heard on the grapevine how hot I am and tracked me down, yeah?'

Juno stared at a vaguely familiar, red-haired figure at a small table towards the rear of the room. He was holding up a glass of wine to the light and peering at it critically.

'It does look a bit like him,' she agreed.

'It frigging well *is* him, yeah!'

Juno stared in awe. Gary was right. It was.

Tall, lithe and urbane, Piers Fox cut an utterly incongruous figure amongst the studenty, pub-going crowd around him. He was wearing a tailored white linen suit and had the hollow-cheeked look of disdain that comes from finding oneself totally out of context.

'What the hell is he doing here?' Juno gaped. 'He represents film stars and supermodels, not door-split comics. Are you blackmailing him or something?' She looked at Gary with newfound respect.

He swaggered perceptibly, brushing a hand over his blond crew cut. 'I sent him a ten by eight and a *very* convincing letter, yeah?' He shrugged coolly.

'You are blackmailing him then,' Juno repeated, rubbing a thumb against her wet forehead. She could feel her Baby Spice pigtails sliding downwards by the second. Piers Fox was one of the hottest, slickest PR agents around. She'd only recently read a long piece about him in the *Sunday Times* Magazine, had heard the well-worn rumours that Madonna had once asked him on a date, seen his picture in *Cheers!* just this week clinking glasses with Bruce Willis at a première.

Everyone dreamed of being represented by Piers Fox. Young and ruthless, he was the hottest agent on the starting blocks and had carved out careers for starlets, politicians, writers, models, as well as those who were simply famous for being famous.

Juno stared at him in awe, still wondering what the hell he was doing above a theme pub in Tufnell Park. It was like spotting Ivana Trump shopping in Mark One, or Jacques Villeneuve having the tyres changed on his Williams at Kwikfit.

She didn't have long for conjecture, however, as Bob was leaping on stage with his customary velocity and grabbing the microphone from its stand as though it was a live animal intent on sucking his throat.

'Evening, lads and gents, I'm Bob Worth and I'd like to welcome you to Laughing Gear in Tufnell Park.' He waited a spilt second for any cheering – which didn't come – before racing on in his mock-cockney staccato frenzy. 'Now we've got a fucking fantastic line-up for you tonight, but before I get the first life model up here for you to try and excite, I'd like to ask you all a question. Simple one – don't be scared. I can see you looking a little uneasy there, mate.' He picked on Piers Fox with reckless abandon. 'But don't fret, me old gingy square – nice suit by the way, is it made to measure? Yes? Where were you at the time? – it's a multiple choice question. Is Camilla Parker-Bowles a dog. Hands up for answer a) YES . . .'

A very few hands went up tentatively whilst pretending to scratch ears, tweak fringes and rub noses, and were almost immediately lowered again. Only the lads at the front jeered and flashed their armpits as though they knew the answer to an easy question in class.

Accustomed to warming up an audience, Bob's machine-gun delivery was undeterred by the muted response. 'Okay, or answer b) NO – because it's fucking cruel to dogs to suggest she's so good-looking . . .'

When the usual gale of laughter didn't immediately ensue, he maintained his composure. A thin audience didn't throw him. He was accustomed to drawing blood from a stony silence.

'Now Camilla is most often compared to a Rottweiler, isn't

she? Which I think is wrong. You see, I have here my *Observer Book of Dogs* . . .' He proceeded to pull it out of his seat pocket and hold it up to elicit a few cackles of recognition before he started flipping through the pages. 'And I think you'll agree that the Rottweiler in here is quite an attractive beast.' He held the book open at the relevant page to show the audience. 'Whereas the Bloodhound – well, judge for yourselves.' Flicking through again, he opened the book to reveal a large picture of Camilla which he'd glued in.

A few of the small crowd came onside and laughed delightedly at the cheap joke while Bob blasted on, 'There are some others in here . . .'

Having heard the set before – and realising with a pang of disappointment that it was one of his weakest – Juno laughed on cue and puffed urgently on a cigarette, blocking her ears and trying like mad to think of a first line. It would come, she knew it would come; she relied upon this adrenaline rush to make her act work. She no longer cared that Harry Frankel was watching. What did he matter when Piers Fox of all people was in the audience too?

'I live with an American,' she muttered under her breath. 'Wanna swap?'

They were getting worse. It just had to come . . .

She looked up and caught Piers Fox glancing in her direction. Those seen-it-all green eyes flicked over her face like a Japanese tourist moving past his twentieth Constable in the National Gallery. Juno blanched and tugged her pigtails tighter. Bastard! I'll knock your monogrammed silk socks off, see if I don't. Just need that first line . . .

'. . . and she still hasn't given up the day job. Please give a huge – '

Jesus, I'm on! Juno gaped at the stage from which Bob was starting to beckon. No first line, no brain. I'm on.

'The gorgeous Juno Glenn!'

She was ricocheting through the unoccupied tables and towards the stage before she'd decided what to say. Her heart was pounding and her head was on the Tower Hamlets of all mental blocks. Piers Fox was watching; Harry Frankel was watching. She had no first line. Her dress was about to ping off in every direction, perspiration was white-watering through her every crevice, her mascara was doing a Jackson Pollock in the bags beneath her eyes and she was reaching for the mike with palms greased with sweat.

'Hi, good evening. I had a new flatmate move in last week,' she said in a husky, breathy voice which came from her curling toes and rasped through her trembling body yet still sounded as intimate as phone sex, eyes catching those of the audience like a best friend eager for a gossip. 'He's a New Yorker so I thought I'd make him feel at home. On the day he arrived, I bought some bagels, brewed dutch mocha with skimmed homogenous *latte* and then drove past his bedroom at three in the morning, peppering the walls with an Uzi. I think he appreciated the gesture.'

There was a mild titter of laughter from the audience.

Juno adjusted the mike-stand lower. 'Of course, he doesn't speak English. Being American, he linguises in transatlantic dialogisation. This morning he asked me to "evacuate the biodegradable matter from the waste reception unit". So, naturally, I emptied the bin . . .' she paused for the catch-up '. . . into his underpants.' She paused again while the audience tittered, timing her addendum to perfection. 'There was room for the bottles and papers in there too, but I'm ecologically aware so I recycle. He thanked me by saying "I accept your co-responsibility with mutual valuation and humility." Then he plugged me with a semi-automatic and went to Budgen's for more Oreos.'

Juno glanced around the room, assessing its first reaction. They were friendly and responsive, but not entirely in tune with her yet. The snogging couple were examining one another's eyes like two ophthalmologists. She could see that Frank was yakking into his lump of plastic-encased microchip again, and Piers Fox was tapping into a digital organiser. The lads were chattering amongst themselves and pointing at her legs which were just inches from their noses. Juno felt reckless and untethered. She would force them to sit up, listen and beg for more. Going for broke, she threw out a ball-gripping line.

'Americans men love their guns, don't they? Let's face it, they're basically penis substitutes, but they're far more likely to get a woman on her back and begging for mercy than Mr Tummy Banana coming out to play.' Her delivery was as soft as a dough ball but it was aimed right between their eyes.

It worked. They responded. As one, the audience threw her a lifeline of boisterous, gutsy laughter. They didn't expect a soft-spoken, smiling, pig-tailed party girl to say such a thing. She'd given them something totally unexpected and they rewarded her for being brave.

'Think of the benefits of pistol over peenie,' she went on impassively. 'Its aim is better, it goes off exactly when you want it to, it's easy and quick to reload, and those Yankee boys can store it under the pillow at home while they're out so we girls know precisely when they're up to no good, and can even play with it ourselves while they're away. I think the government over here has it all wrong. Don't ban handguns, ban penises, that's what I say. I know which I'd rather be holding in my hand at one in the morning when yet another guy is saying, "It's not you, baby, I think I've just drunk too much tonight".'

More guffaws and jeers. Juno looked towards Triona's table in triumph and caught a momentary expression of discomfiture on her friend's minxy face before she was heckled from the front.

'Get yer tits aat!'

She smiled benevolently at the table of lads.

'Why? Are you still breast-feeding? How sweet.'

The delighted cackles from the sparse audience were all she required to spur her on.

'My new flatmate's penis would be the first to be banned. It's just like him – short, thick and insensitive.' She smiled sweetly until the laughter subsided. 'You may be wondering how I saw it. Well, the truth is, he came into the sitting room the other day while I was reading an article in *Cosmo* about seducing men.' She dropped her voice to an intimate, sensuous purr. 'And I took one look at him and found myself saying, "Take off my bra, take off my stockings, then take off my pants."' There was an embarrassed, giggly hush as the audience pictured the scene. 'When he did,' Juno went on calmly, 'I said to him, "And don't ever let me catch you wearing them again."'

There was another explosion of laughter. Frank was making air traffic control arm gestures for her to wind up this material. Juno ignored him.

She looked over to Triona's table again and saw Barfly in tears of laughter. Although a professed admirer of hers for several years, he was more impressed by her great boobs than by her jokes and she generally expected a more muted response from him at her gigs. This feedback was unexpected and frankly weird. She scanned the table for Triona again and was overcome with icy dismay.

Sitting beside the mirrored pillar, yellow eyes fixed on the rear of the room rather than the stage, was Jay. His golden-syrup hair was clean and uncombed, his faded t-shirt advertised a *Hell's Kitchen Hoodlum's Hooley*, his old Levis hugged those lean, sinewy legs. He was disconsolately shooting out 'don't give a shit', 'not listening' vibes, but there was a muscle slamming against his jaw-bone. Juno flinched and felt the microphone slide like an oiled fish through her damp hand.

The laughter had died now and she knew she had to ride the moment and keep the joke spinning like a plate on a stick. She swallowed a dry ball of air into her lungs, felt it scratch and scrape its way to the pit of her belly, and glanced desperately around the room.

Piers Fox was, alarmingly, giving her his undivided attention now, menthol cool eyes on her face. She found that once she looked at him she couldn't stop, mesmerised by his detached speculation.

The silence could only have lasted one or two seconds, but to Juno it felt long enough to hard boil an egg – plus slice it, arrange the pieces in a fan and pipe ornamental mayonnaise florets on them. Sweat was almost spouting out of her temples now. She could feel it wet in the creases of her ear, moist in the folds of her crow's feet, hot and sodden in the furrow that ran from her cleavage to her belly button. The audience shifted uncomfortably. She shifted uncomfortably. Someone coughed. Juno coughed. She dragged her eyes from Piers to Jay, who was scuffing his toes insouciantly now and looking straight at her with dead-pan lack of interest.

Staring out into the smoky, scattered gathering, Juno was amazed that she had got away with such a long pause and yet her modest audience was still relatively rapt – if rustling crisp packets a touch worriedly and starting to resemble spectators at an execution.

She cleared her throat again. The microphone amplified the sound so that it boomed around the room like the last gasp of a consumptive Brontë. Just as she was about to launch into her 'mad Irish granny' routine in a hyperbolic bid to get laughs, the lads jumped to her rescue.

'You're crap!'

Juno blanched, but was at least glad that the aching silence had been broken.

'Forgive me,' she resorted to a standard response, 'but I think that if you consult your *Bumper Book of Biology for Boys*, you'll find that what you actually should have said is, "You're eighty per cent water, five per cent calcium and only about two per cent crap."'

There was no response. The scanty audience sipped drinks and scraped seats. With a free-falling heart, Juno knew she had lost them. They might be rapt, but they were willing her to die, not live. They'd clearly never seen *Bambi*.

She wanted to say something, anything to get them back onside. If only she'd got her squeezebox to hand, she could launch into a song. Even without it, she'd fluffed and dried before and fought back. But this was different and Juno knew it. If she'd been performing her usual set then recovering from a lapse would have been far easier – her jokes were gentle and self-deprecating, an audience empathised with her, felt she was talking about them and their lives. They weren't threatened by her. But tonight she had tried a different tack, had set out to shock and insult them into laughter. She knew from experience that this required quick-fire rhythm, relentless momentum and nerves of steel. Seeing Jay had robbed her of all of those.

She suddenly felt angry, ludicrously angry. She loathed herself for her ill-judged approach and current humiliation, she hated Jay for being there, wanted to scream at Triona for bringing him. She wanted to hurl the microphone at the inane, brainless lads in front of her, tell the snogging couple to get their hands off one another, yell at the giggling girls to grow up, tell Frank he was a fucking sexist bastard, slap Bob for getting her this gig in the first place. Most of all she wanted to ram Piers Fox's untouched glass of wine right up one of his neatly clipped nasal passages.

She clenched her jaw so tightly for a second that her fillings almost shattered and then, instantly, an eerie calm kicked in, as though an overdose of adrenaline had frozen her nerves. She smiled widely.

Very slowly, she lifted the mike to her mouth again, stared levelly out into the audience and started to speak in a low, luscious voice. 'For the benefit of those of you in the room who aren't mind readers, I told a long and extremely dirty joke just then.'

A peculiar little man standing at the bar suddenly laughed aloud.

'Thank you – it was rather good, wasn't it?' She beamed at him. 'You're wrong, by the way – I am, and they're black M and S ones.' She turned back to the audience again, relieved to hear a few hushed titters. 'Ever hear the one about the female comic who selected a male member of her audience to take home, smother in Nutella and invite all her gorgeous single mates around to taste? No? Then I'll give you a practical demonstration.'

The sweet, sultry smile widened as she realised she was playing Russian roulette with her future career, her dignity and her reputation. She was flying by the seat of her support pants and taking a gamble which might take forever to live down if it bombed, but she had no choice. There was no way her usual style would be effective now that she had started so aggressively and stopped so abruptly. She had to escape and, tonight, that meant taking hostages. She knew that the comic's truism was to work with the audience rather than against it, to read its mood and surf along on it. Well, this audience was embarrassed for her. She had no choice but to make them squirm even more.

'Now I expect you're wondering who the lucky man is going to be. Is it Henry, the mild-mannered janitor? Is it darling little Bob, your host and compère who thinks I'm gorgeous? It could be you.' She pointed to her most recent heckler who cowered and stared into his pint. 'Are you feeling lucky tonight, punk?' She beamed, noticing that the audience was starting to perk up and take notice. 'Want to add an "s" to that baby, and shoot me some . . .' she paused for a suggestive three seconds '. . . punks?'

Crossing the sacred line, Juno stepped off the stage. It was only a six-inch drop, but she felt as though she was taking a running jump off Beachy Head. 'I like the simple things in life . . .' Her victim at the front table shifted to the edge of his seat as she approached him and hopped on to his lap Miss Piggy-style.

'. . . and I'm strangely attracted to you. Believe me, I know how to make a man happy to be alive,' she murmured with Mae West daring, stroking his cheek and making him flinch as his mates fell about laughing. 'But you're just a boy, so I guess you'll have to wait. If I hear your balls drop in the next five minutes then I'll be right back, I promise.' She winked. 'Now over here is a *man*, and what a specimen he is!' She shimmied over to Barfly who sat gaping at her in astonishment. 'There are people in Kent who can smell your pheromones tonight, big boy. Men like you don't grow on trees, do they? They swing from them.'

As she slid on to his lap and started playing with his shirt buttons, she could distinctly hear Triona mutter, 'What the fuck is she doing?'

Juno straightened Barfly's collar mumsily. 'Do you know what we girls call that little area between our vaginas and our anuses, big boy?'

'Er, can't say that I do,' he spluttered in his Rothman's and cheap Scotch voice.

'A chin rest,' she announced cheerfully, to the delight of the women in the audience.

Gently, coaxingly, Juno made fun of him. Not enough to offend deeply, not so little that she looked inept, but her patter was cute enough to get the audience tittering – at first in embarrassment and then, as they realised she was totally nerveless, in genuine appreciation. The sight of a comic walking through the invisible glass wall at the edge of the stage and hopping on and off the laps of the audience startled and excited them. And, doing this, she could adapt her old material and use it with direct examples. She had picked on Barfly early on because she knew he wouldn't be offended.

'No, foreplay is not "asking first", big boy. Foreplay is sitting through an incomprehensible German opera for three hours, buying her a boozy meal at the most fashionable restaurant in London and letting her eat three puddings washed down with buckets of Amaretto, drumming up for the taxi home and stopping several times to let her be sick, giving her a foot massage for an hour, running her a bath, plumping her pillows and then showing her that you can touch your eyelids with your tongue.'

Having dispensed with Barfly, who once again had his mouth open like a dying fish, Juno slithered past Triona, muttering, 'Stick with me, baby, this is going to work,' and hopped on to Horse.

It did work – better than Juno could have dreamed. Within five minutes, she had the lads jeering with glee again, the snogging couple had unplugged their lips and were snorting laughter bubbles into their drinks, the giggling girls were her best friends and Frank was apoplectic.

She had worked her way through two other willing stooges and couldn't believe how well they had taken it – had revelled in it, even the guy whose pint she had drained in one. Somehow she'd stumbled upon a winning formula. She supposed it had something to do with being short, plump and baby-faced; she was unthreatening and cute enough to get away with it without exciting them sexually or annoying their girlfriends. She was almost appalled that it worked so well – it was like discovering that the secret of getting rid of cellulite was nude sky-diving over Stoke-on-Trent. Her confidence was floating towards an all-time high.

Standing in the middle of the room, whipping her mike flex behind her, Juno wondered who to pick on next. She glanced very slowly from Piers Fox to Jay and then back again. Both were steely-eyed and seemingly impervious to the turnaround she had wrought amongst a few North London drinkers in a dingy pub. Both were completely the wrong people to pick on, could easily take offence and walk off or start to kick up a fuss which would kill her punchline. But Juno didn't care. She was riding her wave of audience approval so high she felt like Sean upon the supreme Cornish breaker, feet gripping the waxed board like an octopus's suckers. She would never do this set again, this was the ultimate one-night stand, so she might as well go for broke. Whether that was a broken heart or a broken career barely mattered.

She chose the former. Making her way back towards the stage as though prepared to wind things up, she detoured to the right instead and climbed deftly on to Jay's lap.

She cupped his rigid face with her free hand, breathing intimately into the mike. 'And what's your name, Ginger?'

He ignored her, thighs like steel girders beneath the Lycra-trussed flesh of her bottom, hand gripping a glass of Diet Coke so tightly that the knuckles threatened to burst through the skin of his fingers.

Juno made him look at her. Although she had to flex her wrist hard to do it, he didn't really resist. His yellow eyes fixed on hers like the twin barrels of a shotgun.

'Sorry, I didn't catch that?' she murmured softly into the mike, pressing her ear to his mouth. His lips were cold and rigid.

'Jay!' She turned triumphantly to her audience, eyebrows in orbit. 'An American.'

Oh, what bliss to have them in thrall. They laughed obediently, primed and ready for action.

'What's that?' She kept her ear close to his frozen mouth. 'Oh, I know, Jay sweetheart. I'm sitting on it. I feel like the princess and the pea here.' She shifted awkwardly. 'Am I squashing you? My doctor keeps telling me to cut down on all those intimate dinners for two unless I get someone to join me. I'm a terrific cook.' She turned to talk to the audience. 'I just love kitchen gadgets – I recently got an electric juicer and it's just amazing. I'm trying it out on everything. Ever tried juiced toast?'

They were lapping her up now, but Juno's heart was being nailed to the floor with every giggle. She'd wanted to teach him a lesson, to get back at him for rejecting her, to show him she didn't care. But her anger was fast turning to shame now.

She turned back to Jay and stroked his forelock from his eyes, her voice a husky intimate whisper. 'If you come home with me tonight, Jay, I'll worship the ground you walk on . . .' For a second her voice faltered and almost cracked. It wasn't the irony of it, she realised. It was the sad, lost truth of it.

'. . . you see, I had a particularly attractive wool-worsted carpet fitted last week,' she finished lamely, but delivered it well enough to get her new fans hooting and clapping.

Jay was as motionless as a marble bust. She gazed into his eyes, trying to transmit some sort of apology however pathetically ill timed, but as she twisted away to clamber off his lap, he gripped her wrist.

'You cheap, fucking cooz!' he hissed.

Juno blinked, eyes smarting as though sprayed with Mace.

His hand gripped her wrist like a surgical clamp, amber gaze raking her face.

'Is there a translator in the house?' she said in a small voice.

Still on her side, the audience chuckled sympathetically.

'Triona said I should come tonight,' he hissed, voice too low to be picked up by the microphone shaking in Juno's hand. 'She told me I'd misjudged you, said you were really a great person.

I figured I must be wrong. Guess the joke's on me, huh?' He more or less kicked her off his lap.

When she was upright and facing her audience, Juno explained, 'Jay here has just told me that he has a very large boyfriend called Eric cooking him macaroni cheese at home tonight, so I guess he fails too.' She was grinning at him, but her eyes couldn't meet his and she swung hastily away. 'But wait!'

She hushed the audience and cocked her head. 'Can you hear something? Like a quiet sort of a clang. Listen . . .' They listened. The muffled thud of the juke-box floated up from the bar below plus the low chatter of voices, but no one in the audience made a sound as they watched her intently.

'There it is again – more of a dong than a clang.' She very slowly raised one eyebrow and turned her head to look at the front table with camp, overacted delight. 'They haven't . . . have they?'

The audience started clapping and cat-calling as they realised who she was talking to. Her poor first victim turned as pink as extra fruit strawberry jam as his mates nudged and jeered.

Juno walked slowly and determinedly towards him. 'Congratulations. I think you just dropped a couple of clangers and picked up a belle.' Leaning down to peck him on the mouth, she received a full on tongue sandwich with extra relish, to the delighted whoops of his mates. She pulled hastily away, wiping her mouth and forcing a smile.

'Wow! That was . . . wet. I see you've kissed so many women you can do it with your eyes closed, baby.'

I guess I asked for that, she thought numbly as she headed back onstage to thank her cackling coterie and slip the mike back into its stand. 'I'm Juno Glenn and you've been an audience. I think we should date more often. Thank you. Goodnight.'

As she walked offstage, she was aware that she'd fucked up big time, but she no longer cared. As a final coup de disgrace, she pulled her jam-coloured victim up from his seat and, before he had time to react, hauled him into a fireman's lift over her shoulder, pulling more muscles than a sous-chef preparing seafood salad. The table-banging response from a tiny audience in North London was remarkable. She even heard someone shout 'More!'

Bob came bounding through the tables from the other direction to reclaim the stage and introduce Pete. Normally he patted her on the back after her set. Tonight, he simply shook his head in bewildered astonishment as he passed. As Juno drew level with Piers Fox's table, she shot him a wink and carried her lad out of the exit doors.

'Thanks a lot, you were a great sport.' She dropped him on to his feet as soon as they were out of the room and hastily backed away, her shoulder throbbing with pain. 'I'll buy you a pint later. Excuse me.' Not looking at him, she darted towards the loos.

'Wait a minute!' he called after her, but she was already inside, breathing in deep gasps like a glue-sniffer plugged to a plastic bag.

Chapter Sixteen

Tears coursed down her face like water from a crack in a dam. If she plugged her fingers into her eyes, they simply seeped around the edges, sliding into her nose and mouth, down her throat and on to her loathsome Lycra dress.

'Juno! Juno! Which one are you in? Come out!' It was Triona, rattling the doors like a prison warder.

Juno rammed two hunks of loo roll into her eye sockets and twisted them around.

'There's an eighteen-year-old boy hanging around outside saying he wants your telephone number,' Triona announced loudly. Her voice was cold with condemnation.

Knowing she was in for a lecture, Juno threw the blackened wads of paper into the pan. Her vision was still too blurred from crying for her to see the door in front of her but it was undoubtedly bouncing on its hinges.

'Juno, come out of there! I demand to know what's going on. Are you having some sort of breakdown?'

She found herself smiling sadly through her tears. Classic Triona to assume she was having a mental breakdown after a bad set.

'I'm fine!' She burst through the door radiant with false jollity.

'Well, that's great.' Triona was leaning back against the sink units, glaring at her. 'Because Jay is freaking out, Barfly is convinced he's got it on with you, Horse is threatening to shoot up, and I want to kill you! I think you've justified the entry fee tonight, don't you?'

Juno tried to wash her hands nonchalantly at a basin, but the tap spluttered water in a jetstream straight into her crotch which further fractured her faltering composure.

'You look diabolical,' Triona told her critically.

'Thanks.' Juno winced at her mascara-stained, red-nosed reflection.

'What were you playing at tonight?' Triona leant back against the Tampax machine and peered at her glossy navy blue nails in a strangely schoolmarmish gesture. 'First you start with all that insulting crap about Jay and then you launch into the manic Mae West routine. I've never seen you like that before. Have you taken a line or something?'

'I just thought I'd try something new.' Juno shrugged, splashing cold water on her face. 'And it worked, didn't it? Everyone laughed.'

'And now you're crying your eyes out in the loo.' Triona tapped one blue fingernail against the metal side of the dispenser. 'I don't understand you, Juno. Your material was funny before. This new approach is fucking dangerous. You're lucky you didn't get punched out there.'

'Well, they liked it.' Juno clutched the cold tap belligerently.

'Jay didn't,' Triona said coolly. 'Nor did I come to that. I thought it was tacky, bitchy and puerile. People were laughing at you as much as with you.'

Tears were seeping out again. Hot and salty, they slithered down her face.

'You're normally such a happy, sweet person,' Triona went on, moving towards her. 'I can't figure out what's got into you.'

'Jay,' Juno sniffed listlessly.

'Why do you hate him so much?' Triona stood accusingly over her. 'I thought he was overreacting when he said you had it in for him, but now I see what he means. You took the piss out of him so badly tonight, you might as well have attached a catheter to his dick to save time. I had no idea you could behave like this.'

'Well, I didn't know you were going to bring him tonight, did I?' Juno wailed. 'That material was new, I was trying it out – my act almost fell apart when I spotted Jay. I'd never have used the American flatmate stuff if I'd seen him earlier. Besides, nothing is ever sacred to a comic. You know I make jokes about anything in my life which strikes me as funny – Jesus, I've done enough insulting material about Sean and his friends, even you in my time, to prove that.'

'That's not the same,' Triona persisted. 'All the stuff I've ever heard you do about me or Sean or the rest of your family was gentle and ironic and based on the truth. This was just cruel shock-mocking – the lowest form of humour.'

Juno peered at her from wet, swollen eyes. Dressed in a sharp black trouser suit, patent platforms, a white dagger of pale cleavage and scarlet lips, Triona looked far from mumsy, and yet the tone of her voice was reminiscent of Clarrie Grundy telling William off for poaching. Juno knew that her friend was justified, but her stubborn, wilful pride refused to acknowledge it. She had, after all, just caused a minor sensation in there.

'Well, thanks for sharing your opinions on comedy with me.' She pulled out the bands from her hated pigtails and tipped her head upside down to shake out her hair. 'I'll bear it in mind next time I tell a joke at a dinner party. No American penis joke will ever pass my lips again.' As she tossed back her head she caught Triona looking at her closely, brow furrowing in thought.

'You're missing Pete Jenkins,' Juno said icily. 'I'm sure you'll find his particular brand of observational humour wonderfully gentle and ironic.'

'Don't be mad at me, Juno.' Triona rubbed her forehead tiredly. 'I'm sorry to have a go at you, but you freaked me out tonight. I appreciate that it worked, and that they loved your Divine Miss M routine back there. I just didn't recognise you.'

'You want to know something?' Juno wiped the lipstick from around her mouth and stared into her tiny, red-rimmed eyes. 'I didn't recognise me either. That's why I'm crying. Do you know how terrifying it is to be on stage and suddenly find that there's a stranger in your dress with you?'

'And Jay?' Triona asked cautiously.

'What about him?' Juno bleated, wondering whether Triona somehow knew about their lost weekend. She frantically raked her fingers through her limp rats' tails and simply turned them into whippets' tails.

Triona spun around then, her face incredulous, green eyes watchful. 'This animosity between you and him . . . it's just about the food poisoning incident, isn't it, and the fact he thinks you're a slob? There's nothing *more* to it . . .'

'He thinks I'm a slob?' Juno fumed indignantly. 'Did he actually say that?'

'Has something happened between you two?' Triona evaded the question. 'Jay says it's just a personality clash.'

Juno wasn't sure why, but there was something about Triona's holier-than-thou attitude which made her agree with Jay for the first time that week. 'Yes, it's just a personality clash, Triona. You see, I have one and he doesn't.'

They had missed Pete Jenkins's set entirely and Bob was onstage again when they crept back in, giving his all to the resemblance between William Hague and Elmer Fudd as he wound up for the interval.

Wondering whether to rejoin the comics or get herself a large drink, Juno spotted Frank bearing down furiously from the right and her 'lad' hovering hopefully by the bar to the left.

'Come and sit with us.' Triona gripped her arm with tiny, sharp fingers and started to tow her towards their stage-side table. Backing away in a panic, Juno decided she'd rather confront Frank than her furious, stony-faced flatmate. Frank nudged her towards a quiet corner of the Function Room, lit a fat cigar and waited until Bob had announced a twenty-minute break before he spoke.

'I have never been so ashamed of an act in all my life.' His voice was so sharp and acid it could have cut through diamonds. 'I'm not going to stay and chat, I wouldn't waste my breath, but

I have to tell you that while I live and breathe, I will never, ever use you in a – '

'May I interrupt?' a claret-smooth voice cut in on his diatribe.

'No, you may not!' snapped Frank, looking up then blanching as he realised who had just joined them. Close to, the pale, freckled symmetry of Piers Fox's face was oddly compelling.

'In that case, I apologise.' Piers gave him a cold smile and looked at Juno, verdigris eyes blinking thoughtfully. 'I very much enjoyed your set tonight. I'd like you to come and see me at my office.' He was straight to the point, business card slotted between two fingers and held under her nose. To Juno it was the dream ticket of all business cards. She went cross-eyed looking at it.

'I think you have a lot of potential.' He hastily placed the card on the table before her eyes swivelled right round in their sockets. 'What you did tonight wasn't particularly funny but it was brave and original and I like that. Let's have an informal chat about it soon.' He tapped the card with one long, freckled finger. 'Call me.'

'Thanks,' gasped Juno, vocal cards tying themselves into cats' cradles. She doubted it was humanly possible to have an informal chat with Piers Fox.

'Don't thank me. It's my job,' he said simply. 'Call me.' He glanced briefly at Frank, nodded, then moved away.

Frank stood open-mouthed.

So did Juno, but slammed her jaws together hard as Barfly appeared beside her protectively.

'Is this geezer hassling you, girl?' he rasped, shooting Frank a look which was a nanosecond away from a head-butt.

Frank's mouth opened even wider as he took in Barfly's dimensions, flashing a lot of expensive gold fillings in his yellow teeth.

'No, no, Barfly. Frank is a business acquaintance, aren't you?' bleated Juno, desperate to defuse the situation. Her brother's friend was capable of spontaneous GBH just for the hell of it. He'd been known to punch members of staff out cold at a certain South London Seven Eleven simply because they'd run out of Dime Bars.

Barfly looked sceptical, his banana-bunch hand clumsily laying claim to her shoulder and inadvertently dislodging her bra strap.

As one tit dropped several inches, Juno smiled at Frank with as much dignity as she could muster. 'You were saying . . . ?'

'It can wait.' His eyes flicked worriedly towards Barfly then traced Piers across the room where he was sitting at his table once more, with the same full glass of wine that had been there all night in front of him, snazzy palmtop computer on the go and Gary hovering unnoticed nearby.

'Something to do with living and breathing?' Juno offered helpfully.

'I've lost my track.' Frank rubbed one hooded eye distractedly and gift-wrapped his face in an insincere smile. 'Get back to you later, treacle.' And he puffed off, Lucifer-like, in a gust of Egoïste.

Juno, fizzing with excitement, hurried over to join Triona, who was now at the bar.

'You will never *believe* what's just happened!' she whispered ecstatically.

'You apologised to Jay?' Triona handed a tenner to the barman and shot her a disparaging look.

'What? I thought he was with –' Looking around, Juno realised he was no longer at their stage-side table, but was too excited to care. 'No! Nothing like that. God, Triona, I've just been approached by an agent. And not just any old bod. We're talking *the* most –'

'Save it, Juno.' Triona took her change and threw it into her Vivienne Westwood bag. 'I'm not in the mood. Are you staying for the second half?'

Juno's moment of delirium was punctured like a lanced boil.

'No, I'm going home,' she said flatly.

'You really should apologise to Jay.' Triona shot her a withering look.

'I'll say something at the flat later,' she promised wearily, not relishing the prospect. 'It'd be better somewhere quieter.'

'In that case, I'll give you a lift.' Triona handed her a Budvar. 'Down that fast. We're off as soon as Jay has talked to his contact.'

'His contact? Sounds very undercover. Don't tell me it's a Belfast man in a balaclava carrying an automatic rifle? They'll let anyone in these days.'

A flicker of a smile twitched on Triona's lips, but she quickly quashed it.

'Judge for yourself.' She jerked her head towards Piers Fox's table.

Juno blinked so hard she practically dislocated her eyelids as she saw Jay slouching moodily in a seat opposite the PR supremo. Even weirder was the fact that Piers's urbane, Charles Dance face was wreathed in obsequious, ingratiating smiles.

'Piers Fox is Jay's "contact"?' Juno gulped.

'The publicity guy? Is that *Piers Fox*?' Triona peered over her shoulder with renewed interest. 'You know, I thought he looked familiar. Jay just said "There's this guy wants to meet me", but didn't say who. Christ, he's a sly bugger.'

She and Juno gaped at one another in amazement, the frostiness temporarily suspended in the wake of this new development.

'So that's why Piers Fox turned up here tonight,' Juno squeaked disbelievingly. 'To meet Jay. Why?'

'I haven't a clue.' Triona rolled her eyes. 'You know how bloody evasive he is. All I know is that when I called him earlier to remind him that he was coming to see your gig with us tonight, he said – and I quote – "There's this guy who's been hounding me for a meeting since I arrived in London. I agreed to go see him at some place called the Oxo Tower at eight. Is that, like, near this Tufnell Park joint?"' She laughed, shaking her head delightedly at his innocent abroad miscalculation.

'That's a brilliant impersonation!' Juno shrieked.

'Shhh!' Triona glanced at Piers and Jay. 'Anyway, he rang back later and told me he'd asked "the guy" to come here instead. He seems to be amazingly honourable like that.' She gave Juno a wise look. 'He did mention that the other person wasn't very happy about it. Now we know why. Piers Fox actually coming here. And he had to sit through all that awful . . .' She shut up guiltily.

Glancing over, Juno could see that Jay was hunched intently over a glass of Coke, staring down at the table, golden cowlicks of hair covering his eyes, his bitten fingernails drumming against a beer mat. Piers was doing all the talking, hands moving expressively, body language eager and open, like a salesman trying to close a deal. But whatever he was saying didn't appear to be cutting much ice, judging by Jay's wintry cool. Meanwhile, ladsy Gary was hovering hopefully nearby, slurping at a pint with nervy rapidity and shooting Jay irritated looks.

So Piers Fox was here at Jay's request. That was why he'd turned up at a grotty, low-profile comedy gig – he certainly hadn't intended scouting for talent. Juno wondered what his interest in Jay was. As far as she was aware, he didn't represent IRA terrorists, even the ones who wrote bestselling memoirs and lived on the run, which was something of a relief.

'You are going to apologise to Jay, aren't you?' Triona badgered.

'Yes, Mummy.' Juno rolled her eyes. 'In fact,' she glanced at Piers Fox again, 'I'm going to thank him too. He's done me one hell of a favour.'

'Got a new supplier, slapper?' Bob greeted her as she danced across to say goodbye, his eyes glittering with amusement. 'You were something else tonight. Scared me rigid, you did.'

Juno grinned. 'Just trying out some new stuff.'

'Whatever it is, don't buy it again – and change your dealer. It must be cut with fucking Ajax. You off?'

'Yup.'

'I'll call you.' He lit a cigarette and glanced at the stage, anticipating his return. 'We'll line some more gigs up.'

As she headed back to Triona, she encountered Gary storming past in the other direction. As he drew level, he pulled up accusingly. 'Bloody bastard's left already. When I finally got to introduce myself and asked what he thought of my letter, he said he'd never heard of me. Not even staying for my act, yeah?'

'I'm sorry.' Juno tried hard to feel less ebullient.

'Ginger tosser,' Gary sniffed and stared at her with fierce, hurt pride. 'He says he doesn't represent comics. So why was he talking to you, yeah?'

Juno's egotism was growing by the minute. 'Because he represents stars, Gary.'

'Do me a favour,' he sneered. 'If you ask me it's got something to do with that other ginger prat, the Yank who called you a cooz during your set, yeah?'

Juno stiffened. 'What's it got to do with him?'

Gary acquired the look of The Hooded Claw about to tell Penelope Pitstop that her hours were numbered. 'I overheard Fox telling the Yank he could make him a mint just now, yeah?'

'You did?'

'Yeah – he was really giving it the old hard-sell, something to do with some press scandal or other.' Gary nodded, smiling nastily. 'And the Yank's saying nothing, yeah – just acting all mean and brooding – like he's pulling some old Micky Rourke number, yeah?'

'Sounds familiar.'

'So Piers is giving it all he's got.' Gary rubbed his blond buzz-cut with a sweaty palm. 'And then the Yank suddenly said to him, "Juno talking is the funniest thing. We say the same things over and over and we just won't listen to one another." And then he told Piers Fox to fuck off, yeah?'

'He did what?' Juno laughed in disbelief.

'He told Piers Fox to fuck off. I heard him. Calm as you like, he was.' Gary blew out his cheeks like a bull-frog to denote how impressed he was. Then he gave Juno a sickly smile. 'So whatever it is The Fox wants from you, Juno baby, it ain't the Bette Midler crap. It's the Yank.'

'Thanks, Gary.' Juno patted his arm absently, thoughts reeling. 'You're a mate.'

'Any time.' He swaggered off.

Juno stood alone for a moment, uncertain whether to smile or smirk. Jay had been talking about his relationship with her to *Piers Fox* of all people. What was going on here? Was he obsessed with her or what?

In Triona's battered Saab, the music thankfully drowned out the need for talk. The boom-boom bass from a club dance track rattled the speaker fascias from the upholstered doors as Juno sat in the back, crammed between Barfly and a catatonic Souxi. Jay was in front of her in the passenger seat, slouching so low that his head was lolling against the shoulder rest of the seat, big biker boots up on the dash in front. Horse and his friend, Critter, had stayed on to watch the remainder of the set.

'How much did you earn tonight then?' Barfly asked, stroking Juno's cheek in heavy-handed admiration.

'Nothing.' She jerked her head away as his nails removed several layers of dead skin more effectively than a cosmetic peel.

'That's a crime!' he bellowed indignantly, almost outbooming the music. 'You were fantastic tonight, girl. That agent geezer said so, didn't he?'

'He said I was okay.' Juno tried to shrug his arm from her shoulders but merely lodged it behind the nape of her neck.

As Triona negotiated the speed bumps of the Hampstead lane which was a short cut to the flat, Barfly breathed a flammable mix of whisky fumes and poppers into Juno's ear. 'You know I've always fancied you, don't you?'

'Yup.' She leaned away.

'You're pretty fucking sexy for a big bird.'

'It's very kind of you to say so.' She was almost pressing silent Souxi into the rear door ashtray in her attempt to get away from him.

In front of her, Jay lowered his window with an electronic whirr.

Juno couldn't wait to get away from Barfly and corner Jay alone in the flat to apologise – especially now she knew that he had some sort of fixation on her. Please be green, she begged the traffic lights on Haverstock Hill immediately before her road. They turned red.

'So who was this agent who approached you tonight, Juno?' Triona asked as she tilted her head up to watch the lights. 'I'm sorry I cut you off earlier.' Her eyes caught Juno's for a moment in the rear view mirror before resuming her red-watch.

'It was Piers Fox.'

There was a moment of hush before Jay started to laugh, a hard cynical rattle with a lisping top-note of disbelief. 'Now, you gotta be kidding, right?' he muttered, not looking around. 'That is the only funny thing to come out of your mouth all night.'

'That's because I haven't given you head tonight,' Juno snapped, furiously hurt, all apologies forgotten.

'Oh grow up!' Jay snarled.

'Children, please!' Triona forced a laugh as the car started moving again. 'I can see we'll all have to come in with you and hide any sharp implements.'

'You could start with Juno's tongue,' Jay hissed.

Juno was on the verge of hissing back that when God was handing out arseholes he'd put teeth in Jay's, but she checked herself in time. Biting her Sabatier tongue hard, she stared murderously out of the window and squirmed with shame. He was right. Every time she opened her mouth, she stabbed herself in the foot. No wonder he didn't want to kiss and make up – he was frightened his lips would be cut to shreds.

Chapter Seventeen

When Juno couldn't locate her Taz key-ring in the lucky dip of her bucket-sized bag, Jay took a stack of keys from the seat of his jeans and let them all into the flat with a long-suffering sigh, backing disdainfully away as Juno passed through, like a bouncer admitting a drag queen into Stringfellow's.

The phone was ringing as they spilled into the hallway.

'The machine will get that.' Juno raced for the kitchen to evade Barfly's attentions. 'Who wants what to drink?'

'I'll just pick this up – excuse me.' Jay strode purposefully towards the phone which had already been intercepted by Sean's message. 'It's probably my LA agent.'

In the kitchen, Juno indulged in a voodoo moment of ritually strangling a wine bottle neck, imagining it was Jay's, before scrabbling for the corkscrew in the cutlery drawer.

'Got a bottle opener, girl?' Barfly rattled a carrier bag of Budvar. 'Don't go in for that poncey wine stuff, as you know. I'm more of a *man*.' He punctuated this unsubtle reference to her earlier Mae West antics with a gravelly growl.

'There's one in that pot by the sink.' Juno darted deftly past him and reached several glasses from a high cupboard, guessing what was to come.

'What are you doing for the rest of the week?' He studied her over the Thresher's bag he was carrying. Because his pale grey eyes were set very close together, it was always hard to tell exactly where he *was* looking, but tonight Juno just knew his attention was firmly focused upon her nipples, juggling for space in their Lycra hammocks as she stretched up for a fourth glass. At least he hadn't said 'the rest of your life' she consoled herself weakly.

'Oh, this and that – why?'

'Thought you might want to come to the dogtrack with me one night – up Catford way,' he offered casually, stretching out to pat her arm affectionately and deliberately missing. 'It's quite posh now, got a lovely little restaurant where you can bet at the tables. Serves wine 'n' all.' He clearly thought that was as date-clinching as telling her Marco Pierre White was the chef.

'Thanks, Fly, but I don't think so.' Juno gently removed his hand from her right breast. 'I'm going to the dogs too much as it is.'

'Oh, right, okay.' He shuffled off, as easily deflected as ever.

Juno pressed her forehead to the cupboard door as he disappeared through the arch. He must have asked her out a dozen times, and it never got any easier to say no. She had a great deal of affection for him, and pangs of guilt always stabbed her when she brushed him off, but trying to fancy him was like learning to love one's cellulite.

Jay wandered into the kitchen just as she was searching the cupboards for crisps. Not acknowledging her presence, he opened the fridge to get out a Coke.

As he stooped behind the door, the fingers of his right hand clasped the top, drumming nervily. Juno could still remember how they'd felt touching her body – remarkably gentle and tentative. She could also clearly recall how glorious that bottom – currently poking out beyond the door – had looked without any clothes on.

She suddenly felt even sadder as she remembered how bitchily she had behaved tonight, taunting him, his country and – most unforgivably – that magnificent trouser missile. She hadn't just behaved shabbily, she had set up a one-woman persecution. She'd even driven him to confessing his problems with her to Piers Fox.

'I'm sorry,' she blurted.

Jay didn't immediately respond, face still shielded by the fridge door.

'It was deplorable to pick on you like that.' She kept her voice quiet to avoid being overheard in the next room. 'It was stupid. I don't know what came over me, I've never done anything like it before.'

'Big of you to say so,' he replied tersely, voice muffled by the fridge.

'If there's one thing I am, it's big,' Juno joked feebly, then rushed on in a hushed whisper, 'I also realise I've been a sulky, awkward bitch this week, and I can understand why you hate living here with me. *I* hate living here with me right now. I'm not really such a bad person, you know.'

He backed out of the fridge and let the door swing slowly shut.

'So people keep telling me,' he said quietly, gazing at a magnet shaped like a football.

'I'm just a bit hormonal and stressed at work at the moment,' she rattled on, clumsily tipping tortillas into a salad bowl. 'And what happened between us last weekend was an unfortunate start to say the least. I think we should try and forget about it, keep it between ourselves.'

'I thought we already agreed on that.' He tipped his head towards her, snapping open the Coke can, eyes unblinking and hostile.

'We didn't so much agree as challenge one another,' Juno said gently, dabbing up spilled pieces from the work surface and sucking them off her fingers. 'I think we need to call a truce.' She suddenly felt she had wronged him so terribly she would crawl to Manchester and back – along the fast lane of the M6 if necessary – to make things right between them. She just wanted him to smile at her again.

'You do?' Jay rubbed his chin against his shoulder and looked at her.

'Absolutely,' Juno rushed on, desperate to make amends. 'Obviously I didn't mean it when I said I didn't want you to talk to me. Or that I hated your accent – it's lovely. Very . . . um . . . de Niro.' Then she remembered with a sinking feeling that she'd told him it was like a bad de Niro impression.

Aware that she was digging a grave-sized hole through the kitchen tiles beneath her, Juno crammed some crisps in her mouth and continued, 'In fact, I think we should talk more, try and make friends – find some mutual ground. We've probably got tons in common. I don't mean we should go mad or anything – I'm not saying we should tell one another our life stories, that would be obituary too much.' She shovelled in more tortillas. 'But I need you to give me the chance to be myself, make things up to you and prove I'm a pretty decent person – even though I'm a fat slob who smokes too much and makes lousy jokes at other people's expense.' She tried to finish on a light and self-deprecating note but ended up sounding self-obsessed.

Dodging a flying piece of tortilla chip which she had accidentally just spat in his direction, Jay said laconically, 'So I'm just supposed to forgive you for what you did tonight, huh?' His eyes bored into hers like power-drills. 'Because your little *schtick* was funny that makes it all right, does it? It made people laugh, so I gotta accept the whole *megilleh*.'

'Not because it was funny, Jay.' She looked at him pleadingly. 'Because I'm apologising. Because I know I hurt you and I know I should have stuck to picking on guys like Barfly and Horse who can take it.'

His eyes narrowed to slits. 'Are you suggesting I couldn't take it, being mauled by a sore broad on a pre-menstrual manhunt? Of course I could fucking *take* it, Juno, I just didn't *get* it, that's all. I didn't get why you behaving like a cheap and trashy whore was supposed to be so fucking amusing!'

She looked away in despair. His defences were so high, they threatened to knock satellites off course. She knew there was absolutely no way he'd forgive her and wished she hadn't bothered to ask him to now, the retentive, humourless bastard!

Maintaining a virtuous silence, she picked up her tray of drinks and headed for the others.

He fingered the football fridge magnet as she drew level.

'Tell me, Juno, why did you let that spotty guy maul you at the end?'

She faltered, glasses slipping precariously to one corner of the tray as she turned to look at him, studying his face in surprise. Its expression was typically disapproving and severe.

'As I recall, *I* mauled him,' she said carefully, monitoring Jay's every facial twitch. 'I carried him out of the room. It was part of the act.'

For a giveaway second, his eyes flashed. 'You only did that after he'd rammed his tongue into your mouth.'

'He took me by surprise.'

'You looked as though you were enjoying it.' He raked the hair back from his eyes with a shaking hand.

They were whispering like pensioners in a library, but the tension in their voices merited screams and shouts of accusation. Suddenly Juno realised there was something weird about the situation. They were arguing like a couple. Not a couple of strangers but a squabbling couple having a domestic. Her head replayed the conversation between Jay and Piers which Gary had related: 'Juno talking is the funniest thing. We say the same things over and over and we just won't listen to one another.' They had known each other less than a week, but he'd talked about her like a wife!

'I don't believe it.' She dropped her voice incredulously, a tiny finger of excitement squirming its way into her belly button. 'You're jealous, aren't you?'

He looked for a split-second as though she'd pulled a gun on him, then his expression changed – as though the gun had fired and a flag saying BANG had popped out of the barrel.

His cello-shank lips pursed for a brief moment and then, very deliberately, he smiled coldly. 'Get real, Juno. If you really want to know, the entire sleazy little episode revolted me. I was just curious to discover why you let him do it to you. It was so damned cheap! You only just stopped short of lap-dancing, which is a little inappropriate given your . . .'

'My size?' she suggested in a tight little voice, chin rising.

He didn't answer, simply swigged more Coke and rubbed

his chin against his shoulder again in that irritating gesture which she'd found unbearably sexy just a few days earlier.

Frozen with shame, she refused to let her eyes drop even though her heart was plummeting to earth like a blasted game bird. 'I let anyone kiss me, Jay, however unappealing. You of all people should know that.'

He blew her a sarcastic kiss.

Determined not to react, though it stung like an acid splash, she felt her cheeks pinken. 'So what were you saying about me to Piers Fox?'

'Huh?' His ridiculously perfect eyebrows met in bewilderment.

'You were overheard,' she challenged, 'talking about me.'

'Juno, you're so fucking egotistical it's unreal.' He laughed bitterly.

She opened her mouth to return fire, then closed it again. She swallowed a lump in her throat the size of a house brick. 'Can you say that again?'

'Say what?' He raised his palms, Coke can tilting in one. 'Juno, you're fucking egotistical.'

'Are you saying "Juno", or "do you know"?' she croaked.

'What's it matter?'

'It matters a lot.' Juno straightened the tray she was carrying and turned away, muttering to herself, 'D'you know, talking is the funniest thing? You say the same things over and over and you always wish you'd said something else.'

In the sitting room Barfly was sprawled on the sofa in front of Channel X, a Budvar plugged comfortingly into his mouth like the teat of a baby's bottle. To one side, Souxi was perched like a tiny figurine on an altar stool, her slender legs crossed at both knee and ankle in the peculiar contortionist's twist only the very slim can achieve. Triona was sitting on one of the oak tables chattering into the phone, her six-inch patent platform boots scraping the French polish from the surface as she crossed her ankles beneath her and kvetched about the customers at the shop.

'. . . full of fucking tourists at the moment, like every summer – Marky keeps threatening to garrotte them with a strapless bra. All they do is take fucking pictures . . .'

Juno dumped her tray on the coffee table and listened in to the call for a couple of seconds.

'. . . Bolan's fine. Yes, still in Beverley Hills with Keith . . . all summer, I think – lucky little bugger, yes . . .'

Juno started pouring out wine, but her hand was shaking so much she spilled most of it on to the coffee table tiles. Trying to get a grip on herself, she took a deep breath and chewed her lower lip for a moment, bottle poised at forty-five degrees.

'Is she talking to Sean?' She turned to Souxi, nodding towards Triona and inadvertently dousing Barfly's leg with Pinot Noir.

Souxi seldom spoke, preferring to maintain an enigmatic silence which went better with her pale, Pierrot image than her stilted American English. In response, she simply shook her fragile head and fluttered a tiny hand towards the framed photograph of Juno's parents which stood on a small table beside Uboat's tank.

'Pa?' Juno balked. Her father only called when he was plastered.

Souxi wrinkled her button nose and gave a minimalist head-shake.

'My mother?' Juno handed her a glass of wine.

Nodding delicately, she took the wine and sipped about one cubic millilitre of it through purple-painted lips.

Juno passed another glass on to Triona, who adored Judy and was thoroughly enjoying her chin-wag with her almost-mother-in-law.

'. . . Are you? That's great. Whereabouts? Oh, *muchos mondo*, you lucky bag! So Howard will have the place to himself, will he? Oh, right, I see . . . dull for him, huh? The same day? That's unfortunate . . . I see. Listen, Juno's right here if you want a chat.' She looked up, beckoning for Juno to hang around. 'Oh, no – just me, a couple of old friends and Jay . . . Well, if you're sure, okay, I'll tell her.' She batted Juno away again and carried on chatting.

Judy clearly asked about Jay next.

Triona was unabashed in her reply, even though he was within earshot. 'Sweet guy, doesn't say much, but clever as hell and bloody talented. Yes, very like. No, more Eric Stoltz to look at, I'd say – *Sleep With Me*, *Killing Zoe*, you know who I mean?' She always spoke to Judy as though talking to a great mate, her conversational references cultish and contemporary. Juno reckoned her mother only understood about an eighth of what Triona said, but they doted upon one another nevertheless.

'Did she?' Triona was looking at Juno now, fashionably thin eyebrows raised in accusation. 'No, I wouldn't say ginger – more strawberry blonde. What? "Nicholas Witchell meets Boris Becker without the body tone"? I think you must have misheard her.'

Gazing intently at the ceiling, Juno didn't dare glance anywhere near Jay.

When Triona finally rang off Juno looked at her accusingly. 'Didn't Ma want to talk to me then?'

'Well, she orginally called to see how tonight went, but said that as you have guests, you can ring her from work tomorrow instead.'

'Great.' Juno felt miffed. Triona had chatted for at least twenty minutes, bending Judy's ear about how terrific Jay was. Two minutes of Juno moaning about her life wasn't too desperate an epilogue, was it? She needed to hear her mother's soothing, plumped pillow voice at moments like this.

'She says she's off to Scotland to shoot a Christmas special next week.'

'In July?' Juno was working herself into a minor frenzy of Mummy-need now.

'You know how far in advance they make these things. Your father's heading off on his lecture tour of Germany at the same time so she wants you to dog-sit while they're both away.'

'I'm not sure I can get the time off work.' Juno downed some more wine, then instantly warmed to the prospect of escaping from London – and Jay – for a few days. She could loll in the garden at her parents' house and plunder their gin. She could even ask some of the gang down for a weekend booze-up. 'I'll try and square it with GWC tomorrow,' she muttered.

'Judy suggested I should bring Jay down for supper on Sunday, while they're both still there.'

'She what?' Juno was appalled.

'She's dying to meet you,' Triona told him. 'Howard and Judy are glorious. They're so laid-back you feel like you're in some 'sixties commune with nothing to do but lie in the sun and make daisy chains – or love – or both.'

'I'm sure that would be Jay's idea of hell,' Juno said quickly, rapidly going off her mother. She'd not been the same since starting HRT.

'Sounds pretty cool to me,' he told Triona, ignoring Juno.

'Besides which he'll be far too busy,' Juno added. 'Won't you?' She threw the question in Jay's general direction.

There was a sticky, quicksand moment of silence, interrupted only by a loud self-indulgent burp from Barfly.

'We'll see.' Triona wandered over to the sofa and snuggled into a sleekly upholstered corner beside the gaseous guest, hooking her platforms over his legs. 'You could come too, Fly.'

'Yeah, maybe.' He lit a spliff, eyes not moving from Channel X where two blondes were romping playfully on a bed wearing g-strings and high-gloss pouts. 'I don't like the countryside much, though. Hard to buy a packet of smokes of an evening. Sean's parents' place is a pretty decent gaff, mind you. We've had some good parties there over the years. And she's a blinding cook, his ma.'

'The television chef?' Jay asked with unexpected interest.

'Judy, yes.' Triona swivelled round and pressed her chin to the sofa back to talk to him. 'You don't know what oral sex is until you try her cooking. Howard's incredibly thin considering how many thirds he indulges in. And the house is bohemian rap – a converted Anglo-Saxon church near Oxford. It's so tatty and gothic, I always expect Vincent Price to loom out of a trap door playing an organ. It's even got gravestones in the garden.'

'Wow!'

'It has bats in the attic too,' Juno muttered darkly. 'If you go outside in the evening, you have to take an umbrella to stop them dumping on you. Now, if you'll excuse me, I'm going to have a bath.'

'You are turning into Blanche DuBois,' she told herself worriedly as she lay in a froth of bubbles twenty minutes later. 'You *are* Blanche Du-fucking-Bois! This is too weird. You'll be relying upon the kindness of strangers next. Talking of which . . .' She sank beneath the surface, letting the wet warmth lick her eyelids and swirl through her hair as she pondered the Piers Fox encounter. He wanted to see her. Stardom beckoned. It more than beckoned – it was waving madly to get her attention, flagging her down and slapping her around the hot, pink cheeks. What did it matter if she pissed off a sulky, secretive American brat? Soon she'd be like a kid let loose in a toy-boy shop. She was in show business after all. Her career was about to take off. With any luck her future husband hadn't even been born yet.

Resurfacing, breathless and dripping, she blinked the bubbles from her eyes and felt the scales fall from them too. Piers Fox had given her his card because she had performed an adrenaline-pumped, attitude-soaked set she couldn't hope to repeat – a set fuelled by her encounter with Jay. Only now she'd lost her sense of humour and gained a sense of foreboding. The only reason Piers Fox had turned up at all tonight was because he wanted to 'make a mint' for Jay. Jay who hated her. Jay who thought she was untalented, egotistical and hell to live with. Jay who was the most infuriating, argumentative, enigmatic man she'd ever met. Jay who had made her swear not to love him and then woken in the night to stroke her face like a child reaching out for a comfort blanket. Jay whom she'd poisoned against her – physically and emotionally.

'Juno talking is the funniest thing,' she said aloud. 'She never opens her mouth unless she's got a cheap wisecrack which she can't afford to say.'

Later, she heard Triona call goodbye to her, along with Barfly exiting in a series of clanks as he took his take-outs with him. 'Ta ta, girl. Stay beautiful.'

''Bye!' she called back, soaping her toes with wrinkled fingers and listening as two sets of feet clattered down the communal stairs – Triona's clattering trendily, Barfly's thudding heavily; Souxi's tiny little feet were far too dainty to make a sound.

As she crept across the hallway, wearing Jay's dressing gown because she had yet again left her towel on her bed, Juno could hear an elegant Bach partita haunting the sitting room. Tiredness was pressing its thumbs into her eye sockets and hooking thick arms over her shoulders as it piggy-backed her to bed.

'Juno, can we talk?' Jay suddenly called out, although she couldn't see where he was.

Clutching her door handle, she thought about her scrubbed red face and freshly applied polka-dots of spot cream. She contemplated her bath-reddened, Radox-raisined body. Her teeth might be squeaky but her hair was ratty, her eyes piggy, and she had just applied pongy fake tan to her cleavage.

He's going to tell me I have to leave the flat, Juno realised in a panic. He's going to insist that I move out or else he'll boot Sean out of his place in New York. He wants to corner me now I'm at my most make-up free and vulnerable. He wants revenge for what I did to him tonight.

Darting into her room, she clicked her door shut, turned the key and stumbled to the bed, so weary that she fell asleep on top of her duvet, wrapped into a fluffy green papoose that smelled of menthol shower gel and haunted her dreams.

Chapter Eighteen

The following morning, Juno employed the 'avoiding Jay' tactics she had been plotting between bad dreams all night.

She nipped into the shower as soon as she heard the front door click and trainered feet pound downstairs for his morning run. Ten minutes later, dripping shampoo suds and water behind her, she raced into the kitchen and made herself several rounds of toast and a pot of tea which she carried through to her bedroom, greeting Poirot and Uboat en route with kisses and jammy crumbs.

Indulging in the twenty minutes she knew she safely had to kill, she ate her breakfast sitting on her bed and listening to *Today*. While she was putting her make-up on and dressing, Jay punctually thundered back up from street level and pounded straight into the bathroom. This gave her the chance to nip out of the front door without encountering him at all.

At the office, she found that Lydia was bunking off on one of her regular 'sickies', leaving Juno with twice the workload, a sulking publisher who was missing the temptress temp's blonde glamour and two overdue print deadlines to meet.

Those deadlines crept in upon her like closing walls as she read through her post and e-mails – one of which simply read 'No time to write. Love you, Odette', located lids for all the pens on her desk, then sloped to the smoking room for a fag and a bonding session with the bubbly new trainee journalist on *Working Week* before spending a long time in the loo trying to figure out whether her left nostril was larger than her right one. On the way back to her desk, she had a debate over the relative merits of ciabatta over foccacia with Finlay at the photocopier, read her horoscopes in all the editorial team's daily papers then walked to production to say hi to Uma, the lovely, mumsy secretary, and steal some of her Waitrose stem ginger shortbreads.

Back at her desk, Juno set about arranging her social life for the coming weekend, eager to secure every night away from the flat. She was disconcerted to discover that everyone was either out of London or doing couply things.

'As you weren't around to ask last weekend, we went ahead and arranged to see the latest Patrick Marber with Jules and Flo – I'm afraid it's booked up now,' Ally apologised. 'But you can come along and eat with us at Mezzo afterwards, if you like.' The offer, although cheery, sounded uncomfortably like charity to Juno.

'Oh, no, don't bother.' She felt hurt not to have been invited but hid it well, knowing it was a childish reaction. 'What about Saturday?'

'Taking the sprog to dinner with the in-laws,' Ally told her. 'Babysitters aren't cheap, you know.'

'Well, if you're ever caught short, I'll do the odd stint with her,' Juno offered. 'I have a lot of Saturday nights free this summer.' She tried to make the irony as pointed as a witch's hat, but Ally was innocently delighted.

'Would you? That's really kind.'

Jez and Lulu were both working on Friday and Saturday night, doing gigs out of town.

'What about Sunday?' Juno heard an air of desperation in her voice.

'The band's in Wales playing the Llanadu Festival,' Jez told her. 'I'll get you a backstage pass if you want to come down, but it's a bit of a hippy-shit event.'

The prospect of trogging alone around a lot of hair-braiding stalls and rebirthing tents in a damp Welsh field was not wildly appealing.

'I don't get back to London until after midnight on Saturday, then Sunday I'm seeing my mate Fruity for a boozy lunch in Wimbledon, pet.' Lulu consulted her diary. 'I'd invite you along but he's just found out he's HIV positive and needs to talk, y'know?'

'I'll pass,' Juno said quickly.

'Perhaps we could meet for tea later?' Lulu offered vaguely, but made no promises.

Elsa and Euan were spending the weekend in a friend's Cornish cottage, Odette wasn't answering her mobile but judging from the e-mail would undoubtedly be working away somewhere. Juno was beginning to wish she'd agreed to go to the dogs with Barfly. She wondered whether she could hide very quietly in her room all weekend to convince Jay she was out on the town whooping it up with her millions of friends. She worked her way through almost half her address book without success, leaving messages on the answerphones of friends she had not seen for months.

In despair, she briefly contemplated hiring a male escort before deciding she couldn't afford one and tried Lydia's mobile number instead.

'Where are you?' she asked as she heard a rumble of traffic in the background.

'I don't know – where are we?' Lydia's voice crackled as the reception came and went. In the background, Juno could just make out a soft Irish accent saying something.

'On the M25,' Lydia told her. 'Somewhere near Staines apparently. We're going to have a picnic at Runnymede.'

'How pleasant for you,' Juno bristled. 'Feeling better then?'

'Still a bit chesty.' Lydia had no shame. 'I thought it was safest to take the rest of the day off.'

'Has Bruno got a cold too?' Juno asked sweetly, drawing a large hamster on her doodle pad.

'No, food poisoning! He told Darren he couldn't keep anything down, which is certainly true of part of his anatomy, isn't it, Bru?' There was a loud burst of male laughter in the background.

'Dodgy chilli, probably,' Juno muttered.

'What? The line's breaking up. Listen, I might be off tomorrow too, actually, Joo,' Lydia confessed. 'I feel a bit fluey. Super-fluey, in fact.'

'You'll feel a bit superfluous to Immedia requirements if GWC finds out you're bunking off,' Juno said darkly.

'Oh, you won't tell, will you?'

'Not if you come and see that new Almodóvar film with me on Saturday – we can catch an early showing and have some nosh in town afterwards.'

'Oh, I'm *dying* to see that.' Lydia's gushing enthusiasm brightened Juno's dim view of her. 'Hang on a sec.'

Despite the fact that Lydia was clearly making some effort towards muffling the phone, Juno could distinctly hear her asking Bruno whether he had seen the film or not.

'Um, it might be a bit awkward,' she hummed apologetically as she came back on.

'Tomorrow night then?' Juno suggested, refusing to give up. 'Or an early showing on Sunday? I might be going to my parents' in the evening – in fact, I could be away all next week.' She was certain Lydia would want to meet up for a gossip before then.

'Um . . . I'll call you back on that, shall I?' Lydia was unwilling to tell her straight that she wanted to spend the entire weekend on an exclusive with Bruno – including seeing the Almodóvar together – and Juno was equally reluctant to hear it spelled out, although she knew that constituted damnation in the Best Friend's Handbook.

'Sure,' she said bleakly, wondering if it was pushing it too far to suggest they all see it together that night, and deciding it was. At least the fact that Lydia was wrapped up in Bruno took the heat off her predatory interest in Jay. 'If I'm away next week, can you cover for me here?'

'Sure, piece of cake,' Lydia said airily.

'It's not that easy.' Juno narrowed her eyes and imagined the agony columns jam-packed with spelling errors, split infinitives and advice which bore no relation whatsoever to the problems. 'I'll leave you as much as I possibly can, but you'll have to do some of the copy yourself – and you'll have to come into the office every day.'

'Sure, sure. Whatever,' Lydia pacified her distractedly. 'I'll call you. 'Bye, Joo darling – don't work too hard.' She rang off.

Juno put the phone down and grinned despite herself. Lydia was incorrigible, but she was too damned inspirational to dislike. Juno longed to live for the moment as she did, to be reckless and impulsive and obvious about everything, heedless of the consequences. It was what she had tried, and failed, to do the previous weekend.

Brooding on the eventless three days ahead, she did a few doodles which looked suspiciously like Jay's profile, called the flat to leave a message for Poirot who always appreciated the gesture, Tippexed a couple of her fingernails and finally plucked up the courage to ask GWC for some time off.

His office was a neatly ordered shrine to his family. Their smiling, matt-finish enlarged photographs were lined up regimentally in pebble-grey frames to either side of his computer terminal spire – sentries to a church they could not access. No bad thing, Juno reflected, as GWC had at least three megabytes of pornographic photographs downloaded from the Internet stored on his hard disk, along with a stack of e-mails from his latest mistress. Juno knew this because she and Lydia had hacked their way in late one night. His password was – disturbingly – 'Lydia'. Even more perturbing was the fact that Juno had guessed it on just her second attempt – the first being 'GWC'.

Asking for time off took a lot of huffing and puffing on Juno's part. She couldn't quite kick the memory of the recent official warning from her head.

'No problem . . . er, Juno.' He still struggled over her name despite their four-year working relationship.

In fact, he was surprisingly accommodating. Hot off the phone from his mistress and en route to a long lunch meeting with a new 'advertising client' – the two were not unrelated, Juno suspected – he looked at her from a lofty position in both senses of the word (his leather-covered executive swivel chair with arm-rests and tilt-head support was several inches higher than her low-slung, nylon-covered utilitarian grey one on the opposite side of the desk) and graciously granted her permission to take off some 'thought time', provided she secured someone – anyone – to cover her 'bits and bobs'.

'Lydia's agreed to do it,' Juno told him nervously, certain he'd complain that she wasn't responsible enough.

'Ah – Lydia.' His lascivious little eyes lit up and he beamed at her. 'I'll help her out as much as I can obviously.'

'Obviously's the word.' Juno smiled back stiffly. Luckily he was too distracted by the prospect of his horizontal lunch to notice her sarcasm.

Juno – who liked the idea of being indispensable – was rather disturbed by his easygoing assent. As she sloped out of his glass-walled office, she made it around Xerox Corner and into the cover of Potted Palm Avenue before she started chewing her fingernails and fretting worriedly. In the past he had been known to refuse her a half day off because no one else could duplicate her unique ability to fabricate problems. Now, it seemed, she could ask Bazza the visiting sandwich man to toss off her columns and there was 'no problem'. This worried her. It then guiltily occurred to her that she'd been in the office almost two hours and had written nothing. She was picking up bad habits from Lydia, her attitude to deadlines getting more and more lax.

She sat down at her desk and selected two cranky letters from her depressingly lean *Commuter Weekly* post-bag. It wasn't enough to fill the page; the rest she would have to make up. Fuelled by coffee and M&Ms, she spent the remainder of the morning typing like a demon, thinking of weirder and weirder problems to solve, giggling to herself as she did so.

Ten minutes before her third 'or you're dead' deadline – and on the receiving end of her fourteenth ratty call from the production manager – she was still one problem short for the Claire Frankel column.

She narrowed her eyes and grinned before starting to type feverishly, 'Dear Claire, I fancy my sexy new female flatmate like mad. The first weekend I moved in, she seduced me and we had sex in every room. She is the best lover I've ever had. But I think she's grown bored of me – she is far brighter and funnier than I am, plus she is a sensationally good cook and staggeringly good-looking. Now she more or less ignores me. I've suggested we talk, but she doesn't seem to want to know. She hardly seems to notice me, except to take the piss. The trouble is, I've fallen in love with her. What should I do? Yours regretfully, Jay. London NW3.' To which Claire caringly replied, 'Dear Jay, Why not strip naked, smear yourself from head-to-toe in strawberry jam and walk around the flat complaining that you've lost your flannel?'

Juno ran a spell-check and had a handful of self-congratulatory M&Ms.

On the dot of the deadline, she e-mailed the text files to production. To celebrate, she sagged back in her utilitarian chair, munched her way through an M & S triple helping of prawn mayo, read a *Cosmo* article about finding yourself single at thirty and then speed-dialled her mother's number.

'Hi, Ma.'

'Pusscat! How gorgeous – just a moment, I'm feeding the dogs.' She could hear the phone clank against the kitchen wall (her mother always let it drop from her hand as though it existed in zero gravity, often causing a shattered plastic casing as it ricocheted off the stone flagging).

Guessing that she was currently listening to events from floor level where the coiled flex had dropped, Juno took in the scrabbling of claws against stone, a strange panting, the clatter of metal bowls on tiles and then a revolting flurry of gulps and slurps before the phone was yanked back again and her mother's soothing, sherry-soaked voice came down the line.

'There, all guzzling like hippies with the munchies. Still there, pusscat?'

'Still here, Ma,' Juno sighed, swapping around a couple of pen lids which she had mistakenly placed upon the wrong Biros. Realising she was being as anal as Jay, she hastily swapped them back again.

'How did it go last night, then? Were they rolling in the hay with laughter?'

Juno scraped some of the dried Tippex from her fingernail and smiled. Judy always imagined her stand-up routines as some sort of antiquated Summer of Love festival.

'I think I panned to be honest.' She could never keep a secret from her mother. 'I mean, they laughed a lot, but I offended as many people as I amused and I'll never have the nerve to try the same material again. There was an agent in who wants to see me, though.'

'But that's just delicious!' Judy Glenn had such a honey-coated voice, the telephone receiver buzzed like a queen bee as she spoke. 'Why do you say you panned, puss? If this agent geezer likes you, then you must have cracked open a few beer tabs out there.'

For an old hippy, her mother was a whizz at London colloquialisms, Juno reflected. She was learning fast from Triona.

'I picked on Jay.' Juno scrunched up her face with guilt. 'The American lodger. He was seriously fucked off about it. QED, we're still not talking.'

'Oh, pooz, what's going on with you and this chap, huh? I know you told me he was a bit of a plonker when we last spoke, but Tri seems to think he's a wicked babe.'

Juno started to re-evaluate her mother's grasp of modern slang; it was rather hit and miss at times as she fought to keep up – not helped by her addiction to *The Archers* and Margaret Forster.

'He's just very difficult to live with,' she said carefully.

'Well, Americans can be bloody demanding,' Judy empa-thised. 'Think of Dinny.'

One of Judy's best friends was her editor, Dinny Goldberg, an Anglophile Baltimore virago who existed on a vodka-enhanced macrobiotic diet, lived according to her biorhythms as dictated by a Tantric sibyl in Islington, would not leave her house during menstruation and had five Siamese cats, all called Simon.

Juno smiled and prodded the earth of her potted fig, which was so dry it caused the entire dusty stalk and its dead roots to capsize and crash land on her keyboard.

Then, taking a deep breath and appreciating her mother's tactful silence, she spilled the Heinz. 'Ma, I've slept with him and it all went horribly wrong. What I did last night's made it ten times worse, and he absolutely hates me now. What's more, Lydia fancies him like mad, and I haven't told her what happened. It's such a mess.'

'And you, pusscat? Do you fancy him too?'

'Like crazy,' Juno confessed.

'I guessed as much,' Judy sighed softly, fanning the hot coals Juno was walking over.

'You did?' She was only mildly surprised. Her mother was a bit of a sixth-sense guru. She might airily claim it was part tarot cards, part claret, but Juno suspected her ma of simply being a wise old bird who could read between the encoded lines better than Alan Turing. She should be writing the problem pages for Immedia, not Juno.

'You slagged him off so much, puss. You simply had to be a little bit infatuated with him.'

'Did I?' She blanched at her own obviousness.

'Well, just a tiny pinch. Bear in mind I've had years to learn that you always do the opposite of what you're told, and say the opposite of what you think. Now tell me, was it good sex? Was it worth the knickers in the wash afterwards?'

Sometimes Juno wished her mother wasn't so damned 'sixties about everything.

'Yes and no,' she spluttered awkwardly, anxious not to contradict herself this time.

At this moment, she was uncomfortably aware that Finlay was rapidly advancing from Xerox Corner with a couple of faxes.

'Oh, puss, how awful.' Her mother made all the right noises at the other end of the line whilst Finlay draped himself prettily and decadently in Lydia's vacant chair and – clearly high from a quick sniff from the photocopier where he stashed his angel dust in the never-used envelope tray – wheeled it around to Juno's newly organised pen collection which he started ramming up his reddened, deadened nostrils to make her laugh.

'Couldn't he ejaculate?' Her mother was never one to pull punches, having trained as a psycho-sexual counsellor.

'No, no, he was fine in that department.' Juno cleared her throat and flashed a humouring grin at Finlay who was placing her empty plastic sandwich carton to his ear and miming a phone call.

'So what happened, pooz?' Judy was all ears.

'I can't really talk about it now.'

'Oh, right – is Lydia listening in?'

'Not Lydia, no.' Juno nodded mindlessly at Finlay who was pointing eagerly at the faxes he'd brought over and pulling a daft face.

'Oh, right, someone else. I understand.' Judy sighed disappointedly. 'Well, you'll have to tell me all about it soonest. Such a shame I can't call you at home tonight as he'll probably be there, won't he? You must get yourself one of those mobile things. So discreet. I adore mine, although I keep forgetting to charge the sod up.'

Pre-empting the end of the call with a classic, precipitate change of tack, she added, 'Now, did Triona mention that I'm hoofing off to Scotland while your father's away in Germany, so I'd like you to come down and house-sit next week?'

'Er . . . yes.' Juno was suddenly distracted as she noticed the top fax lying on the potted fig soil in front of her. Written in big, bold font it read: **'Juno. Forgive me. I know my behavior has been nothing short of indefensible. Friends? 9.00 Friday. Central Perk. Let's talk. Love, J xxx.'**

She urgently scrunched it to one side.

The second fax was even shorter: **'Juno. Lovers even? 9.00 Friday. Bar Oque. J xxx.'**

She gaped at the two sheets of A4 in disbelief, flattening the first to read every letter of the thirty-six-point font. No wonder Finlay was hanging around, hungry for gossip.

'. . . So that's okay, pusscat?' her mother confirmed.

'Sure, fine.' Juno scrabbled for the first fax again and read the narrow computer line at the top which identified the sender, but it was a jumble of numbers and digits.

'Computer modem,' Finlay told her knowingly, sticking her Tippex correction tape over the bridge of his nose like a retrospective Adam Ant fan. 'It was sent in to the advertising department's fax, not editorial's, so you've given us all a laugh.'

'Who's that speaking?' demanded her mother in one ear. 'He sounds rather sexy. Scottish, is he?'

'Who's "J"?' Finlay asked in the other.

Juno wished Lydia was around to drag to the loo for a gossip. On the other hand Lydia knew nothing about her relationship with Jay and their lost weekend, and Juno hadn't forgotten her official warning for slackness.

'It's Finlay, Ma,' she told Judy, scanning the first fax.

'It's my ma, Finlay,' she said distractedly as she perused the second.

'Who's Finlay?' Judy asked leadingly.

'Judy Glenn, the celebrity cook?' Finlay was plastering correction tape to his long, pampas grass eyelashes in excitement.

'Is Finlay your type?' her mother asked in a bubbling undertone. 'Isn't he the one in sales who's like Ewan McGregor, but you think is gay?'

'I adore Judy Glenn.' Finlay blinked with coke-enhanced sincerity while peeling tape from his lashes, eyes watering in unfelt pain. 'Lydia told me she was your mother, but I just thought she was trying to make you appear more interesting. Juicy Judy was the reason I took a higher in home economics. That and Kirsty McKechnie, the tartan toast burner with the buttery knees.' He shivered at the memory.

Desperate to sequester the faxes somewhere quiet – like the smoking room – and study every word for significant meaning, Juno clutched them to her chest and seized upon an idea.

'Ma, this is Finlay. He's tried all the same drugs as you, so you can compare notes. I'll see you on Sunday night.'

She thrust the phone at him.

'Have a word with Judy Glenn. She'll give you a few tips on burning knees and buttering toast.' Rendered incoherent by agitation, and completely forgetting her second overrun deadline, Juno absconded to the nicotine-varnished office cell with her faxes.

There was no one else in the smoking room. Flattening her precious pieces of A4 on the table after lighting up, Juno touched the type-face in wonderment. They had to be from Jay, surely? She stroked the words 'Lovers even?' like a talisman and realised that he had perhaps, after all, wanted to tell her something completely different. How typically reserved and romantic to suggest a date somewhere away from the flat to talk things over. Bar Oque was one of the most sumptuous, intimate places on earth. It was also one of the most fashionable bars in London that month. It was also just a stroll down a tree-lined avenue back to the flat . . .

So why tomorrow night? She chewed her lip worriedly, doubt starting to niggle. Why not tonight? I can't sit and watch *Londoners* with him and not mention this.

The *Friends* reference just had to be a hint; she remembered making some cheap joke about it the first time they had spoken, on the evening of her birthday when he had wiped mascara from her cheek and set off libido alarm calls all over her body.

'Perhaps he's busy tonight,' she told herself calmly.

He was always using his high-tech lap top. Surely he could send a fax with it? That was why it had gone to the advertising number, which was listed in all the magazines littered around the flat. He didn't know her e-mail address or the other fax number.

Then she saw the give-away clue which told her the faxes just had to be from Jay. BEHAVIOR. American spelling. That clinched it.

She couldn't stop smiling for the remainder of the afternoon.

'Got a hot date?' Mel asked jealously as she left the office bang on five o'clock.

'Yeah – try the thirtieth of July. That's normally a guaranteed scorcher.' Juno belted off towards Goodge Street tube.

She was disappointed but not surprised to find that Jay wasn't in the flat when she returned.

It was as spotlessly tidy as usual – all the glasses from the previous night had been washed and dried, the ashtrays hidden and her morning toast crumbs wiped from the kitchen surfaces.

For the first time that week, Juno admired the polished, uncluttered appearance of the flat with something close to sheepish gratitude, something that flirted dangerously with affection.

Before sagging down in front of *Neighbours*, she liberated Poirot for a few fly-bys, which he loved. He finally landed on the sofa back and squawked delightedly over Juno's shoulder as Madge Bishop crashed her car in a potentially tragic Ramsay Street pile-up involving a skate-boarding kid, Toadfish, a vacuous blonde who couldn't act and a yellow Labrador who could.

'I think a little quiet sympathy would be appreciated at this juncture,' Juno said out loud, watching in horror as Madge was stretchered away from the scene.

After the news headlines, she wandered around the kitchen in search of culinary inspiration. She flapped open a few cupboards, stared into the fridge until the alarm light came on and her nose started running from the cold, then leafed through the stack of take away flyers by the phone. Nothing appealed.

'I can't believe I'm not hungry,' she told Poirot who was using the studio spotlight as a perch. 'It must be infatuation.'

Time was crawling by. There had been no messages on the answerphone and nothing exciting in the post. She wondered why none of her friends had returned her calls from that morning's phone-blitz.

'At least I've got a date for Friday night now.' She shivered happily. 'Perhaps even Saturday too?' Or was that being presumptuous? Juno was too misty-eyed to care.

She wandered over to the oak table where the paraphernalia from Jay's technical link-up with the Immedia advertising fax lay in neat lines. His little lap top, several cameras and mobile phones were missing, but the chargers and floppy disks were all coiled up, stacked in piles and serried in ranks like a miniature stage awaiting a rock band.

Oh, the temptation to go into his room next and have a tiny, weeny peek. Then perhaps a couple of indulgent sniffs. Maybe she could just pop a few inches over the threshold to absorb the full New Yorker abroad atmosphere. Then perhaps just have a fleeting wander around, stroking a hand across the odd item of discarded clothing or pile of loose American change. He could, after all, have some connection with terrorism. It might be in the nation's interest to take a quick look around.

Firmly quashing temptation, Juno locked herself in the bathroom, where she chipped off the day's make-up with industrial-strength cleanser and a flannel, slapping on a tester face pack she had peeled from an inside page of that month's *Marie Claire*.

Looking like a very cheap extra from *Dr Who*, she settled in front of *Londoners* and started munching last night's tortilla chips (which Jay had thoughtfully placed in a seal-bag in the salad drawer of the fridge).

'The mother-in-law's a moose!' Poirot told her. 'Double carpets, thirty-three to one. Get your kit off.'

'Tempting, but I think the face pack's enough, thanks.' At least, Juno realised happily, it would give her skin like silk for her date tomorrow.

The face pack dried to a crust, the tortillas were chased down by several mini Bounty Bars,. Poirot shared a bag of pistachios with her and she watched every cruddy quiz show satellite television had to offer without once straying into Jay's room. Her only embarrassing moment was when a neighbour waved from an adjacent roof terrace as she spotted Juno puffing a Marlboro Light by the bay tree.

'Sean given up, has he?' she called cheerily, nodding at the fag. 'Goldybollocks has too.' She waggled her own cigarette and groaned.

'In the States,' Juno projected back, cracking her face mask like a blasted cliff face as she smiled widely, grateful for conversation with a fellow human being. 'My new flatmate loathes the smell.'

'Is he the gorgeous-looking guy I've seen coming out of your front door loaded down with kit bags every morning this week?' The neighbour – a young mum with a patterned leggings addiction – leant over her ivy-draped picket fence excitedly. 'Long, dark-blond hair? Wildly romantic?'

'More ginger actually,' Juno sniffed. 'Yes, that's probably him. He's from New York.'

'God, he's divine!' The neighbour gave a cheek-hollowing suck on her cigarette. 'We're all talking about him in the street. It's like a Diet Coke Break every day as we bored Belsize mums lean out of our windows to watch him. Can't say the same for the company he keeps, though.'

'No?' Juno tried to sound coolly knowing. 'Whyever not?'

'Look like gangland criminals to me – especially the man with the ponytail and the mad eyes.'

'Yes, he is a bit unsettling, isn't he?' Juno nodded in neighbourly agreement, wondering what the heck she was talking about.

'And who's the beautiful one with the Armani suits and the scar across his eyebrow? Looks like one of the Gladiators. You know – drives a flash red sports car and has a neck like a tree trunk. He's terrifyingly stud-you-like dangerous, isn't he?'

'Oh, he's not so bad once you know him.' Juno wished she was in a position to ask for more information, but her coolly superior stance had clearly been ill advised.

She was only acquainted with the neighbour from these occasional roof-terrace exchanges, and the Amnesty International prize draw tickets which she tried to flog from time to time. Juno hadn't even got a clue what she was called – just that she was married to 'Goldybollocks' and had a small baby to whom she referred variously as 'Brat', 'Brownbum', 'Bjork' and 'Belcher'.

'So you saw them all together today, did you?' Juno tried the conversational approach, eking out her almost-dead Marlboro Light as she lingered on the balcony.

'Same as yesterday.' The neighbour nodded. 'They gathered around that great tank thing of Sean's, yakked into their mobile phones then vroomed off in their various cars like the vice squad on a drugs bust – most exciting. I must say, he handles Sean's monster a heck of a lot better than your brother does. What is it he does exactly, this new flatmate? We've all been guessing.'

'He drives Sean's Land Rover?' Juno yelped, unable to curb herself.

'Like a demon,' the neighbour sighed admiringly, not picking up on her tone. 'Cecily across the road is convinced he's some sort of professional bodyguard. Now I'm certain he works in films – am I right?'

'Not quite.' Juno gritted her teeth. 'He pyramid sells water filters. Gosh – something's burning. See you soon!' She threw her dead butt into the garden below and scuttled inside with an over the shoulder wave.

It was now ten in the evening; Jay had still not returned. She washed off the face pack then bolted outside and scanned the rows of parked cars to the left and right of the front door. As she tried frantically to remember where Sean's pride and joy had last been parked, she guiltily realised she hadn't checked on her brother's tatty 1970s Land Rover since he'd left. The battered T reg long-wheel-based safari beast, which Sean lovingly called the T-Bird and doted on like a second mother, hadn't entered her thoughts. It could have been broken into, crashed into or clamped and she wouldn't have noticed. He'd expressly asked her to check on it every day.

And now it wasn't even there. She half wanted to report it stolen to the police and see how Jay reacted when pulled over, but instead went back to the flat and took the faxes from her handbag.

Juno re-read every brief word – typical Jay to say so little yet mean so much. He was probably keeping away tonight so that she wouldn't say anything directly about the faxes or have the opportunity to turn him down.

He still hadn't returned by the time she went to bed. Juno lay restlessly awake. She tried reading a couple of chapters of the latest Iain Banks, but had developed temporary dyslexia as the words jumbled and jumped in front of her wandering eyes. She listened mindlessly to a late-night phone-in, but the droning monotones of the callers melted into one long series of 'y'know', 'I mean', 'yeah', 'basically', 'right', 'doncha think?' and she hadn't a clue what they were talking about. Finally, she clicked the dial to a retro music channel and soon found herself passionately relating to every lyric of every sloppy song.

When she finally heard the front door click at two in the morning, Juno dive-bombed the radio to silence it and lay half-on, half-off the bed, frozen in the dark. Some sort of pride was at stake. She didn't want him to know she was moonily stewing in her room listening to The Bangles yodelling 'Eternal Flame' and thinking about her date the next night. As far as he was concerned, she had to be fast asleep and dreaming of the muscliest Gladiators.

She could hear him moving through the flat – the occasional muffled bursts of noise made by someone who is taking great care not to wake others.

After a while, they became more frequent and louder. Quite soon, they had mingled into a series of crashes and curses. She could distinctly hear him pacing about the sitting room, colliding with the furniture and muttering. Was it her imagination or was he calling out a name?

Still clamped to the side of her bed and steadying herself with a hand on her clock radio, Juno lifted her head and cocked one ear in amazed anticipation. Was he on some sort of deranged bender out there, in need of her body? Was he driving himself crazy with frustration and desire? Was he pacing around, calling out her name in carnal craving? Then she let out a disgruntled sigh as she heard him hiss: 'Poirot – Poirot! Come here, you mangy bird!'

Juno clutched the radio guiltily, not noticing her thumb stroke the volume dial to the right. She'd completely forgotten to put the parrot back after his exercise flight.

'Poirot, for fuck's sake, come here!' Jay sounded increasingly exasperated. 'How in Christ's name did you escape, you goddamned waste of feathers? Get in here *now*.'

Juno listened with increasing fascination as Jay clearly began to chase Poirot around the room. His prey was getting thoroughly overexcited by this unheralded attention from the flat's newcomer and started yelling out racing tips, phone impersonations and insults faster than a comic in a working men's club.

Wishing she was in the sitting room, Juno propped herself up so she could hear better. The next moment her bedroom practically fell through the floorboards into the flat below as she leant on the radio's 'On' button.

The sound was so excruciatingly loud that for a moment she thought a bomb had exploded inside the flat.

It was like sitting inside the speaker cabinet of a Beemer cruising up Brixton Hill, only the music had far less cred. A glass of water fell off the bedside table as it jumped beneath the onslaught of sound and Juno felt the bed vibrate violently beneath her to the bass beat of Cyndi Lauper's 'Time After Time'. The humiliation was beyond nudity in public places, beyond getting leg-crossing giggles at a funeral, and far beyond slagging someone off in the ladies only to turn around and spot them exiting a cubicle. This was a humiliation even Juno had not experienced in a long, long personal history of unspared blushes.

She scrabbled madly to silence the din, knocking over her bedside light, tearing several leaves of Iain Banks and losing her duvet in the process.

Once stifled by the 'Off' button, the noise still rang on in her ears along with the gurgling rush of blood through her arteries and thrum of her heartbeat. In its echoing aftermath, she could pick up nothing of Jay's ongoing parrot pursuit. All she could hear drumming through her head was the chorus of 'Time After Time', complete with the 'I will be waiting' line about hanging around like a sad old moose for a lover to return.

As the buzzing subsided, she realised there was an eerie

silence next door. She listened for several more minutes, but Jay had either used the momentary noise-cover to slaughter Poirot and then defenestrate himself, or they had both suffered heart attacks during the impromptu ninety-decibel Cyndi symphony.

Either way, Juno was far too ashamed to crawl to the door and peek out. Recovering her duvet from the floor, she pulled it over her burning face and chewed a hunk of it in anguish.

On Friday morning, despite lurking for a long time in the bathroom and eating her breakfast in front of *Big Breakfast* in the sitting room, Juno failed to encounter Jay and use her painfully concocted story of mis-setting her alarm the night before. Nor did she have a chance to mention in passing the fact that Poirot – on rare occasions – was capable of opening the door of his cage with his beak.

When she hoofed off to work twenty minutes late, Jay was still out jogging.

'He's avoiding me until tonight,' she sighed affectionately, stroking Sean's battered Land Rover as she passed it – and noticing that it had been parallel parked so perfectly between two Golf GTIs that it looked as though it had been air-lifted into place.

'Tonight,' she repeated lovingly as she approached the tube, digging her hand into her bag for her travel pass. Instead she drew out a business card.

In ten-point minimalist font it read simply 'Piers Fox', with an even smaller typeface beneath it bearing a phone number and address in Wardour Street. If she didn't go and see him in his office today, Juno realised, then she wouldn't get the chance until after she returned from house-sitting which was over a week away. To leave it that long was a bit damned flip. She had no choice.

Juno decided that, since she was late already, she might as well go to the Immedia office via Wardour Street.

Chapter Nineteen

Piers Fox's office would have made a padded cell appear disorganised. The three pieces of stark black furniture, two cacti and one telephone within it had been Feng Shui-ed to within a millimetre of their wealth-cornered lives. Such was the Zen minimalism of the place that, in search of visual distraction, Juno found herself gazing in rapt fascination at Piers's right brogue which jerked sporadically as if acting as an earth to the rest of his rigidly upright body.

'I would have preferred it if you had telephoned first,' he told her tightly as he flipped open his little digital organiser.

The pale, perfumed supermodel secretary who had just shown Juno into his office had been equally disapproving of her casual, unheralded arrival. Having been caught in a shower on Oxford Street, Juno was looking damp and bedraggled, her funky purple jacket blackened at shoulders and chest like a two-tone rugby shirt.

'You said to drop by the office sometime.' Juno was defiantly cheery, certain that Piers Fox would perceive any form of apology as a sign of weakness. Her buttocks were squirming with nerves, but she forced a hearty showbiz smile.

'No matter.' He went on typing a couple of words into his electronic organiser. 'I happen to have a relatively free morning, so I'm glad you're here. I must admit, I was rather surprised to see a woman like you doing a slot for Harry Frankel who I'm told is antediluvian. Indeed, I was perplexed

to encounter anyone with genuinely original talent performing in a Frankel line-up. I certainly didn't attend that rather
grim event on Wednesday night to scout for up and coming
comics.'

Juno longed to ask him what he had been in the Cod and
Cucumber for, and why exactly he was interested in Jay. But
her ego got the better of her. 'So you think I have genuinely
original talent?' she asked delightedly, brushing a parrot feather
from her best black satin boot-cut trousers.

He studied her face long enough to reproduce an Identikit
picture from every angle if asked.

He's working out the publicity photographs, the blurb, the
launch, the television appearances, the newspaper features, Juno
decided headily. She widened her eyes becomingly, pouted
slightly and tilted her head winningly.

'You could have talent,' he finally told her with flat-voiced
detachment. 'But you're a long way off success as things stand.
In fact, I didn't really rate your material at all. And I certainly
haven't invited you here on the pretext of putting you up for
television work, if that's what you think. As you stand now,
you couldn't pass muster in a discount warehouse commercial,
so I'm not about to waste my time promoting Juno . . .' he
consulted his electronic organiser for her surname '. . . Glenn
as the new Roseanne.'

'Well, of course not,' she blustered hastily, although a tiny
corner of her recently massaged ego was, in truth, ridiculously
disappointed. 'I mean, I'm hardly known on the circuit. Haven't
cut my teeth at any of the really established venues yet –
Jongleurs, Warm Up Club, Comedy Store, the Ha Ha. I've
done a bit of radio work, but no television at all. In fact, I still
do a day job to pay the mortgage.'

'Quite.' He looked down dismissively.

There was a long pause while Piers scrolled through files on
his palmtop. Feeling like an underachieving pupil waiting at the
headmaster's desk, Juno mulled over the Roseanne reference in
nail-chewing silence. She wasn't sure whether to be flattered or
miffed. She was dying for a coffee but she hadn't been offered

one and felt it was rude to ask. Would Roseanne demand a coffee in similar circumstances?

Suddenly, she panicked that Piers had fallen silent because she was selling herself short. Self-deprecation did, after all, simply diminish a woman's value according to the latest American self-help book she had been reading: *Enriching Bitches: A Modern Women's Guide to Empowering Herself, Ergo Ego.*

'But I am pretty bloody sharp,' she pointed out in a hard-sell voice, 'and the Outing recently described me as "the new girl putting lesser comics' heads on the block. The hair is blonde, the air is blue and, Victoria Wood, your heir is apparent".' So what if Euan had written it? It was still a rave review.

'Did they? That's creditable,' he said vaguely, still tapping away on his dinky executive toy. 'I have to confess, I'd never heard of you before Wednesday.'

Piers was so preoccupied with his electronic organiser, she was beginning to think his indifference signalled the end of their meeting, when he spoke again.

'I don't really represent performers as such.' He didn't look up, his voice as flat as a bored schoolboy's reciting *amo, amas, amat*. 'Less than fifty per cent of my clients are in the entertainment business, less than five per cent are comedy-related, and of those I am publicist rather than agent to all but a very few. I'm more accustomed to dealing with celebrities at the end of their career than at the outset – I reinvent has-beens and smooth over the misdemeanours of indiscreet politicians and businessmen. I'm a damage limitation expert, not a showbiz Svengali.'

That final two-word description was a direct lift from the headline of a *Sunday Times* piece Juno had been reading about him only a fortnight earlier. Listening to him, Juno realised he was giving her the 'don't call me' spiel.

'So, er – ' She cleared her throat and tried not to glance at her watch. She was almost an hour late for work now. 'Why did you ask me to come here?'

He didn't answer immediately.

Chewing her lip in consternation, Juno covertly studied his face. Even his paprika freckles seemed to be painted neatly on the bridge of his nose, like computer-generated polka dots. Jay had red hair too, she found herself thinking, but no freckles at all – just pale, evenly golden skin. Piers's colouring was a darker red than his. More titian. Jay's tones were sunsets on beaches, old frames around masterpieces, Irish setters dashing through ripe cornfields . . .

'I'm contemplating the development of an act of sorts,' Piers said, finally looking up from his electronic organiser, voice brusque with efficiency, eyes focused upon hers. 'It's something of an initiatory publicity nucleus at the moment, and may never gestate into anything fiscally viable. To be frank, it's more of an experiment in the manufactured mass-market media phenomenon on my part than a serious business proposal, but I've already run it past quite a number of established venues, plus key comedy festival promoters and several independent television producers, and I must say their response was far from discouraging.'

'Oh, yes?' Juno was lost in her mental *Business Terms Manual*, looking up words like fiscal. She hadn't a clue what he'd just said, but it sounded good.

'What I have devised,' Piers went on dispassionately, 'is the idea of a manufactured "comedy group" which works along similar lines to those in the pop industry. Think boy bands and girl power.'

'Call me au-Spice,' Juno cracked excitedly as she began to cotton on. 'I'm just the girl you're looking for.'

'The basic premise is,' he smoothly ignored her interruption, 'that I assemble a company – a troupe if you like – of sexy, emerging female comics who work exclusively together – on the London scene, at the Edinburgh Festival, at provincial theatres, on the university circuit, on radio and ultimately television, maybe even a feature film. We're talking individual stand-up, plus combined sketches; team chemistry is essential. We're also talking hard work – at least a year of touring and promotion before anything takes off. And when I say that they work exclusively together, I really mean exclusive. If you're signed by me you work for no one else.' The green eyes glinted for a nano-second with Mephistopholian relish.

Juno was almost demented with the hyperbole of it all. 'Sounds fantastic!' she managed to splutter inanely.

'Thank you,' he said ironically, totally indifferent to her opinion.

'So you want me to be part of it?' she panted eagerly, already composing her resignation letter in her head. 'Dear GWC – your job sucks. Stick it where your crappy magazines won't fit.'

'I'm not sure – you're perhaps too much of a wild card.' He looked at her with cool, calm honesty. 'And frankly I'm uncertain whether you're funny enough, attractive enough or established enough.'

'Thanks for the review – I'll quote "wild . . . funny . . . attractive . . . established" in my next publicity mailshot.' She narrowed her eyes, wondering if this was an ideal juncture to request a coffee and a Danish to go.

'But you're certainly marketable.' He barely heeded her jokey repartee, which was worrying. 'You have an erotic appeal which isn't conventional – I've been searching for an atypical plump girl for a long time, to balance the troupe. There are too many Jo Brand wannabes out there in faded black t-shirts and leggings, ranting about men, models and fashion boutiques. That doesn't equate with the ensemble I have in mind. You portray yourself as sexually desirable, which is ballsy, original and seductively funny.'

'Thanks.' Juno's heart was banging away like a punch ball in her chest. He thought she was marketable. So what if he'd called her plump (being an atypical plump girl was, after all, preferable to being a typical plump girl), he thought she was 'seductively funny'. Piers Fox thought that of Juno Glenn. She wanted to have 'Seductively funny' – Piers Fox tattooed on her forehead.

'It's essential that this troupe is seen as greater than any individual member of it,' he told her with ominous gravity. 'Which is why I'm selecting so carefully. This isn't going to be a group of feminist graduates seeking a break in pub and club comedy, banding together while they await individual stardom. I want no egos, no alcoholics, no drug-addicts, no obese dogs.'

Juno was so insulted she forgot her American self-help bible. 'Well, that counts me out then. Take away the "no"s and you have my CV.'

To her amazement, he shook his head humouringly. 'I think we both know that's not true. Which is why I have just disclosed so much of the project to you at this early stage. I'm confident we may well find ourselves working together in the near future. I would, however, be grateful if you treated this meeting as confidential for now.'

Juno was almost too excited to splutter, 'So am I in?' But she bounced around on her minimalist black Milan-designed chair nonetheless, like a greedy squirrel on a chestnut-roasting brazier. 'Am I?'

'Like any good poker player, I rely upon the occasional wild card.' He glanced at his electronic organiser again. 'I can safely say you are short-listed at this stage. And that list is severely vertically challenged.' A great white shark smile spread across his face. 'I'll be in touch over the next fortnight to let you know when and where we are auditioning.'

'Auditioning?' she gulped. 'You mean, I'll have to do some sort of try-out?'

'Naturally, I cannot recruit the group on the basis of individual performances I've seen,' he said crushingly. 'I need to see potential members interacting together to get an idea of the chemistry. And I have a manager lined up who will need to sit in. As I said earlier, this is an exercise in mass-market manufacturing, not necessarily a viable media enterprise. Once we have a provisional team in place, I'm planning a mini-tour of venues to gauge audience reaction and try out various formats and line-ups. Only then will we make the final selection and consider setting up a full-scale promotional tour.'

'I see.' Juno began to realise quite how formidably far off this lucky break was. 'Who else have you approached?'

'About twenty other female comics so far,' he told her evasively. 'They range from household names to total unknowns like yourself, but everyone will audition, regardless of background and experience. I'm planning to set up a week of workshops somewhere in London later this month. I trust you'll be able to take time off the day job?'

'Oh, no trouble.' Juno conveniently forgot that she had already arranged to take a swathe of time off work the following week. 'I'm pretty much self-employed.'

'That's good.' He flashed his teeth dismissively. 'In that case, I'll be in touch.'

Giddy with excitement, Juno beamed back and gathered her bag from beneath her chair, not noticing that several precautionary tampons had tipped on to Piers Fox's slate grey Axminster. Her period had yet to start.

'Do you want to know my phone number and stuff?' she suggested idiotically, like a teenager asked on her first date.

'I already have it.' He stood up to see her to the door, prodding a manicured finger into the soil of a four-foot cactus as he passed it.

'You do?' Juno turned back to him in the doorway, a smile spreading like melting butter across her lips.

Saying nothing, Piers shook her hand with a brief, tight grip and, smiling thoughtfully, turned back into his underfurnished lair, thick black ash door clicking quietly behind him.

GWC was on the phone and peering through the venetian blind of his office when Juno crept towards her desk at eleven o'clock. She waved cheerily at him, but he just glanced pointedly at his wrist watch and turned away to continue his call.

'Damn,' she muttered under her breath. She had been banking on his being away from the office that morning, as he often was when none of the magazines closed that day, so he could comfortably work from home. It was almost unprecedented for him to come in on a Friday.

Not that she cared much. She was still reeling from her encounter with Piers Fox. The more she dwelled upon his 'girl group', the more she convinced herself that he had been subtly letting her know that she was already in; he had, after all, told her a great deal about it, stuff which he still wanted to be kept a secret. He had treated her as an equal, told her she had a unique talent and thought her important enough to spare her half an hour of his time without an appointment – all of which led her to the delighted conclusion that he was absolutely desperate to mould her wild-card, untamed, sexy (and, let's face it, inexpensive) talent into girl power superstardom.

Dumping her bag on her desk, she sloped off to fetch herself a coffee. Helping herself to sugar, she wondered idly whether Piers's girly troupe would have individual nicknames, like members of the Spice Girls.

'Plumptious Sex Kitten Girl,' Juno murmured aloud, distractedly adding another sugar to her coffee. 'Or perhaps just Sugar Girl?'

Her voice mail-box was crammed with messages. She listened to them as she slurped her coffee, distractedly scalding her tongue when she realised her desperate attempts the previous day to arrange a social weekend for herself had paid off rather alarmingly. An excess of success.

She was now double-booked for every day and night of the weekend. Ally had managed to get her a ticket to see the Patrick Marber play that night, two friends for whom she'd left messages had returned her calls with invitations out, another was eager for her to join a hen night; for Saturday she now had a party invitation, two comedy gigs to go to, a clubbing session with a mob of old schoolfriends, a lunchtime barbecue, a tea-time cinema trip and the chance to join Elsa and Euan in Cornwall. Sunday was even more jam-packed with lunch invites, the offer of a lift to Llanadu, meetings with Lulu and Odette. Her weekend read like a trashy, pubby version of Tara Palmer-Tompkinson's social column in the *Sunday Times*.

Juno scribbled the messages down on a pad and looked at the list in alarm. There was no way she would get to everything and yet the thought of letting everyone down was equally inconceivable. It was in her nature to try to go to everything she was ever asked to, she loathed missing out. Besides which, having begged her way into everyone's social plans, it would be appallingly louche to throw the invitations back in their faces and say, 'Sorry, can't make it after all – far too busy, better offers around, another time, huh?' She already had a reputation for over-committing herself socially, which she had been struggling to shake off in previous months. This would set her right back, and it was all her own fault. Yesterday she'd been convinced she had no friends. Today she decided she had the loveliest bunch around, most of whom she was about to let down.

As ever in a moment of crisis which required quick-wittedness and hasty action to limit the damage, Juno did nothing, deciding instead to wander over to see Uma and demand the low-down on the latest rumour that the office was due to be down-sized.

'Don't quote me on this,' the secretary said in a cloak-and-dagger whisper, handing Juno a stem ginger shortbread, 'but Vanessa Furness says we're in for a redundancy shake-up which will register on the Richter scale.'

Vanessa Furness was PA to the group chairman, and an invaluable source of insider gossip.

'So am I for the chop?' Juno asked bluntly.

Uma squinted doubtfully and tilted her head from side to side in an embarrassed gesture. 'Your name was on the Streamline hit list, child. I'm sorry. But it was pretty far down, and it's early days.'

'There's a list?' Juno choked on her biscuit.

Uma nodded. 'And before you ask, I don't have it, no – I just got a tiny peek in the ladies yesterday afternoon.'

'What's Streamline? Sounds like a pair of control-top tights.'

'Management consultants.' Uma stroked some crumbs from her desk with a broad black hand. 'You remember the men in suits this spring?'

'Men in suits?'

'Reservoir Sniffer Dogs, you called them.'

'Oh, yes – the ones who were thinking of buying Immedia?

Spent a week wandering round asking questions?' Juno had been breaking up with John at the time, and had been too busy spending large portions of the day crying in the loos to take much notice.

'They weren't thinking of buying the company.' Uma tucked her chins in disapprovingly. 'They were on the company's payroll, putting together a report on ways of making the magazines more cost-effective. Now they've delivered their findings, and they're not just saying we should cut down on paperclips. There's been a big meeting going on in the boardroom all morning – GWC is furious because he's not included. It's why he came in to the office today, to try and find out what they're saying about him.'

'You're not telling me . . . ?' Juno's jaw slackened and her forehead creased.

Uma nodded. 'Further up that list than yours, child. Much further.'

'But you're okay?' Juno looked at her worriedly.

'Sure I am,' cackled the secretary. 'Old Mama Uma ain't leaving this chair – I've been here so long my fat old behind is stuck in it. Besides, who else is going to water them damned pot plants in this place or act as a one-woman cookie jar?'

Juno smiled in relief, and wondered whether Cookie Girl would work. It had a nice double-meaning ring to it.

'You're not worried?' Uma looked at her slyly. 'I thought you'd be more upset, child.'

Juno scratched her chin with her half-eaten biscuit and pressed the tip of her tongue to her top teeth as she debated whether to brag about her meeting with Piers Fox. The temptation was ghastly, but she knew it wasn't worth the risk.

'I'll see what happens before I bulk-buy the Kleenex,' she said cautiously. 'I might have something lined up if things don't work out here.'

'Oh, yes?' Uma eked several nosy syllables out of the question. 'The *News on Sunday* finally offered you a full-time job?'

'No, nothing like that.' Juno thought longingly about Piers's girl power comedy troupe and wanted to be rehearsing there and then, ready to head off on tour. A big, excited smile started tugging at her cheek muscles once again.

'I won't ask.' Uma was wise enough to appreciate that Juno was hankering to spill the beans on something she shouldn't. 'But don't worry yourself too much, child – your columns are still the best-read thing in these trashy old magazines, so they're not about to fire you overnight.'

'Thanks.' Juno was so carried away with her fantasy of fame and fortune that she almost wished they would; she knew sacking stories made good publicity fodder.

As she headed back past Xerox Corner Finlay draped himself over the photocopier, blinking his baby blond curls from his big, cutesome eyes.

'Where's Lydia? I miss her legs.'

'Right now, I'd hazard a guess they're wrapped around someone called Bruno,' Juno said uncharitably.

'Shame,' he sighed. 'I was going to suggest we go shop-lifting this afternoon. She's so good at it, and I love choosing women's clothes.'

'Lydia doesn't need to shop-lift.' Juno laughed. 'She's loaded – her father's given her store cards for most of Bond Street. Her purse reads like the Stockists list in *Vogue*.' She sucked in her cheeks and struck a Madonna pose to emphasise her point.

'Trust me.' His eyes glittered as he tapped his broken nose with a long finger. 'I was with her when she nicked your birthday present one lunch hour last week.'

'No way!' Juno was appalled.

'Oh, come on, the girl is addicted to danger.' He eyed her thoughtfully. 'Don't suppose you fancy a jaunt to Selfridge's this afternoon?'

'I'm more of a Top Shop girl, myself,' Juno muttered, walking to her desk to leaf through her post. 'Besides which, I hardly think bunking off work for the afternoon constitutes prioritising my schedule.'

Finlay followed her and sat on Lydia's vacant chair.

'Oh, come on – in half an hour's time GWC'll be out of the office for the weekend. Seeing as we might all be out of a job soon, why not shop? You know what they say: When the going gets tough, the tough go shop-lifting.' His fingers were rat-tat-tatting an eager drumroll on the top of the monitor in front of him. Wired, excitable and impatient, he was impossible to take seriously.

Juno pulled a face then noticed her social schedule sitting on her keyboard. 'I have a lot of calls to make.' She chewed her lip worriedly.

'What about your date with "J"?' Finlay pressed his chin to the monitor top and eyed her pleadingly, seraphic toddler's face totally bewitching. 'Don't you want a lovely new outfit to wear?'

'Who told you it was Jay?' Juno looked up excitedly, wondering how on earth he could know.

'The fax . . . "J",' he mocked her slowness. 'You are going, aren't you? No one could turn down Bar Oque – it's *so* divine.'

'I'm supposed to be seeing the new Patrick Marber play,' she said guiltily.

'Shit, I'm dying to see that! Couldn't get a ticket.' He cocked his head leadingly, gorgeous dimples appearing in both his smooth, pale cheeks. 'I guess it's another night in with a pot noodle and the nail-clippers for me . . .'

Juno brightened. She knew Ally and Duncan would be furious with her for turning down their generous, last-minute offer, but then again if she let someone as glamorous and fun as Finlay go in her place, they might forgive her the slip. They were always complaining they didn't meet new people or get decent drugs now that they had a baby.

'So you're not doing anything tonight?' she asked, flashing her own dimples in return.

Winking one big grey eye, Finlay slid out of the chair and dipped his face beside hers so that his fluffy hair tickled her forehead. 'First, we shop. I'll meet you in reception the moment GWC's cleared off.'

Juno picked up her phone forty minutes later.

'Ladies and gentlemen, GWC has left the building,' came a gloriously camp, Scottish rendition of the *Frasier* catchphrase.

*　　*　　*

Shopping with Finlay was as unexpected as shooting the breeze in a vacuum and as fun as giggling in a pub with a best friend, although persuading him that she really did want to pay for items she tried on was tougher.

'Bar Oque requires a certain *tu sais quoi*.' Finlay burst into a changing room with tightly closed eyes and sucked-in cheeks just as Juno was struggling to extricate herself from a leather halter-necked top which seemed intent upon strangling her. 'What we know being glamour with an emphasis on amour, more and oo-er. This little off-the-shoulder suede number is so Bar Oque, even the doormen would wear it.' He waggled a coathanger at her, from which a small amount of dead skin dangled like a poacher's catch.

'How is it?' he called out from behind a thick velvet curtain two minutes later.

'Fits like a glove,' Juno called back. 'On O.J. Simpson.'

After an hour, she was starting to get seriously fed up with his optimism when it came to sizes. He might be a rack-raking rake with an ability to win over shop assistants as easily as a rock star searching for an impulse-buy dress for his supermodel girlfriend, but his rose-tinted specs were shrink-to-fit. Tall, gangly beauties like Finlay had no concept of the word 'outsize'.

'I really don't fit into a size fourteen,' she told him as she returned a pile of clothes to a cat-eyed, pierced-bellied fitting-room attendant who was regarding Finlay with something close to idolatry. 'Even a sixteen can be a bit tight on me.'

'Rubbish, you've got a fantastic body,' he dismissed her curtly, turning to the attendant. 'Hasn't she?'

'Um . . . er . . . not bad,' the attendant lied unconvincingly, eyes glancing from Juno's bulges to Finlay's beauty in a way that clearly said: Are you mad? What are you doing with the fat dog? Look at my flat belly and weep, pretty boy.

At least that's what Juno was convinced she thought, having worked herself into a sweaty lather of self-hatred with every zip that wouldn't meet across her soft, pliable flesh or button that obstinately refused to meet its intended aperture. Her body image was normally as positive as the nippled end of a battery – occasionally as riotously, lavishly positive as a power station. She accepted her plumptious size and lack of stature. She didn't hate her body, she hated clothes shops. Years of humiliation at the hands, hangers and tills of just such places as this had hardened her against them.

Piers Fox had been wrong to assume she was a woman who didn't berate boutiques which considered a size fourteen to be 'large'. She loathed shops which assessed women's figures on a scale of 1 to 3, when in the real world, 1 was a coathanger and 3 was a drip-fed anorexic; shops which occasionally catered for a size sixteen as long as she was six foot tall and didn't mind wearing sludge green. Yes, the anomaly bothered her, but not enough to use it as material. So what if the fashion industry had an ignorant, insular inability to see the large woman as anything other than a walking, talking tent frame with a penchant for brightly pattered drip-dry nylon? Juno had funnier things to joke about than couture and cake. She could joke about men.

'Look at the symmetry, the femininity, those curves. To die for,' Finlay was squinting at her in aesthetic appreciation. 'I think they've just got the sizing wrong in this shop. Let's go somewhere else.'

Juno panted behind him as he strode towards the door, leaving the assistant open-mouthed.

'We,' Finlay hooked his arm through hers, 'are going to a little shop I know in Soho. You'll love it.'

It was pouring with rain outside. Buying a pink, flowery brolly from a stall on Oxford Circus, he ran whooping through the rain with Juno in tow.

Chapter Twenty

'Finlay, I can't go in here!' she bleated at the door of a tiny, dimly lit shop in a cobbled side-street. In the window, a neon sign in bright pink joined-up capitals buzzed out the word TRANSPOTTING. 'It's for cross-dressers.'

'And you, my grumpy little friend, are a very cross dresser this afternoon.' He dragged her inside.

An hour later, they collapsed into two chairs at the Nero Club, a fat cluster of bags at their feet.

'I'll never wear it,' Juno giggled, nodding at a hovering waiter who appeared to be staring at her rather intently.

'You'll wear it if I have to glue you in.' Finlay cocked his angelic head and looked up as the waiter patted his back. 'Hi, Ralph. How're you doing? We'll have a bottle of something red with a high haemoglobin count, and two plates of the usual.'

'Sure, mate.' With a wink and another curious glance at Juno, Ralph peeled away from the table.

'I didn't know you were a member here,' she whispered, looking around respectfully at the slate walls, eccentric modern art and fat, red velvet settees. 'Isn't this place nicknamed Arthritis because it's such a cliquey joint?'

The Nero Club was one of the most exclusive, members-only media haunts on the little square of Soho roads known as 'Writer's Block' – although the bars, restaurants and private clubs which lined them were more likely to play host to actors, cult television celebrities and Britpop bands than starving wordsmiths. Just to see how the other half lived it up, Juno had visited a few with her more successful friends – Jez belonged to the Groucho Club but seldom used it because he preferred the Cobden or his local pub on Ladbroke Grove; Odette regularly networked in the Union which was largely peopled by the young and the beautiful from the broadcasting industry; Elsa and Euan were both members of the funkier Soho House. Of all the places to star-spot, the Nero Club was reputedly the best, and the hardest to gain entry to. It was commonly thought to be easier to be beatified by the Pope than accepted for membership to the Nero.

'It's nicknamed Arse-writers now, because so many members have newspaper columns,' Finlay said matter-of-factly. 'My brother Calum was one of the co-founders so I'm allowed in on a purely nepotistic basis. They throw me out quite a lot too.'

'You sly crow.' She shook her head in amazement. 'Tell me, why the hell do you sell space at Immedia if you belong to a place like this? Surely you only have to network this bar a couple of times to get a job at Hat Trick or Working Title or *GQ*?'

'It's not as simple as that, sugar.' He grinned easily, flashing his chipped tooth. 'I'm a junkle, I'm a slacker and I'm unreliable. I let people down. Just 'cos my brother's a big boy in this playground doesn't mean I get to join his gang – I just enjoy the perks. He's got me jobs before and I've always fucked up. None of his flash media friends would employ me. Besides which, I don't want a career.' He shrugged. 'It's too much like hard work. I just want to stay up all night doing the clubs and bars. And I don't need the money – Calum's too fucking generous for his own good. He'd buy me the whole of Colombia if it made me happy.' His insouciance was staggering, as was his honesty.

'So why work at all?' Juno scrabbled through her bag for a cigarette.

'I tried sleeping all day but it didn't suit me,' he said simply. 'My father's always saying I'm a waste of space, so I figured I should sell space for a living. I like the irony. I've only stayed so long at Immedia because I much prefer watching Lydia all day to sitting at home watching day-time television. I figure I might as well hang around and chat her up till they fire me.'

'You're incorrigible,' Juno laughed, and popped a cigarette into her mouth.

'She's a lot like me, Lydia.' Finlay took a match-book from the ashtray and lit her cigarette. 'We belong to a club far more exclusive than this one.' He looked around the room as he shook out the flame. 'It's called Generation Ex Gratia. Entrance is free, the drinks are on the house, you can party till late but you get thrown out the minute you sober up and develop a desire to do something worthwhile with your life. Quite a lot of us die on the premises.'

Juno rolled her eyes. 'Is this some sort of Notting Hill trustafarian crap? "My parents sent me to the best schools money could buy, and now they send me to the best rehab clinics".'

'It's no' crap, Juno.' He shook his head, blond curls dancing. 'Life's too easy for freeloaders like Lydia and me. We lack ambition, get our kicks from underachieving and overindulging. Most of our friends have much higher-status careers, but we can easily move in the same social circles as them because we have the parental disposable hand-outs to match their incomes. They like us because we're charming and witty and clever and hedonistic and just a little bit dangerous.'

'Don't forget modest.' Juno rolled her eyes, but he was already turning to talk to the waiter who had arrived with the wine.

'You are a god, Ralph.' Finlay took it from him and studied the label.

'Calum's told me not to let you get drunk in here again,' Ralph warned.

'In that case Juno will get drunk for me.' Finlay filled her glass up to the brim.

'Whoah! I've got a date tonight, remember?' she giggled.

Finlay's eyes fluttered in girlish parody. 'Ah, yes, the sumptuous Bar Oque with the mysterious "J". You used to work there, didn't you?' he asked Ralph who was once again looking at Juno with interest.

'Mmm – great place.' He cocked his head and carried on studying her face intently.

She shifted uncomfortably under the scrutiny. She was certain he was about to tell her she was breaking some sort of strict Nero Club dress code – like not being a size 10.

Suddenly his face brightened in recognition. 'You're a comic, aren't you?'

'Sometimes, yes.' She nodded delightedly.

'I knew it!' He clicked his fingers. 'I caught your act a couple of weeks ago, upstairs at Café Bleu in Highgate. You were the best thing there.'

'I was?' Juno bleated in amazement. She tried to think back. She'd done several gigs upstairs at Café Bleu. It was one of her favourite venues. The manager, Faith Gower, was a close friend of Duncan's from his days at The Delivery and tried to book Juno as often as possible.

'My girlfriend still raves about you.' Ralph laughed. 'She'd only dragged me there in the first place because that good-looking Irish guy was on. What's his name? Jerry something . . . ?'

'Maloney?' Juno stuttered disbelievingly.

'That's it. Nice bloke – comes in here sometimes with Dylan Moran.' Ralph nodded. 'But we thought you were funnier.'

Christ! That was the night she had been on the bill with Lulu, Mick Collins and comedy's flavour of the month, Jerry Maloney. She'd been so terrified she'd rattled through her material in less than five minutes, but the audience had been quick enough to keep up, and unusually responsive. It was one of her squeezebox nights. She remembered feeling incredibly high afterwards.

'I really mean it.' He started to move away. 'You were brilliant.'

'Thanks.' Juno found she couldn't stop grinning, like a rank outsider on a victory podium.

'And that comes from a man who serves drinks to some of the funniest comics in London on a daily basis,' Finlay whistled after he'd gone, taking a great swig of wine straight from the bottle.

'It's the first time anyone's recognised me out of the blue like that,' she realised excitedly.

'Out of the Café Bleu.' Finlay took another swig from the bottle and then poured some into a glass. 'The wine's good. Try it.'

Juno took a sip. It was delicious – as smooth, round and rich as Mohammed Al Fayed.

'Gorgeous.' She shivered happily. 'This is turning out to be the best day I've had in flipping weeks and I've still got tonight to look forward to. I'm going to suffer from happiness overload in a minute.'

Finlay watched her in amusement.

She looked at him with glistening eyes, taking in his dishevelled, seraphic beauty: the crooked nose, sensuous lips, long languid body in foppish clothes. He looked like a picture she'd once seen of Oscar Wilde's young lover, Bosie, lounging on a stone bench wearing a straw hat and a distant expression.

'So do you want to sleep with Lydia or are you gay?' she suddenly asked.

He spluttered into his wine.

Juno smiled at him encouragingly as he wiped his mouth with the back of his hand and looked away in amused disbelief.

She lit another cigarette and watched as he turned back to face her, eyelashes fluttering camply and one corner of his mouth curled in a part-cocky, part-defensive smile.

'D'you really expect me to answer that?' he asked finally.

'Of course.' She nodded, wondering why he was making such a big deal out of it. He'd been so open about his feckless, slacker ways a moment ago that he struck her as the sort of guy who thought a closet was something you kept your clothes in, not your sexuality. Lydia was gorgeous and he clearly doted on her. The answer was either 'Yes, I am one of the many hundreds of men who fancy Lydia Morley', or 'No, I'm gay, but I think she's fabulous'.

'You're an amazing woman, Juno,' he laughed. 'You don't beat about the bush, do you?'

'Not unless it's on fire.'

'Okay, sugar.' He poured himself another glass of wine and topped up hers. 'Give me a cigarette and I'll tell you why I'm not gay but neither do I want to sleep with Lydia.'

He didn't so much smoke the cigarette as play with it, rolling the tip against the glass of the ashtray for several seconds before he started talking.

'I can't get it up,' he murmured almost dispassionately. 'If I can, I can't keep it up. If I still can – and we're talking twice a year here – I can't come. It's not a question of sexuality, Juno. It's a question of insexuality. Junkies are lousy in bed. I love coke more than I love lovers. Call it a conscious choice.' He downed two inches of wine and looked across at her thoughtfully. 'The last time I had sex – tried to have sex – with someone was over a year ago. I've been celibate since then . . . I sell a bit here, sell a bit there.' He smiled ruefully at the joke, cigarette caressing the glass of the ashtray again.

Gaping at him as she absorbed his astonishing honesty, Juno felt a great wave of pity sweep over her. 'Surely you still feel attracted to people? To women?'

He wrinkled up one eye in thought, watching the end of his cigarette. 'Sure, but I'm always aware it's a spectator sport. I might flirt for Scotland, but I know it won't make my dick work.' He took a slug of wine. 'Shit, I don't know why I'm telling you all this.'

'Lydia?' Juno watched his face as she said the name. He glanced up at the ceiling and sighed, like the Archangel Raphael asking his boss what to say.

Juno swigged some wine, letting his story sink in. Part of her thought his shallow, fickle, self-destructive lifestyle thoroughly deserved a sexual punishment like impotence. It was a modern-day Aesop's fable. But for all his self-professed hedonism, he obviously had no sense of self-worth and for that she pitied him.

'You know, you and Lydia are so different.' He blew on

the tip of his cigarette to make it glow. 'I always wondered why you two were friends – it's one of the reasons I made you come out shopping this afternoon. I seriously didn't expect to like you much.'

'No?' Juno was horrified. She'd always thought she and Finlay got along pretty well in a jokey, officey kind of way.

'Lydia worships you, and you snap at her all the time,' he said critically, his ethereal, imperfect face tilted to one side.

'She's my best friend, but technically I'm her boss,' Juno defended herself hotly, slugging back some more wine. 'I adore her, but sometimes when she doesn't pull her weight I have to throw mine around a bit.' She flinched as she realised she was skidding on the banana skin of a Freudian slip.

'Like I say, you're such opposites.' Finlay was decent enough not to laugh, but he'd spotted the joke straight away. 'Lydia shows off that gorgeous, flawless body and hides her mind.' He paused to take a long drag at his cigarette and blow several perfect, smoke rings before completing the epigram. 'You cover your body self-consciously, and show off the fact you're witty and clever.'

'Ever heard of emphasising your best points?' Juno helped them both to more wine, then spilled a great splash on the table as she realised she had inadvertently insinuated that Lydia's mind wasn't her best point. She opened her mouth to splutter a hasty rebuttal but Finlay had already started speaking.

'It's funny, but something happens when a man knows he can't make love to a woman he desires – especially if that was once his only *raison d'être*.' He shifted his elbows forward on the table, looking at her gravely. 'He starts seeing her differently. Don't get me wrong, I still wonder what her body's like under her clothes, what it would be like to undress her, to touch her, to make love with her. But when you can't follow that through, pretty soon you find you're not just thinking about climbing inside her body all the time, you're starting to try and see inside her head.' He dropped his gaze and smiled thoughtfully at the ashtray. 'Lydia's body is so perfect it's unreal, but her head's a fucking ugly mess.'

'She's a fantastic woman!' Juno instantly defended her dearest, most frustrating friend. 'Okay, so she might be a bit wild and screwed up, but she's the most generous, honest, giving sweetheart alive. She's my best friend. And she's as clever as anyone I know.'

'I couldn't agree more.' He looked up at her again, nodding in agreement. Then he laughed harshly. 'Can't you see that I might not want to sleep with her, Juno, but I fucking adore her? I haven't got much of a working knowledge of love, but I guess this is as close as I've ever come to it.'

The scales dropped from her eyes.

'You've got to understand something,' he said urgently, taking hold of her hand. 'I'm not about to tell her how I feel, or make a move on her. The last person in the world she needs to get involved with right now is me. This afternoon is not some sort of teenage "ask the friend" session to find out what she thinks about me.'

'So why are you telling *me* all this?' The idea of keeping his confession from Lydia was almost unbearable.

He shook his curls from his eyes. 'I made up my mind today. Just now, when I decided I was going to tell you all this. I made up my mind to do something. Thing is, I'm really going to need your help.'

'To do what?'

'I'm going to straighten myself out.' He stared directly into her eyes, and Juno didn't doubt for a second that he meant it. 'I'm going to cure the white line fever, exodus Ex Gratia, and then try to rescue her too.'

'Oh, Finlay, that's so romantic!' She felt tears in her eyes and longed to call Lydia on her mobile straight away.

'You think so?' He laughed cynically, then drained the last of his wine. 'You've been reading too much chemical fiction, sugar.'

'I know, I mean, obviously it won't be easy . . .' Juno blustered, embarrassed by her lack of cool.

He stared at the ceiling. 'I've been through rehab twice. I've attended the group sessions, studied the diagrams, read the leaflets, drunk the tea, smoked the cigarettes, met the sad bastards who tell you their life-stories before they tell you their names. I've eaten the bland food, walked in the bland gardens, sat in the television room watching the bland quiz shows. Anything to take my mind off the only thing which could take away the blandness of it all. D'you know, you don't really appreciate what irony is until you sit in a nicotine-stained room full of strangers watching *The Price Is Right* and hear Bruce Forsyth saying "Come on down!"' He laughed bitterly. 'I've done rehab, Juno. I know how to make them believe you're clean, how to make yourself think you're clean. I just don't know how to *stay* clean for longer than a week afterwards.'

She blinked, uncertain whether to make some crass comment like, 'My brother's friend, Horse – geddit? – was a bit of a hype once. He kicked it.' She wisely decided to stick to silence.

'When you're in rehab,' Finlay went on, 'they occasionally make you say these really cheesy things like, "I respect myself", or "I respect my body" or "I love myself more than I love cocaine". And you know what? I can't wait to stand up there on some patterned nylon carpet in some big, old drawing room in Kent or wherever and say "I respect Lydia more than cocaine". I truly can't.'

'That's so fantastic!' Juno was totally caught up in his determination. She felt so evangelically anti-drugs at that moment, she even stubbed out the cigarette she was smoking. In her fervour, it didn't even occur to her that this was the first time she'd reacted to one of Lydia's plethora of admirers pledging his troth without the slightest itch of jealousy nettling her skin.

Finlay looked at her, a curious half-smile playing on his beautiful lips. 'It's going to take some time, some doing. Until then I'm going to stay as flippant Finlay, the office flirt who may or may not be gay, who she talks to about her crushes, her dates, her love affairs, and then goes shop-lifting with to cheer herself up when they end. And if you blow my cover, if you repeat a word of this conversation to her, I'll deny it ever happened and push off for good. I couldn't talk to her again if she knew what I was doing.'

'So what am I supposed to do in the meantime? Subtly insinuate that you two are made for one another?'

'No.' Finlay sighed impatiently. 'I said I needed your *help*, Juno.'

'I don't understand?' She had terrifying visions of visiting him daily in a discreet Kent clinic to make reports on Lydia's love life.

'Your date tonight.' He folded back the spills of the matchbook in front of him, making a flammable hedgehog. 'With "J". He's your new flatmate isn't he? The sexy New Yorker Lydia fancies?'

'Did she tell you about him then?' Juno chewed her lip worriedly. The question was too rhetorical to require an answer. Finlay just broke off one of the wooden spills and twisted it between his fingers.

'Why haven't you told Lydia there's something going on between you two?'

'It's complicated.' She closed her eyes as she thought about the past week.

'I do complicated.'

This is the return pay-off for his honesty, Juno realised as she haltingly told of her disastrous weekend with Jay and of Lydia's predatory interest in him, trying to ham it up for his entertainment but making herself look like Miss Piggy in the middle instead. Finlay didn't laugh once, listening to her sorry little tale with one eyebrow cranked. The matchbook in his hand was systematically shredded as she admitted that she'd told Lydia that Jay was free for her to try and seduce if she grew bored with Bruno.

'So do you love him?' He pressed a match to his cherubic mouth.

'Of course not!' Juno scoffed. 'I hardly know him. He's only been in the country a week, and we haven't been on speaking terms for most of that. The rest of it we spent plugged together.' She looked away in embarrassment, smiling at the irony.

Finlay was staring at the match at such close range now that his big grey eyes were crossed. 'Lydia has him firmly in her sights, you know.' His focus snapped back to Juno.

'Oh, I know she was attracted to him when she met him.' She played with her wine glass. 'But she's all wrapped up in Bruno at the moment. It's weird, but he's the reason I slept with Jay in the first place, *and* he's the reason Lydia hasn't made a move on Jay yet. I guess I have a lot to thank him for.'

The match snapped between Finlay's fingers. 'He won't last much longer. We both know that. Particularly as his heir is already apparent. The moment he gets too keen, too mean, or too routine, she'll be knocking on your door, sugar. And she won't have come to see you.'

'And what am I supposed to do about that?' Juno laughed hollowly. 'I don't flatter myself I stand a chance with Jay if she decides to make a move. I know how irresistible she is, and you should have seen his face when he first saw her. There was so much mutual attraction there, they could open a building society together. It's not as though telling her what's happened between me and Jay will make a whole lot of difference. You know what she's like.'

He shrugged. 'I guess you're right, sugar. That's what I've always loved about her – she's totally, innocently sybaritic. She thinks a moral is a picture painted on a wall. She'll go after him sooner or later. I was just hoping you could put her off for me.'

Juno winced. 'So what d'you suggest I do? Tell her he's lousy in bed?'

It was Finlay's turn to wince then. He stripped off another match and lit it, watching the flame at close range. 'And is he?'

Juno was blushing to her roots, which badly needed retouching. 'He's the most sensational lover I've ever had. He's spoilt me for life.'

'In that case, you've got to go out there tonight and make love with him again.' Finlay dropped the flaming match in the ashtray and looked up. 'Make him love you, sugar. It's you he's asked out, after all. He might even be in love with you already.'

A loud snort of laughter from Juno. 'I'm sorry, but you are *so* off beam there, Finlay. He's only been here a week, and I've behaved atrociously for most of that.'

'Ever heard of love at first sight?'

Juno laughed even more. 'The first time he caught sight of me, I was raiding the fridge in nothing but a pair of knickers and odd socks. And that was when I was on my best behaviour.'

'There you go! Charming!'

'Oh, Finlay, you don't know the half of it.' Juno wiped tears of laughter from her eyes. 'But thanks for cheering me up.'

He was undeterred, slouching back in his chair and looking at her seriously. 'If you really do fancy him as much as you say, then tell him tonight, and ask him how he feels about you.' He pulled a nanny-knows-best face.

'Do you self-destruct in ten seconds? Because this *is* Mission Impossible you're talking about here, you know. He's so secretive, he hasn't even told me why he's in England.'

'Hey, look at the fax, sugar. He obviously wants to make things up with you.' Finlay's eyes were wide with belief, the telesales voice at its most alluring. 'You're halfway there already. Tonight's your chance to cut darling, irrepressible Lydia off at the pass, by making a pass of your own. You've got the dress, you've got the shoes, you've got the attitude and you've got the advantage.' He smiled easily. 'The man's putty in your hands.'

'I give up.' Juno held up her hands. 'Okay, so it's true, he's madly in love with me. I'm that irresistible. I just have to crank on my new dress, jack up my boobs, shimmy into Bar Oque and he'll be gibbering in his seat declaring his undying passion. So what? It doesn't mean Lydia won't still make her move, does it?'

'Of course it does,' he chided. 'She'd have no qualms if all you'd done is have a one-night stand with him, you were right when you said that, but if you and this Jay character become an item, well then . . . whole different love story.' He drained the glass, smacking his lips. 'There's a Mills and Boon subtext hidden in that Bret Easton Ellis lifestyle, y'know. Lydia's an old-fashioned romantic at heart.'

Juno pressed her fingers to her mouth and looked at him – a blond, nervy, desperate, hopelessly mixed-up master of generalisation. She so wanted to believe what he said was true, but she was too much of a cynic.

'Yeah!' she scoffed good-naturedly, reaching for her wine. 'A drag queen dress won't make Jay fall in love with me, Finlay.'

'Your address might. You have *so* much in common.'

Juno burst out laughing but his face became still and watchful.

'Don't tell Lydia about this conversation,' he made her promise. 'Don't tell her how I feel. Just believe what I've told you.'

Juno grudgingly agreed, but kept her fingers crossed beneath the table as an insurance policy.

Ralph chose that moment to sweep across the room with two large orange plates centred with high-rise stacks of haute cuisine.

'Chow down.' He winked at Juno before melting smoothly away to serve Emma Thompson, Colin Firth and Jack Davenport at a nearby table.

Juno hadn't noticed the number of celebrities who'd infiltrated the room since she and Finlay had arrived, popping in for an early-evening drink with friends. She swung her head around as though she had a crick in her neck, eyes out on stalks. 'Christ, Johnny Vaughan is sitting in the corner with . . . blimey! . . . that bloke from Blur. Sandra from *Londoners* is standing at the bar. And isn't that the male model over there . . . whassisname, Felix something? He's gorgeous. My god! He's having a drink with Winona Ryder.'

Finlay followed her gaze and laughed. 'That's not Winona Ryder, that's his girlfriend, Phoebe.' He raised his wine glass to them and they waved back.

'You know them then?' Juno was seriously impressed and gagging for an introduction.

'Vaguely.' Finlay shrugged, too busy tucking into his food to offer one.

Suffering from honesty overload, the conversation eased into trivia and office bitching. Together they worked their way through the rest of the wine and stuffed their faces with bangers and mash.

'I had no idea poncey places like this served good grub,' Juno enthused as she wolfed hers back, hoping her dress would still fit that evening.

Finlay chuckled. 'Well, they call the dish "herbed wild boar and water buffalo *cervelat*, twinned with olive oil *pommes purée* and a timbale of minted *petits pois*", but it's basically bangers, tatties and mushy peas.'

'So are your parents terribly rich?' she asked cheekily.

'Terribly.' He grinned, mocking her home-counties vocabulary.

Juno turned pink. 'S'weird because I always thought you were some sort of back-street Glasgow hooligan who made good academically then went bad after university.'

'Have you got a sticky label with that written on?' He forked up some fluffy, olive oil potatoes. 'I'll pop it on my forehead.'

'Sorry.' Juno blushed even more.

'No, you're right.' He laughed. 'I could have been – would have been, I guess. I was brought up in a council estate in Falkirk. My father's a welder. That's a job which involves attaching one piece of metal to another.' He grinned condescendingly.

Juno flicked a *petit pois* at him.

He ducked. 'Then he won two million on the Pools fifteen years ago. Bear in mind, that was before the Lottery ever existed. It was a fucking fortune. My father thought he could "better" us with money. I went from being practically the only bright kid who wanted to learn something at an underfunded state school, to playing truant from a stuck-up boys' boarding school in the Borders. Imagine that, if you can.

'I didn't know how to speak "posh", let alone Latin. I was bullied so much, I fought my way into detention every day with my fists because that was the only way I knew to protect myself. Calum – my brother – was already at university in England, so he didn't suffer the same culture shock. I guess that's why he's still got this working-class chip on his shoulder about getting on in life, whereas I think the world owes me a living.'

Halfway through a second bottle of wine – which Juno had only just noticed was a Pauillac and probably cost as much as a week's rent – she shuddered as though doused in cold champagne. I'm going to meet Jay tonight, she thought dizzily. I'm going on a date with him.

Finlay watched her and laughed.

'I've got to go home and tart myself up,' she told him excitedly.

'You'd better wear that dress, sugar,' he ordered. 'It makes you look like something I once used to twist myself inside out to try and fuck.'

'If you just said it made me look slim I'd be happy, but thanks.' Juno stood up and swayed. Daytime drinking always affected her badly. She could skull more beers than Barfly over a long, gassy evening, but a couple of glasses of wine during office hours made her feel as though her inner ear had gone to sleep.

'Have a coffee when you get home,' Finlay recommended, kissing her on both cheeks. 'I'll call you at your parents' next week. Find out what happened, and let you know how it's going my end.'

They regarded one another slightly drunkenly – unlikely conspirators thrown together in an underhand quest for happiness.

'Good luck,' Juno told him.

'You too.' He winked.

It was only when she was slithering around in the back of a black cab with her shopping spilling from bags beneath her as they spring-boarded off speed bumps that Juno allowed herself to close her eyes and think of Jay.

She shuddered excitedly as she realised she would be meeting him in the sexiest bar in London in just a few hours' time. Hours which would be pleasurably occupied with frothy baths, eyebrow tweaking, body-scenting, mouth washes, toenail varnish and vigorous depilation. She knew he'd stay away from the flat during that time, just as she was certain he'd be nervous, uncommunicative and moodier than a teenager later on. But he wanted her to be there, and he wanted her to be his lover. She hadn't felt this excited since Jared Williamson – the shy sixth-form girl-magnet she'd gazed at for five terms – had slipped a note into her locker asking her to the 1987 Summer Ball.

Chapter Twenty-One

The flat smelled of furniture polish and Windolene when Juno returned, because Simmy had clearly nipped in earlier for her two hours of hoovering up the floor and the vodka, dusting off the surfaces and the biscuit tin, polishing up the furniture and the loose change in the bedrooms. There were no messages on the answerphone, so she'd probably wiped those off too. Breathing in cleanliness and godlessness, Juno decided she'd have a little lie down on the sofa before she started her tartathon.

She fell asleep in front of *TFI Friday* with Poirot on her shoulder and Uboat in her lap. She awoke with *Brookside* heading for a commercial break, her eyelashes stuck together with sleep, mouth tasting like a pub's slop-tray and her body lagged like an ancient, spluttering boiler. Uboat was poised on a cushion looking dry and fed up; Poirot was perching cheerfully on top of his cage squawking at her. There was parrot poo all over the sofa.

'Christ!' Juno peered at the digital clock on the video. It was twenty to nine.

She leapt up, clutching her pounding forehead, and raced into her bedroom to pull the contents of the carrier bags out on to the floor. The dress she and Finlay had chosen was divine, but it would take her a barrel load of Courtney Love confidence and a vat of carefully applied make-up to get away with it.

'Perhaps it's too much, even for Bar Oque?' Juno dithered, glancing at the clock beside her bed. She had less than a quarter of an hour to tart up; the walk to Primrose Hill was at least ten minutes – longer if she wore the Pied à Terre six-inch gold velvet platform mules she'd bought today.

But selecting an alternative outfit would take even longer. Juno knew herself well enough to estimate the average decision time for what to wear on a hot date was generally far longer than the date itself.

To the accompaniment of The Pretenders singing 'Sassy', she put on her most dramatic party face in record time. It was only when she was applying her third coating of mascara that she remembered Jay telling her she wore too much make-up.

'Bollocks to that.' She looked at her reflection. The transformation from the red-eyed, dry-lipped liver-failure patient she had peered at pre-application, to the doe-eyed, plump-lipped temptress in front of her now, told her all she needed to know. 'I need make-up to kiss and make up with Jay. He's already had more than enough of my bare-faced cheek.'

She had no time to wash her hair, but it looked rather sexy pulled up into a tufty, sexy Zoe Ball bun, a style which slimmed her face and hid her roots. Going for it, Juno selected a pair of big, dangly earrings which she usually regarded as too outrageous to wear; they were gold Chinese symbols; one translated as 'shag', the other 'me' – Juno could never tell which way around they went. There had also been a matching pendant which read 'sideways', but she had thankfully lost it. Tacky and tasteless, Juno adored them but seldom wore them as many of her nights out on the town with the gang had a tendency to end up in late-night Chinatown restaurants. A particularly unpleasant experience in Wong Kee's had put her off them for months.

Doubting that Jay spoke fluent Mandarin, she plugged them in and embarked upon the lengthy process of levering, wedging and pouring herself into her outrageous dress.

She didn't have long to contemplate her reflection in the mirror before she set out, but what she saw filled her with excited, anticipatory confidence. What man could resist?

Sometimes when Juno had very little time to get ready

for a big night out, the end result felt far better than after hours of meticulous preparation and preening. She doubted it looked any different, but it *felt* better. When changing in a hurry, particularly into a brand new outfit, the adrenaline of urgency and confidence-boost of newness combined to give her ego a mini-fix, and she saw a prettier, sexier version of herself in the mirror; if she dressed slowly and carefully, checking every angle, every facial expression, smoothing every hair, seeing herself as a man would, she had plenty of time to spot every imperfection.

Juno had always loved dressing up – as a small child she had raided her mother's wardrobe and jewellery before she could walk. She knew she was a lazy stylist; she wore her tops too tight because it meant they didn't need ironing, and she didn't own a pair of socks that matched, but she was a natural born exhibitionist. Her clothes weren't always the best fit, or colour-co-ordinated or complete with their full quota of buttons, but they were never dowdy.

Tonight's ensemble was pretty sophisticated by her standards, but Juno adored it nonetheless. The dress was superficially demure – a one-shouldered, figure-hugging cream number which was probably intended to reach mid-calf but fell to Juno's ankles. Cut to make a man look like a woman, it made Juno's buxom curves resemble Jessica Rabbit's. Inside, it was discreetly boned to create the impression of a hand-span waist, Jayne Mansfield hips and pneumatic cleavage. The effect was Anna Nicole Smith stunning. With her gold mules and earrings, oodles of bangles and favourite antique cream lace jacket, she felt sex-kitten glamorous.

About to leave her room looking like a tip, Juno had a sudden, presumptuous tidy up, sprayed herself from head to foot in Escape, sprayed the room with 'Amour' aromatherapy air freshener, sniffed her duvet to check it was passably fresh and plumped her pillows invitingly. Then, forgetting that both Poirot and Uboat were out, the television on and the answerphone off, she dashed towards Primrose Hill.

The wolf whistles and horn beeps which followed her down

Haverstock Hill were all the encouragement she needed. She paused at the Midland cashpoint and smiled to herself as a man fell over a dog lead as he turned around to eyeball her. *Hello* sex appeal! She pressed the button corresponding to £50 on the screen. Scrap sex kitten – we're talking *lurve* vixen here. Watch out, Jay boy, I feel carnal tonight!

SORRY – YOU HAVE INSUFFICIENT FUNDS IN
YOUR ACCOUNT TO
COMPLETE THIS TRANSACTION.
PLEASE SELECT AN ALTERNATIVE AMOUNT
OR PRESS <CANCEL>
TO RETURN YOUR CARD

'You what!' Juno tried £40, then £20, then £10. All were rejected with the same pompous, impersonal message. She suddenly longed for a cash machine that spoke her language – something like 'Sorry, babe, you're broke again.' Furious, she ignored the disgruntled queue behind her and demanded a balance enquiry.

'Oh, honestly,' she grumbled to the woman behind. 'Isn't that typical? I have almost five hundred quid in my account and the machine won't let me have any. I'm afraid it's faulty, everyone.' She pressed to get her card back.

'You're five hundred pounds overdrawn, love,' the woman told her helpfully. 'Didn't you notice the D after the sum?'

'Huh?' Juno spun around to the machine again, but it was already poking her card out of the slot like a jeering tongue.

Cashless, and twenty minutes late, she marched angrily towards the legendary Bar Oque. She supposed she had spent rather a lot over the previous few weeks – especially now that she was paying rent to Sean as well as half of the mortgage, insurance and standing charges on the Clapham house. Drat! She had forgotten to call the estate agent's again. Double drat! She stopped directly outside the discreet, clustered front door of Bar Oque and groaned as she realised the money she had spent with Finlay today – most of it on her Switch card – wouldn't have registered yet, so she was even more overdrawn.

Because it was a warm night, the drinkers at the popular little bar were spilling out on to the street, gathering around the few dark red wrought-iron tables placed there, leaning against the walls or just getting in the way of passers-by as they clustered in gaggles and yattered over the loud, raunchy music. Bar Oque had once played nothing but muted Vivaldi and Bach over its wall-mounted, gold-framed speakers, but nowadays it was better known, had a brasher, younger, funkier crowd, and pandered to them with classic make-out tracks or the latest indie ballads.

From her vantage point in the street, Juno peered through the open doors to see if she could spot Jay – knowing that once she was inside she would be buried in a mass of armpits and shirt fronts because she was so short. His golden-treacle hair had to be pretty recognisable from here.

But she could see nothing except trendy buzz-cuts, tufty buns, citrus-coloured fabrics and exposed, tanned flesh jostling together in a hot, sweaty orgy of laughter, chat and eye-meets. The crowd was impossibly self-confident and glamorous.

And then she saw him, leaning back against the bar, sipping a pint of bitter – a drink currently as unfashionable as a Piña Colada. His eyebrows were beetling together as he scanned the room with those big, long-lashed eyes. He was wearing a Yorkshire cricket cap, a Leeds United away shirt, white jeans and vast desert boots with red laces on his big feet. Juno's breath was punched from her chest as she regarded him for a minute as she would a stranger, realising afresh how stand-back good-looking he was, how unbearably handsome she'd thought he was when they'd first ever met in some god-awful club in Camden.

It wasn't Jay she was looking at. It was John.

For a split second, she wondered if he was drinking in Bar Oque by some quirky coincidence of fate. She scanned the room again for Jay, but her mind was already working overtime. 'J' was John. So ludicrously obvious. It simply hadn't occurred to her – John was a techno-buff who e-mailed everyone, but she supposed he could just as easily fax from his whizzy computer at work. And his spelling was atrocious. 'Behavior.' It hadn't been an American spelling, it had been a mis-spelling.

Juno couldn't believe how debilitating disappointment could be. She wanted to lie down on the dirty pavement at her muled feet and adopt a foetal position. She wanted to close her eyes and not open them again until she was deep beneath her duvet in smothered privacy, ready to bawl them out. Jay hadn't wanted to meet her after all, hadn't asked her on a date, didn't want to be 'lovers even?'.

She contemplated dashing home before John spotted her. She was totally overdressed and underprepared. She hadn't seen him in two months, hadn't taken his calls for over a fortnight. But even though she knew it was weak and wet, she couldn't bring herself to turn and flee home. And a lot of the reason for that, she suddenly realised, was because Jay might have returned there, still hating her, just wanting her out of the flat and out of his life. The realisation was horrific after two days of such giddy self-delusion.

With a leaden heart, she walked inside and dived through the clusters of rowdy drinkers to the quieter end of the bar where John was standing. The speakers were appropriately belting out Garbage's 'Stupid Girl'.

At first he watched her approach with the admiring, las-civious look he would afford any attractive female stranger, a wide, toothy smile spreading like spilt milk across his face. Then he recognised her with a loud – and unpleasantly cocky – wolf whistle. Far from feeling flattered, Juno wished more than anything that she was wearing her old jeans and a t-shirt.

'Well, I'll be buggered,' he chuckled, swivelling around to put his pint on the gilded bar and then opening his arms wide. 'You look fantastic, our Juno!'

'I'm going on somewhere afterwards,' she improvised quickly, side-stepping his attempt to hug her. 'I can't stay long.'

'That's a shame.' His eyes trailed up and down her corseted curves in leisurely admiration. 'I've booked us a table at your favourite restaurant – I know it's a bit presumptuous and that, but I was hoping you'd turn up tonight, seeing as it's close to home.'

Juno gaped at him. 'You booked a table at a restaurant?'

'S'what I said.' His creamy Skipton accent was at its most Hovis-and-flat-caps endearing. 'I had to ring them last bloody week to get the reservation and even then they could only offer me a table three hours after dinnertime. But I know you like it there, flower.' John always wanted his evening meal at seven. Any later and he developed stomach cramps.

Juno was thrown for a moment – her favourite restaurant was a tiny bistro in Soho which was never booked up, but she was too amazed by John's admission to dwell on it.

'But you hate restaurants.' She blinked in astonishment. 'You used to say going to a curry house once a month was eating out regularly.'

'That's 'cos I loved your home cooking so much.' He beckoned a barman over with a proffered tenner. 'No poncey Michelin-starred wanker could ever beat it.'

'C'mon.' Juno was instantly on the offensive. 'We ate takeaways almost every night.'

He chuckled delightedly. 'Aye, it's good to see you, Juno flower. Pint of cider, is it?'

'No, I'll have an orange juice and soda, thanks. I'm not drinking.'

John laughed uproariously. 'Good one, that. You always were a funny lass.'

'Orange juice and soda,' Juno told the approaching barman.

'And another pint of this,' John added, pointing to his half full pint of bitter. 'Plus two bags of nuts and a couple of those packs of crisps over there.' He nodded towards a box of pretentiously labelled 'Vinnegan's deep-fried celeriac and olive chips' before turning back to her. 'You haven't seriously given up drinking?'

He got out a packet of Marlboro from his bum pocket. 'Don't tell me you've packed these in too?'

Juno's hoover bag lungs were weak with exhaustion after her walk.

'Yup.' She watched his reaction, awaiting a supercilious estimate of how long she'd last. 'It's funny how little you miss things you once thought you couldn't live without.' She flashed him a pointed smile.

But he simply looked impressed, a little 'well, I'll be damned' smile of his own tugging the corners of his mouth as he scratched beneath his cricket cap, readjusted it on his head then put the packet back in his pocket without taking one.

Juno was slightly disappointed as she'd been planning to breathe in his second-hand smoke for a quick fix. No one nearby appeared to be smoking – they were all trendy, gym-mad health freaks on Ecstasy. Juno's untoned legs were feeling weak from just a short walk. She glanced around for one of the gold-seated, wrought-iron bar stools but they were all either taken or being jealously guarded while the occupant was in the loo.

Bar Oque was as flamboyant and stylish as the drawing room of a seventeenth-century French château, its blood red walls covered in ornate, peeling gilt picture frames, its high ceilings dripping with chandeliers, its oil-slick marble floor covered with sumptuous dark blue and green velvet sofas and distressed, gilded tables. The press were always raving about it, but it had recently started to suffer from being just too damned cool and trendy. The City Suits with their loud ties and even louder champagne-ordering voices had arrived to sniff out the gaggles of beautiful young things who drank there. Now it was just another loud, cliquey twenty-something haunt. The men were too brash, the women too young.

'Lovely this place, in't it?' John said awkwardly.

'A bit showy.' Juno wrinkled her nose.

'We can go somewhere else, if you like?' he offered eagerly, turning to glance at the pint-pulling barman.

'It's all right, I'm only staying for one drink anyway.' She had no intention of tramping off to some dingy pub with him.

It was weird being with him again – so familiar yet so awkward. Juno found herself assessing him as he paid for the drinks and crisps. He was so tall. Being around Jez, Duncan, Sean, and most recently Jay had made her accustomed to shorter men – still far taller than her, but nothing to John. Euan and Horse were over six feet, but Jarvis Cocker skinny. John had shoulders as broad as David Seaman, wide wrists, big hands and feet. He seemed a species apart. She had always loved the fact he was so big, he'd made her feel fragile and doll-like by comparison.

'I've put on a bit of weight lately.' He caught her looking at him, and turned to pass her the orange soda.

'You look okay.' She shrugged indifferently, guessing he'd been on a beer-and-barsnacks diet since Double D's departure. She glanced around for a stool again.

'And you look just sensational.' He gave her his most roguish smile, keeping hold of her glass as she took it. They stood wrestling for possession for a moment, looking into one another's eyes, Juno frowning, John smiling.

She had almost forgotten how blue his eyes were. They were ludicrously blue – like the colour of Angel Islington on a Monopoly board. So much so that she had been convinced for the first few weeks they'd dated that his contact lenses were tinted, even though he'd adamantly denounced this as 'poofy'. She'd searched his bathroom for evidence of them the first night she'd stayed over at his all-lads Lavender Hill flat, but had just found disposable clear ones. It was only when he'd shown her photographs of himself as a young boy that she'd finally believed him.

In adulthood, he still looked so like those photographs it was uncanny. The body had grown rangy and muscular, but the face was still strangely wide-eyed and innocent – not in Finlay's beautiful, corrupted Cupid way, but in a thick-lashed, big-eyed 'I know not what I do' way. It was why he could get away with so much without arousing suspicion. It was why he had been able to shag Double D all those weeks behind her back.

Juno narrowed her eyes at the thought and won possession of the glass, slugging back some orange soda. It tasted revoltingly healthy. She wished she hadn't come in. Seeing him again was such an intense emotion-kicker it was almost physically painful.

'Peanuts?' He offered her a packet.

'No, thanks,' she said frostily, suddenly spotting a bar stool being vacated behind him. An experienced bar-goer, Juno recognised the need to move quickly. A pack of hyenas was already gathering on the other side of the stool as its departing occupant shrugged on her jacket. A young, gym-freak fashion victim was edging in for the kill from square leg, another had spotted the movement with eagle eyes and was lurking at first slip.

Juno lunged.

Thinking she was making some sort of spontaneous romantic move, John opened his arms and gasped, 'I've missed you too, Squidgypud.'

'Get out of my way, you prat!' she wailed, ducking under his arm and grabbing the barstool seconds before the fashion victim. Unfortunately the previous occupant was only halfway off and crashed into the bar as Juno whipped it away.

'Sorry!' she gasped, keeping a tight grip on her bounty.

The girl gave her a dirty look. So did the fashion victim and her rival. So did John when she dragged her catch back to him.

'You called me a prat,' he said with deeply insulted pride.

'You called me Squidgypud.' Juno positioned her stool at a safe distance from him and hopped on.

'You used to love me calling you that.'

'I used to love you enough to put up with you calling me that,' she corrected, finding that sitting down in the dress had the unfortunate side effect of cutting off the circulation to her lower body and preventing her from breathing in more than two molecules of air at a time. The hidden boning clamped her ribs to her lungs like a Heimlich manoeuvre and jacked her boobs up so high, she could almost rest her chin on them.

As luck would have it, this agonising posture seemed to

make John instantly forget the 'prat' comment as he gawked excitedly at the twin orbs rising in front of him in total, awed silence for several seconds, big blue eyes filling up with dilating pupils.

Juno liked the feeling of power and sipped her orange soda demurely. I'm going to make the faithless bastard sweat a bit, she decided cheerfully.

She glanced at his watch. Half-past nine. She'd stay until ten, she decided.

'Like I say, you look totally gorgeous tonight, flower,' he told her breasts lovingly.

'Thanks.' Juno longingly eyed the peanuts on the bar.

'Gorgeous,' he breathed, gazing into her eyes. Then a big, knowing grin spread over his face. 'And you're wearing the earrings I gave you!'

Damn! Juno wished she'd had the foresight to take them off before she'd come in.

'They go with my shoes.' She waggled her mules so that they kicked his shins. 'I don't have much gold jewellery – it's not really my taste.' She wrinkled her nose as though implying it was rather gaudy and ostentatious.

'Don't you?' He looked genuinely surprised, and mildly hurt. 'You should have said, our Juno. What about that watch I got you?'

'Never wear it,' she said in her best throwaway, Kristin Scott-Thomas manner.

'And the brooch shaped like a microphone?'

'Lost it.' She shrugged.

'By heck, I'm sorry.' His thick eyebrows met above his Mel Gibson eyes. 'I thought you liked them, flower. I spent ages choosing them.'

Juno felt a pang of guilt, but said nothing. Instead she shrugged airily and concentrated on breathing, which was getting tougher and tougher as the dress cut into her chest like a strait jacket.

John was smiling at her again, the cocksure look of victory re-establishing itself on his tanned face.

'So you got my fax.' He moved closer. 'And what's more you came. I didn't think you would.'

'And I wasn't sure who "J" was.' She slid back on the barstool until she was dangling off the rear. Sometimes the truth made the saddest of cheap jibes, she realised.

'I thought I'd be supping pints all night on my own.' He adjusted his cricket cap again, then brought his forearm down to rest on her shoulder.

'You were confident enough to book a restaurant table.' Juno shrugged it off.

'Yeah, well, I thought I could pick someone up here if you didn't turn up,' he joked nervily, laughing at his own gag as always.

Juno dead-panned him to see how he'd react.

'No, I didn't really!' he retracted slightly desperately, hastily seeking to change the subject. 'You still knock around with that mad gang of yours?'

'You know me, "all I do is keep the beat and the bad company".'

He laughed in recognition. 'Dire Straits. "Romeo and Juliet". 1980.' It was a favourite game of his – quote the lyrics, name the tune. The songs had to be pre-1990 and mainstream, but he was a whizz at it. Juno had once revelled in testing him. Now she realised it was just one of her many John-indulgences; things she'd done from gratitude simply because he'd loved her, made her feel safe, been a fully fledged boyfriend after all those years of single insecurity.

'Why did you send a fax to the office?' she asked suddenly. 'Why not just e-mail me like you always used to? You dropped more Es than East 17.'

'I lost your address, flower,' he groaned, rolling his eyes in genuine frustration. 'I lost most of my mates' e-mail addresses. My computer went down on me last month.'

'Sounds compromising.' Juno gritted her teeth. 'Did you respect it afterwards?'

He didn't get the joke. He seldom had. 'It was a nightmare. The work that's crashed is bloody job-threatening, and I've lost all my personal stuff from the database. I had to look your office fax number up in a back copy of one of your magazines that was lying around the house.'

'You still read my columns?' Juno felt an involuntary belly-lurch of affection.

'No, I've just not tidied up since you left, flower.'

She wanted to punch him, the tactless sod.

'Stop calling me "flower",' she muttered sourly. '"Don't need a sword to cut through flowers".' Damn! She was playing his game again.

'John Lennon. "Whatever Gets You Through The Night". 1974,' he chuckled, then eyed her excitedly. 'Give me another.'

Juno lifted her chin defiantly. '"How it hurts – deep inside, when your love has cut you down to size".'

He thought for a moment, fingers tapping against his mouth, then smiled in recognition. 'Queen. "It's a Hard Life". 1984.'

She gazed at him levelly. 'How can you do this to me, when I love you so much? How can you kick me out and move her into your heart?'

Scratching beneath his cricket cap, eyes scrunched in concentration, he pondered for a long time before shaking his head in defeat. 'You've got me there, lass. Is it the Police?'

She shook her head, 'Juno Glenn. 19 Elford Avenue, Clapham. This April.'

For just a brief moment, his boyish face looked contrite. That was as good as it got before he smiled resiliently, once more on the guileless charm offensive – very offensive, Juno found.

'I was glad those magazines you write for were still in the house.' He slurped his pint and leant his thigh against hers, warm and familiar. 'It made me feel you were still there – part of you, anyroad. Debbie was hopeless at housework. She didn't tidy, she redistributed. She'd just shuffle all the little piles of stuff into one big pile so I couldn't find anything, like a one-woman JCB. I kept finding myself missing your junk everywhere, flower. At least I knew where I was with that.'

'Don't call me "flower",' she snapped, realising that hearing him bitching about Double D, however well meant, hurt too much to endure. It was like listening to a deaf orchestra cranking out Stravinsky's Rite of Spring for a charity benefit concert. Well meant, but agonising nonetheless.

John was rubbing her arm now, his huge, square hand enfolding the butter-soft flesh between armpit and elbow. It felt nice; Juno didn't immediately pull away, but she was still determined to pull ahead.

'So you two broke up over *housework*?' She attacked his innate sexism – which she'd once found so sexy – with familiar venom. 'Wake up and smell the coffee, John. Because you will do soon, believe me – and it'll be hot and scalding and poured all over your privates. Housework is like any work – there's a sexual discrimination bill in place these days. You won't find Cherie Blair massaging Tony's piles into place.'

'She left me because I couldn't stop talking about you,' he sighed.

'You what?' Juno wrinkled her forehead in disbelief, not certain if she'd heard him right over the bar noise.

'I love you, our Juno,' he suddenly spluttered, blue eyes blinking so furiously he was clearly battling against either conjunctivitis or tears. 'I fancied Debbie all the time but I didn't love her. I never loved her, I can see that now. I loved you, flower. I didn't always want you around, but I loved you then and it's never stopped. I've tried to stop it, believe me. I've tried not to call you at midnight. I've found myself pacing round that phone willing myself not to use it, just like you used to with the fridge.' He dipped his head and laughed fondly. 'I know you, love, and I miss you.'

Then he kissed her, and to Juno's eternal shame she let him, on and on. She let him because she wanted to remember what it felt like. She let him because she needed the reassurance of that familiar, thick tongue exploring her mouth. She let him because he wanted to. She let that delighted, plunging dolphin tongue dance with hers because it showed that John – big, brawny John whom she no longer wanted – had chosen her over Double D. And she let him because Jay wouldn't kiss her now if she paid him.

She pulled away finally. It didn't matter that her heart still banged fast, her hands registered an itch to touch his skin, her groin turned over and over like a car engine on a cold morning. She might not be entirely cured of John yet, but she now had a disease whose symptoms far eclipsed these.

She had caught Jay-fever. And the fact that this moody, uncommunicative, sexy New Yorker was the only reason she was in Bar Oque tonight allowed her to pull away dispassionately. A fortnight ago she'd have kissed John back with desperation, frantic to prove that she was sexier than Double D. A fortnight ago she'd have tried to kiss her way back into two years of laughing and snapping, yawning and scrapping, domesticity and romance. She'd have done it for old times' sake, not for better or for worse, forsaking all others; it would have been a litmus test to see how much better or bitter she was still feeling. Tonight, kissing him was just an embarrassing mistake. She'd known Jay a week but he'd stolen her heart like a street mugger, snatching and running, not caring about the destruction he'd left behind. And she, meanwhile, had kicked him in the balls, sprayed his face with Mace and flashed a laser pointer in his eyes to show him that she wasn't vulnerable. Oh, no, not Juno.

'Like I say, I'm so glad you came tonight, flower.' John's liquorice pupils and pink, animated lips showed how turned on he was. He'd always been hopelessly easy to please. 'I miss you so much.'

'So much you forget my e-mail address after two months?'

His eyes darted away for a second.

'So why fax me at work?' she asked matter-of-factly. 'Why not at Sean's flat?'

'Didn't want that bloody Yank reading it, that's why.' His voice was a pastiche of northern disapproval and his blue eyes flashed warily. 'The one who's always answering the phone when I call. Who is he then?'

Juno looked away. Thinking about Jay made her face burn and her dress tighten so much against her chest that she could almost hear her ribs creak like a tall boat in a storm.

'Some American photographer Sean's swapped flats with for six months.' She shrugged casually, lungs almost rupturing.

'You mean, it's just you and him living there?' John was appalled at the idea.

'Yes.' Something weird occurred to her. 'Are you saying you've spoken to Jay more than once?'

'Is that his name? *Jay?*' John sneered. 'Bit poofy, innit?'

'You've talked to him on the phone more than once?' Juno persisted, ignoring his jealousy.

'Yeah – a few times this week.' He nodded. 'I was trying to ask you out tonight, but he's a bit bloody sharp, isn't he? Just says "She's not here" and puts the phone down. That's why I had to send you a fax at work in the end.'

So far as Juno was aware, Jay had only spoken to John on the night of her birthday. He certainly hadn't passed on any other messages. She had been in most nights that week, sulking in her bedroom, had heard the phone ring several times and let him answer it. Come to think of it, she had been slightly surprised that none of the calls were for her. It had also struck her as odd that she had received so many messages on her voice mail at work, yet no one had called her at home. Was Jay deliberately blanking her calls to spite her?

'So why did you come tonight?' John was asking seductively, his thighs brushing against her knees as he closed in further.

She wanted to scream: Because I thought that fax was from Jay, you bastard! The one who drops your calls, doesn't pass on messages, doesn't care about me enough to bother; the one who made me swear not to love him and then made love to me like he had a price on his head.

'I wanted to know what was happening with the sale of the house,' she said lamely, twisting her knees away from the pressure. Then she remembered the second call he'd made on her birthday, that stumbling, post-pub message which had interrupted the long, weird stare-off between her and Jay. 'And I thought you might bring my birthday present along with you.'

'Sorry, flower, I left it behind.' His eyes didn't quite meet hers.

'You didn't get me anything, did you?' She laughed bitterly. 'That message was just an excuse to get me to Clapham.'

For a moment he was all big blue-eyed misunderstood umbrage. Then he laughed too. 'I'm a transparent bastard, aren't I?'

'No, you're actually quite a dense bastard, John.'

He stopped laughing, cleared his throat awkwardly and downed the remainder of his first pint.

'No one's been to see round the house for a couple of weeks, to be honest.' He pulled an apologetic face, sucking froth from his upper lip. 'I think the agents are losing interest.'

'Meanwhile I'm paying the interest every month,' she said with stiff-jawed irritation.

'I'll give them a call on Monday, flower,' he soothed. 'Chivvy them on a bit.'

The bar was literally heaving with people now – Juno's barstool was rocked around like a kingpin as they jostled to get to the gilded bar, knocking John against her knees so often he was almost straddling her lap, muscular white denim thighs rucking up the fabric of her dress. She could smell his aftershave and feel the heat coming off his body. Suddenly he was jostled so hard from behind that he leant in against her, almost knocking her off her stool. He instantly took his chance to envelop her in his arms and press her to his warm, protective chest. The sensation did nothing for her at all. It was just a body against hers. The speakers overhead were thumping out 'Stuck In The Middle With You'.

She pulled hastily away and glanced down at John's wrist-watch. It wasn't yet ten.

He grabbed her hand and squeezed it tight. 'You're not going already, are you?'

Juno looked at his face – open, expressive, wide-eyed with emotion. His sporadic, clumsy attempts at reconciliation were by turns appealing and infuriating. This one was by far the most concerted yet, but it affected her no differently from the others – those pleading, husky-voiced calls late at night asking her to come over. They angered her, saddened her, tempted her. But not enough for her to react with passion one way or another.

He was the ultimate kid in a sweet shop – wanting everything and throwing a tantrum when he realised his pocket money had run out. He never played mind games, but his unthinking hedonism made him the sort of man who broke hearts without even knowing it. John was someone to whom 'playing it cool' meant calling a girl twenty minutes after *Baywatch* rather than as the titles went up, yet equally he would forget to phone her entirely if a match went into extra time or a mate called round with a four-pack and a Chinese takeaway. On Christmas Day he would give a girlfriend a thousand kisses and a hand-made card, but then he would forget her birthday a week later. He was lazy, easily distracted and careless.

'I can't forgive you yet, John.' Juno pulled her hand away from his. 'It still hurts too much.'

'You said "yet",' he breathed. 'Does that mean you will one day?'

'What?' Juno couldn't hear him over the background din.

He repeated it as loudly as an *Evening Standard* vendor announcing the West End Final. Several people close by turned round to stare.

It was hardly the ideal setting for a quiet heart-to-heart. They were surrounded by hot sweaty bodies queuing at the bar, the babble of conversation meant that they had to shout at one another, and the jukebox was now belting out Oasis's 'Don't Look Back In Anger'.

My life is conducted to a backing track of unpleasantly pertinent pop music, Juno realised sadly. Next time she met up with an ex, she'd take her personal stereo and a Gloria Gaynor tape.

'I've got to go.' She looked around for her bag.

'Stay just a few more minutes,' he begged. 'Or come to The Ratz. You can choose whatever you like off the menu. You were always badgering me to take you there.'

'The Ratz?' Juno looked up in surprise. An unpleasant memory had popped up from the Pandora's Box of her mind, the place she kept all those best-forgotten nights of tears and torture as she started to realise her relationship with John was over.

'Yes, I know you love it.' He puffed out his chest proudly, convinced he'd done well. 'Like I said earlier, it was bloody hard to get a table but I wouldn't take no for an answer. It's my treat. I'm paying. Please, Juno. I've never been there before.' He was like a small boy begging to be taken to Thorpe Park.

The Ratz was one of the trendiest restaurants in North London. A pastiche of its near-namesake, it was a brattish, snobby, fash-trash haven of good food and silly dress codes, adored by young media luminaries and spoilt trustafarians alike. Juno loathed it.

She gazed at him in awe, wondering how he could have got it so cheerfully, thoughtlessly wrong. It was Sean who adored The Ratz with its rude door staff, fuck-off waiters, ultra-cool diners and gorgeous food, not her.

'Oh, John, you don't even remember, do you?'

The hyenas were already gathering behind Juno's stool as she struggled to stand up in the posture-clamping dress which now seemed to have moulded her body into a permanent seated position.

'Remember what?'

'Sean's birthday in March?' She tried to jog his memory, let him guiltily second-guess her accusation.

'March . . .' He scrunched up his face as he thought back, then shook his head in defeat.

Yes, fucking March! Juno wanted to scream. Literally in your case, seeing as you were doing so much of it at the time. And not with me.

To the frustration of the seat hyenas, she leant back on the bar-stool, Dave Allen-style, and started her anecdote with easygoing charm, although she had to project her voice more than she'd have liked.

'Triona had booked a big table at a restaurant . . .' she pressed him gently.

'That was good of her.' He nodded eagerly.

'And we were really late . . .'

'Sounds normal.' He touched her cheek lovingly.

'It was a big surprise – Sean was led in blindfold at nine and found all his loved ones sitting round a table holding champagne glasses in the air.'

'Oh, yeah, yeah . . . it's coming back to me now,' he lied unconvincingly, snorkelling up his pint and glancing at his watch.

'You remember it then?'

'Of course I do, lass,' he agreed, stroking her arm. 'Do you want to come for a meal at The Ratz now? We can talk about this there. Reminisce.'

'Do you really think you stand a better chance of getting in this time then?' she snarled.

'Huh?' he looked puzzled.

'It was The Ratz that night, John. Sean's birthday party was in The Ratz.'

'No!' He seemed genuinely astonished. 'You must be mistaken, flower. I swear I've never eaten there.'

'You didn't eat with us then,' she muttered flatly.

'Huh?'

'When we got to the restaurant they wouldn't let you in because you weren't wearing a tie.' She looked at his Leeds United shirt with blurred eyes, Packard Bell logo coming in and out of focus as she struggled against the tears.

'Wouldn't they?'

'They insist that customers wear ties.' She stared at the tufts of hair emerging from the V-necked nylon. 'It's a bit of a stupid joke, along with women not wearing trousers and no one being allowed in with sunglasses on their heads. I was so worried about making it on time I'd forgotten to check if you were wearing one.'

'And I wasn't?' He was the perfect, dumbfounded fall guy to her story.

'No.' She shook her head. 'You were wearing that t-shirt where Taz the dirt devil is saying "Dirty Harry made my sandwiches".'

'God, I loved that t-shirt!' His eyes widened in delighted recognition. 'Whatever happened to it?'

'You pretended to be really insulted that they wouldn't let you in without a tie,' Juno's jaw was aching from the effort not to cry, 'but you insisted I go in without you as it was Sean's birthday. You said you'd go back to Clapham and change into your dinner jacket and dickie bow, then cab it back just to show the pompous bastards.'

'I did?' He looked impressed with himself. 'Pretty political that.'

'But you never did come back.' She ignored someone to her left asking if her barstool was free. 'And when I got home after midnight, you weren't in the house either. I stayed up for hours, thinking you'd been mugged or had some sort of accident. When you rolled in at two, you were too pissed to explain where you'd been.

'The next day you told me you'd popped into the Windmill for a quick pint before you went back home to change.' She looked up at the ceiling in an attempt to contain the tears. 'That you'd bumped into some mates, got talking and not noticed the time. That you'd ended up at a party in Battersea.'

The hyenas were starting to listen in now, distracted from their barstool quest as they became absorbed in Juno's tale, relishing the prospect of a domestic.

John cleared his throat anxiously. 'Did I?'

'Yes.' Juno gritted her teeth. 'But you hadn't been at a party at all. Debbie lived in Battersea then, didn't she? You'd been with her.'

He hung his head in shame.

'You don't even remember that night, do you?'

'Well, not the restaurant bit, no,' he said with blistering honesty. 'Now you mention it, I do recall some bits. I remember that wanker telling me I had to wear a tie. Shit, I should have worn one tonight, shouldn't I, flower? Stupid of me to forget.'

Juno looked up at the ceiling again, by now familiar with its glittering chandeliers.

'I'm sorry, John, but I can't go to The Ratz with you tonight,' she said flatly, dropping her head to look him in his little boy face. 'Like the song says, "I can't go on just holding on to ties".'

'Phil Collins, "Separate Lives", 1985,' he recognised sadly.

'Dear John.' She sighed, kissing him on the cheek. 'Dear John . . .' She smoothed down the gorgeous dress, turned on the high, fuck-me heels bought especially for 'J', and clattered out of the bar.

Chapter Twenty-Two

In her desperation not to go straight back to the flat, Juno tried to take some cash out of the hole in the wall with her credit card – despite the astronomical interest rates – but realised at the last minute that she didn't know the pin number, and that she was already over her credit limit anyway. She wished she'd had the nerve to borrow some money from John before her hasty exit from Bar Oque. Scrabbling through her bag as she teetered up to Chalk Farm tube station on her mules, she found she had three pound coins, a handful of loose change and her monthly travel pass. The station clock told her it was still only five past ten.

She caught a south-bound train fully intending to go into the West End and wait for Ally and Duncan's mob in Mezzo. She could just about afford a mineral water. Once they all turned up from the theatre, she was certain she could borrow some cash off one of them, and squeezing an extra chair in at the table wouldn't be much trouble. Finlay was bound to want to see her in her glad rags, and she was dying to know what they all thought of him. Ally had, admittedly, been a little surprised when Juno had called – rather drunkenly – from the Nero Club that afternoon to tell her that she couldn't come to the theatre after all and was sending a complete stranger in her place.

'But who is he, Juno?' she'd asked, baby China gurgling in the background as she spoke. 'Is he the one from Immedia you're always telling us looks like Ewan McGregor? The one Lydia gets on so well with?'

'Yes, and I want to know what you think of him because – '
Juno had been gagging to tell her that he was in fact madly in
love with Lydia, and planning to try and win her, and wasn't it
romantic? but for once in her loose-tongued life she'd exercised
discretion. It was about the only exercise she'd had all week.
'Because I think you and Duncan will really like him,' she'd
finished lamely.

Ally had laughed, as sweet and forgiving as ever. Most friends
would flip, complain that they had bent over backwards to get
another ticket, that they had other people they could invite
along, thank you very much. Most friends would demand to
know what she was doing that evening instead. But Ally was
the most easy-going person Juno knew, and simply agreed, albeit
with a baffled sigh.

'Okay, tell him to meet us in the Cottesloe bar at seven,
wearing a pink carnation and carrying *Exchange And Mart*.
Although if he really does look like Ewan M, I guess he'll
be easy enough to spot. You do lead the most complicated
life, Juno.'

Gazing at the overhead adverts opposite her in the tube
carriage, she wondered how they were getting on, how her
newfound, foppish, wastrel friend was coping amidst the thirty-
something sophistication of a couples night at the theatre.
The incongruous image was difficult to conjure up, but Juno
suddenly had a mental picture of Rab C. Nesbitt making a guest
appearance in an episode of *Melrose Place*.

A minute later, she jumped off at Camden Town as she also
remembered she owed all of them bar Finlay at least twenty
pounds – and that she had promised him she would try and
make Jay her lover tonight. She knew which was the greatest
debt. Juno was always running out of cash and borrowing it,
and always paid people back – eventually. The problem was
that she tended to remember what she owed to whom only
when she needed to borrow more. By contrast, she had never
before promised to try and make someone fall in love with her
on borrowed time.

Juno was always changing her mind – and consequently

changing platforms – at Camden Town. She'd nicknamed it her boob tube station because she so regularly realised the error of her ways there. She trudged up the familiar, grubby steps, through the clubbers greeting one another by the central information boards and across to the Edgware platform.

Ignoring the attentions of a flirtatious drunk, she sat on a wooden bench, closed her eyes and wondered whether Jay would be at the flat. Over the past two days she'd spent so much time mooning around thinking he fancied her – assuming he was too shy to face her before their 'date', admiring his incredible self-control for keeping out of the way until then – that she'd had a reality by-pass. He'd just been avoiding her. He was still truculent, secretive, moody Jay Mulligan who'd been in the country just one week, had tidied up the flat and turned her life upside down while he was at it.

Sitting in a tube carriage which smelled of doner kebabs and spilled lager, she picked up a discarded *ES* magazine and leafed through to her horoscope.

'Your house of love is in Uranus this week,' she read, then sagged back in her seat, muttering, 'You can say that again.'

As she came out of Belsize Park station and walked towards the pedestrian crossing, she could see all the couples sitting outside Café Flo on the opposite pavement, leaning together across guttering candles as they talked and laughed and held hands. She wondered how many of them were on first dates. Were they nervous and eager to impress, babbling a little too much about themselves, asking too many questions, wondering excitedly what it would be like to kiss and touch and be touched by the person opposite whose body was still only an imagined harbinger of pleasure? Did they think their date was a hunk or a nerd, a babe or the back end of a bus?

Pressing the 'Wait' button, Juno leant against the traffic light and felt her eyes mist over as she wished that tonight had been her first date with Jay. She wanted to be watching him across a flickering candle on a pavement table, listening to him talk and babble and ask questions, secretly yearning for him to make a move.

Juno suddenly realised she wanted him to babble to her more than anything. She wanted him to touch her skin again, wanted to taste his tongue again, to slide a bed-time arm across his moist, warm, post-lust chest and fall asleep beside him again; but more than that, she wanted him to babble to her.

A sharp beeping made her jump as she realised the pedestrian crossing was showing green and that a whole host of people was surging across Haverstock Hill ahead of her, anxious to catch the final showing of the new Almodóvar at Screen on the Hill.

As she listlessly crossed the road after them, she wondered why she had told none of her friends the truth about what had really happened with Jay. It would make a classic Juno anecdote. She had an uneasy feeling it was because whenever she shared her love-life with her friends, it somehow cheapened and weakened it. And Jay was no joke, as her disastrous set in Tufnell Park on Wednesday had proven. Perhaps that's why she had behaved so crazily with him. On the very first night they'd slept together, he had said, 'Don't fall in love with me.' And Juno was a girl who reacted badly to being told what not to do. It tended to have the opposite effect.

As she trailed distractedly past the tables outside Café Flo, she eyed a group of men and decided she should develop a new crush, try to fall in love with a complete stranger, not a taciturn, secretive American who hated her while sharing the same bathroom. One of the men eyed her back appreciatively. Chunky, funky, dressed like a club promoter and built like a spin bowler, he had cheeky brown eyes and a pudding basin haircut which made him look like a medieval knave. He was certainly worth a passing smile. Juno mustered her most radiant beamer, received a blinding spread of ivories in return, then almost broke into a sprint as she spotted who he was drinking with. Sitting with his back to her, silken butterscotch hair poking out beneath a down-tilted baseball cap, faded t-shirt rolled up to reveal the Celtic band tattoo on his bicep, was Jay.

Juno didn't hang around to observe whether he turned to see who his friend was smiling at, but as she bolted around the corner on her noisy mules she was pretty certain he hadn't spotted his bane of a flatmate tripping hastily past in a hopelessly sexy dress which she'd bought especially for him.

In the flat, she found Poirot strutting around on the oak table where Jay normally kept his computer, squawking a delighted welcome. The computer thankfully wasn't in situ, but Poirot had chewed through a couple of wires leading to chargers of some sort and thrown all Jay's floppy disks to the floor in a fit of neglected pique. Juno hid the damage as best she could before putting him away in his cage, tossing the Peruvian birthing smock over it and tracking Uboat down to the bathroom where she was sulking in the damp patch behind the wash basin.

'Sorry, baby.' Juno carried her guiltily back to her tank, kissing her on the top of the head and stroking her flippers. Beavis and Butthead were cackling on the television, which had been left on all evening. When she tracked down the remote to shut them up, Juno noticed that the answerphone had switched itself on, but only managed to listen to the first message before the street door slammed far beneath her and someone started scaling the stairs.

The message was from Sean, and he'd just got as far as 'Juno, Jay – it's your landlord here. I'll call you la—' when she punched the 'Stop' button and froze, listening to the footsteps.

But it was just one of the pretty Italian girls from the first floor, coming up one flight to her flat, accompanied by a man with a deep voice.

Juno listened as the voices were muted by another slamming door. Friday night is pulling night, she thought sadly, heading to the kitchen for a biscuit, the other phone messages forgotten as she dwelled dejectedly on Jay and the date that never was.

She raided the fridge for supplies, made herself a vast pot of tea, located her *Enriching Bitches* self-help book and an armful of magazines, and retreated to her locked room with just a low-wattage angle-poise and a muted stereo for company.

The phone rang in the sitting room and was picked up by the machine. Juno wondered guiltily whether it was one of her friends, but she was too certain that Jay was about to come home to rush through and intercept.

Once ten minutes had passed with no click of the door to herald his return, she considered it safe enough to creep out and check the answerphone. The figure five was flashing in the digital display. All the messages were for her, confirming her theory that Jay wasn't passing them on when he had the chance to intercept them first. Not that they brought her any joy – merely shame that her life was so thoughtlessly disorganised, and embarrassment that she had yet again let down so many people as a result. They were all 'where are you?' calls from anxious mates who had expected her to swell their ranks that night. The background noise was of pubs and parties, chatter and music, as hasty calls were made from mobiles and pay-phones in the heat of the Friday night action. Listening to them in the gloomy silence of the flat, Juno suddenly felt achingly lonely and mildly paranoid that everyone was talking about how slack she was for begging to join in the fun and then failing to turn up. If only she wasn't so stony-ground, profligate son, biblically broke.

She listlessly jotted down a list of people to grovel apologetically to the next day then retreated back to her lair to nibble biscuits and read a chapter of her self-help book which left her convinced she was orally fixated. She smoked a couple of fags, swigged some tea and sucked a biscuit to console herself.

Listening to *Book at Bedtime* on Radio 4 – a depressing spiel about a lonely Eleanor Rigby-type spinster who went insane during her prolonged spells of solitude – she began obsessing that she hadn't quoted Phil Collins correctly to John. Was it really 'I can't go on just holding on to ties'? Or was it in fact 'I can't go on just holding on to lies'? It was ages since she'd heard the bloody song. The line could be 'I just can't go on holding up my flies' for all she knew. Damn! Had John been humouring her by acknowledging the quote? In that case was he now harbouring the sweet victory of one-upmanship?

There was nothing for it – she had to venture into the body of the flat again and look through Sean's sad but extensive collection of vinyl. The cooler indie and punk records from his student days and beyond were kept on open display; the sadder ones, bought during his spotty, nerdish teenage years when taste was a maturity yet to be acquired, were hidden from public view, although sometimes very late at night Juno had distinctly heard strains of Chris de Burgh or Queen playing in his room. Somewhere amongst them was an alphabetically organised ensemble of Phil Collins LPs, nestling no doubt between Joe Cocker and Cool and the Gang.

The only drawback, Juno realised as she raced across the dark depths of the hallway, almost colliding with the Day-glo thruster surf-board, was that Sean's record collection was kept in Jay's bedroom.

It smelled strange inside the room – tangy and unfamiliar. Determined not to snoop, she didn't switch on the lights and headed straight for the big laundry cupboard which housed the cheesy collection (or as Sean euphemistically called it 'ironic anthology') and speedily started flicking through them, squinting to see in the mean half-light provided by the full moon and the street lamps outside.

'Christ, he's got Go West in here,' she wailed, leafing backwards. 'Fun Boy Three, Sheena Easton, Duran Duran – gorblimey, Dana!'

At last she found the little baldy one's collected works. Whipping out a Greatest Hits, she was about to dash from the room leaving no perceptible sign of entry when she realised that the only record player in the flat lived on the dressing table in front of her.

Juno didn't want to hang around in this Jay-scented haven of snoopaholic temptation, but she was desperate to check that she'd quoted the song right. It was a matter of honour, dignity and long-term self-respect. She walked to the window and scanned the sleeve for lyrics. None – not even on the dust sheet. Just a big, moody photo of Phil with more hair and fewer ex-wives.

She stood impala-still for a few moments, checking there was no sound from the stairwell. Then, squinting hard in the dim half-light, she checked which side of the record she needed and slipped it on to the turntable before pressing the power button.

God, she'd forgotten how hard DIY track selection was on LPs. When she picked up the needle head and plonked it down roughly halfway through the album, it skidded its way to the centre with a furious hiss. Trying again, she managed to locate 'It Must Be Love'. Within seconds, it was tippy-tapping its languid, introspective sentiment into her head.

Poised to lift the needle closer to her track target, Juno hesitated.

'I haven't heard this in years,' she told the darkened, unfamiliar-smelling room, almost as though its occupant was lying on the bed awaiting her.

The tune skipped and twisted around her. It reminded her of close-dancing in Oxfordshire village halls during under-eighteen parties (or more likely watching her friends close-dancing), swigging Thunderbird Blue in the back of battered 2CVs, possessing fierce crushes on gorgeous sixth formers who never once glanced in her direction, dying her hair pink and her eyelashes black. She could almost smell the memories, they were so vivid. Her pertinent backing track was playing again – only this time it was a flash-backing track.

'He's rather clever, old Phil.' Juno perched on the end of the bed and started twitching her toes in time, all thoughts of nosing around the room forgotten as emotion swelled her chest and threatened to ping her dress's corset wires into the walls like thrown knives.

Soon afterwards 'One More Night' was pleading for a lover to drop her kit a final time. Juno snivelled quietly into a corner of the duvet and rather wished she'd taken John up on one of those after-pub curry sessions in Clapham for old times' sake. There was no way she'd ever do it now, not when Jay had lifted the dusty fire curtain on her libido and made her realise what she'd been missing out on all these years.

Sex with John had never been the full five acts but it had become a *Fast Show* comedy sketch in the end, she remembered miserably. They'd hardly made love at all in those last few months, and when they had, she'd started noticing that they were doing it in the same order every time, as though they had perfected a routine – kiss, suck, tweak, 'does this feel good?', twiddle, stroke, lick, twiddle again, 'that's fantastic, flower, don't stop doing that', kiss, lick, 'you're beautiful, flower', stroke, separate, enter, plunge, pump, tweak, pump faster, 'I'm coming!', thrust, gasp, arch back, shudder, gasp again, kiss, exit, roll over, reach for tissue. And pretty soon that routine started getting even briefer as they took more and more short cuts, left more and more out. The kisses were the first to go, then the strokes, then the conversation, then the licks, and finally practically everything that preceded 'enter'.

In Jay's darkened room 'Leaving You Is Easy' made her smile and cry at the same time as she remembered walking over the porch tiles of the Clapham house for the last time with Uboat's tank in her arms, forced to kick the co-habiting habit and talk in the first person singular once more.

Loving and living with John had for a time made Juno feel like the swan she'd always longed to be, but it had also made her realise that she was much happier swimming against the tide after all. It was only now it was well and truly over that she could see that. She'd longed for years to have a hunky, demonstrative boyfriend – one of the floppy-haired gods she'd had such fierce crushes on for all those years. And that's what John was. Hunky, and charming, and shallow as a puddle. She'd always thought ugly ducklings liked puddles, but it turned out she was looking for something deeper after all. And she didn't have to look very far – he'd moved in and was living under the same roof as her. She was sitting in his room right now.

At last, 'Separate Lives' started echoing its way into the room.

Sitting bolt upright and eagerly awaiting her quoted line, Juno's ears burned as she realised the pertinence of it all. Did John see it too? She suddenly envisaged him sitting in the cluttered Clapham house right this minute, record covers spread like confetti around him, listening to the same track in synchrony from the other side of the river, feeling the same sadness, the same sense of irrevocable loss – only far more immediate desire for her body, she secretly added.

She shuddered with relief as she heard her little excerpt sung verbatim.

'This girl never forgets a line!' She punched the air victoriously.

Feeling rather proud of herself, she listened on for a couple more tracks, deciding as she jiggled in time to the beat that it was about time modern chart stars started a Phil revival. He had, after all, belted out some killingly good tunes. Surely Boyzone could cover a couple and cash in? Even better if Liam and Noel decided to try a bit of a Collins retrospective to lend him well-deserved kudos. The man was basically a god.

She was just cuddling into Jay's duvet and gurgling dreamily along to 'In the Air Tonight' when she heard the street door slam far below her. Voices floated up from each stairwell, approaching fast.

Surely Jay hadn't asked people back?

He surely had, and they appeared to be taking the stairs two at a time.

With a great scratch of diamond across vinyl, Juno dragged the needle back to its rest and punched out the power switches. There was no time to take the LP from the turntable, so she flipped the tinted anti-static lid down above it and kicked the sleeve beneath the bed like an adulteress hiding the milkman's Y-fronts.

She had just made it to the hall, panting as the corset steam-pressed her lungs, when the front door started to swing open. Her bedroom door was on the other side of it. She dived into the bathroom instead.

Chapter Twenty-Three

Sitting on the flipped-down loo seat, heart racing like a greyhound, Juno tried to distinguish Jay's quiet, throaty voice amongst the sudden babble of male conversation. But the rushing of blood in her ears made it impossible. She could hear them moving into the sitting room, discern a mobile phone ringing and a male voice laughing, but her heartbeat was far louder.

Oh, the shame of being caught swooning around his room in the dark, crying to Phil Collins's Greatest Hits. Thank God she had evaded them. The only problem now was getting back into her room undetected. She had to cross the hall in front of the sitting-room doorway. She had a sudden vision of herself in the sculpted Jessica Rabbit dress, creeping out of the bathroom and along the hallway – flat against a wall, like Emma Peel in *The Avengers*, then executing a perfect commando roll across the foot of the sitting-room doorway before slipping silently into her room. She had a feeling it was a bit of a tall order for a short, tubby and monumentally unfit woman.

As the thrumming in her ears subsided, she could hear her favourite Prodigy CD starting up loudly in the sitting room. Juno narrowed her eyes proprietorially. They'd better put it back in the case afterwards.

Ever the unconscious hypocrite, she prayed Jay didn't notice the Phil Collins album lurking on the turntable in his room before she had a chance to creep in and remove the evidence over the weekend.

Crouching on the loo seat and chewing her nails, she realised she had to make a move soon before someone out there felt the call of nature. Judging from the sound effects there were at least three of them besides Jay, their voices an overlapping puzzle of different accents and tones. None, as far as she could make out, was female. She hated herself for feeling so relieved.

She decided there was nothing for it but to brazen it out. So what if she was home alone before closing time on a Friday night wearing her party frock? There was nothing odd, sad or uncool about that. She'd just swan regally past the sitting-room door with a cheery wave and an enigmatic smile.

She checked her reflection quickly in the mirror above the sink. Her war paint was still intact apart from the lipstick, and her hair was looking cutely dishevelled. She had biscuit crumbs in her jacked-up cleavage and had lost one of her earrings but convinced herself she looked pretty spectacular nonetheless.

Humming 'In the Air Tonight' and holding her chin high, she flushed the loo as an alibi and shimmied into the hallway.

As she passed the sitting-room doorway, she turned casually to scan the room over her shoulder, a carefully composed 'what-have-we-here' expression on her face.

Three men were huddled around Jay who was sitting at the nearest oak table, tapping away on his laptop like a preppy kid showing the school rugby team his Super Mario 8. At least whatever cables Poirot had chewed through earlier didn't seem to have stopped it working, she realised with relief. They all had their back to her. It was, Juno surmised, a pretty Sad Lads scenario. She almost laughed as she loitered in the shadows to study the newcomers.

'Great view you have here, mate,' said one in a funster, Essex-lad drawl, gazing through the window to the fading London skyline. Even from behind, Juno could tell he was the spin bowler with the pudding basin haircut and the big, cheeky smile whom she had eyed outside Café Flo. Great bum, too, she spotted with a well-trained eye.

Standing beside him was a tall man in a very expensive suit, who didn't need to turn around to make Juno catch her breath in excitement. He was built like a cartoon superhero, had thick, glossy coffee-bean hair cut very short at the nape of his long, broad neck and gelled back on top in rigid waves. A plume of cigar smoke floated above one sharply tailored, pin-stripe shoulder. Juno could almost smell his money and sex appeal across the room.

Crouching at screen-height on Jay's other side – and by far the most interested of the three in the computer – was a shorter and much thinner man, whose curly, receding black hair was scraped back into a pony tail. He was the only one talking, and his whiny, nasal, mosquito-buzz voice set Juno's teeth on edge even on the other side of the room.

'So you've just sold that shot of Michael Caine to fifteen different countries, less than two hours after it was taken on a Friday fucking night?' he buzzed in disbelief.

'So far, yeah.' Jay's voice was a soft, breathy balm to the ears compared to his companion's. 'Face it, Dormouse, it's a great photo.'

'Agreed,' the man whined rather resentfully. 'I just don't understand how you can syndicate it so fast. My agent would take days to do that.'

'Digital cameras, Dormouse. They're the future. No film, no lab, no slides, no bike courier, no wait,' Jay explained smoothly. 'I sent the Caine shots to my L.A. agent using my laptop, a modem and a mobile phone ten minutes after I took them.' He pronounced mobile 'mobul'. 'If it had been earlier in the day, I'd've let the East Coast guys have them too, or even the Brits. It's a time-zone thing. Most often, I send a shot direct to a picture editor if I know he's hungry enough to pay for an exclusive.'

Juno jumped nervously as the spin bowler's mobile phone went off, but he moved to one side to answer it with his back still turned away from her snooping presence, so she lingered for a few more moments.

'Now I see why you're always crouching over that little

box of tricks of yours.' Dormouse was scratching his bald patch. 'Shame you don't know who's who over here.'

'It's not a box of tricks,' Jay said curtly. 'It's my livelihood. And I know who makes newsprint.'

The suited superhero turned towards Dormouse, revealing a profile as straight-nosed and noble as the bust of a Greek god, flawed only by a straight white scar through one perfect, Michael Praed eyebrow. Juno caught her breath even more as she realised he couldn't be older than twenty-five. 'Surely some of your – er – compatriots use digital technology like this, Parker?' His voice was American too, but far deeper and bolder, without the New York twang to it. He even *sounded* like Captain America, she realised in awe.

'Yeah, a few of the Royal specialists do.' Dormouse sniffed disapprovingly. 'We're more old fashioned in the celebrity line – the front line. I personally prefer to hold the finished product up to the lightbox before I offer it for sale, if you know what I mean. I let my agency deal with the electronic gizmos.'

'You're antediluvian,' Jay laughed, but not unkindly. 'I've met at least half a dozen guys over here already who work digitally. Admittedly they're not as well hooked up as me, but they don't need to visit a lab. Pretty well every picture desk accepts stuff on-line these days. Some demand it.'

Standing in the shadows of the hall, it suddenly occurred to Juno why the darkroom was still full of Sean's clutter. Jay didn't use film. She'd read about it somewhere – digital cameras which stored the pictures in a memory chip and could be plugged into a computer to be transferred to its hard disk and viewed on screen, then downloaded anywhere in the world via a modem.

She chewed her lip thoughtfully. So he was in England to take pictures after all. It was a relief to know it. But why Michael Caine? Perhaps he was here shooting portraits of famous film stars, she mused as another mobile phone rang in the room. She backed hastily away from the door before she was spotted.

As she slipped into her own room, she could distinctly hear the funster, Essex-boy drawl saying: 'D'you see that bird standing in the doorway just now, Timon, mate? No? She your girlfriend, Jay boy? Tasty, in't she?'

'You gotta be *kidding* me, man,' Jay laughed caustically.

Kidding that I'm his girlfriend? Naturally very amusing. Very ironic. Or kidding that I'm tasty? Not so rib-tickling. Downright insulting in fact. Bastard!

Juno prowled furiously around her bedroom, hungry to be included in what was going on in the flat's sitting room and to prove – to Jay more than anybody – that she was, in fact, very tasty indeed. So tasty that John wanted her back. Barfly adored her. Even Finlay had said he'd once have fancied her in this dress – gorgeous Finlay who loved Lydia to distraction. Now that, if anything, proved she was tasty.

If she met Jay's friends, they might persuade him that she was tasty too – the spin bowler already thought so. She decided he had to be extremely successful and intelligent. Jay should respect someone like that, take his opinion seriously.

She could hear the conversation burbling on, mobiles ringing, male laughter – that sexiest of all sounds when responding to your joke, most insulting when making you the butt of theirs.

Juno wanted to go out there and fight her corner. She longed to be introduced, wanted to know who they all were, what they did, most especially Timon the superhero who looked so ridiculously John Kennedy Jnr gorgeous that he had to be some sort of international playboy with a string of yachts, apartments and blonde girlfriends. The thin-voiced Dormouse – who struck Juno as more of a sewer rat – was obviously another photographer. And the flashy Essex spin bowler had the barrow-boy, wheeler-dealer manner of one of Bar Oque's gorblimey City brokers who ordered champagne by the magnum, but judging from the club promoter's outfit – John Richmond leather jacket, sexy black flat-fronts, Patrick Cox suede loafers – he did something considerably funkier than that. They were such an incongruous bunch, Juno was dying to know what linked them to Jay.

Knowing who and what they were would be a huge piece

of the jigsaw puzzle towards constructing a clearer picture of what made Jay tick. Christ! Juno rubbed her forehead with the heel of her palm. She hated him for making her feel like this, yet she was so desperate to be close to him, to be involved. She loathed missing out.

She could hear two mobiles ringing at once in the sitting room – one shrilling a repetitive trill, the other playing some sort of tune. A moment after they were silenced another rang in a completely different tone. In her experience people only called late on Friday nights to announce that they were at a great party/club/bar and to offer an invitation to come along.

Any minute now they might all leave. Jay might never ask them back and he'd consequently keep his life as secret from and inaccessible to her as it had been so far.

Juno caught sight of her Anna Nicole Smith reflection in the mirror.

This was the 'fall in love' dress Finlay had helped her choose. She had bought it for Jay and, for all the racking disappointment of discovering he had not orchestrated a date at all, she suddenly wanted him to see her in it. In the past week, he'd seen her in her Peruvian birthing smock more than anything else. This would knock his eyes out. She wouldn't bow out of her love-pact deal with Finlay without a fight. So Jay might not exactly fall in love with her the moment he clocked her but at least he could see what he was missing out on. She'd show him just how tasty she could be.

She needed a ruse. An excuse to go out there which would make her look both fascinating and elusive, captivating yet unavailable, sexy yet very, very choosy. She needed a ruse to make her look . . . tasty.

Then it occurred to her that they didn't in fact know she was alone. She could have anyone in her room, and what better excuse to be in the flat on a Friday night wearing a divine dress? She'd pulled! Simple, obvious and guaranteed to make Jay think about her in a different – possibly even wildly jealous – light.

Without pausing to think of the greater significance of her strategy, Juno fired up the Soul Seduction cassette in her stereo (she liked the ironic touch), dragged a couple of matching wine glasses from the clutter of dirty mugs, plates and assorted crockery on top of her chest of drawers, and – checking in the mirror that she was still looking sexy, mildly dishevelled and lipstick-free – swung her way out of the door to the strains of 'When a Man Loves a Woman'.

Her mendacity was almost immediately blown as she walked straight into the designer leather back of Spin Bowler who was standing in the gloomy hallway talking into two mobile phones simultaneously.

Juno hastily shut the bedroom door so he didn't get a chance to glimpse her empty room, clutching the handle behind her with one hand, holding the stems of the two glasses with the other and smiling guiltily.

'Well, hello!' Spin Bowler swung around in a well-practised Leslie Phillips manoeuvre, huge cheeky smile in place, although he immediately recommenced his calls as his naughty brown eyes drank her in. 'I can't go below fifty, mate – these things are like gold dust. It'll be a hundred come tomorrow night, mark my words . . . You live here then?' He eyed Juno's cleavage. 'No, Justin, I don't want twenty. A dozen, tops. Nice frock. I'm Will.'

'Thanks!' she said brightly and breezily. 'I'm Juno. I can see you're busy, excuse me.' As she darted past him and into the sitting room, she heard another mobile phone ring from within his leather jacket. Three! Now that wasn't just extravagant and flash, it was suicidal. He had to be a Stock Exchange whizzkid on the verge of a breakdown. That or a mobile phone salesman.

On the oak table, Jay's computer lay folded up like a sleeping mussel, plugged into its charger. To her right, Dormouse was peering into Uboat's tank in fascination while her beloved turtle studied him impassively from the prow of her sunken ship, hooked snout cocked to one side. There was a distinct physical similarity between them – the nose, the squinty eyes, the receding chin. To her left, Timon the dreamboat superhero was sitting on the rust silk sofa, crouched like a chess player over the coffee table and tapping something against it, although

Juno couldn't see what or why. Jay was not in the room at all. Faltering in the doorway, glasses clinking nervously in her hand, Juno suddenly panicked. What *was* she doing?

Behind her, she distinctly heard a fourth mobile phone ring – this one with a tinkling rendition of the first bars of Beethoven's Fifth. Four! Will the Spin Bowler definitely worked at People's Phone.

At that moment, Dormouse looked away from Uboat's unblinking gaze and spotted her.

'Who are you?' he asked rudely.

'I'm Juno. I live here.' She smiled winningly. 'Who are you?'

'I know Jay,' he said as though that answered it. He had big, close-set Ryan Giggs eyes which gave him a faintly psychotic air.

Juno nodded and advanced a few cautious feet into the room, feeling like an intruder even though it was her home. 'Is he here?'

'On the bog.' Dormouse squinted critically at her dress.

'Are you another photographer?' she asked graciously.

'Do I look like one then?' His gaze finally landed at her bare feet and shot back up to her eyes with a sneer. 'Your nail varnish is chipped.'

'I've run out of this colour – it's my favourite.' Juno glanced down at them lovingly. 'These are my mementoes.'

Dormouse grinned broadly, which rendered him unexpectedly attractive as it revealed a set of Hollywood-straight white teeth and wrinkled the mad eyes into harmless creases of amusement.

'You're quite funny,' he said, as though this was absolutely astonishing.

'Thanks. So are you all friends of Jay's?' Her eyes darted towards Timon the dreamboat who was still tapping out a rhythm on the coffee table, long, broad body arched intently over his task.

'Only met him a few days ago,' Dormouse sniffed. 'Nice bloke. We're in the same line of business. Timon introduced us.'

The superhero glanced over his shoulder, rendering Juno speechless for a moment. He was just *beautiful*.

'You Jay's bird then?' Dormouse wheezed with a knowing cackle.

'Not exactly – not at all in fact. Jay and me? You must be *kidding*!' Juno was still staring at Timon. Christ, but he was spellbinding. Those heart-stopping black peat eyes, mocha hair, butterscotch skin. He was a binge feast of a man. She was back in the school playground, the university campus, the raucous twenty-something party, staring at a hunk and feeling as though her lungs had developed slow punctures.

Then he turned away without interest and Juno found that the feeling vanished as instantly as it had arrived, like a momentary left-the-oven-on panic quashed by the memory you'd switched it off after all. It had just been *déjà vu*, she realised. A brief glimpse of the life she had left behind. She glanced over her shoulder, looking for Jay, knowing he was something new – not that old, well-worn path of unrequited hunk crushes she'd blistered her feet on for years, but a terrifying bobsleigh run of snatched breath and broken limbs. Not so much a crush as a crash. But only Will was in sight in the hall, still chattering on one of his phones, winking at her flirtily.

As Timon resumed tapping on the coffee table – more scraping on it now that Juno listened again – she turned back to Dormouse and smiled ingratiatingly, about to ask precisely what line of business he was in.

'Thought so!' he declared victoriously, ratty eyes fixed on Timon's broad shoulders. 'All you girls are the same, aren't you?'

'Meaning what exactly?' Juno gulped. What was this man? A mind reader? Could he tell she'd experienced a brief, fickle moment of lust? It had gone. She was a mature woman these days, as Jay would find out the moment he wandered back into the room to find her enchanting his friends.

'Meaning what?' she repeated in a far more relaxed, mature and tasty way – adding a naughty, knowing smile.

'You want a bit of the action.' Dormouse flashed his

expensive teeth and nodded towards Timon once more. 'You can sniff it a mile off, huh?' He looked impressed, although Juno had no idea why. She was appalled he could think her so fickle and shallow.

'I want no such thing.' She laughed lightly. 'Now, if you'll excuse me,' she waggled her glasses, 'I have a guest waiting.'

In the refuge of the kitchen, she dumped the glasses in the sink and flipped the kettle on. As she waited for it to boil, she heard Jay come back into the room on the other side of the arch and felt her pulse start to race. He was his usual laconic self.

'What the fuck are you doing, Timon?'

'Drawing up the battle lines,' the Captain America voice purred, as deep, silky and confident as a Persian cat twining itself around ankles.

'Not in here,' Jay said gently. 'I draw the line around here – and that's the wrong side of it, buddy.'

'Hang on, Jay boy!' buzzed a mosquito whine. 'Let him keep his chopper out a while. There's a girl in the kitchen wants to scratch and sniff old Timon's gear. Chunky little blonde thing – looks like a Teletubby.'

'I mighta guessed,' Jay groaned.

Face flaming at the double-barrelled insult, Juno busied herself gathering two clean mugs and searching for the cafetière, awaiting Jay's angry arrival in the kitchen. She couldn't wait to see his face when he clocked the dress, spotted the brace of cups, and realised she'd pulled. That'd teach him to deny she was tasty.

Suddenly a figure appeared in the archway to her left and elbowed the fridge door. 'So, live here with Jay, do you, sweetheart?' Two brown eyes assessed her body all over like a masseur. 'Lucky old Jay.'

It was Will, pudding bowl hair tickling the bridge of his nose, wicked smile creeping across his face. He couldn't have been more obvious if he'd had 'untrustworthy, sex-mad bounder' tattooed across the laughter lines on his forehead. He was one of those men who just lived to flirt, fibbed to flirt and ad-libbed to flirt. He reminded Juno instantly of Lydia – madder, badder and more dangerous, but essentially hewn from the same small precious diamond mine of hedonistic self-confidence.

'I think Jay might argue that point,' she said lightly, dumping some more coffee into the jug.

'Some caffeine habit you've got there, darlin'. I take it you don't want to sleep tonight?' He moved towards her, looking at the cafetière but heading for her body. Then he saw the two mugs lined up on the kitchen surface and stalled, elbowing the microwave instead, smile still dancing.

'Got company then?' His eyebrows rose. Fairly decent eyebrows, Juno noticed, but not a patch on Jay's.

'Just thirsty,' she said breezily, realising that the only way to dig for information was to flirt. It wasn't something she was very adept at, but if it made her appear tasty – and learn something about Jay into the bargain – she'd have a shot.

'Shame. Pretty little thing like you. Should have a nice big fella to cuddle up to of a night.' He cocked his head and stroked the inside of his cheek with his tongue.

Tempted to say 'tell that to Jay', Juno laughed. 'I get by.'

'I'm sure you do. If you ever fancy getting one by me I'd be happy to oblige.' One brown eye winked to emphasise his meaning.

'I'll bear it in mind,' she gulped, unaccustomed to being chatted up quite so obviously. It must be something about this kitchen, she decided, remembering Barfly's advances earlier in the week. Perhaps Sean's hash-plants hidden amongst his herb pots gave off an aphrodisiac aroma? If so, why didn't they work on Jay?

'I could take you somewhere nice.' Will edged forward with slow, steady confidence. 'Name the gig and I'll get us in, guaranteed. If you like a bit of opera, I'm your man. If you want to see some celebs, I'll take you to a première.'

Juno's eyes widened in surprise as a link fell into place. 'Did you say your name was Will?'

'The best Will in the world, that's me, sweetheart.' He winked a cheeky brown eye, his one-liner as off-pat as a farmer's gumboot.

'Will Pigeon? The Dream Ticket tout?'

The smile broadened like an oil slick in a fast tide. 'Hey, the girl has class. I'm your Dream man all right. What can I do you for, darlin'?'

This was it. This was the break she needed. If she played it really cool she could find out what Jay was keeping from her.

Juno was sober and quick, and knew she hadn't much time. 'I like Tag Heuer watches.' She smiled cheekily. It was the only thing she knew which connected them.

'Then we'll go to a jeweller's, sweetheart.' He didn't miss a beat, moving closer as he registered the green light, like a Formula One car growling away from the front of the grid – still on the warm-up lap, but supremely confident of success. 'The morning after I take you out, I'll buy you a little Tag if you fancy.'

He was in her space now, breathing the same small pocket of air in the kitchen, eyeing her spectacular cleavage. Juno felt claustrophobic, cornered, clammy-handed, but desperate to find out more without awakening his suspicion. She had no idea what she was letting herself in for here – guns, drugs, debenture seats at the Oval.

'A watch with "Surf, Shag and Shit" inscribed on it.' She jumped as the kettle whistled at last.

A smile crept across his face as he reached out to stroke one finger along her shoulder. 'I like a woman with her own style, but doncha think that's a little bit unfeminine, darling? I prefer a more romantic inscription myself.'

His finger trailed up to her neck. Close to, Juno could see scars on his face – not as obvious as Timon's eyebrow slash, but far more sinister. There was a hair-line scar on his lip, another by one twinkling brown eye, and – most daunting – a heavy slash, still healing, ran from one pointed sideburn up under his fringe. That must be why he had the pudding basin haircut, she realised.

Suddenly, she started to feel frightened. For all she knew, Jay, Timon and Dormouse could all be part of the same cell of which Will was operational leader. She remembered the snatches of that phone conversation she'd overheard Jay having – 'I don't want to shoot her unless I have to' – 'someone's on my back'. She could be playing blind man's bluff in a mine field for all she knew.

Jerking away, she turned off the gas beneath the kettle and stood facing the hob, mustering courage. She refused to be intimidated by a few scratches. Jay had bullet holes in him, for chrissake. That was far nobler and scarier. He couldn't be a terrorist, surely? She just wanted to know what he *was* doing in England – and what he was doing with her brother's watch. He'd denied he'd given it to Will, pretended he hadn't even met him. There had to be a reason . . . and as he wouldn't tell her, she was going to find out for herself.

'A mutual friend of ours gave you a Tag like that in a deal about a week ago.' She winced at the story, hoping he wouldn't rumble her uncertainty. At least, facing the tiled wall behind the hob, she didn't have to look him in the eye any more.

He moved in behind her so she could feel his breath on her neck. 'Might ring bells . . . might not. Remind me.'

Juno flinched as she felt a warm hand slide around her waist. She was desperate to find out how he'd come by Sean's watch, how come he was in the flat tonight when Jay had denied he'd ever met the Dream Ticket, but she was aware that Will's cocky, evasive, flirty manner had to be matched as lightly and carelessly as possible. She didn't like him touching her, but was certain that he would lose interest in the subject if she shrugged him off.

'You got it in a deal.' She poured boiling water over the coffee grounds, watching them foam, smelling the hit of the aroma. An idea occurred to her. 'I might want to make a similar transaction.'

'You might?' He laughed uproariously, and the other hand moved around her waist as his designer flat-fronts were pressed against her rear, demonstrating a far from flat front beneath.

'Yes, why not?' Juno nodded, pouring water so shakily now that most of it washed over the zinc surface. She resisted an urge to kick back like a mule.

'So you know all about it then?' He whistled into her ear, clearly impressed by whatever it was she was supposed to be a party to. The resulting Michael Caine impersonation was impressive. 'Not a lot of people know that. You must have insider info. They're really hard to get hold of, those buggers. Don't come cheap.'

'I can pay,' she croaked, realising she was so broke she'd have to offer him a post-dated cheque. What was she trying to buy here? she wondered worriedly. A Kalashnikov? She could hardly go to the bank manager for a loan.

'In that case,' he laughed on delightedly, leaning harder against her and talking into her ear on a warm, intimate breath, 'I'll make a few calls and – '

'Time to go, Will,' muttered a soft Bronx drawl from the doorway. 'Timon wants to hit the road.'

'I'm just doing some business with your charming little flatmate here, Jay boy.' Will didn't even look round, just carried on pinning Juno to the oven with his hard, stocky body.

'*Now*, Will!' Jay snapped irritably.

With a regretful look at Juno, a wink of one eye and a blown kiss, Will swaggered out of the kitchen. Breathing out with relief that he'd stopped mauling her and frustration that she'd almost found out what the deal with the watch was all about, Juno backed away from the hob and wiped her damp forehead with the back of her hand. She turned to see Jay still standing in the doorway.

Aware that she'd been caught in a compromising position, was pink in the face and that her dress was riding up fast, Juno licked her lips nervously and straightened her skirt. Jay watched her in silence, taking in the dress, the embarrassment, the two mugs. Juno felt an awkward smile flicker on her lips then die.

Still, he said nothing.

Staring at him was doing absurd things to her heartbeat; it appeared to be tapping out the percussive rhythm to M People's 'Moving on Up' – the speeded-up, Europop version. She was almost tempted to sing along.

'Hey, Jay buddy!' called a silky smooth Captain America

voice from the sitting room. 'I gotta red roll-mop here. Wanna help us wipe these marks from your coffee table?' There was a cackle of male laughter which reminded Juno of the Beavis and Butthead snorts and honks she'd zapped from the television earlier.

Shooting her a split-second look of contempt, Jay went out.

Not very tasty, Juno realised in a panic. Not very tasty at all.

They were all moving towards the hallway, back-slapping their farewells by the time she tripped hastily out of the kitchen with her cafetière and two mugs.

'Nice to have nearly met you, sweetheart.' Hanging back in the sitting room, Will Pigeon eyed her curves and pulled a cheeky, regretful face. He nodded theatrically towards the cafetière. 'Hope that keeps your man up tonight. If it doesn't, you call Will here. Jay boy's got the number. We'll finish that little bit of business . . .' One of his mobiles rang, cutting him short.

'Have we met?' asked a creamy, Jeff Colby voice.

Juno realised that Timon had turned back to look at her now, one scarred eyebrow curling towards the other perfect one in classic soap-opera style. He was holding up his finger like a doubtful cricket umpire calling 'Out?', eyes narrowed in concentration as he tried to place her.

Despite herself, Juno was too awed by his incredible hunk-factor to answer.

'Do you live here?' He looked even more confused. Actually he looked as though he was trying to divide six hundred and seventy-nine by thirteen, but Juno dreamily envisaged more depth to him.

She nodded, still rendered speechless by his looks. Opening the front door to usher them out, Jay looked positively minuscule beside him; Timon was bigger than John and far, far better looking.

'Did you mention her?' He turned to Jay, dipping the raised finger towards Juno as though she was a house pet.

'Juno Glenn – Timon O'Kelly,' Jay grunted unwillingly, husky Bronx voice almost a hiss.

'Good to meet you, Juno.' Timon nodded then turned away to study his reflection in the hallway mirror, leaving her mouthing silently, like a yodeller with laryngitis.

Will covered the mouthpiece of the phone he was talking into and smiled wickedly at her. 'Don't be fooled by that smooth old patter of his, darlin'. He's really a shy old Herbert at heart – ain't that right, Ti?'

'Huh?'

'Come and tell little Juno here about yourself, Timon.' Will did a quick double-click of his tongue against the roof of his mouth then, taking his hand away from the mouthpiece of his phone, he turned his back on them and resumed his call. 'Yes – I've got it right here. What? No, I'm off to Café Frog. Yeah, maybe later – say, three in The Washroom? I'll give it to you then.'

Juno swallowed in disbelief. Will Pigeon – whom she'd met for less than two minutes and who'd chatted her up for one hundred seconds of those – had just played Cupid.

'So, Timon – um – O'Kelly.' She racked her brains for something incredibly original and witty to say, leaning back so that she could look up at him. 'That's an unusual name.' Great one, Juno!

'My father's Irish, my mother's Greek.' He shrugged, not smiling.

'Oh . . . right. Fascinating.' There was a long pause. Juno stared up at his chin. She'd never stood directly beneath John Travolta but imagined the view from this angle would be pretty similar.

'So h-how do you and Jay know one another?' she spluttered, noticing that he smelled overpoweringly of Hugo Boss. It reminded her of John and made her feel slightly sick.

'We met in L.A.' The chin moved up and down above her head. 'We used to work together way back when – before Jay went crazy on us all and started walking in front of bullets. He called me up about a week back.'

'Wanting to catch up on old times?' Juno perked up at the realisation that she could do some more hasty delving.

'He won't talk about those days.' Timon shook his head. 'He was a natural then. Totally focused. The best.'

Juno felt the blood drain from her face. Focused on what? Timon had just mentioned he was half-Irish, hadn't he? Was he the person Jay had met on his first night in England, the one he'd spoken to on the phone about needing to get past someone's heavies? Had she stumbled upon some sort of cell meeting taking place in Sean's flat after all?

'I thought you fellas had to go,' Jay muttered tersely.

Juno looked across to the hallway where he was still holding the front door open in the vain hope that it would encourage his guests to leave, but no one was taking any notice. Will was standing by the fireplace tapping numbers into one mobile while still talking into another; Dormouse had disappeared inside the darkroom, his whiny voice just audible as it made snide comments about the mess. As Timon stretched up to pat his stiff, glossy hair again, Juno peered at Jay from beneath his armpit and realised he was staring at her with such ferocity that she blanched.

The next minute, Dormouse called him into the darkroom.

'A natural at what?' she asked Timon in an urgent hiss the moment Jay was out of sight.

'At what he does,' Timon said, clearly thinking she was dumb. 'Covert photography.'

Covert! Juno was baffled. What were they talking about here? Secretly photographing terrorist targets?

'Do you like my hair?' he asked suddenly, tilting down his head and looking at her intently.

'Your *hair*?' Juno balked in surprise.

'Yeah.' He touched his crisp, glossy executive cut with a tentative hand and stooped even lower so it was level with her face. 'Does it look okay?'

Juno pressed her lips together to stop herself laughing and nodded earnestly. The temptation to throw out her 'Did you swim here tonight then?' line was itching away inside her. 'It looks . . . sensational,' she said sincerely.

She glanced at the hall where Jay and Dormouse had re-emerged from the darkroom. Those guarded yellow eyes caught hers for a brief second and blinked contemptuously before he looked away and laughed at something Dormouse said. Juno felt her heart drop in her chest. Dormouse was cackling loudly now.

Suddenly Juno stiffened as she distinctly heard the words 'Benny' and 'Abba' in that nasal mosquito's drone and remembered that most of Sean's photographs from the holiday camp talent contest were still littered around the darkroom. They'd obviously been falling about together at her kipper-tied, fake-bearded expense.

'You don't think it's too short?'

'What?' She blinked up at Timon again. Christ, he was still going on about his hair. The deep, rumbling voice was pure Robert Mitchum, the looks Cary Grant, the conversation Philadelphia Girl. He dipped down to her level so that she could give it her full attention. His after-shave at close range was like a punch in the nose from a Christmas edition of *Elle*.

'No, it looks just great that length,' she assured him.

He scrutinised her face through long sooty lashes. 'You sure? Definitely not too short then, huh?'

She nodded, adding loudly for Jay's benefit, 'The shorter the better. I loathe long hair on men. So girly.'

Timon seemed delighted, suddenly flashing a toothpaste smile. 'What d'you say your name was again?' he asked, straightening up to look at his reflection in the mirror above the fireplace.

'Juno.'

'So, Juno, are you coming to Café de Paris with us?' It was a matter-of-fact inquiry, not an invitation. 'Because we gotta shoot off now.'

Wow! She'd obviously made more of an impression than she'd imagined. It must be the dress. She looked nervously at Jay, who was glowering again, totally unimpressed. 'I don't think – '

'She can't, mate.' Will, his calls curtailed, had swaggered over. Giving Juno's bum a friendly pat, he nodded towards the cafetière and mugs which she'd propped on Uboat's tank. 'Can't you see the girl's got company tonight? The poor bloke in her room must think she's had to go to Brazil to fetch that coffee.'

Juno had completely forgotten about her ruse.

Biting her lip in embarrassment, she glanced nervously towards Jay in the hallway. He was still looking at her, but his face was an expressionless mask.

'Oh, right.' Timon didn't seem unduly bothered. He glanced at his watch, checked his reflection once again, and wandered towards the door without saying goodbye.

'I think you're in there,' Will whispered in her ear. 'Old Ti takes a bit of warming up, but he's a demon bloke. Not as good as me in the sack, granted, but decent enough when it comes to getting rounds in. Funny thing is, I was certain you'd be Jay's bird when I saw you. A sexy little jay-bird.' His brown eyes twinkled. He stood far too close and sounded far too suggestive for their two-minute acquaintance.

'Are you always like this?'

'Like what?' His flirtatious smile was still in place.

'So . . .' Juno thought about it for a second '. . . intimate.'

'One good turn-on deserves another.' His cheeky gaze raked her body, then he picked up the cafetière and the two mugs and handed them back to her. 'And you, my sweetheart, are one hell of a turn-on. No wonder old Jay's kept you such a secret. Give Uncle Will a ring about that bit of business, yeah?'

Juno suddenly remembered Sean's watch. She opened her mouth to say something but he was already heading towards the door, one of his phones trilling urgently.

'See you, fellas.' Jay's fingers were drumming against the latch.

''Bye,' Dormouse droned, heading out first, followed by Timon who punched Jay lightly on the shoulder, then Will, who blew Juno a kiss.

'T'care, darlin' – till next time.'

The door closed with a thud.

Juno stood in the sitting room with her two 'I have pulled' mugs, one cafetière and Jay. She knew for certain that this was not the scenario Finlay had had in mind.

Quick as a flash, she thought of a way out.

'Coffee?' she offered, racing towards the coffee table and suddenly seeing what Timon had been tapping and scraping there. On one tile, like chalk scratches on a prison wall, were four neat, parallel lines of cocaine. Beside them, he'd left behind a tightly rolled fifty-pound note – the 'red roll-mop' he'd referred to earlier. Casually leaving fifty pounds behind in a friend's flat like a half-finished packet of cigarettes was beyond Juno's comprehension.

'Christ!' she gulped. 'Talk about laying it on the line.'

Jay didn't answer.

Turning around, Juno saw that he was leaning against the arch to the hallway, eyes narrowed.

'Interesting bunch, your friends.' She cleared her throat. 'Nice, though – very, um, friendly.'

'So were you,' he muttered. '*Very* friendly.'

'Mmm.' Juno cast around for a suitable way forward. The watch. She had to ask him about Will and the watch while it was still fresh in her head. 'Will Pigeon's certainly a character. I thought you said you hadn't met him when Lydia asked you?'

To her surprise, he smiled, ducking his head away and looking towards Uboat's tank.

Juno waited for an answer, but none came.

'And what's that supposed to mean?' she asked lightly.

'What's what supposed to mean?' He turned back and regarded her insolently through his lashes.

'That smile?' She heard an involuntary note of accusation in her voice.

'You liked Will, huh?' He looked at her levelly.

'Is this one of those conversations where we just ask questions?'

'Would you like it to be?'

'Would you?'

'What d'you think?' He cocked an eyebrow almost playfully.

Christ, are we flirting here? Juno wondered giddily. But then Jay stuck a pedantic, pragmatic boot in.

'Your friend Lydia only asked me if I knew Will because you told her to.' He shrugged. 'You told her I was a thief, Juno.'

'I did not!' she fumed. 'Her boyfriend shares a house with Will – she found the bloody watch there; stole it from *him*, if you must know. Besides which, you bloody well denied knowing Will Pigeon that night when you patently do.'

'I hadn't fucking met him then, okay!' Jay's voice climbed the scale of angry impatience.

'Ah.' Juno savoured her knowing smile, feeling like Miss Marple cracking a tough suspect with her sweet, persistent charm and acumen. 'But Timon says you got in touch with him last week. And,' she paused for effect, 'our neighbour has seen you with those three every morning so far.'

'What is this? Fucking *Colombo*? I need a Coke.' Jay laughed in disbelief, storming into the kitchen.

'There's some in here,' Juno joked feebly, looking at the lines in front of her. She had a desperate urge to sneeze on them just to cheer herself up, but her bloody sinuses were far too healthy. She had to stop scrapping with Jay, she realised, and start talking.

Damn, oh damn, oh bugger, this wasn't going according to plan at all. She sagged back on the sofa and stared at the fifty-pound note. It would get her into a mini cab to find her friends and party the night away. She still had her list of fixtures; it was still early. She had at least three places she could choose from to escape this flat, meet her mates with a whoop, an apology, and the offer of a round of drinks. But all she wanted to do was race into the kitchen after Jay and beg a truce, tell him that she was only prying because she wanted to know if what had happened between them was a cheap sham or an expensive mistake, because she had never met anyone as disturbing as him in her life, because she wanted to kiss and make up. In fact either would do right now. To make friends would be nice, but to kiss would be just as nice. Better even.

Yes, kissing seemed like a very good idea, now she came to think about it.

'Listen, I'm sorry,' she called out, kicking the coffee table so that Timon's coke lines jerked into Zs. 'I just want to . . .' Want to what? Juno wondered. 'Make friends', 'know all about you', 'find out you're not a terrorist', 'kiss you until our ears pop'. What?

There was a pause. In the kitchen, the fridge door sucked shut and a can fizzed open.

Juno picked up the tightly rolled fifty-pound note from the coffee table, turning it around in her fingers, holding it like a cigarette. Fifty pounds. She sniffed it indulgently, inhaling its freshly printed, cash-machine-heated smell. A large lump of white powder, hidden in the folds, flew up her nostril like dust into a vacuum cleaner.

Juno blinked in shock, eyes stinging, nostril burning. What had she just done? She threw down the note in horror and rubbed her nose violently, like a child with a cold.

'I never denied that I knew who Dream Ticket was.' Jay emerged from the kitchen. 'I told your friend that. It freaked me out when she mentioned his name, I'd only just heard it myself.'

Juno blinked again. Christ – he was opening up. Now of all times. When any minute she might start talking non-stop. She had to concentrate. Had to be calm and logical.

'So Timon introduced you to Will?'

'Yeah – on Wednesday. I met Timon for a drink when I first arrived, and he said Will was a good fella to know in London.'

Juno's head was beginning to spin like the drum of a washing machine, thoughts jumbling and tangling, thrown together, the white powder starting to dissolve into her system. She tried to concentrate. Lydia had found Sean's watch in Will's flat on Sunday afternoon, days before Jay had met him for the first time. If that was the case then how could he have done a deal with Dream Ticket? There was no doubt that Will had acquired her brother's watch in exchange for something. When she'd probed him in the kitchen, he'd more or less said so. It didn't make sense unless . . .

'Last Friday night? You met Timon for a drink then, didn't you?' Still feeling pretty okay, Juno realised. Good. Still making sense.

'Yeah? So what?'

'That was the night Sean's watch went missing.'

'What?' He seemed bewildered for a moment.

Juno was certain she was on to a winner here. She suddenly felt like Wilma in *Scooby Doo*, piecing the vital – and often ludicrous – clues together at the end of the cartoon. She wanted to don a red wig and 'fifties specs, reach forward and unmask the villain. 'That's the one mistake I was making all along, wasn't it? You gave the watch to *Timon*, not Will. You don't have to be embarrassed. I won't tell Sean. I don't even like the watch very much. I've always thought that inscription was pretty tac—' Aware that she was gabbling, she shut up.

'Jesus, Juno! How many times do I have to spell it out?' Jay laughed bitterly, swigging from his can. 'I never set eyes on the frigging watch.'

'I don't believe you.' She swivelled around so that she was kneeling on the sofa, elbows propped on the back to face him. She was starting to feel distinctly focused now, mind quick, intentions clearly prioritised in her head. Two missions: solve the watch mystery and win a kiss. Still feeling okay, still making sense. Good.

'You don't, huh?' Jay looked at her curiously, yellow eyes searching her face.

'Will knew all about the watch.' Juno realised she was smiling flirtatiously and tried to stop. Mustn't muddle up missions, she told herself. Watch first, kiss second.

'Oh, he did, did he?' Jay shouldered the kitchen arch this time. He was good at standing in arches, Juno decided. It must be the photographer's instinct – self-framing. Either that or he had a down-and-out streak. She felt like pointing this out, but knew she had to stay focused. She was starting to feel more and more confident that the watch was somehow behind all his uptight secrecy. Watch first, kiss second . . .

'What did you exchange it for? Was Timon the go-between?' she asked, pressing her chin into her palms as she hung over the back of the sofa.

He shook his head, eyes darting away in disbelief. 'You are too fucking unreal for words, Juno. You're fucking with my head.'

'Nice to know I haven't just restricted myself to your underpants region.' She tilted her face and smiled with as much gall as she could muster.

For a moment he looked utterly contemptuous and then, to her surprise, he laughed. Not a belly laugh, admittedly, but it sounded and looked genuine enough – diaphragm engaged, eyes smiling.

'You're driving me insane, Juno.' He shook his head, laugh sliding away. 'I don't want you involved in this – I mean it.'

'In what?' She was fascinated and more than a little excited by the sudden, salty tang of fear in her nostrils. Her elbows slid off the back of the sofa as she craned forwards.

He walked towards her. 'In why I'm here, in what I'm doing in England. Or in who I'm hanging around with. I mean it, Juno, leave it alone. It's none of your business. You'll only get hurt – and, believe me, I don't wanna hurt you.' He reached the back of the sofa and squatted down parallel to her, so close she could feel his breath on her cheek.

Kiss me, kiss me, kiss me, Juno thought dreamily.

'*Capisce*?' He pulled back his head to stare at her, yellow eyes earnest, wolf's tooth dancing on its taut thong in the hollow of his throat. It was the closest he'd come to her in days.

'Kis— *capisce*,' she corrected herself, nodding madly. '*Ca* – totally – *pisce*.'

They smiled at one another – actually smiled. Juno grinned and grinned and felt her heart lap her chest. It's like *The Crying Game* without the twist, she thought dizzily. Oh, God! He's going to kiss me.

Then he looked over her shoulder. 'Hadn't you better get back?' he asked.

Juno carried on smiling at him – almost leaping over the sofa-back to grapple him to the floor in a sexy embrace.

'Back to what?'

'Back to whoever it is you've made coffee for.' He stood up swiftly so that her eyes were level with his crotch. Her grin slipped.

'Ah – no – you see, I only made it for . . .'

'G'night, Juno.' He walked out of the room.

A couple of minutes later, she was slurping a mug of diabolically strong, cold coffee by the mantelpiece and admiring the still-intact Crackerjack pencil which Sean had won as a ten year old and which he kept proudly in the Malibu bottle miniature he'd drunk that same night then thrown up on the Paddington–Oxford train.

She looked at her reflection thoughtfully, eyeing a stranger. A fat little face with smudged make-up looked back – not the tasty sex-pot she had seen earlier. Jay must think she was such a tramp, she realised. She'd flirted with his friends, flirted with danger, and – to complete the hat-trick – tried to flirt with him. She pressed her forehead to the crusted wax on the mantelpiece and closed her eyes tightly.

If only he knew I can think of nothing but him at the moment.

'I think this is yours.'

A light, tinkling noise behind her ear alerted her. A moment later Jay was dangling something over her shoulder.

Juno's eyes snapped open and her head jerked back in time to see his face in the mirror – beautiful, threatening and unfriendly, inches from hers.

'You left this earring in my room.' He dropped a tiny, glittering Chinese symbol on to the mantelpiece. 'Next time, ask first and I'll give you a guided tour.'

Juno's face burned as she watched it come to rest against a blue candle. 'But I wasn't snoo—'

'Save it,' he snapped. 'Why don't you take that coffee

through to whoever's waiting for it? Christ knows, he probably needs it to get through a night with you.'

Cheeks flaring with colour, Juno grabbed her cafetière from the coffee table and stormed past him.

An hour later a phone call was picked up by the machine in the darkened sitting room.

'Hi, Juno, Jay – it's Sean again. Don't you guys ever pick up? Listen, forget looking for my watch. I admit it, I'm a complete muppet. I've just remembered that I left the bastard on the rim of Triona's bath, not the one at home. Sorry, guys, I hope you haven't been searching too hard. I've just left a message on her machine asking her to bring it over when she visits – she's coming in a couple of weeks. D'you know where she is tonight, by the way? Her mobile's switched off. Remind her she's got it when you see her this Sunday – I gather you're all dining with the Jurassics. Give them my love – and change the bloody greeting on this machine! That's all, folks. Hi, Poirot, baby – Daddy loves you. Put a pony on old Pridwell in the first hurdles outing next season for me.'

From deep beneath the birthing smock, a small, avian voice muttered, 'Love you, baby. The mother-in-law's a moose.'

Chapter Twenty-Four

Juno lay awake in a shaft of sunlight which spilled through the gap in her curtains and moved slowly up the bed towards her torso like a sawmill blade towards a victim in a Vincent Price movie. She heard Jay come back from his jog, take a shower then go into his room. She dragged a pillow over her face and groaned into it. Last night had been such a total Juno cock-up, it had to rate as one of her best.

The front door slammed and feet pounded outside. Peering blearily through her window, Juno was just in time to see Jay's shock of butterscotch hair disappearing into the dusty cab of Sean's T-Bird. He exited the tight parking space in two deft movements and roared off along the street.

Getting up at ten, she searched through pockets, scrabbled through the mess on her chest of drawers, dug down the back of the sofa, and located almost fifteen pounds in loose change. Timon's fifty-pound note was still sitting temptingly on the coffee table but Juno ignored it. It hadn't done her any favours last night and she wasn't about to half-inch it given her persistent accusations about Jay and the watch. She had a feeling she'd gone on about it far too much last night, become a bit side-tracked. She hadn't even started to ask him about the covert photography Timon had mentioned. The lines of coke, she noticed, had been neatly wiped away.

As she was slurping tea and counting out her booty on one of the oak tables, she noticed the message indicator flashing on the answer machine and played it. A tall pile of ten pences toppled over as she listened to her brother apologising about the watch mix-up.

'Oh, God – Jay really did have nothing to do with it,' she whispered, gnawing a thumbnail which tasted of old coppers and sofa dust. Jay's cameras and computer were missing, she noticed. A Post-it note beside his chewed-up charger cable read simply, 'Do you know anything about this?' Juno turned it over and scribbled an equally polite, 'I think we have mice.'

She then blitzed the phone for an hour and a half, apologising to friends she'd not met the night before, hearing all the gossip, and arranging to see others throughout the day. She decided to keep out of Jay's way as much as possible and let him cool down. She was looking forward to catching up with some old mates – friends she barely saw from one year to the next. Jay had done her a favour.

Bracing herself, she called Ally and Duncan's number last to find out whether Finlay had behaved himself at the theatre.

'We all loved him!' Ally laughed. 'What a sweetheart. He had Jules and Flo in stitches all night and I seriously think Duncan is in danger of developing some sort of homo-erotic crush. I, meanwhile, just have a straightforward crush on him. Thanks for getting him to come along, Juno. It was a hoot – best night out I've had in ages.'

'My pleasure.' She wished her own night had been as much fun.

'After we'd eaten at Mezzo, he took us all along to some late-night drinking bar in Soho called The Washroom, d'you know it?'

'Only too well.' It was one of Sean, Horse and Barfly's favourite haunts. 'Wasn't it a bit rough for your taste?'

'No, it was a scream. Full of drag queens and hooligans.'

'Sounds delightful,' Juno laughed.

'And you'll never guess who we spotted drinking together?'

'Lily Savage and Mad Frankie Fraser?'

'No – Sean's girlfriend. What's she called?'

'Triona?'

'Yes, Triona and this bloke Finlay recognised. He says he's a complete shark – some sort of dealer by all accounts.'

'Not Dream Ticket?' Juno faltered, gnawing her lip. She was certain she'd heard Will Pigeon arranging to meet someone at The Washroom during one of his many mobile calls the night before. And Triona had, it turned out, been the one who'd had Sean's watch all along.

'You know him then?' Ally gasped, confirming her fears.

'We've met briefly.' Juno didn't like the way her life was closing in on her, trapping her in a net of interconnections between supposedly random acquaintances. It left her feeling as though something major was going on which she knew nothing about.

'Finlay says he's a seriously dodgy character,' Ally told her conspiratorially. 'He has gangland connections, Juno. Triona should be careful. I was chatting to Duncan about it this morning in bed and he's convinced it's to do with a protection racket – after all, her shop's bang in the middle of Soho, isn't it?'

'Isn't that a bit far-fetched?' Juno was doubtful. 'She probably just wanted VIP passes for some club night or other.'

'Maybe,' Ally humoured her. 'Unfortunately we had to push off just after they arrived, so couldn't listen in. Our baby-sitter was furious we were so late back. She says she's not working for us again. So we might take you up on your offer to look after China sometime, if that's okay?'

'Sure,' Juno said vaguely, her head full of protection rackets, money laundering, drug deals, arms deals. How could that possibly link up with Triona, Sean's watch, Jay, little Bruno and photographs of Michael Caine?

After she'd rung off, she closed her eyes and tried to play join-the-dots with the connections, but the only picture she could draw resembled a child's crayon scrawl of a spider. The key to it all lay with the loquacious Will Pigeon, she knew that. But the key to what? Whatever it was, Jay and Triona were tangled up in it. Juno felt horribly left out, and killingly guilty for misjudging Jay so badly – for all she knew he was trying to help Triona out of some sort of dangerous corner by befriending Will, and she could have blown it all for him last night with all her wink-wink references to watches and doing business. If only they were on speaking terms!

She scribbled out her note to Jay and wrote instead, 'My fault. I left Poirot out. Sorry. If they're ruined, I'll buy replacements. Also, I now know you had nothing to do with Sean's watch disappearing. Sorry again. And I promise I wasn't snooping in your room yesterday, I needed to listen to –' Damn! She'd run out of space. Finding the block of Post-its, she wrote 'sorry' on each and every one. Then she ran around the flat sticking them on every surface – the mirror, fridge, microwave, every door, the television, Sean's surfboard, the loo seat.

It was only when she was plastering a few on Uboat's tank like an over-zealous bill-poster campaign that she noticed a rival collection of differently coloured Post-it notes neatly fanned out on the little table beside it. Between the framed picture of her parents and another of Triona with mauve hair and a leather bra, were half a dozen neatly written messages. Juno peeled one off and examined it.

'John rang, 8.05 p.m., Monday. Will call again.'

She whipped off another, clearly more recent.

'Odette rang, 9.00 a.m., Saturday. She got your message – suggests you make it lunch tomorrow instead. Her place. Call her to confirm.'

A third read, 'John rang, Thursday 9.30 a.m. Will fax you at work.'

Juno sagged guiltily on to an altar stool. He'd been writing down phone messages all along! She felt terrible for assuming otherwise. Of course someone as punctilious and pedantic as Jay would log every call neatly and leave them somewhere he thought she'd notice them. Only she hadn't.

She peeled off all the remaining messages and plastered her Post-it apologies all over the table.

On something of a roll, she changed the answerphone message, starting out with: 'I'm afraid Juno Glenn and Jay

Mulligan are away from the phone right now, and Sean Glenn is overseas. Leave your message or fax after this', and working her way through every permutation of 'Juno and Jay' (God, how she loved stringing the two words together in that couply way) with increasing embarrassment until she finally opted for, 'We can't pick up your call, so leave a message'. Satisfied at last, she stuck a couple of Post-it apologies on the phone and, armed with a bottle of red wine and her duffel bag crammed tight with spare shoes, a change of outfit, *Enriching Bitches* and her personal stereo, she left the flat at lunchtime looking as though its walls were developing bright yellow scabies.

It was a hot, sweaty midsummer Saturday in London; the tube was packed with tourists, the pavements crawling with beautiful young things showing off flat brown bellies, the air thick with pollution.

First stop was Shepherd's Bush where an old university friend was having a barbecue. The last time Juno had seen her was at the wedding six months earlier where she'd promised to 'support, respect and nurture' a tall, bearded man who taught at the same comprehensive in Acton.

'Joonee! I didn't think you'd come. This is fantastic! We must have a long gossip later.' She kissed Juno hello with a plate of tofu kebabs in one hand and a barbecue prong in the other then disappeared into the crowd.

Juno knew no one else there. The other guests were almost all teachers, almost all vegetarians, almost all married and almost all not drinking because they were driving. Several babies wailed from carry-cots and a few toddlers roamed around at ankle level, looking up skirts and down molehills – all being ignored by their parents. No one seemed to smoke at all.

'Surely one of you can have a drink?' Juno asked a couple of geography teachers in matching Greenpeace t-shirts.

'We don't think it's fair on the twins, do we, Tony?' One t-shirt turned to the other lovingly and reached out to cup a wedding-ringed paw.

'Fabian and I don't want to bring Mississippi and Prussia up believing that in order to have fun, one parent must get sloshed at parties,' Tony said earnestly.

'Teaching geography must come in handy when choosing your children's names,' Juno said sweetly, swigging some wine and wondering if she could sneak behind the garden shed for a fag. 'Is your school in London?'

Standing in a sunny, overgrown garden trying to get to grips with the national curriculum, self-funding crises, NUT action, inner-city deprivation and abused children, she drank too much, stuffed her face with veggie sausages, developed sunburn on her nose and wondered why she'd come. She had nothing in common with these people. The university friend had been a dope-smoking crony ten years earlier, but now a whole phase of twenty-something evolution divided them. Looking around at the sweet, make-up-free faces of the women and the sincere, naive faces of the men, Juno felt like a different species, and suddenly realised that a part of her envied them their settled, suburban liberalism, their issues and their sincerity, and their wailing, puking babies.

'"These are my salad days slowly being eaten away,"' she said to no one in particular as she pronged an organic radish with a biodegradable fork. 'Spandau Ballet, "Gold", 1983.' She closed her eyes as she remembered lying on Jay's bed the night before listening to Phil Collins. She was truly cracking up.

She'd come out today to take her mind off him, and now found she could think of nothing else. His face danced in the sunlight that dazzled her, his eyes peered up at her from her paper plate, his voice hissed from the sizzling barbecue, 'You're fucking with my head, Juno.'

She decided she needed a change of venue to escape. She was already running late as she'd promised to meet another friend outside Baker Street tube at three.

'But we've not spoken at all!' wailed her teacher friend, galloping past with a tray of wholemeal garlic bread and a bowl of green salad as Juno was leaving, her face puce from barbecuing nut cutlets. 'I always love hearing all your wacky news. Your life is so much more exciting than mine.'

'Another time,' Juno apologised. 'Great party. And I think your life's gorgeous.'

And so the day went on – always running late, always feeling detached, constantly thinking of Jay. Her Baker Street friend – a former Immedia trainee journalist who was now a staff-writer on *Dentistry Monthly* – wanted to give the latest Almodóvar a miss and see instead a new Will Smith sci-fi fantasy, which just left Juno perplexed.

'Why did he keep saving his cat when tens of thousands of Americans were turning green and melting all around him?' she asked over tea.

'It shows what a lovely caring man he is.' Her friend shrugged and then proceeded to bitch about everyone at *Dentistry Monthly*, moaning how much she loathed her job and missed the 'lovely, crazy crowd at Immedia'. Juno remembered a similar tea session a year earlier when she'd called everyone at Immedia 'no-mark tossers who wouldn't know journalism if it typed the news on their arses'.

Her face made the right expressions, her mouth the right noises, but Juno was thinking of nothing but Jay. She wondered if he'd found the Post-it notes yet, if he'd laughed and forgiven her or sighed tetchily because she'd simply created more mess for him to clear up.

'You're so talented, Juno,' her friend raged. 'It should have been you who left, not me – you should be a famous stand-up by now. Oh, Christ, I hate it there so much.' The friend started crying. 'If I have to write "caries" one more time I'll crack up. I keep dreaming that all my teeth are falling out.'

'You need to go to a caries adviser,' Juno joked feebly.

Wiping away tears and making all the right noises took time, and Juno was late again to meet up with her stand-up pal Alicia who performed in a duo with a friend from drama school under the stage names Sue Denim and Vera Go. Together they were collectively 'The Supermodels' and were following a recent glut of female double acts into stardom. They were regulars both at the Ha Ha House and at Jongleurs, could fill a regional venue, had written their own Radio 4 sketch show and were appearing with increasing regularity on television.

'Channel Four want us to write a pilot for a possible series,' Alicia said excitedly as they downed hasty pints in De Hems before sussing out the early show at a new club, Stand-up and Deliver, in Brewer Street. 'I only heard yesterday – can't wait to tell Carol but she's in Corfu for a week with Silo at the moment. Christ, I hate being single. You and John still going okay?'

That was the problem with occasional friends, Juno realised. You occasionally had to fill them in on six months of your life in five minutes.

The acts at Stand-up and Deliver were depressingly routine, with no women on the bill at all. The one good moment was seeing Pete Jenkins, the nervous English teacher, try out completely new material to terrific effect.

'That was simply fantastic!' Juno bounced up to him during the interval. 'You do characters so well – the French exchange student was a gem, and the Oasis fan was priceless.'

Pete grinned delightedly. 'It was you who gave me the idea, actually.' He blushed. 'When you did that tart with a heart stuff on Wednesday night and turned the audience like that.'

Alicia was less impressed. 'I heard about your little turn on Wednesday night.' She handed Juno another pint as they moved away from the jostling bar. 'I met Bob last night for a drink in Streatham and he seemed to think you were on something hallucinogenic.'

'I was trying to impress a bloke I fancied in the audience.' Juno sighed sadly, suddenly realising it was the tragic, mis-judged truth.

'And did it work?'

'Not exactly.'

'Shit, Juno.' Alicia shook her head with a bitter laugh. 'Face it, you're too funny to be sexually attractive to most men. Women like us can't resist wise-cracking during sex. We're spinster-doctors for life.'

The second half was starting. Juno was aware that she was more than a little tight. She found herself thinking about Jay again. Obsessing about him, in fact. She tried to concentrate on the acts, told herself she was supposed to be having a day away from the flat to clear her head, but all she could see was his cold yellow eyes the night before as he'd told her to get back to the fictional 'lover' in her room. A lover she was too funny to attract.

Rushing off before the end, promising Alicia she'd be in touch soon, Juno changed into a creased dress in the pub loo and panted off to a party in Earl's Court being hosted by a mate from a journalism course years earlier.

The party was held in an immaculate mansion block flat, full of high-powered, sharp-witted, power-dressed national newspaper reporters discussing politics. They were almost all single, under thirty, chain-smoking heavy drinkers, but Juno felt no more comfortable than she had at the barbecue. She hated being introduced as a walking joke. 'Come and meet gorgeous Hal – he's a political reporter on *The Times*. Hal, this is Juno – she has the funniest job. I'll let her tell you all about it.' Out of her depth, too tight to remember who was in the shadow cabinet, and embarrassed by her free-sheet agony-aunt status, she drank even more, thought about Jay even more, used the loo to repair her make-up then raced back to the West End to meet a bunch of old schoolfriends who were intent on a night of clubbing. She was an hour late as she staggered down the steps of another throbbing bar to find them, and now possessed less than fifty pence to her name.

'We'll buy you drinks,' they all insisted, poo-poohing her embarrassed insistence that she'd just stay and chat until they left for the club, then catch the last tube home. 'And we'll club together to get you into Emporium. C'mon, Juno – we hardly ever see you, you're not getting away that easily.'

Tears of gratitude filled her by now slightly bloodshot eyes, although in her secret, lovelorn little heart she just wanted to go home and see whether Jay had received her apology. She'd mixed too many drinks and too many people into one day. Her four old schoolfriends, whom she saw less and less as years went on, were a pretty high-energy bunch of single women (two divorced, two unmarried) who spent an entire week building up to a night like this – they'd been waxed and conditioned and clay-wrapped and aroma-massaged for tonight. Juno was acutely aware of being dog-tired, stale and badly dressed by comparison.

And so she found herself sitting alone on a fake fur banquette in a dark, sweaty club at three in the morning, sucking on a plastic Evian mini-bottle which she'd filled up at the sink in the loos because she couldn't afford the three pounds it cost to buy an ice cold one at the bar.

She hated night-clubs – Hades for the overweight woman, Heaven for the underage girl. They were a paradise of paradox. People turned up in gaggles looking fantastic, then took a small pill with a logo stamped on it which made them dance alone and sweat profusely all night. Juno didn't need an E to dance alone and sweat profusely. She should be offered free entry.

Of the four friends, three disappeared to dark corners with suspiciously young-looking men, and a fourth got so drunk that Juno had to hold her over a loo-pan, stroking her damp hair until she managed to evacuate four Margaritas, two Orange Hooches, a Long Island Tea and a Sea Breeze.

'You're sush a good mate, Juno,' came a small voice, echoing around the porcelain. 'I'm shorry you din' pull either.'

Juno tucked a strand of sweat-sodden brown hair away from her friend's mouth and shrugged. 'It's okay. The only thing I'm trying to pull tonight is wool from my eyes.'

A Between The Sheets came dribbling out between retches.

As the Vomit Queen straightened up, she reached for a hunk of loo roll to wipe her mouth and looked blearily up at Juno. 'I think Tina's gone back with shomeone. I'm not sure I can make it to the flat on my own. Feel bit wobbly. Will you come back with me? Shtay over? I'll pay for the cab.' Her reddened eyes were coming in and out of focus.

Juno thought about Jay, about the Post-its. She remembered that she was meeting Odette for lunch and Lulu for tea the next day, that she still had to pack to house-sit, that she'd planned to re-touch her roots in the morning. She wanted to check on Poirot and Uboat, longed to sleep in her own bed.

'Christ, I feel shick. It's Tina's bloody fault. She went after the same man as me and got him – ash usual. Bitch.'

'I'll make sure you get home.' Juno reached up to flush the loo. 'Let's get your coat and go.'

She was always crashing over at different people's flats and houses – a habit she'd picked up as a kid. Nowadays it was more often because she couldn't afford a cab home than the teenage excuse that her parents were both too drunk or lazy to drive out and fetch her from whatever Oxfordshire party or pub she and her friends had landed up in.

The Battersea flat was a typical girls-together rented slumbox, with pants drying on the radiators, *Four Weddings and a Funeral* prominently displayed on the video rack, Klimt prints and photo-collages on the walls, tasteful patchwork throws hiding the Dralon three-piece suite. Compared to the sterile bleached wood floors and white sofas of the Earl's Court mansion block Juno had quaked in earlier, it felt comfortably familiar, if a throw-back to the days of student loans and Value brand food. Tina and her flatmate had lived here years – Juno remembered pre-John parties which she'd attended, dolled up to the nines in the hope of scoring, only to find twenty other women far better dolled, and just five men in situ – four of them with someone, the other gay.

Once on home territory, her friend went on to auto pilot, staggering straight to bed and conking out.

Juno sat up and drank a mug of tea, thinking about Jay, imagining him tucked up in bed in the flat – a bed she'd shared for just a few hours, but long enough to know the way he tossed and turned as he slept, haunted by his own demons. She longed to be back there, sleeping under the same roof. She only wished she could afford a taxi home. Tomorrow night she'd be in her little single bed in Oxfordshire, far away from Jay and his secrets.

At four in the morning, just as she was nodding off fully dressed on the sofa, Tina crashed into the flat, hit the lights and screamed as she spotted Juno.

'Oh, it's just you!' she giggled, pitching sideways into the dining-room table. 'What are you doing here?' Her face was stubble-rashed and happy and her lace shirt buttoned up wrong. She lurched forward, knocking over a cheese plant.

Tina had been the one girl at school whom all the boys fancied – she'd counted her Valentines by the score, and scored with most of her Valentines. Her Age of Aquarius had been at eighteen when every boy in their progressive Oxford school's upper sixth had wanted to get into her ultrabrite white M&S tanga briefs. She'd never been particularly academic, and had dropped out of university to go to a posh private secretarial college. While her old schoolfriends skulled pints at the union bar and raved about the Socialist Workers' Party and indie bands, Tina wore little power suits, had a tights allowance, dated older men and stayed late at work in her role as PA to the MD, serving champagne to directors in the boardroom. It was only after they had all graduated that the salary scales of her school contemporaries gradually started to outweigh hers, their boyfriends seemed younger and more glamorous than her thirty-something divorced computer programmers, her own job suddenly mundane and repetitive. Ten years on she was still PA to some MD or other. The older men now wanted younger girls, and Tina resorted to younger men. Much younger.

'Nineteen!' She flopped on to the sofa beside Juno. 'He still lives with his mum. Fantastic kisser, though. I thought about asking him back here, but I'm a bit off sex at the moment so we necked in Bar Italia for a couple of hours and I gave him a made-up number. You still living with whassisname? John?'

Juno was shattered and hungover and fed up with playing catch up.

'No. I live with a guy called Jay.'

'Wow! Quick mover,' Tina whistled, kicking off her court shoes. 'And you were the girl who was so shy she used to bully the men she fancied at school.'

'I what?' Juno stifled a yawn.

'Remember Jamie Hickson?'

'Christ, Jamie Hickson.' Juno blinked in recognition of a

name she hadn't heard for years. 'That was when we were upper thirds, Tina. I was fourteen. He gave Gabby Alsopp a love bite and I cried for a week.'

'You bullied him,' Tina hiccuped, made honest by drink. 'You fancied him like mad – you told us all often enough – but when you were near him, you teased him and flicked him with your ruler and made him blush because you couldn't tell him you liked him.'

'I did?' Juno could only remember the sleepless nights spent crying over him.

'Yeah, we all used to reckon it was the only way you thought you'd ever get him to notice you – by making his life hell. You did that a lot to boys. Most of them were scared of you, but liked you too. You did it to Jared Williamson as well but it really paid off that time. I was so jealous when he asked you to the A-level ball.'

'You were?' Juno was starting to wonder whether she was dreaming this. Jared Williamson – her heart-stopping date to the last school summer ball – had behaved like a perfect gentleman all night, pecked her on the cheek afterwards, told her she was special then never called her again. Juno still half-believed that her mother had paid him to take her to the ball. During the summer holidays that followed he'd started dating Tina – a relationship which lasted until they all went off to different universities in the autumn. They'd even Euro-railed together, which at the time was almost equivalent to marriage.

'Mmm. He was such a god, wasn't he?' Tina pulled her legs up on to the sofa. 'I remember the way you'd just bound over to him in the common room and challenge him to a game of Triv which you'd rigged so you'd win and he'd look dim. Or you'd impersonate him dancing at parties. Or there was that time when you had to read aloud an essay in Eng Lit and compared him to Edmund in *Mansfield Park* and everyone fell about.'

'I thought they were laughing at me.' Juno rubbed her eyes tiredly, painful memories being pulled like teeth from her Pandora's Box. That one was a killer – the laughter mocked her to this day. She'd been made to read the whole thing aloud, a privilege preserved for the top essay. It should have been a golden day – her first A-grade essay. Instead it had marked a moment of madness as she'd stuttered out her Jared Williamson metaphor in front of twenty cackling seventeen year olds. It was the first day she'd ever smoked a cigarette, puffing tearfully on a JPS with Dawn Ryder, the school punk, in the loos during second break.

'Of course we were laughing,' Tina snorted. 'Everyone knew you were taking the piss – you always did. He was so embarrassed. His mates called him Eddy for weeks. He fancied you rotten by then, but was too tongue-tied to ask you out so he sent you that note.

'Christ, I was jealous!' Tina sagged back on the sofa, eyes drooping. 'When you dragged me to the shops to suggest what you should wear, I wanted to pick out the dog-ugliest dress in that old hippy shop in Little Clarendon Street you liked. You were so fat,' she was almost talking to herself now as sleepiness kicked in, 'and you always looked a mess. I couldn't understand it. Why he fancied you and not me.'

'But you ended up going out with him, Tina,' Juno pointed out.

'Mmm, so I did,' she sighed sleepily. 'I was a bitch, wasn't I? He came into Browns with some mates the day after the ball – remember I waitressed there as a summer job? – and asked me whether I thought you liked him or not, because you hadn't seemed to the night before. And I – forgive me, Juno, I was such a cow in those days – I told him you'd only gone to the ball with him as a joke, that you'd been dared to, that you thought he was thick.'

'You didn't?' she gasped.

'I gave him my phone-number and knocked twenty quid off his table's bill. I'm sorry, Juno.'

'So he fancied me all along?' The lump in her throat was back. 'He really did fancy me?'

'For a bit, yeah,' Tina hiccuped. 'You see, you aren't – weren't – pretty,' she corrected herself too late, 'but you were always so fucking popular. And, you know, it's like powerful men attracting beautiful women – popular women attract gorgeous men, don't they? Look at you now.'

'I'd rather not.' Juno was aware that she was on the stale and ragged end of the popular bag-lady scale.

'Tonight you turn up late – as always, broke – as always, looking a bit of a mess – as always.' Tina hiccuped again, eyes shut now, her stream of consciousness threatening to break its banks. 'And when we ask what you've been up to today, it turns out you've been all over London meeting people and partying and being Miss fucking Popular. D'you want to know what I did before we met up today? Bought a lottery ticket, plucked my eyebrows and phoned my mother.'

'I have lots of Saturdays like that,' Juno insisted.

But Tina was rambling on drunkenly, 'And now it also turns out you've junked in drop-dead-gorgeous John whom we all fancied like mad on the rare occasions you bothered to ask us to a party in your busy-busy life these past three years – and you're already living with some other guy. I should hate you, Juno. You're so bloody . . . *sorted*.'

Juno offered a tentative hug and was immensely grateful when it was accepted. Tina's fragile frame slid into her arms like a child's.

'I'm not sorted, Tina.' Juno kissed the top of her head. 'I promise you, I'm hopeless. Today was awful – I was late all the time, I had no money, I wanted to see people that I like and hardly ever get a chance to see, but didn't have enough time to do anything but literally just *see* them before dashing off. And John went off with someone younger and prettier. Jay's just my flatmate – he hates me, if you must know.'

'Do you fancy him?' Tina sniffed sleepily, sinking deeper into Juno's soft bulk.

She closed her eyes and thought about him for the hundredth time that day. 'I bully him. I bully him very badly indeed.'

Even if a decade of differences divided them, there was still a shorthand between old friends which led straight to the heart.

'Don't worry – I bet he fancies you rotten too.' Tina

cuddled into Juno's stomach and fell asleep, the tears from her face soaking into Juno's cheap, creased dress.

She sat awake for hours, watching dawn steal into the room, dwelling on her weird, back-tracking day. She'd seen herself from all angles as reflected in other people's eyes and suddenly started to realise that she wasn't cracking apart – she was fitting a jigsaw puzzle together. And the picture it presented was far from flattering. She was a wacky, chaotic, unmotivated bully. No wonder Jay wasn't falling at her feet. It would take more than a few Post-it notes to make things up with him. A post-bag full of letters couldn't make him respect her now.

The morning brought cricked necks, dead legs, hangovers and embarrassment. Juno didn't want to stick around for a post-mortem of the night before, but she needed to borrow a fiver to get her through the day and first had to pluck up courage to ask. It was only after three cups of tea, a bowl of Special K and a foul ultra-low cigarette provided by Tina that she made her guilty request.

'Sure.' Tina handed her a tenner, squinting across the dining-room table, mascara-stained bags propping up her tired eyes. 'Have this, I've nothing smaller.'

'I'll send you a cheque,' Juno promised.

'Whenever.' Tina rubbed her eyes, distributing the mascara further. 'Keep in touch more often in future, huh?'

Juno nodded and they smiled at one another, both knowing it would be months before they saw one another again. Such was the nature of some friendships, Juno realised sadly as she waited for a bus to take her to Islington to meet Odette for lunch. There they were, little buried mines of shared experiences and emotions that you trod on every so often, exploding a painful memory or two before limping away again. And it was only when you were skipping and dancing through the daisy field once more that you stumbled upon one again. Some friendships, however precious, were too painful to maintain at the same intensity all the time.

Her closest cronies – the gang – were a solace and a haven

of shared humour and ideals, but their friendship possessed none of the bitterness which she and her schoolfriends hefted around on their shoulders like satchels from bygone days to swing at one another on their occasional meetings. The gang had shared far greater traumas and tragedy, had seen one another through agony, ecstasy and more broken hearts than Guy's Hospital, yet to an outsider their relationships appeared divinely shallow; the support network was a vast, cast-iron structure which held up the little paddling pool of frivolous mundanity in which they splashed. The schoolfriends had only shared petty bickering and teenage jealousy, yet the residual resentment and hurt from those *Jinty Album*, ra-ra skirts, *Just Seventeen* days filled a huge, black quarry of competitiveness into which they inevitably slipped every time they met.

'Shit, you're looking a bit rough, babe,' Odette greeted her cheerfully on the threshold of the vast, immaculate Zen Den.

Wearing DKNY joggers, a Nike sports bra and CK trainers, Odette was glistening lightly through her tinted moisturiser, short, dark hair scraped back from her face by a black stocking acting as an Alice band.

'I've been working out, trying to shift some flab,' she panted, leading Juno through the open-plan flat to her canteen-sized kitchen. 'We've got a communal gymnasium in the basement here, but I prefer to use me own equipment. I bought a load of gear from Lillywhite's a while back, but I only had the time to unpack it last week. Impressive, huh?' She nodded towards an industrial array of weight machines, press-benches and stair-masters which were scattered across the shiny floorboards of the flat like medieval torture apparatus.

'You don't need to lose weight.' Juno looked at her in amazement.

'Too many corporate lunches, babe.' Odette patted her enviably flat stomach and then proceeded to produce lots of high-cal M&S goodies from her restaurant-sized fridge. 'I 'fought we'd have champagne.'

'Are we celebrating something?' Juno laughed.

Odette winked, expertly peeling foil from a bottle of Taittinger. 'I packed in my job on Friday.'

Juno's jaw dropped at the same moment as the cork popped. 'Your job?'

'I'm fed up of never seeing anyone, Juno.' Odette poured bubbles into two oversized champagne flutes. 'I'm tired of working from seven till ten and thinking that's good 'cos I'll get an early night for once. I hate travelling overseas, eating foreign muck and drinking alone at mini-bars. I'm pissed off with earning all this dosh and never having time to spend it. I'm sick of meeting men I fancy and never getting as far as the first sodding date 'cos I've never gotta free night and if I have I'm too shattered to go out, or I want to see me mates or me mum. I want to know what lying in feels like, Juno, not lying my teeth out at another power-breakfast.'

'But what are you going to do?' Juno was staggered. Odette had been the archetypal career girl for so long that one hand was constantly callused from carrying her briefcase.

'I gotta load of dosh saved up.' Odette grinned, clinking glasses. 'I'm gonna bum around London for a coupla months having fun, then I'm gonna set up a restaurant with a bar downstairs and a comedy club upstairs. Simple, innit?'

'You what!' Juno shrieked in delight.

'No joke, babe.' Her friend grinned. 'This isn't some sort of pipe-dream bollocks. I've got a well-sound business plan and everyfink. It's totally boss. I've got a couple of big investors secured, even possible premises lined up – an old fire station up the road here which comes up for lease in October. I mean it, babe. I've even got Calum Forrester to agree to help me launch it. Now that,' she took a swig of champagne, 'is a class act.'

Juno sagged down on a 'fifties kitchen stool in surprise. 'Finlay's brother?'

'Who?' Odette shook her head. 'No, Calum Forrester, babe – he's a big restaurant and club promoter, knocks around with Marco Pierre White and Damien Hirst and that lot. He's the business.'

'Founded the Nero Club?'

'That's the geezer!' Odette raised her glass. 'He reckons he knows this hot-shot young chef who's gonna be a real celebrity soon, wants to put him in charge of the restaurant. We're talking the business nosh-wise. The bar's gonna be fucking trendy – Calum knows an artist who'll do the decor. The comedy club's gonna have top-ranking acts, its own bar, food too maybe. The place'll be a launch legend, babe. I've got sponsorship offers coming out of my ears. Have a prawn won-ton.'

Juno started guzzling happily, listening to all Odette's plans.

'Calum reckons we'll rival Jongleurs in a year or two. We're pitching it as a fusion of Comedy Store and Quo Vadis, with a bit of Atlantic Bar tack thrown in. Downstairs, the bar's totally fuck-off trendy, yeah? We're talking drag queens on the door, totally arsey dress-codes, drinks at least a fiver each – it'll be packed every night. The restaurant's more money and media, attracted by the hype and the star chef's food. City Suits, Channel Four, PR, music industry – plus the idiots I know in advertising. It'll be booked up weeks in advance. Upstairs is more right-on Islington guilt-trippers, but wealfy – no student tossers. We'll pay well and book big names. Some nights it'll be five acts, others it'll be one touring star doing an extended set. We'll try for a TV tie-in too – I've got the contacts. At weekends we have early and late shows, maybe lunch-time open mike slots . . .'

It was only when she was cramming back her fifth prawn won-ton and washing it down with her second glass of champagne that Odette let drop the real clanger.

'I'll need a resident emcee.' She looked at Juno slyly. 'Know anyone decent?'

Juno thought about it. 'Bob Worth's good but he wouldn't come cheap,' she said. 'There's a guy called Pete Jenkins I really like. I saw him do some cracking stuff last night, but I'm not sure he has the confidence yet.'

'Interesting.' Odette nodded. 'We need a big personality – someone who's part maître d', part compère – maître emcee if you like. Someone who works all three spaces, but primarily the top floor. They've gotta have a lot of charisma, and they've gotta be fucking funny.'

'In that case, I'd suggest someone like Mick Collins – he's very sexy, and he's great at ad-libbing.'

Odette shook her head. 'Too well known, and too busy. Besides he's out of London half the time. Whoever does it has to be there at least four nights a week for the first six months. Plus, we're really looking for a woman. Possibly two to share the workload.'

'The Supermodels?'

'We thought about them. Same problem as Mick Collins – too established. C'mon, you thick cow, get your brain in gear.'

Juno started on the gravadlax, face starting to flame in excitement. 'Well, if you're stuck, I suppose I . . .'

'We're not stuck, babe,' said Odette curtly. 'We want the best. I insist upon it.'

'Oh.' Juno chewed her lip in embarrassment.

'You're seeing your mate Lulu later, aren't you?' Odette eyed her.

Juno nodded mutely, disappointment pressure-hosing her body.

'Well, ask her if she can think of anyone.' Odette grinned wickedly. 'Now let's watch the *Londoners* omnibus – and don't you dare tell me what's happened!' Some things took precedence over discussing life-changing decisions after all.

Juno had seen two of the four episodes that week, and spent the first half-hour's repeat imagining herself floating around a glamorous restaurant, charming the tables of celebrities who had come to see her legendary compèring. Some of them might be from the cast of *Londoners*. She'd always harboured a quiet crush on the brutish but sexy Wayne Jones who played Liam Sullivan.

'Rumour has it she's for the axe.' Odette nodded at the television as Lily Fuller pulled up the sash of the Man and started screaming at Liam in the street below.

'Belle Winters? Never!' Juno was appalled. It was like

hearing the Queen Mum was going to be put in a retirement home.

But Odette nodded, eyes wide with shared horror. 'A mate of mine's a script editor on the show. Says that Belle's contract's up for renewal soon and she's demanding double the salary or she walks. Or rather, her new agent's the one demanding the dosh – some West End hotshot she's hired to get her more press coverage, 'parently. The production company's freezing them both out.'

'It wouldn't be the same without her.' Juno looked at that familiar, fiery face and felt tears spring to her eyes. 'Lily *is* *Londoners*.'

'I know.' Odette sniffed, swigging back a gulp of champagne. 'The one thing I've been looking forward to about packing in my job is watching it before anyone can tell me what's happened. At the restaurant, I'm gonna have a thirty-inch telly in my office and I'll be unavailable for half an hour, four nights a week.'

'What are you going to call the place?'

'Remember my old nickname at college?'

'OD?' Juno laughed.

'Simple, innit? The OD. Can't fail – drug culture being boss and all that.'

Juno was late to meet Lulu for a hasty pot of tea and a Danish in Patisserie Valerie. Bubbling over with excitement, she babbled out Odette's plans so quickly she developed hiccups. She tried not to sound too jealous when she explained about Odette's ongoing search for a resident maître emcee.

'You're so thick, Juno pet,' rasped Lulu, spiking up her blue hair with one tiny hand. 'Odette wants you to do it, doesn't she? It's frigging obvious.'

Juno shook her head. 'She didn't ask me.'

'Juno, I despair of you!' Lulu howled, banging her Danish on the table with such a thump its cherry fell off. 'You *always* wait for bookings to come to you. You think because you don't have a manager or an agent, you haven't a chance at any of the bigger venues or out-of-town gigs, and that's bollocks. You just need to push more for the work. You have to sell yourself. Can't you see, Odette wants you to do just that to her? She might be your mate but she's also a businesswoman. She probably has promoters and sponsors and all sorts of other buggers to win over before this thing gets off the ground. And you've got to be able to win them over too.'

Juno's little ego boil throbbed irritably at this insinuation that she was gutless. 'I have impressed someone recently,' she boasted, unable to resist telling Lulu about Piers Fox's plan. She knew it was wildly indiscreet, as Piers had asked for her confidentiality, but swore Lulu to secrecy too.

Her friend swore quite a lot after she'd heard the story. And laughed. And rubbed her hand through her blue hair, eyes narrowed critically.

'It's bollocks, pet. Comedy won't ever be pop culture. The lust factor's missing. Look at Newman and Baddiel. Played Wembley Stadium and then what? It's the love-child of Ringo Star and Sandra Bernhardt who's made it big. The pretty one wrote a book and disappeared back on to the pub circuit. Comedy can make an ugly bloke sexy, but a guy who's drop-dead sexy in the first place finds it twice as hard to make people laugh. For women comics, triple that, square it and add your own age to the power of your bust measurement. Piers Fox's babes are doomed.'

'Oh,' said Juno in a small voice. 'So you don't think I should audition, then?'

'I think you should tell Odette you want to be her maître emcee – insist upon, in fact it,' Lulu growled. 'And don't you dare go all stubborn and mope around waiting until she asks you like you do with men, pet. You'll only miss out, I promise you.'

At half-past four Juno yelped, grabbed her bag, kissed Lulu and fled.

She didn't make it back to the Belsize Park flat until almost five, by which time Triona had arrived and was pacing around in a state of angst.

'Thank Christ you're all right!' She pounced upon Juno at the door. 'We were convinced you'd had an accident.'

'An accident?' Juno raked one hand through her dirty, dark-rooted hair. The Post-it notes had been cleared away, she noted with a hollow feeling in her chest as she walked into the flat.

'Jay says you didn't come back last night.' Triona's super-thin eyebrows rose enquiringly.

Juno found she couldn't look at him. She could see his legs nearby, but only managed to meet the eyes into which his bootlaces were threaded. Any higher was impossible.

She looked at Triona again.

'I slept over at a friend's place.' She was aware it sounded like a line.

'Oh, right.' Triona let one eyebrow drop, the other angled tellingly. 'So are you ready to set off? We're going to be late as it is.'

Juno knew that she must look awful – slept-in clothes, greasy face, eau-de-night-club wafting around her. She hated the thought of Jay's seeing her looking so shabby, but guessed it was the least of her problems on the charm-offensive front. After all, she was the bullying tramp who flirted with his friends, accused him of theft, pretended to have a man in her room (he still thought she had, come to that), nosed into his private life, and – in his words – fucked with his head. Now he was being forced to meet her mad parents.

'Er – no. I think I might have a bath and pack first. You two go on.' She shot another glance at Jay's boots. 'I'll catch you up.'

'How are you going to do that? Charter a helicopter?'

'I'll drive the T-Bird of course.' Juno edged towards the bathroom. 'I'll need it down there.'

'But Jay's using it.' Triona marked her as far as the bathroom door.

'Sean said *I* could use it while he was in New York,' said Juno, feeling like Blanche facing up to Stella.

'Don't be childish about this, Juno.' Triona held on to the

bathroom door. 'I'll give you a lift down. You can use your father's car while you're there.'

'I can't drive it,' she bleated truthfully. 'It's German.' She managed to wrench the door from Triona's grip and shut it.

She raced to the taps to set them gushing and obliterate any argument that she smelled over the limit, that they were hugely late and that there were a stack of messages for her on the answermachine which she needed to listen to before they left. 'And now you're having a bath! Are you feeling yourself, Juno?'

'Don't be obscene!' she squeaked, before realising she might have misinterpreted the question.

Scrubbed and loofahed, she felt far better. She even managed to catch Jay's eye and smile as she raced around the flat, throwing a few dog-walking clothes into a kit bag and apologising for her lateness at least twenty times to Triona, who was tapping one very high heel on the ash floor and tutting about the time.

'You can listen to these as you pack,' she muttered, pressing 'Play' on the answermachine.

Oh, God. Juno gnawed her lip as she ferreted through the boiler cupboard for some clean underwear. More guilt to load on to her already stricken conscience.

There were several messages from friends she'd let down this weekend, and one from Finlay asking how Friday night had gone.

'I hope the dress worked, sugar – oops!' he laughed as he clearly realised the message might be heard by Jay. 'I'm going away next week. I'll try and call you, let you know how it's going. Find out your exciting news.' The final sentence was deliberately cryptic but loaded with innuendo. 'I'm sure you tasted the fruit again on Friday night – feel it in my bones, in fact. If not, alas, in my boner.'

The next message was from John. The unfortunate juxta-position of the two was lost on Juno as she hunted out a pair of socks.

'Juno, flower,' he mumbled awkwardly, at least half a dozen Ruddles up and feeling very down. Tom Waits was droning in the background. 'It's Shaturday. I know you probably don't want to talk to me again after what happened last night, but I can't shtop thinking about it. I want to – hic – talk to you again. I hoped you might come over, I've made a curry. You love my – hic – curries, don't you, our Juno? We could – hic – talk things over . . . Bugger, I've got hiccups! Back in a – hic – minute.' There was a long pause as he went to fetch a glass of water, clearly falling over several items of furniture as he went.

Juno kept her head in the boiler cupboard, eyes clenched shut. As John picked up the phone again and slurred on penitently, she felt guiltier and guiltier for making him feel so bad.

'I'm so shorry about what happened last night, flower. About forgetting to wear one again, you know? I just didn't think. I was so made up that you agreed. And you came, didn't you? You came? That meant something, surely? Oh, bugger, my curry's burning . . .' There was a clunk and the time stamp cut in: 'Seeernday – tweaaalve-fifty aaa-eeem.'

As she scuttled into her room to fetch her wash bag, Juno didn't notice Jay's eyes following her sadly.

Chapter Twenty-Five

Having insisted upon driving, Juno found to her shame that she couldn't manoeuvre the T-Bird out of its tight parking space. She glanced in the wing mirror and saw Triona's ancient Saab already waiting in the street behind, its two occupants expecting her to lead the way via a short cut she knew to the M40. She only wished she knew a short cut out of a ten-foot parallel parking space which didn't involve edging backwards and forwards for half an hour under Jay's critical gaze.

Damn! Why hadn't they gone on ahead? Juno thought wretchedly as she crunched gears, cranked the huge steering wheel around and tried not to feel sick as highly revved diesel fumes swirled around her in the cab. She slid the window shut and craned around as she inched the big heap of steel backwards – straight into the bumper of a parked Audi which let off a car-alarm shriek and started flashing its lights angrily.

A small queue of traffic was building up behind the waiting Saab now and a couple of impatient motorists tooted their horns. Juno gestured Triona to drive on, hoping they would go around the corner and wait out of sight of her appalling demonstration of parallel unparking. The T-Bird let out a loud groan as she wrenched its steering column around and edged it forwards – slap into the rear bumper of a Mazda whose car alarm joined that of the Audi, wailing in unison like a couple of competing scream-queens on a bad B-movie. Sandwiched in between, Juno was almost deafened.

Crunching the gears into reverse once more, she jumped as the driver's door was pulled open and Jay appeared beside her.

'Move over,' he ordered.

'Can't you see I'm trying to do that?' she complained. 'This Mazda in front has obviously hemmed the T-Bird in since you parked it here. It's impossible to get out.'

'Move over into the passenger seat, Juno,' Jay sighed irritably, stepping back as she almost ran over his foot. 'I'll get her out.'

'Be my guest.' She slithered over to the passenger side and picked sulkily at the plastic tax disc holder, deeply ashamed of her own feebleness. Yet another black mark against her.

To her utter humiliation, he coaxed the old Bird out of its space in three easy movements.

'It's the first bit that's hardest,' Juno mumbled defensively. 'I must have got the angle for you.'

'Sure.' Jay slid open the window and gestured for Triona to follow.

'I can drive from now on, though!' Juno bleated. 'You go with Triona if you'd prefer.'

But they were already heading west out of Belsize Park, sunlight hanging over the high corridor of white stucco houses like a blinding chandelier.

Juno felt terrified and claustrophobic alone in the cab with him, certain that anything she said would only dig her more deeply into his bad books – and he must have a library of them now, all neatly indexed 'Glenn, J'.

'I keep getting lost in this damned city,' he said, keeping his eyes on the road. 'The more I drive, the better I get to know my way around.'

'Well, I suppose if it helps you out . . .' Juno cleared her throat, not looking at him. 'I know London pretty well. I can show you the best route.' She guessed there was some pride to be salvaged after all.

They drove along Wellington Road in heavy traffic, where she watched the early-evening joggers pant past as they headed for Regent's Park. The din of competing car stereos all around them floated in through the open window on Jay's side, dominated by the Top 40 countdown.

She would have liked to maintain a dignified, discreet silence, but was obliged to give monosyllabic directions for the M40. 'Turn right at the lights – past Lord's Cricket ground.'

'That's a cricket ground?' Jay glanced through his window at a high wall. 'I thought it was a prison.'

'It's hidden from view.' Juno glanced warily at him although she pretended to be looking at Lord's too. His eyes were invisible behind a sweep of hair but the set of his chin was far from friendly. He was wearing a remarkably smart outfit, she realised. Dressed in conventional cream chinos, a soft leather belt and crisp white shirt, he looked terrific. She quickly looked away in case he caught her gawking.

'Jesus, the traffic's appalling.' Jay squinted as bright sunlight danced on the tops of cars and cyclists' helmets, stretching ahead in a long, blinding line to a set of traffic lights whose signals seemed to be having no effect on the static clog of idling engines gridlocked around them.

'I think a Sunday League match has just finished.' Juno's heart sank as she realised the mass exodus would slow them up so much it would have been easier to do the conventional slog around the North Circular. Damn! She'd just showed off about knowing London, completely forgetting that St John's Wood turned into a cricket spectators' car park on Sunday evenings. Every copy-book in the 'Glenn, J' library was being blotted by her ineptitude. Couldn't she do anything right?

Jay tapped his fingers impatiently on the wheel as they moved five yards in as many minutes. 'This is fucking ridiculous! I thought you said going this way saved time?'

'It's all right, I know a back route.' Her eyes glittered as she realised she could guide him through what she and Sean had nicknamed the 'Black Run' – an even quicker short-cut to the Westway than their usual one. A taxi-driver mate of Sean's had taught it to him, but it was normally far too narrow and twisting to contemplate in the lumbering T-Bird. Still, if Jay wanted to show off how well he handled the car, and get to know London better, then who was she to deny him?

He followed her instructions to head left, cutting through the back streets of Lisson Grove towards Little Venice. As they lurched over speed bumps, rattled around mini-roundabouts and pelted through deserted roads lined with solicitors' offices, Juno grudgingly admired Jay's skills behind the wheel. He handled the Bird as though she was a Mini Cooper: pulling her tightly around corners, accelerating through straights, judging distances like a rally driver. Pretty soon Juno stopped feeling grudging and started feeling downright excited. This was fun.

'Turn right here.' She tried not to notice that a deliciously spicy aftershave had replaced the usual dieselly smell in the cab.

'Now left,' she instructed, starting thoroughly to enjoy this ride.

'Are you sure you know where we're headed?' he asked warily as they nipped through a mews and along a slim back alley so narrow the walls almost grazed the wing-mirrors. Behind them, Triona was looking decidedly nervous as she tried to keep up.

'Trust me,' Juno said airily, pointing the way like Bodie directing Doyle in *The Professionals*, not looking at him once. 'Straight ahead at the lights, then cut through that garage forecourt there to avoid the no left turn.'

'Jesus!' Jay did as he was told. 'You really *do* know London, don't you?'

'Right over the bridge.' Juno found herself smiling. 'Then follow the blue signs on to the A40M.' She checked the grotty digital clock which was stuck to the dash – the Bird had none built in. 'Ten minutes. Not bad. Well driven.'

He didn't respond to the compliment, but Juno sensed a thawing of the atmosphere in the cab and stole another glance at him.

He was checking his mirrors to confirm that Triona's red Saab was still following them as they climbed up on to the Westway and Juno noticed for the first time that he was wearing glasses – trendy little elongated owl-specs were balanced on his straight nose. He obviously needed them for driving. They made him look ridiculously intellectual and just a touch nerdy, and rendered him far less intimidating.

Sitting beside him, she suddenly felt illogically cheerful. She'd always adored travelling as a passenger – it took away any sense of responsibility, reminded her of setting out on holidays as a child or on weekend breaks with her friends. The loud rattle of the T-Bird's engine was comforting, her solidity felt safe as an armoured tank's, and Juno finally had to concede that Jay was a great driver.

She gazed out over Notting Hill, drenched in sunshine, and perked up even further at the prospect of seeing her parents for a few hours. She was also looking forward to her lazy week – planning to touch up her roots, eat nothing, sunbathe in the garden, take Rug and her parents' dogs for long rambles and plan the menu for a spectacular 'gang' lunch the following weekend.

As they sped over Ladbroke Grove towards White City and Wormwood Scrubs, Juno wished there was a car stereo, but the Bird had been designed to drive over sand-dunes and through scree, not cruise along Western Avenue belting out The Verve.

The wind from Jay's open window was whipping her hair across her face, into her eyes and mouth. Juno tipped down the ripped shield in front of her to stop the sun blinding her and sat in silence as they left the city behind and hit the suburbs, pelting through Ealing and Greenford, past the Northolt Airfield with its low streetlights and military fencing, and finally out on to the M40.

As the suburbs melted away into the hills and fields of Buckinghamshire, she felt the warm, cuddly 'going home' sensation familiar since her first trips away in childhood, when the M40 hadn't even existed and she had belted back to Oxford from Paddington Station after shopping expeditions or parties in London.

She suddenly turned to Jay as a ghastly thought occurred

to her. 'Will you look after Poirot and Uboat while I'm away?'

He nodded unenthusiastically. 'I guess so. What does it involve?'

'Oh, just checking they're okay, feeding them twice a day.' Juno practically had to shout to be heard over the engine, spitting out clumps of hair as it was blown into her mouth. 'Poirot needs his water topping up, and his cage might need a bit of a skip out. You have to check that the filter and heater in Uboat's tank are both working – there's a red dot on the thermometer at the right temperature. She's a bit off her food at the moment, so keep a close eye on her. If there are any problems, you can call me.'

'What do they eat?'

'There's a big bag of parrot food by Poirot's cage, but he sulks if he doesn't get at least one piece of fruit a day. Uboat has chopped chicken liver – there's tons in the freezer – plus some prawns and hard-boiled eggs occasionally. There's some calcium supplement by her tank which you can sprinkle on whatever you give her. And she loves cheese – but not Cheddar. She loathes Cheddar. Do you think you can remember all that?'

'Sure.' Jay nodded reluctantly.

'Thanks. That's really kind of you,' Juno sighed in relief, swallowing a lot of her own hair and spitting it out again.

Jay looked at her curiously for a second, but said nothing.

Using her hands as an Alice band, she screwed herself around to check that Triona was still with them. She had been to Church House lots of times, but Sean usually drove her there and it was a bit of a marathon getting around Oxford then threading through the lanes into the Vale of the White Horse. Dinner-party guests were constantly getting lost and being talked into Uffcombe village via their mobile phones.

But Triona was still right behind them, her bleached blonde head bouncing around to some drum 'n' bass track she was listening to in her car, fingers tapping against the steering wheel. Settling back in her seat again, Juno realised that the wind had dropped considerably and the cab was far quieter. Beside her, Jay had slid his window closed.

'I got your apology,' he said suddenly. 'I appreciated it.'

Juno blushed as she remembered the Post-it notes. 'I hope they didn't take ages to clear away?'

'No – they made me laugh.' Even with the window closed, it was hard to hear his soft voice over the Bird's groaning rattle.

The smell of his aftershave was stronger now, and Juno was acutely aware of his cream-covered thighs stretched beside her far shorter, wider ones.

'Good.' She cleared her throat uncomfortably, realising they had the chance to grope their way towards a fresh footing – something more amicable. 'I guess it's no bad thing I'm away this week. At least I'll be out of your hair.'

When he didn't immediately answer she ploughed on, 'I'm sure you'll enjoy being able to spread all your stuff out around the flat without worrying about me seeing anything. Not that I've snooped – not at all. No.'

'No?' He moved into the middle lane to overtake a horse-box.

'I mean, I totally respect the fact that you have to be discreet about your work – photographing stars and everything.'

'Who told you I was photographing stars?'

'Oh, no one,' she gulped, trying to sound light and airy. 'I just got that impression.'

'I'm a photojournalist, not a portraitist,' he muttered.

I will not wind him up, Juno told herself determinedly. I will not ask nosy questions. I will be calm and serene. I will say nothing, in fact.

Ahead, their first glimpse of Oxfordshire appeared between the high corridor of man-made verges – a shimmering heat-haze of bucolic beauty.

They sat in silence again, listening to the drone of the engine, watching as the Chiltern cuttings quickly fell away and the exquisite checked upholstery of sun-drenched fields surrounded them. Hello, Oxfordshire, Juno thought lovingly. It happened every time she visited home, this heady realisation that there was an England outside London, that it was beautiful and crisp, that the skies were black as pitch at night and blue-white as Spode by day, not glowing with differing pollutant yellows in a twenty-four-hour cycle. She cranked open her window a fraction and breathed in, to be rewarded with a lungful of diesel fumes.

'Did you have a good time last night?' Jay suddenly asked, raising his voice to be heard.

Juno looked at him in surprise but he was watching the road, face impassive. 'It was okay.'

Pulling her hair from her eyes, she stared fixedly at the primitive air vent in front of her – its cumbersome lever wearing a faded Comic Relief nose from years ago, the one with little hands waving out to either side. It rattled in the wind like a wired dancer in a club.

'Actually it was a bit stressful.' She shrugged, remembering the intimidating Earl's Court journalists and pissed schoolfriends. 'I'm sorry I didn't let you know I wasn't coming home. I didn't think you'd notice. Sean never does.'

'You could have called – left a message.'

'It was the early hours.' Juno remembered with a half-smile that John had called the flat at that time, offering her a curry. Boy, was she in demand last night!

She assumed they were lapsing into silence again, but he glanced across at her, the glasses making him look serious yet strangely sexy. 'You have a lot of friends, don't you?'

Juno thought about it. 'I suppose so – but only a few really close ones.'

'Lydia?' He said the name cautiously.

She felt her teeth clench together like a stuck stapler as she realised he was about to start digging for information like a teenager with a crush. Think calm, think serene. 'Yes, Lydia's one of my closest friends.'

'D'you stay with her last night?' His voice was husky and hopeful now, clearly eager for some information about the beautiful, flirtatious blonde.

Juno glared at the Comic Relief nose jealously. 'No, someone else. An old mate. We used to be very close, but it's turned a bit sour.'

Jay slowed as a caravan swayed in front of them. His voice was throaty with regret. 'So I guess it was another lost weekend then, huh?'

Still thinking he was probing about Lydia, Juno didn't quite understand what he was driving at, but suspected he meant he'd lost out on seeing her friend this weekend. Well, tough. She was tempted to blurt out angrily that Lydia had probably spent most of it on top of Bruno, but knew that would just add to his image of her as a childish, petty monster who was jealous of her prettier, sexier friend. Think calm, think serene . . .

'If you say so.' She shrugged.

'You two used to live together, didn't you?' he asked, voice strangely tight and embarrassed. Juno guessed it took a lot of pride to ask her of all people about Lydia. He had to be desperate, probably bitterly regretted not agreeing to meet her for a drink when she'd asked him. Now he had the flat to himself for a week, he'd have plenty of opportunity to take up her friend's offer of a chat.

'For a while,' Juno sighed. She was determined to stay cool, but the last thing she felt like was telling him all about Lydia. She'd been through this routine with so many men before, she had the answers off pat. But with Jay it would hurt too much.

As if reading her thoughts, he let the Bird trundle slowly behind the caravan and rubbed his chin awkwardly on his shoulder as he drove, clearing his throat.

'I don't mean to criticise, but don't you think your relationship is kind of dysfunctional?'

'I *beg* your pardon?' Juno said pompously, as insulted as a primary school teacher asked by a pupil if she had regular anal sex. Oh, God, she was rising to the bait again, she realised. But if he wanted the low-down on Lydia, he was coming from entirely the wrong direction. She frantically tried to calm herself down, stop feeling jealous. Think calm, think serene. 'We adore each other,' she said smoothly. 'It's a great friendship.'

'Friendship?' Jay said lightly, carefully overtaking the caravan. 'Nothing more than that? I thought you two still got it on from time to time?'

Snapping her window shut in order to be heard, she turned to him in amazement. What was he suggesting here? That they both fancied the same woman? Great! Now he thought she was a nosy, bullying, trampy, slobby *dyke*. Could her profile get any worse? Perhaps she should subtly hint she had a prison record too?

'We lived together for a long time, and I can assure you I wasn't in the slightest bit tempted in that direction,' she spluttered, raising her voice over the Bird's drone. 'Take the next exit – junction eight.'

'Are you serious?' Jay checked his mirrors before signalling. He sounded astonished.

Juno ground her teeth.

'Of course I'm serious – if you don't turn off here we'll end up in Birmingham.'

'C'mon, Juno, you know what I mean,' he sighed tetchily as they turned on to the A40, pelting in a long, straight line towards Oxford. 'You're not telling me you lived together all that time as *friends*? Didn't John get kinda frustrated?'

Jesus, what was he insinuating now? That John had egged them on to have three-in-a-bed sex romps together in the Cam Den? This was all getting way too personal. How dare someone so pathologically secretive probe into her past so offensively, just to satisfy his all-too-predictable craving for Lydia?

Well, if he wanted the truth, he could bloody well have it. At least it would shatter his lesbian fantasy.

'John always fancied Lydia.' She removed the faded red nose from the ventilator and played with it like a worry bead. 'It used to drive me mad, but I got used to it – it's not as if he'd ever have done anything about it, let alone suggest we all sleep together. I'm sure he dreamed about it a lot – he's pretty basic like that. But it never happened. I've never slept with Lydia. Satisfied?'

'Jesus! Where did that come from?' Jay burst out laughing

– shocked, astonished laughter which almost sent them off the road as the Bird swerved dramatically to the left.

'You asked me.' Juno looked at him doubtfully, chewing on the corner of the Comic Relief nose. 'Didn't you?'

He cleared his throat, suddenly very red in the face as he stared fixedly at the bumper of the car in front. 'No! God, Juno. It's just I thought you said . . . that is . . . you seemed to be telling me that you and John . . . when you lived together . . .'

Suddenly she twigged. 'Me and *John*? You were talking about him, not Lydia?' She started to giggle.

'What's Lydia got to do with it?' He shook his head. 'You were the one who started talking about you guys all sleeping together.'

'We didn't!' Juno squeaked. 'Never. The only kinky thing about me are my boots.'

He started to laugh again – this time a lovely, husky laugh of delight. 'Jesus, Juno, what makes you such a crazy person?'

'What d'you mean?' She played with the red plastic nose, unsure whether this was supposed to be flattering or not.

'I've never met anyone like you before. I can't figure you out at all. You seem so together, but you're not really, are you?' he said without a hint of sarcasm. He sounded strangely cheerful. She couldn't read his mood at all.

She put the nose on and tapped it thoughtfully with the end of her finger. It smelled foul – a noxious mixture of plastic and mildew.

'I guess I'm too busy joking apart to be very together.' She shrugged, voice distorted and nasal as though she had a cold.

Jay turned to glance at her, catching sight of the red plastic nose.

'C'mon, there's a lot more to you than just jokes,' he muttered. The next moment, he'd stretched across and removed it, his warm thumb brushing her upper lip.

Juno looked up in surprise and for a second their eyes locked.

There was a toot from behind as the T-Bird swerved dangerously towards the avenue of trees to the left. Jay hastily corrected the wheel, facing front to watch the road once more.

Juno was astonished by the conversation – and by the gesture. They were both unexpectedly intimate. Stripped of her jokes, she felt new-born naked and thoroughly flustered by the frisson that Jay's sudden interest in her personal life had given her. The fact he'd almost lost control of the Bird saved her blushes but only added to her confusion.

Another road-watching silence elapsed before she spoke again, daring to lift her voice above the engine. 'I really am sorry about Friday night.'

'What about it?' His jaw stiffened.

Juno hoped he wasn't going to make her list her mistakes: letting Poirot chew up his cables, sneaking into his room to listen to records, trying to be 'tasty' in front of his friends, pretending she'd pulled, probing into his life, accusing him of stealing a watch he'd never seen, then lolling over the back of the sofa making eyes at him on an accidental coke-bender. She decided the safest bet was to apologise for the lot in one foul swoop.

'I guess we all have nights we'd rather forget – where you want to take a rubber and wipe it all out, start again with a clean sheet.'

'It's none of my business what you do with rubbers, Juno,' he said curtly, his tone as unfriendly as she'd ever heard it. 'Just don't involve me in it, okay? I couldn't handle that.' He looked furious.

'Turn left on to the ring-road,' she muttered. 'Follow the signs west to the A34.' How could I even contemplate falling in love with this beast? she thought wretchedly. He's totally emotionless. He can't even take an apology.

Her directions-only communication lasted for half an hour. They circumnavigated Oxford on the ugly ring-road, dived south towards Newbury and then turned off at Didcot, where the fat, mutant loo-roll chimneys of the power station belched man-made clouds into an otherwise flawless blue sky.

'Right – left – right,' she muttered at lengthy intervals, like a drill sergeant issuing instructions. Finally, they were heading west again, out into open countryside which grew more familiar to Juno with every passing mile of the gently meandering road to Wantage. She'd travelled along it twice a day for five years, on the bus to and from her Oxford school.

Beside her, Jay was taking in the scenery with interest, his thunderous expression starting to lighten.

Gorgeous, golden fields of ripe wheat spread out to the left of them like mother nature sunbathing on a nudist beach. To their right, vast stretches of rough emerald grass were patched with smaller grazed areas edged by electronic fencing where piebald Friesian cows or gaggles of newly shaven sheep twitched ears and swatted tails as they stretched out to snatch at moist greenery beyond the wire.

As a school commuter, Juno had thought of this road as a long changing room which transformed her from the streetwise city teenager who stopped overnight at her friends' houses in order to stay out late, to the cossetted daughter who needed to be hugged all the time and never wanted to leave home. She'd never really rebelled as a teenager; she'd simply adjusted.

She turned to Jay excitedly, too happy to be close to home to let their brooding silence last a moment longer.

'Thanks for coming today – I know you probably didn't want to.' She felt the warmth of the sun soaking through the windscreen. 'My family are a lot nicer than me, I promise. They'll spoil you rotten.'

Beside her, he nodded in silence. They were skirting the edge of Wantage now – speeding past the off-putting suburban welcome mat of modern housing estates which belied the ancient beauty of the town.

Juno suddenly felt incredibly relaxed. More so than she had in weeks.

'King Alfred the Great was born here,' she said proudly, eager to make up for her long, grumpy silence. 'There's a statue of him in the middle of the town. He defeated the Danes.'

'No kidding?'

He was talking to her again, thank God. Juno cheerfully

directed him on the final leg of their journey, pointing out sights as they went.

Oh, the bliss of climbing through the familiar tunnel of trees out into the curling heartstring of a lane that led towards the tiny villages at the foot of the Ridgeway.

'Wow – now I know I'm in England!' Jay whistled as they passed a village cricket pitch scattered with men in white fielding the last few overs of a match. 'Is Lord's like this behind that wall?'

'Not quite.' Juno grinned, looking across at the cricketing wives huddled around their picnic tables and baby buggies beyond the boundary.

The narrowing lane swerved and tilted with stomach-punching irregularity now. To their right, the flat plains of Oxfordshire stretched out into a miasma of early-evening mist, appearing in enchanting glimpses as the verges dropped away then loomed up again – thick, choked hedges walling in the hilly, bending lane like a bobsleigh run.

The landmarks became increasingly familiar to Juno as they drove into weirder and wilder landscape. They pelted in and out of dappled light, climbing higher into the hills, blinded by sunlight as the old Bird angled upwards, then blinded again by shadow as she dipped into a wooded hollow. They crossed the perilously twisty Lambourn–Childrey road at the point where Sean had written off his first car. They passed footpaths Juno had traipsed along; the Star Inn at Sparsholt where her parents used to take her for birthday meals; Blowingstone Hill which she'd once free-wheeled down so fast on her mountain bike that she'd flown through a hedge and landed upside down in a cattle trough.

'Jesus, this is staggering.' Jay almost drove into the thick, banked verges as he gazed through his window. Voluptuously sculpted chalk hills rose and dipped to either side of them now – a violent, earthy sea which had been moulded by centuries of storms. Blond waves of ripening crops were ridden like surf by the odd brave oak at their highest breaks and paddled by dark, choked woods in their shallows.

As the Bird groaned at the climbs and sighed through the descents, the landscape divided. To their right, tiny villages huddled amongst the big square, agricultural fields; to their left the ancient Ridgeway rose to its crest, creating a natural amphitheatre of grassy chalk hills like the giant green shanks of sleeping foals – angular at their peaks, sinewy in their midst and leggy in their folds.

Half a mile from home, Juno pointed proudly through her window.

'That's the White Horse that the area's named after – right on the very top of that hill.'

Looking across, Jay slammed on the brakes so that Triona, following closely behind, almost shunted them. The booming bass from the Saab was killingly inappropriate for such eerie surroundings. Staring out of Juno's window, Jay's yellow eyes searched the landscape then blinked as though hit by a sandstorm.

'Jeesh!' He breathed in sharply, gazing past her, his head tipped so that he could see it all. 'It's awesome. Is that some sort of man-made fortress?'

Following his gaze, Juno laughed with the insouciance of long familiarity. 'No, not that. That's Dragon Hill. St George slayed the dragon on it, according to legend. There's a bald white patch at the top which never grows grass because the dragon's blood burnt it away for ever. It's a natural chalk mound – pretty amazing in itself, but nothing compared to what's behind it. It obscures the view from here. Drive on fifty yards and look again.'

There it was: a huge stick-drawing of a horse etched out in chalk on the brow of a hill. Primitive, simple, exquisite.

'It's at least three thousand years old,' Juno told him, proud to introduce an old friend whom she loved to bits. She'd spent so many evenings sitting beside it, drawing strength from it, tucked in its bum-cosy eye and gazing north to where the fields, woods and villages stretched as far as you could see. It was part of her childhood, part of her muddled head. 'Drive on half a mile –

my parents' house is just round the corner, you can look at it from there.'

The lane twisted acutely to the left and dipped between the distinctive rippling haunch of chalk hill known as the Manger and a scrubby wood which Juno and Sean had nick-named 'bran mash', then it climbed through high hedges into a tiny village which nestled away to their right. A tourist had added an 'M' to the rectangular Uffcombe sign as a joke – it happened every year and the locals no longer bothered to white it out until September.

Uffcombe was more of a hamlet than a village; it dated back to the Domesday Book and was close enough to a National Heritage site to be rigidly listed and protected from the outbreak of red-brick bungalows and phallic grain silos which marred other local villages. It was edged by two sagging little eighteenth-century red brick cottages – 'the kennels' Judy called them – then past the crumbling sandstone farm was a row of terraced farm cottages and the single-track no-through-road lane which led to a scattering of old brick-and-stone village houses. Juno could name every occupant of every house, even though most of them were now weekenders. The lane curled past the Smithy Inn pub, now a tourist monster ('B&B available. Cream Teas £4.99 in season. Beware of the Alsatian'), and finally, as it climbed more steeply out of the village past the sandstone rectory, the grey stone church loomed into view, almost hidden behind its three fat yew trees. A narrow track cut acutely away from the lane to a tree-veiled lych-gate where coffins would once have awaited their pall bearers. In front of it, Howard had widened the hoggin surface into a circular sweep and his big black Merc sat beneath a veil of weeping willow branches like a forgotten hearse, covered in bird droppings.

Juno glowed happily. Home at last.

'This is it.' She shuddered contentedly, drenched in familiar nostalgia.

'Jesus – it's a church!' Jay said, stating the obvious and signalling right.

Chapter Twenty-Six

As the Bird groaned up the overgrown gravel track, crunching through the pot-holes, Judy Glenn appeared in the roofed porch of the lych-gate, drinking a gin and tonic. She waved delightedly, wild grey curls spilling out of their chaotically lop-sided hairclip. Dressed in a voluminous green sundress which showed off her gardening tan, she was as huge, curvy and enveloping as the surrounding hills. The Glenns' two overweight Mastiffs had their paws up on the gate behind her, bellowing a welcome, while Sean's little dog, Rug, jumped up and down between them like a pop-babe between two bouncers, scrabbling excitedly at the wooden slats.

'Ignore them!' Judy laughed in her booming contralto, billowing towards the Land Rover as Jay cut the engine and jumped from the cab.

'Mrs Glenn.' He held out his hand formally.

Judy batted it away, engulfed his face with her bread-kneading hands and kissed him heartily on both cheeks.

'So lovely to meet you, Jay – for Christ's sake, call me Judy. God, you smell divine . . . Ah, Juno, pusscat!' Dropping Jay, she surged forward, arms aloft and flesh swinging from them as she bore down on her daughter, who was tumbling out of the passenger door with her weekend case.

It was the ultimate mother-hug. Judy was a whizz at them. Juno wanted to stay there for ever, squashed in those warm, spongy, sweet-smelling arms. She was a comfort-wrap of Penhaligon's Jubilee Bouquet and 'missed you, pusscat' endearments. But Judy was also a thoroughly modern and wise old bird. 'How's it going with him?' she breathed into her daughter's ear.

'Ma!' Juno hushed her hastily, noticing gratefully that Jay had wandered out of earshot.

'He's very dishy.' Judy tucked her daughter's bra strap beneath her sun-top then her eyes creased in amusement as she glanced over her shoulder. 'Oh – Tri's made it up the drive!' She started clapping.

It was a long-standing joke that Triona's car always got stuck in a pot-hole, which was why she seldom brought it to Church House.

Shrouded by willow leaves, Jay stood watching the red car bump up the track from the other side of the high-tech Merc which he'd been peering into admiringly.

Triona parked in the space beside the Bird, branches scraping along the Saab's roof like chalk against a blackboard, and Judy leapt upon the car so that Triona was embraced half-in and half-out of the door.

'God, you're so gorgeously slender, Tri, I feel as though I'm hugging my scarf,' Judy grumbled, squeezing her tightly. 'I can tell you're not adding to my royalties.'

'You're too rich, and I'm too thin.' Triona kicked the door shut behind her. 'Thanks for asking us down here, Jude.'

'I'm so excited you could make it – especially Jay.' She beamed at him over her broad brown shoulder. 'I adore Americans.'

'Thank you, ma'am.' Emerging from the willow fringe, Jay caught Juno's eye for a brief second.

Was it her imagination, she wondered excitedly, or was he smiling at her with an expression that was almost friendly? Cursing herself for feeling so shy now that she was home, she fought a sudden mad urge to run and hide behind a gravestone playing 'he loves me, he loves me not' with a daisy as she'd done so often as a kid. Naturally, she'd always cheated. Only today it would be 'he hates me, he hates me not'. She guessed she'd still cheat.

Judy was beaming delightedly at him.

'Now poor Howzat – that's Howard, my sexy husband.' She gave him an earthy wink. 'Poor Howzat is madly trying to orchestrate a score in his study, so supper's going to be wonderfully late.' She hooked as many arms as she could gather and towed them towards the lych-gate. 'Which gives us all lots of time to get tight first. I'm trying out my Scotland special on you, so we're all pretending it's Christmas. Come and try my new *apéru* – a mulled Bartesol cocktail. I gather being "ironic" is all the rage at the moment.'

The dogs were leaping all over the gates as they tried to edge their way through.

'Down, kids!' Judy ordered to no effect whatsoever. 'Jay, these are the twins – Eff and Blind.' She pointed out the slavering Mastiffs which were already pinning him to the lych-gate bench in compromising fashion. 'Effie's the bitch – the smaller one here. The fat one's Blind. Used to be called Linus, but he lost an eye a couple of years back. Don't worry, they're terribly affectionate. There – they like you already!'

They had both now rammed their snouts into Jay's crotch and were inhaling like glue-sniffers. Rug, meanwhile, was trying to take his leg from behind.

'That's Sean's little monster,' Judy laughed as Rug – a small white mohair missile on legs – tipped over on to his curly white shank and started shagging Jay's foot in spoons position as he tried to close the gate behind him. 'He's being a randy little sod because Effie's in season and he can't reach up. Blind's had the op, thank God. Good journey?' She whistled the twins away from Jay's flies.

'Fine, thanks, Mrs Glenn.' He tried to limp up the path with Rug wrapped around his calf, humping away in knee-trembler position. Following behind, Juno rather admired his repertoire.

'Call me Judy!' She thumped Jay affectionately on the shoulder, almost propelling him into a gravestone.

As they headed towards the house, strains of piano music could be heard floating from an open skylight, interspersed with a male voice muttering 'bugger' at regular intervals.

'What's Pa writing?' Juno asked her mother.

Judy paused to pull a few weeds from the path. 'Oh, he's finishing something for a natural history programme on dolphins – listen.' A few looping arpeggios danced around the gravestones. 'Very wet and jumpy. He has to get the orchestration done before he goes to Germany.'

'Sounds great.' Juno noticed Jay gazing in wonderment at the gravestones around him and the church in front which had a square Anglo-Saxon tower to the left with a tiny row of round, button-hole arches at the top from which long fronds of yellow ivy trailed like Rapunzel's hair.

Juno always thought it looked like a much-darned, hand-knitted sock. The tower's rough rubble walls were patterned with long, thin stone uprights and smaller criss-crosses, the edges stapled at regular intervals by primitive corner stones which looked like fat blanket stitches. The foot of the sock was dotted with pin-hole arches at odd levels, and the toe – added on in recent years – was made of a paler, more even stone.

'This place is magical, isn't it?' Triona was hauling Rug away from Jay's leg.

'I thought you were kidding about the gravestones.' He paused by a crumbling stone cross sinking into the ground at a jaunty angle.

'That's wonky Walter.' Juno nodded at it, still tongue-tied with infuriating shyness. 'He was run over by a coach and six in 1707.'

Judy laughed. 'Juno and Sean gave all the graves names when we first moved here, although there are only two or three that are still readable – the rest are far too eroded. The last burial here was at least two hundred years ago.'

'You're kidding?' Jay whistled. 'Boy, people around here must live a long time.'

Juno gaped at him, realising that he was making a joke.

Her mother just laughed uproariously.

'The church was a ruin for over a century,' Triona told him as they stepped down into the wooden porch. 'Only the tower is original.'

'Oh, right.' Jay hung behind, gaping up at the ancient, tapering square tower. 'What's the story behind it?' He looked straight at Juno, but her mother was already reciting the well-worn tale.

'Uffcombe was once a feudal village.' Judy heaved open the heavy oak door. 'The church was built in the tenth century, and was the local place of worship for almost six hundred years, by which time the village had changed beyond all recognition. It became part of the estate of Uffcombe House – a great pile constructed as a gift to one of George II's favourite generals. A far grander church was built in the next village and this was turned into a folly. Then the big house burnt down and this became a ruin. Only the tower and part of the east wall were intact when we bought it seventeen years ago.'

As ever the house smelled of cooking. It was a scratch and sniff paradise of haute cuisine – every wall, beam and rug infused with twenty years of sublime Judy Glenn recipes. Today the unmistakable berry, booze and spice aroma of Christmas overpowered the subtle fragrances of freshly picked summer fruits and herbs spilling from wooden trugs on the seats of the porch.

They walked into what had once been the south transept. A thickly beamed ceiling weighed down on them from above as they picked their way through a cool, shady entrance hall full of wellies, coats, dog leads, bottle-filled recycling skips and two incongruous, heavily laden Welsh dressers. (Both had belonged to Howard's long-dead mother, and he hadn't the heart to throw them out although they were universally loathed.) Triona's heels rang against the bare flagstones. Ahead, in the rebuilt north transept, was the vast, modern kitchen and conservatory which had been the setting for three successful series of *Judy Glenn Cooks the Books* on terrestrial TV – its sparkling marble surfaces and jungle-thick house-plants the envy of millions of viewers who had no idea of the dusty, messy state of the rest of the house, just out of camera shot. It was drenched in tree-dappled sunlight which sliced in from the left.

'The north side was completely derelict when we converted the church into a house,' Judy told Jay. 'So we decided to get our architect and builders to reconstruct it as it would have been – only using glass and wood instead of rubble and stone. You can see the original walls this side are as thick as forearms and have mean little windows, so we needed to make the remainder as light as possible. But it's a bugger to heat and our window-cleaners are practically millionaires.'

Ahead of them the walls were all glass – small, arched panes, vast rectangular ones, tiny square ones – all cross-hatched with black wooden beams to form an extraordinary lattice, like a rough sketch by Mondrian. Light danced through leaves beyond, showing how smeary and rain-dirtied the glass was.

'Must have a wee.' Triona cut off to the left and clattered up the rickety tower staircase followed by Rug's scrabbling paws.

'Watch out for the bats, pusscat,' Judy called after her, looping her arms through Juno's and Jay's and towing them off to the right into what would once have been the nave and was now the family dining room. Its monastic refectory table was as long as a cricket wicket and covered with old newspapers, unopened post, gardening books and dirty mugs. Above them piano music thrashed out chaotically.

'Tuna fishermen catching dolphin in their nets.' Judy looked up, pausing by an oak settle table littered with unironed table linen. 'The string section, I think. Bugger – I must baste the goose again! Go through to the sitting room and I'll fetch you sexy young things a drink while I'm at it.' Patting them both playfully on the bottom, she turned on her heel, pursued into the kitchen by the twins.

Not daring to look at Jay, Juno led the way beneath the vast round stone arch to the chancel – double height, hazy with dust, and faced by an east wall which was also ninety per cent glass. Between the thick, dancing yews it looked out across the village towards the Manger and the White Horse.

Jay walked to the window and leant against it in awe.

Glad to be home, Juno slumped into a vast, lumpy tapestry sofa. All her parents' furniture was tatty and oversized. She peered up at the minstrel's gallery, from which a door led to her father's study, half open and emitting more 'wet' music and occasional 'buggers'.

'This is like a dream,' a low voice whispered.

Juno turned to Jay in surprise, but he was still staring out over the Manger in rapt concentration.

'Did you say something?' she asked.

'Huh?' He glanced at her.

For a moment their eyes locked and Juno was certain she saw the strangest look pass over Jay's face – totally unexpected and too brief to be certain. But just for a second she almost thought he looked afraid. Then he turned away as Triona came noisily into the room, trailed by Rug. She raised her eyebrows at Juno as she entered, face questioning as her eyes rolled towards Jay and back.

Pulling a cushion on to her lap, Juno ignored her.

'This place is just so fantastic.' Jay turned back to face the room, face as excited as a small boy's. He gazed around at the fat, comfortable furniture, the musical instruments of every conceivable description, the towers of books rising like pillars from the floor because there was no space left on the shelves, the strange, tribal artefacts from all over the world crowded together on shelves like a United Nations store cupboard.

'I told you it was incredible, didn't I?' Triona sank into another vast sofa and a second later Rug hurled himself on to her lap, paws slithering on her PVC trousers. 'Now you know why I insisted you come here. I freaked out the first time I saw it.'

'It's so bohemian, man.' Jay wandered around, staring through the glass walls at the rear garden – a walled haven of ancient gnarled fruit trees and shag-pile clover. Every oak joist in the wall had paintings or etchings hanging from it – some so densely that they appeared to be suspended in mid-air. Amongst the host of local artists' landscapes and stylised etchings was an eclectic collection of modern art and a mass of cartoon originals just like those in Sean's flat.

'Howard's father was a collector.' Triona tickled Rug's ears and watched Jay stretching and stooping to study each framed sketch. 'He had a great big pile in Wales that was literally wall papered with cartoons, didn't he, Joo?'

'Huh?' She jumped, having been dreamily admiring Jay's bottom in the cream chinos.

'Howard's father?' Triona gave her a knowing look.

'Oh, yes, he had thousands.' She nodded, hugging the cushion tightly. 'Lots of them are stored in the barn here – there's no room for them on the walls. Sean has loads as you know. When Grandpa Glenn died we found a huge ledger cataloguing every one in neat copper-plate handwriting.'

'He was an amazing man,' Triona sighed, sinking back in the sofa and stretching her arms above her head. 'I only met him once but he made a lasting impression.'

'He certainly had a good eye.' Jay whistled, spotting a long row of Gerard Hoffnung cartoons.

'For women as well as art,' Judy laughed as she re-emerged from the kitchen with a jug on a tray. 'He was married three times and had countless affairs. A total roué. Here, try some Punch Line. I named it in Juno's honour. I was going to call it Yule Be Sorry, but my producer thinks that's too depressing.'

Chewing a corner of her cushion, Juno winced in embarrassment. 'Jay doesn't drink, Ma.'

'Nonsense – it's Christmas,' Judy scoffed, pouring a large glass of lethal-looking red liquid and shoving it under his nose. She ruffled his hair as he took it. 'Exquisite colour – like safflower – and natural too, you lucky thing,'

Jay made no protest. He merely gazed at Juno's mother in wonderment. 'You and Juno are real similar.'

She loved her mother passionately, but considering Judy was wearing a green tent-dress the size of a hot air balloon, had hair like a nuclear mushroom and was at least ten stones heavier than her daughter, she wasn't as flattered as she'd have liked. Judy, meanwhile, was simply delighted.

'Aren't we just? People are always saying that.' She passed a glass to Triona who was trying not to laugh. 'I think we have the same bone structure.'

Juno took her glass grumpily, tempted to point out that no one had seen her mother's bone structure since the sixties.

'Is this you?' Jay had found the overcrowded muddle of framed photographs on the scuffed grand piano. In their midst was a black and white one of a round-faced girl with huge, shining eyes and a smile that could melt an igloo.

'Yes, I was ten – ten years, ten stone, tenacious, but tender-hearted. And quite *the* most adorable child in Suffolk.' Judy dumped her jug on a vase-cluttered, ring-stained harpsichord and padded over to him on her gold flip-flops. With her brown shoulder pressed companionably to Jay's, she started to name the vast, eclectic assortment of Glenns and Arnolds, boasting about how much better-looking her side of the family were.

Juno swigged some Punch Line, expecting it to be revolting. It was in fact delicious.

'That's Juno as a baby – she was so cuddly,' Judy told Jay.

Juno gazed at the ceiling in despair. Great. Bloody baby photographs. She knew for a fact she'd looked like William Hague until the age of two.

'What's that on her forehead?' Jay was asking.

'A flower. Howard liked to paint on her because she was so plump and pink.'

Juno closed her eyes. Plump and pink. Thanks, Ma. Very damned sexy. At least she didn't say it was the number of the beast on my forehead. That was one of Judy's favourite jokes.

'And that's one of her as a toddler – look how plumptious and giggly she was even then, but very, very naughty with it. And *such* a sulker if she didn't get her own way. Mind you, I was just the same at that age.'

'What, thirty?' Jay said lightly.

As her mother let out her booming laugh, Juno looked up sharply and caught Jay watching her, the tiniest of smiles playing on his lips.

Triona had polished off her Punch Line and was help-ing herself to seconds from the jug. 'This is divine, Jude – what is it?'

'It's my version of winter Pimms.' Judy wandered over from

the piano and settled into a fat leather armchair, the Mastiffs at her feet. 'It's basically mulled fortified wine and bags of fruit, with cranberry juice and rosemary sprig ice cubes dropped in at the last minute, so the cubes melt as you drink it. Hugely naff, but the viewers will love it. What do you two want?' She looked down at the twins who had their chins on her feet, solemn eyes watching her longingly. 'Blast! *Howzat?*'

The piano music stopped.

'Yes, poodle?' came a faint response from the gallery.

'Have the dogs been for a walk yet?'

'No, poodle.'

The piano music started again with a vengeance – the dolphins appeared to be having a pretty rough time of it.

Judy looked at the tatty long-case clock which was wearing a deerstalker above its dial. 'Blast! Nearly eight . . . I have to make the green peppercorn sauce for the oysters. Can you lot be angelic and trog the canine gang across a couple of fields for me?' She looked around the room imploringly.

'Juno and Jay can go.' Triona flashed a smile as she drained her second Punch Line. 'I'll stay and gossip – these heels would plug me into the ground before I got to the gate.' She waggled her strappy carpet-stabbers.

Why do I get the feeling this has all been planned? Juno thought worriedly as she stepped into her wellies a minute later. In the hallway, Judy was busily kitting Jay out in Howard's well-patched, dog-walking layers.

'It's very warm out, Ma.' She watched as her mother tried to persuade him to put on a shooting waistcoat.

'It gets windy on the hill.' Judy wrapped a scarf around his neck.

'Who says we're going up there?' Juno was planning a quick lap of the village.

'Of course you are,' her mother laughed. 'You can't bring Jay all this way and not take him up to see the horse. The view is spectacular.' She crammed an old gardening hat on his head. 'Don't rush back – dinner's at least an hour away. You take Rug, Jay. Juno can have the twins, just in case anyone tries to rape the bitch and she needs protection. She is *such* a flirt, then gets terrified when it comes down to the business.'

Juno caught Jay looking at her in total horror.

'She's talking about Effie – the Mastiff on heat,' she muttered, stomping out of the door. 'Not me.'

They walked in silence across the lane and on to the footpath which led them up to the crest of the Manger. Dressed like a real-ale enthusiast, Jay had Rug trotting devotedly alongside him on a short lead within seconds. Juno, meanwhile, was towed along by the Mastiffs like the girl in the tampon advert minus the roller skates.

Within minutes she was fifty yards ahead of Jay and panting heavily. The only good thing about it was that they dragged her up the hill so energetically, she barely needed to use her leg muscles. Glancing over her shoulder, she saw Jay mooching along far behind her in his hippy rambler's outfit. He looked so divertingly silly that Juno didn't notice the dogs criss-crossing in front of her, tying their taut leads together.

Judy had been right. Despite the hot evening sun, it was ear-strippingly windy on the hill. Eyes watering, Juno was propelled against the gusts as the twins charged side-by-side along the familiar path to the horse. The footpath cut through a field of shaven sheep which bleated away into a far corner as the Mastiffs ploughed their way towards a wooden stile, slamming Juno against it as they dived through the rectangular dog hole beneath and strained on their tangled leads for freedom. Forced to crawl through the hole after them rather than climb over the style, Juno almost got stuck, ripping the side pocket from her jeans as she struggled to slide her hips between the two wooden uprights before Jay could witness the humiliating, big-bummed struggle.

Dusting herself down afterwards, she untangled the twins' leads and waited for him to catch up. Her bruised, grazed hip-bones throbbed in pain.

'You okay? You looked as though you fell over just now.' When Jay finally climbed over the stile, he'd stashed the flower-pot hat and his specs in his pocket and was looking far more like the old Jay, although there was a decidedly sexy touch of the Mellors about the green moleskin waistcoat.

'No, I'm fine!'

Pocket flapping, Juno crossed over the single-track road which led to the tourist car park and led the way up the narrow, high-sided chalk path to the horse. Now that she knew he'd spotted her spat with the stile, she was so embarrassed by her fat bottom that she clenched her buttocks the entire way to try and make them appear smaller, which meant she walked like the Penguin from Batman. She was certain Jay was staring at them in horrified wonder as he followed close behind.

It was only when they scaled the hill to the first plateau that the long, flat stretch of Oxfordshire plains came into view to the north, spreading out into the mists of the horizon. The wind once again bit into their cheeks, throwing their hair to one side and lifting the dogs' ears.

'Wow!' Jay stopped in his tracks and gazed around him.

One or two late-evening walkers were heading back to the car park, nodding as they passed by. Juno marched on in her awkward waddle as far as the angled sign which told tourists about the history of the horse, Dragon Hill and Uffington Castle – the large, raised hill fort. Looking over her shoulder, she saw that Jay was still standing at the top of the path, hair blowing around in the wind, Rug sitting obediently at his feet. He looked like a rock star making a video. The tortured hero image wasn't even dimmed when he reached into his pocket and pulled out his glasses.

God, her legs hurt from the climb, and her hips were still throbbing like mad. Juno sat down by the horse's head and lay back on the grass, closing her eyes and ignoring the twins who were snorting excitedly, eager to race back to the tourist sign and sniff the messages left at its base by other dogs.

A moment later Jay came to sit beside her, little Rug panting like an asthmatic jogger as he was reunited with his friends. Juno felt one of the Mastiffs lie down against her arm, warm fur settling against her goose-bumped skin.

She was grateful for the insulation, wishing she'd worn a jacket.

'This place is something else, man,' Jay murmured from a couple of feet away.

'Isn't it?' Juno found she was less embarrassed talking to him if she kept her eyes closed. She supposed she must look pretty odd lying beside him like a ritual sacrifice, but her hips were throbbing now and lying flat on the ground seemed to be the most comfortable recovery position.

'I guess you've seen it too many times to bother looking?' he muttered.

'I think it's best viewed alone the first time,' Juno said, keeping her eyes tightly closed. 'That's when it's at its most magical. It's a healing place.' She only hoped it'd start working on her aching legs soon.

'So you used to come up here as a teenager? When you were low?'

'All the time. It seemed like a better place to sulk than my room – especially in winter when there was no one around up here and the weather matched my mood.'

'Sounds kinda romantic.'

'It wasn't really.' Juno wrinkled her face. 'Especially when it rained.'

'I used to go to a deserted tenement near where I lived and kick the shit out of a wall,' Jay said. 'But then a crack gang moved in there, so I stole a basketball from a store and started shooting hoops – taking my anger out on the cage and the backboard.'

Juno held her breath. He had told her something about himself at last. It wasn't a lot, but it conjured up an instant image in Juno's head – a fiercely angry teenager in a run-down area. She longed to know more.

'Hard to steal a basketball, I should imagine,' she said lightly, sliding her arm across her closed eyes as the sun burnt into her lids.

'I could hoist anything as a kid,' he muttered, voice oddly strained.

'What did you do – shove it up your jumper and pretend to be pregnant?'

When he didn't answer, Juno winced into her arm and wished she hadn't been so flip.

'You had a real idyllic childhood, didn't you?' he asked eventually.

'I don't know. I suppose you could call it that, compared to some.'

'Yeah.' He let out a sarcastic sigh.

'Okay, so it was idyllic.' She conceded the point, although she would have liked to argue that being a fat kid with boozy, hippy parents was not entirely without its problems when it came to peer pressure from teenage conformists at school.

'I used to have this picture on my bedroom wall,' said Jay. 'I ripped it out of a library book. It was of some place in Ireland – I don't know where. It was of all these green hills and trees and shit. This place reminds me of it. Real beautiful, you know?'

'Ireland's lovely,' Juno agreed carefully.

'Yeah.' He let out a short, bitter laugh. 'It was real beautiful, my picture. I used to imagine it was where my ancestors came from. I'd ask my old man about it all the time, but he just laughed, said how the fuck should he know? He'd never left New York State in his life. His daddy died when he was five and my grandma was never sober enough to tell him anything.'

Sliding her arm from her eyes, Juno squinted up at the blue sky. She couldn't believe he was telling her these things. Her mother's Punch Line cocktail must have acted like a truth drug. She daren't look across at him in case she broke the spell.

'I used to look at my picture of Ireland and wish I lived there,' he went on. 'It was one of those trashy postcard shots, taken with a purple filter to make the sky look bluer and the grass more emerald. Of course I didn't know that then. I just thought it was so beautiful and peaceful compared to a damp apartment in a shabby neighbourhood, where the walls were so thin you could hear a television a block away, where everything was so fucking grey and dirty and cheap. I'd stare at that creased little picture for hours, listening to my sisters arguing, my parents arguing, the neighbours arguing. For years I never knew people talked to one another, I just figured that shouting all the time was natural. That's why I pick fights now. I find it easier to argue than to talk, y'know?

'My old man couldn't help shouting.' His voice quickened. 'He was a construction worker. A union foreman – really respected, you know? One of the boys. I guess you'd say he was a man's man. He was a bully, too, but he meant well. Before he got sick, he used to – '

He stopped talking abruptly and Juno stared at the sky until her eyes watered, willing him to go on, waiting to hear that soft, drawling voice pick up the story again. She watched a hot air balloon floating far overhead, its burner letting out the odd muted hiss.

Finally the silence was too much for her. 'What did your father die of?'

There was another aching pause before he spoke.

'I guess you could say I killed him in the end,' Jay said quietly.

Juno went very, very still, her heart crashing so violently it almost broke her ribs. 'You murdered you father?'

'Of course not, Juno,' he muttered. 'But I was responsible for his death – or my behaviour was. I can never forgive myself for that. Never.'

The dogs stirred impatiently after lying in silence for several minutes. Juno thought of a hundred things to say, more to ask, but said none of them, certain that they were the wrong things and he would clam up totally if she said them.

After what seemed like an eternity, he started talking again. 'I don't think he ever forgave my old lady for all those daughters – one after the other. Six girls who cost a fortune to feed and clothe, when all he wanted was a son. It broke his heart. And my old lady, she never forgave him for not loving his daughters as much as he loved me.' For a moment the soft, lisping drawl cracked with emotion.

Unable to bear the pain in his voice, Juno tilted her head to one side, but he'd leant back on his elbows and she couldn't see his face beyond Blind's shank – only the curve of one cream-covered knee.

'He must have loved you a lot,' she said tentatively.

'He did.' Jay's voice was flat and dispassionate again. 'But it was a twisted kinda love – especially when he had to quit his job. That broke his heart. He changed afterwards.'

'Why did he stop working?'

'Someone was killed on a building he was working on. Got crushed when a joist gave way and a metal girder fell on him. Dad was standing right beside him, saw him die but couldn't do shit about it. It wasn't my old man's fault, but it really screwed him up. He'd known the guy for years – was godfather to one of his kids. Afterwards, he started drinking, picking on my old lady, staying out all night, beating up on me when I misbehaved.'

'He beat you up?' Juno was appalled.

Jay didn't seem to hear. 'Nowadays they have a name for it – post-traumatic stress. But then it was just seen as weakness. The other men thought he was wimping out. When he lost his foreman's job, he cracked up big time – started hitting the bottle at work. Pretty soon he was fired altogether.'

'How old were you?'

'I dunno – twelve, thirteen, I guess.' He sat up again, his profile silhouetted by the dying sun so that his face was in shadow, the wind lifting his hair from his face. 'He'd just sit at home all day, watching TV and reading gossip sheets. He loved those fucking gossip sheets so much. They were his life – that and the liquor.'

'And he beat you up?'

'He didn't really hit me hard – he just used to get so angry. He hated staying home with a bunch of women. It made him feel inadequate, emasculated, y'know? He had to borrow money off my old lady to drink. My sisters' bickering got on his nerves. I was the only other guy around to pick on. And you gotta understand, Juno, I was a monster when I was a kid. I was a no-good piece of shit even then, and my old man knew it.' He turned to look at her, chin rubbing against his shoulder, yellow eyes burning with shame.

Between them Blind lumbered into a stiff-legged stretch then shook himself vigorously, hoping that they were about to move on.

'I just want for you to understand something, Juno,' Jay muttered, turning away again. 'You need to know . . .' he rubbed his forehead with his thumbs, summoning the words '. . . that I never had what you had. I belong to a different planet. There's something about this place, I don't know if I can handle it.' His voice shook. 'I don't want to flip out on you here, but I feel kind of crazy right now. I gotta get outta here.'

'It's okay, we'll go back home.' Juno watched him dip his face into his hands.

'No! I mean the house – your family, the whole deal here. You. It's messing with my head. *You're* messing with my head.' His voice was taut with emotion now, knuckles so white they almost looked as though they'd broken through the skin of his hands.

'I don't understand.' Juno sat up, shoving Blind out of the way. 'Are you saying you want to go back to London?'

'Yeah, maybe. I dunno,' he muttered.

'If you really hate it here, you can take the Bird. You don't even have to say goodbye.' She didn't want him to go, hated the thought of him running away from whatever demons this place had summoned up inside him, but she could see how close to the edge he was and it terrified her.

'I couldn't do that to your family.'

'Of course you can,' she insisted. 'I'll say you remembered you had to meet someone. Or if you like, I'll say we had an argument – that I told you to piss off. I don't think they'll find that too hard to believe, given my history.'

'I dunno what to do, Juno. This feels so fucking weird.' He ran his shaking hands through his hair. 'I'm sorry – you must think I'm such a kvetch. I hardly know you. Shit!' He pressed his forehead into his wrists.

Juno stared at his hunched back, not knowing what to do. He'd let go of the plastic dog lead and Rug was creeping away from them. Not caring, Juno let go of the twins too and crawled forwards on her knees, wrapping her arms around Jay's shoulders like a scarf and hugging his taut, hunched back to her chest. For a moment he stiffened against her touch, then he gripped her hands and pulled her arms tighter around him, his own alongside in a strange, double-armed straitjacket embrace which was so tight and comforting that neither one of them let go.

'You must think I'm fucking *meshuggah*, huh?' he muttered.

'I might if I knew who *meshuggah* was.' Juno pressed her chin to his shoulder. 'Have I met her?'

He laughed nervily. 'It means crazy, y'know? Nuts?'

'I don't think you're crazy.' Juno shook her head. 'I just wish you'd tell me why – '

'You don't want to know, Juno,' he interrupted, fingers tightening around her wrists. 'You wouldn't like me if you knew the truth. That's why I freak out when you keep asking questions all the time. You wouldn't like me at all.'

'So you do want me to like you?' She felt her heart crashing against his back.

'Yeah,' he muttered.

'Without knowing you?'

He didn't answer. Just kept his arms on hers in their strange hug, his mouth pressed into the crook of their elbows. In silence, they stayed like that for what seemed like hours. Insulated from the wind, but isolated from Jay's mind, Juno hugged him for warmth and comfort, feeling his shoulders slowly relax, his hands loosen their grip on her wrists, his breath lengthen from short, nervous gulps to steady, even intakes.

'Thanks for listening,' he said at last, voice artificially light and brisk. 'I dunno know what came over me just then. Must be that cocktail your mom gave me. I said some dumb things. I don't wanna go back to London yet.'

'No?' Immensely relieved, Juno pressed her cheek to his cold ear and stared out across Dragon Hill to Uffcombe. The tiny church was just visible through the trees.

'Heck, I gotta try your mom's cooking for one thing.' Jay tried to make a joke of it, but his voice was nervy and defensive. He let go of Juno's wrists and removed her arms from his shoulders as though taking off a coat that had started to stifle him, hastily standing up and putting his glasses back on.

Sitting back on her haunches, Juno rubbed her sore hips and looked around, trying not too feel resentful that he could brush her away so easily. The fact that he'd accepted her comfort in the first place was astonishing given his fierce pride.

She suddenly realised that they were alone. 'Shit – where are the dogs?'

'Oh, Jesus.'

Their search broke the bleak mood, lending them a fragile unity as they ran up to the highest part of the chalk slopes – Uffington Castle – screaming for Rug and the twins.

They didn't have far to look. The Glenn pack was terrorising an elderly man and his King Charles Spaniel. Leads trailing, they had formed a canine ambush party around the little pooch and were nudging him with their noses in tail-wagging synchrony – like a bunch of big L.A. homeboys saying a friendly 'Hi' to a lost British tourist. The dog's owner was waggling his walking stick at them angrily.

'They're yours, are they?' he barked, far louder than his yappy little charge. 'Get them off! Bloody wild animals – and you're no better, the pair of you.' He eyed Juno and Jay furiously as they gathered leads and made apologies. 'Don't think I didn't see you – feeling one another up in a public exhibition of immorality while your dogs run wild. Should be bloody ashamed of yourselves!' He marched off, stick jabbing into daisy heads.

Juno burst out laughing and, reeling in Effie's lead, turned to Jay, but he was looking horrified.

'Christ, he thought we were making out!'

Juno's laugh petered out and she cleared her throat nonchalantly. 'Easy mistake – his eyesight's probably not so good.'

'But we weren't.' Jay tugged Rug away from Effie's bottom and looked deeply insulted.

'Well, no, of course not.'

'Too right we weren't.' Looking relieved, Jay pulled Rug and Blind to heel and walked up to the plateau of the hill fort.

What's that supposed to mean? Juno wondered as she hobbled after him, hips aching. That the thought of kissing me again is truly repulsive?

But five minutes later, as they trudged down the sharp hill towards Uffcombe again, she tripped and almost fell. As she pitched forward, Jay grabbed her arm to steady her. After she'd regained her balance, he slipped his hand into hers. Their fingers interlaced tightly for a moment. Then, not looking at her, Jay let go and walked on in silence.

Juno didn't understand him at all. She had no idea where he was coming from. But she did know, with a grateful twist of her heart, that he wasn't going just yet.

Judy and Triona had polished off the jug of Punch Line by the time they returned. Dolphin music was still splashing and warbling its way from Howard's upstairs study, but the 'buggers' were noticeably absent as Juno wandered through the dining hall, leaving Jay to pause by the table and admire the decorations.

'Good walk, pusscat?' Her mother gave her a huge wink. 'You've been gone ages.'

'Fine, thanks.' Juno shot her a warning look as Jay came into the sitting room. 'The table looks great.'

'We've been creative in your long absence.' Judy blew him a welcoming kiss, filling her chair like a sexy Beryl Cook lady. Her green dress had slipped down to reveal a deeply tanned, mountain-pass cleavage, her eye make-up had run into her smily crow's feet, and her hair had fallen totally from its mooring now, spilling around her face in greying pre-Raphaelite splendour.

'Pusscat – your trousers are ripped.' She'd noticed the torn pocket. 'Don't tell me you rolled down the Manger to show off to Jay?'

Sitting cross-legged on a sofa like a fashion victim pixie, Triona let out a snort of laughter.

'She was always doing it as a child – broke her arm once,' Judy told him. 'She'd just lie down and race off downhill like Cleopatra spinning out of her carpet – all the way to the bottom. Completely reckless.'

'Of course I didn't,' Juno sighed, offering to take the waistcoat and hat which Jay had been holding out politely to his distracted hostess. 'I – er – had a slight run-in with a gate post.' She caught his eye and smiled nervously. Just for a second, his lips twitched in response, but his face was pale and haunted. He had yet to say a word and a muscle was twitching in his cheek. Juno found herself automatically stroking his arm as though comforting a jumpy dog.

'How boring.' Judy was sighing theatrically. 'I thought you'd been having a bit of a roll around out there.' She directed another Dick Emery wink at her daughter.

'I'll just put these away,' Juno hissed, marching out and calling over her shoulder, 'Diet Coke, Jay?'

'Sure,' he muttered, glancing at Triona who was welcoming Rug with semi-focused delight. He cleared his throat. 'Am I driving you back to London later?'

'No need, I've got my car here, remember?' She looked up and patted the seat beside her. 'Come and tell me all about your walk.'

He stayed put.

'I'll drive it for you,' he offered, noticing that her high-boned cheeks were already flushed pink from drink, green eyes glittering like malachite.

'Why don't you all stay the night?' Judy offered eagerly. 'We've got plenty of beds – single and double.' She laughed throatily.

'I can't,' he said hastily, looking around for Juno. 'I gotta be somewhere at eight tomorrow morning.'

'Jay's looking after Uboat and Poirot.' Juno marched in from the kitchen with a glass of Coke. 'He has to get back, Ma. Besides, Triona has to be in the shop tomorrow morning, don't you?'

Triona and Judy exchanged a very blatant look of comic

disappointment, like teenagers who'd been angling for an extra hour before bedtime.

'Party pooper,' Judy chided her daughter.

Juno caught Jay's eye as she handed him the glass and he blinked gratefully. He was still on edge from the walk.

'When's Pa leaving for Germany?' she asked her mother as she collapsed into a fat sofa with a glass of red wine.

'His flight's at ten, I think. *Howzat!*'

The dolphin music halted above. 'Yes, poodle?'

'When's your flight tomorrow?'

'Ten, poodle. Be out in a min.' The music started again, with a tell-tale 'bugger'.

'Better finish that green peppercorn sauce then.' Judy heaved herself up from the armchair. 'You young things have a chat and a couple of reefers while the fogeys are out of the room.'

'Just her idea of a joke,' Juno told Jay hastily, shooting Triona a wary look in case she took Judy at her word, but she appeared to be drifting off to sleep, bleached blonde head lolling towards the sofa arm.

Chapter Twenty-Seven

Howard Glenn was a gentle, self-effacing man with a wit as sharp as a Kitchen Devil, a patience as immutable as Mr Bennet's and a faith as lop-sidedly lovable as a very old oak full of New Age road protesters. He emerged from his study at close to ten, by which time both his wife and his son's girlfriend were extremely tight – their customary condition whenever they met up.

His lined face curved instinctively into a smile as he saw his daughter – a scruffy, pretty, round-cheeked Queen Mab with her mother's face and her own mind. She might be thirty, but to Howard she was the same little dryad he'd taught to play the flute and the lute, to recognise pine from fir, to make corn dolls and crop circles, to sing a hundred different folk tunes, of which she no longer remembered a single air. It didn't matter; they were still in her head along with her dreams.

She was sitting with a red-haired boy who possessed an extraordinary aura. Howard recognised his nervous energy immediately, sensed his disquiet, saw the purity of his spirit. He and Juno were not looking at or talking to one another, but Howard knew that they were communicating. His chakra unwound as though he were being stretched on an osteopathic rack. No wonder he had found working so difficult that evening.

Watching them from the gallery, he stroked back his mop of white hair and cleared his throat.

'Merry Christmas, everyone!'

'That's the spirit, Howzat – even druids celebrate Christmas!' Judy laughed, getting up and blowing him a kiss. 'Now get your beautiful arse down here and meet Jay. He's living with Juno now.'

She got up to hug her father.

'You look well, wildcat.' Howard cupped her face in his bony fingers and looked into her eyes. 'The lotus flower is blossoming, huh?'

'Cut the spiritual crap, Pa.' Juno kissed his nose fondly. 'I'm great, thanks. I liked the dolphin stuff. This is Jay – he's swapped flats with Sean.'

'Good to meet you, Jay.' Howard gave him a double handshake then patted his back for good measure, assessing the young man's cosmic ambience. It was as fierce as a forest blaze and quite the most exciting aura he had encountered since meeting Jim Morrison in '69.

Jay eyed him back sceptically.

Hugely tall, thin and bearded, Howard looked like a cross between George Bernard Shaw and John Cleese. He was wearing a faded denim shirt and linen shorts which showed off his twig-thin legs. Despite the hippy paraphernalia – beaded bracelets, woven sandals, amulet on a leather thong – he was a strikingly handsome, noble-looking man whose height and booming voice intimidated many, although his manner could not be more docile and peace-loving.

'I hope my daughter isn't driving you too mad,' he laughed, nudging Juno on the shoulder. 'We lived with her for eighteen years and it never got any easier.' He eyed Jay wisely.

'We're getting along just fine, sir.' Jay cleared his throat.

'Are you now?' Howard laughed joyously.

'Now, Howzat, I think you should put some suitably Christmassy music on so that we can all go through and eat,' Judy told him. 'Haven't we got a "Festival of Nine Lessons and Carols" CD floating around somewhere?'

'Have we?' he said vaguely. 'I'll have a look, poodle.'

'Poor Howzat's had Christmas dinner six times since May.' Judy ushered them through to the dining hall. 'I've been testing things out on him. Tonight's menu is his favourite, so blame him if you hate it. Now, Triona – you're on Howard's left, I'm on his right, and Jay and Juno are here.' She pointed to two chairs facing one another several feet away from the trinity at the top of the table.

Juno caught her mother's eye. Judy couldn't have made the pairing more obvious if she'd suggested they take a tray up to the spare bedroom together.

The long table looked spectacular. The Glenn silver was out, along with a host of novelty decorations which the viewers would 'love'. As the female answer to Keith Floyd, Judy had a reputation for outlandishness, occasional drunkenness and constant eccentricity. Her food was universally declared sublime, but her table decorations were something of a national joke. Sadly, this didn't stop them from adorning the dining tables of half of suburbia every Christmas. This year she was going in for a Scottish theme; everything was tartan – the napkins, table-cloth, place-cards and crackers. A bowl made of ice, with sprigs of heather and rosemary in it, was filled with chilled water in which scented petals floated alongside ice-cubes containing coloured beads. Fat church candles were propped up by pebbles in tartan-covered clay pots. The centrepiece was a vast sphere of leaves and berries, all sprayed silver, some tied with tartan ribbon.

'It's a haggis,' Judy announced proudly. 'I tried to make a sporran toothpick holder, but it didn't quite work out.'

Suddenly the room was filled with eerie music floating out of the overhead speakers which fed through from the hi-tech stereo system in the sitting room. It was more Jesus and Mary Chain than Jesus College, and seemed to consist largely of a tooting long-horn and the clattering of dustbin lids against small animals.

'Found this glorious recording of Norse anthems.' Howard wandered through. 'A chap I know has been researching ancient northern European music for his doctorate. Sent me this tape last week. It's recondite but not inaccessible, I think.'

They sat down to what sounded like the noise of a cow in labour.

The food was sublime, the conversation a non-stop babble of family anecdotes, gossip, politics and local scandal. To the accompaniment of the increasingly tortuous Norse anthems, Howard flirted mildly with Triona and Judy flirted mildly with Jay, but most of all the senior Glenns flirted with one another on their last night together for a week.

Juno sucked up her oysters in green pepper sauce and wished the food wasn't quite so aphrodisiac. The starters were all slithery fingers and probing tongue food, requiring the maximum of hands-on contact as shells had to be ripped from seafood, sauces dipped into and long, hot loaves torn to shreds. Huge scallops sat in their shells, drenched in sour lime marmalade; fat king prawns resembled the pink legs of synchronised swimmers as they kicked up from a pool of saffron-chilli mayonnaise. A warm and ludicrously phallic salsify, scorzonera and haricot salad made summer asparagus look positively demure.

'The key to it all is simplicity,' Judy was telling Jay who had politely asked her how she devised her recipes. 'I steal all the best modern trends from Michelin-starred restaurants and bastardise them to make them easy. Top London chefs think I'm a terrible old granny, but I don't care because their books can't touch mine in the bestseller list.

'Boozy goose!' she announced proudly ten minutes later, in between screaming at Rug and the twins to get into their beds.

The main course was a Judy special – a fat goose stuffed with Calvados-soaked apricots, nuts and whole shallots. She moaned about the fact the bird had been frozen and was vastly inferior to a fresh one, but even the oak table seemed to sigh in wonder at the glorious aroma clouding over it. With it was potato and parsnip purée, rich with cream and chives, and a sour apple sauce of sublime runniness. There was exquisitely rich fried forcemeat with prune and port sauce, spiced cranberries swimming like lava in a deep bowl, sweet potato crisps glittering with rock salt, mountains of stir-fried celery, carrots glazed with star anise caramel, and broccoli unadulterated by anything bar a knob of butter.

'No sprouts?' Triona laughed as Judy swept out of the kitchen with a big bowl of slow-roasted vegetables.

'Not quite cooked yet.' She banged her bowl down and scanned the table. 'Now I think that's everything – wine, Howzat.'

'Oh, yes – straight away, poodle.' He removed two empty champagne bottles from the table and headed into the kitchen, sandals creaking.

'Good. I can change this bloody din while he's getting it.' Judy winked at them all conspiratorially and nipped through to the sitting room. A few seconds later, Clannad was flooding the room.

'Not much of an improvement,' Triona whispered to Jay.

'I thought you young things'd appreciate some pop music.' Judy floated back through and danced for a few bars – a strange half belly-dance, half limbo which looked uncomfortably muscle-pulling. But she bounced back to the table with no apparent ill-effects, although she'd silenced everyone completely.

'Still life in this old bird, huh?' She gave a shimmy and started carving the goose.

'It looks quite dead to me, ma'am,' Jay said straight-faced, watching her blade skim expertly through the crusty skin.

Judy laughed heartily. 'You are so witty – I can't believe Juno said you were humourless.' Thin slithers of meat fell into a neat stack on the serving platter and then her knife shot up in alarm, slicing several silver leaves from the haggis. 'Oops! Did I say that? Bugger.' Without a word of apology, she carried on carving, leaving Juno with a flaming face, totally unable to look at him.

For just a second she felt a light pressure against her ankle and glanced up in surprise to see Jay looking at her. Was he playing footsie? Why, when he'd just been told that she'd insulted him to her mother?

But Jay looked away and the pressure disappeared. Juno guessed it must have been one of the dogs brushing past.

Howard brought back a heavy decanter of a Cru Bourgeois so dark it appeared almost black.

'I'll stick to Coke, thanks, sir.' Jay cleared his throat awkwardly.

'I'll fetch you some more,' Juno offered, desperate to cool her face in the fridge.

'Can you get the sprouts out while you're at it – top left oven, pusscat?' Judy called after her.

As Juno piled ice-cubes into a fresh glass, she noticed that the dogs were all in their baskets, looking solemn – still banished there by Judy, who loathed them begging at the table. So the movement under the table earlier couldn't have been them. She pressed an ice-cube to her hot cheeks as she realised that Jay – secretive, truculent Jay – must have been pressing his leg against hers.

'Probably wanted you to pass the salt or something,' she told herself firmly, lobbing the cube into the glass with the others and filling it up with Coke.

In the oven was a shallow dish of sizzling green purée, dotted with olives and latticed with prosciutto.

'Ah – that's the business!' Judy reached for it as Juno tried to carry the Coke into the dining room at the same time, almost dropping the lot. 'Pease Pudding Italiano, made with sprouts. Only way I could think of to make the buggers palatable.' She slammed the dish on the table and fired it towards Jay. 'Help yourself.'

It crashed into his plate, the serving spoon almost stabbing him in the arm. As Juno leant across to put down his Coke, she could see his eyes blinking nervily again, that look of panic returning.

She gave him a reassuring smile and heaped some of the Pease Pudding on to his plate for him.

'Thanks,' he muttered, starting to wolf back food at his customary speed.

'Good to see someone with a hearty appetite,' Judy declared. 'Now what's the verdict?'

A round of 'deliciouses' followed amidst much chomping.

'Merry Christmas then!' She raised her glass again. 'To the sexiest cook in England, huh?'

'Certainly, poodle,' Howard chortled, raising his glass too and blowing her a kiss.

Cheeks bulging, taste-buds purring, Juno realised it did feel like Christmas. It was dark outside now; the candles danced light into the room. Even the melancholy naffness of Clannad reminded her of that charitable season when one indulged aged parents in bad-taste records, old cine films and parlour games.

'Shame Sean isn't here,' Triona sighed, filling up her glass with mineral water. She was back-pedalling on the booze now, having got far too tight too quickly earlier.

'He's here in spirit,' Howard said sagely. 'Jay is his representative. He shares the same tree of life – I can see it in his aura. His roots lie close to ours.'

Jay looked appalled at the prospect, gulping his Coke and accidentally elbowing his knife from the table.

As he dived beneath to retrieve it, Howard got into his hippy trip swing.

'I recognised a soul cousin straight away.' He rested his bony elbows on the table, waving a fork full of forcemeat around. 'The inner karma is so raw, the search for a spiritual family incomplete. It's like looking into the eyes of a newborn infant.'

Juno could feel a hand grabbing her ankle beneath the table, bitten-down nails digging urgently into her flesh.

'That's enough, Pa,' she bleated. 'Tell us about Germany. Whereabouts are you lecturing?'

'Wait – I feel it is very important I say this, wildcat.' Howard twirled his fork theatrically and the forcemeat flew into the haggis centrepiece. 'Jay is very much alone in England, on a spiritual journey as well as a physical one – I can see that. I think we should have another toast to welcome him to the family as an honorary son.' He put down his fork to raise his glass, enthusiastically followed by Triona and Judy who had their heads cocked and were watching the head of the family with loving indulgence – King Arthur addressing his knights in Avalon.

The hand was tugging at Juno's trouser leg now.

'Welcome to the clan, Jay – your heart is amongst kinsmen!' Howard intoned loudly, glass aloft. 'Where's he gone?'

'Um.' Juno pulled a face, wondering how to explain that he was hiding under the table and clearly having some sort of nervous breakdown at her feet. 'I think Jay's feeling a bit overawed by your love, Pa. He's – '

'I'm afraid I'm kinda trapped, sir!' called a husky voice from beneath the table. 'My shirt seems to have gotten attached to something down here.'

He'd been speared through the collar by a huge iron nail, hanging down from the underside of the ancient table.

'I told you we should do something about that nail, Howzat,' Judy grumbled after Jay had been extricated. 'It lacerated poor Libby Figgis's tights last week. I'm sorry, Jay – you and Juno both seem intent on ripping your clothes off tonight.' Her mother's winks were coming thick and fast now, Juno noticed worriedly. She looked as though she was developing a lewd facial tic.

A flaming Christmas pudding was brought out and devoured, along with nutmeg hard sauce, wild hazelnut biscuits and Amaretto ice-cream.

'One thing you can't make trendy is Chrissy pud,' Judy told them, dolloping out third helpings. 'Although I do have a cinnamon and sweet horseradish soufflé with devilled plum sauce up my sleeve if the producer thinks it'll help ratings. Now, Jay, we've been terribly rude and not asked you anything about yourself.'

'Odette's thinking of opening a restaurant,' Juno interrupted quickly. 'With a comedy club above it.' She shot Jay an anxious look. To her surprise, he smiled back at her – a slow, wide, sexy smile. What were they here, co-conspirators in some sort of cover-up? Juno fretted. She could be harbouring a terrorist, a patricidal maniac, a Bronx mass-murderer for all she knew, and yet she was protecting him simply because he didn't like talking about himself.

'Oh, I adore Odette. So motivated,' Judy boomed. 'What's she planning?'

As she told her mother about the proposed OD Club, Juno caught Jay's eye again. Yellow, direct, challenging.

'Well, she's hoping to get the lease on an old fire station in Islington . . .'

Christ! That pressure was back against her leg. It couldn't be, could it? He was concentrating on his pudding bowl now as he wolfed up a fourth helping of Christmas pud like a hungry red setter puppy, golden hair falling over his eyes, mouth chewing extra-fast in order to get the next mouthful in as soon as possible. But the pressure remained – not nudging or groping just constant.

Juno rather lost the plot on her description of The OD as a consequence – muddling up which floor would be which and repeating herself like a badly made corporate video until Judy interrupted.

'Sounds fab, pusscat.' She winked, topping up her glass with Sauternes. 'Now you take Jay through to the sitting room, and Triona and I can rev up some coffee while Howzat raids the cupboard for *digestifs*.'

Juno elbowed some lights on to illuminate the far side of the arch. The vast east window was a shiny black looking-glass of panes now that darkness had stolen the glorious view.

'I'm sorry, my parents are a bit epic,' she muttered, flopping down on a sofa and looking up at Jay.

He sucked his lower lip thoughtfully. 'Y'know, that wasn't as bad as I thought. I kinda like them – no, scrap that – I *really* fucking like them. They're so,' he searched for a word, 'loving. They're something else, man. I thought they'd ask loadsa stuff about my family and shit, but they didn't.'

'They're pretty self-obsessed.' Juno shrugged, hooking her feet up beneath her. 'Now you know where I get it from.'

He cocked his head and looked at her for a moment, starting to smile. 'I dunno. You're always asking questions.'

She stared back at him, wondering whether he was going to make some comment, some indication of how he felt about her, but he turned away and walked to the fat sofa opposite hers and sat down.

'I'm glad I came.' He stretched out his arms along the sofa back. 'It's sorted a lot of things out in my head. You were right about this place being kinda magical.'

'That's good.' Juno was determined not to ask any questions. She looked at him across ten yards of flagstones. They could hear laughter and clattering in the far kitchen, Rug yapping and Howard breaking into a deep bass rendition of the 'Wassail Carol' soon accompanied by an improvised percussion of wooden spoons against pan lids, and yet more laughter.

Still Juno stared at Jay, trying to work him out. But it was that classic post-prandial moment at Christmas, gazing raptly at a cracker puzzle, knowing you could stay up until midnight trying to solve it and still be no further on. There had to be a simple solution but until you fathomed it out you simply grew more and more maddened with frustration.

Pulling a cushion into her lap, she looked at his mop of hair, his beautiful eyebrows, cello-shank mouth and lean, sinewy body. A body that had been inside hers long before she'd tried to get inside its head. With every day that she'd known him, he'd grown more enigmatic and contradictory. Each day had revealed another twenty pieces of that complicated, mind-bending, three-dimensional jigsaw which was Jay. Yet she knew she'd never wanted anyone quite so much in her life. More specifically, she had never wanted to know someone as badly as she wanted to know him.

'Thanks.' He lifted his chin and smiled across at her – a shy, blinking smile which gradually widened and softened. It was that sunny valley smile she longed to run towards.

'For what?' She winced as she spoke. Damn. A question. He hated questions.

'For not laughing at me when I freaked out on that hill earlier. For checking I was okay tonight. I know you think I'm a pain in the ass. You don't owe me any of that stuff, and I appreciate it.'

'You're the one who thinks *I'm* a pain in the arse.' Juno picked at the cushion.

'No, I don't.' He shook his head, voice quiet and earnest. 'I think you're real special, Juno.'

'You do?' she gulped. Damn – another question. She bit back an additional 'After the atrocious way I've behaved all week?' and settled for staring at him excitedly instead, hugging the word 'special' like a warm friend at a cold bus stop.

'Yeah.' He nodded seriously, gaze burning into hers. 'You're demanding, argumentative, infuriating, manipulative, contradictory . . .'

'Oh.' Disappointment cracked the shell of her heart and gnawed away the soft centre like a fox with an egg. He'd meant 'special' as in special needs, special school, go see a specialist. Not so good. Pretty bad in fact. Oops – tears alert. Down, boys. Juno doesn't cry in public. Juno is going to make a grand, conciliatory gesture. Juno is going to lie.

She stabbed her cushion with her finger. Her father was singing 'All You Need is Love' now, accompanied by her mother in warbling harmony and Triona on the saucepan lids. 'I just want us to be friends, Jay.'

He chewed his lip and smiled again, eyes sliding away from hers. 'I was afraid you were gonna say that.'

Juno's head said, *What was that? What do you mean? What's happening here?* but she could hear Triona's heels clacking through the dining hall towards them and her voice calling out cheerily: 'They're snogging over the cafetière – so sweet!' She appeared through the arch with a tray laden with bottles. 'We've got everything Oddbins would never dare to sell here. I vote for the *eau de vie* which dates back to the 'seventies. How 'bout you guys? Ribena?' Her pointed face creased into smiles as she shimmied over to sit beside Jay, placing the tray at her feet. 'I think I might need that lift after all, Jay. I just found myself agreeing to post Howard something from our novelty pouch line.'

'We'll go now, yeah?' He stood up.

'What? Well, I wasn't meaning . . .' Triona watched him march towards the arch. 'Still, I suppose if you're keen to get back.'

'I am.' He felt through his pockets for the Bird's keys and threw them to Juno. 'There you go – she's all yours.'

Juno caught them and clutched on tight. 'You're leaving?'

'It's past twelve.' Jay shrugged. 'I gotta lot to do tomorrow. I'll just say 'bye to your folks.'

'But –' she gasped, watching him stride away.

Putting her palms up in defeat, Triona pulled a regretful face at her and followed him out.

Juno raced through to the kitchen just as Jay was climbing out of one of Judy's killer hugs.

'So great to meet you at last.' Judy pressed his face between her hands before he could back away, squeezing his cheeks lovingly so that his mouth popped open like an orchid.

'I've only been here a few days, ma'am, but thanks – it's good to meet you too.' Jay spoke through protruding lips before ducking politely away and shaking Howard's hand.

'I'm sure you'll find what you're looking for,' Howard said with cryptic emphasis before looping his thin arm around his wife and nuzzling her ear. Christmas always made him feel sexy.

'Thanks.' Jay turned away, catching Juno's eye as she watched from the doorway, mouth hanging open in bewildered frustration.

While Judy and Howard kissed and hugged Triona, Jay walked past Juno as though heading outside without a parting word. For a moment she felt hopelessly hurt, then he caught her hand and towed her along with him, through the south transept and out into the roofed porch. Tripping over the steps, she was propelled on to the lawn where Jay came to an abrupt halt by wonky Walter and stared at the blackened sky.

Juno waited excitedly, expectantly, her breath as short and quick as her temper. Please let him kiss me, she prayed silently. I know it's a long shot, God – especially as I'm an atheist – but let him kiss me. A quickie. No tongues or anything. Just let him bend his head towards mine, let those yellow eyes look straight into mine and let him –

'So, the parrot needs feeding once a day, huh?' he asked.

Juno nodded mutely.

'And I'll call you here if there's a problem?'

'It's number one on the speed-dial.' She carried on nodding, feeling like a lunatic rocking backwards and forwards to comfort herself.

'Okay. Take care.' He headed towards the Saab.

Minutes later, she was standing with her parents, waving numbly as the tail-lights of the car bounced along the pitted drive and disappeared into the distance.

'God, he's bloody sexy, pusscat.' Judy hooked her arm through her daughter's and led her inside. 'Fancies you like mad, of course. Very shy, isn't he, though? Listen. Howzat and I are bushed – going to hit the sack. Night, pusscat.'

Juno stayed up for hours, sitting in the darkened sitting room and staring out at the moonlit Manger, trying to figure out what Jay had meant. Special. Was that a special person he didn't want to be friends with – or a special person he wanted to be *more* than friends with?

Chapter Twenty-Eight

The kitchen was an absolute bomb site when Juno tried to find her way to some breakfast cereal the following morning. She'd been unable to sleep for thinking of Jay and had finally conked out at five in the morning. Searching for breakfast at almost midday, she found notes from both her parents saying their farewells – both apologising for not having cleared up or walked the dogs. The dogs – far from looking fed up because they hadn't had their morning leg-stretch – were guilty-faced and fat-bellied from polishing off everything they could possibly steal from the surfaces: goose, forcemeat, Pease Pudding, Christmas pud. Juno had more or less to tow them across a field and back to relieve themselves.

Oh, the bliss of being home alone. She ignored the piles of washing up and grew dusty-fingered, digging out old teenage tomes from her bedroom bookcase – *Love Numbers – Romance Through Numerology, Astrological Compatibility, Test Your Love Life With Playing Cards, The Essential Runes Guide To Love Prediction.*

Armed with a pen and a pad, Juno indulged herself in a long and scientific romance analysis. The news was good. She and Jay were made for one another. Okay, so she'd had to tweak the results around a little – change the odd card, flip over a rune or two, spell his name differently – but there was no doubt that the overall trend was positive.

Feeling good, she wandered around the garden and tried to

locate a suitable position for sunbathing – planning to lie down and write a few sketches, some new squeezebox songs, and a dream resignation letter to GWC. But it was too hot, there were too many flies around and *Countdown* was starting. She ended up inside with the dogs sprawled at her feet, infuriated that she could only get 'bog' when some sixteen year old with a dodgy haircut got 'toboggan' for eight points.

The evening dog walk was upon her before she knew it. Juno meant to revisit the spot where Jay had revealed his vulnerability, to sit and dwell upon his words, but she was too lazy and ended up circumnavigating the foot of the Manger before returning home. She wanted to catch *Neighbours*. Malcolm might come back from Europe, after all.

It was a good night on the box – *Londoners*, followed by a documentary on bad drivers (there was some 'eighties footage of a lunatic in a Reliant Scimitar who she was certain was her grandfather), then a sitcom set in a print shop she rather liked, then a Coen Brothers film.

Too good a schedule to waste on writer's block. Juno decided to give sketch-jotting a miss. It was, after all, her first official day off work. Having fed the dogs, she took a tub of taramasalata from the fridge, located a vast bag of Kettle Chips and settled on the sofa in front of the box. She'd start to get tanned, lose weight, write sketches and dye her roots tomorrow, she decided.

Three days later Juno knew the television schedule backwards. The dogs were growing accustomed to shorter and shorter walks – and more and more treats to make up for it. Juno herself was developing a strange penchant for frozen peas mixed with vinaigrette, eaten out of a mug with a dessert spoon. Her skin was still pasty, her roots still dark, her sketches still unwritten, Christmas dinner pots still lay underwater in the sink along with her own washing up, but she'd done every quick crossword in *The Times* that week, and her Saturday lunch was coming together nicely.

Bored and lonely, she had hugged the phone to her ear

during the breaks between decent television programmes. What had started out as an intimate gathering of her closest cronies was rapidly turning into something which required hired glasses and portaloos.

She wanted to ask Jay. More than anything, she wanted to ask him. But, while she plucked up courage, she ended up asking everyone else instead. The gang was coming, of course; Lydia was being driven down by Bruno (still together, thank God), Ally and Duncan were getting a lift with Elsa and Euan, Jez was picking up Lulu and Odette and had a space on offer. Triona was delighted at the idea of a second trip to Church House within a week.

'Jez'll pick you up,' Juno told her. 'That way you can be driven to drink, not drink and drive.'

Triona gave a cheery two-tone sigh, recognising the gentle dig. 'I said I'd meet Souxi for lunch, but if I drive – and stay sober – I can just bring her along, can't I? It's not as though she ever eats anything.'

'Sure.' Juno gnawed her lip, realising that there were four men – one gay – to eight women. Great. She was thirty years old and still the sort of woman who had no straight platonic male friends apart from her friends' partners.

'Are Barfly and Horse free?' she asked rather desperately.

'I should think so.' Triona sounded surprised. 'I'll ask them along if you really want – they can come with us. Shall I invite Jay too?' she added casually.

'I'm not sure if he'll fit in.' Juno had an attack of nerves at the prospect.

'I'm sure I can squeeze him in the back of the Saab. Or Jez can bring him. Didn't you say he had a space in his car?'

'I'll call Jay myself,' Juno promised, silently adding 'just as soon as I've had a snack, watched *This Morning* and checked my horoscope on Teletext'.

'Still too many women,' she calculated in a panic, as she totted up the numbers on her much-doodled list. Most of the doodles looked suspiciously like Jay. She added a moustache and glasses to them all to make herself feel less girly, and nipped into the kitchen for a snack. Now what did she fancy?

Peas and vinaigrette. Unusual but not untasty. Quite moreish in fact. She had several helpings before settling down by the phone again.

She phoned Immedia on the pretext of checking that Lydia was doing okay, but also to suss out Finlay's availability.

'I'm doing fine, Joo, looking forward to Saturday,' Lydia told her breezily. 'Hang on a sec – ' the phone was partially muffled as she spoke to someone at her desk ' – yup, that's fine as far as lay-out's concerned, but I'm not happy with the Americanisation in the spelling. Look at it, will you?' The phone was released from her palm again. 'Still there, Joo?'

Juno was flabbergasted. She'd never given a toss about the nationality of the spelling. Come to think of it, wasn't 'Americanisation' an Americanisation?

'Still here,' she puffed and explained her lack of men problem.

'I'll ask Nat along, if you like?' Lydia offered. 'Finlay's been off sick this week. We all miss him – and you too, of course – but the weird thing is it's far easier to work without you two around the place. Listen, I'll put you through to sales. They've got his home number. See you Saturday, Joo.' Her voice was cut out by a ringing tone as she transferred Juno's call.

Juno was astonished by her curt efficiency. It was like talking to herself three years earlier.

She got Finlay's home number which was answered by a far gruffer and more unfriendly voice than her newfound chum's. It just had to be his elder brother.

'Calum?' she asked nervously.

'Yup.'

Juno realised he wasn't a man to take to introductory courtesies – not even of the 'you know a friend of mine who's setting up a restaurant' variety. So she ploughed straight in.

'Which clinic's he in?'

There was a long pause. 'Who is this?'

'Juno – a friend of Finlay's. C'mon, are you going to tell

me or not? 'Cos I'll find out some other way if not. I need to talk to him.'

Two minutes later, she was dialling a number in Henley.

Finlay wasn't hard for the receptionist to track down. He was draped over her desk chatting her up at the time. Juno was flattered that he recognised her voice straight away.

'Juno, sugar! Am I glad to hear you.'

'How are you doing?' she asked.

'Murder, sugar. I'm so fucking bored! I feel like the school swot – they keep using me as an example in class. Please come and visit.'

'Would they let you out on Saturday?'

'Unsupervised? Unlikely,' he laughed.

'I'm having a lunch party. Lydia's coming.'

'*Very* Hyacinth Bucket,' he cackled camply. 'Don't tell me you've got uneven numbers and you need a spare man?'

Juno burst out laughing, suddenly relaxing into the new friendship again. It was as easy and pleasant as realising one was wearing a new, unfamiliar, but delicious perfume. 'Can you come? I'll get you a lift.'

There was a long silence in which she could hear someone freaking out in the background, screaming that he had to have a drink. It sounded suspiciously like the voice of a famous panel show host she'd been watching just that afternoon chairing *Celebrity Pets*.

'I don't think I can do it, sugar. I gotta stay here. I'm serious about this, you know.' Finlay sucked in his breath as he lit a cigarette. 'Is Lydia bringing . . . ?'

'Bruno? Yes.'

'Still together? Fuck. I take it you've invited your American? How'd the date go last Friday? Pretty hot, huh?'

'Oh, quite heated at times, yes,' she hedged.

'That's good then. The Marber play was fantastic, by the way. I adored all your friends – especially the beautiful blonde bookends. What a perfect couple, huh? Will they be there on Saturday?'

'Ally and Duncan? Yes.' She could hear more chatter in the

background at the clinic now – someone insisting that it was an emergency.

'Oh, God, I really want to come,' Finlay growled sexily, camping up his envy. 'I'll see what I can do.' There was a male voice in the background, and Juno distinctly heard the words 'taking liberties' and 'receptionist'.

Finlay cackled again, delighting in some unheard joke. 'Shit, I gotta shoot . . . metaphorically speaking. Sorry, I probably canna come to lunch. Call me soon and let me know how it went, sugar. And visit me, huh?' He hung up.

Juno listened to the tone sadly. She wanted Finlay to come. She liked his directness and his flippancy.

Eight women, seven men. If she asked Jay that would even things up.

She read her runes, flipping a few around to take destiny in her hands, not caring that three were missing because Sean had made them into wire-encrusted medallions when he was heavily into Marillion. They were good. Very good.

Juno dialled the Belsize Park flat and then hung up before the tones rang through. *Londoners* was starting. She fetched herself a mug of frozen peas and decided to shelve calling Jay until later in the week.

By Friday, she was no further on in her quest for men for the following day's lunch. She finally washed up the last pot from Christmas dinner – the Pease Pudding dish – and took the Bird into Wantage to raid Waitrose.

It was only when she was debating whether two or three packets of smoked salmon would do that it occurred to her that she had no money in her account to pay for the trolley-full of goodies she'd just spent half an hour amassing.

'I'll put it on Switch,' she said aloud, tossing three packs on top of the pre-washed luxury salad selection and wheeling her way towards the ready-cooked chicken.

Somewhere near the fresh bakery display, she started having a guilt attack mixed with a panic one.

'Don't they check your credit via the computer for amounts

over fifty quid?' she muttered to herself as she squeezed a foccacia.

'No, my love, they don't,' a soft voice assured her as two hands grabbed all the other foccacias – plus the garlic ciabattas – from the shelf.

A pair of kindly eyes twinkled at her over a heaving trolley-full of party food.

'Are you sure?' Juno asked worriedly.

'Certain, my love.' The woman grinned chummily. 'Just don't ask for too much cash back – that's when they start getting suspicious. You need to keep your strength up when you're eating for two, don't you?' She patted Juno's stomach affectionately and steered her Mother Courage cart of food in the direction of the deli.

Holding in her tummy, Juno sulkily put the loaf back on the empty shelf, selected six Nimble baguettes and wheeled off towards Condiments to choose some new low-fat vinaigrettes for her frozen peas.

Her shopping came to over a hundred pounds. Appalled, she bought a lottery ticket from the tobacconist's booth on her way out. She always used the same numbers – 40, 30, 42 (her vital statistics), 36, 22, 38 (the thin woman inside waiting to get out).

It was only when she was sitting in the cab of the Bird in the car park, ripping into a fresh bag of peas for a quick fix, that she remembered she needed hair bleach.

'I'll buy the cheapest,' she told herself firmly.

In the chemist, Juno marvelled at the choice, fantasising herself honey whisper, ash promise, harvest gold and almond majesty – all colours which she was convinced would miraculously transform her into the Timotei girl the following day – floating through the garden in a haze of pollen, serving Pimms to her friends and flicking her hair around as though she had a bee in one ear.

She plumped for d'Orleol's 'almond majesty' bleach, because, although a tad pricier than the rest, it seemed the simplest to use and the woman on the front of the box looked brighter than the others. With it, she bought razors and body scrub to pare herself smooth again, some fake tan, an aromatherapy bath oil that was guaranteed to make the cleansee feel like a sex goddess, a pot of herbal pills called 'Irrigation' which claimed to flush out toxins, a face mask, some jaunty nail polish for her toes and a pregnancy kit.

The last was an impulse buy. She was hardly aware that she had added it to her basket until she was back in the cab of the Bird, shovelling back some rapidly melting frozen peas and reading the instructions.

It was the pea fetish that had done it. All week, a terrifying fear had lurked in the back of her head, telling her that the motivation behind her newfound snack was more than pure greed. It was getting out of hand for a start – she'd got up three times the previous night for a green veggie and vinaigrette hit. She didn't even like peas that much. If it had been chocolate, she'd have understood, but *peas* . . . now that was weird.

Her period still hadn't come, although she was convinced the food poisoning had mucked up her system. She'd certainly felt menstrual enough – crying during *Londoners*, retaining water like a camel, sprouting spots. Her boobs had been aching so much she'd taken advantage of her strange eating habits by pressing bumper packs of chilly Bird's Eye VIPs to her chest.

'Waste of a tenner,' she said, shoving the kit back in the plastic bag and patting her tummy. 'Eating for two, my arse. I'm just fat.'

Back at Church House, she was stalled from an immediate dash to the loo to pee on the little mascara wand by the presence of Mrs Puffet the cleaner, who was grumbling that Juno hadn't watered the hanging baskets outside.

Mrs Puffet (known to the Glenns just as Puffball) was a short marshmallow of a woman who had been clearing up after the messy occupants of Church House for over a decade. Hopelessly forgetful and vague, she was inadvertently extremely loyal to Judy, who suffered the celebrity pitfall of being gossiped about locally. Puffball adored the Glenns, and loved boasting about her famous employer to her friends at the British Legion, but always forgot the specifics of any exciting news she'd been a party to – muddling up names and places. The only thing she could ever remember to pass on about the nation's favourite large, drunken, effervescent cook was that she and her husband were the untidiest people on earth.

Today, the house was littered with old newspapers folded down to the crossword or the television schedules, open dictionaries, mugs swimming with peas, playing cards and runes, and pieces of paper with names and numbers scribbled all over them. The huge Belfast sink in the kitchen was brown with coffee grounds, the kitchen surfaces dusted with crumbs, and the beds upstairs coated with dog hairs.

'Place is looking much neater than usual, dear,' Puffball complimented Juno. It was the truth.

'I'm sorry about the hanging baskets – I meant to do them tonight,' she apologised, putting away her shopping while Puffball Jiffed the surfaces and chattered companionably.

'Too late for some of those petunias on the porch.' Puffball eyed the several bottles of Cava Juno was trying to fit into the fridge. 'Having a knees up, are we?'

'Just a few close friends for lunch tomorrow,' Juno told her, well aware that she and Puffball had spent the best part of three days clearing up after the last party she'd thrown whilst house-sitting, although Puffball had no doubt forgotten about the spliff ends on the flagstones and condoms behind the gravestones by now.

'Well, dear, call me if you need any help afterwards.' Puffball winked, loving the idea of a cleaning emergency. She thrived on drama – even the sort provided by a dozen twenty-somethings leaving incriminating rubbish in the shrubbery. 'Now let's have a sherry and put our feet up for half an hour, shall we?'

She stayed until evening, wanting to hear all the gossip about Juno's life in London, which she secretly thought gloriously depraved if only she could remember the details. In turn, she passed on plenty of news about her own family – each story repeated several times. Juno missed *Countdown*, *Ricky Lake*, *Pet*

Rescue and *TFI Friday* as she listened to several repeated stories about Puffball's grandson's GCSE results, which changed from two Bs and eight Cs to ten As with the second take.

Juno tried to get on with preparing some food for tomorrow's lunch while she listened. She boiled pans of rice and pasta for salad, chopped vegetables and drained cans of beans, made pastry for a roast pepper and goat's cheese flan and baked it blind. But all the time the thought of the pregnancy test took the edge off her concentration. She added so much garlic to the butter for the baguettes that it mixed up to the texture of suet, she threw away the hard-boiled quails' eggs for the *Salade Niçoise* and kept the shells, and made a huge mascarpone cheesecake which she put in the oven instead of the fridge, melting it into a foul, sizzling pool.

'Still not got your mum's touch, have you, dear?' Puffball sympathised. 'If I were you, I'd buy it all ready done from Marks. Can't beat their strawberry Pavlova. We had one last week. Now was it the Wednesday or the Thursday? It can't have been the Tuesday because I had to take old Mrs Gilbert to have her gall stones lasered – or was that the week before . . . ?'

Juno mindlessly spooned compôte into her summer pudding bowl before realising she'd forgotten to line it with bread.

At last a toot from outside signalled that George Puffet was waiting in the lane in his spotless beige Metro. As Puffball headed into the south transept to fetch her handbag, she spotted the crumpled chemist's bag on the floor.

'Oh, you missed this one, dear.' She picked it up and peeked inside.

Juno turned purple and snatched it from her. 'Thanks.'

'Got yourself into a spot of bother?' Puffball tucked her arms beneath her bolster breasts and eyed Juno wisely. 'Or do my eyes deceive me?'

'Wh-what?'

'Spotted your little pot of laxatives in there, dear. Now I swear by syrup of figs – or is it prune juice? I always forget. Oh! I think someone telephoned earlier. Now who was it?' She pressed a finger to her mouth in concentration.

Juno was so relieved that Puffball had only copped the 'Irrigation' detox pills that she hardly cared. It was bound to be Lydia consulting her on what to wear the following afternoon, or Odette saying she'd discovered she was double-booked and was going to have to cry off.

'No . . . it's gone.' Puffball shook her head in defeat. 'See you soon, dear.'

After she'd cheerioed, Juno headed for the phone, but found that Puffball had left it off the hook and it was wailing quietly to itself. Juno dialled 1471, but the number stored was Puffball's own. George always called her at work to check when she wanted to be collected. The handset smelled strongly of Pledge.

Juno traced the pattern of the Belsize Park number on the keypad with her fingers, not pressing hard enough to dial. Jay wouldn't want to come down tomorrow. She'd left it far too late to ask him. He was bound to be busy.

She dialled 0171 and then experienced another overwhelming desire for a mug of frozen peas soaked in Paul Newman's Own Recipe.

Leaving the kitchen full of half-prepared dishes, she took her chemist's bag up to her parents' plush bathroom, but although she spread all her purchases out in a prioritised line – pregnancy test first, hair dye last – she decided to take them in reverse order.

So she was wearing a Waitrose bag on her head and eating peas in front of *Wheel of Fortune* when she heard a car draw up outside. Juno wondered for a moment why the dogs didn't bark. She hadn't seen them for at least half an hour. But she was far more concerned with the fact that she couldn't let anyone see her looking like an extra from *Casualty* lying in a bay awaiting assessment. Her face was red-raw from a sugar scrub and eyebrow-pluck and she had Jolen bleach on her upper lip. She was dressed in a stained T-shirt with FRANKIE SAYS RELAX on the front – an ancient fashion-statement-turned-nighty which dated back to her teens. There were tissues wedged between her toes from applying polish to her nails, and she was doing an Immac patch-test on her bikini line. Juno decided there was only one thing for it: she had to hide upstairs.

The dogs started barking at last as she duck-stepped on her heels up to her parents' bedroom. To scale the tower stairs which led to her own bedroom required passing several windows that faced on to the drive. By the time Juno was lurking in the darkness by her mother's dressing table and trying to peer out of a skylight, the dogs sounded like occupants of Baskerville Hall and the bell was jangling beneath her.

Standing on a button-back chair to see out of the skylight, Juno could just make out a flashy green sports car parked on the gravel sweep in front of the lych-gate.

It was bound to be one of her mother's racy London friends popping in for a drink before going out to dinner locally. That was probably what the call Puffball had forgotten earlier was about.

As the bell rang again, Juno flicked on the television that was mounted on the wall and flopped on to her parents' vast, oak-framed bed.

Wheel of Fortune was still on. The category was a title and author – N . . CH . . L . . S N . . CKL . . B . . , CH . . RL . . S D . . CK . . NS.

A puddingy brunette with bad teeth and a CKJeans t-shirt on looked blank as Jenny Powell flipped over the second K.

'I dunno, Bradley. Can I buy a vowel, please?'

'*Nicholas Nickleby*, you prat!' Juno wailed, wondering whether there were simpler ways to earn money than buying lottery tickets. She'd apply to be a contestant on a television quiz. If she won a Hyundai off-roader, she could always advertise it in *Exchange & Mart*. She must remember to send off for some game-show application forms, although she might start small – entering Uboat for *Pets Win Prizes* or something.

Damn! The bell was still ringing downstairs, the dogs still going mad.

She crept back to the button-back chair and clambered up to peer out of the skylight.

The flashy sports car appeared to have its boot tied ajar by bungee ropes and contained some large article which was impossible to identify through its tinted windows.

A delivery. Juno groaned. Her mother hadn't warned her about this. Who delivered something at seven-fifteen on a Friday night? And what exactly were they offering?

Juno splashed her face with cold water in her parents' bathroom and stole a dark blue towel to cover up the head bag, plus a cream silk dressing gown which was far more sophisticated than her t-shirt, if acres too wide and emblazoned with 'Sexy Mother' – anything was preferable to FRANKIE SAYS RELAX. Listening to the increasingly demanding shrilling of the bell, she dabbed a little Jubilee Bouquet bath oil on her pulse points (one never knew, it might be Marco Pierre White) and checked her teeth for pea skins in the mirror before creeping downstairs.

'I'm sorry – I was in the shower!' she announced breezily as she wrenched the door open and came face-to-face with Michael Stipe from REM. 'Christ!'

The dogs crammed their way out through her legs and jumped all over him.

'Juno!' He fought them off.

It wasn't Michael Stipe. It was Jay with no hair – or at least not much hair. The golden-treacle tresses had been shorn to a mean number two cut all over.

Juno took several seconds to gather herself, the 'Sexy Mother' dressing gown practically combusting. Christ, he looked *gorgeous*.

'Don't tell me you've joined the army?' She tied her dressing gown tighter, trying to hide the slogan.

'Thank God you're here,' he gulped. 'The turtle's ill.'

Chapter Twenty-Nine

'What?' Juno gasped, not really taking in what he was saying because she was staring at his hair. It still, on closer inspection, looked damnably sexy.

'The turtle – Uboat. She's real ill,' he said, grabbing Juno by the hand and dragging her towards the lych-gate, pursued by the pack of dogs. 'I called earlier. That woman who answered said she'd get you to call back, but you never did. Then when I tried again it was engaged.'

They were racing through the lych-gate now, Juno's bare feet stinging as the gravel cut into her soles.

'You brought Uboat with you?' she gasped as she realised that the object in the back of the sports car was a large tank. As they passed under the lych-gate, the dogs raced out on to the gravel parking sweep too and sniffed their way eagerly around the unfamiliar car.

'I had no choice – I think she's dying. I called a veterinarian, but he said he couldn't come over till tomorrow. I figured it might be too late by then. Look.'

Two protruding reptile eyes peeked sadly at Juno from the boot of the car as Jay released the bungee ropes. The tank was so huge that even with the two rear seats flipped down, it was poking out an alarming amount. Uboat was cowering as far into the car as she could. Juno wasn't certain, but could almost swear that the turtle rolled her eyes and sighed in relief as she spotted her.

'She started acting real weird last night,' Jay told her, hauling open the boot. 'Kicking up water and racing around her tank and stuff. Then, this morning, she was lying in a corner like a dead weight. When I got back at lunchtime to check on her, she'd dumped all over the tank – real golf balls, man. I think she might have been prolapsing. She's hardly eaten all week.'

Uboat was looking extremely car sick and fed up. She'd never been a great traveller, and Jay hadn't realised that her tank needed to be almost empty for transportation to stop her from drowning, so she was gripping on to the only dry land still available – her battleship. The castle and her rocky outcrop had both tipped over into the water, which was now a soup of stirred-up pebbles. In its depths was a small pile of white, sprout-sized spheres.

'See what I mean?' Jay lifted the lid and pointed them out. 'I promise I haven't fed her anything weird or nothing.'

Uboat craned out over the rim of her tank, defending her ruined home, mouth snapping angrily. Then she dived into the soup and started trying to scrape the little sprouts into a neat pile.

'Those are just eggs.' Juno rubbed gravel from her feet and peered closer. 'She's been laying eggs, Jay.'

'Eggs?'

Juno nodded, holding on to the towel on her head as she stooped closer. 'She's just feeling broody. It happens every few weeks, but that's a bumper crop.'

'No shit.' Jay stared at them in alarm. 'Eggs?'

Then he started to laugh. Watched in surprise by both Juno and Uboat, he gripped his belly and creased over, shaven head dipping towards the ground as he cackled.

'Shit, Juno – you don't know how scared I've been.' He wiped his eyes as he straightened up. 'I thought you'd never forgive me if she died while I was looking after her. I thought I'd done something wrong, y'know? Made her ill. I drove here like a maniac.'

'Well, the journey might have shortened her life, but there's nothing wrong medically so far as I can tell.' Juno reached into the tank and felt the water, hastily removing her fingers as Uboat lunged for them. 'We'd better get her inside and give her home a spring clean. We'll take the eggs out while she's not looking.'

They took one end of the heavy tank each and carefully walked it towards the house. It was incredibly cumbersome, the size of an office desk. Uboat didn't help by racing around pulling angry faces at them as she tried to head-butt the lid off and leap out.

With the curious dogs ordered to stay in their baskets, Uboat splashed irritably around in a washing-up bowl while Juno and Jay drained the messy tank and refilled it with fresh water, carefully taking the eggs out and putting them in a saucer. Juno then rearranged Uboat's playpen while Jay plugged in the pump and the heater, checking the thermometer to see that the water was the right temperature. It felt strangely domesticated working together. They didn't speak much – but at least they didn't argue.

Scratching beneath her head towel, Juno retrieved the quails' eggs she'd thrown away earlier from the bin, rinsing them under the tap for Uboat. Exhausted from her broody period of starvation, the de Bergerac-nosed turtle gobbled them back greedily, almost taking Juno's fingers off.

'Isn't that a bit insensitive, given her condition?' Jay asked. 'I've got some chicken livers in the car.'

'She loves quails' eggs,' Juno insisted, looking around for the big packet of prawns she'd been defrosting from the freezer.

'What's that funny smell?' Jay wrinkled his nose.

'The purifying tablets probably.' Juno noticed it too – a sharp, ammonia-like pong with undercurrents of burnt hair. She wondered if she'd left something in the oven. Where *were* those prawns?

'Been doing a lot of cooking, huh?' Jay looked around at the bowls of boiled rice and pasta, the pastry bases and dirty chopping boards.

'Yes, I'm – ' Scanning the kitchen surfaces too, Juno suddenly noticed that there was a strange demarcation zone of cleanliness between the edges of the marble work tops and the messy, food-covered middles – a zone that was just about the right size for a large dog with its paws on the edge to reach with its tongue. Along with the prawns, the garlic-butter bowl was missing. And where was the goat's cheese she'd got out for the flan?

'*Twins!*'

They stayed in their conservatory baskets, foreheads creasing into furry plough lines as they pressed their chins to their forepaws and looked up at her innocently.

Marching over, Juno located the garlic-butter bowl under Blind's blanket. His one eye watched her with mournful regret and he burped, mouth salivating. The reek of garlic was asphyxiating. A moment later he stood up, stomach heaving, and was sick into a cheeseplant pot. Ten quids' worth of tiger prawns landed on a terracotta automatic plant feeder.

Effie's nose was white with goat's cheese. Even Rug had got in on the act and was shredding the plastic prawn bag behind a veil of trailing vine.

Blind was sick again on a rush mat.

'Not my marinated tuna!' Juno wailed, instantly recognising the second vital ingredient of her acclaimed *Salade Niçoise* to be ruined that day.

Jay started laughing again. What's got into him? Juno thought sourly as she tucked her towel in at the nape of her neck and fetched a dishcloth. She preferred him sombre and sulky. God, what *was* that pong? Despite the garlic fumes, she could still smell something revoltingly chemical.

Clearing up dog sick was hardly her favourite occupation. She was, however, quite adept at it given the inherent greed of her parents' pack. She was so busy that she didn't notice one tit had popped out of the 'Sexy Mother' dressing gown until she was trailing to the sink with the dish cloth for the third time. She tucked it back in discreetly, noticing that Jay was staring fixedly at the clock on the microwave.

It was only when she paused to offer him a Coke that she realised her scalp was burning.

'Shit – I've left the bleach on!' she wailed.

There was no time to lose. She ripped off the towel and supermarket bag and stuck her head under the kitchen taps.

'Ow, ow, ow!' It felt as though her hairline was being fried in acid.

The bleach had started to dry crustily on her hair, matting it like chicken soup on a beard. It smelled atrocious. The ammonia alone seemed to burn every hair from her nostrils. In her haste, Juno clumsily splashed diluted chemicals in her eyes and mouth.

'Oh God, I need the special sachet of shampoo!' she realised, groping in front of her for the towel to blot her stinging eyes.

Jay handed her a tea towel from the Aga rail. 'I'll get it for you – where is it?'

'In my parents' bathroom – up the stairs from the sitting room and through the bedroom.'

She could hear him pounding upstairs as she tentatively felt the frazzled rat's tails on her head. They were as rough as the hairs on an onion bulb. Great. Yet again Jay had witnessed her in a complete state of incompetence. Not only that, but she was destined to look as though she'd had her hair styled at the local garden centre – by weedkiller.

She couldn't help herself. She started to snivel. Pretty soon she was letting rip with great, shuddering hiccups. Her hair would probably all fall out in broken clumps now. She'd have to wear a wig until it grew back. She'd look like a freak.

Her nose filled up as she stayed bent over the sink, snorting and sobbing, sore eyes watering with pain and crying with shame at the same time.

Jay was back in next to no time, his voice incredibly soothing given her fit of vain histrionics.

'Bend over further – I'll wash it out for you,' he ordered, stretching past her to mix the taps to a steady, tepid flow. 'You can't see what you're doing. If you do it yourself you'll damage it even more. You gotta be real gentle.' He started massaging the shampoo into her still-burning scalp, keeping the water deliberately cool so as not to aggravate the reaction further.

Juno snivelled and hiccuped some more, letting him get on

with it. She felt incredibly foolish. And, as ever when she was humiliated, she started firing out the jokes.

'Not too much off the back – yes, Benidorm . . . have you? I prefer the Costa del Sol myself, but I hear the paella's better there . . . yes, he's called Gary. Works at B&Q. Lovely bum.'

Jay ignored her, just stretching over her and slowly working up a lather to get rid of the stinking bleach. She gulped back some more tears and tried not to notice that the entire length of his body was pressed against hers, making the silk dressing gown slide up and down her skin with every movement as he stretched over her.

'Don't tell me, you served as an apprentice with Vidal Sassoon during your mysterious past?'

'I used to bleach my hair when I was a kid,' he said, 'to try and look like all my sisters. I used real cheap shit which you had to leave on hours to stop it going orange, so I know how to deal with the burn. It's not damaged too badly, y'know.'

'No?' Juno hiccuped.

'You'll be fine.' His soft strokes moved around to the back of her ears, making her shudder with involuntary pleasure.

'Water too hot?'

'No – no, lovely!' she bleated. 'Are you sure it won't all break off?'

'It's OK,' he assured her. 'It might be a bit lighter than usual, but I reckon it'll be as glossy as ever. Guess we've both had bad hair days today, huh?'

'Yeah, I noticed you'd had a bit of a trim.' Juno spoke into the sink, staring at the foam sliding into the plughole.

He let out a caustic laugh. 'I told the guy to lose the length and the next thing I know I look like a military cadet.'

'It'll save on shampoo,' Juno said sympathetically. 'Why d'you have it done?'

'Oh – someone I know said something about long hair looking girly on men.'

'What a shallow remark,' Juno huffed, her stinging eyes blinking like mad.

He fell silent, concentrating on his task as he scooped water into a mug and started rinsing. Water streamed into Juno's eyes and he quickly handed her a towel to hold over them.

'This is the second time I've washed your hair.' Jay applied more shampoo, his fingers kneading more confidently now as her scalp grew less sensitive and her hair less matted.

'Is it?' Juno was genuinely baffled for a moment, and then felt her face blasting cracks into the sink as she remembered the shower they had taken together, when he had taken her so gloriously from behind. How could she possibly have forgotten?

She hadn't, of course, it had simply been living in a separate pocket of her memory, tucked in the 'moments to savour' file, not the 'Juno makes large fat tit of herself again' one which she was currently taking the minutes for. But now that she thought about it, the two files became hopelessly mixed together as Jay's fingers worked through her hair with delicacy and patience. Her silk dressing gown was falling open at the front, heavy with water. She could feel his chest pressing down on her shoulder blades as he reached forward to tease shampoo through her hair line, his breath stroking the nape of her neck as he worked.

He rinsed again, and Juno bit back a groan of pleasure as warm streams of water stroked her earlobes and slithered along her neck like a silk scarf dropping to the ground. Then the conditioner started. Now *that* did bring back memories. The rich cream seeped towards her scalp, cool and soothing at first, them warming to skin temperature as Jay worked it through every inch of damaged hair, fingering it into the shaft, teasing it from root to tip.

Juno would never lie back into a hairdresser's basin again without a small, knowing smile flickering round her lips as she closed her eyes and relived this moment. She'd ask for every type of conditioner on offer, beg for it if necessary.

Suddenly she realised that this was a far more intimate moment than they had shared in the shower. This wasn't hot, urgent, non-verbal sex. However ludicrous the circumstances, this was something far more exquisite and far more of a turn-on.

'Tip your head a little lower,' Jay said, reaching for the rinsing mug.

He worked the conditioner from her hair for what seemed like hours, rinsing and re-rinsing. Juno stared at the plughole and decided she hadn't felt so utterly horny in a life-time of shampoos, cuts and blow-dries. Her pelvis had never dissolved like this amid the heat and perm fumes of North London's cheaper hair emporia. She was aware of every point of contact between their bodies, every wet hair on her head slithering between Jay's fingers and every dry one on her body standing up on end like a startled hedgehog.

After a few minutes, he set the cold taps on full over her head.

'Ouch!' She ducked away. 'What the – '

'It helps the shine,' he insisted, forcing her head back under.

Spluttering furiously, Juno clenched her eyes shut and shivered with discomfort until the chilly blast was abruptly curtailed as Jay wrenched the tap closed and wrapped her head in a warm, fluffy towel.

'Don't rub it dry,' he warned her, backing quickly away and walking over to check on Uboat, who was bobbing around in her tank contentedly, admiring her new vista. The tank was sitting on top of the chest freezer, which afforded her a glorious view of two humans standing several feet apart, deliberately not looking at one another.

Leaning back against the sink, Juno tucked the ends of the towel in behind her head and tugged together the sodden, gaping front of her 'Sexy Mother' dressing gown. She wondered whether Jay had realised how turned on she'd just been? She felt ludicrously shy and flustered as she started to suspect that he'd only doused her in cold water to calm her libido.

'Do you want that Coke now?' It seemed such a banal offer, but she felt she had to fill the silence with something.

'Not right now,' he muttered, turning away from the tank and heading towards the front door.

'You're not going, are you?' she bleated.

'No – I just gotta lock the car.' He disappeared outside.

Juno stood on one foot in the kitchen, mindlessly scratching the back of her calf with the shiny pink toe-nails of the other as she surveyed the debris on the surfaces. Then it occurred to her that, if she was quick, she could get dressed. Seeing her in the wet 'Sexy Mother' dressing gown might be putting Jay off a bit.

She raced up the tower stairs to her bedroom, tripping over Sean's old electric guitar in the narrow landing lobby as she pelted over the threadbare carpet to the tiny room at the far end – still a shrine to her former adoration of The Cure and Morrissey. Unfortunately most of the clothes she kept in the lop-sided, sticker-covered wardrobe dated back to the same era. The clothes she'd brought with her were all practical, well-worn, dog-walking stuff, the only touch of glamour being a powder blue Chinese-style dress she had earmarked for her lunch.

This was ridiculous, she realised. She'd been throwing on any old thing all week, and now that Jay was here she suddenly longed for Richard and Judy to pop up from behind the wardrobe and offer to air-lift her to the studio for a quick make-over. Where was that timeless little black dress when you needed it?

'Juno, you coming down?' Jay called up from the foot of the tower stairs. 'The phone's ringing.'

'Can you answer it?' she yelled back cheerily, sniffing a dark green dress and then noticing it was full of moth holes. 'Or the machine'll turn on in a minute if you don't want to.'

'Ah, ha!' She tracked down a favourite old last resort. A long, flattering denim button-front dress with only one lower button missing, a small stain on the bum and no distinguishable smell as such. Thank God it still fitted reasonably well – if a little strained over the bust. She couldn't think why she'd left it down here and not taken it to London with the rest of her decent stuff.

When she pounded downstairs, Jay was in the kitchen, tidying the surfaces, clearing away food and wiping the marble tops where the dogs had licked them.

'You don't need to do that,' Juno told him, heading for the fridge. 'Who was on the phone?'

'The answermachine switched itself on.' He wiped a little pile of rice into the palm of his hand before throwing it in the bin. 'It was your friend Lydia so I didn't bother to pick up.'

'You didn't?' Juno turned to gape at him, secretly delighted by the idea that Jay wouldn't want to pick up Lydia.

'I don't think it was an emergency or anything.'

'What did she say?' She took a bottle of wine from the fridge door.

'I wasn't really concentrating. Why don't you listen to the . . .' His voice trailed away as he watched her pour a glass of wine. 'Should you be drinking that?' He eyed her closely.

Juno shrugged. 'Well, I'm over eighteen.'

For a moment he seemed about to say something else, but then he reached for a pile of letters on the butcher's block.

'These have all come to the apartment while you've been away.' He handed them to her.

On top, a thick cream envelope was marked with a discreet 'Piers Fox' logo.

Juno ripped it open eagerly. It was a photocopied letter about the auditions for the all-female comedy troupe. She had to attend at least one of three workshop sessions the following week, hosted by the comic-turned-promoter Frank Grogan, who would then select the line-up for the final auditions on Wednesday night, which he would emcee while Piers made the final decision. She read the times in alarm. *Mon, Tues, Wed,* 10 am till 4pm. It would mean taking more time off work.

The Wednesday night auditions were being held under public scrutiny at one of London's top comedy clubs, the Ha Ha House. If she was selected to appear, Juno had to prepare five minutes' worth of material to perform live in front of a paying audience. On the bottom of the letter, Piers had scribbled a personal note.

'Juno – It was good to meet you last week. Please perform as you did at Laughing Gear. Will not be at workshops, but fully expect to see you there on Wednesday. Good luck.'

'Christ,' she muttered, re-reading all the requirements. It sounded more like an audition for a West End musical than for a stand-up ensemble. As well as wearing dance clothes (she had a horrifying image of herself prising a g-string leotard over footless tights), it seemed singing would be required – plus playing any musical instruments with which one was vaguely au fait. The workshops also included improvisation, clowning and fight training, and she had to bring along three ten-by-eight publicity stills.

Juno's publicity photographs were four years out of date, and she only had photocopies left because she hadn't remembered to badger Sean to take some more before he left for the States. She wondered if she could dig through her parents' photo albums for some flattering snap-shots.

'Good news?' Jay watched her as she read.

'An audition,' she murmured. 'Next Wednesday.'

'Wednesday?' His forehead creased. 'With Piers Fox? It can't be.'

'Says so here.' She handed him the letter, and started to rip open the others – several credit card bills, a rude letter from the bank, a council tax bill and a set of greetings cards from IFAW.

'I don't believe this,' Jay hissed, scratching his crew cut as he flipped through Juno's letter. 'There has to be some mistake.'

'I don't imagine Piers Fox is the sort of guy who makes many mistakes,' Juno said lightly. 'Why?'

Jay didn't answer. Instead he picked up his mobile phone and tried to dial out on it.

'Damn' battery's flat.' He pointed at the wall phone in the kitchen. 'May I use that one?'

'Feel free.' Juno slugged some wine and wondered what Jay had to do with the audition. Was he taking photographs or something? Perhaps that was why Piers had wanted to meet him. It seemed pretty small beer by Jay's standards, but Piers was, after all, a very persuasive man.

He took her letter with him, reading a number from the header to call Piers Fox at his office.

'Shit – it's an answerphone.' He hooked the receiver under his chin and flipped through the letter. 'There's not a home number. Hi – this is Jay Mulligan.' His tone abruptly changed as he heard the beep at the other end. 'Can you call me urgently? I'm on . . .' He read the number off the face of the Glenns' phone and then hung up. 'You got Piers Fox's home number, Juno?' he asked, lifting the receiver again.

'Of course not.' She started eating cooked rice out of a bowl. 'We're not exactly social friends.'

'It's okay, I got it on my computer.' He dropped the phone back on the hook and headed for the front door.

'What's this all about?' Juno called after him, but the door was already slamming behind him as he crunched along the gravel path.

Juno ate some more rice (could do with a splash of vinaigrette, she decided) and wondered whether she had the nerve to ask him to stay for supper. She was pretty certain he'd refuse given her previous cooking record, but the prospect of his dashing off without an explanation was wildly frustrating. As he walked back in through the porch with his computer bag, his short hair still unfamiliar, she felt her heart form itself into a tight fist and use her lungs as punchbags. She knew that there was a far more basic reason to want him to stay. She liked the way she could barely respire when he was around. It made her breathe heavily, and feel light-headed.

While Jay was revving up his little laptop on the butcher's block, she wandered into the dining room and unravelled her towel, daring to look at her damp hair in the tall, arched mirror above the fireplace. Jay was right, it hadn't been damaged too much, although it was shockingly blonde – almost as platinum as Lydia's. She rather liked it.

Gently fingering it into place, she was amazed by how soft it felt. Jay's hands had worked wonders, she realised, listening as he left another message for Piers – this time on his home number. A few seconds later and he was leaving a message with what had to be a mobile phone's answering service. When she went back into the kitchen, he was standing by the phone chewing his nails distractedly.

'I can't track him down.' He gnawed his thumbnail. 'I think the bastard's gone away for the weekend.'

'What's the deal with him?' She located her wine glass again and was astonished to find it empty. She was certain she hadn't drunk it all.

'You and me, Juno,' he rubbed his chin on the shoulder of his faded blue t-shirt, 'we're just tiny pawns to a fella like Piers Fox. We're pawn stars, baby.'

'How d'you mean?' She swung around, hearing the 'baby' echo in her ears. It all sounded hugely sexy – if a little sleazy.

'I can't talk about it.' He shook his head, face shuttered as of old. 'We have a meeting arranged for Wednesday night, that's all. It's kinda important.'

Juno swung open the fridge door in search of the wine bottle, but it seemed to have disappeared. Even odder. She fetched some juice instead and splashed it into the glass, trying to sound as casual as possible.

'I don't suppose you want to stay for supper, do you?'

'Sure.' He tapped a couple of keys on his computer. Besides the laptop, he'd brought in his pile of camera bags, a zip-up portfolio and his battery pack which was charging at the toaster socket.

Moments later, he was plugging his mobile phone charger into the food processor socket.

Well, that was easy, Juno realised happily, not pausing to wonder why Jay had brought so much stuff down with him on his emergency dash. Now all she had to do was engineer the conversation so that he opened up to her again. She wished her mother had left the recipe for that Punch Line cocktail.

They munched omelettes in the sitting room, plates balanced on their laps as they shared the same sofa.

It was only when she sat down that Juno realised why she hadn't ever taken the denim dress to London. The front buttons slithered undone with the slightest movement – crossing legs, leaning forward, turning to look to either side. She had to sit in a perfect Alexander Technique position to keep them together, which didn't exactly aid her attempts to relax Jay enough to make him talk. The only thing that was opening up tonight was her dress.

'Your hair's turned out fine – a little light maybe,' he said as he took her empty plate and stacked it on top of his own.

'Thanks to you.' She reached up to feel it. Blissfully silky. She then hastily did up the top two buttons of her dress which had popped open during her preening. 'I need it to look good for next week. This audition's really important. I suppose that's thanks to you too.'

'How come?' Jay looked wary.

'Last week at Tufnell Park. Piers Fox only came to see the show because he was meeting you there.'

His yellow eyes slid sideways disparagingly and he ran his hand over his stubbly hair. 'I don't trust the guy. You should be careful, Juno.'

'Why?'

He scrunched up one eye in thought. 'He uses people. People like us.'

'He makes people famous.'

'Maybe.' Jay shrugged. 'But sometimes fame isn't worth it. I used to be a little like him. It doesn't feel too good after a while. It feels even worse to be on the receiving end.'

'Is he trying to make you famous too then?' Juno tried to lean forward on the sofa, but buttons started unpopping from both ends of her dress, so she had to slouch back again, which made her question seem far more casual and off-hand than she felt.

He blinked uncertainly, opened his mouth to speak then closed it again, leaping up and heading into the kitchen to put the plates in the sink.

'Have the dogs been out for a walk this evening?' he called over his shoulder as his footsteps echoed through the dining hall.

Realising he might want another confessional session on

top of White Horse Hill, Juno bounded forward on the sofa, buttons popping. 'Not yet.'

'Mind if I take them?' Jay reappeared in the arch. 'I could use a walk.'

'Don't you want me to come too?' She turned to look at him, feeling so hurt she didn't realise the top buttons of her dress were gaping open to reveal a jaunty purple bra.

'I can manage.' He rubbed his chin on his shoulder, and stared fixedly at a small Ralph Steadman cartoon above her left shoulder. 'If you don't mind, I'd appreciate clearing my head a little. I got some stuff to think over, and I kinda like it round here.'

'Well, if you're sure you can manage with them,' Juno agreed doubtfully. 'I don't suppose they'll be too raucous considering all the grub they've scoffed.'

'Thanks.'

After he'd set out, she headed back up to the tower to change yet again, pulling off the hopeless dress and plumping for the safer option of brightly patterned leggings and a baggy sweater. It was feeling a little chillier now that the evening was drawing in, so she hoped her face wouldn't turn too pink.

Then she stood despondently in the kitchen, looking at her half-prepared lunch food, plus the mess from cooking omelettes. Uboat eyed her wisely from the top of the freezer.

Why hadn't Jay wanted her to walk with him? she stewed. He'd come all the way here on a turtle mercy dash, washed her hair, turned her on, mystified her, eaten her food and then gone for a walk on his own. It didn't make sense.

Remembering Lydia's message, Juno listened to it with half an ear as she started grating some cooking Cheddar for the flans, which she would now have to improvise.

'Hi, Joo, s'me. I guess you're out with the dogs. Nat can't come tomorrow, I'm afraid. He's gone off to Milan to look at furniture – don't ask me why. He's been a bit funny this week. Anyway, I know you're desperately short of men for your lunch, so Bruno has asked a friend of his along. You'll never *guess* who it is! I'm going to leave it as a surprise. Um

. . . that's about it. Everything's fine at the office – er – well, sort of. Actually there've been a few changes. Thing is . . . oh, I'll tell you tomorrow.'

The slab of cheese was too big to handle, so Juno wandered over to the butcher's block to fetch a knife. Jay's computer was sitting on top of it, still switched on.

She stared at it for a moment, sucking her cheesy fingers. The screen saver had come on and fish were swimming across the little rectangle which had been displaying information about Piers Fox just a few minutes earlier. All she had to do was nudge the rollerball mouse by accident as she reached for a knife and it would come back.

No, that would be prying, she told herself firmly, fetching a Sabatier from its wooden slot without touching the computer.

She grated the entire slab of Cheddar in a frenzy of guilt, knowing that she wouldn't be able to resist much longer.

She sidled back to the computer and brushed against the mouse. A little box flashed up demanding a password.

'No!' she yelped, realising that unless she cracked it, the box would remain there until Jay returned.

She chewed her lip anxiously. Juno had a bit of a reputation around the Immedia office for being a whizz at cracking passwords, but she knew this would be one of the toughest. She recognised the screen saver programme – it was the same as the advertising director at work used. The damn' thing only let you try six different words before it threw up a brick wall which required the computer to be switched off and rebooted so that the DOS could be program-edited.

Cracking her knuckles, she thought hard. Now Jay was the sort of secretive – some might say anal – guy who would choose something horribly obscure.

She tried Bagel, the name of his cat in New York. Wrong. Much more anal than that.

Peeking in his camera bags, she located his prize toy – the digital camera which was worth over seven thousand dollars – and typed in its model number: RDC-175. Wrong.

Damn! Two good guesses foiled.

Wiping a bead of sweat from her brow, Juno thought hard. Heck, it was worth a try. She typed 'Juno'. Wrong again. Just three left – her fit of vanity had cost her another life.

Okay, she had to be logical about this. The password was probably far too obscure for her to guess. She might as well give up, pretend she'd brushed it accidentally and that the window had popped up over the screen saver without her noticing. That way Jay could just type in his password when he returned without knowing she'd fiddled with it.

Then she read the message on the screen. It no longer said simply 'Enter password'. Damn! It said 'Incorrect password – try again', making it obvious that she'd already tried to enter at least one. Damn! Damn!

Juno pulled off the jumper and tied it over her shoulders to cool herself down. She then tried entering 'Diet Coke'. Wrong.

She only had two guesses left. It just went to show how little she knew about him, she realised forlornly.

Drumming her fingers on the butcher's block, she tried to think of the oddest thing that had struck her about Jay since she'd met him. Many sprang to mind, but only one occurred to her as really unusual. It was something that any Brit would consider common or garden, a national pastime, part of the popular culture. But for a Yank it was an oddity.

'Londoners.' Damn! Access denied.

Feeling like Sandra Bullock in *The Net*, Juno swept her arm across her moist brow and typed out what felt like her suicide note: 'The Green Man'.

Bingo! The fishes gave way to a lovely crisp white screen lined with typeprint.

'Thank you, God!' she whooped, giving the air a high five and winking at Uboat. 'Okay, what do we have here, you sexy, secretive bugger?'

She scrolled down from Piers Fox's address and telephone numbers, past a list of others, most of which were New York-based with the classic 212 Manhattan area code.

Great, she realised bitterly. After all that effort, she had simply accessed Jay's electronic address book. He had some impressive names in it, but it told her nothing. There were no personal notes attached, no indication of why he knew Piers.

Then she saw something which made her neck heat up – followed by her face and chest as an excited blush slicked her torso. After 'F', neatly stored in the 'G' section before her brother's mobile number, was 'Glenn – Juno'. Beside it was the Church House number and three little asterisks. Juno hadn't a clue what they meant, but as far as she was concerned they were as romantic as three little words and three coins in a fountain. Scrolling up and down, she couldn't find another name with those three asterisks beside it. She suddenly felt very tasty, very special and very, very hot.

She longed to snoop further, but was terrified she'd lose the file and be caught trying to access it again. It wasn't worth the risk. Besides which her back was already crawling with guilt tics.

By the time Jay returned, the screen saver was once again showing swimming fish and Juno was lounging in the sitting room. The dogs rushed in to leap all over her, scratching her legs with their claws and dabbing her hands with eager tongues as they announced they were back.

She waited for Jay to appear through the arch, but there was no sign of him.

'Hi there – good walk?' she called out, but there was no reply.

She gnawed her lip anxiously, certain he'd somehow guessed she'd been playing with his PC and was seething in the kitchen, sizing up the Sabatiers.

It was past nine and starting to get dark outside. Juno rubbed the back of her neck and stood up uncertainly.

'Jay?'

Still no reply.

Then she spotted him on the other side of the glass wall. He was wandering between the fruit trees in the walled garden, the knuckle of one finger clenched between his teeth.

He looked so different with his hair short. Less vulnerable, less poetic, but infinitely more sexy.

What was he doing mooching around her parents' garden at twilight chewing his finger?

Juno chewed her own finger in sympathy, and then made up her mind to find out once and for all why Jay Mulligan had come to England and crept into her life, and why he'd left three asterisks beside her name on his computer.

Chapter Thirty

She found him leaning into the cleft of an old Bramley apple tree, squinting out towards the Manger.

Juno picked up an early windfall as she walked towards the tree – a tiny, misshapen runt that had been dropped from the branch long before it could ripen. Like her relationship with Jay, she thought. A little, twisted, bitter non-starter that would be left to rot under normal circumstances.

She hurled it over the garden wall, watching it spin through the dappled evening light.

Jay turned around in surprise.

'I used to sit in that tree as a kid and pretend to be riding a pony,' she told him, reaching out to stroke the smooth cleft as she approached. 'You get a lot of splinters when you try to rise to the trot.'

'You shoulda ridden Western-style.' He stapled a tiny cushion of his lip with his teeth, pinkening the flesh.

'The only spaghettis I knew then came in a can with mini-sausages.'

The yellow eyes watched her warily, waiting for the banter to turn into an argument.

Wood pigeons were roosting noisily in the trees overhead. The twins sat on the lawn staring up at the branches, willing one of them to miss its footing. Rug lifted his leg at the foot of Jay's apple tree and trotted away to root for moles in the vegetable patch.

'I can't believe you've only been in England a fortnight,' Juno sighed, picking at a lump of bark on a low-hanging branch. 'It seems much longer.'

Jay looked blank. 'What's a fortnight?'

She smiled, pulling hunks of bark from the tree. 'We don't have a lot in common, do we? Not even a language.'

He lifted his hand to brush his hair from his eyes as he had so often before, only to find it wasn't there. Instead he scratched his stubbly head and shrugged. 'I guess we're just coming from different directions.'

Juno longed to say something hugely cheesy like, 'But are we running towards one another or just passing like ships in the night?' Thankfully she got a grip of herself in time and nodded in what she hoped was a sage and mature fashion.

She decided it would be easier to talk if they were involved in some sort of task together. She looked around the garden for inspiration, but apart from the wheelbarrow leaning against the barn and a metal bucket sitting on a garden chair, there didn't appear to be much in the way of ongoing gardening jobs at hand.

Then she remembered the croquet set. Perfect! It was buried in the barn somewhere. Together, they could dig it out and set it up, and she could casually chat her way into his confidence.

'Could you help me find something in the barn?' she asked, already setting off towards the old stone outhouse, her mission decided.

He followed her in silence.

Damn! Another fat bottom moment, Juno realised as she clenched her buttocks together and hurried towards the tall black-stained wooden doors. Thankfully the padlock was still open from her recent forays to collect garden furniture.

Inside, it was dingy and dusty and smelled of petrol from the lawn-mower, and of compost from the open bags which were spilling out their contents on to the cluttered floor.

The Glenns were appalling hoarders, hating to throw anything away that 'might come in handy one day'. Consequently, the barn was ceiling-high with old furniture, children's toys, garden implements, rusty bicycles, pots and pans, suitcases, camping equipment, mildewy books and black bin bags full of old clothes, curtains and linen.

'What are we looking for?' Jay peered around the dim space.

'A croquet set.' Juno flicked the light switch and the neon strips buzzed into life overhead.

'What's a croquet set?' He was peering at a pile of old music scores which were yellow with age and curled from damp.

'It's a sort of game with hoops and mallets.' Juno lifted the lid of an old, warped ottoman. 'I think it's in a wooden box about the size of a guitar case.' She dropped the ottoman lid as she saw Randy Andy, the deflated sex doll, tucked beside a pile of her grandfather's old 78s. 'It should be pretty close to the surface – we had it out last summer.'

Jay picked up a couple of black bags and looked underneath them. 'Jesus, there's a stuffed goat down here!'

'Oh, that's Beardy Weirdie – he died years ago; Grandpa had a girlfriend at the time who was a taxidermist.' Juno opened an old wardrobe and stepped back as several footballs fell out and bounced away. 'She did Beardy as a freebie. Gave him cross eyes and a lumpy bottom. Kind, but misdirected.'

'Scary.' Jay dropped the bags back on top of the Glenns' former lawn-chomper.

'She stuffed a couple of Grandpa's roadkill pheasants as well.' Juno searched through piles of old board games in the wardrobe. 'He drove like a maniac – used to joke about how many birds he took out a month. They're around here somewhere.'

'He sounds quite a guy, your grandfather.' Jay flipped open the doors of an old sideboard and encountered a choked pile of old computer keyboards, monitors and printers.

'I was a bit frightened of him,' Juno confessed without thinking as she spotted a ouija board and wondered whether to dig it out for tomorrow's lunch.

'Frightened?' Jay removed a stack of lampshades from on top of an old chest.

'I doted on him.' Juno rejected the ouija board, deciding it was tempting fate. 'But he never really liked me. He thought I was undisciplined and headstrong. After he died, Pa said the reason we never got along was because we were too alike, but I don't buy that.'

'But you *are* like that, Juno,' Jay murmured thoughtfully.

'Am I?' She turned to stare at him, but he was nose-deep in old frames. Then when she turned away to prod through a pile of old toys, he spoke again.

'I thought you went for guys who were like that too? Big macho types.'

'Like Grandpa?' Juno gaped at an old orange space-hopper, experiencing a giddy head-rush of opportunity. 'No, not at all! I – er – prefer quieter types. More self-controlled.' She almost added 'ginger-haired' but decided that would be too obvious.

The space-hopper's toothy, cartoon mouth leered at Juno knowingly as she awaited some sort of comment. But, still flipping through canvases, Jay didn't react at all as she'd hoped.

'Where's the rest of his collection?' He looked up and gazed around. 'You said there were a stack of other cartoons in here?'

'Upstairs.' Juno pointed at the rickety ladder which led up to a hatch through to the second level. 'It's less damp up there.'

'May I look?'

'Be my guest.' She watched him climb up, uncertain whether to follow. She knew that the croquet set wouldn't be up there, but she had to keep the casual conversation going somehow, steer it towards Jay. All this talk of Grandpa Glenn was making her feel maudlin and vulnerable, and she wasn't sure her hint about preferring quiet men had registered.

Just as his legs disappeared through the hatch, Juno spotted the familiar wooden box sitting on top of the wardrobe. Bingo!

She'd just have to pretend she hadn't seen it and grasp the opportunity to probe further. Undisciplined and headstrong. Hmm. Well, if he thought it, she'd be it.

She hated climbing the barn ladder – two of the rungs were missing, and the others were full of woodworm. Years ago, when the Glenns had first moved to Church House and lived in a caravan while the builders worked on renovations, she'd fallen off it and broken her wrist. She held tightly on to the uprights and tried to pull herself up as much as possible so that she didn't put pressure on the rungs.

She was halfway up when Rug bounded into the barn and scrabbled at the foot of the ladder, eager for a bunk up.

'Forget it, little beast.' She looked down at him. 'Ugh!'

He was clenching a dead rat in his teeth. Juno almost fell off the ladder in revulsion.

The last few rungs were the ones she dreaded. She carefully inched her way up, clinging on to the uprights so tightly she could feel the grain of the wood indenting her palms. As she stretched up so that her head was through the hatch, she caught sight of Jay's legs nearby as he squatted low to the wooden floor to flip through a stack of folders.

'Find anything interesting?' She lifted her foot to the next rung and admired his bottom from her low angle of approach.

Jay looked at her over his shoulder. 'I can't believe there's a Max Beerbohm sketch here — and a loada Mark Boxer originals.'

'You seem to know a lot about British cartoonists.' Juno tried for a super-casual tone, but it was hard when climbing a deadly ladder. Nearly there. She inched a little higher.

'A friend of mine's a cartoonist for the *New York Post*.' He picked up another folder. 'He'd go wild about this stuff, man. He has books in his apartment all about these people.'

'You must miss your friends.' Grabbing hold of the top of the hatch, Juno elbowed her way up so that her feet were almost on the top rung.

'I guess.' He looked over his shoulder again and then grinned. 'But I miss Bagel the most.'

Yes! Juno smiled at him victoriously. Here we go at last. I'll get him talking about his cat and before he knows it we'll be on to some serious psychological profiling.

'Tell me about Ba— aagh!' The top rung gave way and Juno plummeted downwards, scrabbling madly as she tried to clutch on to the edge of the hatch, but it scraped past her fingers and belly as she dropped like a sack of corn to the stone floor below.

There was a shriek of canine outrage as she landed in a sprawl at the foot of the ladder. Something warm and soft and dead was directly underneath her.

For a moment, Juno was so stunned and disorientated that she thought she'd landed on top of Rug. The horror of the notion made her burst into instant, noisy tears. It was only when he bit her on the ankle that she realised he'd jumped out of the way in time and was standing by her feet, baring his teeth at her angrily. She'd landed on the dead rat. Juno could feel it squashed under her left thigh. Rug was simply livid that she'd flattened his recent kill and started to savage her plimsoll in a revenge attack.

'Juno!' Jay's face appeared in the hatch, white with shock.

'I'm okay,' she sniffed, tears rapidly dissolving, burnt away by a fierce blush. Her coccyx was throbbing and her hands were full of splinters, but Juno was too mortified to care. It seemed vital to appear ultra-casual about the whole episode. Clutching on to the ladder, she scrambled up, wincing as she tried to put her weight on her left ankle. 'Ow!'

'Watch out — I'm coming down.' Jay backed hurriedly through the hatch, lowering himself down with his arms then dropping the last few feet.

He grabbed hold of her shoulders and looked at her worriedly. 'You okay? You hurt yourself?'

'Hurt my ankle a bit,' she said through gritted teeth, determined not to blub again. 'It'll be all right in a minute.'

'Nothing else?' His eyes met hers urgently.

Juno found his concern deeply embarrassing. She was certain he thought — as she did — that the ladder had given way because she was so overweight.

'No, I'm fine, honestly.' She pulled away and hopped towards an old kitchen bench.

'You shouldn't have climbed up there in the first place,

Juno.' Jay followed her, starting to sound almost angry. 'You gotta be more careful now that you might be – '

'Get off, Rug!' Juno yelled as the terrier continued savaging her injured foot, yanking at a lace and growling furiously.

She sat on the bench and eased off her plimsoll, screaming as pain shot up her leg like the stab of a harpoon slicing through her heel. As the shoe fell to the floor, Rug leapt upon it with glee, killed it barbarously and then dragged it away by the lace.

'You can't go putting yourself in danger like that.' Jay stood over her. 'Not in your condition.'

Juno chewed her lip with humiliation. My condition being out-of-condition fatness, she realised wretchedly.

'It was just a little slip,' she muttered. 'Don't make such a big deal of it.'

'Let me have a look.' Jay dropped to his haunches and took her foot in his hands.

'Careful!' Juno yelped, although she was aware that the shooting pain she was experiencing came almost wholly from trying to hold up her foot so that Jay didn't realise how heavy her leg was. In the heightened perception that pain brought, it suddenly occurred to her that she had not felt this fat when she first met him.

The ankle was badly grazed and already starting to swell up, but when Jay gently manoeuvred it from side to side the pain was no worse than a constant, dull throb.

'It's just twisted.' He lowered it to the floor and smiled. 'Like the person it's attached to. Put your arms around my neck and I'll carry you inside.'

'No!' Juno yelped, arms staying stapled to her sides. 'I'll be fine.'

'Well, if you're sure you can walk okay . . .'

'Walk?' She laughed breezily. 'I could tap along to *Riverdance*, no trouble.'

Juno was pretty certain that any attempt to move from the bench she was sagging upon to the house would be extremely ungainly, and require a large amount of stooping, groaning, limping and hopping. She had no wish to be observed by Jay so stayed put and started removing the splinters from her hands, although she knew she was tempting septicaemia.

'Shouldn't you disinfect them and use a set of tweezers?' he muttered, watching her in alarm.

'I'll clean them up later,' she said airily, yanking out a shard of wood the size of a tooth pick. 'Shouldn't you be getting back to London soon?'

'I'm in no hurry.' He leant back against a broken old pianoforte which was piled high with magazines tied up in string.

Damn! Juno was in no fit state to get up and shamble out with him watching. She realised she needed a diversionary tactic.

'Oh, look!' She pointed at the wardrobe. 'There's the croquet set! Would you be an angel and reach it down for me?'

While he had his back to her, she made an almighty effort and managed to get as far as the door unobserved, hopping and limping like a ham actor playing Richard III, and almost biting her tongue off as she battled not to shriek and squeal in pain. By the time Jay had fetched down the croquet set, she was leaning heavily on the latch and smiling victoriously. He looked mildly surprised to see her there, but made no comment.

Juno was relying upon the door for support, so could only open it a few inches.

'After you.' She made a doorman-type gesture, waving him through the very narrow gap.

As Jay shuffled out sideways, the twins greeted him eagerly. He bent down to talk to them and Juno had the chance to hobble the few agonising steps after him and lean heavily against the wall of the barn.

It was almost dark. Midges danced overhead and the automatic light had come on at the side of the house.

So far, so good. Jay didn't seem to have twigged that she could barely walk. She couldn't bear the idea of him putting his back out trying to carry her.

There was twenty feet of gravel path between the barn and the conservatory doors. The twins were lumbering around her restlessly, presenting another obstacle. Juno was certain that the moment she moved, they'd bounce up and trip her over. Her ankle was throbbing like mad and her hands were agony. She hadn't a clue how she was going to get any cooking done for tomorrow's lunch when she couldn't even make it as far as the kitchen.

'Lovely evening, isn't it?' She breathed in deeply and appreciatively.

'Sure.' Jay nodded.

'Sometimes I just like to stand outside for a while and drink it all in,' she carried on enthusiastically. 'I could stay here for hours enjoying the peace and quiet.'

They stood in silence for a few seconds, both pretending to drink it all in. All Juno wanted to drink was a large Scotch to deaden the pain. Her ankle had already almost doubled in size.

'Don't let me hold you up if you're dying to get back to London,' she told Jay, although she didn't want him to go at all — just go away for a minute or two. 'I think I'll stand out here for a bit longer.'

'I'm not going back to London tonight.' He opened the barn door again and reached in to turn off the lights.

'You're not?' Juno clung on to the wall.

'No, I think I'd better stay here and look after you. Unless, of course, you actually *want* to stay out here all night soaking in the atmosphere.'

'I told you, I'm fine.'

'Okay,' he sighed impatiently, pulling out the wheelbarrow and rolling it behind her. 'So let's say we're just doing this for fun. Now sit your ass down in this thing and I'll take you into the house.'

Before Juno knew what was happening, she was through the conservatory and being rolled like Ironside towards the fat leather kitchen sofa. She dragged herself on to it before Jay could offer to pick her up and drop her there. Minutes later her ankle was propped up on a bag of frozen peas, a cup of tea was pressed into her mitts, a pile of magazines deposited on the floor beside her, and Jay was trying to pull off her leggings.

'What are you doing?' Juno yelped, trying to pull them back up.

'You've got a loada rat fur and blood on your ass,' he told her.

'It's this season's latest look.' She kept a tight hold on the waistband, acutely aware that she hadn't shaved her legs all week apart from the fronts, and that was two days ago. Her splinter-filled fingers stung like crazy as she tugged.

'Juno, you don't have to be embarrassed,' Jay sighed, sitting back on his heels. 'I've seen your legs before, remember?' His attitude was clinical, impatient and detached. Mortified, she let him get on with it. She felt like a naughty, besmirched toddler being wiped up by the baby-sitter.

While the leggings were being thrown around the drum of the washing machine, Jay took a pair of tweezers and a bottle of Dettol to Juno's hands, perching on the side of the sofa as he worked, head bent in concentration.

'Jesus, there are hundreds of the little fuckers in here – some real deep.' He studied her palm. 'This must hurt like hell.'

'Well, it is a bit sore.' Juno shifted uncomfortably. His thigh was alongside hers and he was holding her hand. Why was it that the only times she got to touch him were during moments of extreme humiliation – like performing her Mae West act, having her crusty hair washed, and falling off a ladder?

'You're something else, you know that?' he laughed, tweaking splinters out expertly. 'I'd be screaming my head off if I'd done this to my hands.'

'Oh, c'mon. You've been shot.'

'And I screamed my head off then.' He looked up at her face for a second, his expression suddenly serious.

'What was it like?' Juno asked.

He shrugged, concentrating on her hand again, this time far less gently. 'I wouldn't recommend it.'

'Sorry.' She winced as he yanked out a fat splinter of wood. 'I know you hate me asking questions.'

'It's not that.' He shook his head, dropping her hand and picking up the Dettol. 'It's just that I did some really stupid things around that time – getting shot was one of them. I hate it when people glamorise it. I wasn't a hero, I wasn't doing it so that the world saw photographs from the front line or any of that shit that was written about me at the time. I just didn't care whether I lived or died. And that,' he splodged Dettol on to a cotton wool ball, 'is truly dumb.'

Juno dared another question, feeling like the pontoon player who's holding a king and a queen and still says 'twist'. 'But you don't feel like that any more?'

'Sometimes.' He dabbed the antiseptic on to her hand. 'I used to think I was a worthless piece of shit, y'know? I really fucking hated myself.'

'Why?'

The cotton wool traced the length of her thumb. 'It's complicated, Juno.'

'Are you saying I won't understand?' she bristled.

'I'm saying you wouldn't like me if you did. And believe me, Juno, I don't want you to hate me.'

She dared herself to say 'twist' again, even though that would probably just mean twisting the knife deeper into her self-inflicted wounds.

'But you don't want me to love you either.' She closed her fingers tightly around his. 'You made me swear not to love you. Remember?'

He stared at their hands for several seconds, seemingly fascinated as the hunk of cotton wool oozed its pungent chemicals on to Juno's jumper. She was desperate for him to look her in the eye, but his gaze remained fixed on her splintered little paws.

He pressed the nub of his thumb to the tips of her fingers.

'You bite your nails.'

'It's a new diet I'm on. They're low in fat and the shorter you keep them, the easier it is to stick your fingers down your throat.'

'You shouldn't be so screwed up about your size.' He pressed her hand to his mouth. 'I think you're beautiful.'

Juno's heart didn't just miss a beat – it missed several bars before giving a massive drumroll of excitement. His lips were soft and warm against her palm, his breath stroking her life line.

'You do?'

'Yeah.' He patted her hand kindly and let it go, reaching for the tweezers again. 'I thought you were beautiful the day I saw you dancing with the parrot. Your birthday, huh? Craziest thing I seen in years, man.'

'You did?' Juno felt as though the splinters had been drawn from her heart, not her hand. She wanted to whoop and giggle and nuzzle her nose into his neck, telling him she thought he was beautiful too. But something about the way he was acting – like an efficient emergency nurse, not a lover – made her stop and hold herself in check.

He picked up her left hand and examined the little shards of wood stapled deep in to the reddened flesh.

'When I flew to this country I thought they'd make me pay excess for all the emotional baggage I was carrying with me. I never counted on collecting a whole lot more on arrival. I should never have slept with you, Juno.'

She felt as though he had suddenly lunged forward and given her an unwanted tracheotomy with a Biro.

'No?' she wheezed.

'It's really thrown me, man.' He stared at her hand so intently, he could be reading the lines of her palm. 'I came to this country to find someone who's real important to me, and I stumbled across you instead. Funny thing is, I've almost thought more about you than her this week. Crazy, huh? She's my life. You're someone who came along by accident, then made me feel like I'd been in a car crash.'

The Biro was digging around in Juno's neck now, lancing her ego boil, stabbing around in her wind-pipe.

She looked at the wolf's tooth hanging around his neck, protecting the little lock of strawberry blonde hair. She remembered him telling her that a woman hadn't given him the chance to love her, remembered the phone call from the soft-voiced American begging him to come home.

Juno suddenly knew why Jay took so many risks, why he valued his mortality so little. It was the French Foreign Legion mentality: risking life and limb because of a broken heart.

'Who is she?'

He didn't need to ask her to qualify at question. He understood straight away. With a short sigh, he nodded but he didn't answer.

Juno knew she had no real right to behave like a jealous girlfriend. But she still felt as though someone was nailing tacks into her heart and pulling them out again via her throat.

'Is she in England?'

Carefully teasing a wafer-thin shard of wood from her forefinger, he twisted his mouth and shrugged non-comittally before dabbing her finger with antiseptic.

Juno knew he was trying to tell her to stop asking questions, stop digging, but she was already six feet down and could feel her spade clanking against metal. The trouble was that it felt like the lead lining to her own coffin.

She realised it was unrealistic to expect Jay not to have a history, but his tight-lipped secrecy had allowed her to build him up in her imagination as an enigmatic loner. She'd seen him as a Clint Eastwood character arriving in a one-street town; a character with no name, narrowed eyes and who spoke his few words with his teeth clenched around a cheroot. Now it turned out Jane Fonda had been waiting for him in the saloon bar all along, chest jacked up in a corset, hair piled up in kiss curls, leg slung up on a card table to reveal white stockings and frilly garters.

'The truth is,' he drew his tongue across his teeth, unable to look her in the eyes, 'I'm not exactly sure where she is. Or who.'

'What's that supposed to mean?' Juno snatched her hand away.

'Let me finish this and I'll show you.' He gently reclaimed it and completed the laborious task of removing the splinters while she contemplated all manner of scenarios. A woman with a mysterious past? A spy who lived under hundreds of aliases? A Mafia moll? A glamorous Nikita working for the Cause?

It was only when he was dabbing the last of the antiseptic on to her punctured palm that he spoke again. 'I don't tell people about her, Juno. I don't like them knowing. I'm having a lot of trouble dealing with it.'

'Dealing with what?'

He sucked his lip and looked at her. His eyes were huge, almost child-like.

'You really want to know?'

She nodded eagerly, torn between bitter jealousy and desperate curiosity.

'You promise you won't judge me?'

'Yes! I mean, no!' she bleated, beside herself with anticipation. 'I promise I won't judge you, Jay. And I've already promised I won't love you. What more do I have to promise? To hit myself over the head after you've told me and hope to get amnesia?'

He shrugged, still stalling for time.

Almost hyperventilating at the intolerable wait, Juno decided she had to give him a cue. 'It's the woman who called the flat last weekend, isn't it? The one who begged you to come back to New Yor—' She bit her lip. Damn! That didn't make sense. She wouldn't have called from New York if he'd come to England to find her, would she? Why hadn't she thought of that before?

Jay sighed wearily, staring at her splinter-free hands. 'That was Maria. She's my sister, Juno.'

'Oh.' She looked down as he traced her life line with his thumb before finally letting her hand drop.

'Okay, I'll show you.' He stood up. 'My old lady tried to throw this out when my father died, but Maria kept a hold of it and gave it to me a coupla months back. She'd been made to promise not to breathe a word about it while my old lady was alive – they all had.'

He fetched his portfolio from the other side of the room

and unzipped it. Hidden amongst the glossy plastic pages of shots taken all over the world, some award-winning, was an old scrap book, dog-eared with age. He handed it to Juno.

The pages had faded from dark blue to dusty grey, the newsprint was yellow, the ink brown, some of the cuttings had fallen out, but as Juno took it she knew she was touching something that to Jay was as valuable as the Dead Sea Scrolls. He walked to the far side of the kitchen and stood in the shadows, watching her while she leafed through the creased and torn pages.

It was a pure *Dynasty* moment. Juno had never known what it felt like to experience high drama until she looked in that book, which had a harmless-looking picture of a pink elephant on the cover and one word written in felt tip pen: 'Jay'. It was so innocuous that at first she assumed it was full of clippings about his career as a photojournalist.

Then she read the first newspaper piece, taken from the *Daily News* with the huge b.o.w. headline NEW ARRIVAL LEFT IN DEPARTURE, and she realised that Jay's secret was far more bizarre than she had ever imagined.

It was dated 15 September 1970 and reported that a new-born infant had been found hidden in a flight bag, tucked beneath a seat in an airport departure lounge. There was a grainy black and white photograph of a smiling air stewardess with Karen Carpenter flicks holding a tiny, big-eyed tot. The headlines on the pages that followed ranged from the practical to the sensational – 'Baby Abandoned Airside at JFK – mother believed to have left country', 'Flyaway Mom Sought', 'Left Luggage Baby Still Unclaimed', 'International Appeals fail to find Baby Jay's Mother', 'All She Left Him Was a Locket of Hair'.

Reading on, the clippings became shorter, reporting that the likelihood of tracing the baby's mother was slim and that he was to be fostered and then adopted if she didn't come forward within six months. After that, there were pages of curling old photographs of the baby playing with a huge stack of toys, or being bounced on the knee of a huge, blond beefcake of a man with seventies side-burns, flared jeans and a long-collared flowery shirt.

'Your father?' Juno picked a loose photograph from the crease of the book.

Jay nodded.

'So they weren't your real parents?' Juno knew it was a dim question but she was having trouble believing her eyes.

'Nowadays foundlings can't be adopted in the State of New York – only fostered, in case their birth mother ever tries to make contact,' he muttered, spewing out facts to avoid emotionally engaging. 'But back then, an abandoned kid was treated like an orphaned one. My father wanted a son more than anything, but my old lady couldn't have any more kids after Jadine was born. She agreed to take me on just so long as I was never told where I came from. She couldn't handle the fact that I was someone else's reject, that I wasn't from good Irish American stock, that I was probably a bastard. Not that she ever breathed a word to a soul. They even moved neighbourhoods when I arrived so that the secret would be safe.'

'They never told you that you were adopted?'

He shrugged. 'I started to suspect it around the time my old man lost his job. I overheard arguments – caught the odd word or phrase about me. I certainly couldn't have guessed I'd made news headlines, but it seemed a pretty safe bet that I was somehow different. The weird thing is, I didn't much care – I guess I was relieved if anything. It seemed to make sense that I wasn't related to these people. I'd turned pretty bad by that point, so it gave me an excuse just to get worse.'

'But didn't you want to know for certain? To look for your natural parents? Your birth mother?'

He rubbed his mouth and walked towards her. 'All I cared about in those days was getting out. I was fucking merciless, Juno. I stole anything – credit cards, car stereos, liquor, cigarettes – and sold it for cash. The only person that mattered then was me. I skipped school and enrolled in every photography class I could get to. I used my money to buy equipment and film – it's weird but I could never bring myself to steal those. I'd hung around the shops on Canal Street for years, I knew some of the guys who ran them. It seemed dishonourable somehow to thieve off them, yet at the same time I'd take a neighbour's stereo without thinking twice.'

He sat down on the sofa again and took the scrap book to look at, leafing through the pages.

'If my old man had given me this then, I honestly think I'd've thrown it back in his face and laughed. I just didn't give a shit about anything except photography. On my sixteenth birthday, he gave me the lock of hair I'd been found with – told some lie about it belonging to my Irish grandmother. He was real ill by then, in and out of hospital. I think he was frightened my old lady'd never give it to me if he died. It was in a gold locket, a real fancy one with engraving on it. He made me promise never to lose it. I sold it that same afternoon. Can you believe that? I got two hundred bucks for it.'

'But you kept the lock of hair.'

'The guy in the shop was going to throw it away.' Jay fingered the wolf's tooth. 'I figured it might bring me luck if I kept it, so I got this at a stall round the corner. I thought it made me look cool. The weird thing is, I've mislaid so many things over the years – watches, rings, cameras. I've been stranded abroad with nothing but the clothes I was standing in. When you travel a lot, you expect to lose stuff in transit; it's not as though you can fly Pan Am to a war zone, or leave your valuables in a hotel safe. But this fifty-cent piece of junk just stayed with me.'

He picked up the photograph of his father holding him up in his arms, his big, square face utterly doting.

'He'd still be alive if it wasn't for me. His liver packed up when he was fifty-two. I'll never forget how yellow his face turned. The hospital discharged him because he refused to stop drinking; he didn't qualify for medical insurance. He used to sit at home watching endless TV – he just loved those stars, man – and reading all the gossip in the trashy mags. He drank himself to death, y'know?'

'But you said he had a breakdown? After the accident at work. You weren't responsible for that.'

Jay's yellow eyes looked into hers, burning with shame. 'He wanted a son to be proud of, Juno. He didn't care if I was a scholarship kid who was good at sport, or a street fighter who stood up for himself, he just wanted me to be a man's man. Instead he got a secretive, sensitive little runt.'

'But you're doing something sensational now,' she argued, picking up his portfolio and flipping through it. 'These pictures have appeared all around the world.'

'You don't know how I got to take those shots, Juno.' He looked away. 'What I did to earn the right to take 'em.'

'So tell me.'

'D'you wanna hate me?'

'No.'

'Well, you will if I tell you.'

'Try me.'

He shook his head, looking away. 'I don't know if I can. I ain't never told no one about that. I cut that part of my life away like a cancer, Juno.'

'Please tell me, Jay,' she pleaded.

He scratched his chin on his shoulder, forehead creasing as his eyes blinked rapidly – yellow hazard lights warning of danger ahead.

When he started talking, he didn't look at her once. He spoke quickly, in staccato bursts that she could only punctuate with the odd 'yes?', 'so?' or 'go on'. The monologue was breathless, compulsive, and delivered in such a pacy monotone that it undercut the raw emotion contained within the story.

'I left New York the day of my old man's funeral and didn't look back. I took all my photographic equipment and hitched to the West Coast. It took weeks. I'd never been out of the state before that. But I had it all planned out. When I got to Los Angeles, I bought a scooter and worked as a freelance paparazzo. I had enough money to rent a room for a few weeks, and I learnt on the job. I was so aggressive in those days. The other paps laughed at me – a scraggy, speccy kid trying to work in a man's world – mostly arriving hours too late or getting in people's way. They thought I was a fucking tourist. I had no contacts, no agency, no commissions. They humoured me at first, passed on tips, and the stars smiled at me because I was just a kid. But I hated them all. I didn't care who I hurt to get those shots – who I bribed, or lied to, or elbowed outta the way. Pretty soon, I was one of the best. I took my first hundred-K picture when I was nineteen. By then, my shots were being wired to countries I'd never even heard of.'

'You were a paparazzo?' Juno gaped at him.

'For seven years.' He nodded. 'When I came back to New York to work, I didn't even look up my family. You gotta believe me, Juno, I was not likeable, I was not personable, I was not a human fucking being – I lived to work. I'd sit in the car outside a hotel for a week to get one shot. I didn't have lovers or friends – I had money. I didn't trust anyone I couldn't pay. Then one day I stopped wanting to do it, and I just wanted to die.'

'Why?'

'Your favourite word, huh?'

'I never wanted to do or die unless I had a bloody good reason.'

'You remember Dorca d'Ermine?'

Juno's eyebrows shot up. 'Of course I do. She was bigger than Garbo. I thought she died in the 'seventies.'

'No, she became a recluse when she grew old. Lived in a mansion in Riverdale – that's like the Beverly Hills of New York. It had walls round it like a state penitentiary and gates as deep as a limousine hood. Rumour had it she was ill, but no one could get near. There were guards and cameras everywhere. We knew she was heading off to a clinic twice a week, but there was no way of catching it on film – they kept changing the times she went, the limo had blackened windows, the clinic had underground parking and a private lift. Everyone wanted a shot of her. She hadn't been photographed for over a decade. I was determined to get it first so I laid fucking siege to that woman. When I got the shot – as I always did – she was yellow. Just like my old man. Fucking yellow. And she was yelling at me in French, waving a stick around with these feeble hands. Just a little old lady, so frail and helpless.'

He buried his face in his hands, talking through the bars of his fingers like the man in the iron mask. 'She died a week later. It should have been a noble death. She deserved it – she was a big star, a gracious lady. The obituaries ran with photographs of a beautiful actress. They listed all those Oscars she'd won, the charity work, the lack of scandal in her long life. But all that week, before she died, the whole fucking world had seen a photograph of an emaciated old woman with liver failure. An icon reduced to skin and bone by old age, and exposed to public voyeurism by me.

'I made a mint outta that picture. I remember taking twenty thousand bucks out of my account in cash and sitting in my apartment shredding it up, note by note. The networks were all rerunning old d'Ermine movies and I sat watching them, hour after hour, surrounded by torn-up hundred-dollar notes.' He looked up at her, eyes tortured. 'D'you hate me yet?'

Juno didn't know what to say. She had wanted Jay to open up since the moment she met him, but now that he was doing it, he appeared to be ripping himself apart in the process.

'I guess that means yes.' He looked away, rubbing his forehead. 'I sure as hell hated myself. I called my old lady that week – first time in maybe five, six years. I couldn't stop crying. Like a kid. Crazy, huh? She hung up on me. Y'know, the way you're told to do to a crank caller? "Just hang up."

'That's when I went to work abroad. Became a hero. Big fucking deal! When you've sold your soul, you can't buy it back. I saw things that make men go mad, that fuck up people's brains, and yet I just checked the light, framed the shot, pressed the button and walked away. Shoot and walk. Shoot and Jaywalk. I felt nothing – not even when I was fucking shot in return by a bullet. Nothing.

'Last fall, I was in New York for a coupla weeks. I had an exhibition going on – other stuff I've done. Good work. Stuff I'm proud of. Maria came along. She was just curious – didn't know I'd be there. I hadn't seen her in nearly ten years. She told me how sick our old lady was. I wanted to go visit, but she said it wasn't possible. You see, my old lady thought that I'd killed her husband. She blamed me for his death until the day she died. I wasn't even allowed to pray for forgiveness at her graveside on the day they buried her. I was banned from the funeral. She hated me that much.'

'But you weren't responsible for his death!' Juno protested.

'Maybe not, but my old lady wanted me to suffer just as I'd made her suffer – just as I was going to make her suffer after she died. She needed a reason to hate me. Later, Maria told me our mother felt real guilty that she had never behaved like a good Catholic and tried to love me as her own. Maria says that she talked about it a lot when she knew she was dying. She believed that God wouldn't forgive her for not loving me. She died believing that her soul was headed for Hell. Maria begged her to let me visit, but she still hated me too much to wanna see me, to try and make things right between us, to try and save herself – and me – from God's judgment. It's the only time she's ever wanted to take me along for the ride. She damned me to join her in Hell.

'I've never really believed in God. She was so fanatical, my old lady. Maria says she had a lotta secrets we'll never know about. One of them was my birthright. She didn't know Maria had the scrap book, although I guess she knew I'd find out the truth one day. In dying, she gave me a reason to live. I guess there's a kinda of divine justice in there somewhere, although I doubt my old lady'd see the joke. I was supposed to go back overseas after that exhibition, but I hung around New York instead. It probably saved my ass from being blown away in some godforsaken war zone. Maria kept in touch – the only one of my sisters who'll talk to me. Let me know when my old lady died.'

'And gave you this?' Juno picked up the scrap book.

He looked at it with a sad smile.

'Who wants to find a mother that left her kid at an airport?'

'But that's why you're in England, isn't it?'

He chewed his lip as he fought not to let out the tears. 'I always wanted a proper family, y'know? I wanted a mother who'd read me to sleep when I was a kid. The only stories my old lady told were from the Bible. Her family was God's family. When I was little, she used to read me *Revelations*. I remember being so fucking scared of the army of horsemen with scorpion tails coming to get me!' He laughed, a strange laconic hiss. 'She used to do this thing where she'd read aloud from the Bible and I'd close my eyes and count the pages turning. I'd learnt how many there were between chapters one and nine, and I always pretended to be asleep long before the bit about the key to the bottomless pit. But if she shut the Bible before she reached it, I'd breathe out in relief, thinking she'd finished. And then she'd carry on – reciting it by heart, knowing I was still awake.

'I came to England to find my birth mother.' He nodded at Juno. 'But I found something else. I found retribution.'

'Retribution?'

'For what I did, Juno. For what I was. I remember you making a joke about Americans not understanding the meaning of irony. Well, I think I've just discovered what it is.'

Chapter Thirty-One

Sitting at opposite ends of the sofa with Rug lying in between them, they stayed up talking until five in the morning. The bag of frozen peas on which Juno's foot was resting melted to a warm mush and was replaced by frozen sweetcorn; cups of tea and cans of Coke were downed, the twins snored in their baskets and Rug had yelping dreams. As the hours crept past, the bowls of boiled rice and pasta on the kitchen surfaces dried and light started seeping in through the windows.

Juno wasn't surprised that Jay had been so reticent about his visit to England. It was hardly the sort of thing you could drop casually into the conversation, especially not if you were having casual sex at the time.

It wasn't always easy to keep him talking. He seemed to think that every word would condemn him, every confession lead Juno to hate or pity him, neither of which he wanted. He spoke without emotion or self-pity, in a voice so calm and quiet that he could have been reading out share prices on a quiet day in the City.

But as she listened, Juno was aware that she was hearing a story that had never been told in full before, that Jay had never shared with a fellow human being. He'd lived a life so isolated from compassion that he saw opening up as something wounding – as though it literally involved cutting through flesh and pulling oneself apart. His aloofness was deliberate, an anaesthetic he required in order to talk at all.

'I was such a lousy drop-out as a kid.' He raised a sandy eyebrow as though talking to a complete stranger, about a complete stranger. 'I was so driven. It was like I was always being chased, and running away in the wrong direction. I can't explain it. I never seemed to fit in, never belonged anywhere . . . and now here I am, back on the hunt again, searching for someone who probably doesn't wanna be found.'

'But you do want to find your mother?'

'I dunno. I just want to know who she was, who she is now. It's weird, but I really wanted the clothes I'd been dressed in that day – a Babygro, a little rug, a bonnet. They'd been thrown out years before, of course, but it seemed so important that for a while I was fixated on them. When I first got the scrap book, I used to stare at those pictures of me for hours on end, wondering where she'd gotten the baby clothes from – if it had been before or after I was born – and whether she'd dressed me any differently that day 'cos she knew I was gonna be found in those clothes.' He rubbed the palm of his hand over his stubbly hair. 'I can't believe I sold that locket. You know, whatever was written on it wasn't even filed in the police report when I was found? I hired a private investigator in New York, and he couldn't believe that so little had been done to trace my birth mother.'

Juno's eyes were full of tears, but she blinked them away. He seemed to hate any reaction which showed emotion. Whenever she started to cry or tried to touch him, it made him clam up. 'How much do you know about her?'

'Practically zero.' He chewed his lip, stroking Rug's upturned belly. 'All the staff who worked in that section of the airport were interviewed, but no one saw anything unusual. It's a restricted area. Somehow I was brought through passport control unnoticed. The bag I was hidden in can't have been checked; they didn't have X-ray machines in those days. The authorities assumed that whoever left me there flew out of New York immediately afterwards.'

'And you know what flights left that day?'

He nodded. 'Abe, the fella I hired in New York, turned

up the original investigation report. It had flight details and passenger lists on it. I was found at three o'clock. A flight left for London Heathrow at a quarter to the hour. Apart from that there was a Paris flight at one-thirty – which was believed to be too early – and a departure to Zurich at four, but it was delayed when I was found.'

'So your mother definitely flew to London?'

He shrugged. 'There are no definites, Juno. It's too long ago, too little information was gathered. The passenger list I got is just a loada names – some were traced at the time, but there are huge gaps. Abe tracked down a coupla people who were on that flight and they didn't remember much, it was too far back, although they knew the story of the baby. But one guy remembered something else. He'd travelled first-class and was blown away because there was a movie star aboard that day. An English actress.'

'You're not saying your mother is a famous actress?' Juno gasped, enthralled by the notion despite herself. This was beyond *Dynasty*. This was *Falcon's Crest*, *Dallas* and *Soap* all fused into one. 'Who?'

'I'm not saying she's my mother, Juno. I seriously doubt that. But she was certainly on that flight. Look.' He reached into one of his kit bags and drew out a glossy hardback book with a Post-it note marking a place.

Juno took the book. It was entitled *Take a Bow Belle*. Twinkling from its cover was a soft-focus photograph of one of the nation's most famous household stars with a stellar system of diamanté glittering in her equally famous cleavage.

'This is Belle Winters's autobiography!' She gaped at the legendary, familiar face of the little blonde bombshell who had once been a B-movie Hollywood star and now graced Britain's small screen in *Londoners* four times a week as feisty Lily Fuller.

'Read the page that's marked.'

'"I remember that day like it was yesterday",' Juno read aloud from the book. '"I confess I wasn't sad to be leaving America, even though it had made me such a star. I was desperate to see all my family again, now that I'd gone through detox and beaten the bottle. For all its glitter, America had taken away my childhood, had turned me from a sweet-faced girl to a boozer with two failed marriages under her belt, and I couldn't forgive it for that. So many bad memories. And the worst was yet to come . . .

'"While we were landing in England, there was a huge commotion and we were made to stay on the plane for ages. It turned out a little baby boy had been abandoned just a few feet from where I'd been sitting in JFK airport. I can't tell you how shocked I was that a mother could do that to a child, and so sad for that poor little mite. I only wished I could remember something to help the police, but I had been too wrapped up in my own thoughts at the time to notice anything.

'"In the years that have followed, I've often thought of that poor child and wondered what became of him. I still do today. Did his mother ever come forward? Did he find America a kinder place than I did? In a way I feel a bond with him. I myself had been abandoned in that big, big land of hope and opportunity as little more than a child and had been swallowed up and spat out. I hope he fared better."'

The chapter ended with a photograph of the same headline that Juno had read earlier in Jay's scrap book. The next chapter was entitled, 'Thick and Thinning' and chronicled her legendary fourth marriage to a wig-wearing chat-show host.

'It couldn't be her, could it?' Juno closed the book and stared at Jay.

He rubbed his chin and shrugged. 'Unlikely, although I gather she was a pretty screwed-up broad in those days. I'm just hopin' she'll remember something, however insignificant. It's one of the few leads I have. When Abe showed me that book, I flipped out. I was so excited, man. We couldn't find out where she lived in the UK, so we tracked down her agent and sent a letter via his office. He called me a week later – arranged to meet me in London.'

Juno groaned as she guessed. 'Not Piers Fox?'

'That's the guy.' He narrowed his eyes. 'And, boy, was he a happy man.'

'So have you spoken to her?' Juno was agog. 'Does she remember anything?'

'Juno, I can't get fucking near her – Piers has made certain of that.'

'But why?'

'He only took on Belle as a client recently.' Jay tickled Rug's chest. 'She had some trouble with the press he needed to sort out, and like the pro he is, made a real media star of himself. Now you can't talk to Belle Winters without Piers Fox checking your breath first. The guy's a shark.'

'Oh, God.' Juno snapped her fingers as she remembered. 'There's a rumour floating around that she might be axed from *Londoners*, isn't there?'

Jay nodded. 'And I guess you've heard of a programme called *Your Life in Front of Your Eyes*?'

'I love it!' Juno confessed without thinking.

'Belle Winters is next Wednesday's star victim. Her life is gonna be chronicled live on air. It's been planned like a military operation. They're catching her by surprise on the set of *Londoners*.'

'No way!' She was momentarily blown away by mindless excitement. 'I'll set the video.'

'Juno, they want to bring me on at the end. You know, the kid she's always wondered about?'

'Wow – I mean, whoah. Hmm. God.' She was brought up short by the thought.

'That's why Piers has been stalling me – and chasing me too.' Jay rubbed his eyes tiredly. 'There's some deal he's trying to swing with Belle Winters's contract, and he figures the publicity will blow the *Londoners* producers away, especially if the programme succeeds in reuniting me with my birth mother.'

'But surely it's the best opportunity to get in touch with her?' Juno thought about it. 'You can do a live appeal on air, asking for her to come forward.'

'Shit – you and Piers Fox should get together.' Jay looked away in despair. 'The only person who's gonna get good publicity around here is Belle Winters.'

'So you both get it, so what? She wins her new contract, you get the biggest audience for a national appeal you could ever hope for.'

'Juno, this isn't *Oprah*.' He closed his eyes. 'I've talked to the agencies, read the books, asked the authorities. The likelihood of an adult foundling in this country locating the mother who abandoned them via media publicity is practically zero, do you realise that? Who wants to admit they've dumped their kid in an airport – especially in front of millions of viewers? Public appeals don't work. Television doesn't work. What's more,' he picked up Belle's autobiography, 'I'm hardly gonna be this lady's favourite person.'

He flicked through it and handed it to Juno, open at an early chapter.

'You see,' he sighed. 'When she finds out what I used to do, there's no way she'll think I "fared better" than she did in America. She'll wanna punch me out. And so will the press if they get hold of the story.'

The chapter was entitled 'Pressing Flesh, Drawing Blood' and told of Belle Winters's destructive relationship with the paparazzi – whom she blamed for driving her from overeating to alcoholism, to drugs and finally suicide attempts.

Juno looked at him worriedly. 'But surely your mother would want to get in touch with you, whatever the media say?'

Jay rubbed his chin on his shoulder. 'Would you wanna risk it for the sake of a soap-star's new contract?'

Without thinking, Juno reached out and took his hand. 'Piers Fox can't force you to appear in the show though, can he?'

He shook his head, looking down at their linked fingers. 'But if I don't, I'm not gonna get near Belle Winters. And you're right. For all my research, I figure it's about the only shot I've got at contacting my real mother. I'm just not sure I can face it. Not like this.'

'What are the alternatives?'

He pulled his fingers from hers one by one. 'I've registered with the right agencies; I've placed small ads in all the nationals; Abe's helped me hire someone in London to check stuff out while he's still working on it in the States, but the outlook's pretty bleak. Our biggest hope was the ads – but it's been nothing but cranks and more cranks so far. Abe doesn't even tell me about them until he's checked them out. I don't really have any alternative but to do the TV show, Juno.

'That's why I'm still playing Piers's twisted publicity game. And the fact that you're supposed to be auditioning for the guy on Wednesday night is kinda freaking me out. I don't trust him. I get this bad feeling that he's stitching me up.'

He reached out to stroke Rug's pink stomach, eyes hiding from Juno's like fugitives from helicopter spot-lights.

'There's nothing sinister behind it, I'm sure,' she assured him, trying to sound prosaic and practical as he clearly didn't want her hugs or tears. '*Your Life in Front of Your Eyes* goes out live at seven, doesn't it?' She was worryingly familiar with the television schedules at the moment.

He nodded, fingers moving shakily across Rug's belly.

'There you go.' She tickled Rug's foot, trying to connect with Jay in some sort of activity – however petty. 'The Ha Ha Club thing doesn't start until nine. There's loads of time in between the two.'

Jay nodded sadly. 'I guess you're right. It's just a lousy half-hour work commitment to a fella like Fox, isn't it? Part of a busy day's schedule. It's my whole fucking future he's got jotted into the seven o'clock window of his diary for next Wednesday!'

Appalled at her own insensitivity, Juno reached out and touched his shoulder urgently. 'I'm sorry. I didn't mean that it's not important.'

He batted the hand away like a wasp. 'Forget it, Juno. You're right. I can see that.'

She bit her lip. She'd been trying to sound calm and pragmatic, to match his cool self-control, but all she wanted to do was stretch across the sofa and gather him into a warm tight hug.

'Listen, if you want some support, I could come along and hold your hand, if you want me to?' Realising how ghastly that sounded, especially as he'd just pulled away from her, Juno went pink and concentrated on scratching Rug's chest.

Rug was in ecstasy now that both of them were rubbing and tickling him.

'You're the first person I've told about all of this.' Jay's head dipped in embarrassment. 'I'm sorry to dump it all on you. I tried to keep it a secret, but I figure it's kinda pointless now.'

'I'm glad you've told me.' She reached out to touch his cheek, but he flinched so she settled for stroking Rug again, rattling on to cover her gaffe. 'I was imagining all sorts of terrible things – I even thought you were some sort of terrorist.'

'A terrorist?' He looked up in horror. 'Whatever gave you that idea?' Suddenly – to Juno's amazement – he smiled. 'Christ, Juno, that's like seriously crazy.'

She hung her head in shame and shrugged. It did seem pretty silly now she came to think of it, but he had behaved very furtively.

'It wasn't really you. It was those men you've been hanging around with.' She chewed her lip. 'Will Pigeon and Timon. And the photographer – Dormouse is he called?'

He said nothing, smile faltering.

Juno looked at his fierce bonfire eyes and knew for certain he was still hiding something from her. 'Are they helping you find your mother?'

He pressed a finger into the cleft of his chin and raised his eyes to the dusty rafters.

Finally he responded. 'I had this dumb idea when I arrived – a kind of sleeping with the enemy thing, y'know? I figured if I hung around with the London paparazzi for a while, I could work out my best line of defence.'

'They're paparazzi?' Juno gulped.

He winced at the word. 'Only Dormouse – and he's such a part-timer he could loan his camera to a tourist and not miss it for a week. Will's a ticket tout – or so he tells people. Truth is, he'd tout his soul for a coupla bucks, but he'd rip his heart out for a buddy too. They're both good guys, Juno. I know it's hard to believe, but they're genuine.'

Juno was gaping at him in disbelief. 'And Timon?'

He twisted his mouth guiltily. 'He used to run a picture agency in L.A. – that's how I know him. He might come across as dumb and beautiful, but the guy's real smart. A year back, he set himself up in business over here. Will and Dormouse are his buddies. We got talking and decided we could do some work together.'

'As paparazzi in London?' Juno was absolutely appalled.

'They're really looking out for me, man. I love those guys.' He sucked in his lower lip gratefully. 'Dormouse is acting like he's seriously pissed off that I muscled in on his "manor" with ten grands' worth of equipment and contacts at all the best agencies in the world. Timon is telling everyone I've gone back to what I'm good at. Will is passing on all the gossip. Who's where, who's who . . .'

'But why are you doing it?' she wailed, unable to believe his stupidity. 'Surely befriending them will just make things worse for you if you go on *Your Life In Front Of Your Eyes* and the press sniff a story? They'll crucify you if they find out you're back on the hunt, driving people like Belle Winters to live behind thousands of feet of security fencing?'

'The story would blow my ass to hell and back.' He nodded, face expressionless.

'So why are you doing it?' Juno wailed again.

'I've got to,' he said with total conviction. 'You see, I've figured out this way of straightening out my head. Of making up for some of the shit I've done in my life.'

'By working as a paparazzo again?' Juno didn't understand. He sounded as though what he was doing was actually a good thing – hiding behind a celebrity's dustbins in the hope of some trashy exclusive. He must be mad.

'I got this idea.' He ran his hands through Rug's curly coat and looked up at her, eyes suddenly alive. 'It came to me last week – when Piers Fox turned up at that seedy comedy dive. The night you pulled that number on me.'

Juno looked away in shame, heart plummeting as she remembered standing up in front of Piers Fox and the paltry crowd in the Cod and Cucumber to announce – quite untruthfully – that Jay had a small penis. Men were fixated about things like that, weren't they? She'd probably driven him to make some sort of suicidal career move which was now going to jeopardise his chance of ever making contact with his birth mother. It was all her fault.

'What idea?' she said with trepidation.

'I felt so sick in my belly – like I was trapped once more, trying to run away but chasing my tail instead. That night in the club, you made me see what a no-good piece of shit I still was. You seemed to see straight through me. I was so fucking angry! And scared. I wanted to tell you about my mother that night, but you wouldn't even talk to me. So the next day I turned the camera around and decided to shoot myself, Juno.'

'You what?' she yelped. Oh, God – she'd almost driven him to suicide! She'd never tell another small penis joke as long as she lived.

'I started taking shots of the paparazzi, not the celebrities,' he said. 'I couldn't believe how easy it was, how good it felt. Sure, I've been hunting with the pack all week, but I'm not pointing my camera in the same direction any more. I'm taking pictures of the fellas around me. I guess you could say I'm in camera.

'I wanna stage an exhibition when this is all over.' He leant back into the sofa, eyes suddenly dancing with enthusiasm. 'A mixture of the shots I took back then, when I was angry and merciless, and new material I'm shooting now – covert shots of the guys who are still doing it. In London first, then I'll go to Italy, France, the States. I don't wanna judge – I just wanna show. But I don't want the sanitised version: shots of press packs penned behind railings at a premiere, standing on step-ladders and yelling at Demi or Uma or Brad. Anyone can do that.

'I know I can shoot the stuff that goes on which nobody

knows about. I've been there, I know where to look. But I have to keep this thing a secret from the people I'm profiling. They've got to think I'm still one of them. It's the only way I'll get the shots I want. I can't rush it. I'm gonna call the exhibition Shooting Up.'

'It's a brilliant idea!' Juno was blown away.

He smiled thoughtfully, scratching his chin on his shoulder and watching her through his lashes. 'Timon, Will and Dormouse are all helping me. Their asses are on the line too. That's another reason for watching out for Piers Fox. I don't trust him – he could stitch me up big time to get publicity for Belle. And Timon's his rival. There's a lot at stake.'

'Christ.' She shifted her sore ankle.

'But you know the weird thing?' He twisted around to plump up her frozen sweetcorn footstool. 'I kinda like them – they're all maverick drop-outs like me. Even Dormouse – who comes over as a sewer rat, yeah? – is a pretty radical fella. You know his girlfriend's a drag queen called Wanda Ringstar?'

Juno snorted with laughter.

The cello-shank mouth smiled at her, and the yellow eyes crinkled. 'I shouldn'ta made friends with them, but I'm glad I have. Here I am in the unfriendliest country on the planet with three guys I like knocking around with – and you.'

'Me?' she bleated.

'Yeah, you, Juno. Now you're something else.'

'Not a maverick drop-out then?'

He shook his head, still smiling. His hand slid in smooth figures of eight across Rug's pink belly and Juno fought a sudden urge to jettison the little dog from the sofa and offer her own tummy as an alternative.

'What am I then?'

'You gotta be something special for me to tell you all this.'

She glowed at the idea of being special. But before she could reach out to touch his hand, he'd jumped up and was stalking over to the fridge to fetch another Diet Coke.

'I'm all talked out, Juno,' he sighed, sounding tense and

nervy again. 'I've got so much shit going on in my head right now, I just wanna forget about it for a few hours, y'know? Think of something else. Why aren't you smoking, by the way?' He suddenly turned to look at her, the open fridge door swinging in his hand.

'What?' Juno was so perplexed by his instant change of tack and mood that for a moment she couldn't take in what he'd asked. 'Oh, I've run out of cigarettes.'

She didn't want to admit that she'd been unable to afford any after her marathon supermarket credit card sweep the previous afternoon. It seemed hugely shallow to mention her broke status after his epic confession – like moaning to the Elephant Man about an unsightly wart.

'I see.' He let the door swing shut and leant back against it, can hissing in his fingers as he pulled back the tab.

Juno thought it a pretty odd question to ask, but she didn't want to get into an anti-smoking debate now that they were getting along so well, had shared such an extraordinary conversation together. Instead, she looked around at the congealing, dog-pillaged food on the surfaces and wondered whether her credit card would stretch to a takeaway for thirteen. Tiredness tugged at her. It was light outside now, although a heavy belt of cloud was pressing down towards the crowded treetops in the garden like an eiderdown sinking on to a lumpy bed.

'Stay for lunch.' She watched Jay wandering back to the sofa. 'If you really mean it about wanting to think about something else for a few hours. I'd like you to stay here, meet my friends. Of course, I quite understand if you don't want – '

'Thanks,' he interrupted hastily, looking as though she'd offered him a winning lottery ticket. He smiled broadly – that rare, devastating smile of his. 'I really appreciate that.'

Chapter Thirty-Two

All week Juno had formulated a work itinerary in her head for Saturday morning. She wasn't the most organised person in the world – her meals invariably started several hours late – but even she realised that cooking lunch for more than a dozen friends required a certain amount of forethought.

Waking up to squint blearily at an alarm clock which said it was half-past twelve was not part of the plan. Outside, thunder was rumbling along the spine of the Ridgeway like bowling balls along a polished alley.

She pulled a pillow over her head and groaned, then remembered that Jay was in the house.

He was probably still downstairs on the sofa with Rug, sleep stealing the tension from his face. The odd thing was that she seemed to recall nodding off at the opposite end of that sofa. She must have sleep-walked to bed later.

She hugged the pillow to her face and shivered. Such an amazing night. She couldn't ever remember learning so much about someone in such a short space of time before, but somehow it seemed right that it had happened that way. It fitted in with the pattern of her relationship with Jay – just as they had tried to pack a month's worth of sex into one weekend, so they had swapped life stories over a sleepless night.

'Juuuno!' he called up the stairs. 'You awake?'

'Not very,' she mumbled, face still pressed to the pillow.

She could hear the tower stairs creaking as Jay climbed them.

'Someone called Finlay just telephoned,' his voice floated up. 'Says he's coming to lunch after all. Wanted instructions on howta get here.'

'What did you tell him?' she asked, peering beneath the duvet to see how respectably she was dressed and noticing in alarm that she was wearing her FRANKIE SAYS RELAX t-shirt. She was certain she'd left it in her parents' bathroom at the opposite end of the house. Had she sleep-walked there too? Now that was impressive somnambulism.

'I told him the way.' Jay's voice was closer to the door.

'But he hasn't got a car.' She sat up, hastily running her hands through her hair and trying to pat the sleep creases from her cheeks.

'I guess he's gonna get a cab.' A tray laden with fruit and toast edged its way in through the door, closely followed by Jay.

Juno stared at him in disbelief for a moment. He was wearing yesterday's clothes, she noticed, baggy and crumpled from being slept in. His eyes were constricted with tiredness, golden stubble grazed his chin and his tufty hair was sculpted into strange crop circles from sleeping with his head pressed to a sofa arm. Yet the smile that curled his mouth was the sweetest wake-up call she had ever received. Jay smiled so rarely that when he did, the paint practically melted from the walls around him.

'I think I've gotten lunch under control.' He carefully placed the tray on the floor and headed towards the window to pull back the curtains. 'I'm not as good as you in the kitchen but I tried my best. And I put the croaky set out. See?'

'Cro*quet*.' Juno twisted around to look out at the rain-spattered garden. A spiral of white hoops led from one colour-fully striped wooden pole to another to form a snail's back. It was the weirdest arrangement of croquet hoops she'd ever seen, and she doubted they'd be playing as it was still raining heavily, but her chest puffed full of sentimental marshmal-low as she realised what he'd been doing on her behalf all morning.

She was suddenly reminded of the laughing, breakfast-making Jay who had taken her completely by surprise the morning after they first slept together.

'You've been cooking?' She looked at him in wonderment.

He nodded. 'I used whatever I could find in the refrigerator, but it's kinda random. The turtle's on top of the freezer chest, and I figure the dogs ate a lot of the ingredients yesterday. Did you say thirteen people are coming?'

'Ish.' Juno pulled a face at the prospect. 'A few more maybe. I've rather lost count.'

'There'll be plenty to go round.' He picked up the tray and put it on her knees. 'I called Triona earlier and asked her to look in on the apartment on her way here and check on the parrot. She promised to bring a loada food with her just in case. How's your ankle feeling?'

Juno was so blown away by his sweetness that for a moment she couldn't even remember which ankle she'd twisted. A quick flex of both brought her down to earth with a wince.

'A bit stiff,' she muttered through gritted teeth. 'Probably because I've just woken up. It'll be better in a minute.'

'You should take it easy today.' He perched on the edge of the bed like a doctor addressing a patient. 'Don't put too much strain on it. Leave lunch to me – you can just tell me what to do.'

'But that's unfair on you.' She played with a kiwi fruit. 'I can't ask you to slave over a hot stove for a bunch of people you've never met.'

'I want to.' He smoothed the duvet cover by his knee. 'It'll take my mind offa things. I really appreciate being away from London, y'know?'

'What about Piers Fox?' Juno dropped the kiwi fruit back in the bowl and selected a peach. 'I thought you wanted to get hold of him?'

'He can wait until Monday.' He picked up a glass from the tray. 'Try the juice – I blended it 'specially.'

What was going on here? Juno thought worriedly as he held

the glass to her lips and waited for her to drink from it. All this Doctor Kildare stuff was lovely, but slightly disturbing. It wasn't the behaviour of a shy lover, it wasn't even big brotherly – it was unsettlingly motherly. She adored being pampered, but she wasn't entirely sure she wanted Jay to see her as a weak, sickly invalid.

'Delicious!' She smacked her lips after she'd taken a sip.

Jay grinned, and started peeling an orange, fingers slipping deftly beneath the skin.

'Your friends . . .' He glanced up from his task, eyes wary. 'D'you think they'll ask a loada questions?'

Juno slugged back some more juice. 'Well, they're not exactly Lady Bracknells, but they're bound to be curious about you.'

He dropped a spiral of orange skin on to the tray and started prising the segments apart. 'As long as you're around, I guess I'll be okay, huh?'

It was such a lovely thing to say that Juno was lost for words. Then, just as she was about to ask him what exactly he meant, he slipped an orange segment between her lips and stood up.

'There. Now I'll help you get dressed,' he offered, starting to pick up clothes from the floor. 'Or d'you want a shower first?'

The thought of Jay helping her hunt around for a clean pair of knickers and then shoe-horning her into her dress with this new found motherly care was too horrifying to contemplate. There was something of the Nurse in *Romeo and Juliet* about his behaviour this afternoon, whereas Juno longed for the tragic young hero she'd talked to until the early hours of the morning. She wanted him to leap on the bed and kiss her, not mop her up and make her health drinks. Moreover, she had no intention of letting him see her in the nug with hairy legs. So what if he'd seen it all before? He'd wanted to caress and undress her body then, not lop a bra and a Tubigrip on it.

'No! I mean, yes, obviously I need to freshen up.' The breakfast almost tipped off the tray as she slid beneath the covers again. 'I think I'll just take a couple of minutes out to enjoy some more of this lovely spread, if that's okay?'

She looked at the fruit which was now bouncing all over her duvet.

'Sure.' He headed for the door. 'Gimme a shout if you need me.'

Juno suddenly realised how ungrateful she must seem. His Mary Poppins act might be freaking her out, but it was far more pleasant than the Mrs Danvers performance he'd frozen her out with in London.

'Jay,' she called just as he was stepping over her discarded dressing gown in the doorway.

'Yeah?' He turned around.

She wanted to ask how he felt about her, but it seemed so childish and banal after his confessions of the night before.

He was waiting patiently by the door for her to say something.

Juno chewed her lip. She had to ask. She'd explode if she didn't. She wanted to be mature and honest and upfront for once. She wanted to say what she was thinking for the first time in her love life.

She took a deep breath. 'You have the most beautiful eyebrows of any man I've ever met.'

He watched her from the doorway for a moment, eyes blinking, said eyebrows curling together exquisitely. For a brief moment he opened his mouth as though about to ask her a question, but instead he smiled, ducked away and started bounding downstairs.

Juno closed her eyes and groaned. Whatever possessed me? she thought wretchedly. She pulled the pillow over her head and heard her words repeated like a mantra in her ears. A peach was lodged between her knees. She longed to squeeze it to a pulp, but hunger took over and she reached down to extract it, digging her nails into its soft skin.

'Well, I guess I've got one over on J. Alfred Prufrock,' she muttered as she sank her teeth into its flesh, juice spilling on to her chin. In fact, reflecting upon it, she decided her little outburst was rather sexy in an oblique sort of way. She was almost proud of herself. Admittedly, it wasn't quite what she'd been aiming for – less direct, more poetic – but it was progress.

She crawled out of bed and hopped to the bathroom which she had once shared with Sean, a tiny square cell in the tower with a phone-booth shower. Her ankle was still swollen, but far less painful than it had been the night before. By clinging on to the shower door, she managed to scrape an old razor over her legs. She'd left her new ones in her parents' bathroom along with her aromatherapy oil and various other descaling and revitalising ablutions purchased the day before. It seemed like weeks ago that she'd applied Jolen to her upper lip and dreamily debated whether or not to invite Jay to lunch, not just a few hours earlier.

Last night had completely changed her attitude to him. Her crush seemed so petty, so irrelevant. He was no longer a flight of fancy she could invent story-lines for and conversations with in her head whilst avoiding in real life. She could no longer fantasise that he was a gunman on the run who had tripped over her and fallen in love. It didn't make the belly-squeezing urges go away, but Juno had them under control. She still remembered the sex with a shudder that threatened to loosen her fillings, but knowing him better had put it into perspective. A perspective which made her realise how insignificant their brief, physical encounter was compared with the rest of his traumatic life.

The truth about him was far beyond her imagination. He had a history which appalled her, a past which terrified her and a future which she couldn't even begin to imagine. But he was a part of her life now, and a part she wanted to cultivate, to protect, to support. If nothing else, she wanted to be his friend. He was real now. He was downstairs in her parents' house, he was cooking lunch, he was infinitely more complex than she'd ever imagined, and, most importantly, she really liked him. The fact that he'd confided in her was far more precious and intimate a memory than the sultry, sweaty hours they'd shared in bed a fortnight earlier.

Juno felt good. Despite the rain, the hopeless lack of

organisation over lunch, the aching ankle and the fact she had no clean knickers so had to go without, she felt good. And, for once, she knew she looked it too. Her skin glowed, her hair glistened, her eyes sparkled, and for some bizarre reason her breasts tingled all over.

It was only when she'd slapped some tinted moisturiser on to her face, wriggled into her Chinese dress (which was a bit on the tight side) and admired her platinum blonde hair in the mirror, that she remembered she'd left something else on the floor of her parents' bathroom. The unused pregnancy test. There was no way Jay could have missed it if he'd gone in there.

When she hobbled carefully down the tower's narrow wooden staircase, Juno was greeted with the unexpected sight of Jay in a pinny, dancing around the kitchen to Underworld's 'Born Slippy' on the radio, a pan in one hand and a tea towel in the other as he sang 'Lager, lager, lager, lager, SHOUTIN'!'

She was so astonished she paused three steps from the bottom and peered around a wooden upright at him.

This change of mood was phenomenal. Juno wondered worriedly whether it was because he'd got the big secret off his chest last night, or whether he thought she might be carrying his baby. It couldn't be the latter, she told herself logically. No man she'd ever known had reacted with elation to the sight of a pregnancy test.

Juno hated herself for a fleeting image of them both as parents, each holding a tiny mittened paw as they jumped a treacle-haired toddler over frozen puddles in the park.

She tried to remember whether he had gone up to her parents' bathroom the night before. After he'd talked himself hoarse and she'd conked out, he might have wandered up there to fetch her RELAX nightshirt and clocked it. No, she preferred her sleep-walking-to-bed theory, for dignity's sake. Besides which she was far too heavy for him to carry. Then her scalp tightened as she remembered that he'd rushed upstairs to collect her special conditioning shampoo when he'd first arrived. Not long after that, he'd disappeared on to the hill with the dogs, saying he had a lot to think about. Had he spotted the test then? Juno tried to convince herself he hadn't. He'd been in a hurry, after all, and it had been littered in amongst a lot of stuff. He could easily have missed it.

'Lager, lager, lager, SHOUTIN'!'

She cowered on the staircase, unnoticed by either Jay or the dogs, who were sitting in a rapt line by the fridge watching the dancing chef at work. Even Uboat was flapping around her tank, entering into the sprit of things.

There was only one thing for it, Juno realised. She'd have to do the test straight away then get rid of the evidence. Waiting until Jay switched on the liquidiser, she managed to shuffle along the solid wall of the kitchen without attracting attention, apart from Uboat eyeing her knowingly.

The liquidiser was switched off to a gleeful wail of 'White thing!'

Ducking violently as pain seared through her ankle, Juno held her breath until Jay picked up the jug of teriyaki marinade and danced over to the chicken thighs to douse them in it. Out of his line of vision, she shambled on, wincing with every other step. But just as she was creeping silently towards the dining hall – not easy with a limp – there was a crunch of tyres on gravel outside and the dogs let off a volley of barks.

'Juuno!' Jay called towards the tower, still thinking she was upstairs. 'You ready yet? Someone's just arrived.'

She hopped back through the dining hall in time to hear a series of toots from a car horn. Only Jez tooted like that, she realised in relief. Of all her guests, he and his travelling companions, Lulu and Odette, were the least demanding. Plug them into a drink and a chair and they'd not notice if she was performing a pregnancy test directly in front of them. Nor would they be thrown by Jay's presence; they were blissfully self-centred. Juno guessed they'd all just try to flirt with him. She hoped he could cope.

'Jeesh – how d'you get there?' Jay looked shocked to see her appearing from the wrong side of the kitchen.

'Secret passageway,' she lied weakly, hopping past the

dogs who had noticed her at last and were crowding round attentively, torn between greeting her and warning off the new arrivals. 'Come and say hi.'

'I gotta wait on the timer.' Jay nodded towards the oven as she hobbled past. Almost as an afterthought, he added under his breath, 'You look real sexy.'

Juno fell over Effie in surprise. Picking herself up, she swung around to look at him but he was chopping chives, fresh and wet from the garden. The knife hammered with tight precision across the glossy stems, and Jay was totally focused upon the board.

Juno hovered for a moment before responding to the calls from outside and hobbling into the porch, letting the dogs out of the front door ahead of her.

Jez was already open-armed at the lych-gate deflecting the twins' wet kisses when Juno hopped awkwardly out of the porch.

'Baby – you look sensational!' he whooped, jumping over the little slatted gate and bounding forwards, followed by Odette and Lulu who came through the gate the conventional way, chatting like mad as they fought through the doggy welcoming party.

Jez gathered Juno into an aftershave and Diesel t-shirt hug, whispering, 'Save me – I've had nothing but potential comedy line ups and cover charges the entire way here.'

True enough, Odette and Lulu barely paused for breath between talking about the comedy restaurant to kiss Juno hello.

'Isn't it just a fantastic idea, pet?' Lulu pulled her tiny hands from the pockets of her great coat for a second to hand over two bottles of Newcastle Brown.

'Lulu's all for it, babe – she's even recommended a boss emcee I'm going to sound out.' Odette blew a kiss at Juno as she dashed inside. ''Scuse me a sec, I'm splitting for the lav.' She rushed into the house without spotting Jay in his oven mitts hovering awkwardly in the kitchen.

Juno held her breath for a second as she wondered whether

Odette – who knew the house well – would turn right to the tower or head through the dining hall for the far plusher surroundings of Juno's parents' bathroom which might or might not still have a tell-tale box on its loo mat. But thankfully she started clattering up the tower stairs.

'Shame about the weather.' Jez ducked inside out of the rain and saw Jay instantly. 'Well, hello there. Juno's certainly kept you a secret. Let me guess – Scorpio, am I right?'

Juno expected Jay to blank him coolly, but to her amazement he laughed. 'I'm Jay – good to meet you.'

Was it Juno's imagination or had he somehow located the iron to lend his slept-in clothes a freshly laundered look? And he was shaven now, his sideburns freshly sculpted, tufty hair sexily even, a faint citrus tang of her father's aftershave wafting around the kitchen. Bathroom alert!

'Excuse the smell of lemongrass,' Jay apologised, wiping his hands on a dishcloth. 'I was just making a Thai dressing.'

Of course he was too well mannered to steal some of her father's aftershave, Juno realised with relief. The pregnancy test stood a slim chance of still being undetected.

Jez and Lulu – who had both been recipients of the jokey anti-Jay tirade from Juno a week earlier – stared at him open-mouthed in admiration.

Oh, the embarrassment of having one's record collection scrutinised by one's closest friends! Not the ultra-cool, cutting edge collection kept in London and constantly passed over in preference for Virgin FM, but the naff relics you've forgotten you possess but which have been lovingly preserved by your parents.

Juno cringed as Jez and Lulu shrieked at her teenage taste. A taste she had long since found too sweet – along with Malibu and pineapple, pixie boots and morello cherry lip gloss. She silently passed an apology across the Atlantic to Sean, whose LPs she'd been sniggering over just a few days earlier. Hers were far more cheesy than anything her brother had ever air-guitared to. Thank goodness Jay was still in the kitchen, mixing up more garlic butter.

'Cliff Richard – Bonnie Tyler – Haircut 100.' Jez shrieked with laughter. 'My life, there's even a Buck's Fizz album in here!'

'Oh, I used to love them when I woz a kid.' Odette appeared through the arch. 'Put it on, Jez, we can all have a bop. Hey, Juno, who's the geezer with his head in the oven?'

'Divine, isn't he?' Jez sighed, pulling the Buck's Fizz album from its sleeve. 'But very shy.'

'It's Jay.' Juno shot him a withering look.

Odette's face adopted a freshly punched look and she mouthed, 'Jay the American?'

Juno nodded, feeling decidedly proprietorial. 'Come and meet him while I fix you a drink. He would come through and chat, but he's cooking.' She limped from the room just as 'Making Your Mind Up' boomed out of the speakers at top volume.

Following behind, Odette gave her a curious look, but was too blown away by the aroma hitting her nose to comment.

'Summink smells good,' she whistled as they walked into the kitchen to see Jay leaning into the Aga, adding under her breath, 'and looks it.'

Jay's bottom did look particularly choice when he was bending over, Juno noticed proudly. Then he turned around, his mitted hands holding on to a large, glossy home-baked pie which was so perfect it could have been a plastic stage prop. It even had a frilly crust and little leaves on it. Juno prided herself on her cooking, but she never bothered adding flouncy touches like that. If he was trying to impress her friends then he was going about it in exactly the right way. Odette appeared to be dumbstruck with admiration. So was Juno, but she managed to splutter an introduction.

'Jay, this is Odette – we were at college together.'

'Hi there, Odette.' He smiled that super-cool, guarded smile of his and Juno could almost feel her friend melt into a pool beside her.

'White wine okay? Or would you prefer Pimms?' She elbowed open the fridge.

'Yeah – thanks, babes,' Odette croaked weakly as she watched Jay expertly turn the pie out onto a cooling rack. 'Will you marry me, mate?'

He laughed shyly, pulling the mitts from his hands. 'I only do meat pie and salad. I think you'd get kinda bored.'

'I'll buy you a recipe book as a wedding present.' Juno flipped the fridge door shut, suddenly feeling childishly jealous.

Jay watched her for a moment, his eyes confused.

'It was a joke.' She unhooked a corkscrew from the rack. 'I'd buy you both a wok, of course.'

'Juno gets everyone a wok for their wedding,' Odette told him, her spiky black eyelashes suddenly becoming strangely fluttery, like two spiders talking in semaphore. 'It's a bit of an in joke. She says it's just wok they deserve.' She beamed at him seductively.

'Wok could be easier?' Juno groaned, opening a fresh bottle of white wine. The wok joke was as old and thin as Lester Piggott now, but it still delighted Odette.

'There's nothing better when you wok down the aisle.' She was slapping her thigh in rapture.

Jay nodded seriously – not getting it at all.

Studying his face, Juno suddenly realised how vulnerable he was, and why he was throwing himself into cooking like Pat Archer at a Harvest Supper. He was doing it to help her out, but also to give himself a prop to get through a day with her friends. Last night had been a huge ordeal for him – telling her so much about himself, stripping his soul bare. Now he was facing a bunch of loud Londoners intent on getting tight and having fun. It must be pretty tough to adjust to the shift in atmosphere.

Odette had lapsed into silence to admire him again.

Juno fetched a clean glass from the overhead cupboard. 'Did I leave my wine in here?' she asked him, looking around.

'Don't think so.'

She shrugged. 'It must be in the other room.'

But it wasn't, and her ankle ached too much to bother fetching another straight away, so she sat on the sofa for a few minutes enjoying the babble and catching up on the gossip.

'Don't fink Lyd's getting on too well wiv her new bloke,' Odette said.

'No?' Juno's heart sank. 'They're both coming down here today.'

'I wouldn't be surprised if she comes on her own.' Jez lit a cigarette and blew a few rings, his battered boxer's face speculative. 'Last I heard, she and Little Brute had conducted a stand-up fight on the communal landing of her flat which involved several neighbours, Nat the twat and, latterly, the police.'

'Christ.' Juno pulled at an unravelling cushion, secretly unsettled by the prospect of Lydia *toute seule*, baring her soul. 'I thought he was the shy, quiet type?'

'Lydia started the fight, babes.' Odette shot her a wink, still slightly fazed from her encounter with Jay. Noises from the kitchen were encouragingly culinary – the food processor, microwave and herb chopper were all whirring away.

Juno thought about Jay and couldn't stop a smile twitching at her lips. What an amazing individual – his whole *raison d'être* hung in the balance and he was adding raisins to the coleslaw! She had to admire the man, even if she had yet to fathom him out.

She settled back in the sofa and experienced a momentary taking-life-for-granted sensation of total satisfaction. For the briefest of split seconds – the sort that divided gold from silver in an Olympic 100-metre dash – she wondered whether being pregnant would be a good thing. Lulu broke into her thoughts.

'I need a piss – is there a bog up here?' She headed towards the gallery stairs.

'Use the one in the tower!' Juno hopped after her. 'I don't think there's any loo roll up here – I'll just check.'

She hurriedly limped up to her parents' bathroom to assess the whereabouts of the pregnancy test. It had been discreetly tidied into the wall cabinet, along with her moustache bleach, razors and aromatherapy bath oil. So Jay had definitely clocked it, she realised with mounting panic. No wonder he was creating a diversion every time she tried to beg a cigarette. She wondered whether he was also responsible for her disappearing drinks.

She sat on the loo pan and leafed through the instructions. You had to wee on the wand and wait five minutes. Just as she was about to embark on stage one there was a knock on the door.

'Lydia's on the phone, babes.' It was Odette. 'They're lost somewhere near Abingdon.'

Grateful for the occasional pelvic floor exercise she'd put in while watching *Countdown* that week, Juno stuffed the test back in the cabinet and picked up the call in her parents' bedroom.

Lydia sounded extremely stressed. There was a lot of background noise and interference on the line.

'We've been driving round for hours, Joo,' she wailed. 'Your instructions are hopeless.'

Juno tried not to feel insulted. Her instructions were, she thought, AA Roadwatch sharp – she'd received eulogies in the past for clarity and forethought.

'Where are you now?'

'What? Turn the music down, Bruno – I can't hear. Still there, Joo? Turn it DOWN, Bruno!'

They were miles off course. Juno carefully directed them to Uffcombe through the lanes, but she didn't hold out much hope. From the noise in the background, there was a minor dispute going on in the car – Lydia snapping at Bruno, who appeared to be shouting at someone else. No one seemed to be listening to Juno's detailed navigational aids and pointers.

'If you don't both shut up, I'll scream gang rape,' Lydia was squawking.

'Who have you brought with you?' asked Juno, but the line went dead.

She debated creeping back into the bathroom to perform the test, but was gasping for a cigarette and a few more minutes' denial. Buck's Fizz was pounding up through the floorboards, and the bass-drowned chattering of voices made her feel left out. Her ankle throbbed as she hopped on to the gallery landing.

She was only halfway down the precarious stairs when Lulu hailed her from below, already plugged into her second bottle of Newky Brown.

'Bumped into that arse of a boyfriend you once had this week, pet.' She was swinging her head in time to 'The Land of Make Believe'.

'Who?' Juno watched her blue-dyed hair waving around. She already knew the answer – she did, after all, have just the one proper ex in existence – but it was nice to ask anyway.

'Whassisname – Jim?' Lulu was deliberately wrong. She'd made a point of never remembering his name.

'John,' Juno corrected gently, making it to the bottom of the stairs with effort. She didn't see Jay moving through the dining hall behind her, collecting extra chairs, the dogs at his heels.

Jez, meanwhile, was eyeing him discreetly as he slapped out the rhythm of the song on his knees and joined in with the chorus. Nice bum, he noticed. Shame he only seemed to have eyes for Juno.

'That's the boy.' Lulu pointed a finger in recognition which inadvertently danced along to the beat. There was something about Buck's Fizz which captured even the most hardened of 'eighties ex-Goths. 'He said he'd seen you for a date last Friday night, pet.' She scrunched her freckled brow critically. 'Y' didn't mention that when I saw you Sunday.'

'Not worth the breath.' Juno sagged into the sofa. 'What exactly did John say?'

'I never understand his accent.' Lulu pointed one finger towards the other elbow as she performed a naff 'eighties dance. 'But I think the gist of it is that he still wants you, pet. And he seems to think he's nearly there. Said you two got quite lippy.' She started head-banging to the chorus.

Juno wondered quite what Lulu meant by that. She knew she'd kissed John in a weak moment, but surely he hadn't told Lulu that? They hated one another. What was this curious syndrome between close friends and ex-boyfriends, that they couldn't bring themselves to exchange a word when the relationship was extant, yet discussed the mutual intimate like gossip column regulars once the love-affair was over?

'So did you shag him on Friday night, pet, or what?' Lulu yelled over the music, characteristically blunt as a truncheon. But she didn't wait for the answer as she closed her eyes in ecstasy. '"Captain Kid's on the sand, with the treasure close at hand". Classic fucking lyrics, huh?'

'You're not going to get back with John, are you, babes?' Odette suddenly stopped singing along too and gaped at Juno in horror. 'I thought you and – '

Jez seemed to be having some sort of coughing fit now, and was pulling strange faces at Odette, who promptly shut up and swigged back half a glass of wine.

'You okay?' Juno watched him worriedly.

'Fine!' He stopped coughing and smiled innocently. 'Buck's Fizz always has this effect on me. I get over-emotional.' He and Odette exchanged a knowing look.

Juno wondered if she was missing out on some sort of secret, but she had too many of her own to care. Besides, there was one very pressing requirement on her mind which blanked out all others.

'Could I scrounge a cigarette?' she asked Jez. 'I ran out a couple of days ago.'

'Sure.' He threw her the packet, but before she could extract one Jay appeared through the arch and called her into the kitchen to show him how the juicer worked.

Jez and Odette exchanged another look. Totally oblivious, Lulu stood up and started dancing to 'My Camera Never Lies'.

'Didn't you use it this morning?' Juno asked in confusion as she limped through the dining hall with him. 'I thought there was freshly squeezed juice on my tray?'

'Glad you noticed,' he snapped huffily, batting the dogs away.

Juno felt her heart plummet. Mary Poppins had clearly left the building, and Mrs Doubtfire had taken over the shift.

'Of course I noticed.' She did a double take as she saw the

kitchen surfaces cluttered with bowls, baskets, flan dishes and plates laden with food that her mother would have been proud to present to a camera. 'Wow!'

She paused for a moment, transfixed. Perhaps Mary was working time-and-a-half after all.

'This is just . . . sensational.' She wanted another word, a better word, but her vocabulary was starved by such calorific excess. It was glorious. Her belly danced in time to Buck's Fizz as it recognised something worthy of an anticipatory lurch.

'You sure it's okay?' He wiped his hands on his pinny.

'Okay?' she laughed, unable to stop herself bounding forward to hug him. 'Jay, you're a star. I can't believe you've done all this. It's sensational. I'm so, so grateful.'

'Hey there – it's cool.' He gently withdrew her arms from his shoulders and pushed her away so that he could look at her, hands clasping her wrists. 'I'm just cooking a meal, y'know? I like cooking. Your folks have a great kitchen here.'

Juno dropped her eyes from his in embarrassment.

'Yes, it's very professional, isn't it? I'll show you how the juicer works.' She cleared her throat awkwardly, but he kept tight hold of her wrists.

'I know how it works.'

'Oh.' Juno's gaze faltered under his as she realised he'd lured her away from her friends under false pretences.

'This is my way of saying thanks, I guess,' he muttered, tightening his grip on her wrists. 'I hadn't realised how much I needed to talk to someone until last night. It's kinda funny, isn't it? You acting as therapist to me?'

'Why's it funny?'

'If I went into therapy right now,' he smiled nervously, 'then you'd be one of the first things I'd talk about.'

She looked into his face again. His mouth was so close to hers she could have blown a kiss and watched its impression land on his lips.

She clutched at an impulse like a child grabbing a thistle blossom wish and stretched up to kiss him.

For a moment those soft lips yielded in surprise, then he pulled hurriedly away.

'Juno, there's something I gotta ask – '

'Juuunooo!' a voice shrieked from outside.

It was Elsa, wrenching open the porch door and frightening the dogs as she burst inside, wild curls flying.

Juno jumped, turning to see her favourite couples fighting their way through the dogs' predictably crotch-obsessed welcome.

In spilled Euan – terrifyingly trendy in a pointy-collared lemon yellow leather shirt and bell-bottomed pony-skin trousers – followed by Ally and Duncan, hand-in-hand on a baby away-day.

'My mother's got her.' Ally hugged Juno hello. 'So we're both going to get obscenely drunk and swear a lot.'

'Hi, pooh.' Duncan kissed her on both cheeks and handed over a carrier bag full of wine. 'You look jolly tasty today.' His eyes wandered tellingly to Jay. 'Hello there – I don't think we've met. I'm Duncan.'

Juno was astonished how charming Jay was with her friends. He was so shy and diffident – not trying to make a big impression and show off as John once had.

Juno eyed him, wondering in a panic whether her lunging kiss had been a good idea. She had a mental image of herself as a projectile octopus, forcing herself upon Jay with the suction force of an industrial cleaner, rendering him helpless. He'd just told her he'd need to go into therapy over all the trauma she'd caused, and then she planted a big wet one on him.

The gang accepted his presence with the breeziness of those who knew they'd met an equal, away from London, amongst friends and close to a non-stop alcohol supply. This was not their usual response to a newcomer. They rarely accepted anyone with such astonishing equanimity.

For the next hour, Juno limped around topping up drinks and popping open bags of Kettle Chips. She gave up searching for her missing glass of wine and poured herself another. But that, too, mysteriously vanished as she circulated at the hop, filling up glasses and offering crisps and olives around, occasionally heeled by Jay who was deputising as host every time her ankle necessitated a quick slump on the sofa. The smile was creeping over his face more and more often, just as the sun outside dyed the garden saffron yellow with increasing regularity as the clouds scudding across it chased one another away.

It was a perfect start to lunch – great friends, cheesy music, wine flowing, and a love interest just a few feet away. As the rain drifted into the distance, so did Juno's worries about the pregnancy test. It could wait. What did a few hours matter when Jay was being so dream-date nice?

The phone rang. It was Triona calling from Sean's flat to say that they were running hugely late and to start without them.

Jez put on Haircut 100 and they all sang along to 'Fantastic Day', feet up on sofas, chairs, tables and one another. The brief kiss she had given Jay continued to dance on Juno's lips like chilli pepper, both pleasurable and startling.

Lydia called at several more intervals – each time from an obscure corner of Oxfordshire, each time sounding more and more distraught. Juno wondered whether she was listening to her instructions at all. The final call was a classic.

'We've run out of petrol!' she cried. 'It's all bloody Bruno's fault. They've gone off to get some from a garage on foot, and left me to guard the stupid car. I have half a mind to trash the silly thing. Every time I say left, Bruno turns right just to spite me – they keep completely ignoring your instructions and trying to read a 1970s road atlas. Damn, I think my phone battery's running ooo—'

As the sun finally came out full-time to scorch the raindrops from the grass, the gang all wiped water from the table and chairs outside and started to carry out the food. But Juno's limp was too much for Jay to bear watching and he ordered her to sit down with her foot up. That shy, winning smile made her want to throw herself straight down on the floor with both legs and arms in the air like a dog longing to be tickled.

'He is just sensational!' Elsa whispered as she carried out the plates. 'No wonder you've been keeping him all to yourself.

Are you two madly in love or what? It's so flipping romantic, I can't bear it.'

Jez and Lulu came out of the conservatory, laughing between themselves as they carried baskets of garlic bread.

'You sly devil, Juno.' Jez tried to find a space on the table. 'Kept quiet about your sexy photojournalist boyfriend, didn't you? No wonder you haven't come out to play with us recently.'

'What a fucking dish, pet.' Lulu sagged into a chair beside her.

'Listen, you've got this all wrong,' Juno whispered urgently. 'Jay came down yesterday because he thought Uboat was ill, and I hurt my ankle so he stayed here to look after me.'

Elsa looked confused. 'But you two *are* an item, right?'

Before Juno could answer, Jay and the rest of the gang had spilled outside, bearing yet more plates of food for the already heaving table.

Juno caught Jay's eye as he settled in a chair opposite her and it suddenly occurred to her why he was behaving so differently. He was relaxed. For the first time since she'd known him, he seemed genuinely relaxed. The smile was dancing on his face like a mirage which seemed to grow closer every time Juno looked at it, but proved to be an optical illusion. That smile – so tempting, yet distant and unreadable. He was sitting on a secret time bomb which only she knew about, yet for the first time since she'd known him, Jay was behaving as though he didn't have a care in the world. She wanted to do an Eric Morecambe and slap his cheeks for a response. As her friends grew drunk around her, she became increasingly desperate for a reaction. She wanted to scream: 'Why are there three asterisks beside my name on your computer? Why, why, *why*?'

Chapter Thirty-Three

The dogs lay hopefully beneath the table as Juno's guests ate, laughed, chatted, and batted away the occasional wasp.

'Juno's taking a long time in the bog.' Odette glanced at her watch. 'Y'reckon she's all right up there?'

'Probably smoking a sly fag,' Ally giggled. 'She hasn't had a puff all afternoon, have you noticed? And she's not drinking much. I think she's pretending to be on one of her health kicks again.'

Juno waggled the little mascara wand once more. No pink dot. She held it up to the light. It was definitely, irrefutably dot-free. The bulge that was threatening to burst the seams of her dress came from eating alone, not sleeping together.

She'd never really understood the notion of not knowing whether to laugh or cry before that moment. She'd always found it pretty easy to decide between the two, and Juno was a girl who preferred to laugh most things off. This was different. The gurgle of relief rising in her throat was having difficulty getting past the huge lump that had formed there.

She threw the wand in the bin along with the box and instructions, burying them beneath several hunks of loo roll so no one would spot the evidence. As she stood up, she caught sight of herself in the mirror: plump cheeks, wide eyes, unfamiliar ultra-blonde hair. It was a baby face. The face of a woman who'd been behaving like a spoilt, belligerent toddler for most of her life. Someone who had almost let herself believe that being pregnant with Jay's child might be the catalyst which brought them together instead of creating another poisonous recipe for disaster.

'You silly cow, Juno.' She pressed her finger to the reflection of her nose. 'When are you going to grow up?'

Lydia was forever telling Juno off for 'projecting'. She had told her endless times that men don't analyse as much as women, that they take things at face value, that they genuinely believe what you tell them unless they know differently. Lydia maintained that women like Juno, meanwhile, try to interpret what men tell them as though it's an encrypted code, instead of a statement of fact.

In a classic illustration of her friend's theory, Juno had told Jay that sleeping with him had been a mistake, instead of admitting it had been one of the most sensational experiences of her life. And he'd believed her, the shallow idiot!

But when Jay himself had said that it was a mistake, she had cleverly interpreted his words to fit her own inverted rules, believing that what he really meant was that he was secretly mad about her. She'd imagined they were performing some sort of intricate, ritualistic love-hate dance around one another when all along he had just meant what he said. And finding the pregnancy test had panicked him into telling her the full, appalling truth about his life to make her aware of how utterly insignificant the episode between them had been compared to the shattering discovery which had brought him to England.

She stared at the mirror and made a mental note to throw out all her self-help books and occult guides, to stop 'projecting', to work harder, stop indulging in crushes and never, ever to seduce a stranger again. At least, not one she had to share a flat with afterwards. Not one she couldn't stop thinking about afterwards.

At the age of thirty, she had finally decided to grow up. And she was going to start by being as honest and supportive a friend to Jay as she could be, without once looking at his bottom and feeling lusty. Standing on her parents' hand-woven ethnic bath mat, Juno knew that she was hardly on the road to Damascus, but it was as close to a moment of revelation as she'd ever come.

Her conversion was put into practice sooner than expected.

Juno almost fell over Jay when she walked out of the bathroom. He was sitting on the gallery landing, legs hooked through two gaps between the banisters, fingers rapping on the polished floorboards.

I'm not ready to be mature and honest, she thought in a panic as he heard the door open and looked up. I need a drink and a fag first.

'It's free now,' she muttered as she headed for the stairs. 'Sorry to take so long.'

'Wait a minute, Juno.' He jumped up and stood between her and the top stair. 'Are you okay? You look kinda pale.'

'I'm fine.' She nodded, unable to look him in the eye.

He scratched his short, stubbly hair agitatedly, still barring her way. 'Really?'

'Really, truly.' She could hear the babble of conversation still going on outside, the clatter of plates, shrieks of laughter, scraping of chairs and the first few chords of 'Summer Loving'. Jez had clearly got his guitar out of the car and was settling down for a sing-a-long. Rug – who loved joining in – started to howl.

It was cool and still inside by contrast. Dust danced in the patches of sunlight which fell through the glass walls, but up on the gallery landing it was shadowy and sombre; the old church had not forgotten its heritage. Juno fought a ridiculous urge to drop to her knees and say a quick prayer to Jude, patron saint of lost causes.

'That's good – good.' Jay was nodding edgily, rolling up the sleeves of his t-shirt and backing away to let her past. 'I really like your buddies, they're good fun.'

She nodded. 'They seem to like you too.'

He bowed his head and studied his feet, reminding her of a shy, gawky teenager.

'Hey, Juno hen!' Euan called up from the depths of the house. 'You got that squeezebox contraption you play here?'

She hopped down a couple of stairs. 'There's one around somewhere.'

'Well, fetch it out here and join the band,' he yelled. 'You two have been necking long enough, you dirty buggers.' With a deep cackle, he headed outside again, singing the chorus to 'Summer Loving' in a very flat bass.

Juno winced, glancing up at Jay who was still standing on the landing, scuffing his feet edgily.

'I'm sorry about that,' she sighed. 'They seem to think we're some sort of item. I tried to put them right, but they're all a bit pissed.'

'Sure,' he mumbled, turning to gaze towards the bathroom door.

'They're always getting the wrong end of the stick and then giving me loads of it as a result,' Juno gabbled.

Jay clearly didn't understand a word she was saying.

The rowdy singers outside launched into 'Perfect Day', with Rug howling along tunelessly. The twins, however, started to bark excitedly. From the opposite side of the house there was the crunch of tyres on gravel and the cheery toot of a horn.

'Triona's here,' Juno muttered as the dogs rattled through the conservatory and kitchen, claws skittering against the stone floor while they barked themselves hoarse.

'I guess you'd better go say hi.' Jay shrugged.

'Yes.' She could feel her opportunity slipping away. The more people there were around, the harder it would be to corner him alone like this.

Car doors were slamming and Barfly's voice was booming out from the drive as he demanded to know where Horse had put the beers.

'You haven't knocked me up,' Juno blurted urgently.

'Huh?' Jay looked confused.

'Hellooo!' Triona called from the porch. 'We're here. Traffic's murder on the A34 and I almost ran over some mad hitch-hiker to boot, but we made it. Souxi sends her apologies – she's under a weather man she met at Cream last night.'

'I'm not up the duff or anything,' Juno whispered to Jay.

'Hellooo!' Triona called again.

'Get off my gonads, you pair of sex-crazed bastards,' Barfly growled in his chain-saw voice.

'You're not ...?' Jay was looking at Juno as though she'd just set light to his nasal hair. 'Up the ... "duff", did you say?'

'That's right. You see, I don't have a bun in the oven after all.' She chewed her lip, worried by his pole-vaulting eyebrows.

His reaction wasn't what she'd expected at all. He sighed irritably. 'You don't?'

Downstairs, Duncan was magnanimously – if drunkenly – acting as temporary host. 'Hello there – it's Triona, isn't it? We're all outside shoaking in the shun. I think Juno is upstairs entertaining her new squeeze, the randy filly.'

Juno was staring worriedly at Jay, who was looking more and more put out by her hurried announcement, his jaw clenched, lips pursed. She was starting to suspect that the mumsy behaviour could have been some sort of misplaced broodiness after all.

'No, I really don't have a bun in the oven,' she assured him gently. 'I'm sorry. Maybe you almost wanted me to, I didn't realise – '

For a moment his eyes blazed so angrily that she flinched.

'I can't believe you're saying this,' he muttered through clenched teeth. 'Talk about taking someone for granted!'

Then he brushed furiously past her as he headed downstairs. 'I made a load more garlic bread. I'll heat it up now.'

Bewildered, Juno watched him stalk away. He must be feeling very broody indeed. He was clearly gutted.

When she went outside again, Juno felt strangely distanced, as though she'd stumbled into a promenade play being acted out around her, when all she wanted was a front seat to watch a Jay Mulligan monologue with a question-and-answer session afterwards.

He was standing by the table with Barfly and Triona, who had dyed her hair black this week and painted her lips and fingernails to match. 'Since Sean's been gone I've tried to blacken my reputation to no avail,' she announced. 'So I thought I'd blacken everything else instead.'

When Juno rushed over to kiss them hello, Jay studiously ignored her.

Barfly wolf-whistled. 'Forget lunch, girl,' he boomed so loudly that Juno suspected they could hear him in Oxford. 'Only one fing I want to eat around here.' The next moment he spotted Odette and did a double-take. 'Scrap that – introduce me.' He elbowed Juno so hard that she thought she felt a rib crack.

'Odette, this is Barfly who originally comes from the East End – Barfly, this is Odette who originally comes from the East End. You'll have nothing in common, believe me.'

Juno caught Jay shooting her a withering look before he gazed pointedly away, pretending to be fascinated by bowl of rice salad.

So it was back to animosity again, she realised sadly. He only told me his secrets because he thought I might be pregnant. He just wants an heir to his air-side start in life to satisfy some sort of strange, rootless, hormonal craving. He's totally screwed up. So why do I still want to throw that rice over both of us in a pledge of happy-ever-after love, and then for us both to jump in a vintage car and drive away into the distance with my friends all clapping and whooping? Why do I want us to vroom up to a secluded spot and indulge in some back-seat sex-driving? Am I just feeling hormonal too?

Deciding she could justifiably get tight now that the pregnancy scare was out of the way, she pulled a bottle of beer from the ice box and drained it almost in one, but just felt vaguely sick and gassy afterwards. It was hopeless trying to catch up with the others or to keep up with Horse and Barfly. She stole one of Ally's super-mild cigarettes and tried to ignore the dirty looks Jay fired in her direction as he huffily followed Triona out to the car to fetch more food supplies.

The sun was scorching overhead now, frazzling flesh like a branding iron, and layers had come off with remarkable abandon. Elsa and Ally were sitting at the table in their bras, to soak in as much of the sun as possible. All the men except Barfly were topless; Horse removed his leather trousers too, wandering outside in just a pair of crumpled boxer shorts which showed his plums through the front vent when he sat down at the table. Odette, who was sitting opposite him and now decidedly tipsy, deliberately dropped her fork beneath the table and stooped to retrieve it, re-emerging in fits of helpless giggles.

'Why don't you get out those great big curves of yours and catch a bit of sun, girl?' Barfly eyed her mountain gorge cleavage hopefully.

Odette clearly didn't know what to make of him. He'd had a new number one buzz-cut – far shorter than Jay's scalping – which made him look both thuggish and almost sexy. Matched with a pair of obscenely baggy surfer shorts and a Hawaiian shirt covered with hula girls, he would have given Travolta a run for his money at a Tarantino casting.

'Why don't you, you fat bastard?' She cocked her jaw, dropping her napkin and diving down for a second look.

Barfly laughed delightedly, waiting until Odette reappeared before his eyes dived in a totally different direction.

'Does anyone want some sun tan oil?' Juno studied the expanses of toned, pale flesh with both worry and envy. 'There's some knocking round in the conservatory, I think.'

'Christ, hen, you obviously need another drink.' Euan handed her a bottle of Bud Ice. 'Suncream's for wusses. Loosen up and get your kit off.' He took another two bottles out of the ice box and pressed them against his silver nipple rings to cool them down.

Remembering she was wearing no knickers, Juno decided to stay fully dressed. She had no intention of burning her bush as well as her boats – today had been biblical enough.

'Juno's right, Euan pet.' Lulu hugged her trench coat tightly around her as she slouched into her chair. 'Melanoma's no joke, y'know.'

'Is she, like, one of the Spice Girls?' Horse asked in his lazy dreamer's drawl, leaning forward to reach for a bread stick and flashing his assets once more. His beautiful, poet's eyes blinked inquiringly at Lulu from beneath their shaggy veil of hair as he dunked the stick in a bowl of home-made hummus.

Lulu gaped back at him from beneath her own thick blue fringe as though he were a different species. 'Are you, like, for real, pet?'

'One short of a full load there, girl,' Barfly told Lulu when Horse smiled inanely instead of answering.

'He's three real then,' Triona said lazily as she wandered out of the house with several bulging carrier bags. They were packed full of Indian takeaway cartons.

'I asked Barfly and Horse to pop out for supplies when I was feeding Poirot,' she announced. 'I meant some bath buns and Cheddar, but they ordered everything off the Balti House menu. Dig in if you want.'

Stacks of poppadoms and naan bread were edged on to the table, along with a breeze block wall of silver curry trays containing lukewarm korma and vindaloo.

'I can't get Jay to come out of the kitchen.' Triona pulled a chair around so that she could sit beside Juno. 'He's got some sort of fixation for making garlic bread in there.'

Juno pressed her finger into the neck of the bottle Euan had passed her so that the froth jumped out. She hadn't even finished the first one yet.

'Are you two getting along any better?' Triona whispered as she piled a plate with food. 'I hear you've been having private confabs upstairs and ignoring your guests?' She winked, her face hopeful.

'Did Jay tell you that?'

'No – the pissed blond bloke over there. Dougal, is it? Jay's like a clam. You know that.'

'He's being really sweet,' Juno said carefully.

'Ugh!' Triona pulled a face as she spooned pasta salad on to her plate. 'When a woman calls a man sweet, the poor sod might as well go hang.'

'No, I like him a lot,' she protested, glancing nervously towards the kitchen.

'Good.' Triona wrinkled her nose delightedly.

Juno knew exactly how to change the subject. 'Have you seen *Londoners* this week? Only I've missed a couple of episodes.'

Thankfully, Triona – who hadn't missed an episode of the soap in twenty years – could talk about *Londoners* for hours. Soon she, Juno and Odette were discussing poor Sandra Fuller's love-life at great length.

For once, Juno noticed, she was dressed quite demurely in a long, floaty Ghost dress – not that it stayed on for long. Soon, Triona too was lolling around in her underwear – a special Fame Fatale line which was guaranteed not to show under diaphanous clothes, largely because there was barely any of it *to* show. With her spiky black hair and her blade-slender body, she looked like a Japanese boy.

With Triona, Barfly and Horse adding their hard-drinking dissipation to the already rowdy gaggle outside, lunch quickly became even more debauched. Jay started washing up in the kitchen, distancing himself from the proceedings. Juno longed to creep inside and curl up on the cracked leather sofa to talk to him, but she had a feeling she wouldn't be welcome. So she stayed and watched her friends, a spectator at the feast. Jez jammed on his guitar – everything from cheesy 'eighties medleys to haunting, melodic compositions of his own. Soon, Duncan joined him as percussion, keeping the beat with two breadsticks and an empty curry box, while Elsa and Ally danced in their bras and shorts. Occasionally, someone sang a bar or two of a tune they recognised and Rug howled along with them. Horse wandered out on to the lawn and lay down to sunbathe beside a croquet hoop. To Juno's amazement, Lulu joined him to share a spliff. Still dressed in her big coat, she stretched out on the grass beside him looking incongruously like a small fruit bat.

Her dissection of the *Londoners* plot exhausted, Triona helped herself to seconds of everything.

'Fucking lunatic hitchhiker on the road earlier. This pie is just fantastic – d'you make it, Juno?' she said between mouthfuls.

'He had a sign that said "White Horse" on it, so we pulled over seeing as this place is so close. He was some crazy Scotsman – a complete headcase. He kept saying he'd escaped and was out to lunch, then giggling a lot. Talk about Not a Care in the Community.'

'Oh, God,' Juno groaned in recognition. It couldn't be, could it?

'What did he look like?'

'Tall, blond – pretty in a dishevelled kind of a way.'

It had to be.

'When Fly told him we were heading for Uffcombe, he got really excited and started raving on about us all being out to lunch too. I decided it wasn't worth the risk giving him a lift, so I put my foot down.' Triona forked up some lemon chicken. 'But the stupid idiot chased after us and I almost totalled him.'

'He wasn't dangerous, surely?' Juno had never known Finlay be violent, although she'd never known him not high. He might be different now that he was in rehab.

'No, the risk *to* him. Barfly was getting a bit agitated, weren't you, Fly? Oi – take your eyes out of there.'

'Huh?' He reluctantly dragged his gaze away from Odette's cleavage. 'Oh, yeah – the loony geezer on the road. I din' like the look of him. Seemed to think I was some sort of nutter too. Bleeding cheek – I could have decked him.'

'See what I mean?' Triona raised her eyebrows at Juno before getting up to wander into the house.

Juno took a gulp of her beer and decided that Finlay, while missing out on a lift, had in fact had a lucky escape. Before Barfly had acquired his current moniker, he'd been known as Headfirst because, if he took offence to something someone said, he head-butted them first and asked questions later.

Right now, he was so overawed by Odette that he was as relaxed as a tree sloth. Snorkelling up bottles of lager at the rate of roughly one every ten minutes, he was so distracted by her magnificent chest that he'd put five Mr Kipling Almond Slices on his plate, doused them in ketchup and was eating them with a knife and fork (little fingers cocked), not noticing his mistake.

'Well, I din' like the look of him,' he grumbled after Juno had explained that the mad hitch-hiker was in fact just a lunch guest trying to thumb a life. 'He'd better keep his distance when he gets here. Blinding grub by the way, girl,' he congratulated her, burping appreciatively and staring at Odette's boobs again.

'Jay did the food,' Juno told him, but she had lost her audience as Barfly chomped on another mouthful of Almond Slice and sighed dreamily towards the happy valley.

Was it Juno's imagination or had Odette undone a couple of buttons? Surely she didn't fancy Barfly?

'Phew, it's hot.' Elsa came back from dancing with Ally. Picking up a poppadom, she fanned herself with it. 'I'm burning in my bra.'

'No offence, girl, but I don't approve of feminists – horrible, hairy old bruisers.' Barfly put on a pair of very dark wraparound shades which made him look like a gangster but enabled him to stare covertly at Odette.

When Triona emerged from the house with a bottle of wine in each hand, she gave Juno a conspiratorial wink. 'I've persuaded Jay to take some piccies. He says he likes you too.'

She closed her eyes and groaned. Put on Buck's Fizz again, she thought wretchedly, I am a teenager. Considering that Triona was a woman who went out to so many VIP gigs she appeared in every annual 'In' list the press could waste space with, she had the social skills of a school perfect pairing up sixth-formers for a barn dance.

No one seemed unduly bothered as Jay wandered around snapping them all. Lulu and Horse carried on sharing their spliff – Lulu even flashed her teeth in a rare smile; Horse flashed something else without knowing. The Couples were caught in action as they carried on singing and dancing to Jez's guitar. Barfly and Odette played croquet holding one leg up behind them as they leant on their mallets in mock 1920s high-jinks. Triona posed in her undies on the stump of an old oak, arms fanned out like a Lalique statue.

Juno stayed alone at the table, wondering why she felt so left

out. Normally, she'd be in the middle of things, pratting about
– posing with a breadstick up each nostril and her tongue out.
She threw the poppadom to one side and watched Jay making
Effie stand up on her hind legs for a shot. He had a battery
pack hanging from one shoulder which looked ludicrously like
a housewife's handbag, she noticed with a sneer.

Suddenly it occurred to her that the reason she was sulking
was because he was photographing the dogs before he'd even
asked her to say 'cheesy grin'. That showed how much he
supposedly 'liked' her now that he knew she was baby-free.
She found Barfly's sinister wraparounds discarded on the table
and donned them dejectedly as she watched Triona tripping
towards her.

'Terrific party.' She sighed her way contentedly into her
chair and started eating again. For someone whippet thin, she
ate like a heavyweight boxer, Juno noticed enviously. 'By the
way, what's the turtle doing on the freezer?'

'Jay thought she was ill. That's why he came down in the
first place.' Juno noticed he was taking shots of the house now.
So he rated her below architecture as well as dogs.

'But I *told* him she was just laying eggs when he called me,'
Triona sighed impatiently. 'Talk about over-reacting.'

'He called you about Uboat?'

She nodded. 'Yesterday afternoon. He was in a right flap
– couldn't get hold of you here. I told him about that time
she laid eggs when you and John were on holiday in Brittany,
and Sean had exactly the same reaction – phoning your hotel
waking you two up to announce she was dying. So I said to
Jay there was nothing to worry about and that I was coming
down for lunch today and I'd let you know what was going on.
He seemed to calm down. We had quite a chat afterwards.'

'So why did he bring her here?' Juno glanced at Jay again,
busy framing up the apple tree. He obviously felt she was less
photogenic than flora and fauna too.

'Same reason he got his hair cut, I guess.' Triona waggled
a piece of bread at her and winked.

Juno was about to ask her what she meant by that, but

the couples 'band' chose that moment to launch into a very camp rendition of 'Dancing Queen' and Triona let out a shriek of recognition. 'I love this! Come on, Juno – let's shake some tush.'

'I can't – my ankle,' she excused herself feebly, desperate for Triona to stay long enough to explain the hair thing. But she was already up and dancing.

Juno watched from behind Barfly's dark glasses as Jay moved forward to take photographs of Triona and the band again, bending and stooping to get the right angle and light source, working quickly and deftly, so unobtrusive that no one seemed to notice he was there. Juno suddenly realised how good he was at his job, could imagine just how he'd managed to capture so many shots without the subject ever realising. Whether it was a sniper waiting for his next target in a war zone, or a celebrity popping out to the shops without his wig for once, Jay caught them on film as quickly as he caught his own breath.

'Dancing Queen' finished with a loud cheer.

'Where's that squeezebox, huh?' Euan pointed accusingly at Juno with his beer bottle and consequently soaked Rug who was still singing along.

'Juuuunooo!' Jez started a football chant. Soon they were all joining in.

She finally gave in to goading and fetched an accordion from the house, collecting together various of her father's percussion instruments to pass around the others.

As she hobbled back through the kitchen, she encountered Jay carrying in a tray loaded with dirty plates from the garden. They drew level in the conservatory.

Act normal, she told herself sternly, staring fixedly at the floor. Mature, friendly and supportive.

'Don't worry about those – I'll do them later,' she said, limping past so quickly that she dropped a bodhrán with a clatter. As she stooped to pick it up, a reco-reco fell into a plant pot and a cymbal crashed on the floor and circled its way to a noisy halt.

Juno hastily gathered them up, acutely aware that Jay was standing over her.

'I'm sorry,' he said quietly.

'Sorry about what?' Juno dropped a tin whistle.

'It's John, isn't it?' he said flatly. 'Last Friday night – the night he forgot?'

She straightened up slowly, hope making her heart crash like a jack-hammer. He was asking about her ex. There was a chance – just a tiny one – that he could be jealous. She had to be cautious over this. He could just be making casual conversation. Be a friend, be mature, but make it absolutely clear that John is no longer in the picture.

'I met him for a drink.' She longed to add, 'because I thought it was you who had asked me out', but stopped herself in time. 'He didn't forget. Not that it was much fun. We rubbed each other up the wrong way and that was that – a bit of a mess. It's a permanent split. These things happen.'

'And does he know?' Jay watched her closely.

'Know what?'

There was an impatient Glaswegian bellow from outside. 'Oi – Juno hen! Hurry up!'

'That you might be pregnant.' Jay's eyes bored into hers like laster pointers.

She gaped back at him in wonderment. He couldn't have heard her right earlier. God! No wonder he was still behaving oddly. But what did it have to do with John? Was this some sort of American thing? That you had to be so open with your exes, you let them know you'd been a bit careless on the condom front with a casual lover?

'I'm not pregnant,' she said, accidentally pressing against the rubber bulb of an old car horn so that it honked with untimely aplomb.

'You're not?' Jay blinked.

Juno shook her head.

'Juuuunooo!' The drunken football chant had started again outside.

'I shouldn't have told you that stuff about me last night.' He looked away and chewed his lip.

'So why did you?'

'I know I don't have a right to think of you as . . . to have any . . . to . . .' He rubbed his forehead impatiently, as though by doing that he could summon a sentence that articulated the thoughts taking place behind it.

Juno felt a set of maracas slipping from beneath her armpit but kept a tight grip, aware she was a hair's breadth away from that oh-so-elusive confession which would enable her heart to start pumping again. She longed to know what he felt about her.

'Juno.' He tipped back his head and found the words at last. 'You're so generous. You can't say no to anyone – you give 'em your money, your time, your heart, your cigarettes.' His eyes slid towards hers almost sadly. 'You expect the same generosity back.'

'Juuuunooo!' the hooligans chanted on.

'Juuunooo,' Jay echoed them in a quiet whisper. 'Listen to those guys – they love you. Look at your family – so close and affectionate. I never had none of that – any of that,' he corrected himself. 'You share everything with the people in your life, I've never even shared a cab. You're upfront and ballsy, I'm cautious as hell.'

Juno absorbed this new information silently.

'Juuunooo's having a domestiiiic!' The chant was developing with giggles and jeers.

She took no notice of it. She wanted her heart to start beating again. 'So why did you tell me?'

'I wanted to share something with you.' He shrugged, gazing at the ceiling. 'I'm an all or nothing guy, so I figured it might as well be my life.'

The maracas fell to the floor with a jaunty rattle as Juno's heart leapt into such frenzied action it thought it was pumping water around an industrial unit.

'Bad idea, huh?' He smiled sadly at the vines overhead. 'I'm just getting in the way. You must hate me more than ever now.'

'Hate you?' She was horrified. 'Why should I hate you?'

Had he just said he wanted her to share his life or was she hearing things?

'You've more or less ignored me since I freaked out that day you cooked me dog food.'

'I haven't ignored you!' she protested.

'Okay, so you've argued with me. But you've ignored me too.' He picked up the maracas and held them out.

Juno didn't take them. She drew circles around his yellow corneas with her gaze, daring herself to be 'upfront' as he'd so deliciously described her. He'd told her that she wasn't allowed to fall in love with him. Well, she was experiencing enough G-force right now to suggest a fairly long fall. She took a deep, empowering breath and decided to be upfront. Forget supportive friend, this was an emergency.

'You're right. I have ignored you. For one, I've started ignoring the promise you made me swear to keep that night we first slept together.' She shivered at her own daring. Lydia couldn't possibly accuse her of 'projection' now. That statement was as transparent as Triona's underwear.

'Huh?' His eyes narrowed suspiciously and Juno had a sudden panic that she'd gone too far, been over-dramatic. Perhaps when he'd said 'share my life' he'd simply meant 'share my life history'?

'Juuuunooooo's having a domeeeestic.' The chant moved indoors as Horse shambled naked inside, giddy on dope.

Noticing Juno and Jay glaring at him, he ripped a leaf from a cheese plant and held it modestly to his groin. He then grinned foolishly as he grabbed Juno's shoulder with his free hand. 'They sent me in to fetch you. Wow! Musical instruments. Like, wow. Can I play the drum?'

He started to drag her outside.

'Come out for a sing-song,' she implored Jay rather desperately as she was edged towards the door then pulled out of it.

He didn't follow. Instead he stood still with his tray and followed her with his eyes, utterly confused by what she'd just said.

Jez – who could play almost anything by ear – led the way,

but Juno found to her relief that sobriety made for very few bum notes. As her fingers flew across the keys, she imagined Jay was listening in and absorbing the fact that she'd just confessed to loving him, ready or not. The music soothed her nerves. Together, they all strummed, wheezed and clanked their way through several 'eighties hits.

Elsa and Ally stopped dancing and ventured on to the lawn to lie out in the sun. They joined Lulu and Horse, and listened in delight.

'I'd forgotten how good Juno is with that thing,' Elsa sighed, dispensing with her bra. 'She was always playing us stuff at college. Her Euro-pop squeezebox Smiths medleys were classics. She was even asked for a demo by an A and R guy once, but she thought he was joking. Wouldn't take him seriously.'

'She should use it more in her act.' Ally listened as Juno and Jez duelled in an energetic Pogues-inspired riff. 'Nowadays she just tends to hold on to the thing onstage like a security blanket.'

'She used to have loads of comic songs,' Elsa remembered. 'She had us all in stitches at the third-year revue. What was that song? Oh, Christ, yes – play that carol you did, Juno! Remember? "Have it Away in a Manger".'

Juno cringed, grateful that Jay was still inside the house. 'I can't remember it,' she said with relief. 'Besides, it's midsummer.'

'Okay – what *do* you remember?'

The sad truth was that Juno knew most of the songs she'd ever composed word-for-word. She often indulged herself in the odd late-night session when she was visiting her parents, long after they had gone to bed. She still used the odd one or two in her act also, although most of those were more recent and topical. The older ones were pure teenage angst – outwardly funny and quirky skits on popular songs, but the wit sharpened on the blades of her own pain.

'What about "Aisle be There", pooh!' Duncan put in a noisy request.

'I could try,' she offered distractedly, staring at the conservatory but unable to see Jay. 'I'm not sure I remember it.'

'Oh, yes, try! That's one of my faves, babe.' Odette waggled her croquet mallet, sportingly ignoring the fact that Barfly had been gazing at her cleavage so intently he was now unwittingly rapping one of the dogs' chew-balls around the croquet lawn, having hammered his own into the shrubbery ages ago.

Jay came back from making a vast jug of coffee in time to hear the last few bars of Juno's song. He stood by the table, listening to the soft, sweet voice and the long, sighing chords. For a moment, he thought it was a love ballad – the sound was so sweet and melodic that he suddenly realised what the hairs on the back of his neck had been put there for. Then the words registered.

It was part Victoria Wood, part Phoebe from *Friends*, but there was no denying the tears of amusement being wiped from eyes all around Church House garden.

A lot of raucous, glass-pinging applause greeted Juno's final refrain, but as she looked up she saw Jay melting away from the table and heading indoors again, back hunched like a pit pony when the mine starts to cave in.

'Oh, shit!' she muttered under her breath. How dumb! How truly dumb! The song was about a distracted mother, stressed out by the supermarket, grabbing the wrong trolley in the frozen veg aisle, so that her baby girl – left behind undetected – grew up as the female Tarzan of Tesco's, lying low for years as she pillaged the pick and mix by night and pretended to be a store detective by day. It was a stupid flight of fantasy which she'd made up when she was at university and barely thought about since. Jay must have thought she'd chosen it deliberately to taunt him.

She limped hastily inside but he seemed to have disappeared. She searched the tower and the gallery – taking ages to climb and descend the stairs – but he wasn't in either. As she hobbled stiffly through the dining hall for the second time, listening to a very drunken rendition of 'Stand By Your Man' floating in from outside, she saw a vision of blonde hair and long, lean body race inside from the porch.

'Lydia!'

'Joo!'

A brief running-together (or shambling lop-sidedly in Juno's case) culminated in a tight hug and lots of squeaky air kisses. For all its apparent superficiality, the hug was as tight as Juno's dress and far more comforting. She knew she just had to tell Lydia about Jay. She felt the waterworks start – tears welled her eyes stung, a couple of splashes and . . .

'I hate him!' Lydia hissed, bursting into very noisy tears of her own. 'I don't want him to stay for lunch. You've got to get rid of him.'

'Who?' Juno gulped back her own outburst.

'Bruno! Who else?' Her friend's beautiful blue eyes rolled dramatically, seeping tears like a marble Madonna. 'I don't care if Will stays – he's okay. But Bruno has to go. T-tell him you don't want him here, Joo. *Please*. I can't b-bear to be in the same room as him. I just chucked him – I had to wait until we were coming up your d-drive in case he made me get out and walk. I'm wearing these, you see.' She waggled a pair of strappy sandals so high and narrow they could have conducted lightning into the Earth's core.

Juno laughed, hiccuped, coughed and then laughed again.

'Oh, Joo, you're such a d-darling.' Lydia hugged her again. 'I can't b-believe you're crying for me. I do love you. I knew you'd understand. You're always on my side.'

'Where is he?' Juno wasn't sure she'd be much good at throwing Bruno out for no reason. She loathed conflict.

'Still in the car, I think. I told him he couldn't come in.' Lydia pulled away, sniffing dramatically. She was dressed in an It girl combination of high heels, spray-on top, lace pedal pushers and petulant pout – all in scarlet woman red. It would look trashy on anyone else; on Lydia it was the Chanel laboratory – experimental, but reeking of class.

'And where's his friend?' Juno remembered that they'd brought someone with them.

'Will?' Lydia pulled a face.

'You called,' chuckled a cheery, Essex-boy voice.

Emerging from the porch was a chunky, smiling figure with a pudding-bowl haircut and more designer club gear layered on his body than the cloakroom hooks at Ministry of Sound.

It was Will Pigeon.

'Well, I never!' he laughed. 'So it *is* you. I thought it must be the same Juno when I bumped into old Jay outside just now. He was taking a bunch of dogs for a walk. Flipping weird sight, that. Never had him down as a dog-lover.'

So that's where he'd got to, she realised wanly. She longed to fly towards the door and limp after him but Lydia was gripping tightly on to her arm, in immediate need of tissues and solace.

'He's very good with children and animals,' said Juno, bleakly, almost adding 'but some of us are just too childish and beastly to tolerate.'

Chapter Thirty-Four

Far above Church House, Jay sat in the chalk eye of the ancient horse and stared across Oxfordshire. He was so lost in thought he didn't realise his mobile phone was ringing at first. He'd forgotten he'd even brought it with him. For one insane moment he wondered whether it was Juno, calling from the house to apologise. But he might have guessed she wouldn't bother. She was wrapped up in her friends and totally indifferent to him, a fact which tore him in two.

'Yeah?' he answered the call. 'Oh, Abe – hi there. Any news?'

Several tourists watched in alarm as he stood up on the eye and started to shout excitedly, voice cracking with emotion.

'. . . You're kidding me, right? Is it genuine? . . .'

An old lady in an anorak edged forwards. 'You're not supposed to stand there, young man.'

Jay ignored her, listening to the news he hadn't dared hope for.

'. . . Jesus, are you sure? . . . Oh, sweet Jesus Christ!'

He let out a howl which sent the old lady scuttling away.

Bruno cautiously ventured inside – wandering through the empty house, then out into a very drunken gathering of semi-naked revellers who were making music, making merry and making eyes at one another. The Couples were dancing to an old 'eighties compilation album now, while Jez took a well-earned cigarette and beer break from the guitar. Barfly had persuaded Odette to join him for a turn on the terrace and was lumbering around her showing off his Madness moves, laughing a lot and gazing down her top.

Bruno stared around in amazement at the scene of debauchery. A girl in a huge black coat was playing croquet with a naked man. He finally saw Lydia talking to her dumpy little friend under an apple tree in the far corner of the garden.

Juno had rather selfishly towed Lydia there so that she could have a good view of the Manger and keep an eye out for Jay.

'I don't *believe* it,' Lydia hissed, sounding just like Victor Meldrew. Her eyes narrowed as she watched Bruno standing forlornly by the table, staring back at her and scratching his head so that all his hair stood on end. 'He has a nerve.'

'Just ignore him,' Juno recommended, hoping Lydia wouldn't demand that she throw him out. He looked so sad, she felt rather sorry for him. She could relate.

Will, who had been chatting with Jez, bounded over to his friend and pulled him into the throng to be introduced, but Bruno quickly backed away and headed towards Lydia.

'Tell him I don't want to talk to him.' Lydia pushed Juno forward so violently that she fell into his arms in an embarrassingly gushy welcoming embrace.

She hastily pulled away.

'Hello, little Marx brother.' He grinned shyly, glancing over her shoulder to Lydia, who had turned her back on him.

'Hi,' Juno said as frostily as she could, and placed a carefully concocted snarl on her face. 'Um . . . she doesn't want to talk to you, I'm afraid.'

'Don't apologise for the fact, Juno!' Lydia hissed behind her.

'I don't understand what I've done wrong . . .' Bruno pleaded.

'Go away!' Lydia hissed.

Bruno gazed helplessly from Lydia to Juno, big brown eyes as lost as an abandoned puppy's.

Juno felt the grimace slide into an apologetic expression. She guessed he'd done nothing wrong. That was half the problem. Lydia had simply grown bored of him, of his niceness and insecurity. It had happened so many times before – a vicious circle entirely of Lydia's own creation. She was like a child twirling a colourful rope, laughing in glee as it spun around her head, and then starting to panic when it coiled around and trapped her.

'I'm sorry I didn't listen to your instructions on the way here,' Bruno told her, his soft voice gruff with emotion. 'It's just, you kept changing your mind, darling – and the farmer wasn't very happy when we drove through that field of sheep, so he wasn't.'

'It was a short cut Juno told me about!'

'I know, I know – and it was brilliant, darling, but I think –'

'What short cut?' Juno butted in huffily. She certainly hadn't directed Lydia through any fields.

Bruno ignored her. 'And that military base we drove through was frankly terrifying – I thought they were going to arrest us, so I did.'

'Military base?' Juno gasped. Where *had* Lydia been directing him to drive?

'You see, you're at it again!' her friend snarled. 'All you do is criticise, criticise, criticise. Piss off!'

'But, Lydia baby,' he murmured soothingly. 'I adore you. I'm not criticising you. It was obviously Juno's fault we got lost and that –'

'Hang on a minute!' she bleated.

'Piss off, Bruno,' repeated Lydia. 'I want to talk to my friend.'

'Yes, piss off.' Juno glared at him.

He slunk away to rejoin Will, who was on a charm offensive, introducing himself to everyone. For a moment, Juno watched in fascination as Triona emerged from the house and – recognising Will – let out a shrill whoop and rushed to hug him.

'Has he gone yet?' Lydia turned back to look over Juno's shoulder.

Bruno had joined Will and was nodding his head towards the drive, clearly eager to leave. But the wide boy shook his head and, letting Triona go, tipped his head to mutter something in Bruno's ear.

'Good, I think they're going.' Lydia started to unlace her strappy shoes.

Juno turned to gaze up at the Manger again. On the ridge of the hill, clusters of people were milling about – the usual tourist crowd plus a few locals taking advantage of the hot, clear day to fly kites or walk dogs. She couldn't identify Jay amongst them.

A sharp pop made her turn towards the garden again. Will had cracked open a bottle of champagne – gratefully received as the alcohol supply was running low – and started filling up glasses as though he was hosting the party. He had so much charm he should be wrapped in foil and sold by Romany gypsies along Knightsbridge. Poor Bruno had flopped on to the grass with the Couples and was looking lost.

'Wouldn't you just know it?' Lydia huffed. 'Bloody Will's persuaded him to stay. I only met that man today, and I don't trust him at all. He's a terrible flirt. He sat behind me in the car and kept stroking my neck when Bruno wasn't looking. I practically had my nose in the glove box the entire way here.'

Juno was too distracted to pick up on the fact that Lydia clearly hadn't flirted back, which was highly unusual when she was planning to sack a boyfriend.

She'd perched on a root of the rocking horse apple tree now, and was patting the grass beside her so that she could give Juno a detailed run-down on Bruno's irritating failings – his lateness, his wimpiness, his closet sexism, his ineptitude. Juno had heard it all before. She often wondered why her friend had such picky taste in men when the very traits she found attractive drove her mad within weeks.

'He's hanging around to spite me,' Lydia growled murderously, downing her own private supply of Pinot Grigio straight from the bottle. Given her low capacity for alcohol, she was plastered within minutes.

If Juno had been more together, she would have noticed that her friend's virtuoso performance of irrational hatred and illogical indignation soon started to slip into self-parody as she knocked back more wine and lost her edge. But Juno's eyes and mind kept drifting guiltily to the Ridgeway and to Jay.

'He's so bloody short,' Lydia fumed to Juno, who was herself on the Lilliputian side of Toyah Wilcox. 'Short-arsed, short-tempered, short of money. His father's worth a fortune, and he does a shitty job as an assistant dogsbody in a post-production house because he thinks it would be dishonourable to freeload. Can you believe that?'

Juno nodded, then shook her head as she realised her mistake. It sounded like a description of herself when she came to think about it.

She tried to listen – she tried really hard. But she kept wondering where Jay was, whether he was marching along the Ridgeway working out the best way to murder her. The other disturbing distraction was the fact that Triona was now nose-to-nose with Will Pigeon on the rickety garden bench, sharing a spliff and a secret.

'And he's so immature,' Lydia was fuming. 'Always banging on about politics and issues like some bloody student, then sulking when I tell him I'm not remotely interested in Banana Workers' Rights or whatever. He irritates the hell out of me. I quite understand how you feel about Jay now. I can hardly bear to be in the same room as him.'

'As Jay?' Juno gazed up at the Ridgeway once more, wanting nothing more than to be in the same room as him right now – locked in it together until she could tell him how terrible she felt about her behaviour.

Lydia looked non-plussed for a moment. 'No, Bruno. I feel the same way about him as you do about Jay. He gets on my nerves all the time now. I just want him out of my life. Poor you, having to share a flat with someone you feel like that about – no wonder you're hiding down here. Thank God I'm not living with Bruno . . .'

Juno thought back to that brief, giddy conversation in the conservatory.

'. . . so much worse when it's your boyfriend,' Lydia was saying. 'He's so unsupportive – just wants to touch me all the time.' She swigged some more Pinot Grigio straight from the bottle and then offered it to Juno.

Juno shook her head. Then she suddenly remembered Finlay. Where was he? It was hours since Triona had almost run him over on the A34. Even if he'd only managed to hitch as far as Wantage, he should have arrived by now. He'd be far better at sorting poor Lydia out than she was in her hopelessly distracted state. He was her knight in shining armour after all, who was planning to rescue her from this self-destructive addiction to sex and shoplifting.

'. . . been working really hard this week,' Lydia was still ranting, 'and he doesn't seem to realise how tired I am. It's been hectic at the office, what with the management consultants' report being put into action and everything. No wonder you and John split up – the job is so absorbing and challenging, you can't think of anything else half the time. I love it. I've even been too shattered for sex.'

Juno scrunched up her forehead as she realised Lydia was talking about the lousy job at Immedia – *her* lousy job at Immedia. 'Am I hearing this right, you love it?'

Lydia was too tight now to realise that this was a question.

'I know. You're right. I do love sex,' she hicupped, 'but I simply haven't felt like it this week. And besides, I've got so much work to do in the evenings now that I've agreed to . . .' She instantly shut up and had a swig of wine, eyeing Juno guiltily.

'Now that you've agreed to what?'

Lydia was suddenly looking extremely shifty.

'Must have a wee.' She struggled up, leaning on the tree for support. 'Back in a sec.'

As Lydia lurched hurriedly inside the house, Juno got up and kicked a few windfall baby apples around, edging closer to Triona and Will.

'. . . better buy it back, I guess,' she was saying. 'You still got it?'

'Sure – I know what you're like, girl. It's around somewhere – I think Bruno took a bit of a shine to it. Hey – sexy!' He called Juno over. 'Small world, huh?'

'Minute,' she agreed awkwardly. 'So you two know each other?'

'We go way back.' Triona cuffed Will's ear. 'This reprobate supplies my ex-husband with all the backstage passes he shows off about to make me feel Z-list.'

'You can talk, Tri. Remember what you swapped that watch for?' he chuckled, then suddenly looked up at Juno, eyes widening. 'Shit! You wanted the same deal, didn't you, sweetheart? You asked me that night in Jay's flat. I was well shocked – wondered how you'd found out about it. So it was Triona told you, was it?' He pinched her cheek. 'I told you not to breathe a word – only offered you the deal 'cos I know you're an addict.'

'I didn't tell Juno!' Triona protested, gazing up at her in total admiration. 'Christ! You sly cow, you know too? I mean, I knew you dabbled, but I didn't realise you were that hooked. This is so fucking thrilling! You've got to get her one, Will. We can do it together.'

He opened his mouth to say something, but was distracted by the ringing of one of his mobiles. As soon as he'd answered it another went off and he moved away to negotiate a price on tickets for a sell-out Oasis gig.

Lydia padded barefoot down the tower stairs and tripped into the kitchen, pausing to gaze at the photographs on the wall. Her eyes trailed the generations of short, cuddly women and tall, thin men.

She adored this house and the people who had created it. It felt almost like an extension of her own family. She'd been coming here for years, since she'd first met Juno. It was impossible to know her for more than three days without meeting her family. Lydia looked at a photo of her favourite rebel renegade as a toddler and chewed guiltily on her lip.

She'd been dreading today, had thought up every excuse under the sun not to come, but Bruno had been so insistent that she'd caved in – especially when he'd pointed out that she should tell Juno what she'd done herself, rather than let her friend find out on Monday morning.

But it was proving harder than Lydia had imagined. As soon as they had set out from London in the car, she'd started to panic that she wouldn't be able to do it, or that if she did, Juno wouldn't forgive her.

Continually giving Bruno the wrong directions had delayed them somewhat, but she might have guessed they'd get here in the end. Deciding to chuck him on arrival had created a valuable distraction, but she wasn't certain how long that would last. Juno already seemed to suspect something. She was in an odd, distracted mood which made Lydia feel even edgier. She almost suspected that Juno knew what she'd done already and was stringing her along until she came out and admitted her shameful secret.

She felt guilty about the Bruno thing too. He was really quite sweet, if occasionally irritating. She knew that she'd have got rid of him sooner or later, but hadn't really planned on doing it today. He'd managed to get two tickets to see the new Patrick Marber play next Thursday, and besides, she normally liked to line up someone new before dispensing with the old.

As if on cue the front door slammed.

She turned abruptly as Jay walked in through the porch, almost falling over as the dogs surged forward on their leads to greet her.

'Oh, hi there, Linda,' he said distractedly, looking breathless and agitated as he scrabbled to unclip the dogs' leads.

Lydia forgave him the gaffe. She adored the way shy men got nervous.

'Wow, I like the hair cut.' She had forgotten how athletic and wiry he was – like a National Hunt jockey. 'I didn't recognise you when I saw you in the drive earlier.'

'Huh?' He straightened up. 'If you'll excuse me, I gotta have a word with Juno. Sort summin' out and say goodbye.'

The dogs raced at her as they were released, flattening Lydia against the wall.

She managed to kick them away before Jay walked past.

'Wait a minute!' She leapt forward and grabbed his arm. 'You're going back to London?'

He nodded, glancing towards the garden.

'Can I have a lift?'

'What?' He didn't seem to be listening.

'I need a lift back to London,' she hissed desperately. 'The sooner the better. Urgently in fact.'

'Yeah, sure, whatever,' he mumbled distractedly, trying to pull away. 'I gotta talk to Juno first.'

'I'm not sure that'd be a wise idea.' Lydia held on tight, not wanting Juno to be alerted to the fact she was leaving too, running away from her responsibilities yet again.

'Why not?'

Good point, Lydia thought madly. Why not?

'Because she's upstairs,' she lied, 'being sick.'

'Being sick?' He scratched his head agitatedly.

Lydia glanced nervously towards the garden. Someone was coming in, pausing to greet Rug who was trotting the other way. She had to get Jay out of the porch before they were seen. Either that or get hold of his keys so that she could steal his car. This called for desperate measures. She looked around for abandoned car keys, but there weren't any lying conveniently on the surfaces.

'I gotta see her.' Jay made to head for the tower stairs.

'No!' Lydia kept hold of his arm. 'I think she'd prefer to be left alone. It's – um – a girly sort of sick.' She hoped that'd put him off. Most men hated the idea of a medical condition which was 'girly'. She'd used it as an excuse herself many a time.

Jay scratched his head again, murmuring to himself, 'But she said she wasn't . . . She must have lied to me.'

Not listening, Lydia was frantic to get him out to his car now. She'd say anything to hurry him along. 'She's like something out of *The Exorcist* when she voms.' She started to drag Jay towards the door. 'I'll never forget that time she had a dodgy curry and was sick at work all the next day – we're talking projectile.'

'It was John all along,' Jay muttered, not really listening to her. 'Last Friday night.'

'You're right!' Lydia remembered. Juno had always been a sucker for John's super-hot curries – the only thing he could cook. 'But not last Friday – long before that.'

'Before that?'

'Ages.' She nodded. 'She's always said John's tasted the best and filled her up the most. She simply couldn't resist, kept going back for more, but boy did she regret it the next day! She never learns, though. The next time he offered, she was straight in there with her tongue hanging out. That's Juno for you. And look at her now – head over a loo again. It's not as though it's the first time.'

Jay was looking more and more appalled.

'In that case I'm wasting my fucking time here.' He shook his arm free from Lydia's grip and stooped to pick up his computer and camera bags. 'Let's go.'

'Yes!' She started to race towards the door.

Jay blinked in surprise as he noticed her feet. 'You've got no shoes on.'

'I left them here.' She jumped into a pair of Howard Glenn's mud-glazed wellies that were lying in the porch.

'Unusual choice.' He sighed sadly, following her outside with a last, regretful look at the tower stairs.

'Cut the calls, Will. Juno wants to cut a deal instead!' Triona trilled. 'She's an addict too.'

Oh, Christ, Juno thought dizzily. What is this mysterious addiction we're talking about? Some sort of new designer drug? I can't even take alcohol any more. Triona has veins like sprinkler hoses and can eat Es like baked beans. If we share whatever it is, I'll die.

'Thing is, I can't really afford it,' she muttered, starting to back away.

'I'll buy it for you,' Triona offered. 'My treat – call it a belated birthday present. I could tell you didn't like the bra much.'

'I loved it!' Juno protested. 'I don't want another present. And, besides, I know you had to trade Sean's watch for yours, so I couldn't possibly put you out.'

'That was just a churlish gesure, Juno,' Triona laughed. 'You know how much Sean despises the fact I'm so addicted to it? The very night he went to the States, Ticket here called me with the offer and I spotted Sean's Tag in my bathroom. I missed him so much, I decided to teach the bastard a lesson for leaving me behind and said I'd buy it with that. I was just telling Will I wanted it back a minute ago. And I insist on buying you one while I'm at it.'

Will cut off his caller and coughed awkwardly as he sat down on the bench again.

'Trouble is,' he stroked Juno's legs apologetically, 'I don't think I can get you one, sweetheart. These things are like gold-dust. Friends and family only, understand? I just had a couple and I sold them straight away.' A phone went off again. 'Hello – oh, hi, mate. Yeah, a monkey, s'right . . .' He looked up at Juno and winked. 'Sorry.'

'Oh, I understand.' She nodded emphatically, desperate to escape the clutches of addiction. 'I quite understand.'

'You'll just have to watch it on telly,' Triona sighed sadly. 'I'll call you afterwards to let you know anything they delayed out.'

'You will?' Juno had a slack-faced moment of confusion.

'God, yes!' She winked merrily. 'I'll tell you everything. I can't believe they're actually recording it in the *Londoners* studio and everything. On the Green Man set of all places. I'm going to freak out when I get there, I know I am.'

Juno's face instantly lost its slack, like a bloodhound puppy picked up by the scruff of the neck.

'Belle Winters?' she said in a frozen gasp, twigging at long last. It was the only healthy addiction she shared with Triona. '*Your Life In Front Of Your Eyes*.'

Triona closed her own and shuddered with delight. 'I can't wait until Wednesday.'

Juno gazed at the Ridgeway again. Will was still stroking her leg, she noticed. Backing away, she fell over Blind who was pigging out on the leftovers from Will's plate, discarded on the grass at his feet.

He yelped in alarm, lips curling, drooling from too much beef vindaloo.

The dogs were back! That meant Jay was too.

As she raced towards the house, she crashed into Jez coming the other way, swinging his car keys between his fingers.

'You're not going to like this, bundle,' he whispered in Juno's ear. 'But I just nipped out to the car for a packet of fags and saw your American friend leaving.'

'Jay's gone?' Juno gaped at him, suddenly feeling as though her eye sockets were housing two ping-pong balls, and her lungs playing host to a couple of wind machines.

Jez pulled an awkward face. 'He had a passenger in that cute little sports car of his. She seemed to be wearing an enormous pair of Wellington boots.' He glanced across to where Lydia's strappy red sandals were still lying at the foot of the apple tree.

The ping-pong balls mutated into tennis balls, the wind machines turned into flame throwers.

'Oh, Christ, not Lydia?' Juno croaked. How could she?

'Not many tall, sexy platinum blondes around these parts.' Jez shrugged, gathering her into a tight hug. 'Although I think I can feel a short, sexy one coming on right now.'

If only he knew the irony of his words, Juno realised, as a period pain tweezered out the core of her belly button.

It took ages to throw everyone out – sobering up the drivers and trying to work out who had come in what clothes. It was an unwritten rule that they all trooped off to the Smithy Inn after one of Juno's boozy lunches, staying there for a lock-in until they passed out, but she wasn't remotely in the mood.

Talking animatedly on one of his mobile phones, Will

Pigeon gave her a thorough farewell grope which Juno was too distracted to deflect. His fudge brown eyes met hers fondly as he chatted to a punter. 'You know those tickets you wanted for the Marber play, mate? I might be able to do you a deal. How's Thursday grab you? . . . 'Bye, sweetheart. Great lunch.'

Bruno pecked her embarrassedly on the cheek as he left, hanging back to deliver a gruff Irish apology for causing such a scene before bolting off in the direction of his rusty yellow TR7.

The Couples – blissfully unaware of anything other than their drunken happiness – kissed Juno gratefully as they left. They all assumed that Jay was still around, keeping the on-off low profile he had been all day.

'I like your new man.' Ally cuddled her tightly. 'Say goodbye to him from us. By the way, can you baby-sit next Wednesday night?'

'Bit busy,' Juno abbreviated tightly, having trouble talking around the lump in her throat.

Jez found that he had an extra passenger on the return journey, as Odette and Barfly were now snogging openly.

'She'll regret that when she's sober and the cold sores start stinging.' Lulu cuffed Juno on the arm. 'Still, I regret being sober when I'm sober.' She dropped her voice to a husky growl. 'I'm sorry. Jez told me what happened, pet. When will you ever learn to act upon it?'

Juno felt tears threaten at that moment, but she thought determinedly of European Monetary Union and the moment passed. Numbly, she hugged Triona and Horse – whom she failed to notice was still naked – and waved them all goodbye.

In a daze, she started to clear up but there was just too much mess. She didn't know where to start, so she redistributed. She was simply moving it from one surface to another. Three broken plates later she gave up.

Instead, she sat by the phone like an obsessive crank caller, dialling Lydia's numbers and the Belsize Park flat in turn. There was no answer at either. She tried so many times that her fingers worked faster than a speed-dial button.

Just before eight, a car drew up on the gravel drive and Juno beat the dogs to the door, not noticing the pain shooting through her wonky ankle as she flew outside to see who it was.

But it was just her mother returning from Scotland with Baz her driver. Three sets of feet crunched through the gravel to the lych-gate. There was someone else with them – a tall, thin figure with a shock of blond hair.

Judy eclipsed the figure from view as she swept through the gate and gathered Juno into a much-needed comfort hug.

'Pusscat!' She cupped Juno's face. 'Did you have a fun lunch? I brought something delightfully Scottish back with me. We found him wandering along the verge near Sparsholt quite by accident. I think he's one of yours.'

The tall, thin figure appeared through the gate and, flicking back his cherubic locks, flashed Juno a broken-toothed smile.

''Lo, Juno – sorry I'm late,' Finlay said sheepishly. 'I had trouble getting a lift. I found these in a ditch.' He held up a pair of familiar-looking Wellington boots.

Juno burst into tears.

'Oh, Finlay, I'm sorry – I think Lydia and Jay have gone off together.'

'I thought they might, sugar,' he sighed.

'We're talking about darling Lydia and that sweet boy Jay, am I right?' Judy draped a warm, doughy arm over each of their shoulders and coaxed them inside. 'Now which of you is in love with who?'

'Your mother's psychic,' Finlay whistled.

'Is in Germany, alas,' Judy sighed. 'If Howzat were here, he might be able to tell you how this will all work out. I, however, can only make you both a cup of tea and offer useless motherly advice.'

When Juno got back to London on Sunday evening, there was a note from Jay on the mantelpiece and a tearful message from Lydia on the answerphone.

Finlay – who'd hitched a lift back with Juno and had helped

carry Uboat's tank back up to the flat – was brave enough to handle both while Juno cowered on the sofa.

They contradicted one another, but neither was cheering.

Lydia's message was accompanied by a lot of background motorway noise.

'I'm sorry I ran away like that. Oh, Joo, I love you but I've done something awful. I don't think you're ever going to forgive me for this. I do love you. Thing is, I think I'm a bit of a kleptomaniac. I just stole something from you – oh God, this is awful. But you did keep telling me that you hated it – that you didn't want it. And I simply adore it. I thought I was doing you a favour, but now I come to think about it, I'm not really, am I? You might rather like it after all. You're such a projector, I can never tell. I love you. Did I say that already? God, I feel awful about this . . . oh, we're going under a bridge in a – ' The line went dead and the machine clicked into Loyd Grossman time-stamp mode. 'Sateeeuurday, seeixx fifty-teuw peee-emmm.' It had been left less than an hour after Lydia and Jay had left the party.

'She always was a fast mover,' Juno said in a small voice.

'*Very* fast mover,' Finlay groaned when he read Jay's note. 'He's fucking well moved in with her!'

'What?' Juno snatched the note and read it.

'J. She's asked me to go visit with her. I'm facing up to my future, I hope yours works out too. I'm only sorry I got in the way. Good luck. J.' The two Js book-ending the little message was almost more painful to Juno than the words between.

'Doesn't think much of himself.' Finlay looked over her shoulder, re-reading the note. 'Tiny handwriting, and he crosses his Js low on the top – look. Very insecure. Darling Lydia will eat him for breakfast.'

But Juno was already racing to Sean's bedroom.

All Jay's things had gone. There was no sign at all he'd ever slept there. It was as clinically empty as the day he'd moved in. Juno threw herself on to the bed and snorted the sheets. They smelled of Persil Automatic.

Chapter Thirty-Five

GWC called Juno into his office the moment she arrived at Immedia on Monday morning.

'I trust you appreciated your break?' he asked as she distract-edly moved his hat stand to one side so that she could keep an eye on Lydia's empty desk through his partition window.

'Depends which break you're talking about,' she muttered darkly. 'Ankle or heart?'

GWC looked non-plussed for a moment before launching into the little speech he'd been practising in front of the mirror all weekend and had been looking forward to delivering with a mixture of relish and terror.

'You're very valuable to us here at Immedia, Juno. We don't want to lose you.' He flashed a smarmy smile, smoothing his tie over his pigeon chest and moving his breath freshener from left to right cheek. 'But we feel it's time you had a change. There's a slot in advertising sales – Finlay resigned at the end of last week. You'd have to train, of course, but they're accepting internal applications. I'd like you to try for that.'

'Advertising sales?' Juno gripped tightly on to the hat stand.

'In the light of the Streamline report, we're restructuring the editorial team.' He'd picked up his executive stress ball and was kneading it between his sweaty palms. 'We think sales would be better suited to your – er – effervescence and bubbliness.' He cleared his throat as Juno's eyes narrowed murderously. 'I think you'll agree that the agony columns have got a little stale of late – need a fresh pair of eyes. Big blue ones, in fact.' He sighed dreamily, before pulling himself together and lying unconvincingly, 'This is a boardroom-level decision, I'm afraid – out of my hands.'

'So who's going to write the problem pages?'

'Well, as I said, the decision wasn't mine but . . .' He backed behind his desk. 'Lydia is.'

'Lydia?' Juno glared through the slatted blinds of GWC's office to her friend's empty desk, or the 'card table' as it was known amongst the editorial team, because all Lydia did there was play Solitaire on her computer.

'Yes.' He licked his lips nervously, not liking the way Juno was eyeing up his hat stand. 'She was most impressive last week. Most impressive. It was noticed at the highest level. And it wasn't an easy decision on her part, I can assure you. She took a lot of persuading.' A very pleasurable lunch indeed, GWC recalled.

'Did she?' Juno snarled.

He backed further behind his desk. 'She felt a certain degree of guilt that she was in effect stealing your job from under your nose.'

Juno opened her mouth to launch a blistering attack and then closed it again. Then, to GWC's utter amazement, she started laughing. She leant against the hat stand and shook her head in delight.

'It was my *job* Lydia was worried about stealing,' she breathed to herself. 'She said she adored it. She'll probably be bloody good at it too – knows far more about therapy than me for a start.' She started laughing again.

'Yes indeed,' GWC brayed along too, delighted that she was taking it so well. 'She's in Totnes attending a three-day psycho-sexual counselling workshop as we speak. She is planning to bring the problem pages bang up to date by turning them into more focused individual case-histories – following a specific issue like impotence with on-going therapy sessions each week.'

'I'm sure you'll find that helpful to your circulation.' Juno beamed at him.

'Ha, ha!' GWC humoured her gamely. 'Very witty. Now can we encourage that sharp mind of your towards sales, that's what I want to know? The salary is admittedly a little lower than you're used to, but I'm certain a bright little thing like you'll make it up in commission in no time. Um – put the hat stand down, Juno, there's a good girl!'

Uma looked up from her monitor as there was a loud scream followed by the sound of shattering glass at the opposite end of the office. The rest of the astonished Immedia staff fell silent and everyone watched as Juno marched towards the lifts with her signed picture of Jimmy Saville under one arm and Finlay's one of Tony Blackburn under the other.

'Juno child, what have you done?' Uma barred her way.

'I tried to break through the glass ceiling, but I missed. I'm going to stand up for myself and do stand-up full-time. I should have done it years ago.'

Uma cocked her head and looked into Juno's excited face, the shiny grey eyes and pink cheeks. It wasn't the expression of someone who bore an instant's regret.

'Oh, child, I know you'll be a success.' She gave her a tight hug. 'You were wasted in this place. But I'm gonna miss you. Come in for a biscuit sometimes.'

'I think GWC would get security to throw me out.' Juno glanced back towards his shattered office, in which he was squawking furiously into his phone. 'Looks like he's trying to right now. Bang goes my reference.'

Uma chuckled. 'I don't think security will oblige.'

News of her dramatic resignation had indeed reached Mel the security guard by the time Juno walked out of the lifts. He was hovering lovingly by the swing doors.

'I hate that geezer. You should have shoved that hat stand where the sun don't shine.' He grabbed her hand and kissed it with a flourish, scratching her knuckles with his moustache. 'Don't make yourself a stranger.'

'I don't think I could get any stranger right now,' Juno

sighed, thoughtlessly rubbing her damp hand on her trouser leg as she walked through the doors. Behind her, Mel's lip trembled as he watched her go.

Her ankle was still blue and swollen, but she hardly registered the pain as she pounded down the steps of Tottenham Court Road tube station and headed towards the Northern Line. Nor did she care for a moment that she'd just junked in her job. All she could think about was Jay. Her eyes searched the crowds of tourists just in case he was amongst them. Wherever he was, she had a feeling it wasn't Totnes. The knowledge lifted her heart a little.

The answermachine had already filled up when she returned to the flat: friends thanking her for lunch on Saturday, her mother checking she was okay, people from Immedia congratulating her for walking out, her bank manager asking her to pop in for a chat. Juno fast-forwarded each one in the hope that Jay had called, but he hadn't. If only she knew his mobile number, but she had never bothered to ask.

She tried Lydia's mobile again, but it was switched off. Juno guessed she was doing it deliberately, thinking that Juno would be on the warpath. But it wasn't an explanation she was after, it was information. She could forgive Lydia anything just so long as Jay wasn't with her. She wished she'd asked GWC whereabouts in Totnes Lydia's workshop was before she'd thrown his hat stand through his partition. She'd always been hopeless at prioritising.

She read Jay's note again. 'She's asked me to go visit with her.' Who? If it wasn't Lydia, then who? Perhaps it *was* Lydia after all. Oh, God.

She slouched uselessly in front of daytime television, not knowing what to do. She knew she had no real right to try and find out where Jay was. Even if he had gone off with Lydia, she could hardly throw herself between them and claim to have bagsied him first like a child with a chair. She picked up the phone, thinking of trying to track down Will Pigeon, Timon or Dormouse in case he'd been working with them today. She thought of calling Sean to tell him his tenant had gone missing. Triona might have heard from him – she and Jay seemed quite close. In a mad moment, Juno even thought of calling Piers Fox. But every time she started to dial she cut off the tone and pressed the earpiece to her forehead, feeling like a stalker, knowing she had no hold over him. If Jay wanted to go Jaywalking then she had no right to try and stop him.

That evening, Finlay called from his rehab clinic. 'Any news, sugar?'

Juno told him about the incident at Immedia, and Lydia's psycho-sexual impotence workshop in Totnes which she had failed to locate despite several embarrassing calls to Totnes Tourist Information and the Impotence Helpline.

'You should have told me you were planning to quit your job too,' he said lightly. 'We could've had a joint leaving party. Where's Totnes?'

'Devon, I think.' Juno watched as Uboat tottered on to her castle. 'Was the clinic very angry that you ran off like that?'

'Quite the reverse,' he told her. 'Apparently the fact I absconded this weekend and *didn't* get high was a positive assertion of my growth curve – an inverse manifestation of my willingness to free myself of old routines or something. They're so impressed with my progress that I'm told I can now survive on ten hours psycho-babble and foul tea a week, just so long as I don't fuck up this time. They're letting me out tomorrow. Calum's coming down to pick me up.'

'What are you going to do about Lydia?'

'Not much we can do until they get back,' he sighed. 'We can hardly storm down to Totnes like offended parents, can we, sugar? And I'm certainly not going to make any big romantic move with that angry little American prowling round – God knows what you see in him.'

'So you think Jay's definitely with her?' Juno's little hope bubble was starting to develop very thin skin.

'Don't you?'

'Why did she leave a message from a mobile phone if she

was on the way here with Jay at the time? Why not wait till she got here?'

'Maybe she hadn't made those irresistible moves of hers by then,' he sighed dreamily. 'I can see it now – sports car pelting along the motorway in the evening sun, roof open, wind in that beautiful blonde hair as she unflips her phone and leaves a tearful message for her friend. Then she turns to Jay, big blue eyes searching his face for comfort as she asks him if he's ever been to Totteridge. What single, heterosexual man could resist?'

'Totnes, Finlay.' Juno's hope bubble popped. She tried frantically to blow it up again, clutching at any straw to wipe away the picture he had just painted. 'But her mobile phone was dead – the battery ran out earlier that day.'

'So she used his – leaving the faintest smell of her perfume clinging to the soft-touch buttons.' He was still sounding unsympathetically dreamy. 'They're probably laughing about it now in Taunton.'

'Totnes.' Juno winced at the thought. 'How can you be so glib at a time like this?'

There was a long pause. When he spoke again he sounded anything but glib.

'Because it's stopping me calling a cab and calling my dealer,' he said. 'Face it, we can't do anything until Lydia comes back on Wednesday, so we might as well joke about it, not hit the coke about it, huh?'

Juno watched the *Londoners* titles come up on the muted television screen in front of her.

Black Wednesday. She knew precisely where Jay would be then. The only trouble was, she couldn't get near him. The *Londoners* set was as well guarded as a high-security prison.

'I'm not sure I can wait until Wednesday,' she groaned, wishing she could tell Finlay about *Your Life in Front of Your Eyes*, but knowing that Jay would never forgive her. He might only have wanted to share his life-story and not his life with her after all, but it wasn't hers to share around.

Finlay was full of irritating advice. 'Do something to occupy your mind. Look for a job, try to set up some comedy gigs . . .'

'Yes, Mum,' Juno muttered, deciding he'd been in far too many therapy sessions recently. Watching Lily Fuller yelling silently on the television set at Derek the dim bookie, she told Finlay about the Piers Fox workshops taking place in the Ha Ha House. She could hardly muster any enthusiasm for the project now.

But he talked her into it. 'Get your arse down there and try. You've got nothing to lose. If you hate it, walk out. If you get chosen, you'll play one gig at the Ha Ha House – doesn't mean you have to join the bastard's gang. It'll occupy your mind. Come and meet me at the Nero afterwards – I'll be there all day.'

'So that's how you're planning to occupy your mind, is it?'

'My mind is fully occupied with Lydia,' he said calmly. 'But I'm patient and I have less to lose.'

'What do you mean by that?'

'You've already tasted the fruit. You know what Lydia's getting. I can only dream.'

After she'd rung off, Juno lay on Jay's bed for a few hours, staring at the ceiling, imagining him in bed with Lydia in Totnes, telling her about his troubles, his awful childhood, his mother, the guilt he was channelling into his work. And Lydia – fresh from her counselling workshop – would stroke his forehead and gently persuade him that he was a good person, a worthy person, a person who deserved happiness and love. Unlike Juno, she would know what to say, how to make him open up yet further, how to keep him calm and support him towards Wednesday's ordeal.

Juno cringed as she remembered her own pathetic offer to go to the Belle Winters recording and 'hold your hand if you like'. She wasn't exactly Claire Rayner. Thank God she'd junked in her job – she'd be sued under the trades descriptions act. Jay had thought he was talking to an agony aunt and all he'd got was antagonistic taunts.

She closed her eyes tightly shut and found herself suspended above Lydia and Jay's bed again. This time they'd stopped talking and were doing exquisite things to each other, two beautifully toned bodies sliding and writhing like a machine.

Juno's eyes snapped open. There was nothing for it. It was going to have to be the Phil Collins album.

When the needle started jumping during 'In The Air Tonight', she remembered something with a groan.

She'd pretended she had someone in her room on the Friday night he'd come back with his friends. The night she'd been listening to Phil Collins. She'd let Jay believe that she spent the night with John in a childish attempt at making him jealous. For all he knew, she and John could sleep together on a regular basis – he'd called the flat enough times since Jay had been living there, offering her a reheated takeaway in Clapham.

She closed her eyes and found herself back in the hotel room in Totnes, where Lydia and Jay were nestling in each other's arms in a state of post-coital bliss.

'Juno was so hurtful to me,' Jay was saying. 'I thought she was a nice person, but she's just a good-time girl who treats men like dirt.'

'It's okay, baby.' Lydia kissed his little icicle tattoo. 'I'm here now.'

On Tuesday morning, Juno reluctantly followed Finlay's orders and attended the comedy workshop, taking her squeezebox and her heavy heart to central Soho. She only went because it was better than sitting at home staring at the walls and thinking about Jay, but she felt about as sociable, dynamic and funny as a wart on a hand model. She had developed an almost pathological hatred of Piers Fox. It hardly put her in a workshopping frame of mind.

'Photographs?' the girl on the door demanded, ticking her name off on a list.

'I don't have any prints,' Juno apologised, passing over her photocopies.

'Your hair's changed.' The girl glanced critically from Juno's smily mugshots to her sad-eyed face.

'I've changed.' She flashed a weak smile and wandered into

the legendary Ha Ha House – the venue that every comic wanted to crack, with its mouth-shaped stage and make-or-heartbreak reputation. It was a disappointingly empty black hull of working lights and stale beer fumes by day, not the terrifying fusion of hushed anticipation, intimate spotlight, smoky air and adrenaline Juno had expected, had hoped would snap her out of her listless mood.

None of the top comediennes whom Piers had assured her were eager to join his troupe had bothered to turn up for this low-key Tuesday workshop. Juno found herself amongst a bunch of actresses and models who seemed amazed to hear that she'd done any stand-up at all. Studying the universal blonde legginess of everyone else as they waited to start, she started to wonder what sort of operation Piers Fox was running. Was he putting together some sort of Benny Hill cast, minus the great man himself? In that case what was her role supposed to be? Bella Umberg? Or the little bald bloke who was always being slapped on his pate? If she wasn't currently unemployed, she'd be tempted to leave straight away.

As the workshop got underway, she grew more and more disillusioned. It was hopelessly disorganised, more like an open audition in a provincial village hall than an attempt to select the funniest women in London.

Frank Grogan, an ageing, once-famous Irish comic, was supposed to be leading the 'bonding session', but was far more interested in trying to get off with Piers Fox's young PA than assessing the comic talent. A Rothman's dangled at all times from his sneering lips and his eyes were so narrowed against the smoke that Juno was surprised he could see anything at all. With a glass of Scotch in one hand and the PA's knee in the other, he asked the various wannabe female comedians to throw a basketball around the room and tell a joke every time they caught it.

Juno joined in half-heartedly, and was surprised to hear laughter whenever she gained possession of the flying plastic globe. She wondered at first whether it was just because she was such a hopeless catcher and kept dropping it. She was hardly on top form – she was coming out with utter rubbish – but something about her dead-pan, careless attitude brushed a feather along everyone's ribs. Even Frank Grogan looked up from the PA's legs to smile at her – and he was a man who no longer bothered to catch the eyes of contestants on the satellite TV quiz shows he hosted.

Improvised sketches followed, and Juno's was so abysmal she was again tempted to walk out. The leggy blonde she'd been paired with couldn't stop giggling. But mercifully Frank barely seemed to notice as he downed his third Scotch and whispered into the PA's ear. Although she was making copious notes, Juno had a feeling they bore little relation to what Frank was saying.

She found her mind drifting again and again to Jay.

When she took her turn on stage, she played her squeezebox. Unnoticed by Juno, Frank Grogan bothered to look up again, the creased lids lifting to reveal three-quarters of his bloodshot green eyes as she sang 'Hopelessly Devoted to Hugh' – a quirky, bittersweet ballad about a girl who has a crush on someone who ends up dating her best friend.

The song made Juno think about Jay. She belted it out so passionately that she almost believed he'd be able to hear it wherever he was right now.

After she'd finished, she sat alone on the stage, utterly played out.

'Name?' Frank took the cigarette from his mouth to speak for the first time that day.

'Juno.'

'No, I don't know – that's why I'm asking you.' He yawned, revealing a lot of yellow teeth. 'Come on, woman, surely you remember it? Think back to when you got out of bed this morning and the bloke you were with said: "What did you say your name was again?" What was your answer then?'

There was some sycophantic tittering amongst the blondes.

Juno was fed up. She knew she wasn't what they were looking for. She preferred to struggle on alone surviving on door-splits and dole cheques than pander to the likes of Piers

Fox and his drunken, letchy, has-been henchman. He was already exploiting Jay. There was no way she was going to allow him to exploit her too.

'D'you know that men with small penises have appalling memories?' She glared at him.

Frank sucked in one cheek and rubbed his mouth with a nicotine-stained thumb, eyes narrowing. Then the PA consulted her clip-board and whispered something in his ear which made him cackle bronchially.

'You can leave – we don't need you here any more,' he told Juno, lighting up another Rothman's with the butt of the first.

So that was it, she realised. Down to the job centre first thing in the morning. She gathered up her squeezebox dejectedly and trailed past Frank and the PA.

'Get here around eight-thirty tomorrow night,' he called out as she reached the double doors. 'You'll be on in the first half. Juno Glenn, right?'

Juno turned and gaped at him in amazement.

'Piers told me to look out for you.' He winked one bloodshot eye, inhaling deeply on his cigarette. 'I was expecting some mouthy Bette Midler type – all tits and no subtlety – but you're quite different. See you tomorrow.'

In a daze, she wandered along to meet Finlay in the Nero where they sat in companionable silence. Juno gazed into a black coffee, thinking about Jay, her feet propped up on her squeezebox as she dreamed up lyrics for a song about what had happened between them.

Finlay was thinking about Lydia and working his way through a match book every few minutes as he ripped off the spills and piled them up in front of him like Pickastix.

After about an hour, he suddenly looked up as he remembered what Juno was supposed to be doing.

'Why aren't you still at the workshop? I thought you said it wouldn't finish till late.'

'I already got the gig.' She shrugged. 'But I'm not sure I want to do it.'

He nodded and they lapsed into silence again. Ten minutes later, he looked up once more, blinking the blond curls from his eyes.

'I'm going to Totnes.' He got up and marched towards the door. Two minutes later, he was back. 'Where did you say it was again?'

Chapter Thirty-Six

Lydia Morley was eyeing an attractive young therapist across the crowded Tom Jones Reception Suite in the Totnes Forton Motor Lodge when there was something of a commotion in the foyer. Ignoring the fracas going on behind the double doors – just as she was ignoring the interminable lecture being given by a worthy Relate counsellor in front of her – Lydia tried to read the name badge on the lapel of the small, dark-haired dish in the corduroy jacket. He look very intense and clever, with a face like a Siamese cat – all cheek-bones and big blue eyes. Hauntingly sensitive.

The argument in the foyer was getting louder. The thickly powdered, thickly lacquered, thickly thick receptionist who had earlier accused Lydia of stealing a novelty cheese display from the lodge restaurant was clearly trying to bar the entrance of a late-comer on the other side of the doors.

'It's fully subscribed, sir.'

Not taking much notice, Lydia noticed a sprinkling of dandruff on those corduroy shoulders and wrinkled her nose. The Relate counsellor was waffling on about couples sleeping together without trying to have penetrative sex now. As if! She caught Corduroy's eye for a wink and he almost tipped over backwards on his chair.

'I want to join the impotence workshop!' wailed a voice on the other side of the door.

'Of course, patience is the key,' the Relate counsellor said in a soothing, Ovaltine voice. 'And patience is the one thing that most of us lack when it comes to sex.'

'Let me past, you Rimmel monster!' demanded the voice from the foyer.

Lydia licked her lips and eyed Corduroy again. He was staring back at her in total wonder now, jaw hanging, ears scarlet. As he glanced nervously over his shoulders to check that she wasn't looking at anyone else, his note-pad slid from his fingers.

Smirking, Lydia looked away. This was getting boring. The argument outside, by contrast, was hotting up. She listened in.

' – can't let you in if your name's not on the list, sir. If you continue to behave like this, I'll have to ask you to leave the motor lodge.'

'I'm going nowhere, sugar,' growled a strangely familiar voice. 'I have to go in there *right now*.'

'They break for lunch in ten minutes. You can have a word with the workshop liaison officer then.'

'I can't wait ten more minutes. I've waited months!'

'I'm warning you, sir – I am about to call security.'

The Relate counsellor was doing her best to be heard above the din. 'Men all too often want to rush things, when the key is "hold back, hold back, hold back" until you cannot hold on any longer. And then you know that you are re—'

'Don't you see, you stupid cow?' the voice screamed, and suddenly the doors burst open, a figure of divine, decadent beauty framed between them. 'I need help!'

It was Black Wednesday. Juno dressed from head to foot in her favourite colour to match her mood. Finlay hadn't called, so she assumed he was using the same method to reach Totnes that he had employed to get to lunch on Saturday. He should really invest in a Railcard.

It was only early afternoon, but she couldn't bear to be cooped up in the flat any longer. Every room reminded her of Jay – they had made love or war in all of them. To add to her tortured claustrophobia, Poirot kept screeching out phone impersonations and telling her that she was a loser. Juno couldn't agree more.

She'd lost Jay, her job and her appetite. The only positive thing to come out of the last three days was the fact that she'd consequently lost several of her spare tyres.

She almost walked over the post in the hall on her way out, there were so many bills addressed to her that she couldn't face looking through it, but a large hand-written envelope caught her eye and she stooped to pick it up.

Inside were half a dozen glossy ten-by-eights. They were all copies of a photograph of her taken at the Church House lunch. Juno stared at it in amazement. She hadn't even been aware of being photographed. She was laughing, head tilted back towards what looked like one of the sitting-room sofas. She looked so happy and animated – almost beautiful. It must have been taken early on, before they headed outside to eat, while she was still in a daze over Jay's amazing behaviour and secretly dreaming about lifting ginger-haired toddlers over puddles. Long before he prowled around the garden snapping pictures of everything in sight except her.

She flipped them over. On the back of one were three little words – the most romantic message she had ever received in her life.

'Let's hold hands.'

She checked the postmark in a frenzy of excitement, but there wasn't one. He'd hand delivered it! He'd been to the flat and not rung the buzzer – just walked up the steps, pushed the envelope through the door and walked away. Juno wanted to scream with frustration. When had it been? Ten minutes ago? Last night?

She clutched the envelope to her chest and bolted outside, hurrying to Fitzrovia so urgently that she screamed at the tube doors for not opening fast enough, and then razored begonia heads from ground-floor window boxes with her rucksack as she hurtled through somnolent garden squares.

Thankfully, Triona was in her flat, having taken the day off from Fame Fatale to prepare herself in body and mind for the Belle Winters life story. She was nose-deep in *Take A Bow Belle*, and eating chocolates from a vast fruit bowl when the doorbell went.

'Do you have Jay's mobile phone number?' a muffled voice hiccuped into the entryphone.

'No, I don't,' Triona laughed. 'Don't tell me you've locked yourself out of the flat again, Juno? You're hopeless. Come in and fetch my spare set.'

She let Juno and her squeezebox into the flat. One look at her puffy-eyed face and Triona uncorked a bottle of Merlot.

When she heard the full story, she handed Juno her *Your Life in Front of Your Eyes* pass.

Juno handed it back. Triona threw it at her. Juno deflected it. There was a brief Henman/Rusedski rally before Juno finally conceded defeat.

'I'll make this up to you,' she promised.

'You'd better.' Triona gave the ticket a last, regretful look. 'That boy has been mad about you since he arrived in this country.'

'He has?' Juno gaped at her in disbelief.

'As if you didn't know!' Triona pulled back her chin.

'Did he tell you then?'

'Of course not – you know how private he is.' She popped a chocolate in her mouth and eyed Juno's outfit critically.

'So it's just a guess.' Juno slumped miserably back in her chair and looked at the ticket. 'He might not even want me there tonight – he hasn't been in touch since Saturday. Just to deliver the photographs.'

'Of course he'll want you there!' Triona howled in frustration. 'You're the only one he's told about all this. "Let's hold hands." You matter to him. He thinks you don't give a fig in return – that all he is to you was a quick fling when you were feeling low about John. You've got to prove differently.'

'Are you sure?'

'You're made for each other, Juno! Talk about protesting too much. You two are like Swampy and Animal. I've been on the blower to Sean every two minutes about it.' She got up and danced through her kitsch, cluttered flat to fetch her make-up suitcase. 'You and Jay are the most hopeless pair of fantasists I've ever met. You both imagine all sorts of dramatic scenarios for each other which aren't really going on.'

'He really was abandoned at JFK as a baby,' Juno assured her. 'And he really did have a lousy upbringing which led him to do a lot of really stupid things. I shouldn't have told you, but I had no choice. Tonight could crucify him.'

Triona hawked her case over to Juno and sat beside her. 'I know, and I shouldn't be flippant. It's going to be torture for the poor sod appearing in front of all those people to bare his soul – which is why you've got to look your best when he gazes out at the audience and spots you waiting to rush up and look after him afterwards.' She clicked open her case. 'I've got an amazing stretchy Herve Leger dress which I'm certain you'll fit into.'

'Triona!' Juno sighed in disbelief. 'Do you actually know the *meaning* of the word "flippant"?'

As he rode up the escalators at Leicester Square, Jay read the adverts to his left – several were for clinics specialising in family planning and emergency contraception, he noticed irritably.

Almost at the top, he spotted an advert which made him walk backwards, treading water on the escalator to stay in one place long enough to read it. FEVER BITCH shouted a plump cartoony headline. Beneath, the poster promised 'London's hottest female stand-ups – so shocking you'd better be sitting down to hear them. Book early'. Another sticker had been strapped across it at a later date and was already peeling off. Lifting it up, Jay read 'Sold Out'.

'Oi, mate – get a move on,' moaned a voice from behind as the upward queue started to buckle.

Jay pounded up the last few steps two at a time.

Will Pigeon was in his usual spot on the corner of West Street, close to The Ivy's stained-glass windows. He was, as usual, talking into several phones at once.

'Jay boy!' He slapped him on the back, still chatting into a phone. 'Yeah – call you later if I see them coming out together, Elbows.' He pressed the 'Cancel' button and ignored another ringing phone as he looked at Jay. 'Where've you been, mate? Haven't seen you all week.'

'Just looking up a few relatives,' he said evasively, feeling through his pockets and pulling out a wad of cash. As he did so an airline docket fell out on to the pavement.

Will stooped to pick it up. 'Don't tell me you're leaving England already?'

'Dunno – it depends.'

'Nice one. So what can I do you for? I don't do flight upgrades, I'm afraid.' He winked, handing it back.

'I wanna buy a ticket, Will.'

'You want to buy a ticket?' he balked, non-plussed for a moment. 'From me?'

'That's what you do, isn't it? Sell tickets? There's a show I wanna catch tonight.'

All Will's phones were ringing now. Different shrills and shrieks and musical jingles were issuing from every pocket of his John Richmond jacket like Jean-Michel Jarre trying out a stint as a one-man-band.

Suddenly Will's big smile wrapped around his face like a snake round a tree and he clicked his fingers in recognition. 'Don't tell me! You want the same thing as that pretty little flatmate of yours wanted?'

'Huh?'

'That's brilliant – even Elbows didn't think of that. Taking shots from inside the *Londoners* studio. *Su*perb.'

Jay blinked. 'Juno tried to buy tickets for the Belle Winters recording?'

'I told her there weren't any more to sell. Gold dust, angel dust and moondust all rolled into one, those things. Terribly disappointed, she was. Got the right hump afterwards – threw us all out.'

'Out of where? When was this?'

'Saturday lunchtime, mate. You were there, remember? Saw you towing a load of dogs around Oxfordshire. Terrifying sight.

Then I walked in the house and bumped straight into little Juno
– a very pleasant experience given her soft corners. What a little
hostess, huh? Sensational food, great people.'

'I thought she was sick?' Jay scratched his short hair.

'Sick?' Will looked confused. 'Looked healthy enough to
me, if a bit down in the dumps when she found out I couldn't
get her a ticket for tonight. Like I say, I'd get you one if I
could, but they're harder to lay your hands on than a cripple
at a healers' reunion.'

Jay winced. 'I don't want a ticket for the Belle Winters
recording, Will. I want a dream ticket. I'm just hoping you
can help out.'

Belle Winters – a tiny figure in sparkling blue sequins – stood
in front of a huge, blown-up photograph of herself, giggling
delightedly and ruffling the hair of her five-year-old grandson.

'Belle Winters,' boomed the deep brown voice of the
show's host, Richard Anson, launching into the classic mantra,
'Tonight, Your Life was In Front Of Your Eyes. Tomorrow,
it will once again be ahead of you. Goodnight.'

'What!' Juno wailed from the studio audience. 'Is that it?'

The final 'and here they are now . . .' section of Belle
Winters's biography of surprises had been taken up by her
grandchildren, who'd been flown over especially from Australia,
tripping on to the stage with wide-open arms and gurgling smiles
to be gathered into that famous tanned cleavage and hugged to
bits. Jay hadn't even been mentioned. Where was he?

The titles were rolling now, a floor manager held up a board
saying 'APPLAUSE' and the invitation-only studio audience –
mostly *Londoners* crew, friends and family – clapped and cheered
tearfully. As the cameras panned across them, they captured a
small, buxom blonde in a very tight dress fighting her way from a
central seat to the exit, carrying a squeezebox under one arm.

'Isn't that the new Page Three girl Wayne's dating?' One
of the *Londoners* make-up artists tucked her chin in critically
and turned to her friend from Costume. 'She's in a hurry to
get somewhere.'

'Cystitis, I'll bet.' The friend offered her a boiled sweet. 'Look at Belle – she's crying. Ah!'

Juno could see Piers Fox disappearing through swing doors into a corridor, his electronic personal organiser held open in front of him, his phone to his ear.

Tripping over a pile of cables, she raced after him.

'Don't leave the studio yet!' A women in headphones leapt forward to try and bar her way, but Juno dodged past her.

She galloped into the corridor, desperately scanning its echoing length for a glimpse of red hair. She finally spotted him making a mobile phone call by a coffee machine. As Juno dashed forward, the super-high shoes Triona had lent her slipped on the polished floor and she flew the last few feet, slapping into the buttons of the coffee machine which started to dispense hot chocolate on to Piers's leg.

He stepped back in alarm, phone still pressed to his ear.

'Where is he?' she demanded.

'Bring the car to the main entrance in half an hour, Mark.' He held up his hand to Juno like a traffic cop, warning her to wait. 'There's some godawful after-show drinks party going on here which I have to put in an appearance at, but I need to be in the West End by nine at the latest.'

'Where is he, Piers?' Juno asked frantically. 'Why wasn't he on the show?'

Cutting off his call, he turned to look at her, dour face impassively appraising the irate little blonde in the hour-glass dress. He knew he'd met her before, but couldn't place where. She must be a relative of Belle's – perhaps one of the daughters. Had they left her father out of the show? If so, which one was hers? The East End villain? The West End restaurateur? The Italian count? The chat-show host with the wig? He loathed getting these things wrong.

'He's probably in hospitality,' he improvised, smiling frostily. 'I'm afraid time was very tight – some guests had to be dropped.'

'Jay was *dropped*?' Juno looked up and down the corridor. 'I must see him. Where's hospitality?'

'Jay?' Piers cancelled the smile.

'Yes, Jay,' Juno wailed, furious that he was being so super-cool about it. 'The abandoned baby whom Belle always wondered about, remember? He was supposed to come on at the end of the show. Now where the fuck's hospitality?'

'I don't know what you're talking about,' Piers said smoothly, ever the PR man. She clearly wasn't one of Belle's mob, but she looked very familiar. She could be press sniffing around the story.

'Don't talk shit!' Juno was fuming. 'I know what you wanted him to do. Such exploitation, but he was willing to go through with it if it helped him track down his mother – and now you've dumped him from the running order because time's too tight.'

'The production team decided that Jay was too difficult to deal with.' He cleared his throat. 'He was highly unco-operative, and there was the threat of adverse publicity con-sidering his previous – er – career.'

'You can talk, Foxy,' shrilled a high voice from the opposite end of the corridor and there was a clacking of heels as two of the most famous legs in show business swung their shapely way towards Piers and Juno. Sequins glittered in the institutional, neon-lit corridor, as incongruous as a tiara on a Rainmate.

Juno gazed at superstardom in the flesh – it looked smaller, slimmer, friendlier, and it was offering her a Silk Cut Menthol like a normal human being.

She shook her head distractedly and it suddenly occurred to her that she hadn't smoked in almost a week. 'No, thanks, I've just quit.'

'You clever girl.' Belle Winters lit up. 'Wish I could. Bloody No Smoking studios. They ask us to go outside, but I say the corridor's as far as I get.'

Juno couldn't believe it. The diva of the small screen was whingeing about the smoking policy like an employee at Immedia. She guessed Belle must assume that she was Piers's assistant or something. He was all obsequious smiles now, trying hard to elbow Juno discreetly out of the way. She stayed put, digging Triona's six-inch parquet-prickers into the mottled grey linoleum, determined to find out where Jay was.

There was clearly something of an after-show party getting underway in the studio. The babble of conversation and laughter grew louder and one or two people started to spill out on to the far end of the corridor to light cigarettes. Two of Belle's many grandchildren charged past, screaming gleefully. Piers, who loathed children, shuddered involuntarily.

'That was a lovely surprise, darlin',' Belle was saying to him, 'so moving. And so clever of you to get half an hour's worth of material out of my life that didn't have a whiff of scandal attached it.' She let out her trademark naughty giggle. 'Now I'm afraid I've got a bit of bad news for you, darlin' – I feel ever so mean about it, especially as you helped organise all this for me.'

'What news?' He looked at her with his squeezed lime eyes.

Belle glanced at Juno apologetically, clearly wanting her to push off. Piers elbowed her again, wanting to her push off too, with no apology attached.

Juno didn't want to be rude to Belle Winters of all people, but she really needed to know where Jay was. It was all very well lurking about in a corridor while the most famous woman in soap chatted to her agent, but she had a mission which she felt superseded celebrity. Besides, she'd got here first.

'Please just say where Jay is, Piers, and I'll go away,' she pleaded. 'When did you tell him he was being scrapped from the show? Is he still here?'

A little bit of starry temper flashed in Belle's eyes.

'Who's Jay?' she asked. 'Come to that, who are you, darlin'?'

'I'm Juno Fan,' she muttered distractedly. 'I mean, Juno Glenn.'

Piers blinked in recognition.

'The ballsy little comic? Of course, I knew I'd seen you somewhere before. You've changed your hair.' He instantly glanced at his watch. 'Shouldn't you be in the West End? You're on the bill tonight, I believe?'

'Oh, you're in *The Bill*, are you, darlin'?' Belle was chatty again, puffing on her mentholated Silk Cut. 'I love that show.'

For a moment Juno was dumb-struck at the notion of Belle Winters sitting at home watching *The Bill*, but then she pulled herself together and crashed on.

'I'm not going anywhere until you tell me where Jay is,' she told Piers. The prospect that he could be in a room just along the corridor from where she was standing was almost unbearable.

'I'm not at liberty to divulge that,' said Piers with some pleasure. It was his favourite sentence.

'Oh, just tell the poor girl, Piers,' Belle piped up indignantly, stubbing out her cigarette with a tiny blue shoe. 'Look how upset she is.'

'Very well, Belle.' Piers smiled sardonically. 'In that case, I can tell you with some confidence that I believe him to be somewhere in the south of Ireland.'

'*Ireland*?' Juno gulped.

Piers nodded his head, pale green eyes narrowing. 'It was decided on Monday that he would not be appearing on the show. A very irritating development, I might say – I had one hell of a job getting all those brats on to a flight from Australi— ouch!' He yelped in pain as his digital organiser was snapped shut on his fingers.

Belle was glaring at him beadily.

'So your friend was going to appear tonight, was he, darlin'?' She turned to Juno, only mildly interested. 'Do I know him?'

Juno was reeling. Poor Jay. His only hope of contacting his mother shattered. Out of his mind with unhappiness, all alone, vacating the flat because he thought she was trying to win back her ex-boyfriend to bring up their child together. So Jay had gone to Ireland, the country he'd always thought his home. He must have flown out there after he'd delivered the envelope of ten-by-eights to the flat as a last farewell gesture. She might never see him again, she realised.

'No, you don't know him.' Piers had started to lead Belle

down the corridor. 'Juno has to leave for a gig straight away, I'm afraid, so can't chat. Let's have that private word you wanted, Belle. Then you can rejoin your family and friends for the party. I've arranged for *Cheers!* magazine to cover it exclusively. They're paying a very tidy sum for the privilege.'

Juno watched them walk away.

'That's nice, darlin',' Belle was saying, 'although it'll be the last twenty per cent you take off me . . .'

Juno dithered, wondering what Jay would want her to do, wherever he was. He had said that Belle Winters was one of his few leads, that she might remember something, however flimsy about the flight. He had been denied his chance to meet her, to appeal on air for his mother, and getting in contact now would be next to impossible. It was hardly every day you bumped into her in a corridor – she was one of the most elusive celebrities in England. But there was Jay's history to think of, and Belle's hatred of the paparazzi. What would he want her to do?

'He was abandoned at JFK airport in 1970,' she blurted out. 'The day you left America.'

Belle turned on one high heel. 'Who?'

'Shut up, Juno! What did you just say, Belle?' Piers was demanding, leaning furiously over the little superstar.

'Jay,' Juno said in a shaky voice. 'As in JFK. That's what he was named after.'

Ignoring Piers who was still spluttering beside her, Belle looked at Juno, big blue eyes as wide as two skimmed milk bottle tops.

'The little baby boy who was left in the airport lounge?' she asked in amazement. 'That's your friend?'

Juno nodded. 'He only found out recently. He came over from America to ask if you remembered anything from that day – anything at all. Piers wanted him to appear on the show tonight as a surprise. Jay was dreading it – all the publicity and razzmatazz – but it was his only chance. Now he's disappeared.' Her voice wobbled.

Belle clicked back towards Juno again. The party was well and truly underway – people kept calling for her. A researcher dashed up to ask her to pose for photographs.

'In a minute, darlin'.' Belle brushed her away sweetly, reaching out to take Juno's hand. 'That poor boy. No wonder you're so worried about him. I'm sure he'll turn up soon.'

Piers had marched up to them and was glaring at Juno.

'You really shouldn't have bothered Belle with this,' he told her frostily. 'She is an extremely busy woman with a punishing schedule. Right now she's – '

'Oh, shut your trap, Piers.' Belle waved him away, cupping Juno's hot cheek in her famous hand. 'Listen, darlin', when you find him, I'll do all I can to help, I promise. Here.' She clicked open her tiny handbag and took out a card. 'This is the number of my new agent. Call her when you find your Jay and bring him to meet me.'

'Your new agent?' Piers asked in a tight voice.

'That's what I've been trying to tell you.' Belle sighed. 'I'm going to take what *Londoners* are offering me for the new contract. It's more than generous, and I never wanted any more money in the first place. Now push off, there's a darlin' – it's friends and family only.' She gave another trademark giggle and turned on her tiny blue heels to click away with the stressed researcher, blowing Juno a kiss over one sequinned shoulder.

Piers's eyes didn't even flicker a response. He calmly placed his organiser in his jacket pocket, took out his phone and pressed redial.

'Change of plan, Mark, I need the car now. I'll have a passenger with me. I take it you need a lift?' he asked Juno.

'Are you mad?' She gaped at him. 'I'm not doing the show now.'

He sighed impatiently. 'Well, that's your choice. I'm willing to overlook your little outburst just now, if you are.'

'My outburst!' She laughed in disbelief. 'I'm not talking about that – I'm talking about what you did to Jay. I have to find him.'

'Juno,' he rubbed his freckled forehead tiredly, 'it's been a very bad week, and I really don't want to go into this at any length, but I think I should tell you that it was Jay's decision not to appear on the show.'

'His decision?' She reeled back in surprise. 'I don't believe you.'

'Why don't you ask him yourself?' He handed her his phone.

Juno looked at it dumbly for a few moments, half imagining Jay's voice would magically speak out of it at any second and say, 'He's not wrong there, baby.'

Sighing even more impatiently, Piers drew his digital organiser out of his pocket again and clicked a few buttons before reading out a mobile phone number. Juno dialled it with shaking fingers.

It rang – long, strumming notes that mimicked Juno's vibrating heartstrings.

'Yeah?'

'Jay?'

There was a long, long pause. Juno could hear music and chatter in the background.

'Hi there,' he said eventually, voice wary.

She cleared her throat, imagining him sitting in a friendly Dublin bar, an ocean away from her. She tried to keep her voice light and conversationally chatty. 'Piers tells me you're in Ireland?'

'I'm in London.'

'You are?' she croaked, the Irish Channel suddenly narrowing to the width of the Thames in her mind's eye.

Then she heard Jay taking a deep breath. 'You're with Piers now, right? At the *Londoners* studios?'

She swallowed nervously, certain that he'd disapprove of her duplicity. 'Um – yes.'

But to her surprise, his gruff, husky voice was as warm and soothing as a hot toddy. 'So you got your ticket after all, huh?'

'I wanted to be here to hold your hand,' she said in a small voice, aware of how silly it sounded. Beside her, Piers looked up from examining his nails, his Listermint eyes rolling impatiently. 'I thought that's what the note on the photographs meant, but you're not here.'

'No, I'm here.' He sighed. 'And I don't think I can reach out that far. I guess we both got the wrong gig tonight, huh?'

Juno was aware that Piers was looking at his watch and tutting impatiently. 'So where are you?'

'I'm in some godforsaken club in central London,' he said. 'Waiting to see a comedienne I kind of dig.' He paused again, his voice suddenly uncertain. 'D'you want me to leave?'

'No,' Juno said in a tight little squeak. 'Stick around – I hear she's rather good.'

Chapter Thirty-Seven

The traffic was agonisingly slow all the way into the West End from the *Londoners* Surrey-based studios. Juno stared fixedly out of the front window, fingers rapping on her squeezebox case in time to her heart.

It was almost ten to nine by the time they arrived outside the popular little comedy club.

Juno leapt out of the car like Daisy in *The Dukes of Hazzard*, desperate to get inside the club and see Jay, but Piers was even faster, grabbing her arm and policing her up to the crowded Ha Ha House door like a bodyguard, refusing to let her go front-stage before the set started. The only glimpse she got of the audience was the long queue outside, which he propelled her past so fast she couldn't even identify the source of a lone cry of 'Joo!' It had sounded suspiciously like Lydia's voice.

The doorman, recognising Piers, let them straight through to the tiny foyer where the box office was doing great business, despite now offering standing room only. A huge noticeboard with the banner ONE NIGHT ONLY – FEVER BITCH, was covered with ten-by-eights of women's faces – some of which, to her astonishment, Juno recognised as top-drawer comics.

Ever the professional, Piers managed to slap one of the glossy photographs which Jay had taken over the tatty photocopy of Juno as he whizzed her straight past the glass doors to the loud, bustling club, and instead led her up the stairs to the private offices.

'But I've got to speak to Jay!' she wailed in frustration as he took her into the packed dressing room and ordered Frank Grogan to keep a close eye on her. 'I've got to tell him what happened with Belle Winters.'

'I'll do that for you,' Piers offered dryly.

'Are you kidding?' Juno gaped at him. He made a very unlikely Cupid.

'I never "kid" – it's a revolting word which should be restricted to the caprine species.' He caught sight of himself in the full-length mirror and noticed the hot chocolate stain on his trousers with an irritated 'tut'.

'He might not want to talk to you.' She glanced around at the exit, assessing her chances of legging it. Not good. Frank was leaning against the door with an easy smile and hard eyes. He might like her, but he knew who paid for his Rothman's habit.

'I assure you, we parted on speaking terms,' Piers was insisting huffily, a certain amount of professional pride at stake. 'Now would you like me to have a word or not? Because we have to get underway in just a few minutes.'

Juno guessed it was her only chance to get a message to Jay before her act. But she didn't trust Piers. Suddenly she remembered the card Belle had given her. Scrabbling in her bag, she managed to locate it in amongst the rubble of chocolate wrappers. She grabbed a pen too and drew a big arrow, pointing to the name on the card before scribbling 'Belle Winters's agent'. Deciding this wasn't clear enough, she added 'wants to meet you'. Realising this could be misinterpreted, she found just enough space to add 'Belle, that is, not her agent'. There! Clear as day.

'I take it you'd like me to pass that little communication on to Jay too?' Piers asked in a stiff voice, deciding he wasn't cut out to play Cupid either. It was too belittling and time-consuming for a man of his stature. But he was eager to get Juno onside. She was the only one of his recommendations that Frank Grogan had let through the workshop selection process. He held out his freckled hand for the card.

'Yes – oh! Hang on,' Juno flipped the card over and scribbled three words before handing it to him.

Shooting her a long-suffering look, Piers headed off, brushing his trouser leg as he went, leaving Frank on the door, a Rothman's dangling menacingly from his mouth.

The functional little room was packed with women dressed in faded black, smoking cigarettes, applying make-up and chatting nervously. Looking around, Juno recognised most as very creditable comics – she'd been on the same bill with at least two before, had seen several others. Frank had clearly been a shrewd operator when selecting the line-up from those low-key workshops. None of them was a leggy blonde. Juno herself was by far the tartiest in her squeeze-me-tight dress.

All the seats and surfaces were occupied by the chain-smoking gaggle – several of whom spotted Juno and said 'hi'. Too distracted to offer more than a nervous smile in return, she perched on her squeezebox and waited, trying to picture Piers Fox singling out Jay for a 'word' in the heaving club bar below her. It wasn't an easy image to conjure. She longed to drill a hole through the floor and peer through it. In fact, cutting a large hole in the floor and lowering herself down there wasn't such a bad idea.

The Ha Ha House had now sold out completely, despite the extra tables and chairs which had been brought in at the last minute. There wasn't even standing room at the bar available. As he descended the back stairs into the foyer, Piers was pleased to notice that the bouncers were turning people away. A tiny, blue-haired female punk in a huge black coat was arguing furiously with one of them.

'Let us in – I've got a comp waiting at the box office!'

'Well, you can fetch it after the show,' said the bouncer, not understanding her Middlesbrough accent. 'Your hair could certainly use it – looks like it hasn't been combed in weeks, titch.'

Peeking through the steamy glass doors to the club proper, all Piers could see was a heaving orgy of sweaty bodies in

sloganned t-shirts and a miasma of cigarette smoke. The sight
– although terrifying – was balm to his eyes as he realised his
girl comics troupe was destined for success. Every table was
loaded down with drinks and skirted by an unravelling hem
of occupied chairs – too many for the circumference of each.
Not that Piers could see much: there were far too many people
in the way, and the glass was dripping with condensation. The
only table in clear view was his own, small, unoccupied one set
very close to the doors – the 'Reserved' sign Sellotaped firmly
to its top to prevent opportunists from whipping it away and
claiming it as their own. He couldn't see Jay Mulligan at all.
Piers took out his mobile phone and decided he should just
call Jay from here. It would be far easier than fighting his way
through all that cigarette smoke and synthetic fibre.

He pressed 'Recall' and turned back towards the foyer,
pinning a freckled finger to one ear to drown out the noise.

A tall, statuesque blonde of quite extraordinary beauty had
been one of the last to get into the club. As Piers heard the
ringing tone in his ear, he was so awe-struck by her looks that
he couldn't remember whom he was calling.

The divine blonde and her companion were watching the
ongoing argument at the door between the midget with electric
blue hair and the bouncer.

'If you don't let me in, you great poof, I'll head-butt you.'

The bouncer laughed condescendingly, catching his mate's
eye. 'Need a stepladder to reach my head, titch.'

'I didn't say I was going to head-butt you up there, did I,
pet? Now are you going to hold on to your helmet, or are you
going to let us in there?'

He let her in. As she marched through the foyer, she shot
a dirty look at the blonde and slammed her way past Piers into
the club, blasting him with the quick rush of hot, smoky air that
escaped in her wake before the doors slammed home again.

He jumped as he realised a voice was talking into his ear.

'Yeah? Who is this? Juno – is that you again?'

He cleared his throat and pressed the 'Cancel' button, still
gazing at the blonde. She was quite, quite ravishing. Delving

in his pocket as if in a dream, he handed her a card with an unctuous smile.

'I'd like you to come into my office. Let's have an informal chat soon. Call me.' With that, he strode upstairs again, his ascent strangely crab-like as he tried to hide the hot-chocolate stain on his trousers from view.

'Who was that?' Finlay asked Lydia as she turned the little rectangle of cardboard over in her fingers.

'Someone called Audrey Gillespie.' Lydia read the type-print and giggled. There were a lot of Biro-scribbles on it about Belle Winters for some reason. On the reverse side were just three words – 'Let's hold hands'.

'The guy's a fucking psycho, sugar,' Finlay laughed.

'My first client then!' Lydia announced excitedly.

'I thought I was your first client,' he grumbled.

'No, Fin.' She kissed her fingers and pressed them to his nose. 'You are my new hobby.' The fingers dropped down to his lips and traced their curves before slipping into his mouth as she shuddered with novel anticipation. 'Do we really have to sleep together for six months without having sex?'

Finlay lifted his hand and pulled her fingers from his mouth in a Groucho Marx impersonation, tapping her knuckles with his forefinger as though tipping off ash. 'So the lady at the workshop said.'

'Better get some good books in then.' She shivered happily. 'I love reading in bed.'

'Like I always shay,' Finlay mimicked Groucho, 'keep your reds under the bed, your well-reads above it. That way you're ready for bed.'

Guarding the dressing-room door like a heavy, Frank watched Juno with a wry smile on his face. 'Wasn't sure you'd come.' He chuckled. 'You didn't seem too enthusiastic on Tuesday.'

'Piers didn't leave me much choice.' She shrugged, gnawing her nails as she wondered what he was saying to Jay.

'He seems to think you have a lot of potential.' Frank admired her cleavage, which Triona's super-tight dress was squeezing upwards like twin air-bags popping out of a flashy sports car. 'You certainly scrub up well.'

'Thanks.' Juno smiled weakly, wondering if she could persuade him to let her out for five minutes.

'You going to sing a song then?' He nodded towards the squeezebox.

Before she could answer, Piers was hastily edging his way back into the crowded room. Freckled nose wrinkling against the thick smoke, he switched off his phone and looked at Frank. 'Front of house say five minutes, okay?'

'What did Jay say?' Juno leapt up.

'Who? Oh, he said thanks.' Piers glanced at her briefly.

'*Thanks*?' Juno wrinkled up her forehead.

'Don't mention it.' Piers smiled coolly, then tilted his head and looked her full in the face, suddenly seeming to remember who she was. 'Now, Juno, I want you to give it the full Mae West chutzpah tonight. I expect great things of you. Between ourselves, you are something of a front-runner.' He didn't drop his flat, sardonic voice at all to say this, and several of the other female comics looked up from gazing nervously at their cigarette ends with narrowed eyes. 'Go out into the audience and frighten them. What's this, by the way?' He kicked at her squeezebox case which she'd been hauling around since they'd met in the television studio corridor. Piers assumed it was some sort of large make-up bag.

'Is that all he said – "thanks"?' Juno was wringing her hands, adding distractedly, 'It's a squeezebox.'

'A what?' Piers eyed it as though it was about to sprout fangs. 'I hope you're minding it for someone else. I'm not looking for the next Victoria Wood, you know. This isn't a regional tour of Midlands civic centres we're setting up here.'

Not listening, Juno remembered the song she'd written the night before. She'd started to compose it in the Nero and written the final verse at three in the morning, sitting on Jay's bed. Piers would hate it, but she didn't care. For this was her chance to see, once and for all, whether Jay Mulligan could take a joke.

Chapter Thirty-Eight

The Ha Ha House was at full capacity, the audience tempted in by heavy advertising, discount door prices and a beer promotion. It was the usual mix of students, tourists, young professionals and rowdy hard-drinking hecklers, but far more of them than ever before for a Wednesday night. Piers had pulled out all the stops to ensure that he had the maximum live reaction from which to judge his selection. The Ha Ha House management was also hanging around front-stage – eager to see if there was any talent to be plucked out. The club was under-represented by women amongst their regular acts.

'This is real make-or-break stuff.' Odette had arrived early to commandeer a table for the 'girls' – herself, Ally and Elsa. 'This place is really buzzin'. I can't wait to get the OD Club underway. They must be raking it in here.'

'If Juno gets into this comedy ensemble, will she still be able to be your *maître* emcee?' Ally asked, hooking her blonde hair behind her ears.

'Bloody hope so.' Odette opened a bag of crisps. 'I can't believe she didn't tell us she had this gig tonight. Piece of luck we were coming anyway, huh?'

'Look who's over there!' Elsa shrieked delightedly, sweeping her springy curls from her face as she pointed out a table on the opposite side of the room. 'It's your man!'

'Oh, no – hide me!' Odette dived down behind her glass, crisps flying.

Barfly was sucking up pints at a table, beergut to the fore. With him was Triona, Souxi the silent fashion accessory friend, and Jay – looking immensely broody and chewing his nails to pieces.

Odette peered around her glass at Barfly.

'What did I see in him?' she groaned.

'Well, whatever it was, you must have liked it,' Elsa giggled. 'Jez told me he kept having to crank up the volume on his car stereo to drown out the sound of slurping.'

'Don't remind me!' Odette covered her face in shame. 'I was so drunk.'

'Jez also says that Juno's sexy American left with Lydia,' Elsa confided in a hush-hush voice.

'Never!' Ally gasped in horror. 'Poor Juno.'

'Blimey!' Odette peered out between her fingers.

'So what's he doing here tonight?' Ally glanced over to where Jay was flossing his front teeth nervously with his thumb nail.

'Check out the bar.' Elsa's big grey eyes swivelled in the opposite direction.

Standing platinum head and shoulders above almost everyone else was Lydia, resplendent in a tiny mini-skirt with an almost indecent split up the side. She was having the usual effect on the surrounding men, who were all vying and joking for her attention. One was admiring her skirt.

'My sides are splitting already!' she shrieked, flashing a length of glossy pale thigh with camp abandon.

The girls didn't notice an even taller, even blonder figure behind her, slouching easily against the bar on his elbows, grinning from ear to ear.

'She's got a nerve – they both have.' Ally bristled and glared at Jay.

The next moment, Frank Grogan strode out on to the famous stage lips and they fell silent, along with everyone else. His dissipated green eyes lifted to half mast as he peered around the room, assessing the tightly packed crowd through a plume of Rothman's smoke. He'd gone to seed so long ago that there was something almost spectacular about him – cultish, potent, and as offensive as cigar smoke in an incubator. He was wearing a crocheted skull-cap to hide his bald patch, a frill-fronted 'seventies dress shirt open to the waist and ludicrously tight leather trousers which strained so much at the waist they were threatening to separate the sediment from the gas in his beer paunch.

'Welcome to Fever Bitch. I'm Frank Grogan. Tonight, I'm changing the habit of a lifetime and coming before the women.' He grinned his lazy, nicotine-toothed smile. 'And if you believe that, you can have my phone number, ladies.'

Barfly almost fell off his seat with booming laughter. The rest of the response was on the embarrassed, tittery side of non-existent.

Hand-picked by Piers for the job, Frank was about as badly placed as Jim Davidson playing the Hackney Empire. Piers settled back at his small, exit-handy table and smirked to himself. If anything was going to highlight his female talent, then Frank would. He wanted a warm-up man who would freeze hell over. That way the female comics had to work twice as hard.

The first two stand-ups on the bill were sharp and well timed, but not original. The huge, rowdy audience responded on cue, but they didn't explode into life; the multitude of hecklers in the packed audience got almost as big a laugh as the comics themselves. The crowd wanted to laugh, but they weren't a charity. Conversations were only slightly hushed as the women fought to be heard over the bustle of the packed club; there was still a long queue at the bar, late-comers darted through tables searching for their companions, the weak-bladdered headed for the loo, others to the cigarette machine, waitresses carried fat burgers and jugs of ale to tables.

Introducing the third act, Frank's voice dropped to a low, gravelly rumble of innuendo.

'A lot of women have squeezed my box over the years, ladies and gentlemen. Quite a few of them have tickled my fancy too, let me tell you. But there's only one that can do both at the same time, and I'd like to welcome her onstage tonight.

She's going to be a star. Put your hands together for the sexy, the squeezy, the ever so cheesy – Miss *Ju*-no Glenn!'

When Juno walked on, there was a flurry of wolf-whistles.

'What *is* she wearing?' Elsa hooted, pulling back her veil of wild curls. 'She looks like Dolly Parton.'

'But does she look sexy or what?' Ally slapped her hands to her cheeks and watched Juno fondly as she slipped the mike down almost a foot to speak into it.

Odette whistled. 'She just has to be my emcee, babes. Forget the stubborn cow business – I'm gonna make her agree.'

At Triona's table, Barfly's pint flew over and Jay jabbed his thumbnail so firmly between his front teeth that it stuck there.

'She is vely beautiful tonight, isn't she?' Souxi said brightly, making Barfly and Triona turn to look at her in wonder. It was the longest sentence they had ever heard her speak. Turning back to watch Juno, Triona saw Jay's eyes out on stalks and smirked. That'd teach Juno to call her flippant.

Juno stared out at the audience, her huge, dark-rimmed eyes table-hopping like a frenzied networker. She smiled sweetly and breathed in her premium-rate voice, 'Hi, good evening. I had a new flatmate move in a couple of weeks ago. An American guy.'

Triona groaned, not daring to look at Jay. What the hell was she doing?

Juno slotted her fingers through the straps of her beloved squeeze box, her gaze roaming the bar and trawling the faces for Jay's, then darting into dark corners and over shoulders. At last she saw him – hunched by the table, yellow eyes narrowed. He was wearing his big leather coat, and looked for all the world the scariest, sexiest Bronx street-criminal to walk into a small London comedy club.

For a moment she faltered, eyes sliding away towards the warmth of the other friends she'd recognised in the crowd.

'Isn't it awful when you suddenly find yourself sharing a house with someone you fancy rotten?' she told them all, spotting Lydia laughing delightedly at the bar and Finlay grinning knowingly behind her. 'You go into best behaviour overdrive to impress them – scrunching down the inner bag in the cereal packet and then actually *inserting* the little cardboard lid tongue in its slot for once . . .'

She saw Elsa and Ally giggling at their table.

'. . . spending ages in the bathroom because you're flossing your teeth for the first time in two years and don't want to walk out and shout "It's free!" until your gums have stopped bleeding like Tim Roth's belly in *Reservoir Dogs* . . .'

Juno's ears were ringing. The audience liked her. They liked her a lot. She dared to look at Jay again. He was staring at his knees, hands raking through his short stubbly hair. Then he looked up and Juno felt every pore on her body tighten in excitement. For a brief instant her mind went completely blank and she almost froze onstage, every word of her act forgotten. The audience around her no longer mattered; there was only one person she wanted to make laugh. She'd touched his body all over, but had yet to find his funny bone. When she spoke again, she was talking just to him.

'. . . you put on lipstick and a seductive outfit to watch *Londoners*, wear high heels to take the bin bag out, and find yourself drying only your sexiest underwear on the radiators.' She looked into those yellow eyes. 'You're so aware of every little thing you do wrong – leaving pubes in the bath or in your teeth, for instance. Or getting home plastered at two in the morning and trying to seduce them. Or poisoning them with your cooking.' She gave her squeezebox a few limbering draws as she spoke, eyes tracing the faces in the audience again, smile widening. 'I gave my flatmate food poisoning a week or so ago. I seduced him too. Here's our story . . . it's called *Hairy Tale of New Yorker*, sub-titled "I seduced an American dude, and then fed him frozen dog-food". Feel free to join in if you know the words. I think you'll recognise the tune.'

As she pulled the first few familiar chords through the corrugated lungs of her favourite old hand-span diva, a few members of the audience let out hoots and claps of recognition. The tune was 'Fairytale of New York', the Pogues classic which

Juno had loved since hearing Shane MacGowan's gravelly butt-end and whiskey voice belting out of her brother's stereo in the 'eighties, accompanied in this irreverent carol by one of her all-time heroines, Kirsty MacColl. Juno had performed it with Jez several Christmases running and knew it backwards. It started with two slow, melancholy verses then flew into a lively gig. As she leaned into the mike, she prayed that the boisterous, easily distracted audience would stick with her until things livened up.

'It was that hot night, babe, in deepest Belsize Park,' she sang, watching Jay rub his forehead in agitation and glance over his shoulder.

'We'd spent the day in bed, humping till it got dark.

And then I cooked a meal, a rare old chilli sauce.

You said it tasted good, but we'd just eaten horse.'

Triona snorted with laughter and looked across at Jay. Was it her imagination, or was a smile starting to creep across his face? Then Juno sang the second, ear-melting verse in her beautiful breathy voice and Barfly whooped with such vocal appreciation that someone from the next table hushed him.

'God, but we felt so ill; no morning after pill

Could pass my lips that day, as passion waned away.

Oh, I fed us dog food; I poisoned our love, Jay,

And it was so, so good. You were a terrific lay.'

With a last sad sigh, Juno launched into a squeezebox riff as the tempo sped up dramatically and the lively, raucous jig began.

Elsa's big grey eyes were almost popping out of her head as she turned to Odette. 'Did you know about this?' she whispered.

She shook her head and winked, laughing as Juno started firing out fast, furiously funny verses.

'You've an arse that's first-class; yes, it's one real cute bum.

But your knack in the sack was rewarded with Chum.

When you woke by my side on that warm summer's night

You were full of dog food, and we had a cat fight.'

Standing by the bar with a bottle of Newcastle Brown Ale pressed to her lips, Lulu threaded her trench-coated arm through Bob Worth's. 'You were right all along, pet. She's going to be famous.'

Bob ruffled her tufty blue hair and grinned as he listened to Juno's glorious bastardisation of one of his favourite songs.

'You were mad, you were sore, you banged the bath-
    room door,
When the puke finished flying, you just howled at me
    more.
When you called me a bitch, I said your peenie's a titch,
So you called me a whore and then we declared war.'

The chorus that followed was so familiar that several of the audience started singing along, then stopped themselves and laughed as they realised that the words were completely different.

'The Lloyd Cole CD on the stereo was singing "Lost
    Weekend",
As I cooked a dog's dinner fit for Man's Best Friend.'

And so the verses flew on, pacy, witty, and occasionally shocking, interspersed with the chorus, which the audience soon caught on to and joined in with rowdy abandon. It was a perfect pub song, pitched just right at the tightly packed, hard-drinking pub crowd.

Sipping a glass of red wine at his table, Piers Fox shuddered with revulsion − at the drink and at the realisation that Juno Glenn was singing a song accompanied by a wheezing musical instrument he thought belonged firmly in small, smelly taverns in Kilburn with sawdust on the floor. She would never, he realised sadly, be mainstream enough to fit into his troupe.

Juno was belting out her story with delighted abandon now, her voice as sweet and tuneful as Piers found her song bitter and distasteful. Piers wondered at the girl's sanity. She was a head-on collision between Pam Ayres and Alanis Morisette. Where she got her ideas from was beyond him; she had to have had a very disturbing upbringing indeed. The song told a totally unbelievable story about two flatmates who fancied one another. The woman sounded like an obsessive lunatic – poisoning the man, imagining he was an IRA terrorist, leading him to believe she was seducing her ex-boyfriend in her bedroom. Juno Glenn was clearly demented. Talented but demented.

'I smoke fags, I eat junk – and I sometimes get drunk,' Juno sang on.

'But I've never sipped wine with hot Winalot Prime. And the Lloyd Cole CD on the stereo . . .' As she launched into the now-familiar chorus, most of the audience joined in.

Piers put his glass down carefully on the table and glanced around him speculatively, assessing the laughing, receptive faces, the tears in eyes and hands on bellies. What was even weirder than Juno's lunatic imagination was the fact that her audience seemed to adore her. As he listened to the delighted hoots and guffaws, Piers started to think. Perhaps she did have potential after all . . . not as part of his ensemble, but as an individual. He'd always found Victoria Wood too parochially shopping-mall for his taste, but there was no doubt she was a money spinner amongst the suburban salad-spinner set. Juno Glenn was slangier, dirtier and more angry, but she had the same touch, the same sensitivity, the same eye for the ludicrously banal. And Piers liked nothing more than turning the tables on popular opinion – turning MFI into Chippendale, Formica into marble, Juno into 'you know!' Looking at her Rubensesque little body, he decided he quite liked round tables. More chance of a good knight. Realising he'd made a mental pun, he laughed aloud. It was such a strange sound that several people turned to stare.

The song was coming to a close. It was kitsch, original and weird, and it had set the audience alight. Only one of them knew that every word of it was true. A few more suspected that it might be. By far the majority were falling about at the zany, self-deprecating imagination of the busty little blonde in the Tubigrip dress.

As Juno reached the end, she had sung her lungs inside out

to the crowded, smoky room, telling of her brief relationship with Jay – from encountering him in the kitchen whilst raiding the fridge in her pants, to letting him wash her hair when she had a root-bleaching disaster. She'd cheerfully told of her raging crush on him, her desperation to make amends and her desire once again to hold hands over the breakfast pop tarts in Belsize Park. But she hardly noticed the audience's delighted reaction. As she slowed the tempo right down again for the final verse, she locked Jay's eyes with her own and, seeing the mirth brimming there, smiled broadly as she sang:

'I've consulted Pru Leith, Delia, Ainsley and Keith
And I've got an idea, which I think might atone.
So I'm asking Jay sweetly, if he'd like to meet me
For a candlelit dinner, of Pal with marrowbone?

The Lloyd Cole CD on the stereo was singing "Lost Weekend . . ."

Her final chorus was almost drowned out by the audience's booming, rugby-team accompaniment: 'As I cooked a dog's dinner fit for Man's Best Friend.'

'Thank you. I'm Juno Glenn. You've been an audience. We should date more often. Good night!'

Juno had never left the stage to table-banging applause in her life. Whoops and cheers on a really good night, but the loud, rhythmic percussion of beer bottles on table tops was a first. As she stepped off the legendary Ha Ha lips, she turned to look at Jay once again. It was the first time she'd seen him laugh to his boots – really laugh until it hurt and ached and cramped and felt delicious all at the same time. His chin fell into his shoulder and dug delightedly into it before he tipped back his head and smiling widely, yellow eyes melting like topaz in a fire. It was the sexiest laugh imaginable. For the first time in her life, she wanted to stage dive like a groupie at a Sham 69 concert – straight into his arms.

Frank Grogan cheered as he came the other way, shooting her a big, yellow grin then blowing a kiss.

'Suicidal – but fantastic,' he chortled, shambling on stage to pluck the mike from its stand.

Juno hurtled around the back of the stage and into the foyer. She waited for a moment, listening to the muffled echo of Frank introducing the next act, which was distorted by the heavy glass doors in front of her. As she moved forward to push them open, they swung towards her, letting out a rush of hot air, noise and cigarette fumes.

Jay stood in front of her as he let the thickened glass swing to behind him like louvered saloon doors. It was a very Spaghetti-Western moment. Juno was glad she was dressed in her Dolly Parton gear. Not that it was going to last out much longer if her lungs continued expanding with trapped gulps of air as she and Jay faced up to one another. Fighting to breathe normally, Juno took in his blinking, uncertain gaze, those white upper teeth stapled into the cello-shank lower lip, the biker boots scuffing the balding carpet. He looked as though he might turn and run at any second.

Very slowly, she held out her hand.

For a moment he curled his beautiful, Beardsley eyebrows in confusion. Then, lifting his eyes from her hand, he smiled and took it, fingers sliding tightly between hers.

'Do I take it that means I have to put up with you writing a song about every bath we ever take together?' The husky Bronx voice cracked with emotion.

Juno hung her head, fingers uncurling from his as she realised he'd been embarrassed by her loud, blowsy description of their short time together. But he held on tight to her fingertips.

'I guess I could live with that.'

'Can you live with me, though?' She stared at the carpet, following the pattern with her eyes until she felt them bulge in pain.

'Right now, I don't think I could live without you.'

Juno lifted up her eyes, then her chin, her lips, and finally her heels.

That kiss! The one that took her breath, pulse, thoughts and knees clean away. She reeled in bliss, adoring the way his mouth moved against hers. It wasn't just a taste-bud sensation, it was a long-lost friend. A taste-buddy. They had kissed only a few times before, yet it was as familiar and heaven-sent as a glass of champagne at a celebration, a cup of tea in a crisis, and a hip-flask of schnapps on a mountain top.

Someone slammed out through the doors of the club, but they didn't break off. Footsteps thundered downstairs, but they kissed on. A voice continually demanded 'A word, Juno', but they closed their ears and opened their mouths yet further, twining tongues instead of lashing them, bodies meeting from mouth to chest to groin to knee to toe in the hope that two minds could meet later.

When they finally broke off, Jay's eyes danced between hers.

Piers Fox, meanwhile, was dancing from foot to foot beside them.

'A word, Juno.' He flashed his emotionless smile.

Juno carried on staring at Jay, the loving, happy, easy grin on his face, the warmth of those fingers that were once again threading through hers, the feel of his breath against her mouth – a warm, sweet prelude to a hundred thousand kisses more.

'I'm feeling hungry,' he murmured.

'Pal with marrowbone?' she offered.

He tipped his forehead towards hers, the smile now dancing from tango to polka as it upped tempo and turned into a laugh. 'I guess we might have gotten the wrong tickets for gigs tonight, but we've both won meal tickets.'

'I hope they're one-way ones.' Juno pressed her nose against his and crossed her eyes to make him laugh again. It was such a delightful sound – as powerful as a Ferrari starting, as husky as a lion cub growling, as joyfully vulnerable as a tickled toddler. She vowed to hear it every day of the year from now on. 'After tonight, I have no intention of making a return journey to eating junk food alone.'

'As you English say, things are looking meal tickety-boo, baby.'

'I'm missing an act by coming out here to talk to you,'

Piers complained, still hopping around beside them. 'Juno, I have an idea. I think we might be able to – '

'Call me.' She winked at him as she and Jay walked out of the Ha Ha House to hail a cab and kiss all the way home.

They talked like a couple of Trappist monks given the day off. By midnight, Juno's throat ached from telling Jay what a paranoid fool she'd been, and yet he was the one who had done most of the talking. Sitting on the rust-coloured sofa in a room lit only by Uboat's luminescent, burbling tank, Juno felt like a child in a magic grotto of confessions and comfort.

'I thought you and your ex were getting it back together.' Jay cupped her face in his hands. 'I figured you just slept with me to get even with him. After all, he called the flat all the time; Triona, Sean and your friends talked about him a lot – it didn't take a genius to figure out he was still a pretty big feature. When he stayed here that Friday night, I wanted to come crashing into your room and tell him to get the hell out.'

'But he wasn't in there!' Juno gasped. 'I pretended to have someone in my bedroom to make you jealous. It was truly dumb.'

'It drove me crazy with jealousy, man,' he laughed. 'You looked so fucking gorgeous that night and it was all for another man – a guy who'd treated you like shit.'

She hung her head. 'I dressed up for you. I thought you'd asked me on a date – when I realised it was just John, I was so disappointed I wanted to get back at you, show you I still had a life.'

'It was a crazy weekend – I thought I was going mad.' He shook his head. 'When you didn't come home that Saturday night, I realised I'd been fooling myself thinking I could live in the same apartment with you and not give a shit. I knew I cared, I just couldn't figure out how to tell you. Then I met your family, and they flipped me out too – they're so beautiful, so friendly, so like you were that first day I met you, before I started aping out on you by trying to hide my past. And then you told me you just wanted to be my friend. Shit, that hurt!'

'But you'd made me swear not to fall in love with you, Jay!' Juno laughed, snuggling into him as they lounged back on the sofa, limbs tangled together.

'Stupid, huh? I thought I was protecting myself.' He pressed his mouth to her forehead. 'That first night, I guessed that you made a pass at me because you were feeling low, that it was a one-night gig, and I figured by making you swear, *I* wouldn't get hurt – so I decided to say something up-front.'

'And put up a front into the bargain.' Juno stroked his Celtic band tattoo, marvelling at the simple fact she could touch him wherever she wanted without incurring his wrath. She started touching some other parts with gleeful abandon.

'When I got back to London and you weren't around to pester me, I just couldn't get you outta my head. I was so crazy, I started talking to the parrot, man. I had to find an excuse to come see you.'

'So you brought Uboat?' Juno's fingers traced the icicle and then started delving lower.

He nodded. 'Triona had told me she wasn't ill, but I needed a reason and I wasn't that sure you'd want me on your doorstep. Our lives have gotten so tangled up since we met, Juno. It was like something was telling me I had to trust you. I know my past stinks. I guessed you might hate me even more if I told you about it, but I had to. I wanted you to take notice of me – to see me as more than just a guy you had a fling with to cheer yourself up.'

'You were never that, Jay.' Her fingers climbed the rungs of his six pack.

'I wanted to explain why I was so uptight,' he carried on, talking too fast to let her interrupt again, his voice urgent with excitement. 'But I'd been so wrapped up thinking about my past that I hadn't really thought about yours – about your break-up with John, about your friends, your career. You were just this crazy little person that I'd suddenly found I needed to have around to make me feel alive. Then I saw the pregnancy test, and I realised that your life was all tied up with other people, other commitments – stuff that was going on long before I walked into this place. The last thing you needed was my troubles on your back.

'I should have left then, but I found I couldn't. I stuck around, hoping you'd say something to give me a little hope. Instead, I saw how much your friends love you, how much you give to them, and I realised I couldn't offer you anything but misery.

'I've always been a loner, Juno. I figured I could cut you outta my life, could run away as easily as I've always done – just pack my bags and move on. But this time I couldn't. I couldn't even leave London, knowing you were going to be here. I've been hanging around outside this apartment for days, like a goofy teenager, waiting for a shadow to move across a window just to reassure me you were there.'

'You've been just outside?' Tears sprang to Juno's eyes as she realised they'd been just a few metres apart for all those lonely days. Her fingers traced the hollows of his throat. 'I didn't even have your mobile number. You could have been anywhere. I even thought you might have gone off with Lydia.'

'Who?' For a moment his forehead creased. 'Oh, yeah – your screwy friend. I just gave her a lift to London, Juno. Her taste in music's diabolical – I almost ripped out the stereo from my hire car.' His eyes suddenly darted away from hers, blinking uncertainly. 'You sure you wanna get involved with a lousy-tempered, reformed goniff?'

'What's a goniff?'

'A thief.'

Juno traced the line of his jaw. 'I don't know about reformed. You stole my heart pretty professionally. Didn't even leave fingerprints.'

His turbulent yellow eyes swung back to hers as the smile spread like a jet-stream stripe across his face. 'It's a big heart. I sure need it around this week.'

Juno chewed her lip worriedly. 'Why didn't you appear on the show tonight? Piers seemed certain you'd gone to Ireland for some reason.'

'I am going to Ireland. I should be there now.'

'Oh.' Her face fell at the prospect of losing him so soon.

He rubbed his chin on his shoulder, reaching out to stroke her leg. 'Instead, I've been up holed up in Timon's flat walking the carpet bald figuring out how I was going to get through this week without you. I had to get Piers Fox offa my back, and he was real good about it considering I pulled out as his main attraction. I told him I was going to Ireland.' Jay's hand found Juno's under a scatter cushion. 'You see, that's where I think my birth mother is.'

'Your mother?' She dragged her hand from the cushion and pressed it anxiously to her mouth along with Jay's. 'Are you serious? Have you found her?' She bit a knuckle and realised that in her excitement she could feel nothing.

Jay gently removed his finger from her mouth and pressed it to the plump curve of her lip. 'Abe placed a load of ads in the English papers a couple of months back – we had a bundla cranky letters, but nothing worth talking about. Then a week ago he got a letter from a lady in Ireland.'

'Ireland?' Juno felt a tiny smile curl her lips.

He nodded, smiling at the irony too. 'He faxed it to me straight away. Christ, I wanted to tell you when I heard about it – but I thought you were still hooked on John, that you might be pregnant with his kid, that I was just a pain in the ass to you.'

'My ass has never felt lovelier in its life since I met you.' Juno gripped his hands tighter in hers. 'I just wish you'd told me. Oh God, is it really her?'

'I think it might be, Juno.' He dug his fingernails into hers as he fought to control his elation. 'And you know how she read the ad? On a load of newspaper packing around a little figurine she mail-ordered from England. Such a long-shot. Such a one-in-a-million fucking chance. Like coming to England and finding myself living with you.'

'And you think she's genuine?' Juno took in the happiness in his eyes and almost dissolved in its heat.

'Oh, yeah – I'm pretty certain all right.' His voice was staccato with excitement. He went to pull his hair away from his face and remembered it wasn't there. 'I spoke to her on the telephone on Saturday night. We didn't talk long – just a half-hour. We were both so nervous we could hardly speak. She cried a lot, kept telling me how sorry she was, over and over.'

'Did she tell you why she did it? Why she left you?'

He shook his head. 'It'll take time, Juno. She was just sixteen, that's all I really know. She's asked me to go visit. I bought an airline ticket first thing Monday morning. But I couldn't leave London without seeing you again.' His yellow eyes drew intricate patterns into hers and he sucked in his lower lip. 'You see, I want you to come with me. To hold my hand. I need you to be with me when I meet her.'

'Are you sure?'

He cupped her face in his hands again. 'She asked me to tell her about my life, and you know what? I've lived twenty-seven years on this planet, and all I could talk about was the last two weeks – what's that word you used for it? Something about fighting for nights?'

'Fortnight,' Juno giggled, blinking tears from her eyes.

'Fortnight,' he nodded, the jet-stream smile turning loop-the-loops on his face as he wiped her tears away with the tips of his fingers. 'All I could talk about was the last fortnight with you. So will you come to Ireland with me, Juno? I know it's kind of an epic suggestion for a first date.'

She nodded so eagerly that his hands moved up and down on her cheeks like the Pope giving a blessing. 'We've slept together, had our first argument, you've met my parents, we're co-habiting. I think it's about time I met your mother.'

Jay pulled her face towards his, eyes drinking her in, his husky laugh filling the room. 'I used to think you used humour as a weapon. Now I see different. It makes people happy. It makes life a better place to be.'

'We did it the wrong way round, didn't we?' She cupped her hands over his so that she had cheeks like a hamster. 'We made love before we made friends. Sex first – talk afterwards. Or lack of talk in our case.'

'So,' Jay leaned his nose against hers, that perfect kiss just millimetres away from her lips, 'let's get it right this time. We've just talked for hours and hours . . .'

FIONA WALKER

WELL GROOMED

'Romantic, intelligent, steamy and really rather wise'
– Bookcase

A dream wedding can turn into every couple's nightmare, when the families start to interfere. But what could be worse than the happy event being planned by accident without the consent of both parties?

When Tash French's potty grandmother mistakes a Christmas cracker engagement ring for the genuine article, a wedding of astronomical proportions is planned. Swept away by everyone else's enthusiasm, Tash and her partner, Niall, can do little but laugh and go along with it. After all, they had meant to marry all along . . . hadn't they?

HODDER AND STOUGHTON PAPERBACKS

FIONA WALKER

KISS CHASE

'Romps along with plenty of self-deprecating wit'
– Sunday Times

Saskia Seaton is the latest romantic victim of Felix Sylvian: a charming, silken-tongued dilettante with the sex-appeal of a school-girl's day-dream and the soul of a poet. He is quite simply divine. But he has one nasty habit he can't seem to break: a sadistic tendency to ride roughshod over any girl foolish enough to fall for him.

Saskia, once a beautiful, precocious aspiring actress, now reduced to a gibbering, suicidal wreck after the whirlwind affair, retreats to lick her wounded pride, and decides to have poetic justice. Her friend Phoebe's the one to get it. She will seduce him, confuse him, delight him until he falls hooked, maligned and blinkered in love with her. She'll open him up like an oyster and then she'll drop him without reason as he has so many women in the past.

The plan is simple; it can't fail – or can it?

HODDER AND STOUGHTON PAPERBACKS

FIONA WALKER

FRENCH RELATIONS

'Raunchy: [an] explosive debut' – Daily Mail

A summer holiday with her eccentric, infuriating family is the last thing Tash French would usually volunteer for. But her mother is insistent and, out of a job and recently ditched by her boyfriend, Tash decides that spending July in the vast rambling chateau in the Loire might have its compensations.

Gawky, shy, funny, intensely bright and talented but completely lacking in self-confidence, Tash finds herself reduced to a quivering jelly in the company of her fashion model sister and assorted hangers-on. The arrival of dishy event rider Hugo Beauchamp and actor Niall O'Shaughnessy sets further cats among the pigeons. And soon it's a summer of lust, bed-hopping, unresolved sexual tension, horses, dogs, bolshy kids – and lots of bad behaviour. And in the midst of all this bedlam, at least two people fall in love.

HODDER AND STOUGHTON PAPERBACKS

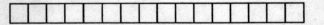